PRAISE FOR *PEARLS* . . .

. . . FROM COAST
TO COAST!

"[*PEARLS*] IS A PASSIONATE . . . NOVEL!"
Richmond Times-Dispatch

"*PEARLS* is a huge novel that captivates the reader from page one. . . . Characters are strong-willed. Each strives with determination against overwhelming odds. Yet, each portrays recognizable human weaknesses and strengths with which the reader can identify. . . . A 'GEM' OF A JET-SET NOVEL!"
[Chattanooga] News-Free Press

"Complex plots and a vivid cast of characters weave in and out. . . . Brayfield's characters and settings are believable. . . . *PEARLS* IS ENGROSSING, SUBSTANTIAL ENOUGH TO KEEP A READER EAGERLY TURNING THE PAGES. . . ."
Macon Telegraph & News

Also by Celia Brayfield:

Nonfiction

GLITTER: FAME & WHAT IT DOES TO YOU

PEARLS

A Novel by

Celia Brayfield

IVY BOOKS • NEW YORK

For Chloe

Prologue

CATHERINE BOURTON WAS SO BEAUTIFUL THAT MEN SELDOM realized that she had any other qualities until it was too late. Her oval face, with its creamy olive complexion, was one of *the* faces of the eighties—so *Time* magazine had said. But her bronze-brown eyes seemed to know much more than they saw; they hinted at the ancestry of the Bourton family, rich Italians grafted to the British aristocracy by Queen Elizabeth I to dissuade them from bankrolling the Spanish Armada.

Such beauty made men vulnerable. Even a man like Mr. Phillips, the Crown Jeweler of Great Britain, whose daily round was largely devoted to considering the effect of the world's most famous jewels on the world's most beautiful women, temporarily forgot the purpose of their meeting in his cramped oval office overlooking Regent Street.

In the concrete canyons around Wall Street, the presence of Catherine Bourton could render innumerate any of the men who had dollar signs where their wives presumed them to have hearts; in a boardroom in the City of London, captains of industry would meander through their agenda muttering compliments and vying for her attention if Catherine Bourton was among them; the two men in Mr. Phillips's gilded candy box at Garrard's were lost the instant she joined them.

The power of her beauty came from the combination of the symmetrical purity of her High Renaissance face with the sensual promise of her mouth. Catherine Bourton's mouth looked

1

soft and crumpled, as if it had just been kissed and would respond favorably to being kissed again. The top lip was a little wider and fuller than the bottom lip, giving her an ineradicable smile. *Time* magazine had called her the Mona Lisa of Wall Street. Catherine had not been surprised. She had been called the Mona Lisa of somewhere or other ever since she could remember.

Nowadays, her reputation went before her. Mr. Phillips had first met her when she was a debutante, pretty, he remembered, but not more distinctive among the crop than one of the spring daffodils in Hyde Park. Like many men after him, Mr. Phillips had misjudged her. She had seldom been out of the headlines since their first meeting, on so many different counts—her marriage, her divorce, her adventures in the City, her glittering connections, and the suspicion that she was the architect of some of the most conspicuous personal fortunes in the world.

Since generosity and fairmindedness were among Catherine's other qualities, she seldom brought her sexual attraction into play unless all other tactics had failed to get her what she wanted. She had found that this was also more efficient. She was dressed to underplay her allure, in a plain black linen suit from Chanel, with her straight brown hair cut in a simple bob.

She wore square-cut diamond earrings, very fine blue-white stones of the first water, because she knew that a jeweler, especially Mr. Phillips at Garrard's, judged people largely on their jewelry. Just as the plain cut of the diamonds only emphasized their quality, so the simplicity of her dress only made her seem more attractive. She considered this Catch 22 typical of many double binds that affect a woman in a man's world; it left her only two possibilities—to win like a man, or to win like a woman.

She liked to win; situations in which winning was neither necessary nor possible disturbed her, and she had come to Garrard's to deal with what she suspected was a major problem of this kind.

"So, Mr. Phillips, what can you tell me about our pearls?" she began, taking the hard, upright chair by his desk. "I've broken with my schedule and flown back to London just to get your opinion. When I spoke to my sister in New Orleans this morning she was dying to know what you've found out. It's not every day we both wake up in the morning and find someone's hidden a pair of pearls under our pillows. Did the tooth fairy get her deliveries mixed up? Or do you think there's a logical explanation?"

She talked about her sister with the same kind of adoration

that Mr. Phillips associated with young brides talking about their husbands; there could be no doubt that this was the most thrilling, the most precious, the most extraordinary person in the world. Mr. Phillips was aware that some of his younger staff, who followed pop music, shared Catherine Bourton's high opinion of her sister, Monty; however, Mr. Phillips himself knew nothing about popular music or its stars.

He was a fine-looking man with the military haircut and shiny shoes of all British courtiers, and he opened his dog-eared file with a nervous snuffle. The August heat made his office stuffy and the plastic desk fan that stirred the sticky air also propelled a lot of dust into the atmosphere.

"I've asked Mr. Jerryman, our chief pearl trader, to join us." He indicated the wiry, white-haired man at his side, who took the pearls in a small polythene envelope from the inside pocket of his black jacket.

"He has examined them and, broadly speaking, the news is that you have a pair of very fine pink pearls, teardrop shape, probably of Oriental origin. . . ."

"And worth?" Catherine knew that when an Englishman said "broadly speaking" and called in a second opinion, she was to be treated to a round of ancient British bullshit.

"The price, you mean?" Mr. Phillips seemed faintly offended that money should be mentioned in the presence of such glorious jewels.

Mr. Jerryman tipped the pearls out of their protective plastic envelope into his hand. Against his papery skin the lustrous gems glowed like living things.

"Pearls are very hard to price, very hard." Mr. Jerryman shook his head and smoothed his slicked-down white hair. "The great pearls, like La Pelegrina, which Richard Burton gave to Elizabeth Taylor, are almost personalities in their own right. They are more or less priceless."

"Well, how do these two compare to La Pelegrina?" Catherine disliked imprecision, especially about money.

"We think they compare very well." Mr. Phillips twinkled at her and took off his glasses for emphasis. "Don't we, Mr. Jerryman?"

The ancient British bullshit began. Mr. Jerryman pulled a cream silk handkerchief from his pocket and spread it on the small table by the grimy window.

"We always look at pearls against a pale background such as this"—he picked the two jewels out of his hand and placed them on the cloth with reverence—"because a pearl is a responsive surface, and it tends to take on the color and texture of whatever it is displayed against. That's why of course pearls look so good against a—er—a lady's . . ." he paused, embarrassed.

"Skin?" Catherine suggested, amused.

"Quite so. Now the first question to consider is whether these are completely natural pearls, or whether they are cultured. And there is no doubt that these are natural pearls because of their size." Catherine gave him her most patient smile. "They each are around one hundred fifty grains, which means they must be among the largest pearls ever fished—and you simply do not get cultured pearls that large. Only the biggest species of oyster, called *Pinctada maxima*, can make a pearl of this size, and that species does not take kindly to interference so they are seldom used for culturing."

"And, apart from the size, of course, there are the X rays." Mr. Phillips unclipped two small plates, no bigger than dental X rays, from the file and held them up against the occluded light of the begrimed window. Catherine saw that each pearl showed a succession of faintly marked rings, like the annual rings of a tree trunk. "A cultured pearl is achieved by seeding the oyster with a tiny pearl bead." Mr. Phillips waved his pen over the X rays with authority. "In consequence, that impurity always shows up on the plates—but in this case there's nothing, so we can be sure they're natural pearls."

"And the third check is on the specific gravity," the older man resumed. "Natural pearls are always just a tiny bit lighter for their size, because they are solid nacre."

"Nacre, what's that?" Catherine inquired pleasantly. Encouraging a display of technical knowledge always gave the boys confidence. Meetings, like everything else about business, were a game to her, and the first rule was to leave the guys their balls.

"Nacre is the stuff the mother oyster makes the pearls with—it's built up in layers around the center. See here on the X ray, these little rings?" Mr. Phillips gestured again with his old-fashioned pen.

"Chemically it is mostly just calcium carbonate—the same as blackboard chalk or the granite curbstones down there on Piccadilly Circus." Mr. Jerryman warmed to his favorite subject. "The magic ingredient of nacre is something called conchiolin, a protein secreted by the oyster's tissues to bind it all together."

"Does it *tell* you anything?" prompted Catherine blandly. "My sister and I are just longing to know about these pearls. They're the most mysterious thing that's ever happened to us."

"Why, yes, it tells us quite a lot. We can get some idea of the pearl's age from the nacre, because it builds up at about one thousand layers a year; but any pearl this size will have come from a bed undisturbed for decades." Mr. Jerryman turned the jewels over on the silk with a gesture of affection. "The color gives us some clues too—it's partly due to pigment in the nacre, and partly determined by the way the light is refracted between the outer layers. These are a very rare color—almost apricot, don't you think?"

Mr. Phillips unfolded his gold-rimmed half glasses and put them on again to peer closely at the pearls.

"Yes, apricot's about right—creamy-golden with a touch of pink in there."

"But what does that mean?" Catherine gave Mr. Phillips's idiotically elaborate ormolu clock a marked glance—for how much of this minuet did she have time?

"These must have been made by the gold-lipped subspecies of *Pinctada maxima*, which narrows down the country of origin for you," the white-haired jeweler explained. "And you only find the gold-lipped pearl oyster off Burma, Thailand and the Indonesian islands. Now, I have some contacts out there, and I've sent a few telexes, but no one's got any information."

"Which I regard as highly significant"—Mr. Phillips removed his spectacles to underline the seriousness of his pronounce-ment—"because when a pearl this size is found—which is very rare, maybe once in twenty years—they know about it in every bar in Tokyo by the end of the week. Fishing up a perfect pair like this ought to have been headline news around the world. I'd be most surprised if these two had been traded on the open mar-ket."

"Are you saying they're stolen?" The idea did not appear to disturb Catherine Bourton as much as the two men had feared.

"Not necessarily, but they must have been acquired by some private means—unless the tooth fairy has taken up pearl fishing in her spare time." They laughed, pleased that the awkward moment had passed.

"And you're sure they're quite new—not antique? My sister and I thought perhaps they might turn up in your records some-where."

"We checked our ledgers, of course." Mr. Phillips was anx-ious not to appear negligently complacent in his expertise. "And I've checked with Sotheby Parke Bernet and Christie's for you as well, but I didn't expect them to find them. We were sure they hadn't been out of the sea very long. It's what we call the luster, you see, that gleam they have that's strong and gentle at the same time; it fades if the pearls aren't worn next to the skin once they're out of the oyster."

"I got these out of our safe to show you what we mean." He

reached into his desk and pulled out a pair of pearl-drop earrings set with diamonds.

Catherine noticed immediately that the large pale pearls were identical to those worn by a prominent European princess whose signed photograph was half hidden by the pile of papers on his desk. She also noticed that the pearls were dull, not shiny like the ones she had brought them. She could see her face in those shiny surfaces.

The Garrard's ledgers, she knew, recorded almost every major jewel in the world. They were large vellum-paged account books, bound in leather the color of autumn leaves, which recorded the history of the world's ruling classes as accurately as any history book. The earliest volumes, from the first entry in 1730, related to the crown jewels of Great Britain, a hoard increased at each dynastic marriage. Then the wealth of the British Empire appeared, in the form of maharajahs' rubies from India or the Koh-i-Noor diamond, which was set in 1853.

From the turn of the century, the once-crowned heads of Europe came to Garrard's to sell what jewels they had been able to salvage from their revolutionary deposers. The ledgers even recorded the shameful affair of the Imperial Russian jewel case, sent for sale on behalf of the tsar's family by Britain's Queen Mary only after she had picked the choicest items for herself.

Of late, many of the ledger entries recorded the creation of state regalia for the new countries of the Third World; but there was still some business accruing from royal patronage—like the diamond and drop-pearl tiara given by the Queen to the Princess of Wales on her wedding.

"See the difference? These were collected by Elizabeth of Bohemia in the seventeenth century. (Mind you, don't say I said that because *she* tells everyone they were the Empress Josephine's.)" He glanced at the princess's photograph. "But she won't wear them, and they'll never get that shine back now." He shook his head, implying that the foolishness of princesses was an occupational hazard.

"Do you think ours have ever been worn?"

"No, frankly, I doubt it. Tell you why—they're the same weight as La Pelegrina, and that used to belong to the Duchess of Abercorn, and I remember her telling me that she had to have it drilled, because it was too heavy to stay in a claw setting, and she once lost it down the side of a sofa cushion in Buckingham Palace. She was always losing it, in fact. These two haven't been bored, so I doubt they've ever been worn. We'd be happy to set them for you, of course. Splendid pair of earrings, had some nice little diamonds in last week, set them off a treat. . . ."

PEARLS

Catherine smiled with polite regret, and opened her briefcase to take out two white leather jewel boxes. She reached forward, picked up the pearls and fitted each one into the little nest of black velvet inside its box, and put them back in the briefcase. "But I'm sure that boring them will reduce their value?"

The two men nodded as she rose to her feet and moved toward the door.

"And my sister and I would like to find out who gave them to us before we do anything else. Now, if I've remembered correctly, we know that these pearls must be newly discovered, from somewhere in Burma, Thailand or Indonesia, and perhaps stolen or at least sold privately, and they've never been worn."

"I'd guess from a small fishery," added the older man, tucking his handkerchief back into the breast pocket. "They'd never have been able to keep the discovery secret in a big operation."

Catherine thanked the two men with such grace that they were at once convinced that they had solved the entire mystery of the pearls. Mr. Phillips escorted her through the blue-walled enclave that the Garrard's staff call the royal enclosure and watched as she walked briskly but unevenly out into Regent Street. She had a very slight limp.

Her office was in Pall Mall, on the sixth floor, high above the gentlemen's clubs and the traffic.

"Any joy, Mum?" her son Jamie called as she closed the plain glass door with CBC Investment Consultants painted on it in small silver letters.

Jamie looked up from the word processor. He had his father's light-blue eyes, all the more startling against his curly black hair.

"A little joy. Curiouser and curiouser, really. How's the bulletin?" Her son spent his Oxford vacations helping out around her office, and this year she had entrusted him with the job of preparing the monthly digest of market trends, which was mailed to all their clients.

"Er—not too bad. Put it this way—I thought an essay crisis was a good excuse for a nervous breakdown until I got into currency forecasts."

She walked around behind him, noticing how broad his shoulders were now as she peered over them at the screen.

"We're calling the yen bullish, are we?"

"I think so; it looks quite strong after oil prices came down last week." He looked up at her, compressing his thick black brows with anxiety.

"And you're sure that's valid?"

"Pretty sure—I'm not basing it all on Chicago if that's what you mean. Don't you agree?"

"Yes, darling, of course I agree. I'm just testing. Can you tone this bit down? Your grandfather will kill us if we talk about the British having a blinkered obsession with short-term credit. You *are* right, just put it more diplomatically."

She patted his sunburned arm affectionately and wandered across to the other side of the office, idly picking up pieces of paper and reading them without taking in their contents.

"What time's your flight?" Jamie spoke without taking his eyes off his screen as he made the corrections.

"Couple of hours—I'll have to leave soon. Make sure the receptionist gets fresh flowers tomorrow, won't you, darling? Those lilies look rather tired." She gazed out of the window at the handsome facade of the Athenaeum Club across the road.

Her son abruptly switched off the word processor.

"You're worried, aren't you? Come on, what's on your mind?" He came over and put his arms around her. "Is it the pearls?"

"Yes, I guess so. It's just so strange, Jamie. Nothing like this has ever happened before. There's no reason, no meaning—I can't understand it. They said they were *priceless* at Garrard's. Who would give Monty and me two priceless pearls?"

"Probably some secret admirer."

"Don't be silly; no one could possibly fancy both of us. No one would dare." She laughed, trying to break her mood of anxiety.

"Didn't they give you anything else to go on at Garrard's?"

She shook her head and shrugged her shoulders. "Nothing much. They just tried to persuade me to have them bored and made into a pair of earrings."

"Well, why don't you do that?" He squeezed her protectively and she smiled with unease. Catherine still had difficulty in bridging the gap in her mind between this brawny young god and the little boy with busy knees in a pedal car, who used to cry when he ran into a tree.

"Go on," he urged. "You and Monty could wear them for six months each, every year."

Catherine gave another nervous laugh. "Listen, I've called my sister all sorts of things in my life, but the twinset-and-pearls-type is something she'll *never* be."

In a cave of light in the middle of the vast auditorium a woman in a pink jacket was punching the air in time to the beat. Twenty thousand voices were roaring for her. Her hips ground to and fro as she stamped the rhythm.

"Was it good for you too?" Monty yelled, and the crowd rose

up like a wave and howled. She flung back her head and felt the sweat trickling down her neck, her back, between her breasts. She snapped her head upright. "Shall we do it again?" Another full-throated roar answered her, and she turned and pulled the band together with a wave of her arm. The crowd was clapping the time, whistling, screaming, stamping the floor, swaying like a wheatfield in a storm as the lights played over them.

Sometimes Monty thought she could die like this, onstage, with her people, all burned up with the noise and the music and the lights. Other times, she felt as if she *were* going to die, right there, as if her heart were going to stop or her brain burst with excitement and exhaustion.

Her voice was raw now, at the end of her third night at the Superdome, but she liked the way it sounded. Raw was good for "Man Beats Woman," her first big hit in the States, the song she always sang for her second encore. Deliberately, she slipped control of her voice and heard the sound tear out of her.

Winston, her drummer, was playing like a madman, his shirt flapping wet with perspiration. She danced across the stage and wound her arms around Stas at the keyboards as he launched into an orgasmic buildup of scales.

The crowd was a sea of reaching hands as she moved forward to the edge of the stage, slipping off her jacket. P.J. and Barbara shared a mike to her left, their legs working like pistons in their long white skirts. Monty whirled her jacket around her head, her whole body whipped into curves by the motion; then she flung it out into the crowd and the arms folded over it like a sea anemone's tentacles.

One last chorus. In a white T-shirt and black trousers, her cropped black hair slick with sweat, she stomped backward and the guitarists moved in from each side to join her for the triumphant final chord. All right! All right. Breath tore into her chest and blood thundered in her ears as she bowed to the tempest of applause.

Better bring them down gently now. A word to Tony, the lead guitar, and then Monty sat down at the edge of the stage and they killed most of the lights. Someone brought her her own guitar and she checked the tuning, gaining time to get her breathing more relaxed. Already the crowd was settling, knowing what was to come.

"This song is very important to me," she told them, aware that most of them knew the story and anticipating the murmur of response. "It's a song about who we are and what we're doing here. It's called 'Broken Wings,' but I always think of it as Joe's song."

She looked away to the right, and there was Joe at the edge of the stage, tipping her an easy little salute with a kiss in it. Then she forgot him, and concentrated on the song; why did I ever write something with such damned difficult intervals? she wondered.

Ten minutes later Monty erupted into her dressing room, filling the small space with the surplus energy of her stage personality.

"Cathy!" she hurled herself into her sister's arms and at once Catherine's white Armani shirt was mottled with sweat and creased by Monty's passionate embrace. "Darling, darling Cathy! You made it! You look wonderful! Doesn't she, Joe? What's the news, about the pearls?"

The veins in Monty's neck stood out, she was gleaming with sweat and her arms were shaking with exhaustion as she hugged her sister closely. Cathy could feel the force of her sister's heartbeats; not for the the first time, she envied Monty her ability to surrender herself completely, body and spirit. Her eyes looked more catlike than ever, their pupils dilated with the high of performing.

"You're coming home with us, aren't you?" Monty continued, talking too loud and too fast. "Say you'll stay, Cathy. I'll scream if you've got to go back to New York to do business. I miss you so much. Did you have a good flight? Tell me—what did they say? About the pearls, what's happening, what are they?"

"Not very much, nothing to go on. I'll tell you tomorrow. You were great, Monty. What a crowd. Are they always like that?" Catherine knew it would be hours before her sister came down and was calm enough to put two sentences together. She was like another person after a concert, jittery and explosive, on an emotional razor edge, ready to plunge from the great high to the great low if she was not handled carefully.

Joe always knew how to calm her. Cathy was never completely at ease in her sister's world; nor was she completely at ease with Joe. Despite her best intentions, she was jealous. The sisters were so close Cathy often felt as if they were twins, psychically connected even when they were apart. Cathy had never found such intimacy with another adult, but Monty had Joe, and now they had a baby, too.

They were carried away in a river of people, swept through the concrete bowels of the Superdome and out into a limousine, then away to an airport and into a jet. Monty at last fell asleep on Joe's shoulder, her lashes curling on her flushed cheeks.

It was still dark when they emerged in the furnace of the

Phoenix night, to be driven through the stark landscape to the home Monty and Joe had built in the mountains. By the time they arrived, Catherine felt as if she were on another planet, and not just because the house was walled with black lava rock; their world was one of extremes—but then so was the world of money, where Catherine lived. The difference was that Catherine succeeded because she remained apart from the craziness, while Monty had won by surrendering herself to it.

Joe, Monty's lover and manager, was one of those men whose sexual aura hung brooding like summer lightning in the atmosphere. Maybe it was because that narrow face, with its black eyes and full, curving lips, had also launched thousands of album covers in its day. Catherine was well acquainted with the power of a public image; that was not the whole story with Joe. He was the most disturbing man she had ever met.

She watched him the following afternoon, patiently feeding some mashed banana to Paloma, his baby daughter, and wondered how it could be that his clothes gave the impression that they covered his flesh unwillingly.

"She's a lovely baby, Monty."

"C'mon—you hate babies." Monty smiled fondly up from the black-leather sofa at the messy tableau.

"Yes, but as babies go she's adorable."

Monty sat forward, dismissing the ritual exchange of compliments. "The pearls, Cathy—we've got to know *why*. Nobody would give us both a present like that for no reason. They've got to have some meaning."

"I know that, Monty—but *what*? What have we two got in common, for heaven's sake? We've lived totally separate lives for twenty years, almost."

"I think that's the key to it." Joe put down the dish and walked down the wide wooden steps to the level where the sisters were talking. "The *only* thing you two have in common is your blood. Sure, everyone knows how close you are, but there's no other link between you at all except that you're children of the same parents. Apart from that, the only thing that's the same in both your lives is just that they don't make any sense."

"What do you mean?" Cathy felt as if she were being criticized, then realized that she wasn't. It was hard to tell with Joe.

"What I mean is, from what Monty's told me, you've both had turning points in your lives where something pulled you back from the edge—and it wasn't anything ordinary."

"You mean, like me and the smack?" Cathy flinched inwardly; she was always disturbed by the matter-of-fact way her sister could talk about being a heroin addict.

11

"Yes, you and the smack, and what about you, Cathy?" Joe's even, velvety voice was devoid of accusation, but Cathy knew she must also make her confession.

"We've never really understood . . ." she paused, not liking to remember past pain. "Well, I've got away with far more than I've had any right to, businesswise, I suppose."

Joe, pitiless, said nothing, hoping to pull a more specific declaration out of her, but the baby, furious that the supply of dinner had dried up, squawked and splashed its small hand into the dish, then hurled it off the tray. The awkward moment passed, and Joe went to wipe up the floor.

Beyond the room's glass wall, the searing colors of the Arizona sunset, bands of orange and neon pink, were intensifying out of the pure blue sky of daytime.

Monty sighed and got up to get her sister a drink.

"Do you remember Daddy telling us that the sun went down with a green flash in the tropics?" She handed Cathy a Scotch and water, half-and-half, with one ice cube, and poured Coke for Joe and herself. "I've seen every color of the rainbow out there, but never green. I'm sure the green flash was just one of those old colonial myths they were all so keen on."

Cathy sipped her drink thoughtfully.

"Daddy never told us anything very much about Malaya, did he? When I think about it, all he ever mentioned were romantic little things like that."

"Wasn't he some kind of war hero?" Joe strolled down into the conversation with a cleaned-up Paloma tucked contentedly into the crook of his arm.

"Yes, but he never talked about that either. And Mummy never told us anything because she hated the place. All I can remember is our amah and her black trousers." Cathy paused, scanning her childhood memories rapidly. She looked at Joe and Monty, now sitting side by side on the leather cushions watching fondly as Paloma crawled around the floor. Sometimes Joe seemed like a cross between Freud and Buddha; he knew the answers to everything. How could her sister live with anyone so disturbingly enlightened? Maybe I just don't like men who're smarter than I am, Cathy thought. Then Monty jumped up, fired by the new idea.

"You're right, Joe! Of course—we've no idea what Daddy's life was like out in the East, and he never told us anything, even what he did during the Japanese occupation to get his DSO. He never even told Cathy anything, and he was so close to her. He never saw any of his old army friends; there weren't even any books in the house about the Malayan campaign. Now I think about it, it's obvious! *And* the one thing the Garrard's people could tell us was that the pearls must have come from the East somewhere—Thailand or Burma, didn't they say? That's just north of Malaya. There *must* be a link.''

Monty's enthusiasm always charmed Cathy, whose temperament was naturally cool.

''Not necessarily,'' she said, ''—but there *might* be some connection.''

''Private detectives!''

''Monty, for heaven's sake, this isn't a soap opera.''

''I know, but there must *be* private detectives.''

Cathy twitched her blue silk skirt as she considered the next step.

''It's so melodramatic, I'm sure they're all bone-thick ex-cops anyway, all thinking they're Humphrey Bogart, and trying to charge one hundred dollars a day plus expenses.'' She recognized that she was being unreasonable, and shook her head. ''Do you know what really bothers me, Monty? I've never felt that Daddy killed himself just because he got into debt. He'd have just laughed it off and charmed someone into lending him more money. There was something worse, I'm sure of it.''

''And you're scared of finding out what it is?'' Monty took her sister's slender, straight-fingered hands in her own.

''I am scared, yes. You're the only person I'd admit it to, but I'm really frightened. I've got this awful feeling about the whole business. My intuition is just screaming NO.''

The three of them were silent. Cathy was always so calm, so decisive, so economically poised as she shifted millions of dollars around the world for her clients; Monty knew that her sister could feel as terrified as any other woman inside, but even she was under the spell of her tranquillity, so this admission of fear was a shock.

The baby tumbled off the bottom step of a short flight that separated the two areas of the vast living space; she whimpered because she had bumped her head. Joe jumped up and scooped the infant into his arms.

''What do you feel about it all, Monty?'' he asked as he sat down again.

She looked into his eyes and Cathy felt the intensity of their intimacy like a spark passing between them.

''I have a strange feeling too, but it's not scary. It's more like I'm being called in, or called home, or something. I feel as if something is coming full circle. Like you, I suppose, I think maybe we'll be able to understand some things that we couldn't before. But I'm not scared—just for once.''

Throughout their lives it had been Cathy's job to look after her younger sister, and the responsibility had become a habit. Cathy resolutely shook off her forebodings.

"Somewhere in the world there must be a private detective who hasn't walked out of a bad film. You're right, Monty, we might as well start by investigating the Eastern connection. And why Daddy died. There might be some link—anyway, that's all we've got to go on." She stood up with a swish of silk, her dark brown hair swinging into place as she moved. "I've got a couple of clients who're big in Hong Kong; I'll ask their advice. I'll brief someone, and get a report when I'm in Singapore next month for the tin-crisis conference, and then we can all meet up at the opening of the Shahzdeh's new development."

Joe and Monty smiled at each other; Cathy had a kind of puritanical guilt about taking holidays, and they had been hoping she would overcome it to accept an invitation issued by one of her oldest clients, an Iranian couple whose multifarious interests included a chain of luxury resort islands.

"Isn't it so typical of my work-obsessed sister to think of a jet-set playground as just another development?" Monty chinked the ice in her drink happily.

"OK, it's a deal," said Joe. "I'm glad you're coming to the Shahzdeh's latest island; it sounds like quite a place."

Monty's butterfly mind had already settled on a new idea.

"Cathy, can I ask you something, sister to sister?"

"If you can't, I don't know who can."

Monty pointed to the baby's neatly diapered rear as Paloma crawled toward the steps once more.

"Did it ever bother you to have that mark on your thigh?"

In the center of the child's plump upper leg was a light-brown, leafshaped birthmark. Cathy involuntarily slid her hand under her own right thigh, where she too had an area of darker pigmentation.

"Only when we were all wearing miniskirts and bare legs, in the sixties. That was the only time it showed. I forget about it mostly."

Monty frowned, knowing her sister's capacity for camouflaging the smallest area of vulnerability. Joe was staring at the ceiling; Monty knew he thought she was obsessed with the baby's birthmark. She'd been fretting over it, and wanting to see a specialist, ever since the birth. Monty's own version of the mark was a much narrower shape, darker, but higher up on her right buttock, so that it was never visible unless she wore a brief bikini or leotard.

"You're sure—you didn't feel it was a disfigurement?" Her voice faltered on the word.

"No, honestly, Monty, I was hardly aware of it. It's something I never give a thought to."

Later, however, Cathy lay awake in the night thinking about the pale-brown stain on her skin.

She had dreamed vividly of watching herself from behind, diving into a swimming pool, with the birthmark showing darker because she was suntanned. Accompanying the dream were feelings of violent emotional disturbance—anger, anxiety and acute insecurity. Monty said that everyone dreamed a lot in Arizona; she had a theory that the elemental landscape, all air, fire and earth, put people in closer touch with their hidden emotions.

Perhaps she was right, Cathy thought, sitting up in bed and pulling the white comforter up to shoulder level. She switched on the concealed lighting in the white wall behind the bed and reached for the folder at her bedside. It contained the draft of the prospectus for her new venture, a private bank. In the years during which Cathy had dealt successfully with some of the wealthiest but most wayward people in the world, she had become convinced that the bank would be a logical development of the service she already provided for her clients. Now other firms were getting to the same place, and it was time to act before her market began to be eroded. Cathy knew she would never be in quite such a strong position again.

She was a wealthy woman, certainly, the richest self-made woman in Britain. But money did not buy friends, it just got you smarter enemies. Human nature didn't change—especially male human nature.

Even the prospectus could not engage her tormented mind and Cathy's thoughts strayed. A name floated out of her unfocused memories of her father—William Treadwell. He was the man to whom her father had been closest out in the East; maybe she could trace him.

Because Treadwell had changed his name and adopted the native religion, Daddy had talked about him as if he had contracted some chronic illness. They must have been close, or her father would never have felt so strongly about the change of faith. She tried to remember more. Treadwell had taught her father to play chess. Cathy smiled with affection for her dead father. She also remembered her husband accusing her: "You don't love me," he had raged, "you can't love me, or any other man. There's only one man you'll ever love, Cathy, and he's dead. That's your little tragedy, darling." The harsh words, spoken in anger so long ago, no longer wounded her. What her husband had said was untrue; she could love. She loved her son more than his father would ever be able to comprehend. There would never be anyone in her life quite as dazzling as Daddy, of course; she had accepted that, but it did not cause her pain. She only felt privileged to have known her father for the first sixteen years of her life.

1

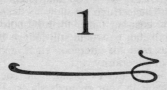

"I SEEM TO BE IN TROUBLE." THE FORELOCK OF JAMES BOUR-
ton's graying dark hair fell into his line of vision as he leaned
over the chessboard. He picked up his one remaining bishop,
moved it halfway across the board, saw danger and retreated.

A few pink petals from the rose that climbed the gray stone
facade of their house fell onto their table on the terrace, and
James picked them off, playing for time. Cathy wondered if her
father was putting on a show of floundering in defeat for her
benefit. She hoped not. She was sixteen, and no longer wanted
concessions of that kind. She watched him with patience, folding
her arms across the bib of her navy school tunic to keep warm.
The heat of the September day was fading.

When she had been a little girl, it had been different. She
could not bear to lose at any game, and had cried and screamed
"It's not fair!" if she was checkmated. Her father had indulged
her, surrendering with a show of despair at the end but putting
up just enough of a fight for her to feel her triumph was genuine.

"Dash it, you've done it again," he would murmur in a pained
voice. "Run off the board by my own daughter!" he would
protest, pretending an agony of disgrace.

"But, Daddy," Cathy would say with childish forthrightness,
which persisted long after she should have learned tact, "I only
won because you were absolutely *stupid*."

"In victory, magnanimity," he advised her, making room for
her on his lap so she could give him a kiss. He smelled of the

17

cologne from his Curzon Street barber, of cigars, and of brandy after lunch. His cheeks were cool and smooth, never scratchy with stubble like Uncle Hugo's.

Cathy began to beat her father for real shortly after she went to boarding school, but he would still lounge back in his chair, blow smoke rings from his afternoon cigar, and give her advice from a position of superiority.

"Always think two moves ahead," he counseled in lordly tones. "Put yourself in your enemy's shoes. Think about what I'm up to as well as what you're going to do about it," he told her, narrowing his bright brown eyes. Then his attention would wander and she would be able to take his queen in two moves.

"That's the spirit, princess. Do as your father says, not what he does." And he would beam with pleasure, tickled pink that his daughter had such ability. His concentration span was short, and, unlike Cathy, he saw no point in winning a game, only in passing his time enjoyably.

The last chess game of the school holidays had become a ritual, as much a part of the process of saying good-bye to home as taking her pony down to the livery stable and kissing his silky nose.

Their mother would leave for her afternoon at the bridge club, and Monty would vanish upstairs to her piano. This was the last precious time that Cathy would spend alone with her father for some months.

"All right, you've got me. I surrender. Hang out the white flag." James tossed the hair out of his eyes and they smiled at each other with satisfaction. "I never mind losing to the most beautiful girl in the world—come and give your poor father a kiss."

From the uppermost window, under the graceful gothic curve of the gable, cascades of notes sounded from the piano. Monty was attacking an elaborate Chopin fantasy much too fast, slurring across the passages she could not remember and guessing the chords until at last the piece collapsed in hopeless dissonance.

Monty said "Hell" loudly enough to be heard outside, slammed down the piano lid, then slammed it up again and started picking out a different tune. James hummed it.

"Isn't that something by those dreadful insects—what are they called?" Cathy knew he was teasing her.

"The Beatles, Daddy. Yes, she can play all their songs."

"They're still the latest thing, are they?"

"They've been number one for weeks."

"Ridiculous name. I suppose you teenagers like that sort of

noise." He tossed the last two inches of Havana into the herbaceous border.

"We're not teenagers, Daddy."

"Of course you are; you're sixteen and fifteen, that makes you teenagers."

Cathy wriggled on the Georgian garden bench. She had a knack of seeing life very clearly, which adults often found embarrassing. "You know what I mean; we aren't *really* teenagers."

What she meant was that teenagers were virtually a new social class. The granddaughters of a duke, educated at the boarding school which was shortly to be attended by the Queen's own daughter, had their position in society predetermined.

Whatever their social background or education, teenagers shared the same interests and rejected everything their parents held dear. Teenagers, by definition, had rows with their parents and wore outrageous outfits. They had jobs that paid them as much as twenty pounds per week—leaving plenty of money to spend on clothes and records—but their attitude to work was irresponsible. They skipped from one job to another, contributing as little as possible and always looking for excitement rather than secure employment for life and a pension after it.

Girl teenagers wore corpse-pale makeup, near-white lipstick and thick black eyeliner; the boys wore hair so long it almost brushed their shirt collars, and Cuban-heeled boots with chisel toes.

At weekends, teenagers hung around coffee bars in gangs. Above all, teenagers liked pop music. They bought singles by the million for six shillings and threepence each, and played them on automatic record players. Teenagers despised BBC pop-music programmes hosted by middle-aged men with patronizing upper-class voices. Instead, they tuned their transistor radios to Radio Luxembourg, a station that transmitted pop music all night from the tiny principality on the continent, beyond the censorship of British broadcasting laws.

James half approved of what he called the teenage thing. He bought Monty a transistor radio for her fourteenth birthday, and silenced his wife with a glare when she objected to the noise. Without ever analyzing his knowledge, James recognized that teenagers were essentially nonconformist, and his two daughters, high-spirited as they might be, were nice upper-class girls, conformist to the tips of their unvarnished fingernails. There was no real danger of their becoming part of the most important change in the British class system in more than one hundred years.

"Why shouldn't they enjoy themselves?" he argued with his

wife. "There's no harm in listening to music. They'll grow up soon enough."

Bettina pinched her lips, making the coral lipstick run farther into the deep wrinkles around her once-pretty mouth.

"Nice young men nowadays . . ." she began, but James cut off her sentence.

"Nice young men nowadays aren't going to want to marry a pair of stick-in-the-muds," he told her, suddenly vicious.

Bettina wanted her daughters married as well and as quickly as possible, so she could consider her duty as a mother discharged. The sisters had sensed their mother's hostility in their earliest childhood, and drawn closely together to protect themselves against her. In those days their father had been a virtual stranger, whose weekend visits were like interludes of dazzling sunlight in a life overcast with their mother's dislike. As they matured from perplexing bundles of childish passion to pleasing preadolescents, James discovered that his daughters were delightful companions. Just as his own lust for living was waning, their enthusiasm refreshed it. Even their faults entranced him; if Cathy was outspoken to the point of rudeness and Monty increasingly rebellious, they were only expressing his own frustrated feelings.

He began to realize that the two girls were the best achievement of his life. They were also the only women whom he could love with all his heart; and he was never anxious to be left alone with his wife, whom he did not love at all.

To everyone but his wife, Bettina, James Bourton was the most charming man you could ever wish to meet. In middle age he was wiry and energetic, with spontaneous good manners and flattering attention for everyone—from the new traffic wardens who put tickets on his Bentley all over the City to the chairmen of his boards.

One enthusiasm after another caught James's fancy, and in consequence he passed on to his elder daughter a broad-based education in gentlemanly pursuits; at sixteen she could hold a competent discussion with anyone about the right trout fly to use, the best claret to drink or the most likely horse to back. She was slow to acquire the ladylike cunning to hide this knowledge, but most of her father's friends found her girlish frankness charming and would only laugh when she earnestly explained exactly where they had gone wrong.

Cathy also learned something else from mixing in her father's world. She learned that he was a failure. He was well liked, and valued for his name and connections, which were worth a great deal in the City of London in 1963. But his colleagues thought that James was a lightweight, lacking in judgment and insufficiently aggressive in business. Every now and then she would catch a patronizing note as someone spoke to him, and she would burn inwardly with anger. Didn't they realize that her father was the most marvelous man in the world?

"Well—all good things must come to an end." James stood up and took her arm as they strolled indoors. "Go and see if your sister's ready. I've got to speak to your headmistress about her and we'd better not be late when I've got to tackle the dragon in her lair."

Nominally, James was a director of a large merchant bank, two new unit trust companies and an old, established insurance brokerage house. Lord James Bourton was a name that looked well on the letterheads, and James himself looked well at board meetings, excavating neat holes in the ends of his cigars with a gold penknife to mask his boredom. He looked best of all in the bank's box at Ascot, or watching polo on Smith's Lawn at Windsor, or striding across a grouse moor, or running a fluent, amusing conversation around the long mahogany dining table of his club.

Any habitat of the British aristocracy was natural to him, and the traditional plumage also became him more than most men; Cathy thought he looked finest in full evening dress, with diamond studs twinkling below his crisp white tie and discreet medal ribbons reminding everyone that this dandy had also served his country.

As soon as the girls were old enough, James took them with him to lighten some of the ceaseless round of entertaining, which was his primary business function. Bettina never spent more time with her husband than necessary; Monty was easily bored, and then became sulky, and soon announced that she didn't want to dress up and go out with her father anymore; but Cathy was delighted with any excuse to enjoy his company.

The road that led to Benenden School was like the road to Manderley, a mysterious private highway overhung with beech trees and rhododendron bushes. Monty always had a sense of foreboding as they drove down the dark green tunnel, leaving the fertile Kent countryside behind in the mellow autumn sunshine. The wall of vegetation enclosed the school completely, cutting it off from life in the real world outside.

She shrank down into the corner of the Bentley as it emerged into the avenue of lime trees that connected the group of redbrick school buildings; the main building was a castellated edifice with Jacobean pretensions. Monty thought it was a hypocritical sham, and held the same opinion of most of the activities promoted within its walls.

Most of all, she dreaded the swamp of boredom that waited behind the diamond-paned windows. The endless afternoons spent acquiring useless facts or redundant skills would, she knew, plunge her into a lethargy that was as painful and exhausting as an illness.

Cathy got out first. Her house, Etchyngham, was a building at the far end of the lime avenue. Etchyngham's color was pink, and Cathy looked extremely pretty with a pink belt and tie on her navy uniform. Monty's house, Guldeford, had orange accessories. She hated orange. It made her look sallow. Monty knew the teachers kept her in Guldeford House because it was part of the main school building and she would be under their noses. The school's biggest troublemaker, Serena Lamotte, who called herself Swallow, was in Guldeford House for the same reason. Monty and Swallow were becoming good friends.

Once the girls had kissed him good-bye and vanished inside their respective houses, James strolled toward the head mistress's study, trying to put himself in the right frame of mind to win Monty the approval of those in authority over her.

James's difficulty in doing this derived from the fact that he felt his younger daughter's spirit was her most valuable quality. He envied her the courage to rebel; he could not help reflecting that his own life would have been very different, and probably far more satisfying, if his character had contained a similar measure of fire. He saw no reason at all why she should obey the school rules. If his bond with his elder daughter was founded on complementary personalities and interests, James's attraction to Monty was the yearning of a reluctantly domesticated personality for one who was fighting to remain untamed. Cathy shared this feeling. They both knew that Monty was in some way special, and protected her accordingly.

In the headmistress's study James began to play the part of the concerned parent.

"Quite frankly, Lord Bourton, I am not at all sure that we will be able to do much more for Miranda." Miss Sharpe began with an expression of discomfort.

Miranda was Monty's real Christian name. Monty, the nickname of Britain's great World War II general, had been the name her father had called her after a holiday at Deauville, where he had listened to his seven-year-old younger girl ordering her sister and her cousins to scramble up and down sand dunes in a game they called Desert Rats. The name seemed more appropriate as

Miranda grew older, more independent, more awkward, and more uncontrollable.

"It isn't just a question of position badges and detentions, or even of the smoking—it's her general attitude. We stress personal integrity here and we have to consider the other girls. Does she smoke at home, do you know?"

"Certainly not." James knew perfectly well that Monty's recent passion for long walks was entirely inspired by the fact that she could smoke undetected out-of-doors.

"We've had some long talks during the holidays, and Monty has promised to turn over a completely new leaf." He beamed with confidence, baring fine white teeth, one of which was chipped. "The smoking, this was just a youthful experiment, I'm sure you'll find." The smile widened and the lines that crisscrossed his otherwise boyish face deepened. Miss Sharpe smiled back. "Monty really lives for her music, and my wife and I are tremendously appreciative of everything you've done for her here. I'm sure you will have every reason to be proud of her. She's quite determined to make a new start." Like all successful seducers, James's blandishing sincerity was due to the fact that he believed every word he said at the time he said it, and Miss Sharpe's shrewd schoolmistress's sense about difficult girls was overwhelmed.

"I've been meaning to congratulate you on your Oxford and Cambridge results," he went on. "You must be very pleased. I think Cathy's rather looking forward to the sixth form."

"Will she be considering university?" The annual tragedy of Miss Sharpe's life was that the parents of so many of her competent girls took them away from the school at fifteen or sixteen and sent them to finishing schools or tossed them into the debutante season, considering any proof of intellect as at best irrelevant and at worst something more damaging to the girl's marriage prospects than congenital insanity. Like many of her staff, Miss Sharpe would have been married herself if her fiancé had not died in the war. Her career was a forced choice, and she was in no position to argue with her girls' parents.

"We'll leave university up to her—I think that's wisest, don't you? I see you've started work on the new house—how *is* the appeal going?" James was subtly reminding Miss Sharpe that his contribution to the fund-raising had been handsome and early, allowing her to approach other parents with a high benchmark to indicate the size of donation required.

Such generosity was to be expected of a man of Lord Bourton's means and social position, but its rewards were expected too and with Monty under threat of expulsion, this was an expedient moment to solicit the school's gratitude.

Having accomplished this delicate negotiation with his usual panache, James stepped out and into the Bentley and ordered his driver to take him on to London, leaving Miss Sharpe with the afterglow of his smile and a sense of obligation toward both his daughters.

"God—another term in this bloody hellhole!" Monty flopped down on her bed with a screech of springs, and scowled across the stack of luggage at the two girls who shared her dormitory. One of Benenden's idiosyncrasies was that girls were quartered in small dormitories of three or four, and their ages were mixed, so now the fifteen-year-old Monty found herself billeted with Frances Graham, the timid twelve-year-old daughter of the British ambassador in Helsinki, and Camilla Carstairs, a devastatingly pretty blonde who was school captain of lacrosse, the apple of the English mistress's eye, and the daughter of a judge.

"Do you have to swear?" Camilla demanded in her strangled drawl.

Monty ignored her.

"Whose is all this stuff?" Monty pointed at six pieces of matching white leather luggage stacked higgledy-piggledy by the unoccupied bed.

"The new girl's, I suppose." Camilla took her brown canvas lacrosse boots, temporarily clean of the mud that would cake their studded soles for the rest of the term, out of her much-mended case and slung them into the bottom of her cupboard.

Most of the girls at Benenden had luggage that was good quality but old, handed down by their parents. The heap of white cases, however, obviously belonged to the girl herself. Each gleaming side was embossed with the gilded initials R.E.E.

Monty sauntered across the room and ran her finger over the monogram on the smallest case.

"Her parents must be loaded."

"Of course they're loaded; they're Jewish. Don't you remember Miss Sharpe giving us a pi-jaw about her at the end of last term?" Swallow Lamotte, skinny and tousle-haired with thick lips like a goldfish, came in and sat on Monty's bed.

"They own half of P and G, don't they?" Pearce & Goldsmith, or P & G for short, was a rapidly growing chain store selling cheap, serviceable clothes of such remarkable quality, considering their price, that every woman in Britain was said to wear their panties. At that moment Camilla was putting a stack of six pristine white pairs of the P & G knickers into a drawer beside her thick blue school-regulation briefs.

"She won't be short on knickers anyway. Did you bring any chocolate?" Swallow rummaged in Monty's tuck box.

The porter struggled through the doorway with the last and largest of the white cases. Monty lethargically snapped open her own case, a scuffed pigskin legacy from James, and began stuffing away her clothes.

"Why are they making such a fuss about her anyway? She can't be any different from the rest of us." She tossed her newly acquired black stockings onto a high shelf, followed by the ferocious girdle that held them up. It was a surgical grayish white, with a flat satin panel in front and wide flanges of rubbery elastic around the sides. Monty was grateful for the way it flattened the obstinate curve of her stomach, but loathed the way it imprinted hideous red weals on her body. To add what the manufacturer hoped was a feminine touch, the suspenders were veiled with scraps of satin ribbon, which frayed unattractively.

"I see your mother bought you a bra at last." Swallow opened a packet of biscuits.

"She made enough fuss about it." Monty showed them the heavy contraption, which, she hoped, flattened her breasts back to nothing.

"She's the first Jewish girl they've had since the war, and they're afraid she'll be bullied—that's why they're making all this fuss." Camilla closed her suitcase and pushed it under her bed, then dragged her trunk toward her and began opening its brass locks. Inside were books, supplies of jam and chocolate, and the filthy one-eared teddy bear she placed proudly in the center of her pillow. "She's seeing the housemistress now and I've got to go and fetch her at half past and show her around." Vigorously, Camilla brushed specks of fluff off the long navy cape the girls wore outdoors in winter, and hung it on the rail of her washing cubicle.

"Look here, Monty, this won't do at all," she said with irritation. "I'm dormitory monitor, I'm responsible for keeping the place decent and I'm not having you turn it into a pigsty on the first day of term. You can jolly well take all those down again and fold them up neatly." She pointed at the crumpled mass of shirts, vests, and underwear in Monty's cupboard.

With bad grace, Monty pulled down the mass of tangled clothes and began folding each garment as slowly as she could.

"Camilla, why do they think she'll be bullied because she's Jewish?"

"Some people are a bit funny about Jews, that's all."

"But why—Hitler hated the Jews and we fought Hitler, so why do we hate the Jews too?"

"We don't. They've just come over here from Europe and made a lot of money and some people don't like it, that's all."

"But if they were going to be put in concentration camps to die it was sensible to come over here, surely?" Monty knew perfectly well what Camilla was going to say next; she was hoping that by spinning out the conversation she could postpone the job of tidying her cupboard. The plan worked. Camilla suddenly checked her watch and jumped up.

"Cripes—I'll be late!" She sprinted off down the corridor on solidly muscled legs.

Swallow pulled back Camilla's bedcovers and sprinkled some biscuit crumbs between the sheets.

"Sweet dreams, Sergeant Major," she said, punching the teddy bear in its stomach.

Monty shoved her clothes back and wondered what the new girl would be like. She didn't know any Jewish people, or anything about them, except what she'd read in English lessons with *The Merchant of Venice* or history lessons with Disraeli buying the Suez Canal with the Rothschilds' money. All Monty really knew about Jewish people was that they were different, and she knew, too, that she was different; she was beginning to look on herself as a lonely, misunderstood figure, forever alienated from quiet, sleek-haired girls like Camilla or Cathy, whose souls were as well ordered as their cupboards, with no tangled masses of doubt shoved away out of sight.

It was easy for the other girls to keep to the stupid school rules, to be quiet, tidy, hardworking and obedient, but Monty found all that impossible. The rules were stupid, and the teachers were too, and what was the point of tidiness as long as you could find your clothes when you needed them?

Half an hour later Camilla returned, bringing with her the Jewish girl.

"This is Rosanna Emanuel," she said formally, as Monty and Swallow looked up.

"How do you do." Rosanna advanced and shook hands with each of them in turn, stepping around her white mountain of luggage as she went. Her whole face was fine and delicate, with a fierce beauty which made Camilla's Anglo-Saxon prettiness look suddenly insipid. Her hair was curly like Disraeli's, and the weight of it was drawn into a ponytail of glossy ringlets, while curly tendrils framed her face.

Her clothes, however, were unlike anything that Monty, Camilla or Swallow had ever imagined. They watched in fascination as Rosanna methodically opened her cases and took possession of the modest allocation of space Benenden offered each student.

From the biggest case came an immaculate array of school uniforms, altered by her mother's dressmaker to fit and flatter. In fact, when Monty looked closely, she saw that the plain navy pinafore was of fine wool gabardine instead of the standard-issue serge from Debenham and Freebody. Rosanna had brought crisp white poplin blouses for every day of the week, and these too had been made for her.

The next case held her cape and "flaps"—an immense circular skirt in the house color, which was worn for the weekly dancing class. Never had Guldeford orange seemed so bright.

"Do we really have to wear these?" she asked Monty, holding up the hideous jelly-bag hat that went with the outdoor cape. Monty nodded.

Next came the velvet dress the girls wore for church on Sundays. This had a half train at the back, and a silk collar. The dresses came in harsh blue, red or green, and most girls had only one. Rosanna had three, one in each color, and the hues were considerably more subtle.

All in all, Rosanna's uniform was perfectly in accordance with the school list, but not quite right. It was better. According to the arcane conventions of the British upper class, better was wrong.

"Did you get all that at Debenham and Freebody?" Swallow asked out of curiosity.

"Oh, no—we hated their things. Mummy bought one of everything and then gave them to her dressmaker to copy. Where do we put empty cases?"

"Under the bed. You can put some of yours under mine if you like." Monty swung aside her legs and drew up her bedcover.

"That's *terribly* kind of you."

It was all wrong—not as wrong as it would have been if Rosanna could not have been expected to know any better, if her father were a workman or a foreigner or something. It was wrong because one shouldn't say "dressmaker" but talk about "this little woman who makes my mother's frocks"; neither should one display emotion, even a mild emotion such as gratitude. "Terribly kind" was incorrect. The right way was to mutter "thanks" and get on with unpacking. It was wrong to be effusive, wrong to exaggerate, wrong to mind so much how you looked that you took care and spent a lot of money and were not ashamed to say so.

Monty, Swallow and Camilla had been brought up in the curious way the English aristocracy raised their children. All but their most basic needs were ignored until they were old enough to be mated.

They had eaten in the kitchen or the nursery with their nannies, seldom in the dining room with their parents; they had been dressed in ugly, practical clothes, some of which were expensive, but none of which were stylish or pretty. Vanity was discouraged as an unnecessary vice, and in some nurseries looking in the mirror was not allowed. There was no question of girls wearing what they wanted; they had to have roomy, heavy shoes, stout tweed skirts and shapeless, heavy coats.

For entertainment they were simply turfed out-of-doors, and for company they had been left to their parents' servants. The girls were encouraged to lavish their emotions on dogs and ponies, thus ensuring that boys and sex were excluded from their interests.

At the age of seventeen these ugly, gauche grubs would be brought indoors, washed, taught the rudiments of social skills, kitted out in adult finery, told that they were butterflies and released to mate in the desperately short debutante season, after which their parents would give them no more money or attention.

"When are you going to wear *that* for?" asked Camilla with a sneer. Rosanna hung up a full-skirted, strapless cocktail dress of black grosgrain.

"The opera. My father's coming to take me to the opera on my first weekend out. Mummy's sure I'm going to be terribly homesick."

"Gosh, you lucky thing." Now Monty was frankly envious. "I've never been to an opera. Is it nice?"

"Some of it is. I like Mozart best, but the singers are all so fat and ugly that I usually end up watching with my eyes shut." Monty laughed, the others did not.

"And is that your fiddle?" Monty indicated the black violin case, the only item among Rosanna's luggage which was not spanking new.

"Well, sort of. I'm not terribly good. I don't practice enough." Rosanna stowed another empty case under Monty's bed and turned to the next full one, which contained only her underwear, packed in crisp sheets of blue-white tissue paper.

First came knitted wool vests and long matching camiknickers, trimmed with pink lace.

Swallow snorted. "You'll certainly need *them*."

"Is it *very* cold here?" Rosanna's eyes widened, fearful of discomfort.

"Bloody arctic," Monty confirmed.

"And is there a lot of lacrosse? We didn't play games much at my last school."

"You haven't missed a thing, I promise. We've got lacrosse every day this term. It's called lax, actually, not lacrosse."

Rosanna smiled, grateful for this tiny measure of initiation into the school customs. "Does everybody have to play?"

"Everybody. Camilla's the school captain. They let you off if you're injured though."

"What about if you're having a bad period—I have awful periods, absolute agony and they go on for days."

"No good, they still flog you out into the mud."

Rosanna shuddered and put away three matching sets of white-lace French brassieres, panties and garter belts. The brassieres were daringly wired to make her already full breasts look even more luscious, and had pink satin rosebuds with green satin leaves sewn between the cups.

Next out of the case was a long white-lace corselette, with bones from breast to hip level and dangling suspenders.

"Gosh, that's *beautiful*. I've never seen anything like that except on Brigitte Bardot posters." Monty fingered the outrageously adult garment gingerly. "Are you really going to wear it?"

"Of course I am, I need it. I've got a horribly fat stomach and no waist at all." Rosanna pulled in her uniform to show them.

By the time the supper bell rang at 7:30, Rosanna had also unpacked thick black stockings of pure silk, not of itchy cotton like Monty's, and an ivory-handled manicure set in a white-leather case. In her washing cubicle was her pure bristle toothbrush and a tiny tube of red toothpaste, which was supposed to make her teeth sparkle. Across the grayish-yellow candlewick bedspread lay a thick red merino dressing gown and a Swiss-cotton nightdress.

Camilla treated each item as a personal insult. Swallow sulked with jealousy. Monty felt as if someone had raised the corner of the dust sheet which had been draped over her future to hide it.

They trooped down to the oak-paneled dining hall, each girl carrying her own napkin in a napkin ring. In keeping with the rest of their possessions, the Benenden girls' napkins were frayed damask squares belonging to long worn-out sets of their parents' table linen, and they were rolled lopsidedly into rings of painted wood or scratched horn.

Miss Sharpe was clearing her throat to say grace as Monty and Rosanna slipped into the last two places at their table.

"Per Jesum Christum Dominum nostrum," she finished, as, one by one, the pupils standing with bowed heads stole furtive glances at the new girl.

Rosanna's napkin was of new Irish linen, with an elaborately embroidered R in one corner. Her napkin ring, on which her initials were engraved, was thick and heavy, and it gleamed with the unmistakable soft intensity of solid silver.

There was a hostile silence at Rosanna's table as the other girls appraised her prettiness, her elegance and her obvious wealth.

"I say," brayed a voice from the table's end, "I thought all Jews had *horns*."

Rosanna looked up and smiled.

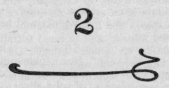

2

Every marriage has a secret contract between wife and man which has nothing to do with any of the purposes of matrimony set out in the prayer book. The unwritten contract between James Bourton's parents required his father to provide the means for his mother to satisfy her ambitions. She wanted to be a great society beauty around whose feet the most powerful men in the country would grovel in adoration.

Since love affairs were the prerogative of married people, Lady Davina chose her husband without delay. The young Duke of Witherham could also give her everything else she needed—entrée to court circles, political contacts, several impressive houses and the wealth to create a lavish backdrop for her personal pageant. She swiftly overpowered him with a barrage of flattery and flirtation, which he accepted as no more than his due.

After their marriage, however, Davina discovered that her husband would not fulfill his part of the matrimonial bargain because he did not understand it; he had no appreciation of the importance of flowers, jewels, love letters and clandestine trysts which would be common knowledge from Piccadilly to Kensington the next day. He rightly assumed that his wife had no intention of rejecting him, his wealth and his title, and was therefore deeply puzzled when she solicited the advances of other men. He did not realize that his wife was an ambitious but cowardly woman who was unable to seek fulfilment outside the traditional arena of feminine manipulation.

The women in her circle understood perfectly the kind of supremacy Davina was trying to establish, and, like her, they counterattacked in the same style, with more outrageous clothes, more notorious exploits and more scandalous liaisons.

The duke turned mulish, and rejected socializing in London for the enjoyment of his country estates. Davina detested the country. She became cold and waspish, and embroiled herself in refitting his country seat, Bourton House, at terrifying expense.

When his wife pressured him toward public life, the duke resisted. With the perverse cunning of a man who chooses to escape his wife's dominion by assuming dullness, he scotched her ambitions by sticking at the social level of a country squire. When she began to launch herself at their male weekend guests in a flurry of seductive sweet talk, he took it as permission to begin an affair with the wife of the local hunt master.

To these injuries, the insult of James was added on a blustery autumn afternoon in 1926. Davina had been convinced that her second child would be a girl. Her Grace at once directed that her second son be dressed in petticoats, and referred to him thereafter as Jane. From the cradle, James Bourton's sexuality was warped.

"I shan't waste any more time having children," Davina told her husband. "We shall just have to make do with what we've got. I've far more important things to think of than babies." She never considered divorce; divorced women were not received at Court. Divorce was for Americans. Davina was determined to shine in society in spite of her husband.

Lord James Bourton joined his brother, Hugo, the three-year-old Marquess of St. Elians, in the nursery, where he was highly popular. As a baby he was plump and smiling; as a toddler he was an irresistible little animal, winning all kinds of concessions from the nurserymaids with his sweet ways.

As a small boy, with a gold watch chain gleaming across the little waistcoat he could wear when his mother was absent, he was the personification of masculinity in miniature, and the stolid Hugo watched with envy as James was bounced and tickled and drawn into romps which grew increasingly less innocent. Virginity was something he never knew about until many years after his own had been debauched by a succession of bored, simpleminded servant girls.

The nannies—and there were so many of them, the two boys could never remember any by name—were tyrannized by Davina, who would descend from London with an avalanche of petty impositions.

"Hugo must always wear green, it suits his complexion," she

would command, "and the children must learn Italian! I shall take them to Venice in the spring." Then she might light on some extravagance. "Why on earth is the nursery fire so high! Are you trying to burn the house down, Nanny? No more than *one* bucket of coals a day, if you please."

Stinginess was followed by generosity. "Nanny, your hands are simply blue with cold. Ask my maid for my old muff as soon as we get back." In another two days, she would forget, and accuse the bewildered servant of having stolen the muff, often in vulgar terms that advertised the blatant greed of her own nature.

Davina, Duchess of Witherham, could never get enough of anything that gave a woman status. She pestered her lovers for flowers and her husband for jewels, wrecked the estate's accounts by requisitioning sums for a swimming pool or a rose arbor, stuffed whole rooms with clothes which she seldom felt flattered her enough. She bought hunters which she could not ride and took lavish holidays in Europe on which she inevitably fell ill, saw nothing and was a whining burden to her companions.

Most of all, she could not get enough of men. Without her husband, the highest echelons of society were closed to her. Instead she joined the vivid coterie of adventuresses around the Prince of Wales. Denied fame, she chose notoriety. Other bright young things might dance on the tables at the Embassy Club, but Davina was to be found underneath, enjoying her latest conquest with insufficiently stifled sounds. One bold man who refused her at the last fence half died of shame when she bit off his fly buttons. It was rumored that at her bedside she kept a silver sugar shaker filled with cocaine, which she sprinkled on her lovers' erections to make them last longer.

When Davina heard this story she played it up to the hilt, carrying a tiny sugar shaker in her purse; most important to her was not to make love, but to be seen as desirable—was not that the greatest tribute a woman could collect?

For a great beauty, Davina was entirely her own invention. She demanded that Cecil Beaton photograph her; the session was lengthy and unsuccessful. "You can't catch the beauty of a woman's soul if she hasn't got one," he said afterward.

Without her repertoire of erotic blandishments she was nothing but a woman with thin brown hair and muddy green eyes, the size of whose hips was accentuated by the swaybacked stance she imagined was regal posture. She had fine breasts in the twenties, when it was fashionable to be flat chested, and by the early thirties, when a soft swelling below the crepe de chine was again fashionable, her bosom had deflated. Nature, at least, would not be ordered to her own ends.

She looked upon her sons as merely two more males whose sexuality could be turned to her advantage. She conducted coquettish inquiries into the progress of their adolescence. Hugo, a naturally prudish creature, found her embarrassing before he was old enough to know why.

James, as an infant, offered her the purest love she would ever inspire. His earliest memory was of standing in adoration beside his mother's dressing table, handing her maid the hairpins as she dressed Her Grace's hair around her glittering tiara. He was about four years old, and if her lovers had noticed a slight wattling of the skin of her eyelids, she was still as beautiful as a goddess to her younger son.

Hypnotized with wonder, James reached up to touch the tiara, and his mother, infuriated, seized a pin from the maid and stabbed it into her son's pudgy hand, then ordered the nursemaid to remove him and pulled her silken skirts away from the bleeding child. James never felt safe with a woman again.

When he was about to go to Eton, Davina ordered his hair to be cut and had him dressed as a boy at last. She then noticed that her younger son had a great deal of charm and worshiped her as lavishly as her adorable new Pomeranian puppy.

Eton, like most other great British boys' schools in the thirties, was an all-male community with a hierarchy of sexual domination like that of a troop of baboons. The older boys buggered the younger boys to reinforce their authority. The juniors were required to act as servants to the older boys to make their submission formal.

James, good-looking, good-natured and piquantly manly even at the age of thirteen, caused quite a stir. He had no fear of his own sex, and promptly escaped into an affair with Cosmo Flett, a cultivated senior boy who was unpopular because of his brains and ugliness. Cosmo protected him, read him poetry, and got a broken nose in the cause of defending their love, after which they were left alone.

In the vacations, however, there was no escape from the hall of mirrors that forever disorients young men of precocious sexual allure and stunted emotional growth. His mother was always waiting for him, with presents, new clothes, and teasing compliments.

"My gorgeous boy," she murmured, messing his dark hair. "I'm too, too jealous of you with all your little friends. Won't you keep your poor mother company just a tiny bit?"

He was paraded through her London life of nightclubs and

cocktail parties almost as a proof of her desirability, as if to show her disenchanted lovers that she deserved only young flesh of the standard she herself had created.

This period of favor ended sharply when James fell deep in calf love with one of his mother's friends, a pale plump woman of forty who hung on his arm, squeezing herself against his awkward elbow and making knowing, I-can't-help-myself eyes at all their acquaintances.

Furious at this double betrayal, Davina raged at the woman, who crumpled before a social *force majeure* and went back to her husband.

James, who had believed himself truly in the grip of romantic passion, stayed in bed at Bourton House for a month, then made a clumsy attempt to shoot himself, blistering the newly painted library ceiling with lead pellets. His mother was briefly concerned, which restored his cheerfulness.

James was young, healthy, sensual and driven by an obscure anxiety about women. However, the more time he spent in female company the more he grew aware of the power of his charm, and he began to use it.

His seductions were initiated by a desperate feeling that a woman was "safe" only if she was squirming helplessly beneath him, gasping that she loved him and begging to do whatever he wanted. Out of bed he was often petulant and jealous, quick to suspect unfaithfulness and eager to make love again to obliterate the suspicion.

He got engaged, then broke it off cruelly, and the duke ordered his newly notorious younger son back to Bourton House, where the housemaids squabbled for the honor of taking up his morning tea. James was becoming more and more attractive to women as hard muscles filled out his small, slim frame and his dark spaniel's eyes learned to plead from below his tousled forelock.

Soon there were a jealous footman and a pregnant housemaid to marry off hastily, and Davina, still seething with rejection, began to demand that James be banished. Hugo, his older brother, whose temperament was placid and pompous, supported her; and James sealed his own fate by paying marked attention to his father's mistress.

His mother maneuvered him toward the army, but James stubbornly resisted. She launched half a dozen different schemes to find him posts in America, India or Australia. He conspired with Cosmo, now a Cambridge undergraduate with remarkable contacts, to have himself rejected by the Foreign Office.

Malaya was James's own idea; he had no idea where it was, but it was somewhere of which his mother had not thought.

"I had an interview yesterday," he announced to his astonished family one Saturday at breakfast. "And I've been offered a job."

"Marvelous, darling." His mother spoke in the threatening tone of voice with which she greeted all bids for independence among her menfolk.

"Exactly what kind of fool has decided to employ you?" asked his father, piling his plate with slabs of ham.

"The fool who is recruiting staff for the Hong Kong and Shanghai Bank." James buttered a piece of toast with precision.

"Does he know you can't add up for toffee?" Hugo's habitual jealousy of his brother had darkened a shade.

"He doesn't seem worried about that. All they did was give me a hearing test to see if I'd be able to understand Chinese. They said I came out of it rather well."

His father grunted as he sat down. "We'd better be grateful there's something you can do, I suppose."

Davina commanded the table's attention with a raised voice. "You can't *possibly* go to a country like that, James. There's a civil war and pirates and heaven knows what. The disease! And the East is an absolute *sink* of iniquity."

"Certainly hope so," James murmured, reaching for the marmalade. "You're quite wrong, Mother," he continued, applying a generous coating of the dark-brown conserve to his toast. "There hasn't been any civil war since Malaya became a British protectorate, in 18 . . . er, well, a long time ago."

"Tosh," pronounced his brother, asserting his challenged superiority. "Own up—you haven't a clue where you're going."

"Don't you bet on it. Malaya is a pear-shaped peninsula slightly smaller than the American state of Florida, which lies to the south of Siam." James rattled on through the information on the mimeographed sheet provided by the Hong Kong and Shanghai Bank. "The country produces half the total world production of tin and four fifths of the total world production of rubber. On the ancient trading routes linking East and West, it is the meeting place of many races where men of all complexions live as friends. Eighty percent of the country is covered with jungle and . . ." At last he paused; the only remaining fact about his destination which he could remember was that there were over two hundred species of dragonfly there.

"You're *completely* mad," interjected his mother. "You haven't the faintest notion of what you're doing. I shall telephone this bank tomorrow and tell them you've changed your mind."

"Leave the boy alone," his father broke in with unusual ferocity. "Let him go to hell his own way. There's damn all he can do around here. At least he's shown initiative."

"I simply thought he might be better off somewhere more civilized. . . ." his mother's voice trailed into an aggrieved silence.

"What are you going to do, anyway?" Hugo was anxious to have the business settled and his distracting brother out of the way.

James bit off the corner of his laden toast with his fine large teeth, and swallowed it almost whole. "I haven't the foggiest idea," he told them.

Despite his bravado in front of his family, James felt nervous about traveling halfway around the world to a new life in a country that was little more than a name to him. When he returned to London he went to the Botanical Gardens at Kew, and walked in wonder from the cool house to the temperate house to the subtropical house until finally he stood below the soaring palms of the largest, hottest, most humid greenhouse of all and looked at a small tree with feathery green leaves before which stood a plaque inscribed FEDERATED MALAY STATES. Beside this tree was a banana plant.

The greenhouse was murmuring with the sounds of water, which dripped incessantly from a million leaves and trickled away under the wrought-iron covers of the drainage channels. James felt his shirt stick to his back and a collar of perspiration form around his neck. This sample of the environment that lay ahead of him acted as a solemn reassurance that he was making a wise decision.

Two weeks later, with a steel-lined trunk containing eighteen stiff shirts, thirty-six stiff collars, a solar topee and a padded jacket designed to protect his spine from the burning tropic sun, James embarked on the P & O liner at Southampton with a sense of release that was the nearest thing to total ecstacy that he had ever experienced.

George Town, the colonial capital of Penang island, delighted him as much as if it had been a toy town arranged entirely for his amusement. The gray stone fort, with its guns pointing seaward, made him imagine distant junks loaded with Arab pirates heaving over the shimmering horizon.

In the solid buildings of the commercial district he felt the pulse of international trade, and saw himself as an intrepid agent of enterprise. He took a rickshaw down Pitt Street and was thrilled at the sight of the Chinese temples belching clouds of incense, the Indian temple painted in pastel colors like a vast ice-cream cassata, and the food hawkers selling green coconuts or tiny kebabs grilled on charcoal braziers.

Even the town clock enchanted him, with its pompous Victorian architecture embellished with Oriental stone fins painted a vivid orange. The exotica of the natives enthralled him; the savagery implicit in the town exhilarated him. The sobriety required by his new profession was a welcome yoke. James felt that at last he was living real life.

At the bank, he supervised a room full of Chinese clerks twice his age. At first he was well thought of, not least because he had an ear for the subtle tones of Oriental languages, and could soon talk enough Cantonese to converse with the clerks in detail.

Within six months, however, nemesis caught up with him.

"Bourton, you have done well, and I don't want you to think we aren't pleased with you," began his supervisor, perspiring in the afternoon heat in the ovenlike office on Queen Street. "But we can't have our chaps getting married the minute they come out."

"I'm not getting married, sir."

"Well, then what the devil are you playing at?" James was genuinely perplexed. He knew, of course, that it was a condition of his employment that he should remain unmarried for his first four years in the East.

The custom, he soon discovered, was for the young British bank employees to work a lot, exhaust themselves in sport, and make forays among the Chinese prostitutes who waited patiently in rickshaws by the port. At the end of their first tour, the men took a six-month vacation in England, in which time the more personable ones would succeed in getting engaged. The poorer, shyer and less good-looking ones would have to wait another four years, for their second long leave. James, eager to do well in his new life, had behaved with perfect propriety and was conducting a chaste romance with a girl called Lucy Kennedy, whose father was a senior civil servant.

"I'm sorry, sir, I don't know what all this is about."

"You've been seeing a great deal of Lucy Kennedy; you don't deny that, I suppose."

"No, sir, of course not. She's a very sweet girl."

"Sweet she may be, but she's putting it about that you're engaged. Where d'you suppose she came by that idea?"

"Honestly, sir, I swear I've never mentioned anything of the sort to her."

His supervisor, a pale Scot with the exhausted look white men of long residence in the tropics often acquire, questioned James's sincerity with washed-out blue eyes before giving a grudging grunt of satisfaction.

"I believe you're telling the truth, but you'd better find Miss Kennedy and get to the bottom of this smartly before I have her father to reckon with. The bank is one of the biggest British establishments in the East, people look to us as an example, and we can't have a pipsqueak like you muddying the water."

"Look here, Lucy," James said awkwardly, stumbling over a fallen palm frond as they walked in the garden of her father's white-pillared mansion, "have you said anything about us?"

"Oh, don't be angry, James, I only told Mummy, I was so excited I had to tell someone." She skipped with happiness at his side.

"But Lucy, there's nothing to tell."

Doubt suddenly fogged her adoring long-lashed eyes. Her plump lower lip quivered and she pulled nervously at her neatly marceled silver-blond bob. "What do you mean, there's nothing to tell?"

James stopped walking and took her hands. "I can't get engaged, Lucy, you know that."

"But you asked me, James." Huge tears suddenly appeared in the corners of her gray eyes.

"Lucy, I swear, I never asked you. There's nothing further from my mind, I promise you."

"But don't you love me, James?" Tears were now pouring freely down her plump cheeks. In another anguished ten minutes the mystery was solved. The previous Saturday James had taken her to the weekly dance at the E & O Hotel, and at the end of the evening they had walked out on the stonewalled terrace above the sea, listening to the soothing splash of the waves and the crickets chirruping in the coconut palms.

"I do love the East, Lucy, don't you?" he had said taking a deep happy breath of the fragrant air. "I shouldn't mind if I stayed here the rest of my life." And Lucy had squeaked delightedly and planted a wet kiss on his uncomprehending cheek. To a girl of seventeen with few brains and nothing but marriage on her mind, his idle words were a proposal.

Lucy howled and screamed and cried her eyes out, and her father angrily attacked James's supervisor, who defended James as firmly as he could without implying that the girl was an idiot.

James, thoroughly frightened, swore to himself that he would not go near a white girl again for the rest of his four years. He drank a great deal of whiskey, played rugger and cricket and a great many games of billiards at the Penang Club and sobered up with long tramps in the cool jungle-covered mountainside reached by a rachet railway from the town.

His luck did not hold. He lodged in a small villa with three other boys from the "Honkers and Shankers."

Next door lived a lanky Eurasian woman, half Russian and half Thai, who was married to the Dutch purser on one of the steamships that shuttled up and down the Straits of Malacca between Penang in the north and Singapore Island in the south. She was bored, lonely and often drunk while her husband was away, though when he returned to their yellow-painted Chinese house they had screaming arguments that sent the chickens in the garden squawking for hiding places.

One evening the four young Englishmen were sitting at their dinner table, gently stupefied with heat, food and drink. The Eurasian woman appeared at their door in a crumpled pink-silk peignoir with a half-drunk bottle of brandy in hand. She sat on the table, began slurring and hiccupping through her life history, then collapsed face down in a plate of melted ice cream.

The four eighteen-year-olds, thoroughly drilled in their duty to see a lady home, rose shakily and carried her around to her door, at which instant her husband returned. The woman's eyes flickered open and she accused the boys of raping her, speaking in Dutch, which they did not understand. The Dutchman stomped into his house, came out with a pistol and fired wildly, wounding one of James's companions.

The police were called and the next morning James was once again protesting his innocence to his supervisor, who shook his head.

"I'm sorry, Bourton, there's nothing I can do. A scandal like this is something the bank will not tolerate. You know damn well it's your duty to observe decent social standards and maintain the reputation of the white man in the community. You'll have to go, I'm afraid. You'll get three months' pay and you'll have to ship home in four weeks or pay your own passage."

"If I decide to stay, sir . . ."

The older man interrupted him with rough sympathy. "If you decide to stay, you'll have a devil of a job finding anyone to take you on, at least in Penang. You might get a civil-service job if you got your father to pull strings for you in London, but you've blotted your copybook pretty thoroughly and you can't expect promotion until you've lived all this down."

James's pleasant features looked as miserable as was possible, and his shoulders hunched unhappily inside his white shirt.

"Don't want to go home, is that it?"

"Not much, sir."

"Got a taste for the East, is that it? Well, if you think you could stand more, you could get yourself taken on at a rubber estate. Nobody gives a damn what you get up to out in the jungle."

A week later a note was delivered to James suggesting that he meet a Mr. C. Douglas Lovell at 6:00 P.M. at the Criterion Tiffin and Billiard Rooms on Beach Street. He found a tall man with thick white hair and moustache taking bets with two Chinese businessmen on the last frame of their game.

"Boy—stengah for my young friend here. Be with you in a moment, laddie, just a bit of business to attend to." He prowled smoothly to the end of the table, lined up the shot through half-closed eyes, and briskly sent the balls clicking toward their pockets. The "boy," a sixty-year-old Chinese with skin the color of a finnan haddock, brought James his stengah, a small whiskey well diluted with water. Lovell collected a handful of dollars from each businessman, the three men bowed to each other, and he joined James at the bar.

"Chap at Honkers and Shankers tells me you've had a spot of bother."

"You could say that, sir."

"Makes two of us. One of my chaps popped his clogs last week. Cerebral malaria, pretty vile way to go." He gulped down half his stengah. "Not afraid of hard work, are you?"

"No, sir." James's leaden mood began to lift.

"Well, you'd better be telling the truth. I don't employ any idle blue bloods on my estate. You'll be up at five every day of the week, including Sunday. Highest-paid form of unskilled labor, my rubber assistants. You'll get one hundred fifty dollars a month plus another ten if you can pass the Tamil exam—got an ear for languages, I'm told."

"They do seem to come easily to me, sir. Where exactly is your estate?"

"Take a day—best way, steamer to Port Swettenham, train through Kuala Lumpur and then it's about an hour. They've promised us a road next year but I'll believe it when I see it. We've got our own club, our own billiard table and you get two free days a month if you want to go down to KL and beat it up. What do you say?"

James was torn between the feeling that he wanted to be at the heart of the country and know the mysteries of the misty jungle-covered hills of the mainland, and the recognition that a rubber planter was looked upon as something of a social misfit.

Although at home he had had no contact with the kind of people who were in trade, and was therefore blithely unaware of the professions which could be considered suitable for a gentleman and those which represented a definite loss of social status, he had heard men at the club talk about rubber planters disparagingly. "The kind of man that marries a barmaid" was the judgment on the white men, mostly British, who marshaled thousands of Asiatics to tap millions of trees to stack the dockside at Penang with neatly packaged bales of latex sheets awaiting shipment to America and Europe.

Douglas Lovell, however, did not look like the kind of man who married a barmaid; his commanding bearing and clipped speech said "army" as clearly as a uniform. James liked his directness and felt the lure of the unknown East call him like a mermaid's song. Only a vague premonition of his parents' disapproval held him back.

"Look, young man," Douglas Lovell spoke in an unexpectedly quiet voice, "you won't get a better offer. I'd heard the story of that Dutchman's wife from three separate people before I'd left KL. I don't doubt it sounded ten times worse than it was, but the point is you're finished out here in the kind of job you came out to do."

"I know that, sir, but it's not fair. It was all a put-up job. . . ."

The older man cut him short with an irritated wave of his glass. "Life's not fair, my boy, and the trick of it is to be in the position to be able to say what's fair and what's not for the other poor buggers, instead of having to take another man's justice. I make the rules of my estate, and I don't give a damn what you get up to as long as we meet our latex quota and the coolies don't shit on the road. Now, d'you want a job or don't you?"

James made up his mind in a rush, swallowing a sense of offense at the implication that he would welcome a relaxed moral climate. "Yes, sir, I do want it."

"Good. I'm told your family have a bob or two but somehow I didn't think you were the type to be a remittance man." James was flattered, puzzled and startled as the older man put out his hand to shake on the deal.

"May I ask what a remittance man is?"

"Young fool shipped out East by the family to save them further embarrassment, spends his allowance on opium and taxi dancers and dies young. Buried one once, found him dead in a shack on the edge of the jungle. Took three months to get the body identified. You're not that type. Ask too many questions."

James was indeed quivering with curiosity about every corner of the thrilling new world for which he departed the next day. With his new job he acquired a tin-roofed bungalow built on stilts, on the edge of virgin jungle. At noon the silence was so profound he felt he could hear the vast primeval forest grow. All day moisture dripped from green leaves and shifting mists mantled the ancient treetops. There was a clean, earthy smell. When he was on his own under the green canopy, James felt as pure as Adam on his own in the Garden of Eden.

3

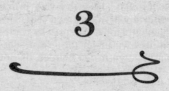

"WAIT FOR ME!" CALLED ROSANNA, RUNNING UP THE AVENUE of lime trees. Cathy and Monty, swathed in their capes and scarves against the raw February cold, were tramping arm in arm ahead of her. Together, they stopped and turned, two figures dwarfed by the massive trees. Cathy, at five feet seven, inches taller than her sister by a generous handsbreadth, rubbed Monty's bare hands to warm them while they waited. Monty often forgot her gloves, no matter how cruel the weather.

"Hurry up, we're freezing," she yelled in the teeth of the blustering wind. Rosanna, brown curls tangled, caught up with both sisters and pulled a sheaf of magazines from under her cloak.

"I've got *Swoon, Honey, True Romance* and *Teengirl.*"

"Fab. Let's get inside before we freeze to death."

In the years to come, the first thing all three of them would remember about Benenden was the cold. Icy winds from Central Europe blew over the flat Kent fields and scoured the school grounds unmercifully, chilling the red-brick buildings.

In the winter mornings the tip of Rosanna's nose would hurt with the cold, Cathy's toes would be blue and Monty would lie like a corpse under her bedclothes trying to conserve the pitiful glow of her body warmth in the clammy chill of the sheets.

Rosanna returned from the Christmas holidays with fur slippers and a thick pink cashmere blanket, which she added to the permitted quota of coverings on her bed with considerable guilt. Unlike Cathy and Monty, she had not been toughened by merciless English nannies and lectured about the virtue of sensual deprivation. Desperate as she was to fit in with the other girls, Rosanna drew the line at freezing half to death.

In every other way she tried as hard as she could to be exactly like the others. At breakfast she ate every scrap of bacon, conscious that other girls were watching her. At prayers in the chapel she could clearly be heard singing "There is room in my heart for Jesus." At Christmas, when there was a candle-lit carol service, followed by an ice-cream and treacle treat, Rosanna sang a solo.

At first Monty and Cathy were enthralled by Rosanna's wardrobe but slightly in awe of her. Rosanna, in turn, did not dare to dream of entering the charmed territory of the sisters' relationship. They were closer to each other than the most devoted friends, bound together by a deep emotion which was like a force field that repelled intruders. They had no particular favorites among their classmates, but spent all their free time in each other's company, talking for hours with such close rapport that their conversations seemed to be in a private dialect.

Sometimes they behaved as if they were a single person; if Monty was penalized for infringing school rules, Cathy would seem pained by the injustice; if Cathy collected a prize for her work, Monty would glow with pride.

A few days after Rosanna arrived, the two sisters united in sympathy for her against the subtle rejection of many of the other girls. They seemed to recognize a kindred spirit, and Monty, as always, acted for both of them and made the first move.

This show of conforming to an alien religion was something Rosanna put on almost by instinct. Her family came from the waves of Jewish immigrants who had fled persecution in Europe before the Second World War; her mother still spoke with a distinct Austrian accent. Their aim was to follow the Rothschilds, Prime Minister Disraeli and other ancient Jewish dynasties in Britain by seeming to be merely English people of Jewish extraction. A Jewish person should be no more conspicuous in the community than were the few acres of wheat which a great banking family reserved for the Chief Rabbi's Passover cakes in the midst of its country estate.

The only concession the school made to Rosanna's faith was allowing her to stay behind on Sunday when the other girls had to walk two miles to the village church. Even then, she was so eager to be the same as the others that she walked through the dank countryside with them, and went to the half-timbered news agent's shop to buy sweets and romance magazines while they attended the service.

They wore thick navy-blue bloomers, called "wovs," which did not quite cover their legs to the tops of their stockings, so throughout the long tramp, there was always a band of icy, naked, goose-pimpled flesh around their thighs.

"Come and join the madrigal society," Monty invited Rosanna abruptly. "I'm sick of being the only contralto who can sing in tune, and they won't let me be a soprano because there are too many of them already," she explained, half apologizing, wanting to say they wished to be friends but shy of making the commitment clear.

As the outcast and the rebel—for however hard she tried the other girls knew Rosanna was different and treated her with reserve—she and Monty were predestined friends. Their love of music settled the matter.

Rosanna was conscientious and quiet and the teachers approved of her; Cathy liked her because she was bright, and in the same classes as she was. Cathy had been feeling more and more isolated by the fact that the things other girls found hard she could do easily, and she was glad of companionship in the top grades. No one in the school could beat Cathy at mental arithmetic, but Rosanna came close.

The rest of the school did not openly reject their first Jewish companion, but they did not accept her either. No one walked with her to the village, offered to partner her in lacrosse or gave her a slice of their birthday cake. They treated her as good English girls treated any other embarrassment—as if she did not exist.

Halfway through the autumn term Swallow Lamotte was suddenly expelled. Monty came in from lacrosse one afternoon and found Swallow, red-faced and truculent, slamming clothes into her trunk. "Just remember, love—they can't actually *kill* you," she called defiantly to Monty as she ran downstairs to her father's car.

"But what did she *do*?" Rosanna asked Camilla in the darkness after lights out at 8:00 P.M. Even the girl who had talked to newspaper reporters about Princess Anne had not been expelled. Camilla knew but found she couldn't quite say the words. *"Elle n'est plus vierge,"* she whispered finally, and refused to say any more.

There was instantly a storm of speculation which roared through the upper school for days.

"But what did she actually *do*?"

"Who did she do it with, that's the point."

PEARLS

"Do you suppose it was—no, it couldn't have been." The Benenden community included only four men, an elderly physics teacher who scarcely counted as a member of the male sex, a young chaplain who played the guitar, with whom three quarters of the girls were in love, and the two plainclothes detectives who shadowed the little princess.

As to what Swallow might actually have done to cease being a virgin, they had no clear idea. Sex was a mystery to them, intriguing because it was forbidden, part of the unknown territory of maturity from which they were deliberately barred. Their biology lessons were evasive. Their schoolbooks were censored; even the word *breast* was expurgated from their editions of Shakespeare. Sex was taboo; romance was considered harmless.

By 4:00 P.M., the magazines had been read, swapped and exhausted, and the three girls drooped around the dormitory, suffering the excruciating boredom of the greenroom of womanhood.

"Do you think people *really* do things like this?" Monty thoughtfully reached for her contraband copy of *Lady Chatterley's Lover* with a frown. They had all read it, especially the page with the word *fuck* on it eight times. They did not understand it.

"I can't see David doing *anything* like that," giggled Rosanna.

"I'd never do anything like that," said Cathy firmly.

Because she had an elder brother, Rosanna was regarded as an expert on everything to do with love, a subject about which all the girls lived in a ferment of impatient curiosity.

They discussed endlessly the right ways to behave when you were overwhelmed by rightful passion.

"Would you let a boy kiss you?" asked Rosanna.

"Yes, if we were in love." Monty rummaged around in one of her drawers for a bag of marshmallows and offered them to the others.

"I bet you would anyway if he looked like Brian Jones," needled Rosanna.

"If he looked like Brian Jones, I'd be in love with him to begin with. I'd let him do *anything* if he looked like Brian Jones," Monty cast languorous eyes up to the picture of the prettiest member of the Rolling Stones, which she had taped inside her wardrobe. She knew it was her role to shock the others. Pinups were forbidden, as were makeup, perfume and letters from boys.

"That's awful. Only an absolute slut would behave like that."

47

Cathy spoke with concern, and Monty, who had intended to worry her sister, gave a chuckle of satisfaction.

"My mother says you must never let a boy touch you or you'll be spoiled and no one will want to marry you." Rosanna listlessly opened another fashion magazine. "She's terrified I'll be a tarnished bride."

"I don't think you should kiss a boy unless you're engaged," agreed Cathy.

"But if you never find anything out before you get engaged, how do you know you really love each other?" Monty flicked through pages of tall blond girls with smudgy black eyeliner, posing knock-kneed in miniskirts.

"You just *know*, that's all. I'm sure I'll know. I'll feel all swoony and weak, like fainting when he holds my hand." There was a silence as the three girls tried to imagine being wildly, passionately in love. They couldn't.

"Let's try that," Rosanna suggested, pointing to a page in Monty's magazine which demanded "Should *you* wear a miniskirt?" in big black type.

"What do you have to do?"

"It tells you—I'll get my tape measure." Cathy ran off to her own dormitory and came back with the measuring tape she used for dressmaking. She measured Monty's legs at the thigh, knee, calf and ankle, then did the same for Rosanna; then Monty measured Cathy's legs and then they lined up in front of the mirror in the corridor and looked intently at their reflections.

"It says here," Cathy read from the article, "that perfect legs should meet only at the knee and ankle." They gazed solemnly forward; Rosanna's plump legs met most of the way down; Monty's legs were also plump, but bowed so there was a tiny gap at the level of her knees. Cathy's legs were perfect—slim, straight and gracefully proportioned.

"But I've got this," she moaned, pointing to the faint gold impression of the birthmark just above the back of her right knee.

"Do you suppose"—Monty pulled in dissatisfaction at her unflattering navy tunic—"that anyone would notice if we put up the hems a bit? Our legs would look longer. We could do it just a little at a time. I bet Grice wouldn't spot it."

Miss Grice was their housemistress, an unsmiling, ruddy-cheeked woman who taught lacrosse. Monty called her the Voice of Doom, because her voice, bellowing "swing, girls, *swing*" across the muddy pitch, could be heard every afternoon throughout the school grounds.

Cathy, who sewed most neatly, took up all three tunics one

inch, and the three friends self-consciously went down to supper. No one noticed.

That night they crept out of their dormitories, leaving pillows under their blankets in case anyone peeped in to check that all was well, and scuttled down the corridor to the laundry room, where they locked the door, jammed towels at the top and bottom to block out the least crack of illumination, then put on the light. Working in a froth of excitement, Cathy pinned, Monty pressed, Rosanna tacked, Cathy stitched and then Monty pressed the tunics for the last time.

"Two inches isn't much, is it?" Rosanna held her finished uniform against her waist and tried to judge the skirt length.

"Look, we've got to be absolutely deadpan at breakfast," warned Monty. "No giggling. Poker faces. We mustn't look as if anything's going on."

Simmering with delicious excitement, they went down to breakfast next morning, feeling as if their newly revealed kneecaps were glowing neon bright. None of the teachers noticed, but two of the other girls shot startled, envious looks at the immaculately raised hems.

Monty grew blasé and crossed her legs with panache as she sat in a deep chintz-covered armchair at morning break. At lunchtime, one or two of the girls tackled them, but they pretended innocence.

"Another inch, Cathy, go on; we're bound to get away with it." Monty's eyes were bigger and rounder than ever with the thrill of challenging authority.

"No," said Cathy firmly. "It's all around the school already; some little sneak's bound to tell on us."

"Rubbish. No one can prove anything. We've just grown a bit taller, that's all. There's nothing wrong with altering your uniform anyway—no one's said anything about Rosanna's being more fitted." Cathy dug her heels in and Rosanna, very anxious not to be conspicuous, agreed.

"We've proved our point, we've got away with it. Let's stop now," she urged, pulling her red dressing gown around her.

"I think you're both absolute *weeds*," sulked Monty, and after lights out, she went alone to the laundry room by torchlight and turned up the hem of her tunic another inch.

As the four hundred girls stood quietly waiting for Miss Sharpe to say grace, Grice, the housemistress, walked suspiciously around the table, eyeing every girl's hemline. As Cathy had predicted, the secret had been guessed and communicated. Monty felt the hairs on the back of her neck prickle as Miss Grice approached, then heard her voice, for once low but still bullying, say "See me after breakfast, Miranda, if you please."

"I suppose you think that tampering with the school uniform's very clever, Miss?" she snapped, walking to and fro across the worn carpet in her study. "Well, let me tell you that it isn't. What have you got to say for yourself?"

"It's the fashion, Miss Grice." Monty's line in disciplinary encounters was what was called dumb insolence—the pretended innocent putdown of the enemy.

"You'll have plenty of time for fashion when you've left school, and we're not bothered with you any longer. While you're here, you'll obey the rules."

Monty's eyes glazed and she looked vaguely at Miss Grice, seeing her as a gesticulating doll about four inches high.

"You'll stay in detention this afternoon and put that hem down, and bring it to me when you've finished. And you'll learn one hundred lines by tomorrow—I've marked the page." The worst punishment that was ever given to a girl at Benenden was to learn poetry by heart.

In the beginning, Monty had simply been given a fat blue book and told to learn a poem from it. She soon became proficient in all the poems of fewer than ten lines in this weighty volume. Miss Grice's next maneuver had been to set a fixed number of lines to be memorized. Monty had countered by picking the most explicit love poems she could find and reciting them slowly, stone-faced, while looking Miss Grice straight in the eye as she intoned, *"Enter these arms, for since thou thought it best,/ Not to dream all my dream, let's act the rest."* She had an excellent memory, despite which her marks for English literature were appalling.

Miss Grice's latest strategy was to specify precisely the lines she wanted Monty to learn, in this case a romantic Scottish ballad with a galloping meter. Thus the girls were even more firmly instructed that romance was right and sex was wrong.

"Rotten old boot," Cathy consoled her sister. "I'll do the hem for you."

"You can't, she wants to stand over me." Monty sulkily opened the poetry book. "Oh, God, what slop. Young Lochinvar."

"Didn't you learn that last term?"

"Yes, the old bat must've forgotten." Monty was rapidly scanning the lines.

"Never mind, Monty." Rosanna huddled thankfully inside her scarlet robe. "She's just jealous. I mean, who'd want to look at *her* legs?" They all shrieked with laughter.

PEARLS

"Ugh. Don't, what a disgusting thought—not before supper, please, Rosanna."

" *'Oh, young Lochinvar is come out of the West,/ Through all the wide Border his steed was the best,'* " muttered Monty rapidly.

"Grice's knees go blue in the cold, you know, and her varicose veins stick out. I've watched them." Rosanna pulled out a magnifying mirror and tweezers and began to tweak at her thick, glossy eyebrows.

"Those revolting divided skirts of hers are shorter than a miniskirt anyway; what's this for?" Cathy picked up a strange implement from the bagful of cosmetic instruments designed to enhance Rosanna's looks without breaking the no makeup rule.

" *'O come ye in peace here, or come ye in war,/ Or to dance at our bridal, young Lord Lochinvar?'* " Monty raced through the poem in a rapid chant.

"Eyelash curlers—look, you do it like this." Rosanna picked the curlers up and demonstrated. "Then you put some of this cream on at night and you get really thick eyelashes."

"You've got really thick eyelashes anyway." Cathy looked at her own face in the magnifying mirror. Her skin was the color and texture of creamy new milk. The natural shade of her lips was cinnamon pink, and above her short, straight nose her eyes gazed out, rayed in shades of brown from dark clove to bright topaz. Cathy liked her looks. For the sake of politeness she echoed the others' moans about their imperfections, but deep down she was prepared to believe she was beautiful. Of course, eyelashes could not really be too long or too thick; and hers might look even better if they curled more. Hopefully, she dabbed on some of the black cream.

" *'She looked down to blush, and she looked up to sigh,/ With a smile on her lips and a tear in her eye,/ He took her soft hand, ere her mother could bar . . .'* " Monty gabbled on as fast as she could, then threw the poetry book across the room with a yell of triumph. "Know it, know it. Can I have some of that?"

"You don't need it either." Cathy handed the tiny pot to her sister.

"I bet you wouldn't do what she did." Monty smeared the cream generously over her lids and studied the effect in the mirror. Her lashes stuck together in spikes, making her eyes look like big black stars. Impatiently, she pushed away the tangle of black curls that hung almost to the wide bridge of her nose. *Why* didn't her hair fall in a sleek curtain down to her eyebrows, like that of the models in the magazines? Like Cathy's did?

"Do what?"

"Run off with your secret lover on your wedding day."

"I'd be marrying my secret lover anyway." Cathy said things like that with a solemnity that never sounded complacent, only serenely confident.

If sex and love were enthralling, marriage was their greatest fascination, and they all felt they knew everything important about it. Except of course, the only important thing—*whom* they were going to marry. There were innumerable ways of consulting fate on this. Although they scoffed loudly at superstition, and dared each other to walk under ladders or leave spilled salt untouched, the girls would carefully peel the skin off an apple in an intact string. Then you had to swing it three times around your head and let it fall behind you. The shape of the fallen peel foretold the initial of your husband's name.

The peel always fell in a wobbly curve so an awful lot of girls seemed to be destined to marry Charleses or Williams. In view of the narrow range of boy's names considered acceptable in their social echelon, it was a probably quite an accurate prediction.

When you ate cherry pie, you carefully nudged the pits to the side of your plate and counted them—"Tinker, tailor, soldier, sailor, rich man, poor man, beggar man, thief." Portions with five cherries, denoting a rich man, were much sought after. After the first rhyme, you said "Silk, satin, cotton, rags" to find out about your wedding dress, and "Little house, big house, pig sty, barn" to determine your future style of living. If you had more than four pits to count, you started these rhymes again, so five cherries won you a silk dress and a big house; everyone knew this, but you still counted cherry pits out loud when you had five, so everyone would know your glorious destiny.

Their romance-sodden languor increased as the weather got warmer. When Midsummer Eve came in the ripe heat of June, they decided to try the ultimate prediction.

"What you have to do," Cathy explained, "is sit in front of a mirror, with another mirror behind you, in your nightdress on Midsummer Eve, with your hair unbound, and a candle on either side of you. Then you look in the mirrors and at midnight you see your husband's face behind you."

"How spooky, I wouldn't dare," said Rosanna, shivering in imagined horror.

"Well, I don't care about getting married anyway. You do it, Cathy." Monty, suddenly annoyed by the complacent way her sister talked about the whole business of marriage, wanted to challenge her. "Come on, where shall we do it?"

"Well, we can't do it in the corridor because someone's bound to hear us—where else is there a big mirror?'' Rosanna was always practical.

"The boot room, but . . .''

There was unspoken agreement that the boot room was much too prosaic. "You'd need a big mirror or you wouldn't be able to see him properly—is there a mirror we could get from somewhere?''

"What about the headmistress's cloakroom?''

"Monty!'' Rosanna squealed in horror.

"There's a big mirror on chains in there—we could take it down easily between us.'' Monty looked challengingly from Cathy to Rosanna.

"We wouldn't be able to carry it very far. . . .'' Cathy thoughtfully chewed the tip of her ponytail.

"I know—what about that room under the stage, and there's the mirror we use to check our costumes—no one would find us there.'' This was indisputable. The room under the stage in the great hall was accessible only from a trapdoor in the corridor outside.

"It's awfully dark down there—maybe we should just . . .''

"Oh, rubbish, Rosanna, anyone would think you were afraid of spiders.''

"Well, I am afraid of spiders.''

"There are millions of spiders under the stage and they'll all be much more afraid of us than we are of them,'' Monty announced decisively. "Now where are we going to get the candles?''

Under Monty's generalship, the prank scheme took on wilder and wilder proportions. The following day they took a pair of three-foot candles in brass candlesticks from the chapel. They synchronized their watches like commandos and met at eleven o'clock on Midsummer Eve at the bottom of the stairs, with their cloaks over their nightdresses, or, in Rosanna's case, over her baby-doll pajamas.

"Walk on the grass; then no one will hear us'' commanded Monty in a whisper. They ran furtively down the avenue of trees; the limes were beginning to flower and the air was sticky and tartly scented with their pollen.

By the dim beams of their pocket flashlights they tiptoed through the corridors to the cloakroom by the headmistress's study.

"Careful—the chains will rattle,'' panted Monty as her sister struggled to lift the heavy looking glass and keep her balance on the old-fashioned porcelain washstand.

With Cathy holding the chains still, Monty and Rosanna carried the heavy mirror crabwise down the corridor. Cathy heaved at the brass ring that opened the trapdoor in the floor, and they slowly negotiated the stairs into the ominous darkness below.

"That torch is useless—light the candles, Rosanna." There was a scrape of a match, a flare of light, then darkness.

"Blast, dropped it. Hang on, I'll try again." This time the wick caught, and when Rosanna held the candle up they could make out the huge wicker baskets that held the costumes for the school's plays.

"Cathy—shut the trapdoor and then no one will be able to hear us." Monty began pulling the creaking skips together. Soon the scene was set according to Cathy's instructions, and the flickering reflections of the candlelight shone around the dark cellar.

Monty found a dusty, Elizabethan-style stool and planted it between the mirrors.

"There you are, Cathy—take off your cloak." Cathy, shivering slightly in her sprigged-cotton nightdress, sat down and Rosanna brushed her loose straight hair for her.

"Move back, you two, I can see you in the mirror." They drew back.

"What time is it? I can't see." Rosanna peered at her tiny enamel-faced wristwatch by the light of the nearest candle.

"Ten to twelve."

A solemn silence fell as they settled down to wait for midnight with mounting apprehension. Cathy gazed into the mirror, trying to concentrate on the black space behind her head instead of her pale, oval face reflected to infinity, with her lips quivering a little with nerves.

She looked like a bride already, Monty thought wistfully, wishing her own hair were smooth and straight, and her nose fine and small, and her skin creamy and absolutely without pimples as Cathy's was. For all she envied it, Cathy's effortless beauty was something she felt vicariously proud of as well.

Rosanna fretted inwardly that she would be unable to find a husband to match her parents' detailed demands; Monty, secretly convinced that no one would ever want to marry a fat, frizzy-haired, bowlegged creature like herself, and utterly determined not to end up like her own mother, had great misgivings about the whole idea of getting married. But Cathy's quiet confidence about her future made her the perfect bride-to-be.

There were noises in the still night. The wicker baskets gave tiny creaks. Above them, the polished oak floorboards settled with occasional groans. A hunting owl shrieked in the park outside.

"What's the time now?" Cathy whispered, her voice hoarse with tension.

Rosanna held her watch toward the light again. "One minute to go."

Cathy gazed intently into the mirror before her. Clearly they heard the distant whirring of weights as the school clock prepared to strike. As if pulled by invisible thread, the three girls leaned forward and stared into the mirror's depth. The candles guttered, the clock struck and a pale shape appeared momentarily in the reflected dark.

Suddenly, Cathy screamed, half jumped to her feet and shrieked again with utter fright. Rosanna screamed too, and fell back against a basket. Monty turned round, wide-eyed with terror, and gazed straight at a furious Miss Grice, who demanded: "What in the world are you girls doing?"

"I've never been so pleased to hear the Voice of Doom, I can tell you." Monty tried in vain to lighten their mood as they sat outside the headmistress's room the next morning. Girls gazed curiously at them as they passed, knowing that they must have done something dreadful to be waiting there.

The oak door opened violently and Miss Sharpe's voice called them in.

"Never in all the time I have taught at this school have I heard of anything so stupid." Her tone was icy with contempt and her blue eyes glared at one of them after the other. "Quite apart from the fact that you have desecrated the chapel, stolen school property and broken school rules, you could have burned the whole school down."

Cathy and Rosanna looked uncomfortably at their shoes. Monty, glaze-eyed as usual, comforted herself with a daydream of the school consumed by flames and Miss Sharpe's charred body tumbling from the castellated parapet.

"I don't know what you were all doing and frankly I don't want to know. Take that smirk off your face, Catherine." Cathy's long, upturned top lip always made her seem to be smiling when she wasn't, and she no longer tried to explain. "I'm most surprised at you all, *especially* you, Catherine. This sort of behavior is quite out of character. And you, Rosanna, you've made a very good start here and I hope you're not going to spoil it." Oh dear, thought Cathy, she's going to come down hard on Monty. "But I've seen quite a lot of you, Miranda, haven't I?"

Why do you always use those mealy-mouthed expressions, wondered Monty with contempt. Miss Sharpe continued, "I'd thought all this teenage rebellion, or whatever you choose to call it, was over, but I can see now that you haven't changed and I'm beginning to wonder if you ever will change, Miranda.''

Same old story, Monty thought. Can't she come up with anything new?

"You will all be confined to the school for the rest of the term," Miss Sharpe announced at last. "I shall be writing to your parents, of course, and if there is any repetition of these escapades, I shall suspend you immediately. As for you, Miranda, I really don't think there is anything more we can do for you here. You will be allowed to sit your exams, but we shall not expect you back next term.''

As if sitting bloody exams was a treat, sneered Monty to herself. As if I wanted to come back here.

Cathy, usually the first to raise the spirits of the other two in times of gloom, said nothing as they walked back to their lessons. Monty, full of brittle bravado, demanded, "So did you see anything in the mirror, after all?''

Cathy shook her head. "Just Grice. It's only a superstition, anyway, isn't it?''

"You really didn't see a thing?'' Monty pressed her sister, sensing that she was keeping something back.

"No, of course I didn't—didn't you hear what I said?'' Cathy spoke with irritation, and Monty let the matter drop. They walked on in silence until they parted to make their way to the classrooms.

Cathy probed her memory, trying to bring back the picture she had seen before the panic of discovery made everything unclear. She had an indelible impression of a man with graying hair and an aura of vitality. The only man she knew who matched the picture was her father.

Arches of bright sunlight, the light rich sun of Paris in summer, lay across the narrow pavement, shaped by the graceful arcades of the Rue de Rivoli. The boutiques selling leather, luggage and elegant but useless gifts pulled their blinds halfway down to protect their stock from the sunlight, but James Bourton's eye was not distracted by the gilded knickknacks on display.

He walked slowly around the Place Vendôme to the Ritz, and ordered himself a whiskey soda at the bar. The barman knew him well. Milord Bourton was almost the last of the real English clientele, elegant, cultivated, free-spending, and a pleasure to serve. Naturally, he always put up at the Ritz. They had had the honor of serving him for almost twenty years.

He seemed a little abstracted today, the barman noticed as he returned to his position midway down the gleaming counter, perhaps even a little pale. Many men need a drink to help them accept bad news, but the barman was not the sort who cared to listen to his customers' troubles; their difficulties were always to do with money or with women, of which neither was susceptible to reason nor really important.

James drank his whiskey rapidly and ordered another, then a third. Had the barman looked closely, he would have seen that his customer was indeed pale beneath his permanent light tan, and that the beautifully manicured hand clamped around the glass was shaking violently enough to make the ice ring against its sides.

After the third whiskey James slipped off the barstool, telling the barman to send the bill to the hotel cashier immediately; he was checking out straight away. Half an hour later, while a maroon-uniformed porter wheeled his bags out into the Place Vendôme, James settled the bill rapidly and took a taxi to Orly airport.

Within three hours he was at his desk in his office in London Wall, thanking his secretary for his afternoon tea.

"You've had an awful lot of telephone calls, Lord James." She gazed over the massive mahogany desk adoringly. All the other secretaries in the firm envied her position; Lord James was so charming, so kind, so good-looking and, at almost fifty, so thrillingly sexy.

The other directors had spreading bellies, dandruff on their collars or pompous ways about them; none of the office girls could quite understand why they all subtly disparaged lovely Lord James.

"Mr. James from the Allied Bank called three times; he says it's urgent. Your solicitors have called twice, and they want you to ring back. And a man came in to see you—he wouldn't say what it was about, only that you weren't expecting him and he'd pop in again."

"I think I know what it's about; is this the rest of the mail?" The letter from Benenden was on top of the pile that filled his correspondence tray. She nodded her neatly groomed blond head.

"Now I want you first of all to go over to Accounts and get me some cash." He scribbled an authorization on a slip of paper and handed it to her. "I've some clients to take out this evening and the banks are shut. After that I'll give you a packet that's got to go by registered post straight away.

"Then I want you to slip over to Piccadilly and pick up an order at Paxton and Whitfield." One of Mr. Bourton's many indulgences was the finest cheese from a Jermyn Street shop.

The secretary didn't ask herself why a man recently returned from France should order Camembert in England. "Don't bother coming back to the office. I'll be gone by the time you get here and it'll be better off in your refrigerator overnight. Give it to me tomorrow." She nodded eagerly, took the paper and tripped down the corridor, returning in ten minutes with two thousand pounds in twenty-pound notes. There was nothing unusual about Lord Bourton's asking for that much folding money. He would often drop considerably more than that sum in an evening when he was entertaining clients with a taste for gambling.

With his secretary out of the room, James fumbled in his desk drawers and found a cigar box that was half empty. He transferred the remaining cigars to the humidor on a sidetable, packed the money tightly into the box, and wrote a card saying simply, "This is for you." He taped the box shut, pushed it clumsily into an envelope and addressed it to a Mrs. Mae Brown at an address in Bayswater.

Once his secretary had left to post the packet James locked his office door and went back to his desk. He raked briefly through his mail with hands that still trembled a little and had difficulty opening the envelopes. For some months now he had asked the girl to leave his mail unopened. He opened the letter from the school with agitation, then smiled and discarded it.

The telephone rang at 5:15 P.M. but he did not answer it. By 6:00 P.M. the office was silent and empty, and the street below full of purposeful bustle as people crowded toward the railway stations to go home. James sat still in his chair, his eyes fixed on the framed citation for his wartime decoration. It was the only thing hanging on the blue silk-papered wall that was not beautiful, but for once he did not want to enjoy his paintings.

When his secretary went to open the office next morning, she found the door locked. No doubt Lord Bourton had not yet arrived. She called his flat in Albany, but the cleaner answered and said she didn't think Lord Bourton had come home from France. Alarmed now, the secretary called the building's caretaker, who came up with a spare key and opened James's office.

Forty-eight hours after punishing the three girls, Miss Sharpe again sent for Cathy, and as soon as she entered the headmistress's office, Cathy knew that something was dreadfully wrong; her first instinct was that Monty had run away.

"Do you know where your sister is?"

There was definitely something amiss. Miss Sharpe's piercing glance was jumping nervously around the room and her voice sounded half strangled.

"No, Miss Sharpe, I haven't seen her all afternoon."

"You must find her at once. I've had a telephone call from your mother. She wants you to come home immediately."

"Has something happened?" Cathy was by now absolutely sure something was wrong. Miss Sharpe suddenly looked directly at her and her voice cracked as she spoke.

"There is, Catherine, but I'm afraid you must wait for your mother to tell you what it is. She will be here to fetch you in forty minutes. All I can say is that I am most dreadfully sorry for you both. Now hurry and find your sister."

Cathy ran out of the square, mock-Tudor stone doorway and around the creeper-covered window bay at the front of the main building. Spurts of gravel shot across the lawn behind her as she raced around the corner, then dodged through a crowd of younger girls packed into the narrow passageway between two wings of the rambling red-brick building.

At the back of the complex was the music wing, where Monty was sure to be. Whenever her sister was worried about something—and for all her outward defiance, Cathy knew Monty was worried about what their parents would say when they got Miss Sharpe's letter—she usually buried herself in the music wing, to play the piano for hours.

She found both Monty and Rosanna on the top floor of the stuffy music building, contentedly practicing a piece by Mozart. Cathy paused for a second and watched them through the glass panel in the door. Her sister's face, for once devoid of cynicism, defensiveness and rebellion, had calmed and was as lovely as a baby's as she followed the line of notes on the sheet music. Rosanna swayed slightly with each stroke of her bow.

Cathy tapped at the door and they stopped playing and looked up. She went in. "Monty, I don't know what's up but Mummy's coming to get us and we've got to pack."

Within an hour their mother was standing awkwardly beside the Bentley as the porter loaded the girls' two suitcases. Bettina Bourton was a dumpy woman with hair dyed a harsh honey brown to hide the gray. Her mouth was set in a thick carmine line. Her vague blue eyes, which always had a look of suppressed anxiety, now registered barely controlled panic.

"Come and sit down a minute," she said, brusque in her agitation. They sat one on each side of her on a stone bench, watching their mother twist the sapphire and ruby eternity rings which cut into her plump fingers.

Suddenly, Bettina caught her breath and began to speak, slurring her words in distress.

"Your father's dead. His office telephoned this morning. They say we've got to go home and wait because the police want to see us. Don't ask me what it's all about because . . ." She gulped air again then spluttered into tears.

Numb with shock as she was, Cathy gave her mother a calming embrace and patted her arm, muttering "there, there" and feeling useless because she had no idea what could be done.

Monty sat in silence. She was sure that the school's letter had somehow killed her father, that her bad behavior was responsible for his death.

Then Cathy and Monty looked at each other over their mother's bowed head, silently sharing the sense of desolation that slowly welled up to swamp their initial reactions. We're alone now, their wide dark eyes told each other. You're all I've got now—don't leave me, each girl's glance implored the other. I won't leave you, each responded; I love you, we'll always be together.

Inside his office, James Bourton's body lay slumped across his desk, a red mess where his head should have been. The blue silk paper of the wall to the left, the leather-bound books in the bookcase, the correspondence in the tray and the blotter were caked in dried splashes of blood and fragments of brain. Clamped in his right hand with the reflexive grasp of death was his army pistol. James Bourton had shot himself.

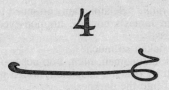

4

Sour whiskey surged in James Bourton's stomach, then died down. When you were twenty-two, a hangover felt good. Standing in the cool predawn darkness in a white shirt and crisp khaki shorts, he supervised the muster of two hundred coolies with the impression that he was enjoying the masculine pleasures of drink and domination simultaneously.

His woman was waiting in the slow-moving line of Tamils that stretched away into the darkness of the muster ground beyond the pool of light from the hissing pressure lamp. Selambaram, the conductor, or overseer, called the name of each man or woman in turn and those who were fit to work answered and stepped forward.

Each tapper carried two buckets for latex; the weeders each held the heavy hoe used to keep the long dim corridors between the rubber trees free of the infiltrating plants that eternally tried to reclaim the land for the jungle.

"Is that right?" James demanded, as Damika, his mistress, impassively answered in her turn and moved away with the kerosene cans she used as buckets; her sari, stiff with dried latex, rustled at each step. James's finger pointed to the line opposite her name in Selambaram's book. The neatly ruled double page had a column for each day of the month, and further columns to note the coolie's total wage due at the month's end, how much of the wages was to be taken in the form of dry rice, and the proportion the coolie had asked for as an advance on the twen-

61

tieth day of the month. Damika had taken half her wages in advance.

"It is correct, *tuan*." Selambaram continued to check the roll of the laborers in James's control, his pop-eyed, almost black face expressionless.

"Why has she taken so much?"

"You must ask the woman, *tuan*. I do not know." James was suddenly agitated by obscure suspicion, which grew stronger as the woman faded into the darkness.

By 5:30 A.M., when the long process of muster was completed, James mounted his motorbike and sped away down the red earth road, riding past the line of coolie shacks and out to a crossroads where he slowed to negotiate the muddy gullies carved by the heavy tropical rain.

From the intersection, the downhill fork led to the railway track, the others to outlying areas of the plantation. James turned uphill. The sad, liquid whoops of gibbons sounded from the jungle to his right. Soon the sun would rise behind the mountains; a smear of colorless light waxed among the dark gray clouds, and the voices of the monkeys were gradually joined by the millions of insects whose calls announced the dawn.

On his left the rubber trees stood in orderly rows, their slim gray-brown trunks all forked at the same level, their leaves mingling at a height of forty-five feet to cast unbroken shadows over the plantation. Each tree was marked with an identical swath of scarred bark, like a sarong wrapped around the bole of the trunk.

On the terraced hillside James saw some of his coolies working. Damika he knew would be farther down, and he bumped and skidded onward until the headlamp picked out the turquoise shades of her sari as she bent intently over her knife and cut into the bark of a tree.

Tapping rubber was skilled work—too deep a cut would damage the tree, too shallow an incision would not produce enough of the creamy sap to fill the cup that was delicately fixed on two wires around the trunk. Only an inch-wide strip of bark could be cut each month. Anxious as he was, James waited until the woman had made her cut, finishing with a twist of the knife that made a curl of bark down which the white sap would run into the conical metal cup below.

She straightened her body and pushed the swath of sari fabric more securely onto her left shoulder, her tinny metal bangles sounding faintly in the quiet half light.

"Why have you asked the conductor for money?" James demanded. His suspicion was formless; there was no logic in it. The woman was poor and powerless, virtually a slave, yet she could raise the fear of all her sex, which was buried in James's subconscious.

"I have earned the money, *tuan*, and I need it." Was her glance startled or guilty? It was too dark for him to tell.

"But I give you money; I have given you a lot of money. What has become of it?"

"The money you give me I give to my husband, *tuan*." Her round black eyes were, as far as he could judge, amiably blank as always.

"You and your husband earn good wages here. You have not been sick. What has your husband done with my money?"

"*Tuan*, he gives it to Chung Li, the labor contractor. We owe him money." James, now in his second tour of duty as an assistant on the Bukit Helang estate, knew Chung Li, the biggest contractor in the district, who shipped in the Tamil workers from South India or Ceylon.

"Why do you owe money to Chung Li?"

"It is according to our contract, *tuan*. We must pay him back the money he has spent to bring us here, for our steamer passage and our food on the journey."

"How much do you have to pay him?" James's eyes wandered to the well-formed brown arms and the band of naked flesh between the tightly wound waist of her sari and the short blouse that covered her shoulders and breasts.

"We must pay him half of our wages for three years. After that nothing, unless we wish to return home."

"Chung Li is the son of a dog. He is paid well by *tuan besar* for finding workers for the estate. I did not know he took payment from the workers too."

"Chung Li is a good man, *tuan*. Before his men came to our village we had no food. My husband and I had no children, because all my babies died. They were too small and we did not have enough to eat." An anxious note crept into her voice at the memory. "Now I have two fine sons, we eat rice every day, and there is enough even for my husband's mother. The *tuan* is also good to us and we are grateful for his kindness." Unconsciously her fingers swung the gold metal earring in her right ear, which James had bought her to match the similar one in her left ear.

James yawned, his anxiety forgotten, and tasted the bile from his uneasy stomach. His obscure fear that the woman was somehow betraying him had faded with the dawn shadows, and he was no longer interested in what she was saying. The faint aroma of the coconut oil she used to dress her long black hair, and the musky odor of her flesh, drifted to his nostrils. He felt the skin around his balls shiver.

The woman sensed his loss of interest and her own anxiety subsided. Then they heard a distant whir; there was a call from the track uphill, and a foreman on a bicycle appeared pedaling fast. As he approached James he braked and jumped off the bicycle as a sign of respect for a European.

"*Tuan besar* asks for you, *tuan*. There is trouble where they are cutting the trees." *Tuan* was a short form of the Malay word *tuanku*, meaning "a prince," and was the usual form of address from an Asian to a white man. *Besar* meant "big," and *tuan besar* meant Douglas Lovell, the estate manager and lord of all he surveyed—and more—in this isolated region.

James mounted his mud-spattered Triumph and roared away. His closest friend among the eight assistants on the estate was Gerald Rawlins, currently on his first leave in England. In his absence James had kept an eye on his coolies and put in hand the work of clearing a new patch of jungle for planting. This ground was now a mass of felled vegetation. A gang of Tamils was hacking the branches off a fallen tree, while another group urged on a pair of lugubrious water buffalo yoked to a naked trunk by rusty chains.

In the midst of the clearing stood the *tuan besar*, Douglas Lovell, in grimy fawn riding breeches and a sweat-stained shirt. Around him in sullen silence waited the band of Malay contractors who had been hired for the work of tree felling. Behind them a single tree, its trunk massively gnarled and covered in flaking bone-gray bark, stretched two hundred feet into the cloudy sky.

"Took your time," grunted Douglas Lovell. "Tell me what these fellas are getting excited about, will you? They're jibbing at the last tree."

James approached the group of Malays, trying to look unconcerned, and asked which one was the foreman. A man of about thirty-five, with a coarse broad face and several missing teeth, greeted him, and James walked with him a little way from the group.

Racking his brains for the right way to handle the situation, James began, "You and your men have done a fine job. You have cleared this area more quickly than I expected."

"Good men work well for a good master, *tuan*," the foreman answered.

Encouraged, James went on, "Maybe if I ask *tuan besar* myself he will give you a bonus."

"*Tuan besar* will not agree. We will be contented with the price on which we shook hands, and as we have worked fast the benefit will be ours, and we will return to our village."

PEARLS

Then this was not a strategy to get more money; James gave the foreman his most beguiling smile and made an oblique request for further information.

"The questions of the *tuans* are as foolish as the questions of a child, I know. I myself am scarcely more than a child," he remarked in a matter-of-fact tone.

The foreman beamed patronizingly at James and laughed. James tried to look grave rather than triumphant as the man explained, "This tree is the home of a ghost. My men will not harm it for fear of disturbing the ghost, which will come in the night and drink their blood."

James nodded and said, "The forest is full of spirits and it is foolish to annoy them." The foreman also nodded, looking relieved, and there was a perceptible release of tension around the men as James jumped nimbly over a fallen trunk and reported back to Douglas Lovell.

"Damn superstitions," the manager muttered, settling his finger-marked topee farther back on his head. "I'd never have employed Malay labor myself, too damn idle." He looked up the vast length of the tree trunk, narrowing his eyes against the glare of the sky. "Any suggestions, Bourton? We've got to get this bugger down somehow."

"Well, sir, the Chinese don't care about the forest ghosts. These men have finished the job otherwise, and in good time. Why don't we pay them off and see if we can hire some Chinese instead."

"Damned expensive."

"If we let the Tamils do it, they'll botch it. And I'll get a good price, sir."

The older man smiled at the slim youngster with brown eyes. "You sound like a bloody Chinese shopkeeper yourself. Very well."

A few years in the enclosed multi-stranded community of the Bukit Helang estate had transformed James from a weak and wary boy into a man. All the sullen resistance that had stunted his abilities at school in England was charmed away by the challenges of a new environment; he had grown steadily confident as he discovered that his name, his lineage and his wealth were of no consequence to his fellow planters, but his quick mind, his sensitive ear and his practical courage mattered and were rewarded by Douglas Lovell's blunt praise and the quick obedience of the men of whom he found himself in command.

Above all, this was a man's world free of the complications of women. Of the fifteen men in Douglas Lovell's employ, only one, Anderson the doctor, was married, and his wife had the

65

flat-chested striding manner of an Englishwoman who has elected to de-sex herself for the sake of convenience.

Douglas Lovell ruled his kingdom like a natural imperialist restrained by his common sense. He threatened to flog bad coolies, but never did so. An army bugle woke the estate every day for muster.

The memory of the rubber slump of the early thirties remained fresh, and Bukit Helang still ran at scarcely half the capacity of the land, filling a fixed quota of production dictated by the rubber company in London. There was a large bulletin board in the white-pillared shade of the estate office, and every day a clerk posted on it the size of the day's crop, the price of rubber, the number of coolies working and the profit made.

James had never before won approval for his abilities rather than his charm, or felt himself to be engaged in useful, productive work. The experience improved his spirit immensely. Above all, he was admired as a linguist. The basis of this gift was his acute and subtle sense of hearing; at Eton he had learned only one foreign language—French—which was taught from books and blackboard by an Englishman with a vile accent that confirmed the boys in the notion that the wogs began at Calais. James had heard a native Frenchman speak only on rare occasions. Now, however, he learned almost instinctively to speak the Oriental languages by listening to the speech of the natives.

"You've got the gift of tongues all right," another junior assistant had observed in admiration, as he came upon James one day quizzing Ahmed, his houseboy, in fluent Malay. James himself had been astonished at the ease with which the new languages around him flowed into his mind. At times he was aware of thinking in a mixture of Malay, Cantonese and Tamil as he gave his men instructions, or of having forgotten the English word for some familiar object as he dined and drank with the other assistants.

His absorption of Oriental speech was instinctive and completely phonetic, however, and when he came to sit the Incorporated Society of Planters Tamil examination for the first time, he failed, because he could speak but not spell.

Douglas Lovell was concerned. "Chap like you saves a manager a helluva lot of bother," he observed from the back of the stocky dun pony on which he made his morning round of the estate.

James walked respectfully by the ambling pony's side. "I'm sure I'll pass next time. I've just got to flog through the grammar, sir."

Douglas Lovell paused to watch a group of Tamils weeding

the avenues between the rows of young trees. "Tell 'em to leave the young grass," he ordered James. "Rain'll wash all the soil away if they clear down to bare earth."

When James returned to his side he continued, "As far as I'm concerned, it's your Malay that's most useful. Never could get the measure of the Malays. Language is easy enough, I'm told, but half the time they're talking in riddles."

"It's their idea of politeness, sir. They think it's discourteous to ask direct questions. And they have these funny little poems that they all seem to know, and sometimes instead of saying something outright, they'll just make some reference to a poem and everything's understood."

"Hrmph. Not by me it isn't. Anyway, as far as the board is concerned, I can't promote you if you can't get the Tamil exam, so you'd better crack on with it." They walked slowly and the pony swished its pepper-and-salt tail in irritation at the flies. Next to the young rubber was an expanse of older, almost exhausted trees, and a solitary Tamil woman crouching as she emptied the half-full cups of latex into her bucket.

"When I first came out here"—Douglas Lovell spoke slowly with light but unmistakable emphasis—"my manager told me the best way to polish up my Tamil was to get myself a sleeping dictionary."

"A what, sir?"

"Sleeping dictionary. Native woman. Best place to learn any language is in bed, y'know." James looked at his boots to hide what he was sure was a blush, and Douglas Lovell looked resolutely between the pony's dark-tipped ears. "Of course, some fellas don't find 'em very attractive." There was a pause.

"I think some of them are quite beautiful, actually."

"You're right. Well, if you see one that takes your fancy, here's how it's done." Briskly he prodded the pony forward, pulled up by the Tamil woman and felt in his breeches pocket for a twenty-cent coin, which he tossed into the half-full latex cup in her hand.

When she looked up, he nodded toward James and indicated with a jerk of his cane that the initiative came from the younger man, who stood by in frozen fascination.

"If she takes the money, the foreman'll have her cleaned up at the end of the day and sent around to your bungalow. Make sure you pick a married woman, or there's a devil of a fuss." He turned the pony. "Best of luck." He cantered fast up the track without looking back.

The woman looked at James with expressionless round eyes,

then picked the coin out of the cup of sticky white sap with a hesitant smile.

Despite his total trust in his new boss, and despite knowing that Douglas Lovell was the absolute monarch of his own domain, James barely believed that the woman would come, and half hoped she wouldn't. But as soon as Ahmed had cleared away his dinner dishes and lighted his Java cheroot, Damika walked gracefully out of the darkness up to the veranda steps.

He was reassured to see that she had dressed up, with a waxy white frangipani flower in her black hair and ankle bracelets that chinked softly at each barefoot step. For a few moments there was no sound except the shrilling of the nighttime insects and no movement but the flicker of a bat across the light from the kerosene lamp. Then Ahmed in the kitchen quarters clashed some pans, as if to confirm his tactful preoccupation outside, and James threw the cheroot away, stood up and led Damika into his bedroom.

She helped him unwind the length of her sari, showing neither nervousness nor attraction, and he felt her flesh cool and firm, where he had anticipated a kind of hot softness like rotting fruit. She was not embarrassed by her nakedness, but sighed quietly as he fished in the knot of hair at the nape of her neck for the restraining pins.

Suddenly James was filled with a huge surge of desire. It came with the realization that this woman was a creature completely in his power. His first instinct was to extricate his throbbing penis from his clothes and plunge into the acquiescent flesh before him, but he paused, wanting to glory in complete ownership, the simple pragmatism of the transaction, the fact that he did not need to charm or flatter, scheme or beg, to get possession of this body, and that when the act was over there was no harm she could do to him.

He made her sit on his canvas stool and spread her hair around her shoulders, feeling its oiled heaviness. He stroked her arms and breasts, moving the lamp closer to see the mahogany tints of her skin. He pulled at her nipples to see if they would harden, licked, then bit them to try their taste.

He pushed her thighs apart, using the commanding firmness of a farrier making a horse pick up its feet, and observed the sparseness of her pubic hair, and the unexpected pinkness of the inner flesh which he probed with his fingers. Where her skin wrinkled, it was velvet black, and the folds were smooth and even. He felt his blood roaring in his veins like a river of fire, which incinerated everything it touched. Unsteadily, he stood up and motioned her to lie down on his bed, then scrambled between her legs and thrust into her with a sensation of instant release like blinding light.

A few moments later he sat up, dazed, and watched her methodically replace her long earrings, check the tiny metal flower that pierced her short straight nose, and coil her hair. Mutely he searched for the hairpins he had dropped on the polished hardwood floorboards and handed them to her, then watched as she folded her sari fabric into fanlike pleats and wound the garment around her. She turned and moved toward the door.

"Are you going?" he asked, clearing his hoarse throat as he spoke.

She looked confused. "I am going, but I can stay if you wish."

"Yes, stay. Sleep here with me."

Without emotion, she returned and unwound the sari. Young, physically healthy and emotionally maimed, James felt the burning river of lust carry him swiftly onward. He also felt a guilty gratitude toward Damika, which he now showed in a fever of caresses that seemed to surprise her. He entered her twice more, then fell asleep. She slept on the mat at his bedside until 4:30 A.M., when Ahmed, quiet as a cat, shook her awake and she returned to her husband's shack to cook their morning rice.

As soon as he had finished taking muster that morning, James tracked her down and dropped another twenty-cent coin into her latex cup.

That had been two years ago. He had discovered, to his amusement, that she was illiterate and no help to his mastery of Tamil. Occasionally he bought her a tortoiseshell hairpin ornamented with gilt metal, or a bangle, with which she was gratifyingly happy. During the day he gave her no thought whatsoever, beyond making the decision to summon her or not.

"Bloody glad you're back, Gerald. It's been a blasted nuisance keeping an eye on your patch for six months," shouted James over the pandemonium of the railway station at the capital, Kuala Lumpur. A swell of people and luggage surged below the pointed arches of white stone. The two men pumped hands and slapped shoulders happily, then turned to follow the porters who were carrying Gerald's battered trunk and two new suitcases through the throng. The length of the train was divided by race, with the Tamils milling around the third class, Chinese families greeting each other at the second class, and Europeans summoning porters at the level of first class; a Malay rajah, his retinue and his polo ponies occupied two special carriages. At the front of the engine a group of Tamil sweepers with baskets and buckets were swabbing the remains of a wandering goat off the buffers amid gently rising steam.

"Not there," bellowed Gerald at the porters' backs as they swerved toward the exit. "James, get them over to the left-luggage office. No sense putting up anywhere if we're to be back at Bukit Helang in the morning."

James passed Gerald the luggage receipts and the two men strolled out into the early evening bustle of Kuala Lumpur, always called simply KL by the British. They climbed into a rickshaw pulled by a sweating Chinese, and Gerald looked fondly around him as he brushed railway smuts from his crumpled white trousers.

"Damn sight prettier than Victoria Station," he said, indicating the cream and white minarets of the railway terminus. "My God, it was cold back home; I'd forgotten how cold. Are we going to the Dog?"

"Where else—the fatted calf for the prodigal son."

"Not prodigal for long now, old boy." Gerald screwed his freckled face into a hearty wink. "There's a little girl back home with my ring on her finger, choosing her trousseau and packing her trunks. . . ." James let out a yell that momentarily startled the sweating rickshaw puller, who half halted and flung them forward.

"You clever sod, Rawlins, you've cracked it."

"Did just what the *tuan besar* advised, old boy. Put up at my aunt's in Guildford, had tea every day in a little tearoom opposite the hospital and bingo! Got myself a nice little nurse in ten days flat." He sat back on the oilcloth-covered seat, grinning, and James thumped his knee in congratulation, knowing how eager Gerald had been to succeed in finding a wife.

At the club, James ordered champagne and they settled into wicker chairs on the veranda. On the playing field a cricket match between two teams of police cadets was drawing to a close.

The Dog, formally the Spotted Dog, or even more formally the Selangor Club, was an ever-growing complex of bungalows fronted with black-and-white mock-Tudor timbering. Its verandas faced the spacious green cricket field, and beyond the far boundary the mellow sunlight burnished the pink and white facade and the copper domes of the palace of the state ruler.

"Spotted" somehow signified the club's character; albeit a smart establishment, it admitted both *tuan besars* and juniors, and was technically open to Asiatic members as well, although they were few in number. Most of the European clubs in Malaya were either strictly for whites or specified either big or little *tuans* only to avoid the embarrassment of social exchange among nonequals. Britain transplanted its class system to the Empire, along with its notions of business, government and social service.

"So when's the wedding?"

"Betty—she's called Betty—is booked on the boat in six weeks' time so she'll be out by October. Mother's as pleased as a cat with two tails, running around Penang arranging the wedding and firing off letters all over the show." Gerald's family, for three generations employed in the East, was scattered across half the globe. "I've bought her a present," he went on, fishing in the pocket of his creased cream jacket.

"Picked it out at Simon Artz in Port Said—you know about this stuff; d'you like it?" He produced a small blue-velveteen case and prized it open awkwardly with his blunt freckled fingers. Inside was a cocktail watch of silver metal, the ornate bracelet strap encrusted with sparkling stones.

"I say, *isn't* that splendid," James picked up the watch and unobtrusively searched for a hallmark. "Your Betty should be absolutely delighted; it's charming, first-class."

The watch was not hallmarked, the stones were marcasites at best and Gerald was yet another of the suckers to have found a glittering bargain at Simon Artz's world-renowned general store on the Suez Canal, but James was too much of a gentleman to say so. While Gerald half worshiped James for his assurance and sophistication, James liked Gerald for his harmless puppy-dog foolishness and saw him, from the lofty superiority of being two years older, as an innocent to be protected.

The cricket match ended in a ragged round of muted applause and the white-coated umpire presided as the stumps were drawn out of the coarse turf. The light of the tropical day faded quickly and they moved into the bar. James saw a familiar figure gangling through the doorway.

"Treadwell! Just the man we need. Come and toast Gerald's future happiness; he's got himself hitched first shot. Boy! another bottle here, if you'd be so kind."

"You'll never get it right, Bourton"—the lanky Australian folded up like a collapsing deck chair as he sat—"your la-di-da manners don't cut any ice with the natives, y'know."

Like many bachelor friendships, the oddly matched threesome passed much time in ritual insult, lest anyone should suspect that there was affection among them.

"When I want a lecture on etiquette from a bloody convict, I'll ask for it. To the bridegroom!" They clinked their tankards of Selangor pewter and gulped champagne.

"Now listen, Bill." James leaned forward, realizing he'd better get important matters out of the way before they were too drunk to remember anything. "I need your help. Can you spare me a couple of your Chinese lumberjacks for a day? Our fellows got spooked by one of those blasted spirit-house trees and I need a pair of decent, sensible men from outside to fell it."

"Sure, I'll find you a pair who'd chop up their own grand-mothers for ten dollars."

"Good man, I knew you'd be able to help."

"Not much good sweating out my life in the lumber trade if I can't help out my pals, is there?" For all his studied lack of pretension, Bill Treadwell was a botanist, an expert in the dis-eases of hardwood trees, employed in a research project for Lon-don University. James, with no desire to get married, had seen no need to return to England for the vacation at the end of his first tour of duty and instead had spent some time in the forest with Bill.

The two men's friendship had been founded on month-long treks into the jungle; they had lived off rice, fern tips and what James could shoot; they had attempted to catalog the hundreds of birds and insects that had fluttered or crawled across their tracks; they had followed tantalizing pathways made by jungle animals, which had abruptly vanished in the walls of vegetation, leaving no clue as to their continuance; they had leaped back in terror from the sweeping horns of a seladang, the Asian wild ox, enraged when they disturbed it at a hidden wallow; they had strained eyes and ears in vain for an elephant or a tiger and surmised that the distant patter of falling leaves was the step of the tiny mouse deer. Humbled in the hushed cathedral of nature, they had shared the natives' superstitions and lain unsleeping in the night telling each other what they knew of the folklore and mythology of the Malayan people. The Australian's erudition and his taste for serious talk had fed James's hungry mind and stimulated the fine intellect his own native culture had stunted.

A boy slipped past with a salver of curry puffs, reminding them that they could drink more if they lined their stomachs. James ordered some.

"So there'll be no tempting you on one of our jungle hikes now, I suppose?" Bill stuffed the corner of a spicy patty into his mouth and bit it off, waving the remaining fragment at Ger-ald.

"No, I'm going to settle down and be an old married man," he replied.

"Shame!" James shouted.

"And there'll be no popping down to old Mary's tonight, I

take it?'' Bill swallowed down the rest of his curry puff, crinkling his shrewd blue eyes.

"Well''—Gerald knitted his pale eyebrows—''I don't think I'll get carried away with this marriage thing just yet—no sense in too much of a good thing, is there?''

"I'm relieved to hear it, mate. You had me worried there for a while.'' Their custom was to meet this way in KL once a month and, emboldened by drink and each other's company, to end the evening at a dilapidated whorehouse in the Chinese quarter, whose official name was the Bright World of Much Happiness, but which was widely known as Mary's.

The curry puffs made them thirstier, and James ordered more champagne, which made them thirstier still, so they ordered stengahs. There was a rowdy commotion as two groups of men started a pitched battle around the doorway of the reading room, spitting whiskey at each other from between their teeth. Behind James, a trio of French planters drew closer together in disapproval and carried on discussing whether sex was more important to men or to women.

"How's . . .'' Gerald belched gently. "How's old Douglas Lovell been struggling on without me?''

"Pretty fair. Got himself a new pony from India and a new mistress from Siam, so he's feeling rather good, I should say.''

"He'll be the last of the uncrowned kings of Malaya. I'm glad I've had the chance of serving under him, y'know. Dying breed, marvelous man.'' Gerald's pale, slightly bulbous eyes misted with drink and sentiment.

"You're a dying breed yourself, mate.'' Bill Treadwell pulled his nose out of his glass and put the drink down with excess precision.

"Don't start. . . . You colonials have always got a bee in your bonnet about something.'' James pulled in his chair as the whiskey-spitting war advanced into the room.

" 'S true. Ten years' time the *tuans*'ll be dying out like dinosaurs.''

Gerald's amiable round face flushed with drunken irritation. "Listen, if we British weren't here, this country would be nothing. There'd be no tin mining . . .''

"Chinese found the tin, Chinese can mine it.''

". . . there'd be no rubber . . .''

"Don't need white skin to plant trees, old son.''

". . . and there'd be civil war from one end of the peninsula to the other. Dammit, man, we're only here because the rajahs asked for British soldiers to stop their people massacring each other.'' Gerald's freckled fist hit the wicker table for emphasis.

The whiskey fighters, now drenched and carrying half-empty bottles, surged forward once more toward the reading room.

Bill Treadwell sat back like a bemused schoolmaster with a particularly obdurate class of dullards.

"The sun will never set on the British Empire, hey? Or the British umpire either?" The cricketers, now bathed and changed, were coming into the bar and acknowledging greetings around the room. Treadwell leaned toward Gerald to give his argument emphasis. "It'll happen all right, but you don't understand why. You don't even understand how much you don't understand. You think that the Malays are like children because they smile a lot and believe that trees have spirits. You can't see what it is that makes them a nation."

"Well, they're not a bloody nation, they're a bunch of bloody savages from every uncivilish—uncivilized race east of Suez." Gerald spluttered more and more as his anger flared. "The Chinese chop each other up in tong wars, the Tamils worship cows and the damn Malays sit in their kampongs doing bugger all. Country would've gone to hell but for the British."

There was a crash, and more boisterous shouting, as the whiskey fighters barricaded the door with an upended leather sofa.

"For Pete's sake, mate, don't you see it doesn't matter? The Malays get their religion from Arab pirates, their art from Indonesia, and half their language from Persia; there are people in the jungle who don't know how to make fire and whose babies are born pink-skinned. They've been colonized by the Siamese, the Portuguese, the Chinese, the Dutch and your mob, and none of it makes any bloody difference. The way the Malays think, all that's totally insignificant. This is their land and they'll be here when you and King George and the British Empire are just another folk memory."

Gerald squirmed angrily in his chair, not noticing that James, who had the ability to hear two conversations at once, had tuned out of the often-repeated argument and was listening to the French planters continue their debate on love.

"You're forgetting one thing," Gerald said finally, stifling another belch, "you're forgetting that we love this bloody country."

The Australian leaned forward, not too drunk to hear the catch of emotion in his friend's voice.

"I know, mate. I know you bloody love it. You shut your eyes on misty mornings and look at the brown cows and the green *padi* fields and you think you're living in England, you think you're at home."

There was a massive roar of drunken triumph as one army

74

succeeded in shoving aside the upended sofa and storming over it into the reading room.

"But you aren't at home, mate. You're in some other blighter's home. And you love it for what you can get out of it, oh, yes, you do." He raised a bony hand to quell Gerald's indignant protest. "You love Malaya because you can live like a king out here and back home you'd be cooped up in a stinking office pushing paper.

"That's rot, Treadwell. . . ."

"But the Malay loves Malaya because the land is part of his soul. Doesn't matter to him who lines their pockets, mining tin or planting rubber, it's his country."

Gerald slumped back, shaking his tousled ginger hair.

"I don't understand. I don't understand you and I don't understand the bloody Malays either."

With an exasperated gesture, Bill shoved his horn-rimmed spectacles back to the bridge of his sun-reddened nose.

"You'll never understand the bloody Malays until you live their life, take their religion and become one of them. That's what it's all about. For Christ's sake, why do I have to explain this to a pair of bloody British? Look at yourselves, man."

The French planters concluded that love was more important to a woman than to a man because a woman had a greater capacity for sensual enjoyment. An armistice was called in the reading room and the whiskey-sodden army came tottering out in twos and threes, laughing uproariously. James suddenly switched his attention to what the Australian was saying.

"What about us, you old sheep-shagger? You two must be as pissed as rats."

"Well, look at you both. You're as swarthy as a bloody Eyetie—where're your folks from originally?"

"Italy, France—my mother's side are Huguenot, my father's came from Florence."

"And look at him"—Treadwell's bony finger pointed at Gerald—"red hair, fair skin—"

" '*The Celt in all his variants from Builth to Ballyhoo,/ His mental processes are plain—one knows what he will do,*' " quoted James. "I get you. You mean that here we are calling ourselves Anglo-Saxon and Church of England and we're no more Anglo-Saxon than a Chinese rickshaw boy; that we've cobbled our version of Christianity together same as the Malays have stuck a bit of Hinduism and a few of their old spirit cults onto Islam. But we're English because we think English and . . ."

"And drink Scotch," Gerald finished defiantly, signaling to the distant boy. "How about one for the road?"

"Well, thank Christ for the upper classes," muttered the Australian, giving James a wink as he emptied his glass.

Later they stumbled under the string of colored lights above the wrought-iron gate of Mary's. Mary, a dumpy Eurasian with skin like yellow leather, shouted to the girls to bring out bottles of warm beer and crank up the gramophone, and as they moved lethargically to obey, she sat down opposite the men at the tin table.

"I got a very nice girl, new girl. . . ." She looked from one man to the other as if trying to hypnotize them into believing her.

"What is she?" James's tone was businesslike.

"She's Malay, but nice, very pretty, you like." The three men shook their heads. "Very pretty girl, you see, I call her. . . ." Mary signaled across the room and they waited uncomfortably.

In a few moments a woman in a tight orange jacket and flowered sarong appeared and stood hesitantly in the side doorway. James judged her to be at least thirty-five, since she had lost the lamblike plumpness of young Malay girls but was not much wrinkled.

"Does she know how to kiss?" asked Gerald, who'd discovered that kissing was quite pleasant during his courtship of his nurse in Guildford. In general, the Malay whores didn't kiss and tended to be uglier and older than the Chinese.

"She do anything," Mary promised confidently. Gerald shook his head in doubt.

"What about Sally?"

"Sally—ah, you mean Sui Lee. She busy."

"Busy long?"

Mary paused for thought. "Not busy much longer, I think. You want her after?"

"Yes, she's worth waiting for." With bravado, Gerald took a swig of his beer.

"And your friend?" Mary looked at James, who was still considering the Malay girl. Her skin was a light walnut shade and she had a neat, high-cheekboned face that argued some Mediterranean blood.

"Where's she from, Mary?"

"I don't ask. She come yesterday, tell me husband die." There was little point in asking further, since he knew he would probably not be told the truth. James liked the girl's diffidence, disliked her maturity, and didn't much care for the Chinese whores who were as skinny as cats.

"She'll do," he said, giving Mary some notes and disappearing with the woman up the house's sloping stairs.

"Since you're so clever"—Gerald turned to Bill—"you tell me this. Why're all the Malay girls so bloody ugly?"

"Easy. Malay women only go on the game if they're widowed or divorced, no male relative to support them, and got no hope of getting another husband. Your Malay, being a Muslim, doesn't care for divorced women because he thinks they know too much. Specially in the little villages—they've got a saying that a wife who's lost her husband is as frisky as a horse that's thrown its rider. The peasants get together and throw the girl out of the village before she gives the married women ideas. But with the Chinese it's all down to money—Chinese girl thinks she can make more money spreading legs than selling mangoes, she's away. Half of them are sold by their mothers, if they're pretty."

"So, what's your fancy? You've been bloody quiet sitting there."

"I'll sit this one out, I think." Treadwell's tone was grim, and Gerald was about to ask the reason, when Sui Li appeared in a skintight pink cheongsam. She greeted him with delighted shrieks, to emphasize her popularity and consequent prosperity to the other girls, and dragged him happily up the stairs to her room. Underneath her cheongsam she was naked, but in the few moments it took her to peel it off, Gerald plumped down on the bed and fell asleep.

Downstairs Bill Treadwell waited, reflectively sipping his beer. For all he had drunk, he felt sober. He took off his horn-rimmed spectacles and put them in the breast pocket of his jacket. Mary's, with its peeling Tiger beer posters and languid, bored whores, faded to an indistinct blur.

5

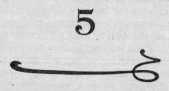

For Monty, the worst thing about her father's death was that it left her alone with her mother. There was her sister, of course, but Cathy was different. She was not a combatant in the unending war with Bettina which was the real focus of the Bourton family's energy.

To a casual friend, it would seem that both the Bourton daughters were caught up in competition for the love of their bewitching father. The truth was much, much darker than that. James and his girls were united in resistance to the hatred of Bettina.

The family had no casual friends, because Bettina froze them off with calculated social inadequacy. She had made an offensive weapon of her shyness.

Their house was a tall gray stone building of exceptional elegance and charm, built to nestle in a spinney at the foot of the downs to the north of Brighton, on the outskirts of a village of red-brick cottages which were so generously decorated that the girls always imagined Hansel and Gretel's gingerbread house to look very much like them. The graceful aspect of the house suggested that life within was all civilized happiness. Very few people ever entered it. Those who did observed that Bettina outwardly followed all the conventions of motherhood, while at the same time persecuting her family with a cold, passive withdrawal that would have made violent hostility come as a relief.

The girls responded by drawing together for emotional support. Before they dared to express in words the conviction that their mother did not like them, they shared the knowledge sub-consciously; it was an awful secret which they kept together.

James all but deserted his home while the girls were small, living his life in London as much as he could. Cathy grew up with the futile notion that if she was as good as she possibly could be, maybe one day their mother would love them and her father would come back. She became a high-spirited girl with great gifts of pleasing, and in due course James began to take pleasure in her company.

Monty scorned to please. She attacked. She wanted more than mere survival. She wanted revenge. By instinct she saw that Bettina's facade of parenthood masked relentless ill-will.

"Witch," she screamed at her mother in her frequent child-hood tantrums. "Witch! Witch! Wicked, wicked witch! I hate you! I'm going to burn you all up."

Bettina never replied. She continued on her daily routine as if she were a planet moving obliviously in its orbit. Her mornings were spent in her room; in the afternoon she would set off for the bridge club and she would not return until late at night. She and James had separate bedrooms. They seldom shared a meal. Rarely, James would suggest an outing for the whole family, in which Bettina would at once refuse to take part. She never ac-companied him anywhere. The family came together only at Christmas.

The wifely duty of decorating the house was also something she avoided, with the result that James and his mother, Lady Davina, had created the interior together. James's taste was for rich, highly colored furnishings and exotic pieces of furniture. Lady Davina introduced fleets of silver photograph frames, col-lections of Sèvres porcelain, wistful watercolor portraits of their distant relatives and odd items which she felt she could purloin from Bourton without Uncle Hugo noticing. One of these stolen treasures was an oil painting of a bright-eyed white lapdog, which, Lady Davina told them with great pride, had belonged to Madame de Pompadour. It was the only one of her additions that could hold its own against James's emerald brocade curtains and inlaid Chinese cabinets.

The girls grew up in a riot of ill-matched luxury. Their moth-er's conversation was a stream of platitudes directed at nullifying all communication. If Monty complained her tennis clothes were sweaty, Bettina would say, "Nonsense. Horses sweat, gentle-men perspire and ladies only glow." If Monty said she was hungry, Bettina would at once tell her, "You can't be hungry. You've no idea what hunger is." If any member of the family attempted to involve her in a decision, Bettina would refuse, saying, "It's no use, I never discuss anything with my relatives. It only leads to arguments."

Bettina also refused to acknowledge either daughter's approach to womanhood. Cathy and Monty knew, from the experience of their friends at school, that they would probably begin to menstruate at some time, and one morning, Monty woke up in pain to find her bedclothes soaked with scarlet blood. Cathy called their mother, who looked at the mess with distaste, said nothing and walked away. Half an hour later the housekeeper appeared to strip the bed, and gave Monty one of her own sanitary towels. They were made to feel they had done something offensive.

"Anyone would think I'd started just to upset her," snarled Monty. "She ought to be pleased. I'll be grown-up soon and then she won't have to bother with me anymore."

Cathy and Monty were sent to boarding schools when they were six and five years old respectively. They passed their summer vacations with their uncle's family at Bourton.

The piano lessons were started in the remaining holidays as a solution to the problem of getting the children out of their mother's way. Cathy was easily pleased with her pony. But Monty was frightened of horses and said that riding hurt her rapidly developing breasts, a ploy she knew would work because Bettina would evade discussion with her on a subject so embarrassing.

Instead, she was put on the country bus to the next village, where an elderly woman gave piano lessons in the church hall.

"I can do tunes now," Monty announced to her sister shortly after her tenth birthday. "It's as easy as anything. My teacher says I've got perfect pitch because I can sing whatever she plays. She says I've got a very good ear."

Cathy looked at each side of her sister's head, pushing back her dark curls to look at her ears.

"Which one is it?" she asked with curiosity.

"Not my *real ear*, silly, ear for music. Don't you know anything?" Proud as she was of her smart older sister, Monty enjoyed mastery of something at which Cathy did not shine.

No one except Cathy had any notion of the pleasure Monty found in music until the teacher by chance met James at a village fete.

"You must be so proud of Miranda's playing," the gray-haired spinster told him, taking the money for his guess at the weight of her almond-paved Dundee cake. "She's such a *pleasure* to teach. She's developing real musical sensitivity, you know— unusual for a child of her age. She needs to practice more, of course. . . . I expect you'll be getting a new piano soon?"

PEARLS

"A new piano?" James was puzzled. He spent so little time at home he could not be sure but his recollection was that there was no piano in his house. The music teacher knew this perfectly well, and had fifty years of experience in manipulating wealthy, philistine parents for the benefit of their talented offspring. Soon Monty was awarded a handsome French satinwood piano with ormolu candelabra.

Monty's joy in the instrument made Bettina feel thwarted and angry; but she could not defy James. She had been outmaneuvered for the first time, and every hour Monty spent at the yellowed keyboard pressed home the advantage.

Now there was no James to save Monty from the cold antagonism of her mother, no champion to ride up to slay the dragon and rescue her. As she took her place in the limousine that drove the bereaved family of Lord James Bourton home from the suburban crematorium where his widow had directed that his remains be summarily reduced to ashes, Monty felt desolate. She was unprotected. She flinched as a group of photographers who had been waiting at the gates to their home crowded around the car, and Cathy pulled down the limousine's blinds with angry force.

Throughout the terrible summer, Monty and Catherine scarcely left each other's company while they watched a succession of small black cars drive tentatively up to the house. Out of the cars climbed dark-suited men, who raised the gleaming door knocker with bowed heads, knowing they were bringing bad news.

They gave their names to the housekeeper in embarrassed, quiet voices, and she showed them into the drawing room where they had long meetings with Bettina.

She would tell the girls nothing, nor discuss anything with them. Her face set in a blank mask; she came and went without saying where she was going or why.

"This is nothing to do with you," she told Cathy with savagery. "There's nothing to do and nothing to tell. Stop pestering me."

In the first few weeks the girls cried a great deal, especially at night when they woke up at intervals and the darkness was full of shapeless horrors. Monty moved her bed into Cathy's room, because anything was better than waking up and crying alone.

"If only we *knew*," muttered Cathy, tears seeping from the corners of her eyes and trickling down her temples to wet her hair. "Why would Daddy do such an awful thing? Surely he must have known that whatever he had done we would always love him? He must have been so unhappy.''

''We'll know next week, it's the inquest.'' Monty realized she was offering small comfort. ''Don't cry, *please*, Cathy, I can't bear it if you cry too.''

''But *when* are they going to have the inquest? It's been weeks now; they don't seem to know anything.''

''I don't believe he killed himself,'' Monty was still haunted by the idea that she had somehow killed her father and was determined to argue herself out of it. ''He didn't have any reason, he didn't have any problems. And he didn't leave a note. They must think someone killed him, or why were the police here?''

''Were the police here?'' Cathy sat up and fumbled for a tissue in the darkness.

''Yes, I asked Mrs. Armstrong and she wouldn't answer. Mummy's told her not to talk to us about anything. But I chatted up the driver and he told me. You could tell anyway—they all wear blue nylon shirts.''

Cathy switched on the light, and at the sight of each other's tear-streaked faces, the girls cried again, hugging each other for comfort.

''It's no good, crying's no good,'' Cathy said at last. ''We've got to wait it out, that's all. Someone's bound to tell us before the inquest. They won't want us to read it in the newspapers.''

The days dragged on, hot and overcast. Their mother made telephone calls behind closed doors. She seemed to age before their eyes, shrinking inside her flower-printed cotton dresses. Her hair collapsed in lifeless strands despite its dye and permanent wave, and the skin of her neck began to fall into slack folds around the sinews. She sat at dinner with them making hesitant rushes at small talk, sipping continually from a very small glass of water, which she would leave the room to refill in her own dressing room.

The sisters saw nothing odd in this behavior, because the very small water glass had been one of Bettina's idiosyncrasies for as long as they could remember. But in the long limbo of anguish, they sought any distraction, and one evening, when Bettina was called away from the dinner table to another hushed telephone call, Monty picked up the glass, sniffed it, then sipped it.

''Taste it.'' She passed the glass steadily to Cathy. ''It's vodka. She must have hidden a bottle somewhere.''

At home the girls were allowed aperitifs before dinner, or a glass of wine, but neither of them really liked the taste of alcohol. Sometimes if James had opened a particularly fine vintage he would insist that they sip it, saying "Never hurts to know a good wine." Neither of them had ever done more than tasted spirits, and they had only the vaguest idea of how drink was measured, how much was too much.

"She can't . . ."

". . . can't be an alcoholic? I bet she's hiding the bottles in her room."

"She can't be. I've never seen her drunk, at all."

Cathy thought alcoholics were people who collapsed in the gutter, not women who drank steadily in secret just to be able to put on a show of being normal.

"Oh, can't she? You know she never kisses us, don't you? She must be afraid we'll smell it on her breath."

"Don't be so dramatic, Monty." Cathy's conviction was wavering. Now that there was an explanation for their mother's odd behavior Cathy's acute mind quickly arranged the evidence to support it, remembering the amount of time Bettina spent isolated in her own room, the occasions when she had not seemed to understand what they were saying or made responses which had not made sense.

"I'll find out, if you don't believe me." Monty swiftly threw down her napkin and ran out of the room. Their mother's muted voice could be heard behind the closed door of the drawing room. Monty ran upstairs and slipped into Bettina's bedroom. A few moments later she reappeared brandishing a half-empty gin bottle in her hand.

"There. It was inside her dressing-table drawer. And there's an empty one in a Harrod's bag in there too." She planted the bottle in the middle of the gleaming mahogany table. Cathy looked at it as if it were a snake.

"So what we know now"—she drew in a slow, shuddering breath—"is that you are sixteen and I am seventeen, our father is dead, and our mother drinks."

"Maybe she'll drink herself to death." Monty immediately regretted speaking so harshly as she saw her sister's eyes brim with tears once more. "Oh, come on, Cathy. She's not going to take care of us, no one ever took care of us, we were all right as long as we had Daddy. But we're both on our own now—it's up to us. We've still got each other, that's the main thing."

A few moments later Bettina came back to find her daughters sitting in silence. She ignored them, and the accusing bottle in the table center.

"If you've finished dinner you'd better go up and pack," she announced grimly. "We're going to Bourton tomorrow."

"Have they found out anything, Mummy?"

"They've found out why he did it, if that's what you mean, and a great deal more besides. It is none of my business. Your Uncle Hugo is going to speak to you."

In the past, they had always gone to Bourton at Christmas and for the summer vacation. Cathy never thought of it without remembering the first time they arrived there, when she was very small and the family had come home from Malaya. In the evening darkness, the car headlights had caught the eyes of a group of deer on the estate road in front of them and her father had wound down the window and lifted her up so she could hear the soft rumble of their hooves as they leaped across the road. It was like driving into the England of her storybooks, a place full of princes and castles and enchantment.

Now, however, it was high summer, and the grass of the park was baked to gold and the estate road was clogged with buses full of tourists. The yellow stone house rose out of the throng of trippers like a square cake rising inside its frill, with a rank of lichen-spotted statues guarding the terrace.

The family lived in the North Wing at the back of the building, which comprised about one third of its total size. The middle third was closed; eighteenth-century hand-painted Chinese wallpaper was boarded over, plastic sheeting filled holes in the roof and dead leaves had collected in the unswept central courtyard.

The South Wing at the front was crammed with paintings that had been too important to sell without scandal and furniture too ugly to sell at a reasonable price; this was open to the public.

The National Trust owned the house; Uncle Hugo, the Duke of Witherham, owned the estate, or what was left of it. With ruthless management it yielded enough to keep him, his wife, Pamela, their two children and the seventy-four-year-old Lady Davina in what they defined as comfort. This meant that the stairs were uncarpeted and the bedrooms unheated, but there were hunters for Pamela, shooting for Hugo, and Lady Davina retained all her jewelry but was unable to afford to insure it.

Cathy and Monty sat side by side in hard chairs in their uncle's office.

"This is a frightful business about your father," Uncle Hugo began. "Your mother just can't cope, so she's asked me to talk to you. I'm afraid you're going to have to prepare yourselves for quite a few changes." He got up from his lopsided swivel chair, and walked around to the front of his desk, on which he perched his heavy, tweed-trousered backside with a clumsy pretense of informality.

"None of us had the least idea; heaven knows how he managed it all without us finding out."

Cathy, whose sensitivity to adult preoccupations made her wise beyond her years, could tell that Uncle Hugo blamed himself for not having known whatever it was, but was trying to cover this up.

"The thing is, my dears, your father wasn't quite as clever as he thought he was when it came to business. He really was rather at sea in the City, you know, and—um—" There was no kind way to say it, and kindness, in any case, was something the value of which Hugo had never known. "He lost rather a lot of money. A great deal of money. Of course he liked to live well."

"But he inherited all that money from our grandfather." Cathy's earnest bewilderment made her uncle even more uncomfortable.

"Not exactly, my dear; you don't quite understand. You and your sister inherited the money, it was in trust for you both. Really your father had no right to it."

"Uncle Hugo, do you mean something has happened to our grandfather's money?"

"Yes, my dear, I'm afraid I do. There are firms which will lend money and which specialize in finding the weak spots in other people's legal arrangements. It seems that your father had consulted one of these outfits, and taken, over the years, a series of loans against your trust. He'd covered his tracks thoroughly, so it has taken the police some time to get all the facts. He was being pressed quite savagely by these people and there's . . ." He paused, wondering if the full extent of their father's agony was something the girls ought to know.

How vividly they looked like their father, Hugo thought as he watched the two bewildered girls shrink together and link arms as if to stand firm against the world. Cathy had that broad top lip that had always made James seem to be smiling, and her hair, though definitely brown rather than James's jet black, had the same heavy texture; and yet, she had a directness, a collected manner, that was nothing like her father's flighty charm.

The younger girl seemed at first glance not to take after her father at all, although she had his unruly curls. She also had his devilment. Hugo could see in her eyes the defiance that he remembered blazing from the eyes of the small brother who had shared the nursery with him many years ago.

"But, Uncle Hugo, aren't trusts supposed to stop people using up all their money?" Cathy had a frustrating sense that embarrassment was making her uncle hold back the most important information.

"Yes, my dear, they are. I promise you, we've thrashed out the whole affair with the lawyers at Pasterns and there's no way round it. When your grandfather set up the trust he was thinking mostly of persuading your father to settle down to a decent family life. He was rather the black sheep in those days." Pasterns was the unimpeachable firm of solicitors who handled all the Bourton family's business, as well as that of half of the remaining landed gentry in England. "The partner who drew the deed up for your grandfather made the firm the sole trustees, which was perfectly correct. Your father was a very persuasive man, don't forget. He deceived us all, I'm afraid. He led us all to understand he'd made a lot of money in the East."

Hugo blamed himself. There was something inevitable about this tragedy; it had been foreshadowed for half a century by James's recklessness and peculiar lack of moral sensitivity. In a sense the rest of the Bourton family had lived as if walking on eggshells, waiting for James, sooner or later, to pay the penalty for his careless hedonism.

Hugo plowed on with his task. "I must tell you this, my dears, because you've got to hear it from one of the family. At the time he died your father had pretty much come to the end of the line. The police know that he had been to see one of these Arab financiers in Paris, and we can only presume he was trying to borrow more money. He was starting to default on some of the repayments on these loans."

Four innocent, questioning dark-brown eyes were fixed on him; a more sensitive man would have wept for them, but Hugo had no emotion to show; he felt only a dogged compulsion to fulfill, as the head of the family, his responsibility.

Cathy met his gaze calmly. "Yes, Uncle Hugo, what else?"

"There is some question of blackmail, I believe, but it seems unlikely that the police will get to the bottom of it because the outfit is based abroad and they're getting no cooperation from the police at the other end. We may never know exactly what kind of mess your father was in."

He means we're broke, thought Cathy. That's why he's rambling around and looking so uncomfortable. The idea did not disturb her. Money, to the sisters, was something you spent on magazines and records and going to the cinema, not something which determined your social position, your marriage prospects, your health or your happiness. Money was the only topic which was more strictly taboo than sex in the girls' artificially prolonged childhood.

"How much have we got left?" asked Monty in a rush.

"Nothing. Nothing at all. I'm very sorry, my dears, but it's all gone."

Cathy's mind was, as always, racing pragmatically ahead.

"We can sell the house. . . ." she began in a constructive tone:

"Your father bought the house with a mortgage from the trust, to provide you all with a home. It has appreciated, of course, but his personal liabilities will more than swallow that up. I shall have to reach into my own pocket to stop his estate being made bankrupt."

"So what's going to happen to us?" Monty's full mouth set in an angry bow. "I suppose you and Mummy have got it all planned?"

"Not quite. We decided to get this business over with before the inquest, then make our plans." Hugo looked awkwardly at Cathy, who was fumbling in the flounced sleeve of her dress for a handkerchief.

"Poor, poor Daddy," she whispered, catching the first tears as they fell. Monty hugged her awkwardly and glared at Uncle Hugo.

"Papa says your father is worse than a criminal. He says he sold your birthright for a mess of pottage," announced their fourteen-year-old cousin Edward in a nasty tone of triumph. "He says you're absolute paupers and we'll have to be kind to you, but I shan't let you ride my new pony because you'll ruin its mouth."

"Shut up, squirt!" Monty kicked him with her new Louis-heeled shoe. "We shan't have to go to school anymore, so think of that when your stupid pony's bucked you off!"

Cathy and Monty always knew they were true blood kin when they were confronted with their cousins. Caroline and Edward were beefy children who lacked all the intelligence, sensitivity and charm of the Bourton girls but were happily too far sunk in bovine complacency to realize it.

The four of them were sitting in the stuffy hayloft above the stables, a favorite hiding place at Bourton.

Monty watched with distaste as Caroline, Edward's older sister, scrubbed a bridle with saddle soap, shoving strands of her coarse brown hair out of her face. She was sallow-skinned and pear-shaped like her father, and her old putty-colored jodhpurs did not improve her silhouette.

"Are you really not going back to school? Oh, damn!" Brusquely Caroline bit off a broken fingernail, then wiped her soapy mouth on her sleeve.

"We've got to go to secretarial college. Then we'll be able to get jobs if we don't get married." Cathy lay listlessly across the highest bales of sweet-smelling hay, watching a swift dart to its nest through a hole left by a missing slate.

"Your mother does go on about you getting married." Caroline was trying to be sympathetic.

"She wants to get rid of us. She always has. She's obsessed with it. She must be crazy—who'd get married just to play bridge all day?" Monty was dying for a cigarette, but could not be bothered to get up and go outside for it.

"Beggars can't be choosers," sneered Edward. "Who'd marry you two anyway, now you haven't got any money? You're a dead loss." He dodged Monty's foot by rolling over on the floor, wisps of hay sticking to his checked shirt.

"I suppose you think you'll be the answer to a maiden's prayer yourself." His sister dunked the snaffle in a bucket of water, then hung the damp bridle up on a nail to dry.

"My mother says your mother won't be bringing you out either."

"I don't think she was very keen on the idea anyway. You know she's terrified of society, as she calls it." Cathy rolled over on her stomach and watched her cousin go to work lathering her jumping saddle. "It would have been fun though."

"Yes, it would." Caroline stood up and hoisted a fallen bra strap back into place under her blouse. "I'll be a frightful bore going to all those cocktail parties on my own."

All Caroline's sentimental potential was absorbed by her animals; by her standards, admitting that she would like to have shared her debutante season with her cousins was an emotional outpouring. Cathy smiled, grateful for what she recognized as sympathy.

"Can I light a fag in here?" Monty already had a Consulate between her lips, and snatched the packet out of Edward's reach. "You're too young. Buy your own."

To one member of the Bourton family, however, a debutante season for Cathy and Monty was strategically essential. Lady Davina had been looking forward for years to piloting the girls through their maiden voyage in society, and the pleasure of instructing the uncouth Caroline in the art of ensnaring the best possible husband was considerably less promising than that of launching her more attractive cousins. She had watched them begin to bloom and longed to teach Monty how to play on her catlike sensuality, and to teach Cathy how to withdraw when her wistful beauty caused havoc.

Now that every trace of her own physical charm had withered,

Lady Davina was enduring an enforced loss of feminine status. She had fought frantically against advancing age, with diets, cosmetics, couturiers and plastic surgery. It was a useless struggle. Once she was no longer sexually desirable, she was not noticed.

She tasted bitter humiliation every time she entered a crowded room and no man registered her arrival. She felt as if she had gradually ceased to exist. Having spent all her life practicing the art of seduction, she was unable to relate to men in any other way, and she despised the company of women. Her pretty granddaughters were her last hope of importance.

"Of course, they must *all* come out!" Lady Davina's bracelets clashed as she reached for her glass at dinner. Hugo glowered up the length of the table at his mother. She was, in effect, proposing that he pay for all three girls, and he knew that with Lady Davina in charge of the operation he would have to find tens of thousands of pounds for dresses and parties in addition to the money he was now obliged to divert to paying James's debts and securing rudimentary job training for his daughters.

"Mother, I've told you before it's out of the question."

"I was not consulted. Caroline can't possibly come out on her own. She's incapable of catching anything with less than four legs. She'll simply be asked to a succession of dreary hunt balls. Hopeless!"

Caroline's mother, a tall, brown-haired woman with the same yellow skin as her daughter, pressed the bell on the floor with her foot and the butler appeared to clear away the gold-rimmed Minton plates. Dinner at Bourton was almost always tinned soup followed by game; Hugo justified the staggering sum he spent on shooting by bringing hundreds of birds back to be hung in the game larder until semi-putrid, then drawn, plucked and stored in the walk-in freezer. This evening they were eating curried grouse. Monty quite liked it. If you mixed in enough chutney you couldn't taste the grouse at all.

"I simply cannot afford to bring out three girls. You must be reasonable, Mother." In the shadowy radiance from the candelabra, which had been converted to electricity but was for economy's sake run on half the right number of light bulbs, Hugo looked exactly like a wicked uncle, with his heavy features, beaky nose and blue jowls.

"I am being reasonable, Hugo. It will be a complete waste of money to bring out Caroline by herself. And three girls will hardly cost you any more than one." Lady Davina's Pomeranian dog jumped off her lap, dislodged by her arthritic gesticulations.

"The money simply isn't there, Mother."

"Nonsense. One can always find money from somewhere. I shall sell some jewelry." This was Lady Davina's ultimate weapon. Almost all her jewelry was what an auctioneer would describe as important; the sale would make headlines. Lady Davina herself, although long past the age of scandalous behavior in nightclubs, was still a name known to society columnists. She chafed in the obscurity of a dowager, and would seize any opportunity to be talked about once more. Hugo sawed into a grouse leg with resignation. His mother was right. Family prestige was the issue.

"On the other hand, it won't look very good if the girls don't come out after all this business." He forked a sinewy morsel into his mouth and chewed it vigorously. "They're on at me to fell some more of the West Wood this year."

"Then that's settled." Lady Davina swiveled her mud-colored eyes, beaded with black mascara, toward Cathy and Monty and gave them an enormous, theatrical wink. "The three of you can have a season next year."

"Two." Monty looked firmly at her grandmother. "You're not trailing me round that cattle market."

"Miranda!" Bettina, sitting in unsteady silence opposite her daughters, spluttered to life. "How dare you be so ungrateful! You wicked child—you'll do exactly as you're told. It's the least you can do, after all this mess. Apologize to Lady Davina this minute." Monty's defiant stare raked around the table like a machine gun.

"Be quiet, Mummy. I'm saving Uncle a lot of money, so you can't complain. I'd rather die than be tarted up in a white frock and led off to be mated like a prize heifer."

Lady Davina scooped up her lapdog and gave a tight, bloodred smile. "As you wish, Miranda. I shall have quite enough to do with your sister and Caroline."

Lady Davina's energy was suddenly phenomenal; she itched to relive the sexual and social triumphs of her own nubile years. Monty's defection made little difference, since she knew that attractive sisters close in age were often invited together, even if only the elder was officially coming out, and what young girl would be able to resist going to glittering balls and riotous parties all summer long?

The endless ill-defined medical conditions which had for years restricted Lady Davina's existence mysteriously abated. Lounging on the blue velvet daybed by the drawing-room fire, with the Pomeranian at her feet and a copy of the *Tatler* on her lap, she telephoned ceaselessly around the country, activating the network of acquaintances she had first made during her own season before the First World War.

"Nancy! Too divine. Yes, we shall certainly see you at Fugborough for Fiona. In May you said?" She covered many pages of thick blue writing paper with notes in arthritic script.

"So sick-making, they can't be presented. Never mind, Thelma darling, we shall make do—now who is this little man with a list?"

She was particularly gushing with the friends she knew to have eligible sons and grandsons. "Nothing makes you more popular than knowing heaps of young men—now where's Marina's number, I'm sure they've got three, but perhaps Charlie is still at Eton. . . ."

Cathy and Caroline were summoned to her bedroom, chilly, stuffy and smelling of stale Schiaparelli scent, and made to try on jewelry.

"Remember, Caroline, never emeralds for you—they make your complexion look like dishwater." Immune to such abuse, Caroline pulled off the necklace and stepped forward to replace it in its box, treading on the dog, which yelped and scuttled under the pink chintz skirts of the dressing table. "Pearls for daytime, of course, and always diamonds for evening, but remember that at your age, *you* must shine, not your jewelry." Catherine tentatively picked up a collar of baguette diamonds, showy in the severely art deco style.

"Certainly not, most unsuitable." Lady Davina took it from her and picked out a modest Victorian pendant instead. She obviously intended to keep the best pieces for herself.

"Thank you, Grandmother, it's really pretty," Cathy held the almost-invisible gold chain against her throat and admired the small rubies and even smaller diamond sparkling on her parchment-smooth skin.

"I think you had better call me Didi, darlings, everyone always does." Lady Davina made this suggestion in carefully casual tones, inwardly appalled at the prospect of being called "Grandmother" in public.

In a week, she had acquired all the vital information she needed to lay the groundwork for the season. Although trained from puberty to present a facade of adorable idiocy, and now able to add the dimension of approaching senility to the performance, Lady Davina had a magnificent memory.

Soon she had stored in it the names of the two hundred-odd girls who were to come out next year, as well as the likely dates for their dances. This data she added to the encyclopedic trove of information she had amassed about the wealth, property, estates and connections of each family. From a society columnist in London she then acquired The List—a roll of young men's names which came with the unwritten guarantee that every one was a sound prospective husband, with a decent family and reasonable wealth behind him and no known social vices.

"*Three* earls," she announced, setting down her translucent porcelain teacup with a tremulous hand. "You should be able to manage one easily, Catherine. I shall be most disappointed if you let me down."

Cathy nodded uncertainly. She felt quite crushed by the responsibility she now had to restore the family's name and fortune by marrying gloriously. Her thrilling romantic dreams were all too quickly turning into frightening reality. "Who are they, Didi—do we know any of them?"

"Sholto Mayleigh Shillingworth—over thirty, I should say. The longer a man stays unmarried, darling, the harder he is to catch. Andrew Downcliffe's people own half of Ayrshire, but you won't want to live in Scotland if you can avoid it. Then there's Charlie Coseley, in banking, I believe."

"He's a dreamboat," said Caroline suddenly, giving her first evidence of interest in flesh that was not equine. "His cousin was at school with us and I saw him once when he came to take her out."

Monty spent three or four days sulking and smoking, wandering aimlessly around the estate feeling irritated by the noisy busloads of tourists. She was not only bored but wrapped still in a blanket of guilty sadness which muffled the effect of the outside world upon her. She was sullen with the adults of the family, contemptuous of Caroline and vilely rude to Edward. No one took much notice of her, except Cathy.

"Please, Monty, won't you change your mind? It won't be any fun coming out without you," Cathy pleaded, finding her skimming pebbles into the lake one afternoon.

"But it won't be any fun for me, don't you see? I'm not pretty like you are; you'll get all the boys and I'll just be stuck with Caroline and the rest of the no-hopers." Monty let fly a stone at exactly the right angle and it bounced across the water much farther than she had intended, frightening a moorhen.

"You won't—don't be silly. You'll probably do much better than I will. Rosanna says her brother thought you were fabulous-looking when he came to take her out from school."

Monty sniffed, unconvinced. They both knew that Cathy, with her slim, coltish legs, her swinging straight hair, beautiful complexion and boyish figure, was so pretty she could have stepped straight from the pages of *Vogue*. What Cathy recognized, but

Monty refused to believe, was that Monty was just as attractive, but in a lush, sensual way that was not, at that time, particularly fashionable.

"You're only saying that to be nice." Monty stooped to pick up some more pebbles.

"No I'm not. Oh, please, Monty. I'll hate it without you."

"But why are you doing it? You wanted to go to university."

"I know, but it's different now, isn't it? Can't you see—if one of us doesn't get married to someone rich soon we'll be stuck living on Uncle Hugo's charity. And everyone will point at us as the daughters of the Suicide Peer." This was the name the newspapers had found for their father. Rumors about his death were still appearing in print.

"Anyway, what good would university do me? I'd only get a lot more useless exams while everyone else was getting the best men. *Please*, Monty."

Monty shook her head. "I'll only do something awful and get you a bad name. All those chinless wonders would drive me nuts. It's your choice, Cathy, but not mine."

A few days later, Monty wandered out of the estate to the side of the main road and casually stuck up a thumb as she had seen hitchhiking servicemen do. Instantly a car stopped for her.

"Where to?" The driver was a plump, golden-haired man of about forty, in tweeds. Monty, thrilled with the sudden success of her half-planned scheme, looked wildly at the signpost across the road. It said FROME 7½, BATH 80, EXETER 110.

"Exeter," she said with what she did not realize was a ripe inviting smile.

"Hop in." He shoved a pile of papers from the passenger seat and flung them in the back, on top of a heap of small brown cardboard boxes.

He was a salesman for a firm manufacturing agricultural pharmaceuticals, jolly, stupid, but worldly enough to recognize Monty straight-away for a posh piece kicking over the traces.

"Live round here? Had a row with your family?" He offered her a strong cigarette, stabbed in the dashboard lighter, then flipped it out and held it for her while steering with one negligent finger. Monty inhaled deeply, feeling fabulously adult.

When they reached the town two hours later, he bought her a hamburger in a coffee bar.

"Seen that, have you?" he asked casually as they went past the cinema where a Beatles film was playing.

"Not yet," she answered.

They sat in the back row and watched John Lennon playing a harmonica in a train. After a while the man's left hand, moving as if of its own volition and not directed by him at all, appeared on her shoulder. Full of delicious anticipation, Monty turned her face toward him; his thumb gently tipped up her chin and suddenly they were kissing.

My first real kiss, she realized with mounting excitement, eagerly parting her lips. Obviously that was the right thing to do, because his hot tongue snaked into her mouth immediately. Out of the corner of her eye she could see Ringo Starr on the screen, with arms outstretched, whirling around like a helicopter rotor, but she was much more aware of delicious, tingling excitement in her limbs. She tried putting her tongue in his mouth, and was rewarded by a crushing embrace.

In the afternoon, the small country cinema was almost empty. The man's firm fat fingers undid her blouse and began stroking her breast over her bra, then dipping experimentally inside the cup. Is he going to take my bra off? Monty wondered, undecided if she wanted him to try but longing to feel him touch her naked flesh.

What she didn't know was that in fifteen years on the road the man had picked up and made love to enough girls to know an overeager virgin when he kissed one and, being fundamentally decent and the father of girls who would soon be Monty's age, he had no intention at all of taking this puss for the hot number she was obviously pretending to be. They necked pleasantly through the rest of the movie, by which time Monty's knickers were damp with excitement. Then he drove her to the edge of the town, and she hitched a ride back to Bourton, arriving in perfect time to change for dinner, at which she was unexpectedly pleasant to everyone.

Monty now had an excited sparkle about her which subtly signaled her craving for sexual adventure to every boy interested enough to read these signs. A youth who served behind the bar at the Bourton Arms, the pub outside the estate gates where she was in the habit of buying her cigarettes, asked her if she wanted to go for a ride on his motorbike and a couple of days later kissed her as they leaned on a gate from which there was supposed to be a view over five counties. He was rather clumsy and smelt of pickled onions.

The French tourist who asked if he might take her picture by the rotunda was much more accomplished and could unfasten her bra with one adroit hand. He was very persistent about trying to pry inside her knickers, which Monty eventually allowed him to do.

By the time the girls had to go up to London, Monty had also tried her newfound allure on a Cockney coach driver, a suave young expert in nineteenth-century militaria who came to value the Witherham collection and one of Uncle Hugo's shooting chums who visited for a weekend without his wife.

She felt slightly ashamed, madly attractive and tremendously powerful with her newly discovered seductive ability. She was more than half regretful that she was not coming out. She longed passionately to find someone she liked enough to lose her virginity. Preferably someone who looked like Brian Jones.

"You remember my brother, Simon." Rosanna Emanuel's demeanor was excessively formal, in order that her brother should not realize how much and how intimately he had been discussed in Benenden dormitories.

"Hello," said Simon, ceremonially shaking hands and hoping that Cathy and Monty would not realize how much and how intimately he and his friends had speculated about his sister's friends in their turn.

"There is not the slightest use in dining with a Jewish family," Lady Davina had warned them. For once, Cathy had argued back.

"We were tremendous friends at school and it would look awful if we didn't see her now we're in London for a year. Besides, Rosanna's a very good influence on Monty."

"Never confuse friendship with social climbing" was their grandmother's reply, but she let them go, knowing that forbidding the association would only make it more alluring.

And so Cathy and Monty had walked across Hyde Park from the Bourton family's small house in Trevor Square to the Emanuels' large apartment by Marble Arch. It was double-glazed and lavishly heated, with carpets your feet sank right into. There were small silver dishes of chocolates everywhere.

Mrs. Emanuel was a tiny, vivacious woman with a strong foreign accent of which both her children were violently ashamed. She had arrived in London in the late thirties from Vienna, one of the hundreds of educated girls from Germany and Austria who had taken jobs as domestic servants to circumvent the British immigration law and escape Nazi persecution. Having married into the Emanuel family, prominent among the rising tycoon class of British Jews, she found fuel for her bottomless feelings of insecurity as well as scope for her limitless social ambition.

It was soon clear that Simon was a major aggravation in his mother's life.

"Why don't you cut your hair?" she asked him bluntly as soon as they sat down to lunch. "You promised me, Simon. No nice girl wants to go out with a boy with long hair. Tell me, Catherine, what do you think?''

Cathy was startled by the directness of this attack and the unembarrassed way that she, a stranger in the house, had been invited to contribute to a personal argument. In her own family no intimate matter was ever mentioned to guests; indeed most intimate matters were never discussed at all. Cathy struggled with the majolica asparagus tongs to give herself time to think.

"Quite a lot of boys do wear rather long hair nowadays," she began diplomatically.

"But not as long as Simon's surely. Look, it's falling right over his collar now."

Simon squirmed in his chair. His glossy black hair covered his ears and the back of his collar in a laboriously groomed bob. His head was neat and his features regular, almost classical in proportion, so he looked like a pre-Raphaelite knight. Nothing like Brian Jones, Monty acknowledged, but pretty groovy all the same.

"I think people don't really mind long hair as long as it's clean and neat. What a beautiful chandelier, Mrs. Emanuel; is it Venetian?" Cathy's attempt to change the subject was defeated at once.

"Long hair, it looks dirty—ugh. You must go to the barber with your father tomorrow, Simon. Joseph, you must take Simon with you. See that he goes. When you are working in your father's office, Simon, you must look decent."

"But I'm not working in the office, and I'm not going to work in his office, ever." Simon glared at his mother from under the coal-black sweep of his eyebrows. Angrily she clutched at the swag of gold chains at her throat.

"And what else are you going to do with your life? You are not such a clever boy, you know. You got yourself thrown out of your school, you don't take your exams, we send you to college for special teaching and you don't do any work. So who will give you a job if your father doesn't?"

Simon shrugged his broad shoulders. "There are plenty of jobs."

"But a *good* job, Simon, Ach, if only you were like your sister, she is such a good girl. Why do you want to go to strangers when your father needs you to help him?"

"He doesn't need me and I don't want to sit in an office all day for the rest of my life."

Mrs. Emanuel's tiny hand grasped her necklace tight in fury. "And what do you want, may I ask? Don't tell me, I know.

You want to be one of those filthy pop singers. Ridiculous! Disgusting! Joseph, you must stop him. . . .''

Simon's father, a pale, quiet man, had picked stolidly through the sumptuous meal as his wife and son continued their squabble. The three girls, all acutely embarrassed, lowered their eyes and said nothing.

Coffee, served in tiny cloisonné cups with petit fours, was taken in the sitting room and as soon as it was poured Rosanna said, ''Would you like to see my clothes?'' and the girls escaped.

Rosanna's bedroom was a tent of white cotton lace; she had a huge dressing room, with racks and racks of beautiful garments protected by plastic bags.

''Will you be getting lots of new clothes now you're coming out?'' she asked Cathy.

''Didi says I need at least six ball gowns, plus cocktail dresses of course. She's taking us to Hartnell next week.'' Cathy pulled a face, wistfully spreading the skirt of a pink flowered gown.

''She can't possibly take you to that ghastly place—why *the Queen* dresses there.'' There was no greater condemnation. ''Come with me to Jane and Jane—they've got such beautiful things.''

''Mmmn.'' Cathy longed to go around to the mushroom crop of new fashion designers whose provocatively pretty clothes filled the fashion magazines. She could already, in her mind's eye, imagine the ghastly thing she would be bought at Hartnell, no doubt with pale-blue chiffon swagged over the bust and sequins everywhere. But there was a problem.

''Oh, do come, Cathy; you *can't* come out in Hartnell.''

''I've got to. Didi gets a discount.''

''Pouf.'' Rosanna had never in her young life owned anything bought for the full retail price. ''I'll get you a discount, if that's all you're worried about. And Daddy says the markup on Hartnell is ridiculous anyway.''

''Are you sure? I've only got the teeniest dress allowance; we can't afford anything really. Caroline's got five thousand for her clothes, and she'll look awful in everything. I do hate being a poor relation.'' She tried on a bonnet smothered in cotton lace flowers. The price tag was still attached—it read twenty-five guineas.

''We'll get you a nice rich husband and then you'll be all right,'' Rosanna reassured her, echoing the advice that her mother had hammered into her, which her grandmother had given her mother, and which had held true for generations of women before them. ''And clothes cost nothing nowadays—look,'' she pulled out a black-and-white flower-printed smock, "from that Laura Ashley shop by South Kensington Station—guess how much? *Two pounds.*"

Monty felt oppressed by the glorious abundance of Rosanna's wardrobe and determined to stamp out the painful wish that she too was coming out. She wandered down the apartment's corridor. Faint sounds of music came from a half-open door—a few single notes, an experimental wail or two, some rhythmic strumming. Curiously, Monty pushed the door open.

"Oh, hello." Simon scrambled awkwardly upright and put his guitar down. "Listen, I'm sorry about my mother."

"She's just as bad as mine, actually."

"*Nobody* is like my mother." Of this Simon was perfectly certain.

"Mine's awful just the same. She drinks, you know." Monty had never told anyone that, or even said the words out loud.

"That's terrible. I think I'd like my mother better if she did drink; then at least she'd have an excuse for being diabolical."

There was an awkward silence.

"What did she mean about you getting thrown out of school?"

"I got expelled."

"They were going to expel me from Benenden, too. What did you do?"

"Oh, smoking and things. And I tried to buy some pot."

Monty was impressed. Buying pot was a very glamorous misdemeanor. Nothing was more effective in shocking the older generation than drugs. She looked at Simon with silent respect. He changed the subject before she asked any more questions that might force him to admit that he had paid twenty pounds for a bouillon cube in a piece of crumpled foil.

"Do you want to hear my new Rolling Stones LP?" he asked.

"Which one is it?" There had been an abrupt withdrawal of money for records since her father's death; even if the Radio Luxemburg DJs had called the *Out of Our Heads* album repetitive and boring, Monty was dying to hear it.

"The Beatles want to hold your hand, the Stones want to burn your town," quoted Simon, reverently placing the disc on his teak-veneered stereo.

"You're really lucky to have your own stereo." Monty made herself comfortable on the end of the bed and looked around. Simon's room was large and immaculately neat, with an intriguing rack of guitars and attachments against one wall and the biggest collection of records Monty had ever seen methodically stored beside them.

"They had to buy me a stereo—they were sick of me playing

Fats Domino in their sitting room. They had to soundproof my room, too.'' Simon sat at the other end of the bed and played along with Mick Jagger's voice. ''Hey, hey—you, you—get off my cloud.''

Groovy chick, he thought, surreptitiously eyeing Monty's clinging ribbed sweater, miniskirt and white boots. Dare I ask her out? What if she turns me down?

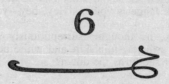

6

When she embarked on the P & O liner *Carthage*, Betty Clare was eighteen years old and full of dreams. From Gerald's descriptions of Penang she imagined an enchanted island like a child's drawing, a heap of green hills piled up in the middle of an azure sea, crystal waves lapping at its sparkling beaches.

"The Pearl of the Orient," she had murmured to herself each night, looking at the small blurred photograph of Gerald posed cheerily on a seaside terrace by a palm tree.

Gerald was the chief part of paradise, of course; so strong, so manly, waiting for her with loving arms and a faithful heart. True, his face was not distinct in the photograph and she could not now remember it clearly. It was six months since their courtship, almost a year since he had come running after her down Guildford High Street, zealous to return the gloves she had left behind in the tearoom.

She remembered how the weak English sun shone on the gold hairs on the back of his hand, and the ruddiness of him in general. He had seemed so vibrant and healthy against the pallor of her existence in a small town whose life was overshadowed in every respect by London, an hour away on the railway.

Betty's family was not wealthy and her cabin on the liner was not large. In fact, the bright-blue metal trunks that contained her wedding clothes, her trousseau and her wedding presents almost filled it up, leaving just a narrow corridor beside her bed. Anxiety that these precious belongings would be somehow lost or damaged made her suffer this crowding rather than send the trunks to the hold. She marked them all WANTED ON VOYAGE, and opened one a little on the first night at sea so that the sight of her pink linen-look going-away dress could comfort her in this strange metal cell which hummed and smelled of oil.

The trunks had another advantage; they put a barrier between Betty and the girl with whom she had to share the cabin. There was no doubt that Heather was "fast." She wore slacks all day, smoked cigarettes at table and painted her nails.

"Getting married, love?" she inquired coarsely at the sight of the bridal supplies. "Love, money or a bun in the oven?"

"Pardon?" Betty had no idea what she meant, but the tone was most unpleasant.

"Skip it." Not bad-hearted, Heather sensed she had given offense. "Oh *ho*!" she crowed as they started to get acquainted. "Padre's daughter, eh? Well, you know what they say . . ." She slapped Betty's knee as if being born the daughter of an army chaplain was something Betty had done on purpose to amuse future acquaintances. "It's a great institution, marriage, so they tell me. I'm just not ready for the institution yet."

"Why are you traveling East?" Betty changed the subject.

"I'm getting out while the going's good, love. Going to stay with my aunt and uncle in Hong Kong. You won't catch me waiting around London for the Germans. I expect that's why your folks are keen to pack you off, too."

"My father says another war is out of the question now the Germans have promised us they won't invade any more countries."

"Well, love, I'm not going to stick around to find out if they promised with their fingers crossed." Heather dabbed another layer of orange powder over her nose and snapped her compact shut. At the end of the corridor outside, a bugle was blown to signify the second sitting in the dining room. "Are you coming to dinner, or what?"

Betty was still wearing her twin set and skirt. Heather had changed into a bias-cut gown with a bolero in some kind of red rayon fabric embossed with flowers. Her scent almost drowned the faint atmosphere of engine oil that pervaded all the second-class cabins.

"I thought one didn't dress for dinner on the first night at sea?"

"*One* may wear what *one* likes, and I can't see any point in looking like a frump myself."

They walked up the narrow tube of a corridor, feeling the odd shifts of the floor as the great ship rode the ocean.

"Your fiancé must be mad to let you come out East alone," Heather offered by way of conversation at dinner. It was well known that aboard ship the combined effect of warm starry nights, the boredom and the great majority of men—particularly young men, setting off to make their fortunes in the colonies, full of high spirits and hearty appetites—made it dangerous for an engaged girl to travel alone to a wedding in the East.

"Isn't he worried you'll come down the gangplank on another man's arm?"

Betty creased her rose-petal lips in a complacent smile. "My father has asked a missionary friend of his to take care of me, so I'll be quite safe. The Reverend Forsyth, he's called. They were at the theological college together. He's sent me a card already." She showed the pasteboard oblong to Heather, who sniffed and dismissed Betty as a dead loss. She's looking at the pan of flaming crepes suzette as if it's going to burn her, Heather thought.

There were two reasons why an Englishwoman should be happy to go East, the men and the luxury. Both were in much more lavish supply than in depression-starved Britain, where a generation of men had been wiped out by World War I. The P & O voyage was just a foretaste of the good life ahead—dancing every evening and attentive servants fulfilling every wish of even the second-class passengers.

"Servants! You will have servants!" Betty's mother and her aunts had exclaimed when she told them her young man wanted to marry her and take her away out East. Not having servants was a greater shame to them than having to keep rabbits. Even the most junior professional man should have been able to afford a cook or a maid, but their household could not.

"You can't get good servants nowadays" was the refrain with which they comforted themselves. Servants were the God-given right of the middle class, of which they had been cheated despicably by fate.

"You must learn how to manage them," her female relations had warned her. "Native servants—give them an inch and they'll take a mile. You must be firm, Betty. Strict but fair. Make them do everything to your satisfaction every time." And her mother had given her a little manual called *The Housewife's Friend*, one of her own wedding gifts for which she had had no use, a slim book written for those unfortunate girls who married in the twenties with the expectation of keeping only one maid.

The three women hated Betty's father for being so inconsiderate as to have been gassed in Flanders and to be a virtual invalid now, not rich enough to provide them with servants.

PEARLS

With every chip of green soap they cut to wash clothes and every dab of black lead with which they anointed the kitchen range, every fire they laid and every mattress they turned, their resentment intensified so that Betty had been raised in a climate of vinegary aversion to all that was male. She did not yet consciously endorse this dislike. She was barely aware of it; but anything that was aggressive, strong, loud or vigorous disturbed her.

The next day they entered the Bay of Biscay, and the liner's vast structure began to stagger and groan like a beast in its death throes. Betty was piteously sick. Heather comforted her, wiping her face and fetching glasses of soda water to settle her heaving stomach. When she was once again fit to stand, Betty disliked her robust cabin mate even more. She was quite obviously one of the wicked who flourished like a green bay tree.

Mrs. Clare had warned her daughter. "You may meet some very strange people on the ship. Traveling throws you together with all sorts and you can't always choose your company. Just take no notice of them, dear."

Mrs. Clare firmly believed that evil ignored would melt away of its own accord, and so it was with Heather, who took up with the junior purser soon after Bilbao and thereafter appeared in the cabin only to change her clothes.

Once the ship was out of the angry gray waters of Biscay and she was restored to health and confidence, Betty found her protector, a short man with absolutely white hair and gray eyes. The Reverend Forsyth was on his way to Shanghai to resume his work at the Christian mission.

"I shall be glad to get back to a city I know," he told her. "I hadn't seen London for seventeen years, and I couldn't get used to it at all. So much building going on. So many automobiles everywhere. My mother's home used to be in the middle of green fields, and now there's nothing but strips of mean little houses as far as the eye can see. Do you play bridge, Miss Clare?"

Betty gave the pack on the table in front of the Anglican priest a doubtful look. "I've never played cards at all. My father is very against gambling."

"Bridge isn't gambling, my dear young lady. It's first class intellectual exercise. Mental calisthenics. Let me explain. . . ." With a supple sweep of his small hands, the Reverend Forsyth scooped up his game of patience and began to deal out the cards anew.

He was a superb companion for anyone, particularly for this shrinking, immature girl on a voyage of alarming sensations.

There was a tradition among the colonists that the old hands initiated the young in the mysteries of the East and the Reverend Forsyth had an inexhaustible repertoire of stories and the sensitivity to select anecdotes which would instruct her in alien ways without filling her with shapeless dread. He was witty but without malice, and worldly without disdain for her ignorance, which was profound.

Her father and mother had taken the greatest care to shield the only child of their house from every influence of the world, the flesh and the devil, and instead of knowledge had filled her head with precepts by which they hoped she would live a virtuous life. As a result, her ignorance was of the most dangerous kind, fortified by a lack of imagination and buttressed by fear of the unknown. Miss Clare, her chaperon realized, had perfected the mental trick of not perceiving anything that might disturb her; thus, for instance, she had no curiosity about the reason why the flashy Heather had abandoned their shared cabin, or where or with whom she might be sleeping.

She had a charming, maidenly serenity which quite captivated their bridge partners, Miss Rogers and Miss Westlake. Betty had no curiosity about them either, and did not remark the unusual enthusiasm with which they insisted she visit them in Singapore, or ask herself why two relatively well-off English ladies should choose to live together abroad, or why two women in their thirties who took care to wave their hair and make up their faces should nevertheless prefer to pass the voyage playing bridge with an elderly missionary and a prim girl rather than amuse themselves in the society of the plentiful young men. Like Queen Victoria, Betty had never heard of lesbians and would not have believed the truth if anyone had explained it to her.

The *Carthage* put into Port Said for coal, and as the ship halted in the harbor, the cheerful warmth of the Mediterranean gave way to a fierce, stifling heat. The ship's officers exchanged their evening dress for short white jackets which reached only to the waist, and in the first class the ladies sent their furs to the ship's cold storage for the rest of the voyage.

In Betty's cabin, a steward came to close all the portholes.

"They say it's to keep the coal dust out, Miss, but tell you the truth, it's to keep out the gippo thieves," he told her. "You'll be all right to open up once we're at sea again." Her cabin was like an oven, and Betty felt nauseated and giddy. There seemed to be no cool place on the whole ship. The decks beneath her feet were like hot coals.

The Reverend Forsyth found her sitting on a steamer chair under a sun canopy.

"I was hoping to take you ashore to see the sights. There's rather an interesting mosque here and ladies usually enjoy the shopping." She shook her head.

"I couldn't, Reverend, you go on without me."

"Not up to it? It's just the heat, you know. You're not accustomed to it. Take a bath and lie down for an hour or so. I'll tell you my adventures at dinner." Deliberately, he withheld his sympathy. This child would withdraw permanently into all manner of fearful illnesses unless her retreat was cut off by someone kind enough to be cruel. At dinner she was wan and ate almost nothing, but he walked her on to the cardroom all the same, using the authority of his quasi-parental position to insist.

Thus impelled, Betty bore up through the smothering heat of the Suez Canal, and once the *Carthage* passed the sunbaked rock of Aden and began to cross the Indian Ocean, the air became more refreshing. The four bridge players fell more and more into the routine of the hot, listless days and cool velvet nights. The endless time was marked by daily rituals—the cocktail hour before each meal, the afternoon siesta, the daily betting on the number of miles the ship had sailed.

The passengers felt a growing sense of freedom, isolated in their own little world of ease and comparative luxury in the midst of the limitless ocean. The tentative attractions of the Mediterranean waters became fierce flirtations, while love affairs begun earlier hit stormy waters.

Heather reappeared in the cabin and started slamming drawers open and shut as she redistributed her belongings.

"You can keep your shipboard romances," she told Betty. "Men are all the same—selfish brutes. I told him, it'll be me that's left holding the baby. Fine start to a new life that'll be. Stuck on the wrong side of the bloody earth, with a squalling brat."

Her resolve lasted only two days, and then Betty had the cabin to herself once more and Heather and the junior purser were again a regular feature of the second-class dining room, where his duties included playing Ivor Novello selections on the piano after dinner while she draped herself adoringly over the back of a chair to watch him.

Betty told her bridge friends the story.

"I think she's awfully silly; how could she have a baby if she wasn't married?" she asked with contempt, and the Reverend Forsyth, Miss Rogers and Miss Westlake glanced at each other from behind their cards. The four had become thoroughly fond of each other, as disparate strangers will when forced together by circumstances.

As soon as Betty said good night, Miss Rogers opened the subject.

"Do you suppose that our young friend knows what to expect from the physical side of marriage?" she asked, putting a pin back into her stylishly rolled hair.

The Reverend Forsyth shook his head. "I think she's as innocent as a newborn lamb."

Miss Westlake nodded, checking her diamanté dress clip to cover her embarrassment. "Green as grass, if you ask me."

There was a pause as they contemplated the implications this discovery had for their little square of friendship.

"There's a certain sort of girl, in my experience, who isn't cut out for a honeymoon. I was dreadfully naive myself and of course, my mother told me nothing, nothing at all. . . . Frankly, it was a beastly experience." Miss Rogers's long crimson mouth puckered in amusement at her own choice of words, and Miss Westlake's willowy figure swayed toward her in sympathy like a sapling bending in the breeze.

"Do you suppose we should talk to her?" the Reverend Forsyth asked with a plain sincerity which acknowledged his own sex's ineptitude in emotional matters.

Simultaneously, the two women nodded. "She looks up to *you* as a father figure," said Miss Westlake, "and I'm afraid if one of us tackled it she might—well, we could—well, you know, our experiences of marriage haven't been very good, I'm sorry to say. And she is such a cowering little thing."

The elderly man of God accepted the truth of what she said with regret. Like most men, he would rather face a shipload of Yangtze pirates armed to the teeth than a woman with urgent emotional needs.

"I'll have a little talk with her tomorrow," he agreed, with resignation.

"Tell me, my dear," he began next day, finding Betty under the sun canopy for her usual siesta, "were you close to your mother? Could you talk to her about life when something worried you?"

"Oh, yes. My mother is a wonderful woman; my father says she's the light of his life."

He smiled, noticing that the only response her creamy complexion had made in two weeks of roasting sun was a tiny dusting of freckles, like toast crumbs, over the bridge of her upturned nose. He thought her a pastel, passive, pretty little girl, made for muted emotions and narrow horizons, hardly strong enough for life at all.

"So your parents have a very happy marriage?"

"Oh, yes."

"I expect your mother told you all the secrets of her success before you set off?"

Betty was earnestly trying to follow the vicar's train of thought. She had been brought up to expect sermonizing from older people, and it had, in truth, seemed strange to her that this very wise adult had treated her like an equal when he was so obviously superior to her in every way.

Now he was beginning to sound like an adult should. Eagerly she followed his lead.

"Oh, yes. She told me always to wear plenty of scent—look!" Quick as a bird, she dipped into her handbag and brought out a bottle of Yardley's Lavender. "And to make sure my husband never saw me doing anything undignified, like cleaning my teeth. She said that being slovenly about that sort of thing killed all the magic in a marriage."

"I expect that's very true. The happiest marriages have always been between people who knew the difference between intimacy and familiarity, I think. One breeds respect and the other breeds contempt. People say that if there's trouble in a marriage, it's usually in the bedroom, but in my experience the rot starts in the bathroom first." The Reverend Forsyth was rather pleased with this quip, but Betty's periwinkle eyes became shadowed with anxiety. He at once abandoned vanity, kicked himself for this besetting sin, and returned to the awkward task in hand.

"Did your mother also mention the bedroom side of things at all?"

"Oh, yes, she was quite frank about it. She said that my husband would make demands on me, but it would be all right, I would just have to not mind, just not let it upset me."

"How very sensible. And did she explain to you what these demands . . . the sort of thing she was talking about?"

"Well, no. I never thought to ask her."

"I'd like to explain, Miss Clare. I have found that some men place great importance on this aspect of marriage, and when their wives can share in it with joyful acceptance there is a great deal of happiness to follow." He spoke with a tinge of wistfulness. The Reverend's own marriage had been ecstatic, but short. His wife had died of malaria three months after arriving in the East.

He proceeded with the utmost finesse, first drawing to Betty's attention the difference between the boy babies and the girl babies in the hospital where she worked. Betty's nursing career had been abandoned instantly after Gerald had proposed to her, and so amounted to only three months of theoretical lessons on hygiene. She had, however, observed that boy babies and girl babies were differently made, but attached no importance to the anatomical distinction. In fact, she assumed that the boy baby's penis was some superfluous fold of skin which would disappear before adulthood.

Next the patient priest asked her if she had ever seen animals mating, which she said she had. Her home had tottered on a knife edge of destitution all her life, with her father's army pension supporting himself, his wife, his two spinster sisters and his daughter. To be sure of eating meat, they had kept rabbits in their back garden, and the breeding, rearing and slaughter of these animals were her father's most meaningful occupation.

Mating the rabbits meant that her father put on big leather gloves, pulled the buck rabbit out of his hutch and tossed him, kicking frantically, into a hutch with a female. They would settle down to munch bran together for a week, and then the buck would be put back in his own hutch. Sometimes he would bite the female, and sometimes he bit Betty's father.

Betty had many times seen rabbits copulate, a process which they accomplished in twenty seconds without any excitement or change of expression. Thick fur hid all the organs employed.

The Reverend Forsyth very carefully explained that mating was mechanically the same process in humans, but that the species to whom God gave dominion over the animals usually went about things with some physical expression of affection. Betty seemed to be following him easily so he mentioned that she might perhaps have enjoyed kissing her fiancé, at which she blushed attractively.

"You will probably find it all rather strange at first," he finished, smiling with relief at a difficult assignment accomplished to the limit of his skill. "Because explanations are all very well but one person can't really convey very much to another. Experience is everything, I've found. Ah—look there—the flying fish have come back." And out on the bright surface of the sea three quivery flashes of light skittered away from the ship's wash. In an instant the silver streaks sank back into the sea, and everything the kind Reverend Forsyth had said to Betty vanished similarly in the morass of her ignorance. The facts of life, without any context of sexual knowledge, held no significance for her at all. She imagined that once married, she and Gerald would, like rabbits, browse contentedly side by side.

At last they approached the island of Penang. The sky was a hazy turquoise and the sea its grayish reflection. The water, Betty noticed, was not clear but opaque and souplike. For twenty-four hours the liner had sailed between green islands just like those of her childlike vision, and now, at last, it was slowly reaching its destination.

Green hills were visible in the cloudy distance. Ahead of the liner was the quay of George Town, with a row of stone buildings, one pillared with a thick square tower which was topped by a dome. Betty liked them; the buildings were solid, and not much decorated, the utilitarian architecture of trade. They looked like the banks at home, only they were brilliantly white, not grimed and soot-streaked. Beyond them was the massive gray stone wall of Fort Cornwallis, with cannon commanding the flat stretch of water between Penang island and the misty, palm-edged mainland of Malaya.

As the ship grew closer to the shore and swung ponderously around into alignment with the pier, she saw a lower layer of buildings, mostly of weathered wood—warehouses and port offices thronged with people. The Reverend Forsyth pointed out to her the settlement of Chinese shacks built on stilts over the water itself.

"Very ingenious people," he explained. "The land is all owned by landlords who want to charge them rent to build on it—so they build their houses over the water for free."

As she docked, the ship was besieged by bumboats full of hawkers selling snacks and curios. Garbage scows moored at one end of the liner and crowlike birds swooped down on the trash like huge flies.

At the mahogany rail the Reverend Forsyth inhaled the tepid breeze with delight. "Smell it," he told her. "That's the smell of the East. Blossoms and spice woods from the jungle, rubber and coconut fiber from the wharf, charcoal smoke, the mist on the mountains—whenever I smell that, I know I'm home."

Betty uncertainly sniffed the breeze. It did have an odor, something damp and almost intimate. It did not seem pleasant to her.

In the crowd of people pressed at the pierside she could not see Gerald and uneasy impatience filled her. Why did everything take so long on this ship? Why did they have to wait for a hundred coolies to scramble on and off before the passengers could disembark?

Below her, three small Chinese boys in a dilapidated sampan were shrieking and performing acrobatic tricks, calling for the curious passengers to throw them money, which some were doing. More urchins were jumping into the water from the end of a vacant pier. As Betty watched there was a crescendo of screaming and violent activity in the boats at the waterside; men began to beat the water with bamboo poles and a dripping child was pulled out and carried away by howling women.

"What are they doing, what's the matter?" she asked the missionary with alarm.

"Sea snake, I expect—they used to have a lot of them in Penang—yes, look, there it is, they've caught it." Betty stepped back and gasped with disgust as the men in the boat awkwardly flung a huge black serpent onto the pier with their poles. It writhed and lashed itself over and over until other men with cleavers hacked at it and eventually chopped it into pieces; then the crowd closed around the dreadful sight and hid it.

"Bit of a shock, isn't it?" the Reverend Forsyth calmed her in his noncommittal style. "You're lucky to have seen it, you know; there are hardly any of them left now."

At last the waiting in the sticky heat was over, the gangplanks were lowered, and Betty said a tremulous temporary good-bye to her friends and walked forward. Halfway down she saw Gerald, eager, smiling, spruce in his white suit and holding out his arms just as she had seen him in her dreams.

The etiquette for a beach wedding was entirely designed to delight the brides-to-be who shipped out from England before they embarked on the hazards of life as a memsahib in the Crown Colony. Gerald and his mother drove Betty straight to the cool palm-shaded haven of the E & O Hotel, where smiling porters in uniform took up her trunks, deft maids unpacked them and her wedding clothes were removed, pressed and returned looking as fresh as they had in Debenham and Freebody's store such a very long time ago.

Gerald's mother, the image of her son and as tall as he, but with more presence, had organized the entire affair and Betty felt the next day as if she were going to be married in a bower of orchids. Her bouquet was the largest mass of blooms she had ever seen, smelling quite violently of jasmine, and with fragile English flowers next to succulent tropical blossoms.

In St. George's Church, two days later, the Reverend Forsyth marched her up the aisle. Elizabeth Louise Clare took Gerald Arthur Rawlins to be her lawful wedded husband according to God's holy ordinance, and posed with him afterward on the white-pillared rotunda in the shade of the huge churchyard trees, surrounded by strangers and half hallucinating with the heat. Her dress was of thick ivory satin, fitted tightly at the sleeves and waist, and on the advice of Gerald's mother, she wore a long cotton slip underneath it to prevent perspiration stains.

"After all," the older woman advised, "you don't want to bring your dress halfway round the world and be photographed in it forevermore with sweat marks round your waist. You'll learn not to buy tight-fitting dresses out East.''

They were photographed again in wicker chairs by a frangipani bush on the hotel terrace, Gerald with his bow tie askew and Betty smiling trustfully at the Chinese photographer. They were both overshadowed by the commanding bulk of his mother behind them; the Reverend Forsyth sat awkwardly beside the bride.

Indoors it was cooler, with fans whirring endlessly to stir the clammy air. The wedding breakfast was a procession of dishes traditional to the colony—fierce mulligatawny soup, hot curry, roast beef and finally ice cream with some horrible white jelly next to it.

Gerald spooned everything down with enthusiasm. He had not had much of a stag night by comparison with an evening with James and Bill in KL, but a few boys from the Cricket Club had got up a party, and he had the kind of minor hangover which made him hungry. He noticed his bride looking at her plate in hesitation.

"It's traditional—mangosteen and ice cream—delicious, try it." He scooped up half the pale fruit and tried to feed it to her. It looked like something unborn, like the most horrible thing Betty could remember having seen, some kind of fetus.

"No, please, Gerald, I'm really not hungry. . . ." she whispered, pleading.

"Nonsense, open wide." Fearful of offending him, she parted her lips and gulped the awful spoonful down. Her head swam and she half stood up, thinking she was going to be sick. Instead she fell limply forward in a faint.

Gerald's mother had her taken upstairs to her room and brought her around with a little bottle of sal volatile. In her overbearing way she was concerned about Betty.

"There are only two types of women in the tropics. Those who cope, and those who don't. If you make up your mind you're going to cope, you will. Take it easy the first couple of days, *always* have a lie-off in the afternoons and whatever you do, don't drink unless you are accustomed to it. You'll get used to the heat, I promise you. Everybody does. But no more fitted frocks, I think." And she went through Betty's trunks and found an afternoon dress of cheap blue and white silk for her to wear in place of the pink linen suit, which had seemed so cool in London but now felt as hot as a blanket.

They were pelted with confetti and driven away in the handsome black Jaguar which belonged to Gerald's father.

Penang seemed to Betty to be divided into districts of three distinct types. There was the crowded, red-roofed hugger-mugger of Chinatown, the stone-built white-washed solidity of the British mercantile quarter and now the area through which they drove, broad avenues shaded by massive trees and lined with immense mansions. These were far more impressive than anything she had ever seen in her life. Even Buckingham Palace, to which her father had once taken her, seemed shabby in comparison.

"Who lives there?" she asked Gerald, as they passed a huge turquoise palace.

"Oh, that's the great Mr. Choy," he told her. "Made his money in lumber and tin. And rubber of course. The neighboring estate to ours is one he owns. All these houses belong to the Chinese millionaires—except that one, that is the governor's." And he pointed out a long building with one square turret.

"They're very grand, Gerald," she said doubtfully, meaning that these huge, colored, decorated palaces awed her. Although their style aped the pale colonial buildings of the British rather than the gaudiness of the Chinatown houses which had upswept eaves and carved, gilded dragons on their roofs, it was still threateningly alien to her eyes. There was too much stucco, too many balconies—the ostentation was blatant, almost savage.

They arrived at their honeymoon hotel in time for the afternoon lie-off, and then Gerald went for a swim in the milky sea. He felt rather lonely cavorting in the waves like a solitary sporting porpoise, but Betty had almost flinched when he said, "Fancy a dip?"

"But the water's *deep*, Gerald," she protested. "Please, please, you must be careful." It made him feel manly to pat her little hand in reassurance before striding down the sand.

He enjoyed showing her the wonders of the country where he had been born, expecting her to feel the thrills he remembered experiencing himself when he was finally returned to Penang after ten years in England, attending school and being farmed out to relatives every holiday. He made her sit on the terrace overlooking the beach and watch the flaming sunset.

"Better than Guy Fawkes Night, eh?" he remarked as the violent orange panorama faded to an apricot blush behind the black clouds.

"Wonderful," she agreed.

"And see the moon's the wrong way up?" he waved his glass at the vaporous crescent rising above the dark hills.

"Lovely," she nodded. Some large insects were flying into the lamplight. The strangeness of everything overwhelmed her and she momentarily yearned with all the power of feeble heart for a clean British sea breeze and the good gray sky of home.

Cheerfully, Gerald prattled at her during dinner, always drinking whisky and water, and then they danced to the gramophone on the terrace. He pressed his cheek to hers and a film of sweat at once formed between them, plastering her hair flat, but Gerald didn't seem to mind.

Betty closed her eyes and tried to recapture the wonderful, melting, giddy feeling she had felt when he had kissed her at home, but it would not come back. Instead she had a pool of apprehension welling up in her stomach.

"Shall we turn in?" he murmured after an eternity of swaying back and forth. In the bedroom he left her to change into her nightclothes alone, as much to mask his own nervousness as out of consideration for hers.

"For heaven's sake, go easy on the girl," his mother had commanded, and Gerald, who had never in his life had sex with a woman who was not a prostitute, was now in a storm of confusion at the prospect of deflowering his wife. He loved Betty so much, he thought; her sweetness and shyness wrenched his decent soul. He wanted sex—sex was what men did with their wives—except it was a filthy, shameful thing he had done only with those creatures at Mary's. Oh, God, why had he ever had anything to do with all that? He was ashamed and he felt drunk, far drunker than he should have been on what he had consumed.

In bed, he held Betty in his arms and kissed her, feeling his desire wavering like the moonlight until finally it subsided. Then he fell asleep, and later so did Betty, content that her duty as a wife had been accomplished.

She opened her eyes in complete darkness, aware that her nightdress was being dragged up above her knees and a weight was crushing her chest so she could hardly breathe. In terror she flailed her arms and legs, but the weight was not dislodged and she heard Gerald urgently whispering, "Betty, oh, Betty, I love you." There was a wave of stale whiskey vapor from his mouth, and Betty lay inert as he pressed his lips on hers with force.

Her husband's body rolled back and forth on hers, and then to her horror his leg shoved between her knees, and he pushed apart her thighs and pulled at the nightdress, baring beneath the sheet that nasty part of her body for which she had no name. Why did he want to expose the place where disgusting bodily functions were performed? Revulsion paralyzed her. She felt as if she were going to choke.

As he half rolled off her, she drew a gasping breath; then there was something else, some hot, hard, rubbery thing stabbing and hurting at that awful place. Sharp flashes of pain shot up toward her belly. The thing was tearing against her dry flesh. Sweat poured from Gerald's face and dripped onto her, adding its acrid smell to the stink of liquor. In the darkness, her husband was grunting like a beast possessed by demons, and the crushing weight of his body was on her again. There was terrible burning pain, then Gerald cried out, stopped rolling and lay still.

Betty lay shaking under his body, crazed with panic. Was he dead, or ill, or mad? Why had he done that revolting thing to her? What had he attacked her with? Gerald rolled off his wife and drifted obliviously toward sleep. At the back of his fuddled mind he realized that something had not been the same as doing it with the girls at Mary's, but perhaps, he reasoned, white women were different.

From Gerald's descriptions, Betty had imagined the rubber estate like the plantations in *Gone With the Wind*, a vast acreage of orderly vegetation dominated by a gracious white house. She saw herself, like Melanie Wilkes, with a pony and trap and a loyal native servant, performing charitable deeds among the plantation workers.

At first her expectations were fulfilled. After the Malay kampong with its dark wood cottages like gingerbread houses, the red dirt road to Bukit Helang curved between attractive fields of saplings and broadened at the hilltop into a spacious compound. Some amiable brown cows grazed in front of the plantation house; the buildings were creamy, pillared and shuttered, and shaded by a row of royal palms. But the ox cart which carried them and their belongings continued past the main settlement and on to a single-story, tin-roofed bungalow a quarter of a mile beyond, on the edge of the towering jungle.

Two young Asiatics in starched white jackets stood beside the front steps to welcome them. "Ah Kit, my—our—boy," Gerald presented him, "and Hassan is the gardener." They bowed and Betty nodded at her servants.

Jungle she had conceived as a kind of endless flowering shrubbery. Instead it was an impassive gray-green wall all around them, tall and dark and full of unseen life which gibbered incessantly, by day and night. It sounded to her as if a million banshees were cackling with glee at her unhappiness. There was no animal ever to be seen, and few birds. No flowers ever bloomed, except some unearthly dead-gray orchids flopping from a high fork of a tree.

When the lamps were lit at night, great bugs would blunder into the bungalow unless the long rattan blinds were pulled securely down around the balcony rail. Even so, Betty at first saw a spider under every cushion and a scorpion in every corner. She suffered tortures of continence in the night because the bathroom floor was slatted and she could not look at it without fearing that a snake would slither through the gaps.

There was only one other white woman on the estate, Jean Anderson, the spare, middle-aged wife of the plantation doctor. They were a kindly couple who took Betty under their wing at once. Dr. Anderson was short and plump, with round cheeks that flamed rosily through his deep tan, and thinning fair hair. They had a gramophone and a selection of lovingly preserved recordings of popular ballads and light opera, and in the evenings they preferred to sit quietly enjoying each other's company and the music, rather than join the boisterous company of the other planters. Betty sometimes heard snatches of Gilbert and Sullivan wafting through the trees on freak currents of air.

The Andersons' bungalow was the nearest, and every morning, when her husband had left after his breakfast, Betty would hear the rattle of Jean's bicycle and her brisk greeting to Ah Kit.

"There's a sort of tradition that we speak Malay to the servants," she told Betty after watching her struggle in vain to tell Ah Kit how to use the refrigerator. This luxury had been Gerald's parents' wedding gift to them, but the houseboy cooked complete meals for a week and stored them in the whirring white box, which distressed Betty's notions of hygiene. "I'll write down some of the basic phrases and if you get into a pickle it'll help you out. Don't be disturbed; they all think the fridge keeps food indefinitely."

"He looks so—well, so sneering and superior," Betty confessed.

"The Chinese are always sure that they are very, very superior people, which makes them first-class servants. You can be great friends with them, and there's never any need to nag them because their standards are terrifically high."

"But whenever I go to tell him something he acts as if I'm insulting him."

"What do you do—go out to his quarters?"

"Well, of course," Betty answered with blank surprise.

"Never do that, dear. You just don't go out to the servants' quarters. That's their home and you don't invade. Call him, always, and he'll come out smiling.''

And Betty did as the older woman counseled, and saw Ah Kit run out of his hut, buttoning his immaculate starched jacket as he did so. He cooked in the open between the two dwellings, on a charcoal fire in a kerosene tin, first chopping his ingredients with a cleaver on a tall wooden block. Betty was quite glad that Ah Kit's domain was out of bounds; once she was sure she had seen him put a frog on the chopping board.

She looked out one morning and saw quantities of their rice and flour spread out on tablecloths on the lawn of coarse jungle grass. She ordered Ah Kit to put the stores back in their tins at once but he fired off a torrent of Malay, then tried to explain to her again, speaking slowly, before giving up and walking away.

''He's quite right,'' Jean told her when she came over. ''When it's a nice hot sunny day and set fair, they ought to take the chance to put the dry goods out in the sun. You can't stop the weevils and maggots breeding in this climate, but if you spread the stores in the sun then the creatures crawl away, and you can sieve it all and put it back in the containers. Housekeeping out here is an eternal battle with the insects, you'll find. I used to think Malaya was built on an ant heap when I first came out.''

Her friendly neighbor could help with household hints, but not with the physical discomfort. Betty soon became accustomed to feeling a band of sweat-soaked fabric behind the belt of her dress, and to changing her clothes completely three times a day. If she wore cool sleeveless frocks her arms were smothered with an itchy prickly-heat rash, and if she covered them up she sweltered. Her toes blistered and her eyelids puffed, the delicate membranes irritated by the brightness and the dust.

Worst of all, much the worst, were the nights. By the time they arrived at Bukit Helang, Gerald had realized that he could not penetrate his wife—at least, not without inflicting an inhuman degree of suffering on her, and Betty had recognized that the revolting thing Gerald did to her in bed at night was what a husband had a right to ask of his wife.

She willed herself not to mind, but it was not enough. Gerald fussed with her and tormented her and only stopped if she cried or told him he couldn't bear the pain anymore. Her deeply instilled ideals of duty made it impossible to hate her husband, and instead she gave way to apathy.

The disaster of their intimate life quickly became a secret that the two conspired to keep, and in company they held hands and kissed like model honeymooners. James with his perception, Douglas Lovell with his experience, Dr. Anderson with his medical training and Jean with her sympathy, all missed the couple's reluctance to be left alone together.

Gerald took to acting the expansive host, and invited James or one of the other young assistants over for meals. He drank more and more, and his humor became sarcastic, while Betty grew thin and listless, sleeping in until after ten in the mornings and prolonging the afternoon lie-off until she did little more than get up and dress for their meals.

Three months after their wedding the news came that Britain was at war with Germany, grinding Betty deeper into her despair. Although she hated the notion of displeasing Gerald, she had lately started rehearsing in her mind a speech to him in which she admitted that she was a failure as a wife and asked to be sent home. Now there was no chance of that. She was condemned to this terrible place.

In the end, it was Betty's feeble temperament itself which saved their marriage. Each evening, the young assistants would play tennis on the two courts which Douglas Lovell had put in beside the plantation office. Betty was incompetent at all physical sports, but she came with Gerald for the distraction and usually sat and drank lemonade beside the court in the shade of the casuarina trees. Even here the jungle was barely held back. Banks of ferns crawled toward the clipped lawn like clawing hands outstretched to repossess their territory. Lassos of blue convolvulus lay over the garden shrubs.

Betty watched Gerald and James play, James darting like a bird across the back of the court while Gerald panted to and fro near the net joking with his opponent. She felt a tickling at the nape of her neck, so light it could have been a falling hair, and put up her hand to relieve it.

With repellent speed a bloated creature clambered down her arm and fell into her lap. Its body was a pallid green bladder covered with spines, its shape so bizarre it seemed to have no head or legs and to propel itself in convulsions.

Betty was stiff with fear. Her lips stuck to her teeth and she was unable to cry out. At that moment, the boy came up with her lemonade and she dumbly implored him with her eyes. Laughing, he fished up the vile creature with his napkin and showed it to her on his tray.

"Stick insect, Madam," he told her with pride. The thing was as big as a dinner plate.

Betty leaped to her feet screaming and scraping at the skirt of her dress as if the animal were still stuck to it. She lost her breath, gasped for air, gasped again, screamed for Gerald, tried to stop, gulped air once more and fell into a chaotic pattern of screaming and gasping which she could not control. Within half a minute she collapsed unconscious.

Anderson the doctor was fetched and Betty was carried home and put to bed. Ah Kit's wife was instructed to sponge her body with tepid water to cool her, and the doctor gave her an injection.

"If I'm correct, this was just a hysterical thing," he told Gerald. "She was hyperventilating, which caused her to pass out, but there's nothing serious amiss. Keep her calm and she'll be as right as rain tomorrow. I've given her a mild sedative, that's all."

After the doctor had gone and he had eaten and drunk dinner alone, Gerald sat on the end of the bed and looked at his wife. Her face was still flowerlike in its innocence, in spite of the weight she had lost in the last weeks. She was loosely wrapped in a sheet, on the doctor's instructions. Gerald had never seen his wife naked, and among the bewildering turmoil of his thoughts about her and their failed love life was that germ of suspicion that white women somehow were made differently from Orientals.

Slowly he pulled back the sheet. Betty stirred but did not wake. Even in the gold lamplight she seemed as pale as milk, and her nipples were the fresh pink of rose petals. With curiosity, Gerald stretched out his hand and felt between her legs. Betty murmured and turned her head, but her eyelids did not flicker. Carefully he felt between each moistening fold, at last deciding that there was no difference. Now he was aroused but perplexed—was it right to screw a woman who was unconscious, even if she was your wife?

In fact, Betty was not completely unconscious. She was aware of Gerald touching her as if it were happening far away. She felt no disgust or fear, and no pain when he eventually unbuttoned himself, got on top of her and penetrated her with a brief yelp of triumph. It all seemed like a dream and of no consequence, but she was aware that he seemed pleased with her.

Neither Gerald nor Betty ever referred to this incident, but the next night Gerald again succeeded in having full intercourse with his wife, and the spasm of fright which had closed her vaginal muscles tight against him never returned. He found, in the next few months, that the process was a good deal easier if he felt around between her legs first. Betty never came to enjoy any of this, but she could appear accepting enough to make Gerald feel happy about doing it.

Six months later, the older Mrs. Rawlins traveled to Bukit Helang to stay with her son and was reassured by the harmony of his household. Betty spoke creditable kitchen Malay to Ah Kit, Gerald was in high good humor most of the time, on the balcony a pied jumbul bird piped in the morning sun and the gardener tended a new row of bright orchids in pots. Little Betty found herself enlisted in the honorable association of the mems who coped.

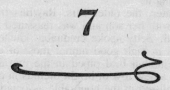

7

GIGGLING WAS NOT ON THE CURRICULUM AT ST. JOHN'S SEC-
retarial College in Kensington, but it was the only activity to
which the students devoted much time. None of the girls really
studied. Many flounced late through the door, signed the register
and ran straight out again to head for Chelsea and the new boutiques full of skimpy minidresses designed exclusively for the
near-pubescent figure.

The teachers, embittered petit bourgeois spinsters with the impossible job of training butterfly-witted debutantes, hounded the
more docile through lessons in bookkeeping and office practice
with grim disapproval. The days after the big debutante dances
the only girls in the college would be the foreigners and one or
two from the suburban middle classes.

By 1964 it was becoming fashionable for a debutante to have
a job. "Hopes to work with children" or "Already signed by
London's top model agency" was the sort of thing to appear
after your name, age and parentage in the caption beneath the
pictures in the society magazines, *The Tatler* or *Queen*.

The students at St. John's adopted these poses without having
the slightest expectation that they might ever want or need a job.
They were content with their destiny as future wives and mothers
who would be maintained as their husbands' most expensive
status symbols. They looked forward to spending money—on
clothes, jewels, homes and amusements—but never, ever, to
making money.

PEARLS

This affectation of work was, to the aristocracy, another amusing pastime, part of the trendy acquisitive spirit of the age. While bank clerks and messenger boys lusted to be millionaires by the time they were twenty-five, the inheritors of the wealth amassed by the young tycoons of a hundred years ago claimed a little of this egalitarian glamor by entertaining the idea of work. It never occurred to most of them that they might actually *need* to work one day, at least in the sense of getting up before 11:00 A.M. on a regular basis.

As they waited every day for the 73 bus to take them down Knightsbridge to St. John's, Cathy, Caroline and Monty saw the signs of the times. When a Rolls-Royce drove past them it might as easily contain a pop-group manager in his twenties, with a flowered shirt, driving himself, as a chauffeur and a silver-haired sober-suited businessman. Grimy workmen's tea bars closed, and reopened as Continental-style pavement cafés serving frothy cappuccino.

Londoners were longing to sit in the sun. In the entire twentieth century, until that enchanted era, no ordinary person in Britain had lived very far from the threat of poverty or death. War, slump, more war, more slump—now the country was famished for pleasure, frivolity and abundance. Now, Britons believed, they could at last afford their hearts' desires.

There was wealth for the making, goods to be bought, plenty of everything for everyone. Foreign countries meant holidays, not battlefronts. The streets were clogged with cars, the shops stuffed with clothes. There was no need to save, no need to deny yourself any longer. Life was nothing but pleasure. "You've never had it so good," boasted the Prime Minister, who was soon succeeded by a Labour government which set out to share the bounty.

Material goods were not the only pleasures that were finally off ration; sex was to be available too, without guilt, shame or danger. Thanks to the Pill, love would soon be free for all.

The debutante season danced to the relentless rhythm of swinging London. Instead of a dance band, girls were starting to demand pop groups to play at their balls. They invited photographers, boutique owners, even their hairdressers to their parties—one girl eloped to Spain with her hairdresser, leaving the rest of his clients fuming with annoyance. "Nobody but Gavin can *possibly* cut my hair!"

Lady Davina was put out to find that, instead of shepherding two demure girls in pastel chiffon through a succession of decorous balls, she must instead release Cathy and Caroline into motley assemblies of men with jeweled cuff links and girls in cotton frocks—full length, high-waisted cotton frocks, pretty in a Bo-peep way, to be sure, but nothing which accorded with her notion of glamor.

Each morning she made them visit her in her bedroom in Trevor Square, a stuffier, more heavily scented reproduction of her chintz-swagged quarters at Bourton Hall. While the Pomeranian wheezed in the folds of her pink satin quilt she lectured them on what she considered to be the art of catching a prize man.

"Never let a man know you are on a diet," she ordered, sipping tepid Lapsang Souchong from a chipped Minton cup. "Men like to see a girl eat heartily; they think it shows *animal appetites*. Of course you don't eat a thing when you're at home, not a scrap! But *he* must never know that."

There was a muffled gurgle, like distant plumbing, from below the quilt. Lady Davina's persecuted bowels, accustomed for decades to a diet rich only in liquids and laxatives, evidently had their own views on her philosophy.

"Never talk to a man about business, money, politics or religion. If *he* wants to talk about those things, of course you listen. Listen properly. Make notes afterward of what he's said." Her pointed red tongue flickered over her dry lips. "But *never* put forward your own opinions. Leave men's things to men—heaven knows why they find them so fascinating. If you must talk, talk about charming topics of no consequence."

"Ask who he hunts with, you mean?" said Caroline.

Lady Davina snorted. "Of course not!"

"What sort of things, then?" Monty picked at a crushed satin rosette on the quilt, trying not to sound as sarcastic as she felt. Lady Davina rallied her quavering voice.

"Gossip!" she exclaimed. "Talk about people you know, tell little stories, amuse him! Think of yourself as Scheherazade, soothing your weary Sultan with tales of a thousand and one nights! And flatter him, always flatter him. A woman should be able to make a man *worship* her."

Cathy, who absorbed these lessons with considerable misgiving since she always had difficulty inhibiting herself from saying what she thought, silently racked her brains for spellbinding anecdotes of typing classes at St. John's.

"I hate flattery—it's insincere," Cathy protested, as she admired her new Sassoon haircut in one of Lady Davina's cherub-infested mirrors.

"Nonsense! In courtship one must always be accommodating—you do *not* need to be sincere."

Yet more embarrassing than these morning lectures were the evening excursions on which Lady Davina occasionally took them. They would go to the Mirabelle or the Caprice, gilt-encrusted, old-fashioned restaurants to which diners still wore evening dress, and whose maitres d' took pleasure in barring a man with long hair or without a tie.

In stiff cocktail dresses, with velvet bands in their hair, Cathy, Caroline and Monty sat beside their overexcited chaperone as she instructed them in the ladylike arts of seeming to eat, seeming to drink and seeming to be merry when in fact you ate no food, drank only water and had a raging migraine.

Worst of all were the occasions when one of Lady Davina's few surviving admirers creakily lowered his shriveled body into a chair beside her. Her animation became more vivid, her voice louder as she whooped and shrieked flirtatiously, heaping ridiculous flattery on the withered specimens of manhood temporarily within her grasp. "Johnnie!" she would simper fortissimo, "you wicked, divine man! How I long for those wonderful weekends we used to have! You were such a *naughty* boy, you know!" and Johnnie or Gervase or Ralphie would twinkle a bleary eye and mumble some chivalrous rejoinder.

"They must be dumb to fall for it—she's as subtle as a brick," Monty disapproved.

"They do fall for it, though." Cathy thoughtfully stroked her hair. "I know it's nauseating, but it works."

They went to one or two London balls in preparation for the Season to come in the New Year, but the real social business of the autumn months was the tea parties, at which the rising debs practiced social skills and sought pledges of support for their planned cocktail parties and dances.

Caroline's strategy was unsubtle bribery.

"Do come to Bourton," she virtually ordered her new acquaintances, "the hunting's first-class, everyone says so, and Daddy's promised he'll turn the heating on for the swimming pool."

"I wish you'd find out who they are first," Cathy complained in the taxi back to Trevor Square. "We don't want a room full of dowdy lumps who haven't got any brothers."

"The girls are only a way to get at the men," Lady Davina had advised them, and Cathy, with single-minded intent, sifted every room for relatives of the three young earls.

Anthea Downcliffe, plump, mousey-haired and totally at sea in London after the enclosed Ayrshire set, was easy to befriend and pathetically grateful for the patronage. Lady Davina, on hearing that Sholto Mayleigh Shillingworth went two or three times a year to a shady health farm for colonic irrigation, removed him from the guest list and refused to explain why. "A dead loss, my darlings. Trust me," she trilled.

The nearest relative of the Coseley clan was the cousin of Charlie the dreamboat, a showy, long-legged blonde who seemed dauntingly impeccable in her Courrèges shifts. Cathy was surprised when, after three or four weeks of tea parties, this girl had come across a Pimlico drawing room, introduced herself as Venetia Mountford, and said vaguely, "I hope you're coming to my dance, and your sister. I hear she's terrific fun."

"I'm coming out with my cousin—weren't you at school together?" Cathy generously indicated Caroline, who was towering over a stockbroker's daughter with teeth like a beaver but who, Cathy recalled with relief, did not have a brother.

"Oh, Caroline," Venetia peered across the room and added with ill grace, "her too, of course. I'll ask Mummy to invite all three of you." This she did, but her dance was almost at the end of the summer and Cathy knew she had to meet Charlie earlier than that to be in with a chance.

The real significance of Venetia's approach, as Lady Davina at once knew, was that Cathy and Monty were acquiring a little mystique in the new Season's coterie. The mothers liked Cathy's beautiful manners, which secured a gratifying array of engraved invitations tucked by Lady Davina into the gilt looking glass at Trevor Square. The society photographers liked her face. She was on the tall side, five feet seven inches, slim, long-legged and well-groomed. Tim Studd, the top society photographer, singled her out at once and spent an afternoon taking pictures which he sent out to glossy magazines.

The debutantes' brothers, however, were attracted by Monty's air of rebellious sensuality, and Lady Davina watched complacently as a knot of slightly red-faced suitors gathered. At the few dances they had attended, Monty was invariably swept on to the floor by one after the other of these, where she danced the Frug or the Twist with increasing abandon. By 10:30 she would have been necking, tousle-haired and conspicuous, with her last partner. Strictly chaperoned as they were, there was no opportunity for more than kissing, but Monty was the picture of erotic invitation and it took only a few weeks for the word to get around that the younger Bourton girl was likely. "I hear she's terrific fun" in fact meant "My brother wants to lay her."

Monty was one of the handful of mildly notorious girls coming out in 1964 who was straightforwardly seeking sexual experience. She knew, with the instinct of a child, that anything so fervently forbidden by adults must be of crucial importance and she yearned with the emotions of a woman to begin what she thought was the real business of a woman's life—the business of love. Most of the debs were less impetuous in moving into the sexual arena—some were scared, some were ignorant, a few were frigid, and most had been taught to preserve their virginity at all costs, because it was the most valuable inducement they could offer a prospective husband.

"Remember, my dear—beauty is only *sin* deep!" Lady Davina roguishly advised them as they set out for their first dates. "No one wants something that's simply given away."

Even Caroline could see, however, that whatever Monty looked as if she might be prepared to give away was a very popular commodity.

However abandoned she appeared, Monty was still in no hurry to explore the mystery of love with any of her overexcited, sweaty-handed dancing partners. Much as she sneered at Cathy's romantic chastity and made jokes about the dream lover who looked like Brian Jones, she too was waiting for the one man whom she could name as the great love. She made more and more daring experiments with her body, while still looking for a man to whom she could commit all of herself, heart, mind and excitable flesh. She felt somehow incomplete as a woman, and reasoned that sexual initiation would supply what she lacked.

In the meantime, all her doubts and worries focused in complete terror on pregnancy. Such was the level of sexual sophistication among her peer group that many of them shared her nightmares when they had engaged in nothing more serious than a kiss. Pregnancy seemed like awful retribution for sex, a punishment for doing what parents forbade. It blighted your life. Quite why getting pregnant would be so catastrophic was hard to define, but it definitely meant the end of everything—fun, good looks, pretty clothes, parties, romance, possibilities and, of course, marriage. Life after pregnancy was never envisaged in detail, only as a black expanse of failure.

In the beginning, Monty never intended her dream lover to be Simon Emanuel, who was not blond, or vaguely menacing, or provocatively thin like Brian Jones, but dark, robust and as sweet as a puppy when he tried to amuse her. The expensive coaching college where he was being crammed for his exams was not far from St. John's, so a few times they met in the Kensington coffee bars, then walked across the park, kicking up the dead leaves, to the Emanuels' apartment, where they played records for hours.

Over Christmas, everything changed. Cathy and Monty traveled to their home, which would be sold at auction in a few more weeks. There were already grimy squares on the walls where some of the paintings had been removed, and some of the furniture had been labeled.

They were hardly inside the door when Cathy mentioned Rosanna's name in conversation and their mother exploded with anger.

"The Emanuels are the scum of the ghettos of Europe!" Her watery blue eyes were livid with a fury of which the sisters had never dreamed her capable. She was in a mood of simmering resentment against her dead husband and, by extension, the two girls as well. Three months alone in the house, undertaking the enforced dismantling of her home and the comfortable life she had enjoyed there, had bred first fear, then anger in her mind. She had drunk even more than usual, and even now the spiritous tang was distinct on her breath. "I can't think what Davina is doing allowing you to associate with those people," she continued. "At school you meet all sorts, you can't avoid it, you have to mix with them. But if this is her idea of bringing you out it certainly isn't mine."

"But, Mummy, it would be awfully rude . . ." Catherine began, astonished at the ease with which an adult would betray her own principles for the sake of prejudices.

"I'm sure they'd *quite* understand. You don't need to say anything. Just don't go there again." Bettina pinched her lips viciously together, lipstick leaking into the wrinkles which grief had deepened around her mouth.

Bettina stuck her nose in the air and walked into the drawing room without answering. Monty flung down the stairs in pursuit of her mother. "I said, *What have you done with my piano?*"

"Don't speak to me in that tone of voice, Miranda."

"What have you done with my piano?"

Bettina rearranged the dried flowers in a silver rose bowl, still silent. It was difficult to believe that she wasn't enjoying wounding her daughter, and Monty was inflamed with rage. Suddenly, she shoved her mother with violence and Bettina fell into the depths of the sofa.

"Answer me, you bitch!"

"Monty!" Cathy was shocked.

"I want to know what you've done with it!" Monty kicked her mother's feet in fury.

"It is not *your* piano, Miranda." The older woman's jaw juddered with anger as she spoke, "None of this is ours anymore, don't you understand?" Her tone was pleading now; she was playing for Monty's sympathy, but where her mother was concerned Monty was pitiless.

"Oh, I understand all right—you and Daddy have spent all

our money so we've got nothing. That's perfectly clear, thank you. Where is it?'' Monty's face was becoming chalk white, her eyes wide. She already knew the answer; inside her anguished mind, she was searching for a course of action, but could find nothing suitable. Rage and frustration seethed like corrosive acids in her head.

"Your piano has been sold, Miranda. And we didn't get very much for it, either. Everything in this house has been sold."

"But not everything has been taken away, has it?'' Monty's tone was ugly. "Only my piano. *This* hasn't gone, for instance.'' She kicked the occasional table over, sending the rose bowl and dried flowers flying. "And this hasn't gone yet, has it?'' She seized the chintz frill around the sofa and ripped it. "And we've still got bookcases, haven't we?'' She grabbed the poker and smashed the glass front of the bookcase. "Who are you trying to kid, Mummy? You got rid of the piano because you'd like to get rid of me, didn't you? Well, you've succeeded. I'm going. And I'll never speak to you again.'' She ran out of the drawing room, slamming the door loudly enough to rattle the windows, and bolted out of the house, leaving the front door open to the chill of the December air.

Bettina gave a satisfied sigh, and patted her hair into shape as she got off the sofa. Catherine looked at her mother with astonishment, realizing that Monty's ridiculously dramatic words were perfectly accurate and that the sale of the piano had indeed been a calculated stab at her sister's only area of vulnerability. Cathy suddenly had an insight into the side of her sister she found difficult to understand; she realized that Monty's pose of rebellion was not just self-dramatization. Her sister had simply decided to fight hate with hate.

Monty's fleeting footsteps could be heard with diminishing volume as she ran coatless down the gravel drive.

"Shouldn't we do something?'' Cathy asked, feeling uncomfortable.

"I think quite enough has been done for Miranda already,'' their mother replied. "You girls think you know everything, I'm sure, but you can't begin to understand . . .'' She paused as if she had lost the thread of what she wanted to say, then started on a different tack. "I haven't started on your rooms, so you'd better begin packing up directly.''

Miserably, Cathy went upstairs and began to take down the row of rosettes she had won with her ponies, which were pinned to her picture rail. Without her father, the house seemed to be a horrible vacuum. She felt desperately alone; but there was work to be done, the whole of her childhood to be packed up and stored away. Then she must get on with her grown-up life, which meant making the marvelous marriage which everyone expected of her.

She scraped her sleeve across her cheeks to wipe away the tears that refused to be held back, and reached for the framed photograph hanging below the rosettes; it showed her winning the first prize in the novice class of the Pony Club gymkhana, which her father had presented. James stood smiling at the pony's head, and Cathy was holding up the little silver cup in a gesture of innocent triumph. The pony stood square and still, its ears forward and eyes alert. It was a picture of perfection. Should I keep it or throw it away? Cathy wondered. She put it with the rosettes on the pile of things she intended to throw away. She had to think of more important prizes now.

Monty strolled down the lane, not caring that her shoes were letting in water from the rivulets streaming from overfull ditches. She felt peculiarly exhilarated, almost light-headed. Without the burden of obligation to a parent she loathed, she felt as weightless as the seagulls planing over the bare plowed fields. She had no money, no coat and no idea what she was going to do, and it was thrilling. She stopped a delivery van which was going to Brighton, and at Brighton ran on to the station platform in time to jump on the London train. She hid from the ticket collector in the lavatory, told the man at the barrier she'd lost her coat and the ticket with it, and then walked to Trevor Square. The house was dark and shuttered; Lady Davina and the staff had gone to Bourton Hall. Still elated, but by now very cold, Monty walked on, across the park to the Emanuels' apartment.

"But she will worry, your poor mother," Mrs. Emanuel looked like an anxious pullet uncertain where the fox was lurking. To get involved in the Bourton family squabbles, and on the wrong side, was no part of her social game plan. "You must telephone her at once."

"I'd much rather not, I'd only be rude to her." Monty felt her fingertips ache as they thawed in the heavy warmth of the apartment.

"But what will you do? Where will you go? You can stay here, of course. . . ."

"I love the way my mother says you can stay here when what she means is you can't." Simon slouched by the window, pretending to look at the gaslights reflected in the distant Serpentine.

"Simon! Don't put words in my mouth. That's not what I said; of course Monty can stay. You're very welcome dear."

Mrs. Emanuel was angry with herself for being outmaneuvered, but disguised this by fussing, "You poor girl, you must be frozen to death." She pressed the brass bell push and an immaculately uniformed maid appeared.

"Please draw Miss Bourton a bath. And, Rosanna, go with her and see if you can find her something to wear." Given the extent of Rosanna's wardrobe, this was hardly a heavy imposition.

Mr. Emanuel, as usual, said nothing, while his wife fretted. "It will all blow over in the morning, my dear" was all he contributed to soothe her distress.

In the end, Cathy, Lady Davina and Mrs. Emanuel negotiated a compromise. Cathy, still shocked by the realization that her mother had deliberately provoked Monty's rebellion, telephoned later in the evening.

"Look, you can't impose on Rosanna's family—what do you want to do?"

"I don't know, Cathy." Monty's voice was unusually quiet. "I'm not ever going back to the house, or ever living with that woman again."

"Mmm—but you'll stay at St. John's?"

"I suppose so."

"Well, we'll have to go back to Trevor Square next term anyway, because Mummy's flat won't be ready." Bettina had bought a tiny apartment in Brighton, where she would be able to keep up attendance at a bridge club.

"But what about Christmas?" Cathy was anxious for herself as well as her sister. "You *can't* not be with your family at Christmas."

"*What* family? You're the only family I've got, Cathy. You're the only one who really cares. Isn't that what a family is—people who care about each other?"

Eventually Cathy telephoned Lady Davina, who in turn rang Mrs. Emanuel and patronized her so lavishly that she was reassured about her role in the drama and agreed to have Monty until the Trevor Square house was open again in mid-January.

The Emanuels were acutely uncomfortable with their guest, but hid the fact by spoiling her. Behind closed doors, Rosanna wrangled with her parents over the best way to integrate the stranger into their household at Chanukah—the Jewish festival of lights, which the Emanuels, like many liberal families in British Jewry, used as a pretext for following the secular forms of Christmas.

The apartment's vast sitting room looked like a Hollywood set for Queen Victoria's Christmas, with a massive fir tree smothered in swags of ribbon and gifts wrapped exquisitely by Rosanna. Monty adored the lavishness of it all, and the genuine religious feeling she detected in the domestic ceremonies of lighting the candles and singing songs. The Emanuels seemed to her to be much more like a real family than her own, even if Mrs. Emanuel did make monstrous attempts to direct her children's lives.

Fifty people, all related, sat down to Christmas dinner. Monty looked on enviously as a succession of uncles, aunts and cousins crowded through the door for the week of banqueting which followed Christmas Day.

"You've got an awful lot of family," she said to Simon one morning as they were awaiting the newest influx of relatives.

"Too much," he stood sourly by the window. "I'm sick of them all asking me when I'm going to join the business. My mother puts them up to it—it's just another of her ways of pressuring me."

Mrs. Emanuel anxiously spoiled Monty, fearful that she was in some way a spy in their midst who would catch the family out in its great pretense of fitting into British society. Monty was taken to the opera, to recitals, to concerts, to half a dozen parties whose extravagant elegance dazzled her.

"Rosanna—have you done your practice?" "Rosanna—go do your practice now, later you will be too tired." Every day Mrs. Emanuel unnecessarily nagged her daughter toward perfection. One evening a famous soprano came to the house to hear Rosanna sing and both parents anxiously questioned her about Rosanna's training—should she study in Paris? in New York? Vienna? How good was she really, no, really, how good?

Monty was entranced. Accustomed to Bettina sneering "Must you play that ghastly piano" or "Stop banging that damn piano, for heaven's sake," it seemed like a dream of good fortune to be born into a family where music was a valued talent, not a dangerous vice.

"Now, Monty, you must play with Rosanna," Mrs. Emanuel commanded one day.

"Yes, play for us, we want to hear you—Rosanna is always better with her friends," Mr. Emanuel added, and so Monty sat down at the velvet-black grand piano and accompanied Rosanna in one of their school pieces.

"But you play beautifully—doesn't she, Mother?" Mr. Emanuel became talkative with surprise and indignation. "Why don't your parents make you study?"

The fact was that neither her mother nor, when he was alive, her father had the faintest notion of the value of art, talent or study. Monty sensed that her present audience would not understand that. Instead she said, "We aren't a very musical family, I suppose."

Mr. Emanuel shook his head in wonder.

"She sings beautifully too, don't you, Monty?" Rosanna was full of encouraging enthusiasm.

Before Monty had time to feel embarrassed, Rosanna played the introduction to one of the madrigals they had sung at school and took the soprano part so that Monty had to sing in the lower registers which showed off the mature tone of her voice. It was an idiotic song full of "hey-nonny-nones" and Monty hated it, but Rosanna's parents applauded them with admiration.

"Wonderful! What a wonderful voice you have! Doesn't she, Joseph?"

"Lovely, my dear, quite lovely. And you haven't studied at all?" He plainly found this an extraordinary example of parental neglect. The next day, after a secret conference with Rosanna, Mr. Emanuel suggested that Monty join his daughter at her singing lessons during the holiday, and for a fortnight they shared a daily session with the Covent Garden soprano who came to the apartment to teach them.

The Emanuels treated her as a charity case, a poor child deprived of music. Except Simon. Simon treated Monty as young men often treat women they are acutely in love with; he barely spoke to her, fidgeted when she was around and stared at her when he thought she wasn't looking.

"Do you want me to show you how to play the guitar?" Simon appeared in the sitting room one afternoon. The weak winter sun streamed in from the leafless park outside. Rosanna and her mother had gone to Fortnum and Mason to exchange unwanted Christmas presents and Monty was amusing herself at the piano.

"Fabulous!" She got up and went to sit beside Simon on the sofa, taking up the Spanish guitar he handed to her. By now, Monty knew enough about men to know that this was one of those invitations not to be taken at face value.

"Press harder," Simon ordered, positioning the fingers of her left hand. "Use the tips of your fingers." He put his arm around her to show her how to press the strings against the frets in the neck.

"But my fingers aren't strong enough," Monty complained. She smelled the faint, rich aroma of his body and the vague scent of aftershave, felt the warmth of his flesh through his cashmere sweater, and her interest in the guitar began to evaporate.

"Your fingers will get stronger in time, and the tips will

harden. Here, feel how mine are.'' Obediently she touched his fingers with hers, then looked up toward him as their hands interlaced. Simon put the guitar down on the floor and pulled her toward him, breathless with elation. Monty opened her lips under his and lay back on the sofa, her senses swimming.

The warm silence of the apartment seemed to roar in her ears as she surrendered to the responses of her body. Whatever it was that had held her back with the boys at the dances, it had gone now. Kissing Simon felt right.

"I feel as if I've known you all my life," she muttered as they finally drew apart.

"Me too. You've got fantastic eyes."

"They turn up, though."

"That's what I like about them." Monty smiled. All the boys said she had fantastic eyes. Whatever dumb magic they had, she was glad it worked on Simon too.

They kissed again and she felt his hand hover over her breast, not daring to caress, so she arched her back and pressed her body against him. Simon, used to the elaborate teases of the "nice" girls he had kissed before, felt ready to explode with lust and gratitude.

For an hour they reveled in their new conspiracy, then tidied the sofa and went to make coffee in the immense kitchen, where Rosanna and Mrs. Emanuel found them on their return. Monty and Simon put on what they thought was an Oscar-winning performance of innocence, in which their complicity was blatantly apparent.

Monty could not sleep that night. She went into the marble-tiled guest bathroom and looked at herself in the mirror. She felt different, but she couldn't see it. Somewhere on her face it must show—how could she look the same when inside she was in love for the first time?

At the first opportunity, Mrs. Emanuel said to her son, "Monty is a very nice girl, Simon, but you won't get too fond of her—promise me?"

"Of course, Mother, I promise, don't worry," he answered lightly. It wasn't a false vow. No degree of fondness would be too great for Monty, Simon thought.

"I'm in love," Monty told her sister three months later. They were back at college, and back at the Bourton house in Trevor Square under Lady Davina's critical eye. Simon had taken Monty out as often as he dared, while Cathy had stayed in, with a borrowed sewing machine, painstakingly copying some of Rosanna's prettiest dresses; she had discovered that even at wholesale prices the frocks she liked best were too expensive.

PEARLS

With great care, Monty zipped up her sister's white dress for Queen Charlotte's Ball.

"With Rosanna's brother?" Cathy pulled up the long white gloves, which reached over her elbows.

"Yes, with Simon. Oh Cathy, don't you think he's dishy?"

"I suppose he is good-looking but Mummy'll never let you marry him." She pulled critically at the thick garland of artificial gardenias around the dress's scooped neckline.

"I don't want to marry him; I'm in love, that's all. You look fab. The chinless wonders won't be able to resist you." Monty accepted Cathy's ambition although she did not share it. Her sister's marriage had become the preoccupying business of them both.

Cathy studied her reflection in the murky depths of the glass in her room at Trevor Square. Under the white silk gown her figure was as slender as a model's—in fact, Cathy had already been invited to model some clothes in a society magazine in a special feature on model debutantes. Her glossy dark hair, cut in a geometric bob by Vidal Sassoon, swung against her faintly hollow cheeks, contrasting with her pale pink lipstick. Her eyes seemed smoky and enormous.

"I think I'll do." She smiled with satisfaction and gave Monty a hug. "You won't do anything stupid, Monty darling, will you?"

"If you mean don't get pregnant, don't worry. We're being very careful. Aren't you dying to be in love, Cathy?"

Cathy sighed. She could see her sister glowing with excitement and longed to feel the same way, but she knew that her own emotional makeup was different. In the bottom of her heart, Cathy wondered if she was capable of the sort of violent feelings her sister had.

"He'll come soon, I just know he will," Monty promised her.

"Who will?"

"Mr. Right."

"*The Earl* of Right, you mean."

They caught each other's eyes in the mirror and giggled.

Queen Charlotte's Ball at the beginning of April marked the official start of the debutante season. Cathy joined forty other selected maidens in white gowns to pull a vast cardboard wedding cake across the ballroom floor with white ribbons. William Hickey of the *Daily Express*, the most influential gossip columnist, tipped her for the Deb of the Year title, and to Monty's fury, printed a picture of both of them with a caption reading "Cathy and Miranda, daughters of the suicide peer, Lord James Bourton."

Caroline, ignored by the photographers and not selected for the cake ceremony, stamped grimly off to college next morning while the Bourton sisters were awarded breakfast in bed by Lady Davina.

"And Charles Coseley has accepted!" she triumphed, waving a sheet of blue embossed writing paper which bore two lines of the electrocardiograph handwriting boys acquired at Eton. "Now don't let us down, Cathy. We're relying on you."

As the autumn tea parties had progressed, Lady Davina had decided on a late July dance for Cathy and Caroline. The funds from the felling of the West Wood would provide for a thousand guests; and as she had watched Cathy quietly charm and manipulate the girls who were prime targets, Lady Davina had realized that there would be no trouble in pledging a handsome number of return invitations.

There would be no trouble, either, in making the Bourton dance one of the grandest of the season. After sympathizing with Caroline's mother over the strain and bother of organizing it all and hearing Lady Davina make all manner of old-fashioned suggestions, Cathy calmly took control of the operation. She hired a young cousin of the Queen to organize the affair and between them the dance was planned in elaborate detail; a discotheque, a pop group, an immense dance floor laid over the priceless parquet of the ballroom, garlands of flowers around every table, a small fun fair set up in the home paddock and a second dance floor of Perspex built over the tip of the ornamental lake. Ever thoughtful, Cathy saved the estate almost a thousand pounds by having the foresight to ask the gardeners to force hundreds of white lilies into flower in the greenhouses.

"Darling, you're simply marvelous," Lady Davina praised her with increasing astonishment. "I don't know where you young people today get all your ideas."

"I just asked everyone about the best dances last season and did the same—it was quite simple." Cathy frowned over a letter from the National Trust demanding that the Bourton family take out extra insurance to cover damage to the Trust's property. "I think Uncle Hugo can deal with this, don't you?"

"Darling, aren't you the teeniest bit nervous? I was simply shattered with nerves before my dance." A germ of doubt nagged Lady Davina as she watched her protégée approach her great day so calmly—was this completely normal? Suppose all the serenity suddenly collapsed and she cracked up at the last moment?

"I suppose I should be wound up, but I don't feel it, honestly. We've planned everything for months, there's nothing we've forgotten, I've done everything you said, now . . ." Cathy didn't finish. She couldn't think of an elegant way to say that the only thing she cared about was getting Charles Coseley to ask her to dance.

She had made a close friend of his cousin Venetia, scanned the society magazines for snippets of gossip and subtly but relentlessly turned every conversation to the end of finding out everything she could about her target.

Charles Coseley, the Earl of Laxford, was twenty-nine, and personally worth £15 million; when he succeeded to his father's title of Marquess of Shrewton, he would get with it houses in London, Wiltshire and Yorkshire, with a total fortune of over £200 million. There was a villa in the South of France, and a yacht; Charlie Coseley liked gambling, dancing, polo, shooting, crashing his E-type Jaguar and, most of all, girls. He'd been out with all the most glamorous girls of the previous season and none of them had lasted more than six weeks.

"Charlie's awful really; you must warn your sister," Venetia told Cathy one afternoon after they had returned to Trevor Square after an exhausting afternoon scouring the Chelsea boutiques. "He just goes for one bird after another, drives them crazy with flowers and phone calls, then as soon as he's got them—bang, finished, all over."

"How odd." Cathy widened her eyes inquiringly at Venetia; she knew all she had to do was look receptive and she'd be told everything she needed to know.

"He pesters them to sleep with him and then as soon as they do, he's off. His parents are getting rather worried, actually. He is the heir, after all."

"Mmmn." Cathy passed Venetia a dark-blue china mug with OPIUM written on it in large gold letters. It contained tea. They had bought it in Carnaby Street. "And he goes a bit far, really," Venetia continued contentedly. "He's so good-looking he can get any girl he wants and they're all heartbroken. Some stupid little dolly tried to commit suicide when he dumped her last year."

"Good heavens. Does he sleep with *all* his girlfriends?"

"Absolutely."

"Sugar?"

Following Lady Davina's advice, Cathy read the polo reports in *The Field* every week and demanded that all her dates should take her to the Garrison and the Saddle Room, the nightclubs Venetia said Charlie frequented. She saw him once or twice, always with a different, stunning girl, but he obviously never noticed her. She realized that she was not his type of girl at all.

135

He went for the girls in the shortest miniskirts and the most transparent dresses, with the longest blond hair and the most heavily made up eyes. Cathy felt awkward in very revealing clothes and knew that she was best suited to the understated, natural style of dress.

"How the hell am I going to get him when he doesn't even know I exist?" Cathy asked herself in desperation as she watched Charlie's elegant limbs vibrating through the Shake on the Saddle Room's dance floor. Opposite him was yet another rangy blonde, wearing a gold crochet dress over a hideous flesh-colored bodystocking.

"What are you looking so moody about?" Cathy's date drawled rudely. "I hate moody birds, come on and dance." They edged into the crowd and Cathy flung herself into sensual gyrations, hoping to catch Charlie's eye at last but succeeding only in winding a young guards officer at her left.

"How much money do you think she paid for that old rope?" she bitched as Charlie and the blonde left the floor. The glittering crochet dress attracted everyone's attention.

"Well, it won't be enough to tie old Charlie down, whatever it cost," her date answered with envy.

In the taxi home afterward Cathy sat inertly while her date half smothered her with kisses. She felt nothing except rather sticky around the face. She was deep in thought, pondering the impossible problem of Charlie Coseley, the man she loved, whose fortune would save her family.

Simon took Monty to the Ad Lib Club, a dark penthouse high in a modern skyscraper where the pop groups played, and those who were not playing came to drink Scotch and Coke and mingle. It was the exclusive haunt of the new meritocracy. Everyone was hustled or being hustled. Like a shoal of piranhas the success-hungry crowd fastened on the stars—George Harrison in a pair of jeans, Mick Jagger in a flowered shirt, Simon Bailey with Jean Shrimpton.

Simon, his arm around Monty, was there to fix a niche for himself in the music business. Since the name Emanuel meant money, there were plenty of two-bit hustlers to take him on, but Simon was after the musicians and that was harder.

"They think I'm just a rich Jewish kid trying to buy into the scene," he told Monty. "I know they'd change their tune if they heard me play, but I can't just get on stage and jam with the Stones."

"Why not?" said Monty. "Everyone else does." It was one of the Ad Lib's unique attractions.

"Yes, but they're different." Simon meant that the Stones,

the Animals, the Kinks, and all the rest were lean, mean, work-ing-class kids, who were even more hostile to outsiders than the traditional elite were. From the perspective of the music busi-ness, he was on the wrong side of the class barrier.

Monty and Simon would leave the Ad Lib at three or four in the morning and stay together in the dangerous darkness of Tre-vor Square, kissing and petting until the dawn. At first, they were frightened of discovery, but then Monty realized that Lady Davina took a sleeping pill every night.

"She wouldn't wake up if the house was burning down," laughed Monty, sinking into Simon's arms with abandon.

"But what about Cathy and Caroline?" Simon unbuttoned her satin blouse.

"They sleep like logs and anyway they wouldn't tell on us, I do love you, Simon." The satin blouse slithered to the floor, to be joined by Monty's black boots, white tights and the eighteen-inch-wide strip of plum velvet that was her skirt. They undressed each other little by little, then embraced on the threadbare Turk-ish rug in front of the warm ashes of the fire. To be together, to touch and hold and caress each other—it was all ecstasy, but they dared not make love properly in case Monty got pregnant; they dared not even tell each other how much they yearned to go all the way.

"Why do you love me?" Monty asked, snuggling close.

"I don't know; you're not like other girls, that's all." He stroked the soft curve of her hip, gingerly slid his hand between her thighs.

"You're not like other boys, either; that's why I love you." Monty reached into the darkness and held the shaft of eager flesh as it swelled in her hand, wondering how it would feel to have it inside her body. It seemed silly to be so close and to love each other so much and to deny themselves the ultimate intimacy. It did not occur to either of them that the most powerful force binding them together was the disapproval of their families. Monty would have been outraged at the suggestion that she cared enough about Bettina's opinion to flout it.

By the time the crocuses in Hyde Park were fading the 1965 Season was under way, and the mirror at Trevor Square was half obliterated with invitations. All over England and Scotland, houses were filled at the weekends with extraordinary mixtures of people whose only common link was some connection with the aristocracy.

Unregenerate landed gentry, their faces reddened by the win-ter's hunting, rubbed shoulders with long-haired *jeunesse dorée* in velvet jackets. Elderly men who had danced with girls who had danced with Edward VIII frowned at youths in hipster trousers and lace shirts. Women with legs as thick and knotted as ancient oaks smiled wistfully at girls whose sapling thighs were displayed in patent-leather boots. Dior swirled disdainfully past Biba; diamonds blazed at plastic flowers; and whiffs of marijuana percolated into the musty folds of tapestries.

There was a ball every Saturday, and besides the dance itself, there would also be the house party, a raucous random selection of revelers billeted on the home of a guest who lived near the host, who were given dinner before the dance and a bed for the night after it, with the requisite amount of chauffeuring and chaperonage. In the Season the entire British upper class conspired to get its young mated without undue incident.

The race was on among the young girls to see how far they could go with drink, drug taking or sexual experiment without spoiling their chances with the wealthiest men in the pool. In six months or so their social careers would be determined, and many would have acquired newspaper-cutting files which would pursue them the rest of their lives.

Cathy and Caroline went first to a couple of dull dances for Caroline's hunting chums at the other side of the country, where they sipped fruit punch that was virtually alcohol free, panted through the Benenden repertoire of Scottish reels and were in bed by 2:00 A.M. and up the next day in time for a scavenger hunt. These were childish, boisterous and inelegant affairs, no preparation for what was to come.

Next they went to the first big ball of the season, for the daughter of a wealthy Member of Parliament in Cornwall. Monty was asked as well.

"Six hours on this bloody train." Caroline shoved her suitcase onto the luggage rack and plumped down to read a riding magazine.

"It'll be worth it. Lucy knows an awful lot of people, and we're terribly lucky to be invited. Half the college is sick with jealousy."

"Hmph. You mean Lucy knows Charlie Coseley so we've got to struggle up the length of the country so you can chase after him."

"Oh, come on, Caroline—we'll be staying in a castle. It'll be really romantic." Monty gazed out of the window at the gray London suburbs.

"I suppose you've got Simon invited." Caroline flicked over a page of light hunters.

"I didn't need to get him invited." Monty complacently turned toward her cousin. "Lucy Limpton's dying to get her paws on him because he's an Emanuel."

Cathy gazed wistfully out of the window. In her heart of hearts she was beginning to admit that she might be stupid to pin all her hopes on landing the catch of the season; but when she compared Charlie's flashing smile and crisp golden curls to her slobbery, importunate dates so far, she shuddered. She was beginning to feel nauseated by the mere smell of them.

Catching Charlie was also a question of pride; Cathy smarted at all the patronizing expressions of sympathy she got from well-meaning acquaintances: "Such a shame about your poor father—nothing in the stories, I suppose?" was the line, vulgar curiosity masquerading as good manners. She smothered flaring anger every time she passed a knot of strangers and they exchanged comments in low voices, and she heard, or thought she heard, the words "suicide peer" yet again. She wanted to show them all that she was a force to be reckoned with, not just a minor figure in a shameful scandal.

It was a small gray castle, taller than it was wide, built at the tip of a steep inlet of sea. On the steps, Cathy straightened her immaculate camel miniskirt, glad now that she had shortened it as much as she dared, and aware how fine her legs looked in their cream tights and white boots, and how her superbly cut hair would fall silkily back into shape no matter how the relentless wind from the Atlantic whipped it about her head. Was *he* watching, perhaps, from the narrow windows?

"For heaven's sake, stop mooning," snapped Caroline. "I'm turning blue."

"The wind is a little fresh today." Their host, Sir John Limpton, appeared to lead them indoors. "We're so lucky here in the West—the Gulf Stream keeps the sea warm so it never gets really cold." He was a tall, thin man with hollow cheeks and thinning dark hair. The girls looked at each other and smothered laughter as he led them down dank corridors whose stone walls seemed to be sweating chill. What was the man's notion of real cold?

Sir John lingered just an instant, supposedly waiting for the footman to bring up the last suitcase but really wanting to look at Cathy's legs.

In Chelsea, there were many girls, and they all wore a skirt no more than halfway down their thighs. But what Chelsea girls considered mere fashion, older men interpreted as invitation. Sir John's life was lived in Westminister and the country where there were few girls, and none who showed so much as their knees. He was virtually hypnotized by the pale, slender limbs before him; Cathy was gratified and disturbed simultaneously as she noticed him directing a furtive glance at her thighs while pretending to supervise the footman with their cases.

The dance was dazzling, and even Caroline admitted that the journey had been worth it. There was champagne, a piper at dinner, salmon and venison from the estate and then half the Opposition front bench seemed to be in the ballroom demonstrating their skill at the Frug or the Watusi.

Young couples who were already paired off but by tradition lodged in separate house parties made their way down the icy corridors looking for a convenient place to make love before getting dressed again and scampering down to the ballroom in time for the toast to the debutante and her future.

Charlie Coseley arrived with the first house party; he had had a row with the red-haired actress who came with him, danced with four or five different girls, then swept Lady Limpton onto the floor for an abandoned smooch. This was not unusual—it was considered good form for the men to flirt with the hostess.

Simon arrived late, ran from hall to crowded hall like a seeking gun dog until he found Monty and then pulled her outside. On the gravel stood a sleek dark car. "Get in!" He pulled open the passenger door with care. Monty looked at him, not understanding.

"But whose is it, Simon—have you borrowed it?"

"Nope. I've bought it."

"But it's an Aston Martin!"

"So what?" He ran around to the other side and climbed in beside her. "My grandmother left me some money. It's been in trust for me for years, until I was twenty-one. So now I'm twenty-one!" He dragged her uncomfortably toward him across the gearshift, kissed her with a new mastery, then broke off and started the engine with a roar.

The powerful headlamps caught the stone parapet, the drawbridge and the close-pressed firs beyond. Wild with his new freedom, Simon drove them away.

"Where are we going?" Happily Monty settled in the low-slung seat.

"Anywhere! Let's just *go*!" Simon jammed a tape into the player and loud music filled the atmosphere. Monty giggled.

"It's like a little house."

"You can put the seats down to make a bed, too." He reached over and squeezed her thigh.

They sped along narrow stone-walled roads and after Simon nearly slaughtered a sheep, Monty persuaded him to drive less fast. They found a spectacular beach of fine silver sand, pulled off their clothes and leaped into the boisterous sea, exhilarated by the April cold and by the gloriousness of feeling as if they were the only two figures in the landscape.

Later, cocooned in the car with Monty's Biba ball gown as a blanket, Simon said, "There's something I want to ask you." He's going to ask if we can make love properly, Monty thought thankfully.

But instead, Simon asked, "If I buy an apartment, will you come and live with me?"

Monty barely hesitated. She loved Simon, and wanted to be with him forever.

"Can you really buy an apartment?" she asked, testing this wonderful dream.

"Yep. I've got enough money for a deposit, and I went to see an accountant who says I can easily get a mortgage once I go to work for my father."

"But I thought you didn't want to go into the business?"

"I don't, but nothing's happening for me with music right now."

"But you'll get a break soon, Simon, I know you will. It's only a matter of time." Monty felt as if he were proposing to renege on their shared faith. They both agreed that rejecting the world of their parents was the beginning of wisdom.

"Are you saying no, Monty?" His voice shrank to a fearful half whisper. He desperately wanted her to live with him, but knew what her family, as well as his, would be enraged.

"Oh, darling Simon, no—I mean, yes—I mean of course I'll come and live with you. I love you, don't I?" Their lips met for a long, uncomfortable and passionate kiss. Monty felt her skin chilled and gritty from the sand of the beach, and she felt suddenly worried by a new thought.

"Simon, I'm going to have to go on the Pill, aren't I?"

"We can be careful, darling, just like now."

"Uh-huh—maybe *you* can be careful, but I can't. Not if I'm living with you, Simon. Can't you see how awful it would be? We'd just be dying to do it properly all the time. I'll *have* to get the Pill somehow." But where was she going to get the Pill without being married?

At 4:00 A.M. the Rattington castle was still ablaze with lights. The discotheque was quiet, and in the dining hall liveried servants were setting out a line of silver chafing dishes for the breakfast. Cathy and Caroline trudged up the stairs to their room, footsore and dejected.

Ahead of them on the first-floor landing a group of smart London guests were shrieking with merriment at one boy who had taken some LSD. Acid was the new diversion for the more daring men, who gaily ravaged their nervous tissues with weekend after weekend of trips, to the entertainment of the more timid onlookers.

"I think I must be the only girl in the room Charlie didn't dance with." Cathy paused to take off her shoes. "He had a stinking row with that actress, got frightfully drunk and grabbed every bird he could reach—except me." She looked exhausted but still luminously beautiful. Her hair was done up in a cascade of glossy curls and sprinkled with tiny white-silk flowers. Her dress was of the palest pink slub silk with a high waist, long fitted sleeves and rows of minute buttons at the wrists and down the back. It was a dress she had made herself and it had taken hours of labor to cover every tiny button and stitch the exquisite silk flowers onto hairpins.

"Never mind," Caroline consoled her. "He was obviously too sloshed to notice that you were the most beautiful girl in the room."

"I've got a filthy headache, too. I don't think much of Lucy's father's taste in champagne." At the top of the ugly oak staircase they turned along the corridor to their alloted bedroom and opened the door on a self-conscious attempt at an orgy. The air was fetid with marijuana, and ten or twelve people were lying on the floor watching the actress who had come with Charlie Coseley. She was naked except for a smudged layer of body paint, and she was ineffectually trying, with the aid of the mirror, to touch up the design on her buttocks.

"You shouldn't have sat down. April," sniggered a man in a polo-necked evening shirt, passing the joint; "spoiled my work of art."

Caroline stomped undaunted into the laughing circle.

"Look, this is our room. Go and find somewhere else to play."

They laughed helplessly, some coughing in the fumes.

"Oh, cool it, Caro. Siddown and have a smoke."

"No, thank you."

"No, *thank you*!" he mimicked her prim tone, to gales of giggling. The handle of the bathroom door rattled noisily, then there was pounding from the other side and cries of "open up!" Nobody took much notice.

At last the boy in the polo shirt struggled to his feet and tried the door. " 'Slocked. Where's key?" There were louder shouts and more knocking.

"Help! Let us out—Jeremy's having a bad trip."

Another man blundered across to join the struggle and together he and the boy in the polo shirt smashed the door lock with the leg of a massive carved chair.

Three people squeezed simultaneously through the splintered doorway.

"Oh, God, you're all *orange*!" the first man shouted happily, then pitched over the nearest pair of legs and sprawled on the carpet, his limbs rowing back and forth like those of an upturned beetle.

Behind him stood Monty's school friend Swallow Lamotte, her straw-colored blond hair now waist length. Apart from a man's black bow tie dangling loose down to her nipples, she was wearing nothing. The man with her wore only his socks and a mass of shaving foam around his lower belly.

"Oh, hello, you two. I was just trying to trim Jeremy's pubes for him. Terrible vibes in here. What's up?" Swallow's taste for debauchery couldn't overcome her basic common sense, nor her sensitivity to social atmosphere.

"We want to go to bed, that's all." They all sniggered and Cathy bit her tongue with embarrassment at her unthinking choice of words. "This *was* our room, Swallow." Her head throbbed unbearably and she rested her cheek against the chill stone doorway for some relief.

"Plenty of room!" slurred the ginger-haired actress generously. "Join th' party." She waved toward the bed. For the first time they noticed that it was occupied by a couple. The girl was virtually unconscious, and the man, grimly drunk, was grinding his limp penis against her, trying to get an erection. He looked around at Caroline, suddenly cheerful at the promise of more lively company, then rolled off and picked up a half-empty bottle of brandy beside the bed.

"Lots of room—have a drink, you two. Whass yer name?"

"Your best bet is to kip down in the housekeeper's room," Swallow briskly advised. "Ground floor, north wing, the passage at the back of the dining hall. Just take your nightclothes; I'll make sure the rest of your stuff is OK." She stepped over the sprawled bodies and showed Caroline and Cathy out of the room like a gracious hostess. "You can ask the housekeeper for an aspirin; she's bound to have one. See you in the morning."

They walked slowly back to the staircase, too shocked and too tired to say very much. The room they presumed to be the housekeeper's, on the ground floor off a corridor which led to the kitchen, was at least warm, heated by a substantial coal fire. There was one ordinary bed and a sofa, on which Caroline kindly flopped to give the miserable Cathy the better berth.

Cathy first went searching the spartan bathroom for aspirins.

She found these, took the tablets and then roused the drowsy Caroline to unbutton her dress. Miserable as she felt, Cathy searched the closet for a hanger but found that the rail in the closet was too low for the long gown to hang without crumpling and so decided to hang the dress in the bathroom, from the head of the ancient shower fitment which drooped like a sunflower over the tub.

Caroline was already asleep, snoring gently. Cathy was just on the point of drifting into slumber when the door of the room crashed open, and a wedge of harsh light penetrated the darkness. A tall figure lurched through the doorway, holding the door handle for support.

"Fucking buggering hell!" it swore as its unsteady legs collided with Caroline's outstretched calves and half dislodged her from the sofa. Three more staggering steps took the figure to the bathroom door.

"Whatever is going on? What do you think you're doing?" Caroline demanded in ringing tones as the bathroom door smashed into the wall. There was the unmistakable sound of a man about to throw up, followed by the unmistakable sound of badly aimed vomit splattering porcelain. The smell of semidigested food soused in liquor pervaded the room.

Cathy sleepily sat up. "What's the matter?" she asked, her eyes flickering open, feeling decidedly angry. "What the hell do you mean by barging into our room like this! You're smashed out of your skull! How dare you charge into our bathroom! If you've ruined my dress . . ." She scrambled out of bed.

"Now look here . . ." Caroline picked herself up from the floor and put on the room light. She stood like an angry Valkyrie by the open door, her beefy shoulders straining at the armholes of her blue Laura Ashley nightdress.

The intruder was leaning against the bathroom door, extremely drunk, wiping his chin with the skirt of Cathy's exquisite pink gown. The rest of the dress was soaked with the foul-smelling contents of his stomach. Charlie Coseley had evidently drunk a lot of red wine that evening.

"You've *ruined* my dress! You pig! You revolting pig!" She felt as if she were incandescent with fury. Cathy scarcely realized it, but weeks of yearning for this man to notice her had brought her to a state where she detested him so passionately that she was ready to pull out his gorgeous blond curls with her own hands.

"Mishtake . . ." slurred Charlie, letting go of the door and taking a few steps into the room. Ahead of him loomed Caroline, her arms outstretched as if to head off a bolting pony. "Shorry . . ." Charlie turned toward Cathy, making a helpless gesture with his hands.

"You're not getting away with this! How dare you behave so disgustingly! You're not fit to belong to the human race!" Cathy raged, almost enjoying herself.

"Anyone ever tell you . . ."—Charlie advanced one step toward her, pointing a wavering finger—"anyone ever tell you . . . you're beautiful when you're . . . hup! beautiful when you're angry? Whassyourname, anyway? Don' I know you?" He looked mildly confused. He raised the pointing finger again, then fell forward across the sofa.

"Zonked out," Caroline pronounced, inspecting the body with satisfaction.

"So much for the Earl of Right," Cathy sneered, giving the prone form a disdainful prod with her foot. "What an animal."

"Oh, cripes, look." Caroline picked up a messy but once expensive pigskin shaving bag. "Maybe this really was his room in the first place." She opened the closet and pulled out a tweed sports jacket and a pair of cavalry-twill trousers. "Yes, look, here are his clothes."

"Well, that's not our fault. If he'd been nicer to that April bird we wouldn't have been turned out of our own room in the first place." Cathy pressed the bell for the servants with a bravura gesture. Looking like a Parisian soubrette with her tousled hair and her Victorian lace nightgown, she stared miserably at the sprawled body of the man on whom she had set her heart. "I'm bloody well going to send him a bill." She picked up the stinking ruin of her dress between finger and thumb, then sadly let it drop. Caroline belted her ugly plaid dressing gown with a decisive gesture and strode toward the door.

"Caro, where are you going?"

"I'm going to make a scene, that's where I'm going."

A few minutes later an elderly maid appeared, expressed anguish over Cathy's soiled dress and took it away. Two more servants and the housekeeper herself followed to clean the bathroom. Two footmen carried Charlie out of the room. Then Caroline reappeared with their host, Sir John Limpton, who immediately sat down on Cathy's bed, took her hand, and offered an emotional apology. "Your sister has explained everything and I regret most profoundly that this should have happened under my roof. The young fool should have known better. You can be sure that I shall have a few words with him in the morning. More than a few words. Considerably more. I knew your father, of course, don't know if he ever mentioned me. Terrible business . . ." He shook his head and rambled on for five minutes more, then pulled himself together and departed.

"*Caro!* Whatever did you tell him to get him crawling like that?" Cathy now wished desperately that the whole affair was just a bad dream. She felt ravaged with embarrassment, and furious with herself as well as with Charlie. In a few intemperate instants, she had blown her chance of landing Britain's most eligible earl.

"I just said you were really upset, and—ah—well, it all got a bit out of hand, I was pitching it strong for the housekeeper when old Sir John loomed up and wanted the whole story. He was absolutely livid. I think he's got a soft spot for you, Cathy."

Smarting with failure, Cathy decided to scuttle back to London as soon as she could the next day, fearful that Charlie would come around before she left. When he did regain consciousness, which was toward the end of Sunday afternoon, he received a thunderous lecture from his host, who was also a friend of his own father. As a result, Cathy received a large bouquet on Monday, accompanied by a colossal pink-velvet stuffed pig, wearing a white tutu and a label which read "This little pig says he's sorry." Shortly after they were delivered, the telephone rang.

"I wouldn't blame you if you said you never wanted to see hide nor hair of me ever again," said Charlie humbly, "but if you think you could bear it, perhaps you would have dinner with me and tell me how I can make it up to you for ruining your dress?"

8

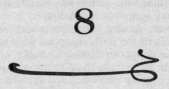

SINGAPORE IN 1948 WAS LIKE A SMASHED WASPS' NEST. HUGE ruined buildings, once creamy colonial white and now scarred with the shrapnel of World War II air raids, awaited demolition. Thousands of people, mostly of Chinese origin, scurried around building sites, gathering up rubble with their bare hands, carrying it away in wicker baskets, driving bulldozers and bullock carts to and fro as they toiled to create a new city.

The water of the harbor was calm as it had been through the preceding centuries, when the ships of five continents had crossed its scummy surface. The corpses of twenty thousand citizens of the city, machine-gunned by the Japanese, lay below the flotsam on the docile waves. Those who lived on remembered the dead with their ancestors but turned their energies to work. While Europe built war memorials, Singapore had decided to construct its glittering future.

The docks were to be rebuilt, the airport resited, the notorious internment camps destroyed but not commemorated. The city at the axis of the East's great trading routes was preparing to welcome oil tankers instead of tea clippers, jet aircraft in place of rusty tramp steamers. Singapore wanted to forget the past and embrace the future.

For the present, there were the British Tommies, thousands of loud, slow-moving men in khaki shorts, their pale northern skins fried red in the tropic sun. They had come to drive out the Japanese, stayed to supervise the repatriation of the prison-camp survivors, and kept arriving in renewed numbers to fight the Communist guerrillas who threatened mainland Malaya across the calm, pale-gray waters of the straits.

The soldiers were mostly conscripts under twenty, eager to sample the marvels of the East, equipped with malaria pills and homilies about the danger of diseased foreign whores. Pencillin had been available for a mere three years, and its power to destroy the bacteria causing gonorrhea and syphilis seemed a claim rather than a reality.

The Tommies' word for a woman was *bint*, from the Arabic name prefix *binti* meaning "daughter of."

Throughout the air raids, blackouts, blockades and invasions, Singapore had maintained its purposeful dedication to business. War was a tonic to trade. The Indian jewelers on Arab Street displayed in their plate-glass cases an unprecedented range of wares: the portable wealth of Eurasian concubines hastily cashed in when the girls' protectors fled the Japanese advance, the slim gold wedding rings sold for medicines by the starving nuns in the internment camps, Dutch cigar cases, Australian watches, Russian icons, Chinese jade. The passport to the city was something to sell.

Into the small curving river which slipped through Chinatown sailed a high-powered Malay fishing boat bringing a few passengers from the mainland. The petrol engine idled and spluttered as the boat nosed to a landing between the ranks of sampans at the quayside, and the fisherman's boy helped the passengers mount the rough steps made from railway sleepers. The last to alight was a woman of perhaps twenty, who climbed with difficulty because of her tight brown sarong. The boy ran down again to collect the palm-leaf bag which bulged with her possessions.

Bemused by the throng of rickshaws and bicycles along the quay, the girl looked wonderingly at the facade of shuttered shophouses in front of her, the three or four-story buildings incorporating warehouses and tea shops behind a shabby arcade of columns. The walls were covered with peeling layers of cigarette posters and advertisements for American films.

"Can I help you—perhaps you have lost your way?" A plump Eurasian woman in a navy print dress spoke to her in English.

"Thank you." The girl turned in relief. "I am looking for a cheap lodging house, if you know of one."

"Singapore is full of cheap rest houses—do you want to stay in any particular part of town? Perhaps you have friends in the city?"

"No, no friends. I have to find work, so I want to be near the center, that's all." She was neatly formed, with a high-cheek-boned, heart-shaped face.

"I rent a few rooms in my house—only young ladies of course. One of them has just left me to go back to her village and get married. Perhaps you would like to see her room?"

The girl hesitated. Apart from the fact that she spoke English well, everything about her indicated a village girl of little sophistication. She had few clothes in her bag, wore no jewelery or accessories of Western manufacture, and her silhouette showed no evidence of a bra. Her figure-hugging black bhaju and printed sarong were in traditional Malay style; the long line of buttons down the bhaju front were, the woman noticed with a covert casual glance, made of braided thread. But village girl or not, she was suspicious of this sudden good luck. Good. She had common sense as well.

"If you wish, I will give you my address and you can call later to see the room. But I am on my way home now and we could take a rickshaw together?" No pressure, not at this stage, not with a Malay. Had she been Chinese the woman would have hectored a little, but the timid Malay girls needed more careful manipulation.

"That's very kind of you."

"So will you come now with me?"

"Why not?" She picked her bag up decisively, and the Eurasian woman hailed a rickshaw.

"My name is Anna Maria," she said, holding out a hand. "Spanish name. My mother is from Madrid." A European connection was always reassuring, she found; in fact, her mother was a Filipino housemaid.

As the rickshaw boy ran through the thronged streets Anna Maria appraised her catch out of the corner of her eye. Slim, graceful but with that bit of extra flesh the British liked; a real little bosom, in fact.

"Excusing me asking, but are you Malay?"

"Yes, I come from Pahang, south Pahang." She had named one of the less developed areas on the east side of the peninsula.

"May I ask your name?" It was an intrusive question, but the girl rallied to answer, evidently understanding that city people were more outspoken than country folk.

"I am Ayeshah binti Mohammed," she answered, as if she had rehearsed the sentence. Anna Maria had heard so many false names she scarcely bothered to register suspicion.

"And are your mother and father still living?"

"My mother only."

"You are very pretty, very nice."

The girl barely reacted. Most young Malay girls giggled at compliments but there was a hard core here, a passive negation in her manner. Yet she *was* pretty, and Anna Maria was sure she had European blood in her family somewhere; her skin was dark olive, her nose slightly upturned but sharp at the bridge, not broad, her eyes round and her hair finer than that of most full-blooded Asiatics.

"A pretty girl like you should have a husband." Another bleak silence. That was it then. Husband had run away, maybe chopped up by the terrorists, who could say?

"What work are you hoping to find?" The rickshaw boy was pacing steadily past the conglomeration of white buildings that formed the Raffles Hotel. A Union Jack hung limp from a pole over the entrance.

"Maybe I can be amah in an English house. I speak good English, I work hard."

Anna Maria drew in a hissing breath and shook her head.

"Very hard work to find. Do you have references? Someone who can introduce you?"

The younger woman's proud poise wavered as she shook her head. References were something that had never occurred to her.

Anna Maria's house was a weatherbeaten turquoise building in the old colonial-Georgian style, with semicircular fan lights above the upper windows. Ferns gushed from the clogged guttering. Ayeshah's room was a small one at the back, with a high window, one foot square, bare floorboards and an iron bed. The Chinese disliked building houses with big windows at the back, in case they gave access to bad spirits. Ayeshah walked around it with an animallike curiosity, agreed to the rent and closed the door behind Anna Maria with a calm finality which inhibited any further overtures.

Next morning, trim and serious in a fresh sarong, Ayeshah asked Anna Maria how to get to the quarters where the rich Europeans lived, and walked off briskly. All day she tramped from one villa to another, knocking on doors with diminishing confidence. In most houses she never saw the owners, only the Chinese houseboys who brusquely sent her away, angry that some stupid village girl should not understand the system of nepotism and introduction which regulated candidates for household jobs.

She had known, of course, that in leaving the village and coming to a town she was leaving a rural Malay life and moving into a harsh, Chinese world, but she had not expected to feel so much of an alien. At night Ayeshah returned, overwhelmed by her failure and by the horrible size of the city, which had been quite outside her ability to imagine. The gray paved streets seemed to extend forever in all directions, crowded with abrupt, busy people who had no pity for her unfamiliarity with their ways.

She bought rice for a few cents from a hawker. It tasted smoky and rancid, as if it had been cooked with dirty oil, and it was expensive, but she was too hungry to care.

"Maybe you will be luckier in the Chinese houses," Anna Maria suggested. While Ayeshah was out Anna Maria had gone into her room, using her duplicate key, and examined her small bag of belongings. The money she found in the pillow lining. There was more than she had expected, enough for a month if the girl was careful, which she seemed to be.

With new heart, waving gaily to Anna Maria as the landlady leaned out of her first-floor window to air her canary's cage in the sun, Ayeshah set off the next morning for Emerald Hill. Again she went from door to door, this time of smartly painted terraced villas with small gardens; she quickly realized that each house had only one or two servants. The houseboys were older and angrier than the others; the doors slammed behind her instead of closing civilly.

At the end of the day she was so tired that she spent precious dollars on a rickshaw back to Anna Maria's street. She had found out that seven other girls also lived there, but when she left in the morning they were all asleep, and none of them were in when she returned in the evening. By the time the other lodgers clattered up the bare wood stairs, Ayeshah was enjoying the sound sleep of a young, healthy and exhausted girl. When she paid the rickshaw boy she asked him where the richest people in Singapore lived, and how she should get there.

Next day Ayeshah took a bus ride out to the prosperous suburb the rickshaw driver had named and continued her pilgrimage in search of work, walking through huge gardens with swimming pools, to knock at the servants' entrances of vast pastel mansions owned by Chinese millionaires. By now, although she did not know it, she had a pleading look in her eye and a plaintive tone in her voice that invited yet more rejection. The butlers were grave, polite but regretful. Returning at the end of daylight she lost her way and wandered the empty streets for hours, panic fluttering in her chest, until at last the slope of an avenue was familiar and she found the bus stop.

From the bus stop in Victoria Street there was only a short way to walk to Anna Maria's house, but it was quite dark and the bars were filling with seamen and soldiers. She passed the junction of Bugis Street, scenting noodles from the food hawkers' barrows, and paused; should she spend more money on food?

A large rat stuck its nose out of the deep guttering by her feet, took fright and retreated. As Ayeshah was counting her money there was shouting in a bar to her left, then fighting men fell out into the street. Chinese and Malays were punching and butting each other, some waving broken bottles. Tension between the two races ran high in the city, needing only an incident to transform hatred into violence. The fighting men crashed to the ground at Ayeshah's feet; totally unaccustomed to both drunkenness and violence, she stumbled away in horror as the bigger man knelt on the other's chest and repeatedly smashed his head on the granite paving stones, yelling a curse at each impact. Ayeshah ran home as fast as her swathed sarong would allow and bolted up the stairs.

Anna Maria sat at her dilapidated rolltop desk on the first-floor landing, with a lean, brown-skinned Chinese man in a black suit. As Ayeshah breathlessly scrambled to the top of the stairs, they turned and rose as if they had been waiting for her.

"Poor girl, have you had an accident?" Anna Maria rushed to her side and made her sit down. Ayeshah regained her breath; she realized that blood from the street fight had splashed her feet and legs. An instant later she remembered that she had dropped all her money in terror.

"No, please. I am quite all right. I just saw some men fighting in the street and it frightened me."

"Sit, please. Have some tea." Anna Maria poured the translucent brew into a tiny rose-printed cup. "You are sure you are not hurt?"

Ayeshah sipped and shook her head. The tea was tepid and bitter, signs of a long wait. She sensed that there was business to be done with the Chinese and looked at him expectantly.

"May I introduce my good friend Hong Seung? He has come here asking my help and I suggested that he should wait and meet you." Hong Seung was courteous. He offered her an English cigarette which she refused with a giggle that seemed to reassure them all.

"My honored friend Anna Maria"—they half bowed to each other—"says you are looking for work. I heard this and thought it was good luck, for I need a girl to work for me. I own a laundry not far from here. My business is good and I need one more girl to wash. Too many boys in my family and no girls. Girls wash better. I think I ask Anna Maria, she know plenty girls." Relief cleared Ayeshah's panic-filled head instantly.

"What will you pay me?" she asked stiffly.

"I am still a poor man, I cannot pay much—five dollars is all I can manage."

It was, she knew, more than an amah's wages, but then she had to pay Anna Maria and buy her own food. Still, it was enough. She nodded. Anna Maria and Hong Seung smiled at each other.

"You come tomorrow," said Hong Seung, showing a mouth full of gold teeth. Stupid girl, he thought, I would have paid her six if she had asked for it.

Hong Seung's laundry was a traditional Chinese shop-house under a stucco arcade, with a slab of granite as a bridge over the deep monsoon drain and a red tin shrine tacked to a pillar with dying flowers and burning joss sticks on it. In the front of the shop four men in singlets and shorts ironed on tables, with modern irons wired to the electric lighting circuit in the ceiling.

At the back of the building was a courtyard where the laundry was washed and dried. At intervals bicycle carts drew up at the wrought-iron gate in the back alley, and huge bundles of sheets, tablecloths and soiled uniforms were dragged inside the yard.

It was not easy work. First the bundles had to be sorted and counted. The washing was then boiled in huge old-fashioned copper kettles, with fragments of soap chopped from big brown blocks with a cleaver. When it was judged to be clean, Ayeshah had to reach into the boiling water with her bare hands and pull the linen out, then rinse it in clear water at the shallow sinks positioned against the wall.

There was one tap at the other side of the yard. The heavy wet sheets were fed through a mangle, and stretched on bamboo poles to dry. There were two children to help her, a six-year-old to fan the fires under the coppers and keep them fed with charcoal, and a girl of eight.

At the end of the first day, Ayeshah's hands were scalded red and her back ached painfully. She was tottering with exhaustion by the time she spread the last sheet on its pole. The courteous Hong Seung was not about, but his mother, a vastly fat woman with gray hair in a bun, glowered at her.

Next morning she was greeted by a screaming tirade from the old woman, most of which she could not understand. What, finally, she made out that she had muddled up two bundles of laundry. There was no system of laundry marks, and she was expected to be able to tell each customer's sheets by eye alone.

The older child went silently about her work, but the younger one watched her with something more than curiosity. Somewhere in her thoughts Ayeshah knew with complete certainty that she was being tricked, that she had been marked as a victim from the moment she met Anna Maria at the quayside. Somewhere else in her mind she was willing to assign her destiny to others. Her will had been drained by a vast grief; while her physical being could be a puppet, her soul was hiding, repairing its wound. It was immaterial who pulled the strings.

At the end of the day a bundle of gravy-stained tablecloths arrived, and Ayeshah left them soaking overnight. In the morning, she found that a blue amah's blouse had been in the bundle, and had stained the entire copperful of white linen, which now included two fine gentlemen's shirts.

"Quickly," she ordered the elder child, "fill the copper with fresh water and boil these again—maybe we can get the stains out." The child shrugged and did what she asked without any sense of urgency.

Ayeshah battered frantically at the shirts on the washing stones, and got them back to an even, slightly tainted whiteness. By the evening the backs of her hands were covered with small blisters from repeated immersion in the scalding water. Larger blisters were swelling painfully under some of her cuticles. When she woke in the morning her hands were crusted where the blisters had wept. When she tried to move her fingers, the pain was like fire.

"Where is Hong Seung?" she asked the fat woman at the week's end. To her surprise her employer materialized at once from the front of the shop.

"Forgive my weakness and foolishness," she began, half muttering words she sensed were useless, "but I cannot do this work. It is too hard for me—now I can't put my hands in the water at all, you see." She held her hands out and Hong Seung made a show of turning on the single naked light bulb to examine them.

"Bad," he nodded. "Hands no good, too soft."

"So I cannot work here anymore." Ayeshah's voice sounded a little more confident once the Chinese had accepted her incapacity. "We agreed my wages would be five dollars," Ayeshah followed up nervously again.

"You want money?" Hong Seung reached into the pocket of his shirt and pulled out a folded scrap of paper. Resting it on a three-legged table, he took a pencil stub from behind his ear and covered the paper with Chinese characters.

"So—look." He motioned to Ayeshah to read over his shoulder.

"Two loads washing you mix up—deliver late, customer angry, not pay. Ten dollar. Tablecloths stain, no good any more. Eighteen dollar. Two shirts no good, very expensive shirt, customer very angry. Forty dollar. Use much soap, we say one dollar. Sixty-nine dollar. You earn five dollar. OK. You pay me sixty-four dollar now, please."

One by one the other laundry workers gathered round. Ayeshah looked in horror at their angry faces. They yammered at each other in Chinese, went over Hong Seung's figures among themselves, nodded and smacked the paper emphatically to express their agreement. Ayeshah caught words she knew: "lazy," "stupid girl," "much money." She began to cry. Finally Hong Seung marched her back to Anna Maria's house.

"Bad girl, she bad girl," he shouted, shoving her up the stairs, "she get money now, pay me."

Choking back her tears, Ayeshah ran upstairs to her room and felt inside the pillowcase. There was nothing there. Frantically she pulled out the pillow, turned the threadbare covering inside out and shook it. She looked under the bed, pulled the sheet off the grimy mattress, turned out her bag, scattered her clothes. Her money was gone.

Anna Maria was standing with Hong Seung in front of the littered desk when Ayeshah came downstairs. She was angry, but restrained by her harbored sense of predestination.

"Anna Maria," she said, trying not to sniff. "Someone has stolen my money."

"Nonsense. You're lying. You had no money," Anna Maria shouted in anger, no longer poised or sophisticated. "You came here with a handful of dollars and now you can't pay me for the room. I've heard that story before, Miss."

"But I had a lot of money—in my pillow."

"You had nothing. I know, I changed your linen. Stupid girl, you think you can swindle me? Or my friend Hong Seung? Prison is the place for girls like you."

Roused by the shouting, two of the other lodgers appeared, sleep-smudged faces leaning over the top-floor bannister.

"Suzie! Get dressed and go and find a constable."

"No, no, please." Ayeshah was so scared she could hardly put the words together. "I'll pay you, both of you. My hands will be good soon, I'll work hard. . . ."

Hong Seung spat. "Hands no good, too soft." A lanky Chinese girl came down the stairs yawning and scrabbling inside a white plastic handbag.

"You want I go to police house?" she asked Anna Maria.

"Yes—tell them to come and arrest this little thief. Hurry up!"

Ayeshah screamed and flung herself at Anna Maria, who furiously shoved her away so she fell in a sobbing heap on the stairs. Three more girls watched from the top floor, muttering excitedly. Hong Seung, Anna Maria and the scrawny Chinese girl talked briskly, deciding something among themselves. Then Suzie helped Ayeshah up.

"OK. All fixed," Anna Maria announced. "You work with Suzie at the dance hall. If you're good and work hard, get lots of tips, you can pay us what you owe. You're very lucky; Suzie is sorry for you, she has asked us to be kind. Myself, I would have you arrested, but she says no. Do what she says and maybe you won't have to go to prison."

There was more discussion between Hong Seung and the Chinese girl, and eventually they seemed to reach an agreement and the laundry owner left.

Suzie pulled Ayeshah upstairs with her and made her sit on her bed while she finished her preparations for the night's work. She scooped up swags of her coarse black hair and pinned them into a chignon like the European women wore, then began spitting into a little case of mascara and stirring up a paste with a brush. Ayeshah was fascinated, in spite of the horrors of the argument with Hong Seung and Anna Maria. She had never seen a woman use makeup before.

Two other girls sat with her, smoking English cigarettes. They pinched her arms and the upper swell of her breast, laughed, and nodded encouragingly.

"Pretty titties," said one. "Tommies will like." Suzie smiled at her in the pink-tinted mirror. "We get brassiere tomorrow. Tommies like brassiere, make titties bigger." She rolled up her pink sweater and showed Ayeshah a white cotton bra of near-surgical strength hanging loose over her own concave chest and forming a bridge of grayish elastic between her sharp shoulder blades.

They took a taxi to the dance hall, an extravagance which hinted to Ayeshah that she was moving into a more lavish world.

The Miss Chatterbox Rendez-Vous was a big, smoke-tainted room with flapping Shanghai doors at the entrance like the doorway of a cowboy saloon. There was a space cleared for dancing in the middle of the room, a modern jukebox, and a row of tin tables, some covered with oilcloth. Each girl planted her handbag by a seat at the table before joining the gossiping group around the jukebox. They played wailing Chinese ballads until the first British soldiers began to slope in, then switched to Western big-band music.

Suzie rapidly instructed Ayeshah in the art of making plenty dollar as a taxi-dance girl.

"Choose young boy only," she advised. "He come quick, no trouble. Be sweet with him; when he say 'Missy, you pretty,' you ask him if he like long time, all night. Ask ten dollar for make love, five more dollar all night. You must get money first— very important."

She opened the white plastic handbag and groped among the mess of cosmetics inside. "Here. Put rubber johnny, then you never get sick." She placed a packet of three contraceptives in Ayeshah's barely comprehending hand, looking at her curiously. Pretty girl, but very quiet. No wonder the Chinese were the best taxi-dance girls; they knew it was important to smile a lot and be brisk and businesslike.

Ayeshah watched blandly as Suzie began work. A meaty middle-aged sergeant approached her with a book of paper tickets in his hand. She tore one out, tucked it into her handbag and danced with him, gazing blankly into space and holding him at arm's length. When the song finished, she returned quickly to her seat and took a ticket from a skinny private with the prematurely aged look of lifelong borderline malnutrition. She snaked her body close to him, grinding her pelvis into his. She gazed vacantly over the boy's shoulder, but her right hand, Ayeshah noticed, was between their bodies, hard at work. At the end of the music they had a short discussion and Suzie triumphantly came back to collect her handbag.

"Be lucky!" she called to Ayeshah, giving her a wink over her shoulder as she tripped out of the door on the boy's arm. Ayeshah smiled a tight, nervous grimace and looked up to see another soldier, slight with curled fair hair, with a dance ticket in his outstretched hand. She took it and, having no handbag, rolled it into the waist of her sarong.

Western dancing was not so different from the Malay *joget*, she found, but harder to do with your bodies pressed together. The fair soldier smelt nauseatingly of beer; he was sweating and breathing heavily; his penis was hardening fast, she could feel it against her body. Timidly, Ayeshah slid her hand to the man's crotch as she had seen Suzie do, wincing with pain as she scraped her blistered skin.

Fortunately, he seemed not to notice her clumsy hesitancy.

"How much is it?" he asked, giving her a smile and pulling away a little to look at her with those funny blue eyes.

She said ten dollars, and he nodded and turned for the door, wrapping her arm over his proprietorially. The men she assumed were his friends shouted things as they walked into the street.

In the taxi he at once unzipped his trousers and pulled her hand to his crotch, not seeming to notice the weeping blisters. He flipped half the buttons of her blouse open, muttering "gor!" as he felt her naked breasts. Was this the time to make him pay for all night, she wondered, fumbling desperately in the mess of unfamiliar garments for the slim, rubbery penis that was already oozing drops of fluid. Suzie was right about choosing the young ones.

In her room, breathing louder still, he helped her undo the remaining buttons, impatiently tugged the sarong off, then tore frantically at his own clothes, in his impatience getting his trousers tangled with his heavy boots.

Ayeshah remembered Suzie's advice, and reached for the packet of contraceptives which had fallen to the floor from the sarong folds. He snatched the packet from her and pulled the sleeve of powdered rubber over his penis with shaking fingers.

"You pay now, please," she half whispered, and he stuffed notes in her hand. Then he was on top of her, stabbing wildly around her soft entrance, muttering incoherently in his fear that he was going to climax before getting inside the body he had hired. Ayeshah felt no pleasure, no pain, nothing beyond the discomfort of the prodding penis. He was much clumsier than her husband and automatically she helped him.

"Easy does it," she said, the English phrase rising like a forgotten memory. With delicate fingers she guided him, and after a few violent plunges it was over.

She slid from beneath him and got off the bed at once, not quite believing that she had done what she had done. The man too sat up, found cigarettes and matches, lit up, doubled over the pillow and lay back, an arm behind his head. He looked at her.

Once, in the village, a Japanese truck had killed one of her father's buffalo. By the time she and her brother had found the stiff-legged carcass, a monitor lizard had already gorged on it and was standing aggressively over the remainder. They had laughed to see the great jungle scavenger, already stuffed with food, greedily raking the meat with its swiveling reptile eyes, too full to eat more but too obsessed with the prospect of plenty to know that it had eaten enough. The lizard had been as big as a man. This man was looking at her now with the same greedy fascination.

"Well, kitten," he said, blowing out a stream of blue smoke. "How about all night, then?"

"Ten dollars." Ayeshah hardly knew she'd said it. He licked his lips, his eyes roaming hungrily over her flesh.

"The other girls ask five." The pained tone in his voice pleased her. So it hurt to give money—well, it felt good to hurt a man, especially a white man.

"I ask ten." She smiled, exhilarated. Ayeshah had animation now, the puppet no longer needed her strings pulled.

"I'll want my money's worth."

"Of course." She walked back to the bed and sat on the hard edge, picked the cigarette from between his fingers, put his hand on her breast and crushed her flesh into his fingers. "Give me all the money now." He gave it to her, feeling a big man, enhanced in his reputation as a jammy sod, having found a more expensive, better-looking tart than those Chinese bints with toast-rack ribs.

Suzie took Ayeshah to the Chinese doctor, who gave her a bottle of blackish liquid to heal her hands. The wound in her soul seemed to mend equally fast, as she acquired the skill of getting money out of men, Western men. Every dollar Ayeshah tucked into her new red plastic handbag seemed to give her more drive. Her aptitude was astonishing, Hong Seung told Anna Maria. His brother (who owned the Miss Chatterbox Rendez-Vous) reported that she was the most popular girl there, making so much money she barely bothered to collect the twenty cents per ticket that she earned for the dancing only. His brother didn't like it when she turned up every few weeks with a stack of tickets to demand her dollars.

The other girls didn't like her either. When they tried to charge her prices the soldiers just laughed. They were in awe of her ability to do business. Ayeshah was so unlike the usual Malay girls; they were never good whores; they always had a bad conscience about the work and a sort of wistful apathy that the Tommies did not like.

"She is more like a Chinese; she thinks only of good business." Anna Maria approved. "But she sees with Western eyes. I have noticed this. I too, see that way. Now she buys clothes and she chooses what pleases the British. But to Chinese I think she looks ugly."

Hong Seung nodded, holding out his cup for more tea. Ayeshah's working dress was a skintight scarlet silk cheongsam embroidered with chrysanthemums, an old-fashioned party dress to his eyes. The Chinese girls mostly wore Western dress, but sweaters and skirts looked wrong on them, accentuating their bow legs or concave chests. The cheongsam made Ayeshah look even less Oriental, setting off the poise of her head and her rounded breasts, but it matched exactly the British boys' vision of an exotic Oriental woman.

In addition, she had developed a proud, mysterious smile which seemed to promise numerous delights. The boys were too young and too drunk to find those delights, but this was not important.

Money gave Ayeshah an almost physical thrill. In the village money had been almost irrelevant. The *padi* fields, the chickens, her little garden had provided a rich abundance of food; anything you needed your husband made, or you traded something you had for it. Before leaving the village she had scarcely ever handled more than two dollars. But in the city, she realized by instinct, money was everything, and so easy to get.

Once or twice, when an unusually drunken soldier had passed out in her room, she had got dressed again and gone out to work Bugis Street, perching at the food hawkers' tables to pick up merchant seamen and taking customers into a side alley for sex in a doorway. They liked you to do it with your mouth, and were older and slower than the soldiers, but she could double her money for the night with two or three of them.

The Chinese doctor gave Ayeshah a medicine she served to her clients as snake wine, the famous Eastern aphrodisiac. It was expensive, and all it did was make them sleep, but they dreamed orgiastically and never complained. The doctor treated her with extreme courtesy because she was a good customer, but in private he despised her as an unenlightened amateur courtesan who had no interest in the medicine which he himself had created which could prolong the rigidity of the Jade Stalk all night.

For the first month, afraid that her new-made riches would go the same way as the money she had hidden in her pillow, Ayeshah carried it in the lining of her handbag. She grew increasingly fearful of theft and wondered where she could hide her wealth. Where did Suzie keep hers? Suzie could not advise her— most of her earnings were sent to Shanghai, to the parents who had sold her to a pimp five years earlier.

Ayeshah dared not ask the treacherous Anna Maria, but she knew she must secrete her rent money somewhere. One week Ayeshah paid Anna Maria a month's rent in advance, then woke early and watched her landlady all day through the crack of her door until she saw her lock her own rooms in preparation for going out. Ayeshah followed Anna Maria, in her distinctive black-and-white frock, through the crowded streets to Orchard Road, where she went into a modern building with heavy wooden doors. A few moments later she came out and returned to her house.

The building, Ayeshah discovered, was a bank. Inside a clerk, a clean and prosperous-looking Chinese boy, explained that banks would store her money for her and even pay her to do it. It seemed too good to be true. At Miss Chatterbox's, Ayeshah asked the other girls, who were scornful and said banks were for Europeans and could not be trusted.

"Stupid women, what do you know?" sneered Ali, the Malay waiter. "Banks are safe even in war, I know. In my village the district officer went to the planters' club when the Japanese came and took all the whiskey and put it in the bank. When the Japanese left it was all there, and he sold the batch for a much higher price."

"But all the banks are Chinese?" Ayeshah was unable to believe in the trustworthiness of such a mercantile race.

"Not all, we have Malay banks too. Bank Bumiputra is very big, as big as the Chinese banks."

And so Ayeshah, with relief, emptied the notes from her handbag lining on the counter of the Bumiputra Bank and opened an account. Because she did not read very well, Ali, the waiter, helped her with the forms. Figures, however, gave her no trouble, and she read and reread her first bank statement like a holy man reading the Koran.

Two years later Ali arrived at the Miss Chatterbox Rendez-Vous at 4:00 P.M. to open up and found the owner, Hong Seung's brother, in bloody joints all over the room. He had been ritually murdered by members of a rival tong, another victim of the endless trade vendettas between the Chinese secret societies. Ali had barely mopped up the blood by the time the first Tommies sauntered through the Shanghai doors. There were more of them than ever now, and on the mainland the Communists were waging a full-scale war.

Ayeshah anticipated that Hong Seung would take over his brother's business, but she returned to Anna Maria's to find her landlady's room stoutly locked and a fat Sikh sprawled on the chair before her desk.

"May I introduce myself?" he spoke elaborately formal English. "Anna Maria is taking a holiday in Hong Kong and you will pay your rent to me while she is away."

Ayeshah nodded noncommittally. "Is there news of her friend

Hong Seung?'' she asked. "On holiday" undoubtedly meant that whatever business had got the brother into trouble had also given Anna Maria a fright, and would certainly implicate Hong Seung too.

"He also visits with his family." The Sikh smiled broadly beneath his crisp white turban, implying that the evil ways of the Chinese always brought them their just deserts in the end.

From habit, Ayeshah and Suzie went to Miss Chatterbox's as usual the next day, and found bamboo scaffolding outside and a band of coolies hacking at the walls. On the opposite pavement, a tall, slender man in a spotless white suit was examining a large plan with a white man. When he saw the girls he quickly crushed the sheet of paper into the white man's arms and called to them.

"Mademoiselles! Over here, please!" He shook their hands in turn. "I am Philippe Thoc and this is now my club. How do you do?" His English had a strong accent they did not recognize, but from his name they guessed him to be at least half Vietnamese.

He bought them tea in a shop across the road.

"Unhappily, it will be two or three weeks, I think, before we can reopen again, but I hope you will consider it worth your while to wait." He offered fat French cigarettes, in a gold case. They took them from politeness and smoked cautiously.

"When we open the club it will be quite different. My plan is to have a club for officers—no more smelly soldiers, getting drunk and making trouble." His eyes sparkled enthusiastically under long ivory lids, and Ayeshah and Suzie felt themselves drawn into his vision without really understanding it. "No more taxi-dance—it's not chic. My plan is for a real nightclub with hostesses, a nice little band, a nice bar. We will serve only champagne. All I need is pretty girls like you, with good English, a little charm. And clean." He lolled back on his chair and watched the girls smile guardedly back at him.

The Eurasian one—and now that Ayeshah's noctural way of life had removed her from daylong sunlight, it was not possible to say with certainty that she was a Malay—was ideal, he thought. Pretty catface, intelligent, you could see it in the eyes, but not tough. Nothing special about the Chinese, but girls had their little attachments and it was wise to respect them.

For two weeks Philippe paid six of the girls half wages to be sure of having a skeleton staff. He hired two more waiters, and a Filipino jazz combo. The outside of the club was painted vivid pink, with the window and door frames in shiny black and a black plastic canopy over the door and over the street. A pink neon sign proclaimed simply CLUB. Philippe lectured the girls for hours on their duties as hostesses, and posted a long list of rules for them in the newly constructed office above the bar. No talking except in English, no fixing makeup at the tables, no girl to wear laddered stockings or clothes needing mending. Evening dress to be worn all the time. Girls must smile. Girls must be polite.

"He's mad," said Suzie flatly. "Where he think we will get money to buy dresses that he wants?" Ayeshah shrugged, pausing as she tried a new eyebrow pencil.

"He's been paying us to do nothing for a fortnight, don't forget. I don't think he's so crazy; he told me he ran a club like this in Saigon and made a lot of money." Philippe talked a lot about his club in Saigon, and about Paris, the place where he had been born. Ayeshah had no idea where Paris was, but he made it sound as if the streets were paved with gold. She was impatient to find out what reality lay behind the talk of elegance, wealth and high society.

Crossly, Suzie stubbed out her cigarette. Philippe wore a heavy gold watch and gold cuff links. His clothes were of a quality neither of them had ever seen. It seemed likely that he had recently made a lot of money.

"If he do so well in Saigon, why he leave?"

"Who can say? I suppose there was some trouble. It isn't our business." Ayeshah kept her eyes on her reflection in Suzie's pink mirror. "Take my old red dress if you like. I'll buy a new one."

What she did not tell Suzie was that Philippe had twice invited her for a cocktail at the Raffles Hotel. He had shown her the immense ballroom with a polished floor gleaming like a lake, and the swimming pool and the terrace shaded by the fan-shaped traveler's palms. Talking nonstop in his curious accent, he opened her mind to the world beyond the island of Singapore, and hinted that if she threw her lot in with him she would have a passport to wealth and enterprise beyond her dreams.

Philippe had three reasons for doing this. One was that he sensed that the other girls admired her and would do what she said. The second was that he saw exactly how her appeal could be marketed. The third was that she attracted him physically. There was something else, of which even this experienced peddler of flesh was unaware. The wider the vistas he painted for her, the better Ayeshah understood what he could do for her and

163

the more uneasy she became about their relationship. She did not want a man to have power over her, any kind of power, physical or financial.

"See that boy?" he asked her, pointing with his cigarette at the Raffles maitre d'hôtel, who was showing a party of Europeans to seats on the terrace. "How would you like to do what he does?"

Ayeshah was puzzled. "Just that?"

"Maybe a few other things. Look after the other girls. Help me in the office, perhaps. It's an easy job—all you have to do is remember the customers, smile at them, keep them happy."

She pursed her lips doubtfully, a mannerism which she had observed that Western men found very attractive. Philippe responded with the leap of interest she recognized. Then he asked her to dance. He moved with a pleasing, confident grace but his hands held her with a faint tremor, like rushes shivering in the breeze. Ayeshah dipped her eyelids, then again caught his glance, and smiled.

Later he took her back to Anna Maria's and disappeared into the noisy Singapore night. Ayeshah pondered. It gave her no trouble at all to open her legs for the Tommies and take dollars in exchange; but this was an involvement, bound up with the possibility of much bigger money, an entrée into a more prosperous world, perhaps a new life far away from this tawdry city. She sensed something in Philippe which was beyond the thrall of physical attachment, beyond the reason of business. Some part of him was out of control, and that was what she didn't like. His neat head, covered in close curls that brilliantine could not flatten, his mobile face and flat, ivory-skinned body, she liked.

The club opened with Ayeshah, in a new black brocade cheongsam with frangipani flowers pinned in her chignon, welcoming the customers and seating them as Philippe prompted. The soft, mysterious allure she projected intensified as her confidence grew. Philippe congratulated himself on his judgment and ached to hold the rounded body which the tight dress simultaneously displayed and concealed. She evaded him with a show of flowerlike modesty which whipped his senses still higher.

She was eager to learn how to cash up the till at the end of the evening, and so be able to evaluate the club's success. The first week, in which Philippe bought his friends drinks all night, was bad. The second week was worse, because few people came to the club. Then one or two friends of friends returned, and a regular clientele was established. Ayeshah was impressed. They were men with gold watches and gold cigarette cases, some in uniforms decorated with gold braid. They spent lavishly. They wore silk socks. They invited the girls to private parties in luxurious mansions, and sent their chauffeurs to collect them.

Ayeshah decided that Philippe's hints of glamour and prosperity had a basis in fact, and calculated that he was an opportunity she could not allow to pass. She relaxed the barrier of reserve she had put up against him. At the end of the club's sixth week, they worked out the accounts together, in the dead of night. When the final figure, a profit well above his projections, was written down, Philippe threw aside his pencil and embraced her with joy.

Instantly they were kissing, something she had not done for years, because she never kissed the Tommies. The feeling was sweet but the memories were painful; Ayeshah stamped them down and let physical sensations swell up to numb her mind. He picked her up and carried her slowly upstairs to his apartment.

Philippe was a delicate, elaborate lover, an erotic gourmet who delighted in finding new sensations for her to try. In his bedroom on the top floor, he nuzzled and nibbled her body with his pearly teeth, laughing with delight. Ayeshah found it relaxing to do nothing and have no concern over the progress of their lovemaking, no need to get it done and get on to more business. It was also curious to have thrilling sensations aroused in her body while her mind was detached. Her deadened senses came to life with feelings that were close to physical pain, as if scarred limbs were bending across their wounds.

It was almost midday when they came downstairs, to Ali's knowing smiles and Suzie's black sulk. Next day Philippe gave Suzie the sack and hired in her place an angular Goanese girl with inch-long fingernails.

Soon Ayeshah identified the section of his soul which was out of her grasp; every night Philippe smoked opium at an expensive parlor uptown. He traded the drug, and others, to wealthy Europeans. The discovery pleased her—now she knew she could destroy Philippe when the time was right.

Philippe had no idea that the captivatingly primitive beauty whom he intended to transform into his ideal companion was already anticipating the day when he would have outlived his usefulness to her. He was not much concerned that her sexual response to him was muted, since in his experience a young whore who had detached herself from her body in this way could easily be reawakened by a patient, skillful lover.

He was momentarily concerned when he entered the club one evening and found her in a state of great agitation, squabbling with Ali and rushing around the small, dark room like a furious cat, too disturbed to register his arrival.

"A man came to see her today, that's what's upset her," Ali told him. "Tall thin European with glasses—I've seen him before. Always the same reaction, Ayeshah's like a witch for hours afterward."

"Who is he?"

Ali shrugged. Philippe assumed that her visitor was an old protector, since many of the taxi-dance girls began their careers in prostitution as the mistresses of European colonists who abandoned them when they left Malaya. He judged that the situation required instant action and, catching her by the elbow, hustled her upstairs.

"I don't care for you entertaining your lovers while I'm out," he told her, shoving her into their room and twisting her arm painfully.

"I have no lover, you're crazy," she told him, struggling with all her strength.

He slapped her face hard, but carefully, so she would not be marked. "It's of no interest to me who he is, but if he comes here again he can take you with him. I shall throw you out on the street, just like that. You belong to me and I won't have you making a fool of me—understand?"

She stopped twisting in his grasp, and although she was shaking with anger, he saw to his surprise a flash of intense calculation in her eyes.

"The man who came today was not my lover. I had a lover once, but not this man. He only brings me news of my village, my family, that's all." There was a hint of desperation in her voice as she continued. "If you think I'm lying, I will make sure he comes again when you are here. But I need to see him—don't you understand, Philippe? How else will I know how my—my family is?"

Philippe was startled. He had expected screams, rage, and attack with her fingernails; in short, a classic jealous fight, a struggle for the demarcation lines of their relationship in which he would assert his strength and Ayeshah would capitulate after a routine display of temperament.

"You little whore!" He hit her again, less carefully. "Don't lie to me—do you think I'm stupid, eh?" He raged on, fighting his own sense of bewilderment as much as Ayeshah, who did not resist him and barely responded. Eventually he tired of the one-sided drama and half threw her down the narrow staircase, commanding her to continue her work.

The next day, she began to insist that they should find somewhere else to live. It was an idea contrary to all economic sense, since the room over the club was cheap, but Ayeshah nagged him remorselessly until he agreed, saying that she could not endure the noise of the family who lived on the floor above. Reluctantly, Philippe decided to believe her. A new baby had recently been added to the family's number, and, ever attuned to Ayeshah's sensual responses, he had noticed that she seemed to freeze whenever the infant cried when he was making love to her.

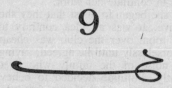

9

"THAT YOUNG LADY WILL BE A COUNTESS BEFORE THE END OF the season."

In the cacophonous bustle of her dance, Cathy's sharp ears picked out the conversation between her mother and a distant Bourton relation. There was no doubt they were talking about her. Everyone was talking about her and Charlie Coseley. The previous week, William Hickey had named her Deb of the Year, printing the picture taken by Tim Studd with a caption mentioning that she was "escorted everywhere by Charles Coseley, 29, Britain's most eligible earl and the heir to the Marquess of Shrewton. Friends expect a wedding announcement soon."

Bettina looked more relaxed than Cathy had seen her for months. She was not drunk; she was conspicuously sipping only orange juice, but that in itself meant nothing. Cathy could tell her mother was sober because the self-pitying mood and vicious tone into which she fell when intoxicated were absent, and instead her behavior was grimly reserved.

"I'm quite sure Cathy will play her cards right—no doubt about that. She's always known exactly how to get her way," she heard Bettina answer with complacent spite.

"She has certainly made the Coseley boy come to heel," the other woman continued. "No more Chelsea tarts and nightclubs so they tell me. His parents must be delighted, after all this time. The only son of course."

Cathy moved out of earshot, hurrying to the kitchen to check that the caterers were coping with the antiquated equipment. They had imported a battery of portable ovens powered by bottled gas to be sure of getting five hundred portions of quail stuffed with grapes to the tables at an acceptable temperature. The old kitchen, fitted out by Lady Davina in the twenties with the latest thing in solid oak cabinets, was as hot and crowded as hell and, she realized, no place for a girl who wanted to keep her blue Laura Ashley gown in milkmaid-fresh condition.

"Darling, where have you been? They're playing 'Pretty Flamingo' and I've been looking for you everywhere. Stop being the perfect hostess and take care of me." Charlie swirled her into his arms and started nuzzling her neck in the way he knew made ordinary girls go limp in his grasp and start begging for sex. He caressed Cathy without any expectation that she would do this. In three months of intensive courtship she had often gone limp in his arms, but steadfastly refused to have sex.

The defense of Cathy's virginity had been conducted according to rules of battle which, had either of them realized it, were as time honored as any principles of military strategy.

Charlie at first had no greater interest in Cathy than in any other pretty, attainable girl. He expected to seduce her within a few weeks and forget her just as quickly. He had taken her to dinner and on to Annabel's twice, frightened her a little by driving his E-type Jaguar at 100 mph along Chelsea Embankment, kissed her very thoroughly at his pad, cursed the invention of pantyhose and said, "Let's go to bed."

"No," said Cathy.

Charlie did a lot more kissing, throwing in a few of the tricks he knew were good for raising the temperature, like squeezing her breasts and tracing whorls in her ear with his tongue. Cathy was far too strung out with anxiety to respond.

"No, please, Charlie," she said, "I don't like it." This was not the correct response. Most girls said no but implied that Charlie should not abandon hope—they said "I don't know you well enough." That was the new code.

Cathy wriggled away as soon as Charlie started snaking his hand under her skirt. At this point, the limited intellectual faculty possessed by Britain's most eligible earl acknowledged the possibility that he was dealing with a girl of little sexual experience.

"You're not a virgin, are you?" he demanded.

"Yes, of course," Cathy replied. He pulled away and took his hands off her.

"But why? Don't you want to lose it?"

"No—not until my honeymoon. I want to wear white on my wedding day and deserve it."

"My God, how can you be so straight? For Christ's sake, it's 1965. Look, don't worry, I'll be very gentle, I promise. You'll love every minute of it." He pulled her close to him again and pulled up her skirt with determination. "Let me make love to you, Cathy. You're driving me crazy."

"No, Charlie, stop doing that."

"Why? Don't you like it?" He trickled his fingers up the inside of her thigh with all the erotic skill he could summon.

"Of course I like it, but what's the point if it's not leading anywhere?"

"Only because you won't let it. Oh, come on, Cathy. Let me turn you on. I'm a fabulous lover, everybody says so."

"Go and screw everybody then, if they like it so much."

"Well, you're certainly a waste of time, aren't you?" he snarled crossly.

Oh, heavens, she wailed inwardly, there I go again. Why, why, why can't I keep my big mouth shut? Charlie angrily marched her out to his car, and drove her home in hostile silence.

But the next day he called her again, and the next evening he attacked her again, this time calling her boring, straight and probably frigid. Cathy was unmoved. She knew Charlie could date dozens of exciting, switched on and undoubtedly unfrigid girls if he wanted to, but it seemed wise not to tell him this.

Then Charlie attempted the soft approach, and told her he loved her, that she was beautiful, that he'd never met anyone like her and couldn't get her out of his mind. The last two statements were perfectly true. He was aroused and challenged by her virginity and his days at the bank were increasingly passed in daydreams about her ecstatic surrender to him. Behind these fantasies was his belief that since she was a virgin she would be absolutely overpowered with grateful lust once he had initiated her into the delights of sex.

"You'll always remember me," he told her with mysterious delight. "Girls always remember the first."

He made a private joke of the idea of her passionate capitulation, but Cathy realized he was half serious and wouldn't play. He sent her flowers, and took her to a chic little jeweler in Beauchamp Place, and bought her a heart-shaped gold pendant studded with diamonds.

On his vast brown-velvet sofa he persuaded her to undress little by little, kissed every inch of her and raved over the perfection of her body. Cathy's anxiety faded and her body began to respond to his caresses.

"You'll be wonderful in bed," he told her. "You're made for it, darling. It'll be like fucking hot velvet. Oh, God, Cathy, *please*."

"No, Charlie. For heaven's sake, why can't you understand that I mean what I say?" She was sharp because it was an effort now to master her senses. Instantly Charlie was angry again, and dumped her back in Trevor Square.

"Fear nothing, he'll call," Lady Davina reassured her, knowing exactly what point in the game her protégé had reached.

"I hope so. I do love him," Cathy sighed.

"What you feel is irrelevant. We must make *him* love you." And Lady Davina made her return the diamond heart, then bought her a new dress and took her racing to Royal Ascot, which Cathy found boring and exhausting. Charlie called the house every day and in desperation called her at Bourton at the weekend. By the time Cathy was found, he was almost angrier than before.

"Where the hell have you been?" he snapped, as if their estrangement had been her annoying caprice alone.

Infuriated as he was, Charlie never used force to get his way because he regarded rape as an admission of failure. He was also coming to appreciate that Cathy had a strength of character which he had overlooked. She also had a sharp tongue and a disturbing propensity for telling the truth. Charlie's sex life was operated for public effect, and he was afraid she might make him look foolish if he broke too many rules. Cathy had a core of still seriousness which a more sensitive man would have appreciated at once. Charlie had come upon it slowly, unsuspectingly, and it drew out of him the unaccustomed emotion of respect.

His frustration he turned into humor.

"This man will self-destruct in five seconds if you don't sleep with him," he intoned like a robot, shuffling along the hall at Bourton.

"Give me your body or I'll join the French Foreign Legion," he demanded, flinging himself onto his knees at her feet in the drawing room.

"If you don't promise to sleep with me now I'll take off all my clothes and dance on the table," he scribbled on a menu card during a particularly dreary house party. Cathy laughed and loved him all the more, and relaxed with him so much that eventually one night in his arms she felt her body mysteriously align itself, tissue by tissue, into a perfect ring of ecstasy, and convulse in an orgasm.

Charlie was almost as impressed as she was. He had never been positively aware of a woman climaxing with him before, having always plowed on more or less regardless of his partners' responses.

"Oh, God, this is such a waste, darling," he murmured as he lay next to her.

Inside her own head Cathy heard the voice of Lady Davina counseling. "*Never* speak too soon. Make it clear you will only give yourself to your husband, then say nothing further. Just leave him to work it out." She sighed, depressed by the sadness following the release of her sexual tension.

And so now she sank reluctantly onto his lap in an alcove in Bourton House and pulled away his fingers as they fumbled with the buttons down the front of her dress.

"Don't undress me here, Charlie. Everyone can see us. Stop it."

"Stopit, stopit, stopit!" he squawked. "Who taught this bird to talk? Can't it say anything else?"

"You know I can't. Oh, please, Charlie, don't start this argument again, not at my dance. I can't bear it."

"*You* can't bear it," he sneered, petulant and rejecting once more. "At least you're getting your oats. Ungrateful cow."

"That's not fair, Charlie."

"Well, *you're* not fair, either."

"Yes, I am. It's my body, and my life, and what I choose to do with them is my affair and nobody else's, and just because you don't like it, you haven't got the right to complain."

He stood up and glared at her. "Who's complaining?" Insultingly he thrust his crotch at her face. "I'm not complaining. Someday you'll find out what you've missed."

And he spun around and walked away, leaving her feeling helpless and angry.

The discotheque was throbbing at full volume in the ballroom, where Charlie hauled a bedraggled girl in a semi-transparent smock onto the dance floor. She'd been had by half the men in London already, he knew. Within three dances she had agreed to leave with him. In the car park he suddenly shoved her down against the body of his Jaguar, and screwed her with violence.

He drove back to London, making her roll joints, and then suck on his penis as he took the car around the block. In his apartment, he demanded that she perform every degrading act he could think of, and a few she eagerly suggested in addition.

In the middle of Sunday morning, he ordered her to leave without warning, and spent the rest of the day drinking vodka by himself. Next morning, he went to the bank with a vicious headache and a sense of self-disgust.

He held out until Tuesday evening, telephoned Cathy and said, "I'm sorry, darling, I behaved like a spoilt child." Cathy said nothing, holding her breath. "Look, Cathy, I want you to meet my parents. Father usually has some people up to shoot at the beginning of August. Will you come and stay?"

"I'd love to." Cathy didn't dare say any more in case he should hear the triumph in her voice. From that moment they both knew exactly where their relationship was heading.

The Marquess of Shrewton, Charlie's father, was an elegant, colorless man whose chilly manner disguised much generosity of spirit. He liked Cathy immediately, which did not surprise her since most older men liked her, and he lost no time in talking to her about her relationship with Charlie, which did surprise her since she had expected this approach from his mother. Engagements, after all, ought to be girl talk. Lord Shrewton evidently saw them as a business matter. He looked at Cathy with intense curiosity.

"I knew your father, of course." His voice clipped and precise. "Terrible tragedy. What was behind it, did anyone ever find out?"

"Money. He didn't have much and he spent much more than he had."

"Didn't the police have some suspicion about blackmail?"

"We were told they did, but they couldn't prove anything."

The marquis was looking directly into her eyes. Suddenly Cathy felt as if she were being interrogated.

"Wasn't there some connection with Paris?" he asked.

"There was supposed to be, because he'd been in Paris on the day he . . ." She paused, the grief making it hard to talk even though Daddy had died over a year ago. ". . . the day he died," she finished, summoning all her self-control. Lord Shrewton said nothing but waited for her to continue. "The police said they didn't get any cooperation from the French, so they couldn't take things any further. We doubted there was anything in it, anyway."

"Why not?"

"Who would want to blackmail Daddy?" she asked, feeling horribly young and naive.

"You couldn't think of anyone who might want to do that, is that what you're saying?"

"Yes," Cathy almost whispered. She sensed an odd, almost obsessive, quality in his questioning, but so many people were curious about her father's suicide and too embarrassed to question her that it was almost a relief to be openly cross-examined. And, she acknowledged, he had a right to know all the material facts about her background.

Suddenly Lord Shrewton stepped back and smiled with reassurance.

"I should think you're probably right. Your father was very well liked in the City, and the police aren't always as clever as they think they are, in my experience. And what about your father's estate—it hasn't been declared bankrupt, I take it?"

"No, we missed that by the skin of our teeth. Daddy's insurance policies were enough to cover what was owing, though they made an awful fuss about paying up. I think the accountants had to juggle the tax around. We had to sell a lot of things, of course. The house and everything."

"That's too bad. But your mother's coping well, I hear."

"She's moved into a little apartment in Brighton." Cathy hesitated. This was not time to confess that if she married into the family she would be extending the blood tie to a chronic alcoholic, but not to mention it seemed like a lie. She compromised. "I think she gets very down sometimes."

"To be expected. Terrible shock. You realize you're nothing like the usual run of my son's girlfriends, don't you?"

"Well, so they tell me."

"They tell you absolutely right." A pale smile shone behind Lord Shrewton's horn-rimmed glasses. "Dreadful creatures, most of them. My wife didn't share my opinion, but I couldn't see any of them settling down to married life very well. Do you like children?"

"In moderation." Cathy had no experience of children at all, but saw herself as a wife with two immaculate offspring in velvet-collared coats shopping serenely in Knightsbridge and feeding the ducks on the pond in Kensington Gardens.

"In moderation." The marquis echoed her answer with irony. "If you want my advice, you'll get your family over with as fast as possible, then get on and enjoy yourself." He made a vague gesture around the landscape outside the windows.

Cathy understood him perfectly. What he was saying was that she could do what she liked as long as she gave him an heir to the title and estates. This implied that there might be something distasteful, or to be avoided, in marriage to Charlie, but Cathy was sure she had already seen him at his worst and was confident that he would change once they were wed. Marriage to Charlie, as she imagined, would be an endless tunnel of soft pink bliss. If only he'd ask her.

The next morning Lord Shrewton telephoned his solicitor in

London and then went to find his wife in the winter garden where she was supervising the potting up of the next year's bulbs. Charlie's mother was a plump honey blonde with a smile as rich as butter, which always seemed a little thinly spread when it was directed at her husband.

He sat her down on the window seat and told her his plans.

"It's all settled," he began, characteristically abrupt. "I want to move quickly or the Bourton girl will think better of it. She's sound and sensible, good family apart from that business with her father; there's no money of course, but she's the best we'll get, in my opinion. Charlie seems struck, don't you think?"

His wife agreed with reluctance. "He's gaga over all of them in the beginning." She disliked Cathy for exactly the same reasons that her husband favored her; the marchioness preferred her son to associate with trashy girls so that she could remain the queen of his heart. Cathy, because Charlie was powerfully attracted to her, represented competition for his affections.

"Well, if he's gaga enough to marry her we can redraw the trust, buy them their own London home and increase his personal allowance quite substantially. The lawyers agree with me that the main concern expressed in the trust document is safeguarding the estate as a whole, and when there's an heir, the entire picture changes again."

His pale gray eyes were gleaming with a relish for the unsubtle strategy he had proposed. Lord Shrewton was disturbed by what he could not control, and the notion that all the care he and his forebears had devoted to the establishment of the Coseley fortune might be dissipated in a single generation by the ungovernable stupidity of his only son had unsettled him profoundly for almost ten years. Like many British families, the Coseleys' wealth was tied up in a tangle of legal arrangements and an addition to the family could provide a useful way of extending this web and restraining the more spendthrift inheritors of the fortune.

He had also observed that his foolish wife took a perverse pride in Charlie's promiscuity. She was happy to see him pursue frivolous attachments with women who could not usurp her position. Although Lord Shrewton had consulted her in accord with his innate courtesy, he allowed her no opportunity to object. That afternoon during the shoot, he paired off with Charlie and made plain the fact that the guardians of his inheritance were prepared to offer him a substantial bribe to marry Cathy.

"Oh, well, I suppose everyone's got to make the same mistake once," Charlie acceded after a thoughtful ten-minute silence in which he balanced the allowance on offer against the money he was accustomed to drop at chemin de fer. "And once I'm hitched you'll all have to stop bleating at last."

The next day the August sun blazed in a cloudless sky and the bracken gave off a rich fragrance in the heat. Long alleys had been cleared in the gorse for the convenience of the guns, and Charlie set off for the most distant of them with Cathy bouncing beside him in an old shooting brake.

Part of Charlie's charm was his confident mastery of momentous occasions; where other, more sincere men were made clumsy and speechless, he was left in control by his lack of feeling.

"Isn't this bliss?" he murmured at midday, pulling her close to him as they lay on the grass. Invisible in the blue heaven above them a skylark was singing. "I'd like to lie here forever with you."

He kissed her lips, then her eyelids, then the hollow of her throat. They had almost finished a bottle of very fine champagne, packed in the lunch hamper in an antique silver cooling jacket so that it remained icy enough to mist the sides of the silver beakers. "I love you, Cathy." He'd said it a hundred times before to other girls but she never suspected the fluent ease with which the words rolled from his tongue.

Cathy nestled in his arms, expecting now to feel his deft fingers slip her blouse buttons undone, anticipating the delicious crawl of a caress on her sun-warmed skin. She could hear bees droning faintly, and, to her left, the gun dog panting in the heat. I can't stand much more of this, she thought, feeling the ache of desire begin again. Why didn't Didi tell me it was going to be such hell? I want him so much I feel as if I am about to burst into flames. Instead of the expected moves, she felt Charlie take her left hand and kiss the palm of it, then sit up, and press the fingers against his cheek. With surprise, she looked up into his chalky blue eyes. "Darling, I want us to be together always, forever. I want to spend the rest of my life with you, Cathy. Will you marry me? Say you will, please, darling Cathy."

"What?" She had visualized him saying the words so often, but now when she really heard them she could hardly believe it.

"Not 'what?' you idiot. 'Yes!' Say 'Yes, Charlie.' "

"Oh, yes, Charlie!"

"Yes what?"

"Yes, I'll marry you."

"And then what?"

"We'll be married?"

"Yes, and then what?"

"We'll have children?"

"No, much more important . . ." He pushed her back on the scented grass. "I'll give you something."

"A ring?"

"More important. Can't you guess? I'll show you. Shut your eyes."

The sun shone red through her closed eyelids. She heard him moving rapidly nearby, then there was something hot and smooth touching her lips.

"Have some to try now," he suggested, devilment in his voice. She snapped her eyes open. He had pulled off all his clothes and was holding the neat, narrow head of his erect penis to her mouth.

"Trust you!" Cathy hit him as hard as she could and jumped to her feet. "Trust you to think of some schoolboy gag to spoil everything."

He capered around her chanting like a Cockney barrow boy: "Try before you buy! Nice 'n' ripe 'n' juicy! Fresh pricks—they're luvverly! Get your fresh prick 'ere!"

The dog, alarmed, scrambled up and bolted straight behind his feet, and the naked Charlie tripped and fell with a yell into the wall of harsh bracken.

Cathy was laughing as she pulled him upright when a group of beaters appeared at a crossroads in the covert and stood stock still with embarrassment. Charlie addressed them with exuberance.

"Don't think the worst of this lovely girl, gentlemen! Allow me to introduce her to you. You should be the first to know! My wife-to-be, the pure, the delightful Miss Catherine Bourton!" To Cathy's amazement the men who were wearing caps tugged at the peaks and the group made a general bow in her direction. "Soon, of course, to be the new Countess of Laxford!"

The months that followed sped past like the landscape outside an express train. A marriage between two great families like the Coseleys and the Bourtons is generally a matter for lengthy and detailed negotiation on a scale which would not be inadequate for the United Nations General Assembly. Mr. Napier, the most junior of the solicitors at Pasterns who dealt with the Bourton trust, spent several afternoons with the Coseley lawyers finding the most advantageous way to join the two of them in law.

"Why is it so difficult? I thought I had no worldly goods to endow anyone with," Cathy protested.

"It's largely a notional issue, of course. The Coseleys are after some fancy footwork to help them, though it would involve the technical bankruptcy of your father's estate, which I assumed you wouldn't want. But there may be other ways we can accommodate them."

Cathy felt at times as if she were being made to do a quickstep in a social minefield. The next delicate matter to be resolved was that there was simply no money available for the wedding and reception from the traditional source of matrimonial finance, the bride's father.

"Why be such a perfectionist, darling?" reasoned Lady Davina, who had lived a life of triumphant extravagance. "You don't need a ghastly gaggle of children following you up the aisle. Two bridesmaids will be quite enough. And you can economize on the flowers . . ."

"I don't feel I want to make compromises about my wedding." Cathy eyed the budget with anxiety. "My wedding day is something I'll remember for the rest of my life."

"But it is only *one* day, darling, and I'm sure you'll be far too busy to remember anything about it. All I can remember about my wedding was the awful smell of the flowers—hyacinths I think they were. Too sick-making. I nearly fainted."

Now that the season was over, Cathy, Caroline and Monty were still living with Lady Davina at Trevor Square. But while Caroline and Monty were reluctantly dragging themselves through the last weeks of college, Cathy had been sent to a cooking school in Chelsea to learn the art of finding her way to a man's heart through his stomach.

"It's quite obvious Lady Davina thinks her job's finished now that I'm engaged," she confided to Monty when they met for a lunchtime cappuccino in a coffee bar. "Do you know, they even tried to make me get married in the chapel at Bourton? You couldn't get more than fifty people in there if you herded them in at gunpoint." Monty sprinkled brown sugar over the foam in her cup, then started skimming it off with her spoon.

"How can you stand it, Cathy? They're treating you like a prize heifer. I bet the Coseley mob will be the same once you've given them their heir. Off to the abbatoir with the useless carcass once the bull calf is weaned."

"Monty! Don't say such awful things. I know you don't mean them."

"You know I mean every word, that's the trouble."

Cathy was half admiring, half disapproving of her sister's talent for outrage. "You're not really going to move in with Simon, are you?" she asked. "There'll be hell to pay. Mummy will go mad."

"Well, he's found the perfect apartment now, and it'll be decorated the way he wants soon. But Mummy is the least of my worries. I've simply got to get the Pill somehow. There's no way I can live with Simon and sleep with him every night and not go all the way.''

"Well, why don't you get married?"

Monty frowned. The truth was that she could not believe a man would ever want to marry her, because she was wicked and rebellious and not as pretty as Cathy. But she told Cathy what she told herself. "You don't understand. I don't believe in marriage. I want to live with a man because I love him and want to be with him, and I want him to live with me for the same reason, and that reason only, not a legal obligation. And I don't want to end up bitter and frustrated like our mother, or an old harpy like Simon's mother. Isn't that enough reason?"

"But it isn't being married that makes them so awful. . . ." Cathy paused. She could think of no apparent reason why none of the married women they knew presented the picture of perfect contentment which she imagined a wife became for life on her wedding day. She changed the subject. "Do you know what I'm really going to hate about marrying Charlie? I'll hate missing you, I know I will."

"But you won't miss me—I'll be around."

"I know, but it won't be the same. You don't like Charlie, do you?"

"I don't have to like him; you're the one that's marrying him. But I won't stay away just because of Charlie. You'll see, we'll have lots of time to be together, probably more than now because you won't be studying. And you'll be able to tell me all about married life." Monty squeezed her sister's narrow, long-fingered hand in sympathy, noticing that she had been biting her nails. This little lapse from perfection was touching.

"Will you do something for me, Monty—a favor? A big favor?"

"What?"

"Don't move in with Simon until after the wedding. Please, Monty. There'll be such rows, and it's bad enough now, with everyone squabbling about the guest list."

Monty agreed. "OK, for you. I wouldn't do it for anyone else, mind. Even Simon can't move in yet. The flat's going to be full of builders for a couple of months anyway." In a matter-of-fact tone, Monty went on, "Have you done it with Charlie yet?"

"Done what? Should you really eat all that sugar, if you're supposed to be on a diet?" Cathy was acting dumb out of hostility. Monty dunked another spoonful of Demerara sugar in her cup.

"I mean, big sister, are you still in a state of maiden grace?"

"It's none of your business."

"Go on—tell. I bet you're not. I bet you've let him have his evil way with you."

"I bet *you're* not."

"Yes, I am. I'd give anything not to be, though." Monty sighed.

Merely thinking about making love launched a visible ripple of languor over her features. Cathy didn't care for her sister's capacity for sensuality, mainly because Charlie had called her frigid so many times that she was beginning to fear that she might be sexually inadequate in some way.

"Well, why don't you go on the Pill?"

"You can't buy it in Woolworth's, you know. You have to get it from a doctor, and the doctor won't give it to you if you aren't married."

"There must be some doctors who won't ask questions."

"But where do I find one?"

Cathy shrugged. "Isn't there something else you can do not to get pregnant? French letters or something?"

Monty gave a pout of distaste. "I want it to be beautiful, the first time Simon and I really make love. I want it to be a way of expressing everything we feel about each other; like a sacrament—the outward and physical sign. Sordid bits of rubber would spoil it."

"Still, at least you wouldn't have to worry about getting pregnant."

"Oh, yes, we would. Simon says half the contraceptive factories have been infiltrated by Catholics who don't approve of birth control so they deliberately put holes in them."

They were talking in quieter and quieter voices. The practical aspects of sexual intercourse were not a subject fit to be discussed in a public place by young women.

"You don't really believe that, Monty!"

"No, of course not—but what I hate are all those awful sniggering schoolboy jokes about French letters. They aren't anything to do with how Simon and I feel about each other. Surely you *love* Charlie; don't you feel the same?"

Monty spoke as if she found it very difficult to believe that anyone could love Charlie Coseley. Her disapproval was so obvious that her sister was offended.

"When Charlie and I go to bed, I'll be offering myself to my husband on our wedding night," Cathy snapped, "It's not the same thing at all."

Monty snatched up the gauntlet. "No, it isn't, is it? You're just trading sex for his name, his title and his money, and he's just out to fuck everything that moves and the only reason he's marrying you is that it's the only way he'll get into your knickers. That's not my idea of love.''

"It's none of your damn business, Monty." Cathy coldly paid for their coffees and stood up, tucking a threepenny piece under her saucer for the waitress. "You're just jealous because I'm getting married and you're not."

They walked along the crowded King's Road to Sloane Square, both aflame with hostility.

"You're the one that ought to be jealous! You must be the only bird in London who doesn't know what Charlie's up to," Monty snarled. "Try going round to April Hennessy's house, and see whose E-type is parked outside!"

As they reached the square, Cathy dealt her sister a ringing slap in the face, then without a word turned and vanished through Peter Jones, the store where the furnishings for her future home were to be made.

She was violently angry because Monty had said out loud something which had been nagging at her as a doubt for weeks. Once he had put the massive sapphire engagement ring on her finger, Charlie's playful resignation had switched to a mood of angry impatience.

"What the hell are you keeping it for now?" He had yelled at her with fury when she again refused him. "You've got the ring on your finger; that's what you wanted, isn't it? What do you think you've got between your legs anyway—the Crown Jewels?"

Once more he had left her on a note of savage petulance, but this time the telephone had not rung again the next day, or even the next week. She saw a picture in the *Daily Express* of Charlie with his polo team in Paris, and told herself this was the explanation.

He had reappeared after a fortnight in a much more pleasant mood, but there had been none of the irresistible apologizing to which she had become accustomed, just an off-hand resumption of the outward show of their relationship, with dates in London and weekends at one or another of the Coseley houses. He no longer pressured her for sex, or tried to cut her out of the herd of their friends and be alone with her at every opportunity. In fact, he treated her as if she were barely present in his life. Maybe Monty was right, maybe there was another woman.

With sudden weariness she made her way to the soft-furnishings department and tried not to think of Charlie at all as she ordered curtains for the impressive house he had bought in Royal Avenue.

Worst of all, Monty was the only person she dared to confide in, and Monty, although she had tried to hide it until now, hated Cathy's husband-to-be with a contemptuous passion. The warm, unquestioning love of her sister seemed to be threatened by the commitment she wanted to make to her future husband. She was dismayed; life without Monty always there for confidences and support suddenly looked bleak.

Cathy sighed as she signed the order form, no longer excited by the twenty-five-foot sweep of turquoise silk curtains she had decided upon for the drawing room, or by the questions of when and how they should be lined, interlined, weighted, headed, hung and allowed to drop before they were hemmed.

One winter weekend, Lord Shrewton led her into the library for a private talk.

"I don't know if you've heard from our people yet, but they seem to have reached an agreement on the marriage settlement and I wanted to have a word with you about it. I don't suppose"—he gave her his wintry twinkle of a grin—"my son has mentioned any of the details, if he even understands them. Briefly, I would have liked to be able to frame the arrangements more precisely so that you would be taken care of if—in the unhappy event of—should it happen that . . ."

"If we ever got divorced, you mean?" Cathy broke in to help him.

"Precisely. It seems a little cold-blooded to talk about divorce before the wedding, and of course we sincerely hope the arrangements are never put to the test. But I wanted to explain to you that the whole thrust of the trust deeds with which Charlie's money is tied up is toward the long-term interest of the family, rather than individuals. I gather the lawyers have decided to continue in the same vein, and detail a separate provision for your heir, assuming you have one."

Cathy grasped his concern immediately. "I think it was just the same for me in my family. All the money was really ours, not our father's."

"Precisely. Rather than make a separate provision for you as Charlie's wife, the lawyers have agreed that everything will go to your heirs. But one assumes the children will stay with the mother so it will come to the same thing if—er—well—"

"Yes, I understand."

"Excellent. You're very quick on the uptake. Maybe you'd

like to come and work for me in the bank one day. Some of our chaps seem to have difficulty getting the gist of a bus ticket.''

He poked the fire briskly and rubbed his hands. ''All the preparations going well? Worse than starting a war, planning a wedding, so they tell me.''

The more Cathy saw of her future father-in-law, the easier she felt with his practical style. She didn't find him frightening anymore; in fact, it amused her to see him snap comments and bark orders, now that she understood he deliberately used his intimidating persona to get what he wanted with the minimum fuss. Cathy felt brave enough to confide at least one of her worries to him.

''Do you think we ought to have the wedding at Bourton? All my family are absolutely set on it, but I know Charlie wants a big London wedding. What do you think?''

''I think it's your wedding and you should have whatever you want. And I suppose you want what Charlie wants, am I right?'' She nodded eagerly.

''Well, I don't see why the Bourton family should foot the bill for my son's extravagant tastes. I don't suppose Hugo Bourton does either, if I know your uncle. We'll see what we can do.'' She darted forward and gave his smooth dry cheek a quick kiss of gratitude, causing the astute marquis to blush.

The next week Cathy got a letter from Mr. Napier at Pasterns enclosing a bundle of legal papers which she dutifully attempted to read, with a final paragraph informing her that ten thousand pounds was being transferred to her bank account as a personal gift from the Marquis of Shrewton to her. He also offered Bettina an apartment in one of the estate's London terraces in Belgravia.

That evening there was also a strangled telephone call from Charlie's mother, suggesting that the wedding reception be held at the Coseleys' London home. ''After all,'' she explained, ''it *is* one of the few ballrooms in London still in private hands, and it seems such a shame that we hardly ever use it.''

In the dreary winter, Cathy learned how to make waterlilies out of tomatoes and baskets out of lemons in the cookery school, and spent hours with Lord Shrewton's secretary checking the list of wedding guests. She addressed five hundred and twenty-three engraved invitations with her own aching hand, and went to Garrard's with Lady Davina to choose a tiara that would sit attractively under her veil without making her feel as if her head were being sliced open like a breakfast egg.

From Jean Muir, she ordered a high-waisted wedding dress of heavy white silk which made her appear slimmer and more graceful than ever, and six small lace-bordered gowns in forget-me-not blue for the bridesmaids. She talked bouquets, posies, buttonholes and table centers with the florists, suprêmes de volaille with the Coseleys' cook, and crowd control with their butler.

All this Cathy did quite alone. She apologized to Monty and the sisters fell into each other's arms with tears in their eyes, promising never to fight again, but Cathy did not dare test her sister's goodwill by asking for her help with the wedding. Bettina abruptly refused the offer of a London apartment, preferring to remain with her bridge-club circle. Caroline was grimly jealous, Lady Davina absorbed with her next charity ball, the marchioness passive and hostile.

Monty kept her word and told Simon that she would not move in with him until after the wedding, but there remained a definite estrangement between the sisters which wounded Cathy more than she would admit. She had decided to have six little bridesmaids and two pages, chosen from the plentiful supply of children in distant branches of their families, but wished now that she had made Monty her bridesmaid as well, to keep her close through the ordeal. Charlie became more and more distant, and arrived an hour late for their interview with the vicar of Holy Trinity, Brompton.

Cathy awoke on the morning of her wedding day with a bleak sense of abandonment which she promptly crushed.

"This *is* the happiest day of my life," she willed herself to believe, and fixed a serene smile under her veil as she took Uncle Hugo's arm and set off along the endless corridor between men in morning suits and women in petal hats. A twinge of panic made her heart jump when she saw no one at the end of the aisle, but then Charlie, looking more handsome than ever, moved into her field of vision, and turned to smile at her. "That's bad luck, he shouldn't do that!" she thought, half expecting the quiet phalanxes of guests to collapse in disarray at this impudent breach of convention; but, glancing from the corners of her eyes through the mist of her veil, she read only bland approval around her.

They halted, Uncle Hugo released her from his arm, and Charlie on the other side at once squeezed her hand and gave her a quick unrehearsed kiss. For once she was grateful of his uncontrollable physicality.

The day went on more and more like a play in which she was both performing and watching, a series of tableaux which she was able to view and experience at the same time. At the church steps the warm June breeze caught her silk tulle veil and she felt it tug at its moorings in the piled coils of her hair. Charlie pulled her into his arms in the car, confetti spilling from the creases in his gray Blades suit, and teased her by tugging open the zip down the back of her dress.

In the ballroom, where the pillars were swagged with garlands of white carnations, Cathy stood in the receiving line until her Louis-heeled satin pumps pinched her toes like red-hot irons. When the last guest had been greeted and launched into the room, she brightened her smile and dutifully worked her way around the circuit of congratulating strangers until, with relief, she saw Monty with Simon and Rosanna in a group apart. Monty looked both decorous and sexy in an Ossie Clark crepe dress printed with tendrilling vines.

"You haven't got a drink." Simon at once halted a waitress and gave Cathy a glass of champagne. "Stop being perfect and talk to us. Do you realize you've got half the Shadow Cabinet here?"

"Of course she does; she wrote the invitations." Monty nudged him affectionately in the ribs as she raised her own glass. "Here's to wedded bliss, Cathy—may it be everything you ever hoped." She spoke warmly, wanting to heal any breach between them.

Cathy surveyed the crowded room, noticing several groups of men whose faces were vaguely familiar from television newsreels and who were set apart by the indefinable aura of power around them. Simon was right. A large proportion of the Conservative politicians recently swept out of office by Harold Wilson's new government had gathered to drink to their health.

"How awful of me, Simon. I must have written the names not realizing who they were."

"Well, I don't suppose Charlie introduced you to the Chancellor of the Exchequer during an evening at Annabel's." Simon gulped down a canapé and licked his fingers. "Mmm—delicious."

"They're not Charlie's friends—they're his father's, surely," Rosanna suggested and Cathy nodded.

"I thought I was just marrying a man—I forgot I was marrying a merchant bank as well."

"Oh, boy—try being Jewish!" Rosanna laughed. "Then you'll really know that family means business. Sometimes my father and his friends make me feel as if they're planning a merger rather than a wedding for me and Jonathan." Rosanna, to the ecstatic delight of her mother, had just announced her engagement to a stocky young man whose mother's cousin had married a Rothschild.

"Yes—but family isn't so important with us. This is more the sort of thing my father used to talk about. When I said I didn't want to be a deb, I remember him telling me, 'Don't write the Season off as mere frivolity—when people reach into their pockets to make a splash, there's always more to it than fun and games. They want the world to know something about them.' "

"Or prove that the upper classes still have the upper hand. Is your eyelash OK?" Monty carefully pressed a straying corner of her sister's false eyelash back into place. "You never dreamed you'd be backing Britain by getting married, did you?"

At last it was almost over. The three-tiered cake was cut, the speeches made, the bride and groom toasted and the overtired tiny bridesmaids led away to grizzle out of earshot. Cathy left the ballroom, kicked off her shoes, and ran up to the bedroom where her going-away dress was ready.

Monty followed her and flung her arms around her.

"I'm sorry I've been such a pig, Cathy. I've been awful, I know I have. I just couldn't bear to think I was losing you, that's all."

Cathy felt light-headed with relief as the anxiety of the past months melted away.

"I felt just the same," she told her sister. "I couldn't bear thinking that you hated me because you hated Charlie. Oh, darling Monty, let's not be so stupid ever again."

To Monty's surprise, she saw tears glistening in her sister's almond-shaped eyes.

"Hey, hey," she soothed her, reaching for the tissues. "Don't cry, your eyelashes will fall off."

A few moments later, the hairdresser arrived to unpin Cathy's false curls and brush out her hair. He was followed by Caroline, who began packing away the wedding regalia with workmanlike bustle; then Lady Davina appeared and finally Charlie who babbled incoherent compliments and fumbled at the buttons on her beige Courrèges shift. At the top of the stairs which led down to the ballroom Cathy looked for Monty at the side of the room and mischievously hurled her bouquet in her sister's direction so the guests surrounding her stood back and she was obliged to catch the flowers.

On the Comet to Nice Cathy and Charlie slept like exhausted children, but when they arrived at the Coseleys' villa at Antibes the warm, flower-scented air of the Côte d'Azur revived them. Charlie carried his bride over the threshold, dumped her in the middle of the vast Art Deco bed, dragged off her knickers and set about consummating their marriage with no further wasted effort. He took about ninety seconds; Cathy felt no pain and was almost delirious with the happiness of being desired.

For the next ten days, Charlie made love to her constantly, in bed, on the floor, on the massive veneered dining table, on the beach, in the water, on the yachts of the various friends who were moored in the enchanting harbor. At dinner he would pull her hand under the table to his crotch, in the car his hand would stray past the gearshift to her thigh and in the powerboat he made her take the wheel and joyfully ripped away her pink gingham bikini while she struggled to control the juddering shell on its crashing course through the waves.

She adored him more than ever. They had one fight, when they had drunk too much, over whether the moon was waxing or waning. Charlie punched her viciously in the side of the head, then collapsed in groveling apologies and made love to her with even more passion than before.

Two weeks after they came home to the impressive house in Royal Avenue, Cathy picked up a lipstick from the floor of his E-type. It was a pearlized apricot shade which she did not wear. Charlie said it belonged to his secretary, and Cathy never considered disbelieving him.

Six weeks after their return, Cathy realized that the box of tampons she had bought before her wedding was still unopened. Two weeks later, she went to see her doctor, who asked her to come back in three days. "Congratulations, Lady Laxford," he beamed as she walked into his consulting room. "You're about to start a family."

10

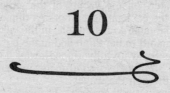

"OUR FIRST PRIORITY IS TO MAINTAIN THE ECONOMY, AND AS far as we're concerned at Bukit Helang that means keeping up our rubber output, meeting our quotas and exceeding them if we can." Douglas Lovell's shoulders, normally braced, were bowed and he spoke seriously.

"In the event of an enemy invasion, Malaya will be defended by the British Army; so will the rest of the Empire, most of Europe and half bloody Africa by the looks of things. The army runs on rubber tires, and our war service will be done better here than anywhere else. So any young fool thinking of running off home to enlist can think again—they're sending back any man who tries it." The elderly manager glared fiercely at the men who had assembled in his office at the hour normally devoted to tennis.

Japanese troops were fighting in Burma a few hundred miles to the north, and all over Malaya the Europeans were anticipating a call to arms.

"Strategically, because of our remote position, we're not as important as the estates near the coast or the border," he continued. "We'll form our own detachment of the Federated Malay States Volunteer Force and organize our people for military training. Bourton, I'm seconding you to the district officer to help organize an intelligence effort—he needs a linguist. Rawlins, Wilson and McArthur—you're to work with the Civil Defense Committee. I want plans for defense works on the estate on my desk as soon as you can. Anderson—pick out a dozen bright boys and give 'em first-aid training. I want parades every Sunday morning, drill in the evening—fight out a timetable among yourselves.''

The tennis nets had already been struck and stored, and within a fortnight the white lines of the courts were all but invisible, and the turf itself worn to its roots by marching feet. Beside the slate on which he marked the rubber prices, Douglas Lovell set up a bulletin board where he posted news of the progress of the war.

''Two battleships of the Royal Navy, HMS *Repulse* and HMS *Prince of Wales*, are sailing to join the Far Eastern Fleet where they will strengthen the defenses of Singapore Island,'' proclaimed a notice which was embellished with a thick red border and star. Gerald Rawlins read it out loud with satisfaction.

''That'll show the Japs we mean business. They'll think twice about sticking their nose in Malaya now.''

''Does it say anything about aircraft?'' asked Bill Treadwell, peering as he scanned the typed lines. ''Not much use sending battleships without some air cover.''

As a European closely involved in Malay affairs rather than an employee of a foreign trading interest, Treadwell had been called to Singapore and given some rudimentary propaganda training, then returned to Perak to whip up support in the largely disinterested Malay community. His weekends were spent touring the state making speeches and distributing leaflets and posters.

Gerald stood self-importantly in front of the bulletin and spoke to his friend as if to a particularly obtuse corporal.

''Don't be daft, man; Jap pilots are all short-sighted. They couldn't bomb a battleship at sea any more than you can read that notice without your glasses. That's if their planes can stay airborne long enough to get out to sea in the first place.'' He picked up a swagger stick and military cap and tucked them under his arm.

The Australian shook his head with a smile.

''What I like about you, Rawlins, is your cockeyed optimism, your pea-green innocence and your astounding ability to swallow any crap that's handed down to you as long as its got Made in England stamped all over it.''

''Careless talk costs lives, old man.'' Gerald did not smile and he glanced uneasily around the office.

''Careless talk costs lives all right, especially if it's written up on the wall and signed C-in-C British Forces, Singapore,'' Bill rejoined, deliberately not lowering his voice. ''If I were you

I'd give some thought to sending your wife away while you still can.''

They walked out into the bright heat of morning and turned toward the parade ground. Douglas Lovell insisted that the Sunday parade take place at 11:00 A.M. in the full heat of the day, to accustom the volunteer soldiers to the worst that the climate could inflict on them.

"Don't think I haven't thought of that already." Gerald flapped his hat at a dog that had strayed from the coolie lines. "Now Betty's in the family way and I'd give anything to have her safe and out of here. But she won't leave. Carried on so much when I suggested it I let the subject drop."

"Women!" Bill spoke in tones of light-hearted despair which alluded to the well-known propensity of the weaker sex for persecuting the stronger with their weakness.

"Said she'd go to pieces if she had to leave me," Gerald admitted with pride. "She's got a point. She can hardly go back home, and if we got her on a boat to Colombo or Johannesburg or somewhere she'd be billeted on some of my family who'd be total strangers to her. Betty just isn't the sort who can take all that in her stride. She's delicate."

On the trampled turf forty men in makeshift uniforms lined up, trailing spades, sticks and dummy weapons carved from plywood packing cases.

"All Chinese?" Bill inquired, at last taking the trouble to put on his glasses.

"Mostly. One or two of the conductors, a few Malays. Most of them don't seem to care." As a captain of this ragged fighting force, Gerald strutted along with greater self-importance as he approached his command.

"Can't blame them—it's not their war, after all. One master's the same as another to a coolie."

"Don't get me wrong, Bill; it's not the Tamils I blame, I'm right with you on that one. But you'd think the Malays would stand up and fight—it's their damn country, after all. They've had nothing but good from the British; now they won't lift a finger." He halted at the edge of the leveled ground. "You're not joining us, I take it? Don't fancy a spot of exercise to whet the appetite for lunch?"

"No fear, mate. In Intelligence, our function is merely to observe, not engage the enemy." And Bill threw him a salute that was only just short of insolent and lounged over to a bench in the shade of the casuarina trees, watching Gerald march stiffly forward as a sergeant called the men to attention.

An hour later, dripping with perspiration, Gerald returned to his bungalow to change, then set off with Betty and Bill up the rutted track to James's house. Gerald's proudest possession was his new car, a dusty Model T Ford bought from another junior assistant at the start of the war. It struggled pluckily up the red-earth lane, bucking over deep channels cut by the rivulets of water which coursed down the hillside after every rainstorm.

"James, you idle bastard—on your feet!" he shouted in greeting as he mounted the veranda steps. But instead of James, Ahmed, the houseboy, came running from his quarters.

"*Tuan* Bourton present his apologies, *tuan*. Gone this morning to Kampong Malim on defense business. Back noon, he say. *Tuan* Anderson has just arrived." The plump doctor and his wife were already settled in the shady interior with drinks in their hands.

"Well, here's a fine to-do! Asks his friends over for tiffin, then clears off!" Gerald flopped into one of the wicker chairs and motioned the others to do the same. "Now I ask you, is that the act of a gentleman?"

"The boy's flapping because James left no orders about lunch, either." Jean Anderson crossed her thin legs primly. "He simply tore off and forgot about us, I suppose." Sunday lunch scarcely required specific instructions from James; the estate community ate in each other's homes in rotation, but the menu was always the traditional curry tiffin—chicken in spiced sauce, rice, and bowls of coconut, banana, chutney and sliced salad vegetables, followed by ice cream and fruit.

Ahmed reappeared with a tray of gin *pahits*, watery lukewarm cocktails of gin, water and pink Angostura bitters which were customary before most of the planters' meals.

"I'll never let him call me an uncouth colonial again." Bill lifted his glass in salute. "Your health, Captain, Doctor. Here's to our future generation."

Betty blushed as he glanced at her. It was only a month since Dr. Anderson had confirmed her pregnancy, and she was not yet accustomed to the role of mother-to-be in her small community. She felt nauseated most of the day, as much from nerves as anything else. Anderson was the only man with whom she felt at ease; bluff and hearty in company, he was comfortingly tactful when they were alone together. She found the touch of his small hands, delicate, confident and cool in spite of the climate, was enough to calm her. He anticipated all the alarms and discomforts of her condition, so that her pregnancy seemed like a delightful secret she could share with him alone.

Anderson was concerned about her. Although she was healthy and followed his instructions with childlike trust, her emotional inadequacy worried him far more than her physical condition. He had directed her to join his first-aid classes and was pleased to see that having work to do calmed her anxiety.

The men's conversation rambled on, by tacit agreement avoiding all issues of importance in front of the women. Betty had the effect of dominating the company around her merely by her timidity; the prospect of alarming this frail creature was so self-evidently dreadful that menfolk automatically talked in nursery terms.

Bill told a rambling story of his one encounter with a tiger, when he had all but fallen over the dozing beast in the deep jungle.

"Dunno who was more surprised, me or the tiger!" he finished cheerily. He always finished the story that way, and Gerald, who had heard it many times before, was roused from inertia by irritation.

"Damn James, how long is he going to be? The kampong's only half an hour on that bike of his."

Boredom settled over them like the clouds of white water vapor that rose from the jungle after rain. To Betty, the life of a memsahib, with its total inactivity, was almost a comfort; the heat, idleness, unvarying landscape and unchanging company held her secure in a blanket of predictability.

They fell silent, and in time became aware of the quiet crooning of a chicken that picked its way around the scarlet canna lilies at the bottom of the steps.

When the boy brought another round of *pahits*, the doctor ordered him to fetch some bread, and in a few moments he returned with some small, half-leavened Malay loaves that were like flattened dinner rolls.

"Ever seen a chicken get drunk?" Anderson asked them, winking his left eye. His sun-reddened face was creased with deep lines already, and when he winked half of it seemed to vanish in a knot of wrinkles.

On the rattan sideboard stood an array of bottles. The doctor selected a full bottle of navy rum and splashed it liberally over the bread, then threw one of the sodden loaves down to the chicken. It ran eagerly forward, gave a wary peck, then began gobbling the treat as fast as it could. Two more chickens scuttled out from under the house and Anderson tossed them another rum-soaked loaf.

"Take it easy, fellas," he advised. "Don't choke on your last supper."

"They love it, don't they?" Gerald was as excited as a child at the spectacle. "Look at them put it away. Go on, give 'em another one."

"Really—you men act just like infants at times," Jean protested, glancing uneasily at Betty in case this cruel entertainment upset her; such was Betty's confidence in a professional man that she was looking with fascination from the birds to the doctor, showing no sign of repulsion.

The first chickens were by now visibly affected by the rum and aimed inaccurate pecks at the latecomer as it struggled for more bread. By the time the loaves were finished, all three birds were flustered and noisy.

"My grandfather used to do this back home," the doctor observed, delighted. "The real joke is when they start thinking they can fly." He walked down the steps and the birds scattered frantically as he began driving them forward with outstretched arms. "Shoo, shoo—chick, chick chick."

"Chick-chick-chick-chick-chick-chick-chick-chick-chicken!" sang Gerald, laughing. Betty began to giggle as the birds scrambled unsteadily forward, flapping and squawking as they went. Anderson lunged for the nearest one, which evaded him with a frantic cry, then fell over its own feet in a drunken panic.

Gerald and Betty laughed aloud as he grabbed the intoxicated birds and perched them on the bamboo fence bordering James's garden. They flapped crazily and plummeted to the ground in untidy heaps, then staggered onto their legs and lurched forward, one dragging a paralyzed wing on the ground.

The first bird, still the least affected, flapped up to the fence of its own accord and evacuated messily over the doctor's boots, an act which looked so much like defiance that Gerald and Betty fell back in their chairs wiping their eyes with mirth. Below them Ahmed appeared, doubled up with laughter and holding his sides.

"Pass me my rifle, Rawlins," Anderson commanded. "Time to get on with the lunch." From the steps he took aim and succeeded in hitting two of the birds. The third flapped in a frenzy of fear toward a length of fallen palm trunk, jammed itself headfirst into a narrow gap between the log and the fence, struggled and was still.

Anderson walked over and prodded the inert bundle of feathers with his rifle.

"Died of fright." He pulled out the body and held it by its neck, then picked up the remaining corpses and handed the three birds to the boy. "There you are. Start cooking and *Tuan* Bourton'll be back before they're ready. That's the trouble with chickens"—he tramped up the veranda steps once more—"no guts. Lie down and die the minute anything scares 'em."

"Chicken-hearted!" Gerald put down his empty glass. "Boy! More pahits!"

Half an hour later the distant purr of James's motorbike sounded through the perpetual churring of the jungle insects and he bounced into the shade of the bungalow apologizing and calling for Ahmed and galvanizing them all anew with his energy. Betty brightened immediately as he fussed over her, inquiring at length about her health.

"What kept you?" Gerald demanded.

"Bad business," James took a gulp of his drink. "Man down in the village came to the police house with his son—real bad hat, off smuggling buffalo over the Siamese border most of the year. Anyway, the boy had been over the border on some shady business or other, and came back swearing that he'd seen the Japs clearing airstrips in the jungle up in the northeast. The old man insisted he tell his tale to the authorities and they got me down to show the flag and put the fear of God in him."

"Do any good?" Bill took out his glasses and began to polish them slowly with his handkerchief.

"Hard to tell, I'm inclined to believe the boy was telling the truth, but it doesn't make any sense, does it? If the Japs come, that'll be the last route they'll choose. It's virgin jungle all the way, right down to the beaches. Totally impassable."

"Monsoon's starting anyway." Anderson, who had lived on the East Coast a few years earlier, spoke with authority. "Landing from the sea would be out of the question—forty-foot breakers pounding the beaches from now until Christmas."

"Fellow was a fifth columnist—you should have had him shot." Gerald stood up with indignation.

"Good old Gerald." Bill pushed his spectacles back into position. "Pax Britannica at any price. Just what we need to turn the Malays against us at the wrong moment."

"What's your reading of the situation, Bill? Are the Malay leaders going to back us? And what's the word from above—any orders for us in case of in . . ." He checked himself from saying the word "invasion." ". . . if the worse came to the worst?"

"I've just sent Singapore a report saying the best help we'll get is probably from the Communists. They're violently anti-British, of course, but my guess is they'll swing round if the Japs do invade."

Gerald snorted with contempt. "Handful of barmy Chinese troublemakers."

"More than a handful, and they can make trouble for the Japanese just as well as for us if it suits them. The Malays will just sit in their kampongs and grow rice, and keep themselves to themselves like they do now.''

Ahmed at last announced lunch and they sat down to a table set with a few small articles of silver from Bourton House and gaudy tropical flowers arranged in jam pots.

"Surely you don't *really* think the Japanese will come?" Betty asked, putting down her fork. She had no appetite.

"They wouldn't dare," Gerald reassured her at once, reaching out to pat her hand.

"Malaya's impossible to invade." Dr. Anderson spoke with his usual confidence. "Mountains, jungle, swamps—the country's a natural fortress. Nothing to worry about, my dear."

"What do you think, James?" Bill was really asking whether they could decently say what was on their minds in front of Betty.

James smiled at her, his wide, frank, irresistible smile. "I'm absolutely certain the Japs will try it," he said gently. "Won't you let us send you away, Betty? This will be no place for a woman when the fighting starts."

Her brow puckering in anxiety, she turned to the fourth man. "Do you think so, Bill?"

"Yup. I've always said it was only a matter of time once Tojo the warlord took over. Malaya's too valuable—they want the rubber, the tin, the rice, everything; to starve us as well as to supply themselves."

"But they say on the radio that the defenses of Malaya are impregnable." Betty looked from one man to another for reassurance.

"They're only trying to keep morale up," James explained. "It's true, no one will ever conquer the jungle. But they will have a damn good try. You see, if the Japs control Malaya, they will control almost all the rubber in the world, which means they can virtually put a stop to any army in its tracks and knock the bottom out of the automobile industry as well. And what's bad for General Motors is bad for America, don't you see?"

Gerald regarded his friends with contempt. "What's the matter with you two—going off your heads? The Japs aren't at war with America; they'll never be at war with America. You're crazy."

They ate on in silence, then dispersed for the afternoon lie-off while James remained at the table to write a report of the morning's interrogation. Soon the even rise and fall of Gerald's snores filled the house.

"What are you doing?" Betty, wan and in stockinged feet, reappeared in the doorway.

"Just a report on this morning's activities." He blotted the page neatly and reached for an envelope. "I'll send it down to Singapore tonight."

"Then you don't think that boy was a fifth columnist?"

"No, I don't. He's not the type. It seems to me if you're going to hire an agent to spread alarm and despondency in the population, the last sort you'd go for would be a virtual bandit." She nodded, marveling at his astuteness; men knew such a lot of things, especially James, who was never ill at ease in any situation.

"You're right, I suppose." Betty sat on the edge of the nearest chair and watched as he sealed the letter.

"Can't you sleep?" he asked. She shook her head and smiled apologetically. "I'll get Ahmed to make you some barley water; that'll perk you up."

"No, please, I don't want to be any trouble."

"It's no trouble. Come and make yourself comfortable on the veranda. You're not just putting a brave face on things, telling us you feel fine?"

"I haven't got a brave face to put on, James." She ran her fingers through her hair with a weary gesture. She pinned up her curls carefully every night, but the heat and humidity of the climate invariably relaxed them, so that by the evening her hair was a mess of lank brown locks which embarrassed her with its disorder.

She need not have worried on James's account; having found extraordinary sexual satisfaction with native women, he no longer had any desire for females of his own race, of whom he had an abiding fear. He treated Betty with all the chivalrous attention he had been trained to show to a woman, enhanced by a neurotically exaggerated respect. This alone, in comparison with Gerald's hearty insensitivity, was more than enough to make Betty half in love with him.

James sent the boy away with his letter and returned to sit by her in the cool of the main room.

"I know it's none of my business," he began, looking intently at the polished floorboards to hide his awkwardness, "but what *are* you going to do, Betty? When the baby comes, I mean. I don't know much about these things, but it's madness to think of staying here too much longer. Won't you even go to Singapore?"

"A wife's place is with her husband, and I shall stay with Gerald." She spoke as if he had offended her.

"But we'll all be called up, all of us volunteers, if there is an invasion."

PEARLS

"I wouldn't know what to do without Gerald." With maddening stubbornness, Betty avoided James's eyes and gazed out of the doorway at the heat shimmering garden and the jungle beyond.

"My dear Betty, you may have to find out in an awful hurry. You need people to take care of you, a doctor . . ."

"I'm sure Dr. Anderson will look after me beautifully."

"But what if he's called up? He may well be, you know."

"I shall manage. I can't leave my husband. And besides, what if the Japanese attack Singapore?"

"Singapore will never fall, Betty. I'm sure you'd be much safer there."

"I think you're being very disloyal, talking like that. There won't be any invasion. There can't be." And she turned to look at him with calm, crazy defiance. It gave her a perverse sensation of power to have so many people expending their energy on changing her mind—above all James, with his good looks, natural superiority and crested silver cutlery.

In the months that followed, Betty rebuffed many more concerned advisers with the same stubborn irrationality.

"My mind is made up; I shall stay with my husband," she repeated as more and more reports came of Japanese preparations north of the Siamese border. "Dr. Anderson agrees with me that I musn't travel," she announced.

She parroted the official line on every new development. "They're on naval exercises—nothing to worry about," she announced with finality when Japanese warships were sighted off the monsoon-lashed East Coast. "They won't come near Malaya." Gerald was driven to desperation by his conflicting impulses to protect his wife and to uphold morale. She was daring him to admit that the official bravado was false.

Betty's vulnerability cowed them all. Even Douglas Lovell had an almost superstitious fear of her, calling her a "stupid little mare" under his breath but never daring to voice his opinions outright. The doctor's wife, as the only other European woman on the estate, acquired a tacit but compelling moral responsibility for Betty, and so the question of either woman leaving was in the end never raised again.

Her pregnancy developed, increasing her discomfort as the baby grew. Worse than the weight of it, the aches and strains and violent flushes of heat, was the shamelessness of her condition, the fact that she could not conceal the ugly swelling that proclaimed her state to all at a glance. She tried to think of the baby, the sweet little mite in its white lace gown, but could not relate that picture to the ugly bulk of her body.

On December 7, 1941, the radio announcer at last dropped his tone of fatuous cheerfulness, and announced that Japanese troops had crossed the border in the northeast, near Kota Bharu, and were engaged in fierce fighting with the British.

Next day came the news that the American fleet had been bombed in Pearl Harbor. A few days later, it was announced that the Malayan peninsula's naval defense, the two battleships *Prince of Wales* and *Repulse*, had been sunk by Japanese warships.

A profound depression settled on the European community, which deepened as it became clear that the Japanese were advancing steadily down the east side of the peninsula. The radio talked of "firm stands" and "strategic retreats" until it became obvious that the defending forces were in chaos and the Japanese army, on foot and on bicycles, using the beaches and the coconut groves, were sweeping down the East Coast.

Then the West Coast, too, began to fall. Penang was severely bombed, and the island's military commander at once ordered all the European women and children to be evacuated to safety in Singapore, making no provision whatever for the Asiatic population.

James walked out of his bungalow for a Sunday parade and did not return; he was ordered to Singapore to join Bill Treadwell in new intelligence work. A week later, Douglas Lovell read out orders for all the planters to abandon the estate and join an armored-car unit bound for the East Coast.

"Time for us to see the little men off," he concluded with relish. Only Gerald was allowed leave to return to his home and say good-bye to his wife, this exception being justified by the need for one assistant to supervise the burning of the remaining stock of rubber.

"You and Jean had best make for Singapore," he told Betty. "You'll be quite safe there until the fighting is over."

Dumb with apprehension, but never doubting that this was merely a temporary parting, Betty kissed him good-bye. Jean Anderson stayed with her that night and helped her pack a small suitcase with clothes for herself and the baby. The next day they were driven to the railway line and boarded the train, heading first for Kuala Lumpur, where they would transfer to the Singapore express.

Ahmed wrapped the Bourton silver in canvas, buried it under James's bungalow and followed the terse order of the British governors to the native population—*Pergi ulu*, Go into the jungle. Ah Kit, Gerald's boy, took the wheels off the Model T and

198

put wood blocks under the axles. He left with Ahmed, the picture of dejection.

"Cheer up, man," Ahmed told him as they turned their backs on the plantation. "There'll always be an England."

On either side of the train as it crawled southward, the sleeping green jungle remained unchanged, but sometimes Betty and Jean heard gunfire or aircraft in the distance and at every halt more Europeans climbed aboard, bringing with them news of Japanese bombers attacking to the north and district hospitals filling with wounded only to empty again when another evacuation was ordered.

Betty, in the seventh month of her pregnancy, sat silently by a window and listened as Jean exchanged news with the other passengers. The weight of the baby under her blue-and-white striped smock pinned her down and inhibited her breathing. Occasionally, the baby moved, thrashing like a big fish in a net and making her gasp.

At Kuala Lumpur, the express was steaming quietly but the platform was a melee of people cramming themselves and their possessions aboard. There was a lengthy delay. The train driver too had obeyed the authorities' command and fled to the jungle.

At last two British soldiers climbed onto the footplate, stripped to the waist, and began to stoke the engine.

Slowly the crammed carriages traveled south, the ominous tranquility of the jungle all around. Night fell, but Betty, more and more uncomfortable with the heat and pressure of the baby, was unable to sleep.

At one station a party of footsore Australian nurses boarded. They were drenched from a savage squall of rain and brought with them a crazy selection of supplies; they had carried hundreds of packets of cigarettes, and a complete Christmas dinner, cooked and not yet eaten, down a branch line from the bombed out station of a coastal town. In the dawn light they heated the meal on the train's boiler, carved it with a penknife and shared it around the carriage. Jean Anderson produced a bottle of whiskey to wash their breakfast down.

"We couldn't let the Japs get their hands on our mince pies," one girl explained. "It's Christmas, after all."

The jungle gave way to the houses of the coastal town of Johore Bharu, which was choked with refugees. Singapore lay a few miles away at the end of the causeway and as the train inched onward, a mood of nightmare gaiety infected the passengers. The nurses stood at the carriage door throwing packets of cigarettes to the huge, disorderly line of people which shuffled across the causeway to safety in Singapore.

There were Malay families riding on oxcarts piled with their possessions, Chinese on bicycles with cages of pullets strapped to the handlebars, and a never-ending line of Morris and Ford cars loaded to the gunwales with white faces which smiled in relief as they approached sanctuary.

Betty slumped against the window, craving air and the coolness of the glass against her burning skin. The baby was still, but her back ached and she shifted heavily to try to find a more comfortable position.

"All right?" Jean leaned across to pat her hand. "It won't be long now."

"It's going so slowly." Betty spoke peevishly, as if the train were dallying on purpose to annoy her.

"There's thousands of people, and they're all walking on the tracks. We'll be there soon."

Betty stared at her dully, with a detachment that made her resemble a small, stupid cow. Her face was quite expressionless, but she had a stricken look which alarmed Jean.

Slowly, Betty looked around to the end of the carriage where the toilet was, then struggled to her feet without saying anything and began to push through the passengers in that direction. There was a patch of moisture on the seat where she had been sitting.

"Are you sure you're all right, dear?" Anxious, Jean pulled at her hand. There was no room for the two of them to stand in the crammed carriage.

"I felt something," Betty said, too embarrassed to say any more.

"What sort of something—a pain?" Jean gently pulled her back to her seat.

"No, not a pain. My back aches a bit. It was something else."

One of the nurses, a broad-faced, competent girl, leaned across toward her. "What kind of something else? Was it like a trickle?"

Betty looked uncomfortably at the two women, not wanting to answer them for fear that they would confirm her worst fears.

"I'm all right really," she told them; "my back aches, that's all. The baby's not due for weeks yet."

The nurse stood up and stepped toward her. "Come on—you don't want to take any chances, do you? What did it feel like—was it like liquid?"

"Her seat was wet," Jean put in, her voice low. Betty shot her a glance of total hatred.

"Have you been having any pains at all, any pains before?" persisted the nurse.

"No, no. Nothing. I'm fine, honestly. There's no need to

worry about . . . uhup!'' She caught her breath as a strong cramp emphatically seized her guts. The nurse quickly put out a hand and felt her belly, then glanced down at the watch pinned to the bib of her crumpled apron. She waited in silence until the onset of the next contraction.

"Seven minutes! Holy smoke—why didn't you say anything before?"

At the end of the causeway Betty, weeping and scarlet in the face with the heat of her contractions, was helped off the train and into a loaded car. With Jean and the nurse gamely hanging on to the running board, they drove through cratered streets to a hospital which was already crowded with casualties of every race who had been injured in the air raids.

"There's nowhere to put her," a Chinese sister spoke with calm authority, as they half dragged Betty into the building. "The best we can do is a trolley at the end of the corridor. The theater was hit this morning, but our equipment is OK, mostly. Lucky for you this was a maternity hospital before."

Betty screamed as another wave of pain engulfed her.

"Try to keep her quiet" were the sister's final instructions. "And when the next raid comes take cover where you can."

Night fell quickly, and Betty began to vomit continuously, bringing up yellow bile and mucus once her stomach was empty. Tears flowed down her cracked cheeks and she began to call out incoherently, no longer able to control herself enough to speak. Her eyes rolled and the lids flickered irregularly.

"She's burning hot all over." Jean quickly tucked a kidney bowl under Betty's chin and supported her as she spat feebly into it.

"Do you think she can hold still long enough for us to take her temperature?"

"She's so far gone, she might bite the thermometer." The nurse shook her head.

"We can try in the armpit, maybe."

The thermometer confirmed their fears.

"She's running an almighty fever—this baby had better not take much longer."

The nurse propped the delirious woman's knees apart and examined her internally. "It's a normal presentation, that's one good thing. But she's so weak and she's getting really dehydrated."

They fetched water, stripped Betty's inflamed body and sponged it to cool her. They made her drink, but she brought back the liquid at once.

The lights failed, then glimmered feebly, then failed again.

An air-raid warning was called, and in a short time, the ground shook and the roar of bombs drowned their voices; at the end of the corridor a window blew out, showering them with broken glass, and all the time Betty groaned and cried aloud.

"I wish to God I could remember my midwifery training," the Australian said, ducking perfunctorily behind the trolley as another explosion shook the building. "There's got to be some way to help her."

They tried to raise the tortured body to let gravity help its weakening muscles, but Betty screamed like an animal and bit Jean's arms in a frenzy of pain. Finally there was an alteration in the tenor of her cries, and the nurse pulled apart her knees once more in time for the small body, sticky and blackened with viscous secretion, to slide head first into her hands. She worked deftly to clean out its gaping mouth and bubbles of dark mucus appeared.

"There's breath in the lungs," she said, "so far so good."

"Oh, Heaven—look." Jean wiped part of the infant's back clean with the corner of the sheet; along half the length of the scrawny body was a visible deformity, an area of puckered flesh along the line of the backbone. "What is it?"

The nurse shook her head. "I've never seen that, but they told us about some kind of spinal malformation. The neural tube hasn't formed properly." Very tenderly she laid the baby down and folded its tiny legs toward its body. She held it upright and rested its feet on the trolley. It hung limp between her hands, snuffling feebly like a kitten. "It's way too early, but it ought to be able to move a little—I think it could be paralyzed."

In the wreck of the operating theater, she hunted for oxygen, but the cylinder was empty. As the noise of the bombing receded, the cries of the injured grew louder, and a new influx of patients crowded into the teeming building. They cleared the baby's throat of mucus and tried to breathe life into the weak lungs, but in a few more moments the infant's slender hold on life slipped and it died.

Betty lay inert on the trolley, flushed with fever, her lips stretched wide over her even teeth. After she passed the afterbirth, she began to hemorrhage and the nurse, at the limit of her own endurance, summoned the last of her control to give her an injection.

"Don't you die on me now, you little cow," she snarled under her breath as she swabbed the puncture. "You die on me now and you'll be sorry."

James saw the Japanese army for the first time as he lay beside the trunk of a fallen tree on the bank of a wide, brown river.

PEARLS

Out of sight of the bridge a hundred yards upstream, he stretched full length in the mud, blinking to keep his eyes focused.

In his line of vision a slender black snake, immobile and straight as a plumb line, hung from a branch over the broad channel. James was distracted by the reptile for an instant before the distant glint of the sun on weapons pulled his attention back to his objective. A disorderly column of soldiers in khaki was advancing rapidly across the wide span of planks.

He gave the signal, then crawled back into the covering jungle and ran along the barely visible track, hearing as he went the roar of the explosion as the bridge was blown. Behind him came the fast, light footsteps of Ibrahim, the man he had charged with detonating the long fuse. Without speaking the two men ran on through the forest, ducking and twisting around low branches, their feet slipping on the litter of damp, leathery leaves and slimy sticks. Finally the light undergrowth of the virgin jungle gave way to a wall of plants with leaves bordered with savage thorns. The razor-sharp fronds and tangled roots disguised pools of mud which sucked at their feet as they followed a hidden pathway.

Their camp was skillfully concealed in this impassable thicket of secondary jungle. At the base of a rocky outcrop Bill, waiting with the Chinese radio operator, greeted them with repressed anxiety.

"What luck this time?" he asked brusquely.

"Sounded good, but I couldn't see much," responded James. He bent down to pull a leech off his leg and the glistening ribbon of black rubbery tissue curled angrily around his hand, searching for blood with its primitive sensory organs.

"The bridge is all gone," Ibrahim confirmed. "I think everything went up. Many Japanese die." He pulled a bottle of iodine from the metal box of medical supplies and handed it to James.

"Did they come after you?"

"I heard shots behind us, but they faded away. You can't hear anything in this jungle, Bill, you know that. Sounds just get smothered." James applied the disinfectant to the bleeding spot from which he had detached the leech.

His friend, now his commanding officer, Major Bill Treadwell of the Special Operations Division, pressed on, "And what about the grenades?"

"Very good," Ibrahim told them. "I saw them go like we think, explosions all up the road. The Japanese were in confusion, running around everywhere like chickens." They laughed together; being trained in the British army ideal of smartness and discipline, the makeshift uniforms and ragged drill of the Japanese amused them.

In a couple of hours two more Chinese members of their party arrived from stations on the far side of the bridge. Their reports were encouraging. The long column of invading troops had halted and bivouacked untidily by the roadside while dispatch riders on bicycles rode aimlessly up and down. Five or six of the enemy had been killed at the bridge and the necklace of grenades strung out along the roads had killed a dozen more and wounded others.

"Did we get any vehicles?" Bill asked. "Or was this lot on bicycles too?

"All bicycle" was the answer, "bicycle or walk. No car, no tank."

"Can you beat the Nips? They're trying to take over the country with gym shoes and cycle clips." Bill laughed in grudging appreciation, but his expression was grim.

The previous day they had seen an Indian division retreat down "their" road, ranks of Punjabi soldiers in turbans pouring southward to Singapore. They had made cautious contact, identifying themselves only as members of the Volunteer Force.

"I'm glad to hear Singapore's sending somebody north," a British officer's voice was weary but tense. "Our orders have been just withdraw, withdraw, withdraw, nothing else for days. My chaps are pretty brassed off, I can tell you."

"Not as brassed off as they'd be if they'd had a few days in the jungle," James remarked to Bill afterward. The Indian regiments had been welcomed when they had arrived as evidence that at last the War Office had accepted the fact that Malaya was vulnerable. Even before the fighting began, however, it became obvious that these soldiers, the finest in the world on their own native mountains, had received no training in the very different techniques of jungle warfare.

Darkness fell, and the noise of the daytime insects was replaced by the strident night sounds of the jungle. They brewed tea, and Bill ordered a tin of pineapple to be opened in celebration.

"Third time lucky, eh?" he said, stirring sugar into his tin mug. "Three bridges in ten days—I think that's pretty good going. Buck up, James."

"Damn!"

"Now what is it, mate?"

"I'm sorry, Bill, I've cut myself on the tin opener. Here, you'd better take over. That bloody wax." Their canned stores were coated in wax as a protection against rust. The jungle air, heavy with moisture all the time, was enough to destroy clean metal in a matter of weeks—even stainless-steel razor blades, left unwaxed, would become spotted with rust overnight.

Flesh itself decayed almost as fast. Every scratch or insect bite had to be carefully treated with disinfectant, and James winced as he dripped iodine on the cut in his palm.

"Haven't smelled that since Matron patched us up after rugger at Eton," he said, taking his share of the pineapple and sucking the juice from it. In fact, the life of a jungle guerrilla seemed to him very much like his time at school. There was schoolboy pleasure in the secrecy procedures of an undercover operation, the code names, the ciphers, the passwords and the manuals stamped "Top Secret."

Every young Briton of the ruling class was trained from childhood to defend the Empire, and the rudimentary military training on the plantation tennis courts was just a continuation of the cadet exercises which James had done on the school playing fields. In Singapore, at the 101 Special Training School on an isolated peninsula, he had sat through lessons in demolition, sabotage, weapons, unarmed combat and jungle survival in the same fog of unfocused boredom in which he had passed his days at Eton avoiding Latin syntax.

Most schoollike of all, however, was the rigid military hierarchy and the absurd, degrading wrangling in which Special Operations Division had been caught up. They had been forced to scheme like desperate spinsters in order to persuade their superiors to order undercover units into the jungle. But while the Japanese army swept down the Malayan mainland like a whirlwind, the military commanders had bickered over niceties of administration, making the final decision only at the eleventh hour. A mixed force of Europeans and a last-minute conscription from the Communist party of Malaya had been hastily trained and sent into the field, but the sense that this effort was too little and too late haunted them all.

Their stores would last them for three months, but Bill insisted that they conserve them as much as possible and start to live off the jungle, so the supplies had been wrapped in gunny-bags and hoisted high in the forest canopy for safety. The canned pineapple was a luxury. They ate fern tips and bamboo shoots, and cheated with rice bought from Chinese smallholders who supported the Communists.

The radio was their only link with what was going on in Singapore; it was an awkward mass of equipment which weighed forty-eight pounds and was best carried on a bicycle because it was almost too heavy for one man. Worst of all, it ran on batteries, and when the batteries failed they would need to be recharged or replaced. Bill ordered minimal use of the equipment—a contact every three days.

The Japanese were offering a bounty for every captured white, and as Europeans they were instantly conspicuous and vulnerable to betrayal. James and Bill adopted Malay dress; Bill dyed his yellow hair black and stained his skin. His height and light eyes made these measures useless except at a distance, but James had been able to transform himself more successfully.

Alone among the undercover parties, they had been given a container of tablets which their instructing officer had discouragingly informed them were "some dope London wants us to try out—supposed to darken your skin. Never had a field trial, so heaven knows how it works. Might come in handy for disguise, if it does any good." The canister was labeled Trisoralen.

James experimented with the drug at once, and found that it darkened his olive skin to an agreeable café au lait, although he felt nauseated and giddy at times. After a month, however, these effects were wearing off.

"Joking apart, Bill, I reckon the dope's pretty good." He pulled up his shirt sleeve and showed a smooth brown arm. "I reckon I can tolerate it, and I'm having to take less and less of it to keep the color up."

"Your own mother wouldn't know you; how many are you taking?"

"Four a day now. I was on twelve at the beginning."

"How much have we got left?"

"Eleven tins, one hundred tablets a tin, plus a handful I've got here." Fearful that the tablets might degenerate in the humid heat, James had meticulously wrapped each day's dose in tinfoil and stored them in an airtight tin which had once held Craven A tobacco.

With his curling dark hair, ready smile and the curve of his slightly bowed legs outlined by his clinging sarong, James appeared a very passable Malay. His British stride had been modified to the swaying, graceful walk imposed by his native dress. It seemed to the others as if he even smelled like a Malay, because the village dogs seldom barked at him as they did at Bill.

With Ibrahim and the Chinese, he could move freely in the towns, unremarked among the crowds of refugees. Communist supporters gave them information, and there was much that they could see with their own eyes. Thousands of enemy troops poured southward, with heavier guns and vehicles landed from the sea on the wide white beaches.

PEARLS

At the end of January came the news that the British had abandoned their last fingerhold on the mainland, retreated to the island of Singapore, and blown up the causeway. The city was under heavy mortar fire as well as air attack, and the European women and children were being evacuated with all speed.

On February 15 they got the news that the defending forces had capitulated. The impregnable fortress had fallen. It was the worst day of James's carefree young life.

"We just cleared out, buggered off. We did nothing, nothing worthwhile." He blew furiously at the sulky fire, making the damp wood burst into flame.

"It's London—London sold us down the river. That bastard Churchill had the East written off from the start." The firelight glinted feebly on Bill's spectacles.

"You know what Malay people call this time?" Ibrahim asked them. "They speak of *tarek orang puteh lari* now."

"The time when the *tuans* ran," James nodded. "They're right."

"Well, we ain't running. We're all that's left, we're on our own, and it's up to us."

"I suppose before this I was proud to be British although I couldn't go along with all that land-of-hope-and-glory stuff of Gerald's." James's voice shook with shame and anger. "But not now, not after this."

"Yeah, well, if you're feeling sick, think how Gerald must be taking it. Poor bastard. I wonder where he is?"

A river of men, defeated troops marching doggedly in unison, flowed eastward across Singapore island, periodically clearing the highway to let through the ambulances which carried the wounded. Once they accepted the Allied surrender, the Japanese issued a general order that all men of the conquered army were to march out to the Changi district, where there were a civilian prison and a military barracks.

The march continued for three days, over bomb-cratered roads obstructed with rubble, twisted tram cables and fallen telegraph posts. The men passed ruined houses and burned-out vehicles, with the ghastly stench of decaying corpses in their nostrils. Every white man on the island from the age of twelve upward, joined the procession, soldiers and civilians in separate groups.

Gerald moved with a blank mind, all his energy concentrated on forcing his shaking legs to walk. Beside him Douglas Lovell strode in silence, his eyes staring ahead. From behind them came the sound of bagpipes and the regular tramp of the Gordon Highlanders.

207

Once they were out of the city the march became easier. The roads were less damaged, and from the villages and coconut plantations people came out with food and water which they thrust into the men's hands despite the angry orders of the Japanese. Every house along the route flew a red-and-white Japanese flag.

Gerald took a tin of lukewarm water from a Chinese boy and paused to drink.

"Don't stop," Douglas Lovell snapped at once. "Stop now, you'll never get started again. Keep moving, man." Obediently Gerald shuffled onward. Neither man had slept for more than a few hours in the past ten days. Exhaustion blurred their vision and dulled their senses, the insistent wail of the bagpipes pushing them forward.

At last they heard an order to halt, and waited in lines in the blazing sun until a subaltern with a clipboard worked his way around to them, asked for name, rank, number and regiment, and assigned them billets in the barracks.

"It's not the Raffles, but it's all we can do for now. We've got more than fifty thousand men here and only space for a fifth of that number. You'll get enough space to lie down in, and that'll be it," he told them. "Report to your CO as soon as you can."

"CO be damned," Gerald muttered. "He can look for me if he wants me." They had no idea of the identity of their present commanding officer; the unit's original commander had been killed during the shelling of one of the many positions they had attempted to hold in their chaotic retreat.

Inside the barracks, a single-story concrete building with a tin roof, Gerald lay down on the dirty stone floor and fell into a heavy sleep, oblivious of the milling men around him who were piling up their equipment and claiming their own territory.

Douglas Lovell woke him the next day. "They're issuing rations. On your feet, Rawlins." Gerald sat up, rubbing his puffy eyes and scratching his unshaven face.

They joined a long, sweating queue of men with mess tins and ate their portions of water rice, boiled without salt, with distaste. It was sufficient nourishment to make Gerald feel refreshed, and thoughts which he had been able to ignore came to the front of his mind.

"I'm going to take a stroll, see what I can see," he told Douglas Lovell. "I've got to find out about Betty. If every man in Singapore is in this damned place, there must be someone who saw her. And if Anderson made it he'll be with the wounded, don't you think?"

PEARLS

With stolid persistence, Gerald began to ask every man in the barracks if he had encountered a brown-haired, blue-eyed, pregnant Englishwoman named Betty in the panic-stricken disorder of Singapore. Douglas Lovell went with him.

They joined a teeming mass of servicemen who were coming to terms with defeat. For most of them this meant thinking the unthinkable. For weeks they had been fired with confidence by propaganda and morale-boosting speeches in which the possibility of a Japanese victory had never been mentioned. Now it was a reality, and the fall of Singapore also implied a loss of faith in their leaders. Immense crowds of captives walked around continuously in search of reassurance for the fearful uncertainty which they shared.

Each man felt as anonymous as a single ant in an anthill, despite their diversity. There were freckled Scots, scrawny Cockneys, fat planters, pallid civil servants, young police cadets and elderly clergymen. Rank, regiment and social standing were suddenly irrelevant. They were all prisoners.

Several of the barracks buildings were in use as hospitals, packed with wounded and dying men. The first medical center Gerald visited was full of Australian troops, but in the second their spirits lifted instantly when they recognized Anderson's small, rounded figure crouched beside a patient at the end of the stuffy room. There was scarcely space to walk between the wounded men who lay on the stretchers and makeshift rope beds, flapping weakly at the flies.

The two men waited until Anderson could be absent for a few minutes. He joined them outside the building and shook hands vigorously, saying "My goodness, my goodness," over and over again.

"Did you get any news of Jean?" Gerald asked at once.

"I saw her for a few hours when we reached Singapore; she got news that our unit had arrived and hunted us down." Anderson still held Gerald's hand and arm, debating with himself whether to pass on the news that Betty had lost their baby. "She'd been with Betty and I'm hopeful they both got away to sea," he added, deciding against passing on the bad news. The doctor had been sent directly to a field hospital from the rubber estate, and during the British troops' flight and the shelling of the city he had seen so many good men die that the loss of an ailing infant to a healthy young couple seemed less of a tragedy than a blessing in the present situation.

Gerald looked at his cracked, mud-caked boots in silence for a few moments, sensing what he had not been told. "As long as Betty's all right . . . ," he muttered.

The following day, Gerald found another group of Volunteers, mostly planters like himself, all of whom were anxious about their families and friends. They sat talking for hours in the meager shade of a squat palm tree, desperate for a hint of the fate of their wives and children. There was nothing else to do and nothing else to think about, except their own unimaginable fate.

"It's damn useless standing here jawing," Douglas Lovell said at last. "The thing to do is post a list of all the relatives. There'll be Red Cross workers of some kind once this place is organized. And there are two thousand women in the civilian camp hereabouts, so I've heard. If we can get in contact with them and get their names, that'll be a start."

"How do you propose going about that?" Gerald sneered, suddenly made vicious by his sense of powerlessness. "Ask the Japs if we can invite the ladies over for tea?"

"Damn your insolence! Don't you know the way to speak to a superior officer?" the older man snarled, and Gerald flinched and looked apologetic, responding instinctively to the military tone of the reproach. Douglas Lovell once more assumed the responsibility of command. He outranked all the survivors of the Volunteer Force, and knew by instinct that if these demoralized men, in their overcrowded, deprived conditions, were not immediately held together with discipline they would degenerate to the level of animals.

"I want all the writing materials we've got," he ordered them, "and all the food. You"—he pointed at a skinny young man whose shoulders were straightening visibly at the sound of commands—"will be our quartermaster in charge of rations. And tomorrow morning, instead of sitting around gossiping like a bunch of washerwomen, there'll be half an hour of physical exercise. We must keep ourselves fit at all costs; there'll be an Allied landing and we must be ready to do our bit. And you, Rawlins, you'll beg, borrow or steal a razor and shave off that fuzz. If you wanted to grow a beard you should have joined the navy."

Soon the other commanders also brought their men into line and the vanquished army began to adapt to the prison camp. At first there were few Japanese to guard them, and while the enemy officers harangued them with barely comprehensible speeches about the shame of defeat and the greater shame of not committing suicide rather than be captured, the Japanese soldiers proved to be peasant types who were seldom wantonly cruel.

Within a few weeks, the Japanese ordered their captives to form work gangs for forced labor in the Singapore docks. Smuggling began in earnest; every man who marched out of the compound returned with food, cigarettes or information pressed upon them by loyal citizens of the city.

With ingenuity which surprised Douglas Lovell, Gerald got himself included in one of the earliest labor gangs and bribed a Chinese youth to ask at the hospital where Anderson told him Betty had been taken for news of their wives.

"They're OK," he told Anderson on his return one night. "They got on a navy ship with the hospital nurses—the HMS *Marco Polo*. They were trying to get to Colombo. Betty and Jean are OK." His ruddy face, for weeks drawn with anxiety, was now creased in a smile and Anderson slapped him on the shoulder, thinking that there would be little benefit to Gerald in speculative talk about minefields and enemy warships. What the man could not imagine could not hurt him.

"That's splendid news," the doctor said in a quiet voice. "Absolutely splendid. They're safe—thank heaven for that."

Betty had been in the water for only twenty minutes, but already it no longer felt warm but icy cold. Her arms and legs were numb, her body so chilled that it felt insubstantial, but in the core of her abdomen an excruciating agony raged like an inner inferno. The waves lapped below her chin, sometimes splashing into her scarlet face. Her lips, deeply cracked after days of fever, were sore and swollen from the salt water. Mercifully, she was scarcely aware of the scene of desolation around her.

The indigo sea was full of floating debris from the stricken *Marco Polo*; like most of the ships at the tail end of the escape fleet from Singapore, she was a rough-and-ready coastal freighter hastily commandeered by the navy to evacuate civilians from the besieged city.

Jean Anderson and Betty had been taken from the hospital with the handful of European nurses who had remained there. After the birth of her child Betty had been seriously ill with an internal infection, but when the announcement was made at the head of the crowded corridor that patients capable of walking would be evacuated, Jean hauled her bodily off her bed and forced her to stand.

They had been bundled first aboard a heavily loaded launch which had plowed from ship to ship in the crowded harbor until the commander of the *Marco Polo* agreed to take its human cargo. They set sail with two other ships, all crammed with women and children, but the desperate flotilla had separated outside the harbor, hoping to ensure by scattering that at least some of the craft would evade the Japanese warships and reach safety.

The unlucky *Marco Polo* had very soon encountered a small patrol of Japanese warships, and the first shell had holed her, tearing the rusty fabric of the ship as if it had been paper.

Now her surviving passengers, Jean and Betty among them, were buoyed up in the water by their cumbersome green-canvas life preservers and bobbed on the waves like so much flotsam among the splintered planks of the old freighter. The Japanese cruiser which had fired on their ship was invisible over the horizon, but three planes, like evil insects, droned louder and louder as they bore down on the helpless survivors.

The ship was listing and her bows were already below the surface. As Jean watched, the rusty stern slowly rose up in the water and the ship poised vertically for an instant before slipping swiftly down below the waves in terrifying obedience to the law of gravity.

"There she goes. That's the end of the *Marco Polo*," gasped Jean, at Betty's side, struggling to point across the surface as the swell bore them up and they saw the last few feet of the vessel's upended stern vanishing into the swirling water. An instant later nothing remained where the ship had been except a pall of black smoke in the air and and a spreading oil slick on the surface of the water. The stink of fuel and of burning debris filled their lungs at every breath, and Betty began to cough.

"Stop it, Betty, you must stop it," the older woman pleaded, keeping a firm hold of the tapes securing Betty's canvas and cork life jacket.

"I can't stop it." Betty miserably wiped a stream of mucus from her nose into the oily water and coughed again and again.

"You must stop it, you silly girl. You've *got* to save your strength, and if you keep gasping and spluttering like that you'll get seawater in your lungs." Jean snapped at her friend without sympathy. In the past few weeks Betty had eroded almost all the gallant woman's patience with her selfish refusal to fend for herself. Too late, Jean had realized that Betty's strategy for survival was simply to demand that stronger people take care of her.

With a roar the aircraft swooped down from the sky and spewed bullets over the water fifty yards away from them. Choppy waves spread out from the impact, washing into Betty's face, and half filling her mouth with a vile emulsion of fuel and brine as if to prove Jean right. The lake of oil which marked the *Marco Polo*'s grave ignited; above the slap of water and the snarl of the aircraft they heard faint screams from the survivors who were burning in the water.

"Thank God they got us off first," Jean murmured to herself, hoping Betty was too far gone in her fever to register the horror around her. Her head was lolling heavily forward now and Jean saw that she was becoming unconscious.

"Here you are, ma'am, catch hold of this." A seaman, swimming strongly, approached pushing a stout wooden door from the ship. "Can we get her on it, d'you think, if we push her up together?" With desperate determination they maneuvered Betty's awkward body onto the half-submerged surface, skinning their hands and exhausting their strength in the process. The seaman's face and neck were burned raw on one side.

The enemy aircraft did not return, and a weird peace settled over the water as the floating survivors fell silent and were separated from each other by the strong currents. The overcast sky darkened, and squalls of rain harrowed the ocean surface. Jean copied the seaman and opened her mouth to catch the sweet water.

"Can you tell which way we're drifting?" she asked him.

He shook his head. "Makes no odds. Whether we're carried back to Singapore or the islands, or swept over to Sumatra, the Japs will be waiting."

"How long can we survive in the water?" Jean's tone was as calm and conversational as if she were asking the time. She no longer felt cold but only tired, but her arms and hands ached from the effort of clinging to the side of the floating door.

"A day, two days . . . we'll be in luck if it rains again."

Darkness settled swiftly over the waves; the moon and stars were hidden behind thick clouds and more rain fell. Manipulating her wet possessions with great difficulty in the faint radiance that persisted, Jean pulled her powder compact from the bag she had tied around her waist and caught a trickle of rainwater in the lid. It cost her a supreme effort of strength to tip the precious fluid between Betty's lips.

Soon after she fell back into the black water, Jean felt the cold, hard snouts of fish butting against her legs. The seaman could feel them too, and she heard him swear under his breath.

"Beg pardon, ma'am. I don't fancy being a fish's breakfast just yet. Keep kicking your legs and the shoal will swim on." Jean did as he suggested and the underwater battering stopped.

Shortly after dawn the seaman pointed to a barely visible black line at the horizon.

"That's land, at any rate," he told Jean, suppressed hope in his voice. "We're getting closer to it and all. Let's pray to God the current will carry us in."

The line thickened quickly and the outlines of palms and other trees became visible, and soon the green of the forest stood out distinctly against the blue of the sea. For a tantalizing hour the current carried them along parallel to the coastline; eagerly they wasted their remaining strength trying to swim to the shore, but the water was too powerful. At last they were borne close to a sandspit and, dragging the unconscious Betty on her makeshift raft, Jean and the seaman waded into shallow water and stumbled onto dry land.

They sat thankfully on the silted strip of gravel, feeling the warmth of the midmorning sun bring life back to their limbs and wordlessly watching white streaks of salt crystallize on their legs and arms. The seaman pulled off the burned remnant of his shirt, squeezed water from it and spread it over Betty's face to protect her from the sun.

Bright as the sunlight was, it was kinder to their eyes on the brownish beach than it had been in the glittering water. Jean picked at the tight knots of her life jacket with weak but persistent fingers, and at last was able to remove the heavy device which had saved her life. Feeling her strength return, and sensing a sweet, muddy smell in the air, she scrambled upright and looked around them.

"Heavens—we're at the mouth of a river!" she exclaimed. "And I can see some houses and boats, quite a lot of boats. And people!"

"Can they see us?" The seaman rose to his feet and strained his eyes in the direction in which Jean was looking. In the middle of the small estuary an elderly Malay fisherman was sculling a small boat out to sea; they watched his slow progress in silence until the seaman at last judged that he could spot them, and began to shout. With maddening slowness the bowed figure straightened above its oar, and finally made a tentative gesture of recognition.

The villagers gave them rice, eggs and dried fish to eat but treated them with embarrassed diffidence; the ocean current had carried them to the coast of Sumatra, but here the Japanese were already in occupation and had demanded that all Europeans should give themselves up. Jean was still pushing rice into Betty's mouth when four Japanese soldiers on bicycles arrived, summoned by the village policeman.

A young man offered to transport Betty in a rough handcart which ran on a pair of bicycle wheels, and in the smothering heat of the afternoon the soldiers and their captives marched slowly along a road by the riverside. Jean became aware that she had a painful expanse of raw flesh like a high collar at the top of her neck, where the coarse canvas of the life jacket had rubbed away her skin.

PEARLS

They spent the night with seventy other wretched Europeans in a derelict wooden cinema, and Jean noticed that Betty was no longer burning with fever. A night in the cold salt water had reduced her temperature. She was conscious and lucid in the morning, but remembered nothing of their escape from Singapore, or of the weeks she had spent in the hospital after the birth of her child. Jean told her very little, believing that forgetting was nature's way of protecting a feeble mind from knowledge it could not bear.

In the morning the Japanese arrived in force, and marched them all onward without pity. The strongest men among the captives took turns carrying Betty between them. They reached the small town of Muntok and were ordered to line up in front of the old prison building, in peacetime a warehouse where spices had been stored.

The men were marched away, the women ordered into the grim, harsh-smelling interior of the building.

"It's like a fish shop—I shall feel like a cod fillet lying down there!" exclaimed a fleshy, gray-haired Englishwoman, pointing at the sloping slabs of concrete on either side of the long room which were the only features resembling furnishings.

Rain began to fall, pattering ceaselessly on the tin roof and dripping down the walls. The captives were of every age and nationality; many were mothers with babies who screamed with hunger throughout the night. In the atmosphere of hellish despair the women's clothing still performed the heraldic function of femininity, and signaled the crucial facts about the people who owned the garments. In the gloom, Jean noticed the tattered gray uniforms of Australian army nurses, the black habit of a nun, and one or two bedraggled silk dresses which had no doubt fluttered elegantly in the mild breeze of Singapore's Tanglin Club a few days earlier while the owners watched the bombing across the bay.

After a week of fetching food and water for her, supporting her as she staggered to the open latrine outside, and silently willing her to recover, Jean was relieved when Betty's strength returned.

"Was there any news of Gerald?" she demanded one day, and Jean told her that she had tracked her husband down at his hospital unit, and he had told her that Gerald and the rest of their volunteer company had reached Singapore safely.

"I suppose he'll be a prisoner of war now," Betty sighed, not unhappily. No one had repeated to her the stories of Japanese atrocities which were circulating through the camp. "We'll just have to wait until the war is over. It won't be long, Jean, will it?'' Her eyes, as blue and blameless as ever, looked for reassurance and Jean reached out a freckled hand to pat her arm. Betty might have her strength back, but she was still living in the mood of unrealistic detachment that had characterized the months of her pregnancy.

The camp had no supplies of any kind. The women slept in their clothes and improvised cooking, eating and toilet utensils from what they had brought with them. The only food was a meager ration of adulterated rice dispensed daily by the guards, and some of the captives began trading with a few daring Chinese who came to the perimeter fence in darkness with food, clothing and drugs for sale.

One day some Japanese soldiers inexplicably threw a whole basketful of bread scraps over the fence of the prison compound, and Jean was pleased to see Betty join the rush to gather the food, and shocked when she realized that Betty was swallowing crusts whole as she pretended to help the other women.

The next day Jean was equally startled to see Betty wearing a fresh, almost white, blouse.

''I didn't know you had that with you—what luck,'' she commented with suspicion. They had boarded the *Marco Polo* with almost all the possessions they had brought from the rubber estate, but, like most the the survivors of the bombed freighter, Betty had seized the nearest, smallest bag before taking to the water. Jean had been exasperated to open it and find nothing inside but a wad of sodden baby clothes.

''Yes,'' Betty agreed brightly, ''wasn't it lucky—I found it in my case.'' Jean was almost sure she had snatched the blouse from the washing lines that now festooned the outside of the building.

''Your friend will make herself most unpopular if she doesn't mend her ways,'' commented the thickset Englishwoman who had compared their accommodation to a fish shop. ''I'd have a word with her if I were you—in a place like this, feelings tend to run very high, you know.''

''She doesn't mean any harm,'' Jean apologized, knowing that the woman's advice was sound but still feeling loyal to Betty. ''She's been terribly ill, she lost the baby she was carrying and she just hasn't got any strength. My husband—he's a doctor, her doctor—used to say she hadn't the strength of a newborn lamb. He meant mentally, of course, not in the physical sense. She isn't strong enough to be unselfish. She can't do anything for herself in life, just survive, that's all.''

The older woman glanced down the length of the prison building, taking account of the sick and injured, the fretful children, the drawn faces and tattered clothes, the shins already blistered with tropical ulcers and the bones beginning to poke through dwindling flesh. "That's all any of us can do—survive," she said, her pale lips set in a grim half smile. "I wouldn't be surprised if your friend turned out to be a great deal stronger than you imagine."

11

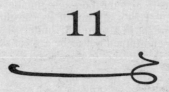

EVERY DAY ON HER WAY TO COLLEGE MONTY PASSED A BRASS plate beside a black front door halfway down an elegant Kensington terrace. The inscription on it read DR. MARY WILSON, M.D., FRCS, FRCOG.

"What do you suppose FRCOG means?" she asked Rosanna one day as they idled past on their way to the coffee bar. "FRCS is Fellow of the Royal College of Surgeons, I know that much."

"FRCOG is Fellow of the Royal College of Obstetricians and Gynecologists," Rosanna told her. "I know because I've got to see Mummy's gynecologist before I get married and he's got those letters too."

Rosanna did not explain, but Monty could guess, that the purpose of this visit was to receive a prescription for the birth-control pill. Already the Pill was so much identified with sexual license that admitting to taking it was rather like wearing a placard saying "nymphomaniac."

Next day Monty went to Woolworth's and bought a cheap ring with one red stone and two white ones. She found Dr. Wilson's telephone number in the directory and made an appointment, saying, "It's because I'm getting married soon," to the receptionist.

A week later she rang the bell and was admitted through the black door and sat down in the doctor's waiting room in the middle of which was a large, battered rocking horse. There was a huge pile of dog-eared comics on the table, and a set of sentimental bunny-rabbit pictures around the walls. Monty felt ill at ease in this nursery atmosphere.

The doctor was a tall, white-haired woman with a beautiful complexion and gold half-glasses. "I came to see you because I'm getting married soon and my fiancé and I don't want to start a family just yet," Monty told her, trying not to sound as if she had rehearsed the speech for a week. "We think we're too young and, besides, my fiancé may be posted abroad soon."

The doctor gave a warm smile. "Well, that's not a great problem nowadays. I expect you've heard of the birth-control pill? Let me just examine you—slip off all your clothes below the waist and pop up on the couch."

Monty felt first the doctor's gentle fingers, then a metal instrument inside her. No one's been in there except Simon before now, she thought.

The doctor removed the instrument and decorously folded Monty's knees together.

"Well, you shouldn't have any trouble at all when you do want to have babies," she said with approval. "All present and correct inside, good childbearing pelvis, plenty of room."

Monty smiled back at her, trying to look sincerely complimented, hoping the doctor was not going to need a reminder about the purpose of the visit.

"Now, I'll write you a prescription," Monty heard her say with relief, "for three months' supply, but I want you to come back after the first month and let me see how you are getting on. Are your periods regular?"

"Fairly regular." She thought of the endless days of anxiety every time her period was late, the morbid scouring through her diary, counting to verify the date she was due.

"You must start taking the pills five days after the beginning of your next period—assuming the wedding isn't far off?" Monty nodded.

Filled with delight and relief, she walked around the corner to the chemist, paid ten pounds, and came out with three pink cartons marked Ovulen in a discreet plain white paper bag. In the privacy of her bedroom at Trevor Square, she looked at the little foil pack, with twenty-one tiny tablets in their plastic bubbles—so neat, so painless, so efficient.

Soon afterward it was Simon's twenty-second birthday. Monty surreptitiously took his front-door key off his keyring for a few hours and had it copied. His parents, pleased that he had started work in P & G's offices, agreed he could celebrate with Monty.

"I'll come round to the flat at seven!" she told him. "I've got a special surprise for you!"

But at four in the afternoon, she called a taxi, loaded her suitcases into it, and drove to the apartment, where she installed all her belongings in the wardrobes. On the bed she put black satin sheets, a gift from Cathy, who had said, ''I don't see why you shouldn't have nonwedding presents as well as wedding presents.''

A great deal of the bedroom space was taken up with tape recorders and stereo equipment. Monty slipped a special tape on the machine by the bedside, and adjusted it to play the instant the switch was pressed. She arranged a giant ribbon and bow of red crepe paper across the bed, with a huge label reading ''Happy Birthday, Simon.'' Then she took a shower, washed her hair, did her makeup and slithered naked between the sheets to wait for Simon.

When she heard the key in the lock, she leaned over and turned on the tape recorder and her own voice sounded out, singing ''Happy Birthday'' and accompanied by a laboriously compiled four-track recording of herself on piano and guitar.

Simon burst into the bedroom with delight, jumped on to the bed, and hugged her. There wasn't a great deal of point in saying anything while the music played, but when it finished Monty managed to speak first.

''Do you like your present?''

''Love it.'' He started kissing her in the slightly cautious way into which they had fallen, knowing that there was no purpose in invoking too much desire.

''You haven't had the best yet.''

''What's that then?''

''Can't you guess?'' He looked around the room thoughtfully, then saw one of the closet doors ajar. When he opened it an untidy jumble of Monty's clothes fell out.

''You've done it! You've moved in! Yippee!''

''That's not all—are you sure you can't guess?'' How could he be so dumb? ''It's something you can't see.''

''You mean that I have got to look for it, you've hidden it?''

''No.''

''I give up then, what is it?''

''Well—come here.'' Monty stretched out a hand and pulled him back to the bed. ''I'm your present, you see, and now you can have all of me. I'm taking the Pill.'' He paused in surprise, then hugged her with tenderness. ''Are you all right—I mean, is it all right—I mean, do you feel OK?''

''Yes, of course I feel OK. I feel wonderful, great, absolutely fab. It's really easy.''

He held her very close and the room seemed to pulse with their heartbeats. At last Monty could bear it no longer.

"Don't you want your birthday present then?"

"Darling, darling Monty, of course. Always. I'll want you forever."

The next day, after agreeing that they wanted to wake up next to each other for the rest of their lives, they set about creating the formal reality of their relationship. Simon introduced her to his cleaning lady, and took the tiny card saying S. Emanuel out of the rack by the doorbells, turned it over, wrote Miss M. Bourton and Mr. S. Emanuel on the blank side, and reinserted it with a flourish. Then he went to the office and spent the whole morning having Monty's name added to his charge accounts. He had no intention of making any announcement to his parents about his new status; the first rule of Simon's relationship with his mother and father was never to tell them anything important.

Monty went to college and used her typewriter to write a letter to Bettina. "Dear Mummy," she wrote "Simon and I have decided to live together because we love each other. My new address is Flat 4, 112 Rowan Court, London W8, telephone Western 2768. I'll come down in a week or two to get the rest of my things." Then she hesitated. "Much love" didn't seem quite right and it certainly wasn't accurate, since she felt nothing but contempt and dislike for her mother. The vision of that pasty, alcohol-drained face under its frill of ill-crimped brown curls made her shudder. Instead she left the space at the end of the letter blank, and merely signed her name.

Two days later she was aware of someone watching her as she opened the door to the house, and no sooner had she shut the apartment door than the doorbell rang. It was Lady Davina.

"Your mother has sent me to talk sense into you, but I don't suppose it will do any good," she began, pulling off her brown suede gloves. "You've always been determined to go to hell your own way and as far as I'm concerned there's no reason anyone should try to stop you. I shan't sit down, I'm not staying. . . ." She peered around the apartment with curiosity, which was obviously the main motive for her visit, and Monty wished that the cleaner had not been in to arrange the cushions neatly and remove the ashtrays. "But you must consider your mother, Miranda."

"Why?" Monty lit up a cigarette and blew smoke in Lady Davina's direction. "She never considered me."

It was a hard assertion to contradict and the older woman did not try.

"And your position, and the rest of the family. We've done

everything we can to get you settled and you're simply throwing yourself away on this Jewish boy. I've no doubt they're perfectly nice people, but this idea of—of . . .''

"Living in sin?" Monty smiled grimly, feeling elated by the nicotine. "That's the difference between me and my mother—I call it love, she calls it sin."

"Don't be so ridiculous. You've no idea what love is. Decent people will cross the street rather than have to speak to you. And you won't get a job anywhere. You haven't a penny to bless yourself with, don't forget. You'll simply be a kept woman."

"Well, I'd rather be kept by a man who loved me than by a man who's only fulfilling his legal obligation. Now would you like to look around our bedroom before you leave?"

"There's no need to take that attitude, Miranda. I'm only doing my best to prevent you from making a dreadful mistake which you will regret for the rest of your life."

As she left, her grandmother fastidiously pulled her coat around her, as if to avoid so much as brushing the doorjamb of this immoral dwelling with her skirts. Monty shut the door with a feeling of triumph, conscious that she had won her first battle with the old order.

As the weeks passed, she felt less and less inclined to fetch her few remaining possessions from her mother's home, particularly since Simon took delight in buying her whatever she wanted. Their Saturdays were orgies of consumption, spent floating up and down the King's Road meeting friends, choosing clothes and hoping to spot Michael Caine or Julie Christie among the glamorous throng which spilled off the sidewalks almost under the wheels of the Rolls-Royces and Jaguars in the road.

Only two of her grandmother's words had any impression on Monty, and they were the phrase "kept woman," Monty's college fees were paid to the end of term and she kept up the farce of her attendance, often asking another girl to sign her name in the register and doing nothing all day but sleep late, meet Simon for lunch, then while away the afternoon window-shopping. But a kept woman, with its connotations of concubinage, was the last thing she intended to be.

"Why not? He's loaded, isn't he?" Swallow, her old school friend, lay back on the floor cushion and expertly sealed a fresh joint with her tongue.

"You don't understand. I don't want money to be part of why we're together."

"You're too pure to live, my girl, that's your trouble." Swallow lit up and inhaled deeply.

"It's like—to live outside the law you must be honest. I just don't want to have to depend on Simon. What to do, though? I'd hate an office job. I'm too fat to be a model.'' Monty looked with distaste at her rounded breasts, which had developed alarmingly since she had moved into Simon's apartment. Her legs had also thickened and her waist was threatening to disappear completely. The scales in the doctor's surgery showed that she had gained ten pounds in the six weeks since she had started taking the Pill. She waved the joint away.

"I'll only get the munchies.''

"Come and help me for a bit,'' Swallow suggested. "We can split the proceeds.''

"Why—what are you doing?''

"Finding houses for chemin de fer parties mostly, but that won't last long, now they've made gambling legal. People keep asking me to help them out, Monty. They think I'm the only person in Chelsea cool enough to know where to find things and together enough to deliver them. I was thinking of making a business of it. Call it 'Something in the City' maybe. Strictly for freaks, you know—no straights allowed through the door.''

Monty felt this sounded too good to be true, but two days later Swallow telephoned. "I've got an office and they're putting the phone in tomorrow. Are you going to come in with me? I've got to do six hampers for Glyndebourne and find a miniature Rolls-Royce for some pop manager who wants it so John Lennon won't have the only one in London. *Please* come in on it, Monty—it'll be a gas.''

And it was. It was the sort of job Monty never really believed could exist, starting anytime between ten-thirty and eleven in the morning and dealing exclusively with groovy people who knew each other only by their Christian names and worked to the ceaseless beat of the new pirate radio stations.

It was also the sort of job she needed to cope with the lifestyle she and Simon fell into as easily as flies drowning in jam. Every evening they would make love, then dress and go out to one of the new raffish rock nightclubs where the music was overpowering. There they would fall in with a crowd of their friends, perhaps go to someone's place to take drugs or listen to music, and then come back to their own apartment in the dawn hours to shower, make love again, and go to work.

At weekends, and in all their unstructured time, they sat around the apartment playing records, making music or experimenting with songwriting. Simon composed long, rambling songs with clever guitar breaks and very few words. Monty found she could write nothing but pretty ballads about love.

When they were exhausted, they either slept or bought some

speed. They smoked marijuana continually in private. If Simon was bored he would take some LSD, but Monty tried it once, was overwhelmed with mad terror and never dared to do it again. Their ideal was a way of life which challenged established authority and the drugs were an essential part of that. Since Simon was known as a rich boy, there was no shortage of people pressing him to buy every kind of mood-altering or mind-expanding chemical. Their favorite dealer was a Cypriot they called Tony the Greek, who got into the habit of dropping into the apartment on Sunday afternoons with a briefcase of samples and a dog-eared pharmacological encyclopedia in which to check out his wares.

Drugs did not interest them nearly as much as sex, although both were new universes to be discovered for the first time. "Before I met you, my life was like black-and-white TV—now it's all color," Monty said one morning as she lay in his arms. "Do you suppose it was ever like this for the people before?"

"It can't have been." Simon thoughtfully propped his head on his hand. "People must have worried all the time about getting pregnant. We must be the first generation ever to make love without any hangups, just because it's beautiful."

"Mmmm." Monty wriggled her naked body against him, remembering how sexy it was. "I can't imagine my mother ever feeling like this."

"Nor mine," murmured Simon, tracing the outline of a nipple with his finger and watching the magic spot of flesh pucker in response. "Rosanna and I used to wonder how we ever got to be born."

"So did we."

They set about exploring the secret realm of sexuality, seeking to elaborate the physical expression of their love and feeling a sense of duty toward the unknown dimensions of human experience which had at last become available.

First they learned what they could from each other.

"What does it feel like when you come?" Monty asked Simon. He paused for thought, screwing up his eyes.

"Like my spine's melting in the middle of an earthquake." It sounded impressive. "What does it feel like for you?"

"Different. It's like waves." It sounded very dull by comparison. "It feels like a giant sea anemone exploding inward." She could see he thought she was exaggerating. "Well, it feels like that sometimes, anyway. It felt like that last night."

"What did it feel like this morning?"

"Bit of a nonevent, really."

"You made enough noise about it."

"Well, I thought you'd be disappointed if I didn't."

"I'm disappointed it was a nonevent." He pulled her toward him and began kissing her nipples. "Let's see if we can catch a sea anemone."

"No, Simon, *please*, not yet. I'm so sore, I can hardly sit down as it is. Darling, don't be disappointed; it just is a nonevent sometimes, that's all."

Guilt about this enjoyment of forbidden fruit stalked them patiently. Every Friday night Simon went home for the traditional Sabbath supper, and sat at the place at the dining table which had been his since babyhood. He listened to his mother call Monty a whore, and defended his love for her silently by throwing a switch in his mind and picturing Monty in his arms, her eyes hot and blank with lust.

As midnight approached Simon would escape his mother's mounting hysteria and drive fast and thankfully to the apartment, to find Monty sleeping sweetly in one of his dirty shirts, which she had taken to bed with her for the comforting smell of him. In a maelstrom of confusion he disapproved of himself for thinking filthy things about the girl he loved, reproached himself for making his mother unhappy and usually ended up rolling a substantial joint to calm himself.

Monty's guilt was a far more stealthy animal, which operated by turning her own emotions against her. She began to worry about what Simon was doing every moment that he wasn't with her, and took to telephoning his office several times a day, "just to talk," as she said. The voice of his secretary preyed on her mind and she couldn't get rid of the idea that she was having an affair with him. "It's ridiculous," she told herself with anger; but the fear would not go away, and she found herself making sneering remarks to Simon about his "office wife."

"No wonder you're in such a hurry to get to the office," she snapped one morning as he dressed. "Not worth wasting time in bed with me when there's a hot little number waiting for you up there, I suppose."

Simon ignored her and started tying his tie in the bathroom. "What am I saying?" Monty asked herself in panic. Nevertheless, she got out bed and followed him. "Why don't you just tell me?" she said with a threat in her tone. "I don't mind you fucking someone else, I do mind you lying to me. We're supposed to trust each other, remember?"

"Monty, for the last time, I'm not fucking anybody else. Yours are the only knickers I'm interested in getting into. For Christ's sake, what's the matter with you?"

Tears began pouring down her cheeks. "I don't know," she whispered. "I'm sorry, Simon, truly I am. I just can't help it."

At work, it was as bad. Monty burst into tears every time she dialed a wrong number on the telephone, or if she broke a fingernail or put down her keys and could not remember where they were.

One morning, she arrived for work at twelve-thirty, unacceptably late even by the relaxed standards set by Swallow. As usual nowadays, she was crying. Swallow closed the office for lunch and took her to the café next door.

"Look, you've got to get yourself sorted out, Monty. What's the matter?"

Monty's face crumpled again and she howled with sobs. Eventually she gained enough control over herself to gasp, "I don't know what's the matter, Swallow. If I did, don't you think I'd stop? I hate being like this. I cry so much it's not worth putting on mascara in the morning. I'm saying such crazy things I don't know how Simon puts up with me. This morning I just couldn't get out of bed, I couldn't. What is it, Swallow—am I going mad or something?"

The next day, Swallow thumped a copy of *Queen* magazine down on her desk.

"Page sixty-three—read it," she ordered. "It's the answer to all your problems. Go on, read all of it. I'll do the phones for a while."

Monty took the magazine around to the café and read through the article. "Side effects of the birth control pill can include skin rashes, varicose veins, weight gain, tenderness of the breasts, nausea and depression," she read. "Depression is a little-known psychological condition which can take many forms including melancholia, lethargy, loss of energy, and the feeling that life is no longer worth living."

She turned the page, her eyes devouring the elegant black type. "Doctors who prescribe the birth-control pill are often reluctant to advise their patients of these side effects in case they experience them through the process of suggestion." She finished her coffee and ran back to the office.

"Swallow! Do you really think . . . ."

"Yes, of course I do. Look, it's everything, isn't it—crying and flopping around everywhere? If I were you, I should go back to that lovable doctor of yours right away."

The doctor nodded wisely, and said, "Quite a few of my patients have reported this type of thing—I'll give you a cap instead. It's not quite as effective, but you and your husband will be starting your family soon, I expect." And she gave Monty a diaphragm that was perhaps a little smaller than the ideal size for her inner dimensions; the next size up would have been perfect, but the doctor did not have a diaphragm of that size in her small stock of contraceptives. Giving the smaller size seemed a minimal risk to run with a healthy young wife asking for only short-term contraception. "Be very careful to check that it is in position correctly," she warned as Monty left.

In two weeks Monty's ankles were delicately delineated once more, her waist was as small as it had ever been, the beginnings of her double chin had vanished and she was ten pounds lighter. The vale of tears through which she had passed seemed like a bad dream, and she kissed Simon good-bye each morning without a pang of the crazy jealousy that had overpowered her before. She did not, however, tell Simon why she had suddenly returned to her old, slender, smiling self.

Their love life, temporarily inhibited by Monty's depression, soon began to reach new heights. Like the well-trained students they were, they tried to read up on their subject. They discovered a small magazine written by doctors with an extensive correspondence section full of letters by men whose wives liked wearing rubber or having sex with Alsatian dogs.

Through an advertisement in an underground newspaper, Monty ordered a book called *The Eastern Encyclopaedia of Erotica* which was rather smudgily printed.

"The Lingam sweetens the Yoni with its tears," she read, puzzled.

"It's got one hundred and twenty-three positions." Simon eagerly took the book away from her. They tried a few positions, and gave up during "The Way of the Enlightened," which required them to sit naked, cross-legged and face to face with their palms pressed together, and meditate until they achieved simultaneous orgasm.

"Maybe it works in a hot climate," said Monty, scrambling into her clothes with a shiver.

"Maybe we weren't meditating properly," Simon suggested.

Next they sent away to Sweden for a pornographic magazine catalog, and ordered three volumes, called *Forbidden Lust*, *Swedish Weekend* and *Rule of the Lash*, which were easier to understand than the *Eastern Encyclopaedia* but still small and grubby.

They scoured the city for erotic films, sitting through endless dreary masterpieces of Czech cinema because the Sunday newspapers had described them as explicit. In a run-down suburb they found a struggling picture house nominated by an underground newspaper as the home of the hottest scenes on celluloid, but they waited in vain for the promised "sexy romps" and "naughty nudes," surrounded by empty seats, one or two old-age pensioners on free passes and an unsmiling Pakistani couple.

Then they discovered a sex shop, with a black window and a small sign saying MARITAL AIDS on the door. They decided to buy a vibrator, having read in the medical magazine extensive testimonials to their erotic capabilities.

"You ought to buy it, you'll be getting more out of it, and anyway I paid for the books," Simon announced, half pushing her toward the doorway. Almost speechless with embarrassment, Monty walked in and hurriedly picked the first instrument she saw in the display. It was black, with gold bands, and the name on the box was Non-Doctor.

Simon was very quiet for a week, until Monty said, "It's different, I suppose, but I think I prefer you, darling. All those women who have multiple orgasms with them must be making it up. I can't manage more than two."

A week later the battery ran down, and they never bothered to buy a new one.

In time, Monty noticed that the weight she had lost was beginning to creep back. Then she became aware of something much more worrying. She had grown out of the habit of watching the calendar, but now there was no doubt that her period was late. At last she could not evade the terrible truth that, vague as she was about dates, she had not had a period for a full six weeks.

"The doctor will give you something," Swallow told her with confidence. "They have a pill that can make your period start if it's late."

"I can't go back to that doctor—she thinks I want to get pregnant. Her bloody surgery looks like a nursery as it is." Monty could just imagine the conversation.

"Well, go to my doctor, then. Old Dr. Robert will come up with something, I'm sure."

Monty shook her head. "I want to think about it. I rather like the idea of having Simon's baby. I can see it inside me, all curled up like a miniature Simon already."

Swallow snorted with contempt. "You'd better think fast, girl. They won't be able to give you an abortion if you leave it too long, you know."

The more Monty thought about the baby, the more wonderful it seemed, especially since Cathy was now pregnant too. She thought how wonderful it would be to share the experience with her sister. By the end of the day she was imagining herself as a triumphantly pregnant bride—or perhaps they could get married after the birth, when their child was old enough to stand beside them in white rompers.

That evening the telephone rang.

"Monty, it's me, Rosanna. Tell Simon the minute he gets in to come home at once."

"What's the matter—you sound terrible?"

"Our father's collapsed. The doctors are with him now."

"Is he . . ." Dead seemed a tactless word.

"He's alive but he looks awful." Rosanna gulped at the end of the line and finished hurriedly, "Just get him to phone, Monty. Our mother is going mad."

Simon came in shortly afterward, and Monty sent him out again as she had promised, sensing that the Emanuel family was drawing together at a time of crisis. At midnight he telephoned from the hospital to say he would not be back that night; he returned next morning, drawn and looking older.

"My father's had a heart attack," he told her, slumping onto the sofa with relief. "They're going to keep him in the hospital at least a month. Apparently it's quite a good sign that he's in his sixties, because there's more hope the later they start. The doctor said he might be dead already if he was forty-five."

The carefree pattern of their life abruptly changed, with Simon now rushing to the hospital every evening to sit at the bedside of the weak, yellow-skinned hulk that looked so unlike his father. Monty barely saw him, and felt wound taut with anxiety as the days stole by and her period still did not come.

One evening Rosanna called in on her way home. "I can't face our mother just yet," she said, dropping her music case on the kitchen work top. "Let's have a quick coffee to give me strength. She's been howling like a banshee for days, she's absolutely hysterical. You can't imagine what it's like."

Mechanically, Monty filled the Italian percolator and set it over the heat. Rosanna talked on as the coffee was made, then said, "You're very quiet, Monty. Is everything all right?"

"Mmm—yes, everything's fine." As she opened the refrigerator to get the milk, she suddenly felt nauseated. She pushed the bottle on to the breakfast bar with haste and ran to the bathroom, fearing that she was going to be sick; nothing happened.

Rosanna looked closely at her friend. "Are you sure you're all right? You look a bit puffy in the face."

The weight of her secret was becoming unbearable, so Monty decided to share the burden with her closest friend. "I think I'm pregnant, Rosanna, my period's not come for weeks."

"My God, I'm so sorry." Rosanna pressed her hands with

ready sympathy. "How terrible for you. What are you going to do?"

Monty shook her head. "I don't know. Simon's so upset about his father, I daren't even tell him at the moment. We'll have to get married, I suppose."

"But I thought you didn't want to get married!" Rosanna looked positively shocked.

"I didn't, but I think it's different if you've got children, don't you?"

Before her disbelieving eyes, her friend was transformed into a dynamic, decisive young woman in whom it was possible to see her mother's ruthless adherence to the dynastic principle.

Rosanna began quietly, "Simon can't marry you, Monty." She put up a hand to quell the indignant question on Monty's lips. "You don't understand, and it's our fault, not yours. Simon can't marry you because he's Jewish, and a Jewish man has to marry a Jewish woman."

"But not nowadays, surely?"

"Believe me, nowadays more than ever. One of our cousins married out and you know what the family did? They sat shivah for him. That's what you have to do when people die, Monty. The idea was that he was dead to his family. They sat in mourning for him for a week."

"But that's . . ."

"That's the way it is, Monty. Didn't you realize? I suppose not. We've tried so hard to fit in, and tried to pretend there isn't any difference between us, and really there is, and this is part of it." She pushed away her cold coffee. "Do you know what I think you should do? Get rid of it, as fast as you can. And don't tell Simon. It'd kill my father if he ever found out, my mother would go mad—madder than she is going already, that is." She pulled a face to acknowledge that Mrs. Emanuel's mental stability was almost beyond prediction.

"But worst of all, *think* what it would do to Simon. Right now, anyway—he'd be in agony. You can't do it to him, you just can't."

Monty nodded in agreement. She loved Simon too much to inflict any more emotional torment on him. Rosanna hugged her and they both sighed.

"Poor, poor Monty. How could you have been so *stupid*?"

That was the question everybody asked her.

"How could you have been so stupid?" asked Swallow's doctor. "In a few months they're bringing in the Abortion Act and there would be no problem. But now, my dear, I'm afraid you're going to have to jump through quite a few hoops. You've got to see one of my colleagues, but he won't be very difficult. Then you'll be interviewed by a panel and they can be a bit sticky."

"What do I have to say?" Monty felt acutely anxious—suppose they refused to let her have an abortion? Now that the happy vision of having Simon's baby had faded, she once more saw pregnancy as a disaster.

"Just look miserable and answer their questions. Cry a bit, if you can. We've got to prove that having the baby will be injurious to your physical or mental health, and since you're obviously in the pink, we'll have to go for the mental angle. Just keep saying you don't know what you'll do, you won't be able to cope, that sort of thing." Monty nodded and he gave her a sympathetic pat on the shoulder.

"Don't worry, they won't turn you down. Now I'm afraid, I'll have to ask you for twenty guineas."

The second doctor barely raised his eyes from his prescription pad to listen to her as he wrote out his recommendation, and at the end of the week, Monty found herself standing in a huge, mahogany-paneled room in a large London hospital looking at four flint-faced men and one woman. The woman was the most vicious.

"You girls think you can get away with anything nowadays," she said in lofty tones. "If you want to know what I think, you're a selfish, irresponsible little hussy."

Monty had no difficulty in crying at this point but in the end the woman's spite defeated itself because her three male colleagues overruled her. Nevertheless, she had the parting shot.

"We have decided, *Miss* Bourton, to recommend that your pregnancy be terminated," she announced, "and frankly I cannot imagine how a girl stupid enough to become pregnant in this way could ever prove an adequate mother. And for the future, remember that the best contraceptive is the word *no*. Fortunately, there's a very good chance you won't be able to conceive again." The doctor believed this final statement implicitly. It was an opinion she based on statistics relating to illegal abortions, which were frequently followed by infection. She felt it was important to punish these girls by scaring them, so that they would be more careful in the future.

Soon afterward, Monty, after telling Simon she was going to see her mother for a couple of days, was admitted into the dingy Victorian hospital where she had been interviewed, and had his child scraped out of her body. She had spent a total of 160 guineas getting rid of the baby she wanted to have. The pain was no worse than the worst period cramps, and she put a brave face on the affair, treating it as just another adventure on the long journey to the promised land of free, true, modern love.

Once the initial relief of not being pregnant anymore had faded, she felt tired. She wanted very much to tell Cathy everything, and could hardly believe the cruelty of fate that made it impossible for her to tell either Simon or her sister, the two people who loved her most, about what she had done.

Cathy was now attractively advanced in her own pregnancy, with a taut oval bulge under her maternity smocks. Her hair was shining more glossily than ever, and she had taken to tying it back at the nape of her neck with a bow of navy-blue ribbon. Her complexion glowed with health and her normal air of serenity was enhanced. Monty was tortured with envy and saw her sister less often because it was very painful to look at Cathy's layette and the wicker crib decorated with ruffles of white broderie anglaise and know that her own baby no longer existed.

The tiredness persisted; Tony the Greek always had an array of amphetamines to sell, and she started taking some speed to keep awake in the evenings. In the beginning, one little apricot tablet would keep her alert. A few weeks later, she was taking three or four of the stronger blue tablets every night. Simon, still preoccupied with his father's illness, hardly noticed that she was either lethargic or jittery. Swallow, however, saw that something was wrong.

"Did you type this?" she asked Monty, passing an invoice across the office. Monty looked at the address and saw that it was a meaningless jumble of letters.

"Sorry, Swallow. I'll do it again right away." She rolled a sheet of paper into the battered typewriter and started to hit the keys, but her fingers would not coordinate properly. Swallow watched her.

"What were you and Simon doing last night?"

"Simon went to see his parents. I didn't do much—why?"

"Seen Tony the Greek lately?"

"Oh, c'mon, Swallow, don't get heavy with me."

Swallow snorted and pushed her tousled blond hair back with an impatient gesture.

"I don't know what dope you're doing, but it's screwing up your mind, whatever it is. I'd give it a rest, if I were you."

Monty knew this was good advice, and was herself concerned that her mind seemed to be falling to pieces and her heart, instead of beating steadily, seemed to be trying to flip-flop and fly inside her chest. She decided to stop using speed, and threw all the multicolored amphetamine tablets in the apartment down the lavatory. Immediately, she crashed into the worst depression of her life. This time she was too anguished to cry. Instead she sat for hours when she was on her own, feeling so abandoned, so lonely and so unlovable that she sincerely wanted to die. She also felt that she was too weak and ineffective to kill herself.

This time Simon came to her rescue, and insisted that she tell the doctor that she was ill.

"But I'm not ill," she protested, "I just feel a bit down, that's all."

"Darling, you *are* ill and I'm sure the doctor can give you something," he insisted, holding her tenderly. "Do you want me to come with you?"

"No, no," she protested, frightened that he would find out about the abortion. "I'll go and see Dr. Robert tomorrow, darling, I promise." Simon's so adorable and kind, she thought, I don't deserve him.

Swallow's Dr. Robert preferred consultations in the bar of the local pub, and dispensed his medicines from a large wooden chest in the back of his car.

"The depression's just a reaction to coming off the speed," he said briskly, counting out some red-and-white capsules into a container. "These will take care of that. Then if you're still feeling a bit shaky, take these—Mother's Little Helper, known as Librium in the trade." He tipped a handful of green-and-brown capsules into another bottle. "But *don't* do any fun drugs while you're taking these, or you'll get some pretty weird reactions. Now what contraception are you using?"

Monty showed him the pills she had taken when she moved into Simon's apartment, which she had just begun to use again.

"Ovulen!" he said with disgust. "No wonder you went off your rocker. There's enough in them to suppress ovulation in a sperm whale. See how you get on with these—they've just brought them out."

Over the beer-stained table he tossed three green packets with another name on them.

The red-and-white capsules immediately made her feel better, but when they were finished Monty felt as if her nerves were as taut as guitar strings. She was snappy with Simon and rude to Swallow's clients, and so decided to take the Librium capsules to calm herself. Immediately she felt normal—at least, she thought she felt normal; it was so long since she had starting taking substances that made her feel different that she could not exactly remember how it felt to be normal.

Simon's father was discharged from the hospital and made a good recovery from his heart attack. Simon paid Monty more attention, and took the doctor's warnings about mixing drugs so seriously that he stopped smoking marijuana himself.

"If you smell it in the apartment you'll just want some. I'm not going to lead you into temptation," he said, stroking her hair. "From now on I'm smoking straights until you're really OK."

"But won't you miss it?" She wound her arms around his waist, noticing that all the meals he had eaten at his parents' home recently had made him plumper. "Why don't I try to make some hash fudge? Then you can just have a little nibble now and then."

He agreed, and on Saturday, while Simon was out, Monty ground some grass to powder in the coffee mill and shook it into a pan of hot chocolate-fudge mixture. She tipped the fragrant sludge into a tray to cool, scraped out the saucepan and licked the spoon. The taste was both bitter and sickly, and she pulled a face. She added some cream, and tasted it again; it was blander but still not very appetizing. A slug of brandy finally made the flavor acceptable. Then, with a couple of hours to kill, Monty left the fudge to cool and took a taxi to Knightsbridge to cruise around the shops.

Half an hour later she was standing in the cool marble cavern of the butcher's department in Harrod's, choosing some steak for their supper, when the smell of meat became so strong that she felt sick. Quickly she walked away into the next hall. This was the fish department; the stink of fish was so vile that Monty began to retch.

She hurried toward the exit from the store, but felt as if the crowds of people were going to crush her. She retreated on legs that felt as if they were made of sponge, and blundered into the cheese department, where the noise of thousands of shoppers' feet clattering on the tiles was deafening. The uniformed floor-walker gave her a hostile look and Monty knew at once that he was going to arrest her for shoplifting and have her ignominiously thrown into the street. He strode toward her with a threatening expression and Monty struggled away from him through the crowds. She half ran into the flower hall, and hid herself, trembling, behind a line of potted palms until he had passed.

Despite her deranged senses, part of her mind was working logically. She remembered tasting the hash fudge, licking the spoon clean two or three times. There must have been more grass in that mixture than I thought, she told herself. Now it's interacting with the Librium. This is what Dr. Robert warned me would happen.

From the corner of her eye, she saw a pool of gleaming red

liquid spreading across the floor from the archway to the meat department. It was blood. She could smell it now. Resolutely, Monty turned to face the archway and willed herself to see that there was nothing there. I'm hallucinating she told herself. As soon as she turned back, she knew that the ghastly tide of blood was rising again and felt full of dread. Desperate to make her mind behave, she shook her head violently.

"Monty! Whatever's the matter?"

Feeling a colossal wave of relief, Monty flung herself into Cathy's arms. She was safe at last. Peering into Cathy's eyes through a chemical fog, she pleaded, "Take me away, Cathy. I don't feel very well. I need to lie down somewhere. Please take me out of here."

Cathy took her firmly by the arm and they walked together out of the store and took a cab to Royal Avenue, where Monty lay down in a dim bedroom with the curtains closed until, four hours later, the effect of the drug cocktail subsided. What remained was an overpowering desire to talk.

"What is it—what made you ill, Monty?" Cathy sat heavily on the end of the bed and stroked her sister's feet in their striped Biba pantyhose.

"It was an accident," Monty explained. "I ate some dope I was using to make fudge for Simon, and it reacted with some tranquilizers the doctor gave me. Thank heaven you saw me." She giggled, still feeling strange. "I was seeing all kinds of crazy things."

Cathy eyed her sister with concern. "What did you need tranquilizers for?"

Monty said nothing, but the truth was burning in her head like a fire behind a door. "Come on," Cathy persisted. "You can tell me, whatever it is. It's OK."

Monty took a deep breath and started to speak, avoiding her sister's eyes.

"I got pregnant, Cathy, and I got rid of it. I had to; Simon's father was ill and he was under so much strain I couldn't bear to add to his problems and Rosanna said that if we got married he'd be dead to his family."

"But why ever didn't you tell me?" Cathy's voice was full of wholehearted sympathy.

"I *couldn't*, Cathy—how could I? You'd have disapproved, I know you would."

"No, I wouldn't, you know I wouldn't. Oh, poor Monty, how awful for you. And I was just chattering on about my baby— you must have felt terrible."

Monty felt tears forming in her eyes. "I thought it would be all over, and I wouldn't feel anything, like having a tooth out, that's all. I didn't realize I'd feel so bad."

Because she herself was carrying a child, Cathy knew exactly how powerful were the emotions which her sister had tried to deny.

Monty looked closely at her sister, noticing that the bloom of pregnancy had faded a little and there were violet shadows under her eyes. Monty blinked to make sure of what she was seeing. Under the serene sweep of her black eyebrows, Cathy's deep eye sockets were tinted an unattractive yellowish green, and there were dark-red contusions around her slightly swollen eyes. Saying nothing, Monty touched her sister's bruised face.

"Did Charlie do that?"

Cathy nodded. "We had a row. It was my fault, I provoked him."

Monty's broad upper lip curled momentarily with contempt but she checked herself from criticizing her sister's husband and simply reached forward to hug Cathy.

"Life isn't too great for either of us, is it?"

"Things aren't how I expected them to be," Cathy admitted.

"The worst thing was not being able to tell you," Monty said. "I felt as if having to keep the secret was pushing you away, somehow."

"Well, don't do it again," Cathy said, with mock primness. "No more secrets in this family."

They spent a few more hours with each other, feeling immeasurably secure just because they were together. When Monty left she kissed her sister warmly and said, "You've always got a home with us, you know, if anything . . . happened." She walked backward down the street, seeing Cathy, a rotund but still graceful figure in cornflower blue, waving from the doorway.

For a month the only drugs Monty took were her contraceptive pills. She felt happier than she had been for some time, but not as happy as when she had first moved in with Simon. He was just as loving, kind and fascinating, but the joy was gone. Monty waited, confident that the magic would return, but the weeks went by and gradually Simon seemed to drift away from her. The secret of her abortion was dividing them, just as it had temporarily separated her from Cathy.

Instead of seeing Simon as the most perfect person in the universe, Monty began to criticize him.

"If you really want to be a musician you should do it," she said to him one day. "Just go in and chuck your job. Quit. Go for broke. Then you'll *have* to be a success." She felt obscurely unhappy when he did exactly what she said and a few days later attached himself to a group of boys whose second-rate band occasionally opened evenings at the Speakeasy, one of the clubs they frequented.

"They're pathetic," she said. "They're only hanging round you because they know you've got money and connections."

"Well, that's as good a reason as any," Simon replied. "At least, they're smart enough to know what I can be useful for, instead of writing me off as some rich kid amusing himself with a guitar."

There were four of them—Rick the singer, who also played lead guitar, Cy and Pete on rhythm and bass, and a drummer whom Monty disliked most of all.

"He smells," she complained, "and he's out of time."

"All he needs is more rehearsals," Simon told her.

"All he needs is a lobotomy," Monty rejoined.

Before long they all agreed with her.

"I'll put the word out," Rick said with finality. "There's a couple of blokes I know might be interested." He was a slim, square-shouldered kid with thick brown hair that bounced in tight ringlets to his shoulders. Monty rather liked him. Although he was no older than she was, he had a sinewy maturity which made Simon appear callow and overprivileged in comparison.

" 'Ullo, darlin', 'ow're yer doin' " was Rick's standard greeting, an amiable exaggeration of his rough accent.

Before long they were approached by a man called Nasher, who played with a jazz-oriented group from Newcastle that had been struggling around the circuit of small clubs and pubs that now lay ahead of them. Nasher was in his late twenties, with a square jaw and a face whose expression seldom changed.

"If I joined you, we'd be the best fuckin' rock 'n' roll band in the world," he announced in his singsong Tyneside accent.

"I like a modest bloke, myself," Rick approved.

"There'll be A & R men coming out of the woodwork to sign us," Nasher told him.

"And besides"—Pete, always the practical one, scraped a thumbnail down his two days' growth of stubble "your lead singer's wrecking himself on speed. He'll be a basket case in six months. You want a clean-living mob like us."

"We aim to make a lot of bread and stay alive long enough to count it." Cy gave the group his most satanic leer. With his lank black hair and hollow cheeks he already looked like a zombie, although his peculiar green eyes gleamed with vitality.

Nasher joined them. Simon bought him a new drum kit for seventy pounds and spent almost a thousand more on clothes and stage equipment, including two amplifiers that were bigger than anything a band of their modest stature had ever used before.

"What are we going to call ourselves, then?" Nasher demanded one evening. Now, instead of going to a smart nightclub every night, Monty and Simon spent their evenings in pubs with the band, mostly the corner pub on the ragged fringes of Chelsea near the house where Rick, Cy and Pete lived.

"What's wrong with the name we've got, The Beat Machine?" Simon distributed the brimming beers around the ring-marked table with care.

"Don't like it." Nasher looked meaningfully over the rim of his glass. He had the most experience as a working musician, and his word carried weight.

"Nah—we've gone off it, 'n' all." Cy and Rick, friends since childhood, always voted together on band policy.

"We're a different outfit now we've got Nasher—and Simon. When people book us they ought to know it's not the same old Beat Machine, but something better." Pete handled the bookings. He was the one with a job; he was a clerk in a big engineering company, and he had access to a telephone.

"Yeah, you're right, we need a new name." Simon took a small sip from his pint. Beer was not to his taste, but to drink anything else would have been unthinkable. Beer was what the boys drank, so Simon drank it too. "How about Raw Silk?"

"How about a smack in the kisser?" Cy bared his gray teeth with contempt.

"Atomic Yo-Yo?" Monty put in, claiming the chick's privilege to be dumb.

"Atomic's nice, I like Atomic," Pete nodded.

"Atomic Pigeon?"

"Atomic Rain?"

"How about The Fallout?"

"Atomic Fireball?"

"Maybe something like The Explosion?" Simon was almost bouncing in his seat with enthusiasm.

"Shaddup, Simon," Rick told him kindly. "We got the balls, you got the juice, remember?"

"Juice." Cy's speckled eyes glittered.

"I like it," Nasher considered, his head on one side. "A little bit rude, short, look great on the van."

"And on a poster," said Pete.

"Right, that's it. The Juice." Rick looked around the table and saw agreement. He raised his glass. "God bless her and all who sail in her."

"One more thing," Nasher put his empty glass down with

satisfaction. "We ain't got a van." This was important. They needed a van to take their mountain of new equipment on the road. All eyes were on Simon.

"I'll buy a van," he promised, "and we can find someone to do one of those far-out paint jobs on it." Since his legacy had been spent at a rate that was beginning to alarm him, Simon decided to sell his Aston Martin in order to buy the van. It was more of a gesture toward thrift than anything else, since more than half his grandmother's money lay untouched in the bank.

"I'll miss the Aston," Simon said as the car's new owner drove it away. "We had some good times in that car, eh, girl?"

"Yeah," Monty agreed, wishing he had not put his arm around her. She did not want him to touch her. She did not want to think about the good times they had had before. She did not once consider the possibility that her love for Simon was dying. She decided to go back to the apartment and roll another joint.

12

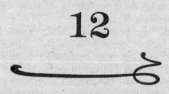

WITH HER BLISSFUL HONEYMOON BEHIND HER AND HER PREG-
nancy confirmed, Cathy expected to be as happy as any woman
could possibly be. She had pictured herself and Charlie in a new
dimension of intimacy, sharing a home, pursuing their social life
and fulfilling the expectations of their families. They would have
their ups and downs, of course, but nothing would seriously
threaten their union.

Instead, Charlie seemed distracted, and shadows of suspicion
began to steal across Cathy's sunny confidence that marriage
would put right everything that was wrong with her husband.
Soon each day brought some new indication of what Charlie was
really doing in the evenings when he told her he was gambling
or taking clients around the clubs.

First the dry cleaning came back with a discreet white envelope pinned to the bag in which were a handkerchief, one of
Charlie's gold cuff links and a love letter signed April. Cathy
burned it and determined to say nothing to Charlie. So what if
that old bag was still after him? Men hated women who nagged;
if she made a scene he'd be angry.

Then one day, she reached down to pull the seat in the car
forward and felt something soft against her fingertips. It was a
pair of red nylon knickers, trimmed with a black silk fringe,
crumpled under the seat.

"Aren't they yours?" Charlie asked blandly as he turned the
ignition.

"Charlie—do they look like mine?"

"No, not your style at all, now I look at them. Yours are boring old white, aren't they?" He snatched them from her fingers, and sniffed them casually. "Mmmmmn. Calèche. Must have been before we were married, darling." And he tossed the scarlet pants out of the car window in Sloane Square.

None of the society columns would dream of ratting on an errant husband, but one gossip writer who often covered Lady Davina's charity functions approached the dowager and remarked, "I hear Charlie Coseley hasn't let marriage change his way of life."

Lady Davina directed a piercing glance at the journalist without altering the width of her social smile a centimeter. "They're blissfully happy according to Catherine. What on earth do you mean?"

"We've been offered half a dozen pictures of Charlie squiring his old flames around town since the honeymoon. I saw to it they were never printed, of course." The elderly woman bestowed a nod of thanks on him, her long diamond earrings swinging against the swagged wrinkles of her neck. "But people will talk, of course," he added, tucking a cigarette into the corner of his blubbery lips. "And I'd be surprised if the shots haven't been hawked around half Fleet Street by now."

A few days later, Cathy received a visit of contrived casualness from her grandmother.

"So how are you finding married life?" she inquired. "Those curtains are simply lovely. Bright, of course, but lovely. The modern style, I suppose, those flowers."

Cathy passed her a cup of tea. "Married life is marvelous, Didi, I love every minute of it."

"Not feeling a little off color—the baby, perhaps?"

"No, I'm fine." Cathy patted the modest bulge under her pink smock.

"Well, of course, husbands to tend to play up a tiny bit at times like this. Charlie's pleased, I hope?"

"Absolutely thrilled."

"I suppose men do feel rather left out when women get interested in babies. Just remember, dear, the best thing in your condition is not to *worry*. Charlie needs you to cosset him, make him feel pampered, let him know he's the most important person in your life. He's still your prince, remember. It would be perfectly natural for Charlie to have a little fling—especially toward the end, you know—and your best course is simply to ignore it. Men need that sort of thing much more than women, in my experience."

What Cathy needed, quite desperately at the time, was not advice but reassurance.

"Do you love me?" she asked Charlie in bed one night.

"Of course I love you," he mumbled sleepily. "I married you, didn't I?"

"But you haven't made love to me for ages, darling. Don't you want me anymore?"

"Mmn. Not getting enough? But what about the baby? Don't want to hurt the baby, do we?"

"The doctor says it won't hurt the baby." Cathy was not very good at recognizing her physical needs, but at present there was no mistaking her body's craving. She was tingling with heightened sensuality because of her pregnancy, and yearned for Charlie's caresses more than ever, even though his brief attentions were seldom very satisfying.

He sighed with resignation, rolled over and twisted her right nipple as if it would unscrew.

"Give me a hand, there's a love." He pulled her hand towards his crotch and she awkwardly kneaded life into his shriveled penis. The instant he was inside her, however, his reluctant erection failed completely.

"Sorry, darling," he said, rolling over away from her again. "What goes up must come down, you know. Try again in the morning, eh?"

But in the morning, he slept late, then ran off to the bank with his tie and a piece of toast and marmalade clutched in one hand, calling over his shoulder. "Client dinner tonight, darling, don't wait up."

As she and the baby grew, the physical yearnings of the first months subsided and mental cravings took over. She waited every night in a fever of anxiety until she heard her husband's key jabbing inaccurately at the front-door lock; then she closed her eyes and faked sleep.

"Is everything all right with you and Charlie?" Monty asked her sister with a transparent pretense of innocence.

"Perfectly. I've never been happier," Cathy answered in a doubting tone that belied every word. She eyed her sister with envy. Monty was now wearing a richly embroidered Indian blouse and velvet jeans. Her hair was long and curling, her eyes, with their drug-dilated pupils, wide and soft. She looked like some kind of gypsy princess, more exotic than ever.

"You are sure? I mean, he's taking care of you and everything?"

"Well, of course he is, he's my husband, isn't he?"

"Husband or not, Swallow says he's always at her gambling parties now, and not on his own, either."

"He has to entertain the bank's clients, and their wives. Just like Daddy, remember? Of course he's always out, and if they want a bit of a thrill at some chemmy party, he knows where to find it."

"Swallow says they don't look much like banking types to her."

Cathy sighed and looked down at her hands, noticing that her fingers were becoming puffy. Her wide gold wedding ring was beginning to cut into her flesh uncomfortably. She stole a glance in the mirror, approving of the fresh pink flush which pregnancy had added to her cheeks, set off by her vivid turquoise smock. She looked the picture of happy motherhood, so why was Charlie neglecting her? She knew Monty's anxiety was well-founded, but she didn't want to continue the conversation in case her own fears were confirmed. "Let's talk about something else," she suggested in a tired voice.

After that, Monty suddenly stopped calling her, and was vague and short if Cathy telephoned her. She doesn't want to talk to me because she knows what Charlie's up to, Cathy surmised, feeling a pang of abandonment and never guessing that her sister was struggling with her own share of misery.

Charlie was uninterested in the progress of her pregnancy, which Cathy found exciting and rather frightening.

"I felt the baby move today," she announced with pride, while they dressed for dinner at Coseley one Saturday. "It was wonderful, like a little butterfly inside me."

"Spare me the details," he joked, opening the closet doors one after another. "Did you see where the maid put my studs?"

Their sex life evaporated completely as soon as her belly was an appreciable size, and to her horror she began to retain water and bloat around her face, feet and ankles. Their housekeeper timidly suggested that she should take off her rings, but the idea was put to her almost too late because she had to rub her fingers with soap and chafe them painfully to do it. She left her wedding ring on. It sat tightly in the crease of her finger with an unsightly bulge of flesh on either side, but she felt that to take it off would be a bad omen.

Charlie made a number of business trips abroad, seldom bothering to telephone and often staying away over weekends. With Monty mysteriously avoiding her, Cathy felt more and more lonely. Every Friday afternoon she was driven down to Coseley, where she occupied her vacant mind listening to the conversation of Lord Shrewton and his business guests. Should she quit their company, she was instantly prey to the marchioness's advice about baby clothes, nursery furniture and feeding the infant.

"We'll send you Nanny Bunting," she said, oozing invasive helpfulness. "I couldn't have managed my boy without her. *Such* a treasure."

Back in London during the week, Cathy had little to do except buy baby clothes and attend the exclusive childbirth-preparation classes of Miss Betty Parsons.

"It's as if I've become the invisible woman," she complained to Rosanna. "You're the only person who ever comes to see me; nobody asks me anywhere. Monty's simply vanished. Just because I'm pregnant I've ceased to exist."

"I'm sure it's nothing to do with being pregnant," Rosanna reassured her. "Monty's having an awful time herself, Simon's distraught about Daddy being ill. She probably doesn't want to bother you with her problems, that's all. She adores you, Cathy, you know she does. You're her best friend."

"But it isn't only Monty—I thought that when we were married everyone would ask Charlie and me round just like they did when we were engaged. But now Charlie spends his whole time entertaining clients and I'm left on my own."

"It's just a phase," Rosanna told her, looking uncomfortable. She suspected that the reason people didn't find Cathy ideal company was because she was wrapped in an invisible cloud of unhappiness. There she was with her serene smile and her brave little bulge, while Charlie was all over town, with a string of models and low-grade junior socialites, acting more promiscuously than he had even before his marriage. "Charlie Coseley only got married so he could enjoy commiting adultery," joked his friends, and laughed uproariously.

Cathy was probably the only person in London who did not know where Charlie went, with whom and to do what. No one told her; the women said nothing because they did not want to upset her, and the men said nothing because they did not want to upset Charlie.

Any evidence of infidelity which Cathy acquired, Charlie explained away with sneering irritation. "*Of course* I took Pat Booth to Annabel's—she's looking for finance for a new boutique. Why don't you do something like that, darling, instead of moping around the house all day?"

Finally the florist's account arrived in the morning mail, and, unthinkingly, he tossed it over the bedcover to her with the rest of the bills. When she read it, Cathy could not contain her anguish anymore.

"Account 1454, the Earl of Laxford, Miss Annabel Scott, 37

Cheyne Mansions, SW3, Mxd ct fls, £15. Darling Hotpants, see you tonight, all my love, Charlie.''

Cathy's heart sank as she turned over the florist's docket and read the next one in the sheaf of half a dozen stapled to the bill. It was the same message. Only the addresses were different. I suppose, she thought to herself, Charlie calls them all Hotpants so he doesn't have to remember their names.

"Read those," she said, pushing the papers into his hand. "Read them and tell me why you're doing this. Why, Charlie?"

"Why do you think?" he snapped back at her, feeling cornered. "I can hardly fuck you in your condition, can I? You're as fat as a cow, it makes me sick to look at you."

"But, Charlie, I'm having *your* baby. It's for you, for us. Why must you hurt me so when I . . .'' She felt tears start in her eyes. "When I love you so much? Don't you love me anymore?''

He finished dressing, lacing his shoes with anger, and stood up. "Love you? Did I say that? I must have been pissed, or something.''

"What do you mean?" she shouted in disbelief, and grabbed his arm. Angrily he flung her from him.

"Don't do that. Don't touch me or you'll be sorry.''

"But Charlie . . .''

"You really are the most stupid woman I've ever met. Can't you see what's in front of you? I couldn't love you if you were the last cunt on earth. Christ, you're so boring, and prim and straight—it's like fucking a bloody board. You're a drag. Grow up, darling. No one's going to be eternally grateful just because you opened your legs.''

"But I can change, Charlie, give me a chance. We've only been married a few months.'' Cathy was crying now, tears trickling down her cheeks. She wiped them away. He ignored her, looked in the glass to brush invisible specks from the shoulders of his jacket, then walked to the door.

"Charlie!" She thumped the bedcover in desperation. "Don't go!''

"Goodbye, darling!" he called sarcastically over his shoulder.

She heaved herself out of bed, wincing as her ligaments strained at the violent movement, and ran after him. "Charlie, please—you can't leave like that.''

"Just watch me!''

Halfway down the elegant curve of the stairway she caught up with him, pulling at his shoulder. He wrenched out of her grasp, a button from his jacket flying off into the stairwell. In the hallway below, the manservant was waiting with his brief-case and umbrella.

"Will you get off me?" Charlie hissed. "Keep your filthy, common money-grubbing little paws to yourself!" He twisted her arm, trying to hurt her.

She had a vision of him throwing her down the staircase and killing the baby, and in the intimacy of their confrontation he guessed her thoughts at once. "*Oh*, no! Oh, no—that's just the kind of vulgar soap-opera stuff you'd like, isn't it?"

He began pulling her back toward the bedroom, finally drag-ging her off her feet, picking her up and carrying her. Once inside he hurled her onto the bed, kicked the door shut and dealt her a vicious backhanded slap across the face.

"Well, this isn't a soap opera, darling, this is real life, and in real life we don't pick fights with our husbands when the servants can hear"—he slapped her again—"and we don't stage vulgar scenes and scream like a fishwife, and snoop into our husbands' affairs. Because if we do . . ." He seized a pillow and she flung her arms over her face, fearing that he was going to smother her. "If you *ever* behave like this again, I'll smash your stupid face to pulp and I'll go out of that door and I won't come back, and the next you'll see of me will be at the divorce court—OK?"

She was crying too much to speak, so he punched her in the stomach. "Say, OK, Charlie! Say, I promise I'll be a good girl. Say it, damn you. And stop fucking crying, I can't stand the goddamn noise." She gasped, trying to control herself enough to say the words, terrified that he would hurt the baby if he punched her again.

"I promise I'll be good, Charlie—*no!*" His arm drew back for another blow and fear snatched at her guts.

"Say it properly, cunt. Say, OK, Charlie, I promise I'll be a good girl."

"Ok, Charlie, I promise I'll be a good girl."

"That's better. Now, was there anything else, my lady?" His eyes were shining with excitement.

"What do you mean?" He hauled her toward him by one leg, twisted it and turned her over onto her stomach. Kneeling, he held her down with an armlock. Her nightdress was almost around her shoulders. She heard his zip, felt his penis stabbing between her spread legs.

"I believe you'd like a bit of cock? Can't disappoint you, can I? Marital duty, and all that?" And he rammed into her, jerked once or twice more until he came and then withdrew and walked out of the room. In the doorway, he paused. "No complaints, I trust? Everything all right now?"

Cathy turned her head away and bit the bedcover to stop herself from screaming with rage. As soon as she heard the front door slam behind him she ran for the bathroom, washed, dressed, pulled some dresses into a suitcase and took a taxi to Monty and Simon's apartment. There was no reply to the bell, and she realized that her sister must already be at work. She told the taxi to take her on to Trevor Square.

"My dear, you really could have been more subtle." Lady Davina spoke with more irritation than sympathy. "Of course he hit you. Men always hit out when you leave them no alternative. You *must* learn to play your cards more carefully. Charlie would be eating out of your hand if you'd only do what I tell you."

"But the baby, Didi—he hit the baby." Cathy's eyes felt sore and she could still taste blood in her mouth from the cuts inside her cheek made by her own teeth.

"Babies are tough little beggars, and I'm positive there's no harm done. Just take care he doesn't do it again, Catherine. Now go back to your home and pretend it never happened. You must *work* at your marriage, dear. Take this as a warning and *try*."

"But it's not fair—he isn't trying!"

"My dear, this is a man's world, but we can do what we like in our own homes. We may be weak but we've got *all* the advantages in our own territory. A woman should be able to make a man her *slave*."

By the time Cathy returned to Royal Avenue Charlie had once again been swamped with remorse. There was a large bouquet waiting for her and he had even had the sensitivity to send them from a florist other than the one he had used to send flowers to the other women.

Charlie came home early from the bank, embraced her tenderly, begged her forgiveness and took her out to dinner at Alvaro's, where they had shared many deliciously romantic evenings before their marriage. He apologized over and over again, calling himself all the names Cathy had hardly dared imagine, and she forgave him.

The next day purple bruising developed around Cathy's eyes and he cheerfully called her "Panda." It was hard to ignore the fact that her wretchedness turned him on. Cathy distracted herself by shopping and so came across the panic-stricken Monty in Harrod's.

With her sister once more by her side in life, Cathy's confidence returned.

"I'm going to fight those birds with their own weapons," she told Monty, her eyes sparkling. "You'll see—once this baby is born, my poor little husband won't know what's hit him."

Their son was born ten weeks later, a little earlier than expected, in the middle of a rainy spring evening. Bettina did not bother to leave Brighton, Lady Davina regarded the whole affair with disinterest, and so Monty stoically took on the job of telephoning nightclub after nightclub until Charlie was found.

Half an hour later he swayed into the ward with a small bunch of tulips. Even his mother and father, who arrived a little later, could smell the sickly combination of brandy and marijuana emanating from their son, but he leaned over the little Perspex crib, making fond cooing noises, and reassured Cathy with hugs and kisses and generally acted the fond father to the satisfaction of them all.

Cathy called the baby James, which was quickly shortened to Jamie. His full name and title was James Charles William Mountclere Coseley, the Viscount Wheynough, but the weight of his lineage did not seem to trouble him. To Cathy's surprise he looked around him with interest, thrashed his limbs with enthusiasm and frequently drifted into a sound, peaceful sleep, his long black eyelashes curled on his round red cheeks.

"Doesn't he ever cry?" Monty asked with interest, noticing that overnight her sister seemed to have acquired a lifetime of maternal experience, and was holding the tiny body with suddenly practiced hands. She never took her eyes off the little being who had so miraculously been created out of her own flesh. Love seemed a feeble description of the emotion that had transfigured Cathy so that she looked almost like a different person.

"He did cry this morning, when he was hungry." Cathy smiled softly as she turned the baby's tiny shoulders this way and that to admire his quarter-profiles. "But he seems quite good-tempered. We're going home tomorrow, aren't we, Gorgeous?" The baby bicycled his tiny legs with enthusiasm. "Look at his dear little fingernails—do you suppose I should cut them?"

"Let me do it." Cathy gave Monty the minute pair of blunt baby scissors and one by one uncurled Jamie's fingers and held them still while her sister snipped off the translucent crescents of nail. The baby snuffled at the sensation but did not cry.

Looking thoughtful, Monty replaced the scissors on the night table and went back to the uncomfortable low armchair provided for hospital visitors. The two sisters looked at each other, both thinking of the child Monty had aborted.

"I should feel sad," Monty said slowly, analyzing her feelings. "I do feel sad. But it isn't important, somehow. He's important; it's like your baby was my baby." Cathy smiled warmly, but searched her sister's eyes to see if she had really looked into her heart.

"Honestly, that's how I feel," Monty protested, sensing the question in her sister's look. "And there's no need to ask how you feel, you haven't stopped smiling all morning."

It was true; although her skin was drawn with the physical effort of her pregnancy and the baby's birth, Cathy's beauty had taken on a full-blown quality. Her finely drawn lips, their natural rosewood-red unobscured by lipstick, were relaxed and seemed softer and fuller than before. Although she was feeding the baby, her breasts were scarcely larger in size, but their skin seemed fine and transparent, with blue veins faintly visible inside her ruffled white lace gown.

A nursery nurse had been engaged for the first month of the baby's life, after which the Coseley family nanny, an elderly, imposing woman with wispy white hair and a low-slung bosom encased in a gray serge uniform, would take over.

With the weight of the baby off her body, the weight of inertia seemed to lift from her mind as well, and Cathy once more took control of her own life, which meant taking control of her errant husband. The first priority was to repair the damage which her pregnancy had done to her body.

The only problem was that she was not terribly interested in Charlie. He seemed a petulant, demanding creature when his needs were considered in relation to those of her baby. She could think of nothing but little Jamie and it was a supreme effort to turn her attention away from her miraculous, adorable son.

Lady Davina, having observed the dangerous phenomenon of maternal obsession before, paid her granddaughter a special visit.

"Whatever you do, darling, do *not* get wrapped up in your child now." The advice was so emphatic it was almost an order. "You'll lose everything if you let yourself wallow in all this baby nonsense. Your husband must be your first priority. Anyone can take care of a baby, after all."

Since Charlie had scarcely returned home for more than a few hours since his son had been born, Cathy reluctantly took her grandmother's advice. She quenched all her inner misgivings, directed the nurses to bottle-feed Jamie, and booked herself into an expensive health farm the day she was allowed to leave the hospital.

The attendants at the health farm scoured her flesh to softness with salt rubs, oiled her face with creams, tightened her slack belly with electric currents and moved her sluggish bowels back to normality with a variety of disgusting but effective treatments.

She passed the afternoons reading magazines, devouring articles called "Your Marriage: Keeping the Excitement" or "After the Honeymoon—Make Sure He's for Your Eyes Only."

A fortnight later the horrible bloating of her body had subsided; her waist was still two inches bigger than it had been before, but she did a hundred situps every morning and was sure it would shrink back soon.

"Look at Mummy, isn't she beautiful now?" Nanny Bunting demanded, propping the baby up in his enveloping white shawl to gaze at Cathy with his vague blue eyes. The old nanny had traveled up from Coseley and installed herself at Royal Avenue in Cathy's absence. The nursery nurse at once took off in a huff but Cathy, wanting to concentrate all her energies on restoring her marriage, was grateful for the capable way the old woman took charge. A massive black perambulator was parked in the stairwell and piles of snow-white diapers filled the laundry room.

Between 6:00 and 10:00 P.M. every evening Cathy heard Jamie crying in his nursery upstairs. "He's a very willful little man," the nanny told her, "exactly like his father at the same age."

Her household began to take on the orderly bustle she had envisaged in her engagement days, with the housekeeper tripping up and down stairs with the nursery's meals and Nanny Bunting wheezing down herself in the afternoon when the little viscount was taken out for a walk in the pram. The servants conducted petty feuds among themselves, squabbling over missing items of laundry and other trivia until Cathy intervened.

She went shopping, glorying in her restored slenderness and buying the kind of clothes she had seen on some of Charlie's other women—tight velvet jeans, virtually transparent lace blouses worn without a bra, long figure-hugging chiffon dresses with tiny buttons and puffed sleeves. She cooed and flattered her husband into a malleable mood and coaxed him into taking her out with him for the next evening of entertainment the bank's clientele required.

"You'll be bored silly, darling; just wiggle your tits and take their minds off business," he instructed her, playfully pinching one of her nipples through its fragile screen of lace.

In fact, Charlie was the one who found business dinners tedious. Cathy discovered that many of his clients were good company; some had been her father's friends and they found it curiously reassuring to meet the daughter of the suicide peer and discover her unharmed by the scandal of her father's death. Others were simply charmed by her, ridiculously flattered when she asked them to explain their conversation, and delighted to talk to a woman who was neither bored nor frightened by the world of finance.

"See that young man over there?" a senior stockbroker said to her in a Chelsea restaurant one evening. "Very interesting fellow—sign of the times, in a way. Most of us in banking have always been looking for the best long-term investment—young Mr. Slater over there says he isn't interested in long-term investments. Six months is all he's interested in. Wants to take the money and run."

"So what does he invest in?" Cathy stole a surreptitious glance at the tall figure with protruding ears who was deep in conversation with two other dark-suited men.

"He's an asset stripper. What his company does is buy up companies who're in trouble and undervalued on the stock market. Then he simply scuppers the company and sells off the assets—usually the property's the main thing. Property's going up, you see, but that isn't necessarily reflected in the company's shares, so he can buy them up for less than they're really worth."

"It sounds rather drastic." Cathy sipped her claret and swallowed it with displeasure. Charlie's taste in wine was eccentric.

"Drastic—yes. But he's not short of companies to buy. Not enough capital investment over the years—there's a lot of rotten businesses in Britain, resting on their laurels and not looking to the future."

One of the other guests joined the conversation, his eyes fixed glassily on Cathy's breasts, whose subtle exposure he had just noticed.

"Rubbish, rubbish—don't believe a word he says, my dear. You're leading the young lady astray, George. Jim Slater's not cutting the deadwood out of British industry, he's just shuffling worthless paper. Don't forget the man was a financial journalist before he got big in the City—he's got the press in the palm of his hand."

At the end of the table Charlie sulked and drank steadily. His business dinners were normally all ribald jokes and hard drinking. His guests complimented him on his marvelous little wife as they climbed into their cars, but as soon as he was alone with Cathy in the Jaguar Charlie snapped, "You stupid little cow, why don't you keep your mouth shut? You make me look ridiculous, asking questions like a schoolgirl. It's bloody bad manners to talk business at dinner. If you want to come out with me you can shut up and behave yourself."

He stamped on the brakes and stopped the car an inch short of a brightly painted Rolls-Royce which was blocking half the road. "Damn!"

"Oh, Charlie, it's John Lennon's car—I saw it in the papers." Cathy watched with apprehension as Charlie got out and walked toward the psychedelic vehicle, his hands in his pockets. He pulled out a half-crown coin and scored a long wavy line through the paintwork with its milled edge.

"That'll show John Lennon—whoever he thinks he is." At the far end of the short street, a policeman was watching them.

"Spiv! John Lennon's a spiv! Jim Slater's a spiv! Gutter-snipes, the pair of them. They think because they're millionaires on paper that means something. They think they're big men because they've made tin-pot fortunes in a couple of years. They don't understand that making money's easy—keeping it's the trick. John Lennon will go bust before he dies and his sons will be right back in the gutter where he started, you'll see." And he reversed inaccurately to the end of the street and roared away, still watched by the policeman, who also respected wealth of several centuries' standing.

The more successful Cathy became at holding her own in his world, the more uncomfortable Charlie grew. He had no justification to exclude her from his business life, and decided to scare her away. He arranged a riotous all-male party in a private room with a dozen call girls hired through the notorious Paris madame, Madame Bernard. This proved vastly popular with everyone but his father, who rapidly heard the news.

"That's not our way of doing things, Charlie. I don't want to hear of it happening again," he told his son at the weekend. "Your private life is your own affair, but I won't have the name of the bank associated with any kind of scandal whatever."

"Sometimes Charlie behaves as if our marriage were some kind of contest," Cathy said, visiting her sister one evening. At this period in their lives they spent many hours discussing their relationships with Simon and Charlie, wondering why love did not make them happy and how they could turn their romantic yearnings into reality. "If something happens that I like, he just wriggles around until he finds some way of spoiling it, and then he's happy." She stretched her legs uncomfortably, stiff from sitting on Monty's Moroccan floor cushions.

"Is he still fucking you?" Monty pulled a cigarette out of the carved soapstone casket from Kashmir which stood on the low brass table.

Cathy smiled with triumph, pushing her glistening curtain of Havana-brown hair back from her face.

"Yes, quite a lot now, thank heavens." She sighed, drew in a lungful of unaccustomed cigarette smoke and coughed.

"Sorry, I'll open a window." Monty did this with difficulty, because she rarely opened the apartment's window. "You don't sound very happy about it."

"Well, I try, but it does get boring."

"Do you have orgasms?" Monty lay back and looked at the ceiling, wondering if a pendant lamp of pierced brass would look good hanging low over the table.

"Well yes, but not very often. He doesn't go on long enough."

"I don't have them from fucking at all, only if Simon goes down on me." Monty sighed. She evaded making love now, feeling guilty and cruel every time Simon accepted her flimsy excuses. Cathy also sighed. She had not had an orgasm since her honeymoon. She went through sex in an odd detached mood now, as if all the sensations were coming through cotton wool. After every brief coupling with Charlie she felt a dull ache in the region of her pubic arch.

"I suppose I could ask Charlie to go down on me, but he doesn't like what he calls fiddling about."

"Maybe you could go in for a bit of sixty-nine?" Monty suggested.

Cathy tried this. It was not a success. Her husband's erection subsided in her mouth and he complained that she smelled.

The only aspect of her life that was wholly delightful was her son, a robust, serious child with dark curls, who crawled excitedly into her arms at every opportunity, twining his plump, starfish hands in her pearls and pulling himself upright on her lap. Cathy adored him with anxious reserve. It was so easy to love her baby son, but increasingly difficult to love his father. She felt confused. Surely, Charlie should be the center of her world?

Nanny Bunting subtly discouraged her from taking any part in her child's care.

"Clumsy Mummy—Nanny do it," she would say, taking the bottle or the toy away from Cathy as if she too were a child.

"We would really prefer it if we could bring baby down to Mummy in the afternoon, rather than her coming all the way up to the nursery," she said one day, and so Cathy received her child every day at four-thirty, and somehow the whole house grew to regard the nursery as Nanny's private kingdom.

In the evening she still heard Jamie cry, sometimes for hours on end, and felt vaguely that this was wrong, but she knew nothing about babies and when she asked Nanny Bunting she was told, "Bless you, Mummy, all babies fret when they're put down for the night. It's nothing to worry about. Crying expands their little lungs."

One evening when Charlie was out she heard cries which she

thought were louder and more desperate than usual, and at last went up to the taboo territory of the nursery to see if anything was wrong.

"Now let that be a lesson to you, not to play with hot things," Nanny Bunting was saying, standing over the tiny figure of Jamie, who was sitting in front of her by the wall, roaring his heart out.

"Is everything all right, Nanny?" Cathy hesitated in the doorway, feeling that she was intruding but alarmed at her son's uncontrollable distress.

"There, see what you've done, you naughty boy? You've disturbed Mummy and brought her all the way up here in the night. Isn't that a naughty boy?"

"Why is he crying so much?"

"He touched my radiator, Mummy, and burned his little hand, but he won't do that again in a hurry, will he? Clever little man knows it's naughty to touch hot things, doesn't he?"

Cathy firmly picked Jamie up and held him close, murmuring soothing nonsense into his ear and wiping the streaming mucus from his nose and mouth with the hem of her white broderie anglaise peignoir. The baby's frantic screams began to subside. Without a word to Nanny Bunting she took the baby out of the day nursery and walked him up and down the landing until he fell asleep on her shoulder. Clucking with disapproval, Nanny Bunting bustled into the night nursery to tidy the cot, and Cathy heard the old woman muttering angrily to herself as she carried the sleeping infant through the doorway. Oh dear, thought Cathy, I've offended her now.

Next morning she told Charlie about the incident.

"My goodness, yes, I'll never forget," he said, tossing aside the *Financial Times*. "She used to do that to us too. Make us hold something hot so we'd know not to play with fire. She made me hold the poker when the end of it was red hot."

"But isn't that cruel?"

"Nonsense. Didn't do me any harm. She's an absolute treasure, Nanny Bunting. For heaven's sake, don't rub her up the wrong way, darling. I know you're not accustomed to managing servants, but what on earth would we do without her?"

A few weeks later the old woman had an attack of gout and could not walk. Cathy went up to see her and found her sitting in state with her swollen foot raised on a stool.

"Can you manage, Nanny? Would you like us to get in a temporary girl to help you?"

"Certainly not!" The old woman glared at her, clearly insulted. "I'm not in my grave yet, by a long way."

However, the inflammation became so severe that Nanny Bunting was taken away to the hospital two days later, and Cathy telephoned an agency for a temporary. A few hours later a very slim girl with hair the color of her dark-brown uniform arrived, and took Jamie upstairs. Monty arrived at the same time, with a bag full of Tibetan amber beads from Thea Porter which she insisted Cathy admire.

Half an hour later the temporary nanny appeared in the drawing room with a naked Jamie whimpering and squirming in a cot sheet.

"Mrs.—I mean, my lady, I think you ought to see this," she said, her voice almost a whisper. She set the child down on the floor and he pulled himself up on the corner of the sofa. The sheet fell away. There were grayish marks on his legs, red weals on his buttocks and a raw rash on his inner thighs.

Cathy and Monty gasped with horrified surprise.

"He's absolutely miserable, my lady." The girl timidly turned Jamie around so they could see the bruises on his chest. "And look at his little hand." She tenderly turned the fat palm of Jamie's right hand upward for Cathy to see the suppurating burn at the base of the fingers. "And just look at his feet. . . ." She picked Jamie up and showed them red marks on the soles of his feet.

"Whatever are they?" Monty asked.

"Burns, I think. He's terrified to have me touch him upstairs. He starts screaming the minute I go into his room."

In the nursery, they were horrified to find that Jamie's cot was cold, wet and stinking.

"It can't have been changed for days." Monty picked up a sodden blanket with an expression of disgust. "Nanny Bunting must have just left the bed when he wet it because she couldn't manage to change it."

"And there's nothing to sterilize the bottles with, and the nappies aren't really clean. No wonder he's a mass of rashes. And look here . . ." Now emboldened, the temporary nanny pulled open a cupboard, and showed Cathy a dozen brown medicine bottles with old-fashioned handwritten labels.

"That's the gripe water she gets from a special chemist in St. James's." Cathy picked up the nearest bottle with foreboding and uncorked it.

"Beg pardon, my lady, but it certainly isn't gripe water. I believe it's some old remedy they used for colic, but she's opened all the bottles and not finished any of them."

"Oh, heavens, my poor baby." Cathy hugged the abused little

body as hard as she dared. "If only I hadn't trusted that old witch. How could I have been so stupid?"

Monty squeezed her sister's shoulders. "You weren't to know—how could you have known? She was covering up deliberately, afraid you'd fire her if you knew she couldn't cope."

Suddenly almost weak with guilt, Cathy called the housekeeper and manservant and asked them to move the new nanny and Jamie into one of the spare bedrooms. Next she asked the doctor to call. He was not only her doctor, but Charlie's as well and the personal physician of the whole Coseley family. He examined Jamie with a frowning face.

"Chronic neglect and ill-treatment," he announced at last. "We'll need to get him X-rayed; it looks as if those ribs have been broken. She can't have had the strength to pick the baby up properly."

"What was the stuff in the medicine bottles?" Monty stood beside her sister and looked at the prosperous physician with mistrust. He seemed to be reacting very calmly.

"It's a sedative mixture, basically. They used it years ago for colic and general fretfulness."

"What's in it?" Monty pressed him, picking up a sticky bottle and screwing up her eyes to read the label.

"Laudanum, I believe, but not in any harmful concentration. It can't have done him much harm, just stopped him crying."

Cathy's eyes, normally so serene, were blazing with rage. "I can't believe anyone could do such terrible things. That wicked old woman is never going to set foot in my house again. Thank heaven we found out what she was up to before she hurt Jamie anymore."

"Don't be too hard on her." There was a bland look on the doctor's round face and he made an ineffectual gesture toward covering the naked baby with his large, gold-ringed hand. "I've seen this kind of thing before, of course. Family brings in the old nanny, not realizing she's past it. Everything's fine for the first six months, but when the baby gets to be a bit of a handful things start to slide."

"I'm sure they don't realize she's past it," Cathy said grimly. "I shall have to speak to my mother-in-law."

"Yes—the marchioness. Well, if you need any help, just give me a call."

"Fat old toad," sneered Monty as soon as the doctor had left the room. "He won't offend the marchioness because he's making a pile out of her—his whole practice is down to him being the Coseley family doctor."

"Come with me at the weekend?" Cathy asked, her neat,

slender fingers deftly fastening the pearl buttons at the back of Jamie's blue-smocked romper suit. "I've got to get rid of the old witch and I know the whole family won't even listen to me."

She was correct. The marchioness was disbelieving, then insulted, then stubbornly insistent that nothing could be wrong with Nanny Bunting's methods.

"Why, she brought up the entire family virtually single-handed," she protested.

"And *haven't* they turned out well," said Monty, alight with gleeful sarcasm. The marchioness glared at them but prepared to accept defeat. Apart from Charlie's well-publicized escapades, his elder sister had just abandoned her husband and children and was living in Tangier with a nightclub owner, and the haughty cousin Venetia had been arrested in Spain and charged with smuggling marijuana.

Nanny Bunting went back to Coseley as soon as she was fit, and was dispatched to retirement in one of the estate cottages. The slim new girl replaced her in Cathy's household, and stayed for three months; then Cathy woke up in the middle of the night and found Charlie and the nanny in a frenzied clinch on the staircase. The girl squeaked like a frightened rabbit and bolted half naked downstairs and out the front door in her nightdress, leaving Charlie with her much-laundered gray-white panties in his hand. Cathy then hired Nanny Barbara, who was a little older, with an air of pious respectability, and black hair in a bun which she was always repinning at the nape of her neck. She was Irish, and amusing, full of silly songs and highly colored fairy tales which Cathy enjoyed almost as much as Jamie.

Charlie took no interest at all in these domestic dramas. He considered servants to be a lesser race, unworthy of his attention.

Cathy could tell when he was again pursuing another serious affair, because he abruptly stopped making love to her. This time, however, she felt calm and determined. She had discovered quite a lot about her weak, foolish husband's susceptibilities, and curiously, the more she adored her baby son, the easier it was to be detached about managing his father.

If Charlie's anybody's, he might as well be mine, she told herself, and set off with Monty for a large lingerie shop in Knightsbridge which had the reputation of supplying all the most expensive call girls in town. They bought a black French bra which was a triumph of engineering, a garter belt and stockings.

"Just think," Cathy said, as she admired her reflection over her shoulder in the fitting-room mirror. "A few years ago at school we couldn't wait to give up wearing stockings."

"Well, they're a lot more practical for sex than for playing lacrosse in," Monty sniffed.

The outfit worked on Charlie like a dream. No sooner had Cathy thoughtfully asked him if her stocking seams were straight than he pulled her down on the drawing-room floor and started pulling off her clothes with complete disregard for the servants' sensibilities.

Her next problem was April Hennessy, who came around one afternoon and announced, "Charlie's leaving you, Cathy. He just hasn't got the courage to tell you himself. He loves me, he's always loved me, and it's no good pretending anymore."

"Pretending what, exactly?" Cathy felt a rush of cold rage. She had no pity for anyone who threatened her home and happiness. "Pretending that Charlie's capable of loving anyone, maybe? He may say he loves you, April, he says that to all the girls. I'm his wife, and I'm going to stay his wife."

"Yeah, but you and Charlie are all finished in bed," the older woman snapped. "You don't turn him on, you never did. He says fucking you's like flinging a wet Wellington boot down Oxford Street, since you had the baby."

"Our sex life is fabulous as always, April. And if I were you, I wouldn't start calling *my* body down—have you seen yourself in the mirror lately? Good thing the miniskirt's gone out—your thighs look like waffles from behind." She marched briskly to the bell push and pressed it.

"Miss Hennessy is leaving now," she told the manservant, whose veneer of noninvolvement momentarily cracked with a hearty "*Yes*, my lady!" as he pulled wide the door.

Now that she had the enemy on the run, Cathy's confidence blossomed. A few days later she cunningly stage-managed a royal fuck in the shower with her errant husband, after which they slumped happily to the floor and let the warm water continue coursing over their tingling bodies.

"How was that for you, darling?" she murmured.

"Wonderful."

"Really wonderful?"

"Oh, God, now what?"

"Was it like flinging a wet Welly down Oxford Street, by any chance?"

He laughed. "Thank you, darling. I wish I'd been there."

"Thank you for what?"

"Getting April off my back. That woman's been such a drag. I couldn't get rid of her."

"I believe you—thousands wouldn't." Cathy skipped out of the shower and flipped the control to cold as she went, deluging

Charlie with icy water. As a result, he leaped after her, decided to smack her bottom and they ended up making love again and being an hour late for dinner.

By the time Jamie was an angelic two-year-old, Cathy had grown quite accustomed to the fluctuation of Charlie's libido, and considered herself well in control of the situation. Lady Davina concurred.

"He's bewitched, the dear boy, simply bewitched," she exulted, watching Charlie cavort around the dance floor at one of her increasingly ambitious charity balls. He was rudely ignoring his partner and blowing kisses to Cathy over her head. "You see how easy it was—all you had to do was keep your head and do exactly as I told you. Men are like puppies, my dear, you simply have to train them. Then they're absolutely *grateful* to you for being firm and keeping them in order. That man's yours for life now, Catherine. Bewitched!"

Cathy smiled in dutiful acknowledgment of her grandmother's praise. In the depths of her heart she now knew the truth about her husband. He was a foolish bag of appetites, the helpless product of overindulgence. She was charmed by him still, but found nothing to respect in him. Cathy would not admit it to herself, but she was struggling to stay the way she thought she ought to be, in love with Charlie.

Rupert Lampeter, Charlie's greatest polo crony and the best man at their wedding, had an airy, gray stone house on a headland in Antigua, and they went there in February.

The party was made up of a dozen or so riotous young hedonists, into whose company a middle-aged American lawyer had plainly been dragged by his girlfriend. Lisa was sixteen, but looked about twelve, even when sunbathing in a tiny leather cache-sexe on a thong, which was all she wore during the daylight hours. Her breasts were tiny little brown buds, and her long brown hair fell straight and smooth to her buttocks. She was sweet, clever and adorable, full of games for whiling away the heavy hours of leisure. Her family were apparently wealthy, even by Texas standards.

They were scuba diving in the next cove when the lawyer, a protruding belly under his mask and air tank, swam up to Cathy in the confusing blue world below the waves and gestured that he wanted to show her something. They finned away from the others, and he led her to an immense fan coral which was certainly worth the trip. Cathy mimed her appreciation, but sensed other business. When they swam back and surfaced, he had led her to a different cove, and the beach was empty.

"Let's go ashore and get our bearings—we could swim around

out there all day,'' he suggested, and they waded in and stripped off their gear. Then he suddenly pushed her down clumsily on the sand and started kissing her.

"Hey, stop it!" Cathy protested, scrambling away. "What on earth do you think you're doing? That's my husband I'm with, you know."

"And that's my date he's banging hell out of every time I let her out of my sight, so why don't we even up the score a little?" He looked at her with hard bright gray eyes, a lock of dark hair plastered across his high forehead.

"What, Lisa?"

"Who else? You mean you didn't know?"

"No, of course I didn't know." She felt angry and humiliated.

"Hey—don't be offended. Lisa told me that he told her that you have kind of an open marriage, so I thought . . .''

"Well, we don't. Open on Charlie's side, maybe. I just don't think it's very important, that's all. Lots of husbands play around.''

"Yeah, lots of them play around with Lisa, too. She's the nearest thing to a nymphomaniac I've ever met. Got started when she was twelve, she told me. Can you beat that?"

Cathy, unused to the values of sexual sensation seekers, gave him a chilling glance. "No—and I wouldn't want to. Now I'm going back—are you coming or not?"

Ignoring Charlie's new attraction in the claustrophobic atmosphere of the holiday was very hard. Lisa sat topless at lunch, munching vast slices of watermelon and letting the juice drip onto her bare buds until Charlie could not resist leaning over to lick it off. If he went swimming, she went swimming, and what they were doing in the water was obvious to everyone on the beach. Her vivacious conversation turned into a series of private, sexy jokes which she shared with Charlie.

On the last evening, Charlie told his wife. "I'm not coming back with you, Cathy. I'm going to Dallas to stay with Lisa for a while.''

"Be good," she told him sarcastically.

In London, the days dragged on and on.

"Why do I feel so tired all the time?" she asked Monty, examining her face in the brightly lit mirror in her dressing room and noticing the telltale shadows under her eyes and the barely visible crease of a wrinkle in the tanned skin of her cheek.

"You're worrying about Charlie, that's all. . . ." Monty led her sister firmly away from the looking glass. "You'll get him back, Cathy, you always did before. You're stronger than he is, he *needs* you."

PEARLS

Cathy sat down heavily on the end of the bed. "Another fight, another campaign to rescue our marriage—that's what I'm tired of, Monty. I'm not strong enough anymore; I just haven't got the stamina to go through it all again." Two large tears crawled down her coppery cheeks.

"Of course you're strong enough—you love him, don't you?"

Slowly, Cathy shook her head and looked up at her sister with despair in the bronze depths of her eyes. "No. If I'm honest I don't think I ever loved him, Monty. Not like you loved Simon, anyway. Charlie was just there, that's all. I was supposed to love him so I talked myself into it. I conned myself, that's all."

Monty sat beside her sister and both were silent. "Love's just one big con all around, if you ask me." Monty looked reflectively at the toes of her pink suede Biba boots. "It's just a game. I don't think I was ever in love with Simon, either."

Cathy jumped up, determined to shake off the gloom that had descended on them like a smothering cloud. "Well, if love's only a game I'm going to win," she vowed, running back to the dressing-room mirror and pulling back her long dark hair. "Do you think I should cut my hair, Monty?"

Next day a letter from Charlie arrived. "I'll be back at the end of the month," she read, "but not to stay, Cathy. I'm sorry, darling, it just hasn't worked out between us. It's better we split now than later on, don't you think?"

She made herself look as beautiful as she could when he arrived, hung on to her poise like grim death and got him into bed with no trouble at all.

"Home Sweet Home," he murmured, patting her mound affectionately before he fell asleep.

But two days later, Lisa arrived to rent a house two streets away and Charlie vanished. He alternated between the two houses for a month, went to Lisa for three months, then returned to Cathy again and bought her a huge collar of diamonds for the heart he had given her when they were courting. He wept like a baby, cursed Lisa, cursed her, went out and got drunk, stayed in and got drunk, started screwing April Hennessy again and behaved so erratically at work that his father sent him on a week's enforced vacation.

Anxiously, Cathy asked her grandmother's advice. "He's just a big baby, remember?" counseled the dowager. "You smile, you're thrilled to see him, you never mention the other woman, you never make a scene—he'll soon get bored with this stupid little girl and come back to you."

Cathy lost weight rapidly, and the elegant sweep of her eyebrows flattened out as tension gave her face a permanent frown.

The rich bloom of her complexion faded and her skin became dry and prone to ugly rashes. Charlie shuttled from Lisa to Cathy for another six weeks, and every day Cathy sank deeper into depression, becoming more and more desperate and less and less confident.

The matter was decided by his mother, the marchioness, who had never ceased to resent Cathy as the first woman to come between herself and her beloved son. "Lisa is a sweet girl, Charlie," she told him, "and she obviously adores you. You owe it to her to do the decent thing, dear. You've made every allowance for Catherine but she simply isn't up to being the sort of wife you need. She can't manage servants—that ridiculous nonsense with Nanny—and she's simply lost in your social circle. We should have expected it, of course, looking at the family."

And so Cathy came back from a shopping trip one afternoon to find another note saying "I'm sorry," and her husband gone. She waited for the inevitable agonized telephone call, but it never came. Instead, a letter from a flashy Mayfair law firm arrived, announcing Charlie's intention to divorce her.

"I can't seem to sleep, but I feel as if I'm ready to drop, I'm so tired." she told the doctor, who gave her some tablets.

"These will help you," he said, handing her a bottle of large white pills, "and these are for the day, in case you need something to keep you going."

She endured another six weeks with nerves as tight as bowstrings. Monty was concerned; she noticed that Cathy's hair was falling out, and she seemed to have no patience with Jamie whereas before nothing the child did irritated his mother. Cathy had become desperately thin, and Monty saw her hand shake as she poured them tea.

"Are you really OK, Big Sister?"

"Of course I'm OK. Why does everyone keep asking me that?"

Monty realized she would need to be cautious. "What do you weigh now?"

"Don't nag, please, Monty. I'll never get Charlie back if I lose my figure."

"But your ribs are sticking out." Above the deep plunge of her raspberry cashmere sweater, Cathy's collarbones were sharp as knives.

"I just can't eat very much, that's all. Food makes me sick."

"Have you told the doctor?"

"No—I only see him for the pills. I'll get well when Charlie comes back, I know I will." She saw the warning look in her sister's wide black eyes. "I'll get him, Monty, in the end. I know it. He's seeing that whore April again. Lisa won't be able to take it when he starts his old tricks."

"How do you know he's seeing April?" Monty demanded.

"I just know," Cathy replied, for an instant hearing in her tone the note of crazy dismissal that was characteristic of their mother. She had no intention of confiding to her sister that she sometimes sat in her car outside the house where Charlie and Lisa were living, spending a whole night watching the lights go on and off in the windows and waiting to see if Charlie would come in or go out.

At last the gossip columns discovered that the Earl and Countess of Laxford were living apart, and Cathy saw her name in the newspapers, and pictures of herself alone and of Charlie with Lisa. She stared at the newspaper for half an hour, realizing that she had to accept the failure of her marriage.

"Nanny Barbara," Cathy said the next day, "why not take Jamie down to the country for a week? His grandparents haven't seen him for ages. I can't go, I've got something on in London."

She gave the servants the whole week off, and on Friday went to Elizabeth Arden for a top-to-toe beauty treatment. Back in the empty house, she locked the doors, then went to her dressing room and put on her wedding dress, which lay pristine in white tissue paper, with all its accessories, in a special mahogany chest.

"Alcohol," she said, "I must drink something." She went down to the pantry and found a bottle of champagne, and drew the cork as her father had taught her. Then she went back upstairs.

At three o'clock on the following Monday morning Monty braced herself against the bulk of The Juice's amplifier as Simon swung their van into Sloane Square. The band had played a gig in a distant northern suburb. In London, The Juice was very much a Monday night band, not big enough to justify the Friday or Saturday gigs, but with enough following to half fill a bar on a slack evening.

They were all running on speed, and they had a bottle of vodka which they were drinking neat. Rick handed it back to Monty from his seat in the front.

"No, thanks." Monty passed the bottle on to Cy.

Rick looked at her at length in the fitful light from the street-lamps. Monty had been quiet all evening, and had played mechanically, which was unusual. Whenever she was upset, she always shook it off when the band went onstage. "What's up with you tonight?" he asked her.

"Nothing."

"C'mon—what's on your mind? You've hardly said a word all evening."

With a squeal of tires, Simon hauled the van out of the square and into King's Road. "It's her sister—Monty reckons she's cracking up because her old man's run off with some Lolita. She's been moping like a wet hen for days."

"I have not," snapped Monty, angry that Simon should intrude on the special bond that she and Cathy shared.

"Don't she live around here, in one of them posh houses?" demanded Rick, taking back the depleted vodka bottle for a final swig.

"We'll pass by any minute," Monty told him, very grateful that Rick at least was taking her anxiety seriously.

"Drive past the house," Rick ordered Simon suddenly. "We can't have Monty getting hung up like this. Let's check things out."

"Don't be daft, it's the middle of the night." Simon held his watch out for Rick to see the time.

"Don't matter—we won't stop unless there's lights on. If it's all dark we'll drive on, no harm done. This is it, ain't it, love?"

Gratefully, Monty said yes, and Simon, unwilling to appear callous or to provoke an argument, slowed the van and turned into the narrow side street that led into Royal Avenue. As soon as they turned the corner they saw Cathy's house with every window ablaze with light. Alarmed, all five of them tumbled out of the vehicle and stood gazing at the bright facade while Monty pressed the bell.

"No answer."

"Gone away for the weekend, has she?"

"She should be back by now; she's always back by Sunday night. Anyway, the housekeeper should be there."

Simon strode up the steps and opened the brass letter box to peer inside. "There are letters on the mat—no one has picked up the mail."

Simon, Rick and Monty went down into the basement, where Rick suddenly assumed command. He rattled the handle of the servants' door, which was also locked, then hammered the panels with authority, calling out "Anybody there? Anybody home?" A gust of raw spring wind blew some dead leaves into the basement area, but there was no sound from the house.

"It's completely deserted."

"On holiday, maybe?"

"There's always someone here. And if they were all away, they'd pull the burglar grille down." Monty looked toward Rick for help, full of fearful premonitions about her sister.

"Good thing housebreaking was part of my education, innit?" In the orange glow of the streetlights Rick smiled at her with sympathy. Then he turned and after aiming a careful kick at the glass panel of the basement door, reached through the shards and released the locks.

With Monty leading, and Rick and Simon behind her, they made their way through the orderly house. In the drawing room Monty pulled the curtains across the naked windows. Simon picked the letters off the doormat and piled them on the marble console in the hallway. Rick kept his eyes intently ahead, refusing to seem impressed by the opulence around him.

In silence they climbed the staircase and Monty pushed open the door of the master bedroom. At once she recognized her sister's wedding dress, apparently flung across the bed. Then she saw Cathy, and instinctively clutched Rick's arm as she stepped back, shocked.

"Oh, my God—look at her." Inside the crushed silken folds of the dress, Cathy lay half on the bed and half on the floor, her left leg twisted beneath her, her face already bluish where the skin was most delicate. At the same instant Monty and Rick leaped forward to the inert body.

"Like Marilyn Monroe," said Simon, pointing to the blue patches on Cathy's skin.

"No." Monty felt her sister's wrist, Rick's strong fingers probed the neck. There it was—a pulse, the merest flutter, but it was there. "Not like Marilyn Monroe—*she's* still alive."

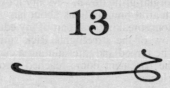

13

ALL SINGAPORE CALLED PHILIPPE'S ESTABLISHMENT SIMPLY "the French club." It had an air of prosperous comfort and an impersonal ambiance which appealed to Singapore's new elite. They were young, hedonistic and cosmopolitan; the war was already a childhood memory, something their parents used to reproach them for their brazen materialism.

Apart from the exotic beauty of the women who worked there, the French club could have been situated in any big city in the world. At the end of the first year, the club had been so successful that Philippe decided to buy the premises next door, combine the two buildings into one complex, and redecorate. Instead of the old, garish plastic, he introduced heavy sofas upholstered in dark-red leather, red café curtains dividing the seating into intimate clusters, air conditioning and brass lamps with green shades which cast pools of soft light. Instantly the rooms acquired something of the atmosphere of a European club, but with a bright, contemporary edge that proclaimed a new order.

It proved a little too sophisticated for the taste of the older colonial types, who did not care to drink their liquor in the company of Malay princelings or the sons of the Chinese tycoon class, however luxurious the surroundings. For the city's wealthy newcomers, who behaved as if Singapore were the South of France and roared through the new suburbs in open roadsters, it was a perfectly congenial environment.

Ayeshah began to emulate the rich Europeans, who wore white

clothes to give themselves the illusion of coolness in the stifling tropical climate. She bought Western fashion magazines at the big hotels, and from them sketched simple fitted white dresses which she had made by a Chinese dressmaker. She wore her glossy black hair in a fashionable chignon with a single starlike frangipani flower, which was the only visible reminder to her clientele that they were still in the East.

On the mainland the Communists attacked the British with increasing ferocity. Shortly after Philippe opened his club, the British High Commissioner was killed in an ambush on a mountain road as he was being driven in his Rolls-Royce to a hill station for the weekend. After that, more and more British soldiers flooded into Singapore, and British statesmen followed them to begin negotiatiating independence for the new state of Malaya.

In the beginning, the Communist war on the mainland was far away and good for their business, but by 1952 the city itself was full of tension and armed revolutionaries had been flushed out of the villages in the rural parts of Singapore island. In the daytime there were frequent angry demonstrations, and when darkness fell to offer cover to an assassin, there were killings in the city's thronged alleys. The Malay police in armored cars patrolled the streets at night, futilely chasing small groups of rioters who vanished into the deep darkness.

The atmosphere of violence and instability seemed to make everyone want to live for the instant and grab what they could while the going was good. Once again, the port at the crossroads of the world's trade pandered to the momentary perversions of its visitors. Old women sidled through the native quarters with children to sell. Bugis Street became a brightly lit gully of vice, through which swooped flocks of gaudy transvestites, shrieking in raucous flirtation with the crowds of seamen.

All this Philippe observed with amused detachment. "I've seen it all before," he told Ayeshah. "Saigon is the same way. Every city gets rotten when an army moves in. And they will never defeat the Communists; they have the jungle on their side."

Ayeshah sensed the changes, but did not see them because she rarely left the club to set foot in the streets at night; Philippe had rented a handsome square bungalow for them in a new suburb, and when they drove home in the pale hours before dawn few people were about. Moreover, she was fiercely single-minded, and no external event concerned her until it affected the flow of clients past her desk.

News of the trouble outside the club's handsome studded doors came to her from Philippe, who spent more and more time at the opium parlor or with his friends, leaving her in charge.

"People come here to see you, not me," he told her, when she suggested he should spend more time in his club. "You are a great beauty, *ma chère*, but I am just a *chop chung kwai* and not important." *Chop chung kwai* was the Cantonese expression for a Eurasian; it's literal meaning was "mixed-up devil."

There was resentment in what Philippe had said, and in the way he pressed Ayeshah to accept the invitations their regular clients would sometimes extend to her to swim at the Tanglin Club or watch the Maharajah of Jaipur's polo team play the British army officers. With a white man to escort her, she was accepted at these exclusive occasions, where he would have been shunned as a half-caste, even though he had been born in Paris, the most sophisticated city in the world.

Philippe was instantly conspicuous in colonial society. His navy-blue blazer jackets, double-breasted and brass-buttoned, fitted his narrow hips too well and their color was slightly too bright; his clothes alone marked him like a brand. Nothing could disguise the Oriental cast of his features, and in his lean, wedge-shaped face, his narrow eyes, triangular like those of a Byzantine icon, gleamed with the predatory intelligence of a man who lived by his wits.

The echelon into which Philippe had a guaranteed entrée was the topmost social stratum of the drug trade, and it was this business that had bought them their bungalow, their servants and the shining Austin Healey sports car which darted like a dark-green dragonfly around the city. Ayeshah, who had always considered opium the exclusive vice of elderly or simpleminded Chinese, was surprised when she discovered that Philippe was procuring the drug for the fast-living, wealthy socialites of every race. He also dealt in cocaine, which was smuggled into Singapore aboard the huge, rusty freighters that were registered in Panama and brought South American beef to the Orient. His merchandise was of high quality, and his service discreet. In a business in which no one could be trusted, Philippe was a safer contact than most, because he was too much of a snob to exploit his customers. He wanted their social patronage more than their money.

He called his customers his friends, and they in turn treated Philippe with as much generosity as they could without drawing attention to their relationship. Ayeshah, at first awestruck by the glamour of this hedonistic cadre, clung to his arm at garden fetes and cocktail parties. Soon she was able to see the pleasure-seekers as the colonial elite saw them—wealthy, dissipated and of no consequence. Nevertheless, she was fascinated by their expertise in frivolity. Avid for luxury, she learned to tell natural pearls from dyed, modern jade from antique, Iranian caviar from Russian and a French seam sewn in Paris from a French seam sewn in Hong Kong. Philippe enjoyed developing her taste, but her hunger for fine things had a desperate eagerness that puzzled him.

In their third year he decided to observe the French custom of a *fermature annuelle*, and closed the club in August. He took Ayeshah to an island which had been put at his disposal by a Malay princeling, a pear-shaped atoll some three hours by launch from a small port on the southeast coast of the peninsula.

Ayeshah was instantly enchanted by this miniature kingdom. They had the run of a tiny pink stone palace, a little yacht, glorious gardens, brilliant white coral beaches, stables and a private zoo. The bathrooms, opulently paneled in yellowish marble with massive gold fitments, pleased her most.

"Whatever are you doing?" he asked her, discovering her seated on the edge of the tub on their first day, her olive-skinned shoulders smooth and bare above the thick, white towel. She had been in the bathroom for most of the morning.

"I'm thinking," she said, with her catlike semi-smile, leaning back to trail her fingers in the fragrant, foamy water. She looked satisfied, which was unusual.

"What about?"

"About washing in the river," she replied.

"When did *you* ever wash in a river?" He sat beside her, full of curiosity. "Come, tell me. I want to know."

"It isn't important." He was irritated. She never talked to him about her past life, her family, or her home; at first, Philippe thought this was merely delightful naïve reticence; but now, after a year, he knew Ayeshah was hiding something from him, a secret so large that it was present in her mind all the time, casting a shadow over all her actions.

"It must be something important if you have been thinking about it in here for the whole morning. Why are you always so secretive? I'm tired of all this mystery. I want to know who she really is, this lovely woman of mine with eyes like a cat. Maybe I've taken up with a beautiful ghost." He smiled, teasing her and stroking the back of her neck lightly with his long ivory fingers.

She shook her head obstinately and stood up. "I am who I am now. It's none of your business, my life before I met you. I have put it away in a box because I can do nothing about it, and if I ever open that box and look, it will be because it is time for me to do something, and then . . . you will see. You will not like me then." She turned toward him, pulling the towel with its massive red monogram more tightly around her. "I'm not interested in the past, Philippe. I want the future, and I want it to be like this." She looked around the opulent room, full of precious ornaments, kept sweet-smelling and spotless by diligent servants; she paused to admire herself in the pink-glass mirror, in which her complexion appeared rose-beige like that of a white woman.

He moved forward to embrace her, but halted. Ayeshah never needed embraces. She never refused them, or showed any distaste, but after months of the most skillful loving of which Philippe was capable, he sensed that while her body responded, her soul was inert. The warmth of her passion in his arms had exactly the same quality as the professional friendliness with which she greeted the club's customers.

This knowledge had bred bitterness in Philippe, which he had focused elsewhere, on his equivocal racial status. He had begun to reject the city that saw him as irredeemably inferior because of his mixed blood and had started to talk about Singapore as if it were merely a provincial port in a country whose capital was Paris.

"When we've got enough money in the bank, this lousy town won't see us for dust," he promised her. "These people are nothing—*nothing.*" He waved his arm around the steamy cool of the bathroom, indicating its owner, his tin-pot court and beyond him their entire acquaintance, British and Asiatic. "They think they are the most important people in the world but they are just barbarians in smart clothes. When you meet *tout le Paris*, then you will know what I'm talking about. In Paris, they wouldn't let a man like that clean their shoes, you'll see."

"When?" she asked him at once. He was taken aback.

"As soon as we've got enough money."

"Haven't we got enough now?" Her eyes were hard; Ayeshah knew that the bank account stood at over ten thousand dollars, and in addition Philippe had a box of large gold coins buried under the bungalow.

Philippe agreed to write to his two brothers, full-blooded Vietnamese who ran a small restaurant on the Left Bank. A few weeks later they wrote back, full of enthusiasm for his arrival but quoting astronomical prices for the kind of premises he needed. Ayeshah frowned and said nothing. She never nagged him, but her will was like a demon's curse which compelled his obedience.

The day after the letter came from Paris, Singapore city was almost brought to a standstill by the largest anti-British demonstration to date, which swiftly degenerated into a full-scale riot. By nightfall, there were rumors that more than fifteen Europeans had been killed, but the announcements on Radio Malaya referred only to minor disturbances; the area around the club was quiet and people were going about their business as usual.

"Shall I open up?" Ali, the barman, asked Philippe as darkness enveloped the teeming streets. Philippe considered the question, smoothing down his pomaded hair with the palm of his hand. From the next room came some soft saxophone phrases and the soft chink of maracas as the Filipino band took their seats.

"Why not? It's quiet enough around here; there won't be any trouble. There's no curfew, is there? Why should we lose business because there was a riot this morning? Who's fighting, anyway?" He took a sip of the tepid black coffee which he always drank throughout the early evening.

"The Malays, they're enraged over this business of the Dutch girl." Ali flicked imaginary specks of dust from the gleaming array of bottles on the glass shelves. "The case was in the Supreme Court this morning, and that's where the crowd gathered first."

"What Dutch girl?"

"Who cares?" Ayeshah was dismissive. "It's only some boring political nonsense, nothing to do with us—until they're outside throwing stones through our windows."

She was wearing a tight strapless dress of gathered white silk, and sat gracefully on a tall stool in front of the bar, a black high-heeled shoe swinging from the toes of one foot. On the bar in front of her was a day-old copy of the *Straits Times*, which she had been half-heartedly trying to read.

"It had nothing to do with politics until the authorities screwed things up. Look, here she is," Ali turned the newspaper over and pointed to a picture of a blond girl with an open, sun-reddened face. "The famous Nadya. She was born of Dutch parents who abandoned her when the Japanese invaded, and a Malay family brought her up as a Muslim and married her to a Malay schoolteacher—but now her parents have decided they want her back and have brought a petition in the courts."

Ayeshah suddenly looked interested and pulled the newspaper toward her. "Can you do that under the British law—claim back children if they have been raised by someone else?" Her wide, smooth forehead furrowed as she struggled to read the type.

Ali smiled, proud as always to show off his education. "Certainly. It has to be a legal adoption with all the right papers and formalities, otherwise it is null and void and the child still belongs to the natural parents. Read it for yourself—there,'' and he pointed to the end of the newspaper article. Ayeshah gave him a sulky look; she still could not read English fluently.

Philippe drained his coffee cup. "It doesn't sound like much of an excuse for a battle to me. There must be a dozen cases like this every year in this crazy place.''

"There wouldn't have been any trouble if the British had not insulted the Malay leaders, who have now taken the side of the foster parents and are stirring up the whole community. There was a very big crowd this morning and the Gurkha soldiers came to break it up, and then there was shooting. . . .'' Ali shrugged again. "I heard that twenty or thirty people have been killed at least.''

Philippe reached for his creamy panama hat. "Nonsense. We didn't see any sign of any trouble on our way here; by now everyone will have gone home.''

Ayeshah quickly put down the newspaper and shook her head. "The worst fighting is always at night. Once it gets dark, people think they can get away with anything, and all the hooligans and looters come out to join in. Let's not open tonight, Philippe. We won't be very busy on a Monday, anyway. Better to lose one evening's business than get involved in any trouble, don't you think?''

He shook his head, glancing down the reservations list by the telephone. "There's a big party booked in; we can't possibly put them off. Once you do that to people they're angry with you and they never come back. And people stop coming to a club if they are never sure if it's going to be open or not.'' He stretched an arm behind the bar and began to snap on the lights. "Business as usual. I'll be back later, *ma chère.*''

Anxiously Ayeshah watched him leave by the back entrance, while Ali went to open the steel gates at the front. She knew Philippe was paying his usual evening visit to the opium parlor and would return in an hour or so in a bland good humor. The place was in the middle of the Chinese quarter, but to reach it Philippe would have to pass close to the mosque by North Bridge Road; if Ali was right, the mosque would still be surrounded by crowds listening to speeches broadcast from the loudspeakers.

She was reassured a few hours later, when the club was full of chattering, dancing people and the street outside seemed to have every sports car in Singapore parked in it. Beyond the line of gleaming jaguars and MGs were half a dozen limousines and a small knot of white-uniformed drivers who stood smoking cigarettes at the street corner.

PEARLS

The event that had filled the club so early in the week was the birthday party of an English girl who was the daughter of a senior British army officer. Ayeshah, temporarily idle but poised like a swallow at the corner of the reception desk, watched the girl as she sat demurely between the imposing figure of her father in his dress uniform and her mother in a fluttering yellow silk gown. She was an ideal European beauty, with golden hair sleek under a velvet headband and a small pink mouth drooping in a pout of boredom.

The soothing hum of conversation and the unctuous flow of the dance music obscured the noise from the street until a sudden squeal of tires penetrated from outside. Two army drivers burst through the club door with pistols in their hands, and an instant later Ayeshah's sharp eyes saw three or four Chinese clients vanish behind the bar, making for the back door.

"Get the shutters down!" one of the drivers ordered. "There's two hundred people at the end of the road!"

The band faltered into silence and one or two musicians surreptitiously put their instruments into their cases. The few remaining Asian clients made for the back door, and Ayeshah saw some of her girls move sinuously toward the toilets, clutching their purses.

One or two couples continued dancing, but the rest shamefacedly quit the floor. There was an air of suppressed panic, and Ayeshah heard the clamor of angry voices growing louder as the mob approached in the street outside. Ali ran back through the door; he had succeeded in running down the steel shutters over the windows, but there was no protection for the door. The panels, thin wood under their covering of buttoned, wine-red, imitation leather, soon began to shudder, pounded by boots and sticks.

"Better get down, everybody," the British officer commanded in an uneasy tone. The rest of the party hesitated. Four sharp pistol shots sounded from the clamoring crowd outside and bullets tore through the door, leaving jagged holes ripped in the fabric. The English rose gave a shriek of panic and her mother pulled her down below the edge of their table.

"Everybody under the tables—for heaven's sake, get down!" her father shouted again, and this time everyone obeyed. The tall white figure of the British officer stood up. "Keep calm, everybody. There's nothing to worry about. Just a little local disturbance."

He signed to the bandleader to continue playing and the music began again, although it sounded thin and uneven because some of the musicians had also left.

Ayeshah crouched behind her desk with one of the uniformed army drivers, who drew his gun from the burnished leather holster at his belt. Outside in the street she heard a violent argument break out in the crowd. A group chanted ''Kill the British'' over and over again in Arabic, their voices harsh with fanatical hatred. There was a violent rattling noise and she realized that the crowd was trying to tear down the metal shutters protecting the windows.

''The shutters! They're trying to pull down the shutters!'' Desperately she turned to the man beside her, her heart leaping with terror inside her chest. ''Shoot back! Stop them! They'll pull the whole wall down!''

The driver raised himself awkwardly so that he was half leaning against the desk, able to take aim at the window. The crowd gave a roar of triumph as one sheet of hinged metal slats gave way and crashed to the pavement, and the man fired a shot into the air. He was a sturdy corporal in his thirties, whose skin was leathery from the tropic sun; his light blue eyes were unwavering and his mouth compressed into a lipless slit.

Stones began to thud on the walls, there was a crash of glass as the window shattered and she saw the men's contorted faces as they began to smash their entry into the club. The pistol was fired again outside and the men at the back of the crowd screamed ''Kill! Kill! Kill!'' The driver fired steadily at the window and hit a man who was already halfway across the windowsill. He fell back with a yell, blood spurting across the floor from a wound in his neck.

While the driver was reloading, Ayeshah heard another disturbance behind her, and turned to see a stream of Malay police in khaki and black running out from behind the bar, their rifles held smartly ready for action. ''Thank heaven, thank heaven!'' she stammered over and over again. ''Thank heaven you got here before they broke in. They're mad! They want to kill everybody!''

The leading constable ignored her, dragged her back from the entry area and took cover behind her desk before opening fire. The rioters fell back in panic, yelling abuse and climbing over each other as they fled down the street.

Then the club was crammed with police and soldiers, orders were shouted and vehicles began to roar up to the splintered door. Within a few minutes all the Europeans had climbed into the police cars or their own vehicles and left, most without even settling their bills.

As the last four police climbed into their jeep and drove away, Ayeshah looked around the club in bitter amazement. None of the officials had taken the slightest notice of her, or of any of the Asiatics in the club. The safety of the Europeans was their sole concern. In their rush to leave, the clients had overturned tables and smashed glasses. The floor was smeared with blood. The door and window were shattered, the protective shutter lay uselessly outside where it had been trampled and she could hear the roar of the mob as they continued fighting a few streets away.

Without waiting to be told, Ali and the bandleader went out to see if the shutter could be fixed, but the stout metal slats had been buckled and the steel fittings bolted to the wall outside were hopelessly twisted.

"We must close the building up somehow," Ayeshah wailed, feeling close to tears as she stood in the wrecked doorway. "There's nothing to stop them coming back and burning the place down."

At the end of the street she saw a familiar slender figure in a pale suit, his panama hat in his hand.

"Philippe! You're all right! Darling, what are we going to do, the place has been absolutely destroyed, they've torn down the shutters. . . ." She paused, realizing as he sauntered toward her that he was insulated by the effect of his drug from any real appreciation of the situation. Philippe had strolled back through the riot-wracked streets with complete lack of concern, no more anxious than if he had been walking down his precious Champs Elysées.

Ayeshah, now that she had no immediate cause for fear, was equally without emotion. A woman with less bedrock hatred in her heart would have been dismayed, resentful or panic-stricken; instead, she was calmly practical.

"Ali—go down to Victoria Street and pull some planks off that building site. You know, where they're working on that old bombed building. Not bamboos; we need good solid wood to nail up the front here. No one will stop you in all this chaos—take a couple of boys from the band with you. Philippe, darling"—she walked forward to greet him and took his arm with a managing air—"go and get the car; then as soon as the club is closed up safely we can go home."

But the Austin Healey, which Philippe had prudently parked in a side alley, had been rolled onto its side and set alight and was now nothing but a burned-out shell. This event succeeded in penetrating Philippe's detachment.

"They knew! They must have known my car—everyone in Singapore knows my car! The bastards!" He stood and trembled beside the charred wreck, and for a moment Ayeshah thought he was going to weep.

The next day Philippe willingly withdrew all their money from the bank, bought a money belt for his gold and purchased their passage to Marseilles aboard an Italian liner.

Ayeshah secretly made an appointment with a lawyer. He was a sharp young Anglo-Indian, the junior partner in a practice that occupied a floor in a new eight-story building on Victoria Street, and his eager interest faded rapidly as she explained what she wanted to do.

"Where is this man now?" he asked her, pulling at the cuffs of his white nylon shirt to hide his awkwardness.

"He has returned to England."

The young man shook his head regretfully. "Not good. You see, in the case of the Dutch girl, Nadya, the adoptive parents had the support of their own people in their own country. That was very important in determining the outcome of the proceedings. The judiciary is not as politically independent as the British always pretend. Now that this man is in his own country, he also will have this kind of support on his side."

She leaned forward, resting her arms on his gray steel desk, oblivious of the film of dust that immediately marked her white piqué jacket. "So what do you think is the best thing for me to do?"

"It is very good that you are going to Europe, because you will undoubtedly be best advised to pursue the case in London itself. But you will need a lot of money, a good social position, influence. . . ." He waved his long-fingered hands, indicating that there was no limit to what she would need to succeed in her aims. "I am sorry to be so pessimistic, but if this man is in the position you describe, your claim will threaten to overturn his entire life, so naturally he will fight you with every weapon he can use."

Paris terrified Ayeshah, in a manner of which Singapore had not been capable. The cold, clammy air at once withered her courage. Kilometer after kilometer of macadamed streets, extending farther than the eye could see, awed her with the arrogance of their conception. The vast spaces of the Étoile, the Place de la Concorde and the area around the Eiffel Tower made her feel cowed.

She immediately had a sense of the overweening pride of the French, their infatuation with the glory of their own creations and their total contempt for all foreign modes of civilization. At the moment of her arrival, the great iron arches of the railway station made her aware that the race who inhabited this land had no fear of natural forces, and saw them only as energy to be harnessed by their omnipotent intellects.

Philippe had taught her a few phrases in French, but the jabber of talk in the streets was incomprehensible. Worse was the dismissive arrogance with which strangers greeted her attempts to talk to them. The French gave shorter shrift to the disadvantaged than even the Chinese did.

They lodged first in an apartment of four crowded rooms above the restaurant owned by Philippe's brothers, a dilapidated, ageless building standing crookedly in a winding medieval alley in the Latin Quarter. In this space lived seven adults, including Philippe's gray-haired grandmother and a large number of children. The grandmother, sensing at once that Ayeshah's attitude to Philippe was less than ideally loyal and submissive, persecuted her with coldness and shrewish observations about her lack of domestic gifts.

Almost immediately Ayeshah fell ill, with a feverish chest infection the grandmother dismissed as *la grippe*, something all foreigners contracted as soon as they arrived in France. For a few days Ayeshah was smothered with misery and clung pitifully to Philippe's arms, too proud to ask to go back to the East but nevertheless devastated by the strangeness of their new environment.

Her healthy young constitution soon began to fight off the illness, and at once fortune dealt them an ace.

"Superb! What could be better!" Philippe sat on the edge of their ancient mahogany bed where Ayeshah lay huddled under all the covers she dared appropriate. "The old shoe mender next door is retiring and he has offered my brothers his shop. It's perfect—perfect situation, perfect size, an enormous basement . . ."

"What about the price?" she murmured, pulling the blankets around her as she sat up.

"My brother says it's fair, more than fair, very good. The old boy hasn't any idea of the market value of his premises so we're getting a real bargain. We're on our way again, *ma chère.*"

The news acted like a tonic to Ayeshah, who quit her sickbed at once and, dressed in black slacks, woolen stockings and one of Philippe's gray-chequered pullovers, accompanied him next door to look over the dusty cobbler's shop.

"I'm going to fit the whole place out in bamboo," Philippe told her as they stood on the cobble street outside looking at the building. "It'll cost almost nothing and we can create a marvelous Oriental atmosphere for a few hundred francs."

Ayeshah looked at him with surprise. "Can't we make it like our old club, European-style?"

He shook his head. "What you don't understand, little flower, is that a nightclub is a place where people come to perform their dreams. It's a fantasy world where they can take off their inhibitions with their coats at the door. Yes, you must offer comfort, relaxation, luxury—but you must take your client out of his daytime life, so he can become another person for a little while. Here in Paris we have an advantage in being Orientals, and we will have a much greater success by offering our clients a few hours in the mysterious East than in trying to compete with the French style of sophistication."

"But I thought you hated being classed as an Oriental?"

"So I do—but one should never confuse business with emotions. And in Paris it's different—the French despise every other race, the Parisians despise everyone else in the world, but it's nothing personal, you see. They think you are inferior but they concede that it's not your fault. But the British think your belonging to another race is some kind of insult to them."

The club was called Le Bambou. Fitting it out took every centime Philippe had and it did not do well in its first six weeks. It was seldom more than half full, and acquired a forlorn, neglected atmosphere which discouraged new clients.

All the prostitutes in the area, from the streetwalkers who posed half naked in doorways, brazenly tinkling their keys, to the footsore young waitresses in the cheap restaurants who might occasionally accept a customer's invitation to a party for two, were controlled by a Marseilles pimp known as Bastien. This thickset individual, whose thatch of coarse, curly black hair smelled of violet oil, visited Le Bambou soon after it opened.

"Very nice." He pursed his lips, setting down his whiskeysoda and looking around the empty room. "Exotic, a little different—I like it. This Oriental style is the coming thing, I'm told. Don't worry, my friend, be patient. Soon your club will be packed every night."

"We need some glamour about the place." Philippe refilled Bastien's glass with an eagerness that was almost contemptuous. Despite his homily to Ayeshah on the danger of an emotional approach to business, he had taken an instant dislike to this squat satrap of vice who had to be placated before the club could employ hostesses.

"Naturally." Bastien's thick fingers closed around the neck of the siphon. He shot a small quantity of soda into the whiskey and half emptied his glass in a single gulp. He looked around again, as if evaluating the club for the first time. "You've got a

lot of potential here. I predict a great success for you. Why don't
we say five thousand francs? I'll send one of the boys around on
Friday."

"Absolutely impossible." Philippe spoke fast, half swallowing the words. "We don't take that much in a week. I can't do
it."

The Marseillais swallowed the rest of his drink and slipped
awkwardly off the high bamboo bar stool to stand up. "Too
bad." He reached for his black felt hat. "Perhaps business will
improve anyway—give me a call, huh?"

He left, rolling like a sailor as he walked, and the two youths
who had waited by the doorway followed him.

Philippe unconcernedly accepted a loan from his brothers to
keep him in business, while Ayeshah became ferociously determined to make the establishment a success.

"Do you think I'm going to stay in that disgusting apartment
with your grandmother one minute longer than I have to? She
hates me, she never stops criticizing me and I can't stand being
pawed by those smelly children with their snotty noses and sticky
fingers. We've got to get out of there, Philippe, or I shall go
mad."

In the daytime, Ayeshah did nothing but sleep late and lounge
in the window alcove of their room, smoking cigarettes and staring discontentedly out into the street. She watched the straggling
crowd of students, like a tide that washed up and down the
pavement, as they went to and from their classes at the Sorbonne. Every day she was amused by the small groups of tourists, conspicuous with their cameras and foreign clothes, turning
their city maps upside down to try to find their way back to the
Boulevard St.-Michel through the maze of ancient alleys.

"Why don't we offer free entry to students?" she suggested
to Philippe. "That way at least the club will fill up and look
alive."

"Huh. Students haven't got any money to spend. They'll be
nothing but trouble."

"Well, let's try a discount for tourists then."

"How shall we advertise—put up a poster at the airport?"

"Don't be sarcastic, Philippe, it's a good idea. Come on, let
me try. Nothing's worse than this—we're losing more and more
money every week."

He grudgingly agreed to her plan and Ayeshah visited the small
print works where the restaurant menus were done. She ordered
one thousand cards and some small posters. Then she systematically visited every hotel on the Left Bank, from the historic to the
anonymous, and persuaded them to allow her to put a card

in every room. After that, she boldly followed the students into the university annex and pinned posters on every notice board. A tiny figure with shining black hair in a ponytail, wearing an overlarge man's sweater and tight black matador pants, she looked so much like one of the students that no one challenged her.

At once a trickle of hesitant young people came to the club and Ayeshah abandoned her characteristic haughty manner and served them slavishly, allowing couples to sit the whole evening over two Coca-Colas and taking to heart their advice about the kind of music the club should play. Within ten days the word had spread through the Left Bank, and on the second Friday after the posters had gone up the club was crammed with kids.

Both Ayeshah and Philippe retreated behind the bar to help the frenzied barman serve drinks. Philippe grumbled savagely as he ripped the caps off Coca-Cola bottles as fast as he could.

"Your crazy ideas. Why don't you think before rushing out to offer cheap drinks all over town? None of these people will ever come back—all they'll do is tell everyone else that the club's overcrowded and it takes an hour to get served."

"At least we'll make some money tonight," she spat back with defiance, then turned with a gesture of mock helplessness to serve a young Italian.

"Money! Five centimes profit on each drink—you call that money?"

Ayeshah decided to ignore him. It was a long, hot, grueling night, and when it was over Philippe had to admit that it had been profitable. By the end of the week he grudgingly acknowledged that the students, although they seemed to drink nothing but Coke, at least filled the club with pretty young girls with whirling petticoats and nodding ponytails, and were enough of a spectacle to amuse the tourists, who had more money to spend. In addition, some of the students were wealthy, especially the foreign ones, whose families mistakenly regarded the Sorbonne as some kind of finishing school.

"But we can't survive on this kind of business," he warned her. "Where will the students be at vacation time? And how many tourists are there in Paris in the dead of winter, eh?"

"So—we make a bit of money this way, we pay Bastien, he lets us have some girls and we go for the big money. Simple."

Philippe scowled and Ayeshah dropped the subject. She appreciated now that her lover was neither a good businessman nor the kind of personality who could fill a nightclub simply with people who enjoyed an ambiance. Sour complaints were his substitute for enterprise, and opium his response to failure. He had always simply used whatever club he owned as a convenient base for his drug dealing, but in Paris Philippe had no contacts except his family. He could always find opium for his personal needs; he went more and more often to a fetid, top-floor room near the Gare du Nord where a dozen elderly Orientals prepared pipes the traditional way, but most of the drug business was firmly controlled from Marseilles and small operators lived dangerously.

Furthermore, as she grew accustomed to the city that was now her home, Ayeshah realized that Philippe would never achieve the easy access to high society that he had enjoyed in Singapore. The film premieres, the jet-set clubs, the glittering balls, the boxes at Longchamp or at the opera were only something to read about in *Paris-Match*.

"What do you expect?" he demanded when she wistfully remembered cocktails at the Raffles Hotel. "When Singapore was just a fishing village with a handful of pirates across the bay, Paris was the greatest city in the world. It's easy to get to the top in a small town that's still growing, much more difficult in a city that's two thousand years old. Of course we're nothing but small fish in a big pond in Paris. It was your idea to come here, don't forget."

"I want money, and I want a social position," she said, her jaw tight with aggression. "And I don't care how I get them. There must be a way."

"Maybe I want to fly to the moon," he replied, putting on his jacket and preparing to go out. "There must be a way to do that too."

Once more he began to leave the day-to-day running of the establishment to her, but he realized that she was becoming his enemy. Ayeshah's energy was directed to mastering Paris for her own, undeclared, ambitions and she no longer took the trouble to weave the elaborate dream of eroticism with which she had previously enslaved him. The balance of power in their relationship had shifted. She refused him in bed and, instead of forcing her to submit, Philippe shrugged off his defeat and compensated by keeping a tight grip on the bank accounts, limiting her ultimate control of the club.

Ayeshah countered by cheating him. She rigged the till, watered the drinks and falsified delivery notes. Within six months, she had extracted enough money to pay Bastien's premium for several months, and she went to the pimp behind Philippe's back and frankly explained the situation.

"Lucky man to have a sensible woman to manage him, eh? We shall do good business, you and I, don't worry. And don't worry about Philippe, either. He won't give any trouble, I assure you.'' Bastien added the notes she gave him to the fat wad encircled by a rubber band which he kept in his trouser pocket. He was generous to her, sending not only a handful of showy tarts with Italian silk sweaters which clung to their mobile breasts and wings of thick black eyeliner emphasizing their smoldering eyes but a few groups of businessmen who normally frequented more established clubs in the area.

There followed an unpleasant few weeks in which Le Bambou's clientele changed; the prices soared, the tourists disappeared, the students complained, the new clients confused the prettier girl students with the whores and there was a fight almost every night. Bastien, who at once took to calling in for a whiskey-soda at some point every evening, loaned the club two young toughs in mohair suits who stood idly by the doorway, ostentatiously picking their teeth with switchblades, and these disturbances gradually ceased.

Philippe, maddeningly, took the credit for the greater profit which they now made with less effort. ''You see, *ma chère*, if you had done as I advised in the first place we would never have had such a struggle. There's no money in students, you can't rely on tourists—businesspeople are the ones with the money.'' Ayeshah and Bastien exchanged glances across the corner of the bar.

A waiter half ran to the counter and called for six bottles of the best champagne.

''You see.'' Philippe took a satisfied pull at his Gitane and blew pungent smoke into the air. ''Six bottles! That's the way to spend money.''

Ayeshah, snakelike, slipped off her stool and helped the waiter set up the ice buckets and distribute the new gilt-rimmed champagne goblets around the table which was occupied by a large group of prosperous-looking, middle-aged men. Their host seemed to be the youngest of them, a fresh-faced man of Middle Eastern appearance with expensively tailored clothes which made the best of his well-covered figure.

''Who is he?'' she asked Bastien, who was personally acquainted with almost all their new clientele. ''He was in here last week with a couple of Arabs; they were drinking champagne like it was going out of style and the girls told me he gave them a good tip.''

Bastien nodded, a solemn expression on his heavy features. ''Make a note of that face, *ma petite*. He'll be the most powerful man in France one day, if you want my opinion. Hussain

Shahzdeh. He's a fixer. You want it, Hussain can arrange it, whatever it is.''

''I like his style,'' Philippe announced in lordly tones.

''Everybody likes his style,'' observed Bastien, his shrewd black eyes watching Ayeshah as she turned away from Philippe with contempt on her beautiful face.

14

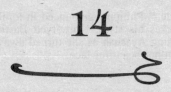

James hitched his sarong casually around his waist and tried to keep his limbs still in the posture of exhaustion appropriate to a laborer slumped on the palm-thatched bamboo bus shelter at the end of his day's work. His watch was rolled into the folds of the sarong around his waist, and he glanced briefly downward to check the time. Thirty seconds to go.

The bus appeared in a cloud of red dust, stopping for the small group of working men standing or squatting around the shelter. James heard the far-off thud of the first explosion as he climbed aboard, and saw, from the rear of the vehicle, a dense cloud of black smoke rising from the dockside in the distance. The first explosion was followed by more, and as the bus left the outskirts of the town behind, the smoke was rising high in the evening sky.

He jumped off the bus as it began to climb the escarpment. Below him the town, the river and the Kuala Lumpur road all lay in a broad valley. The hills on each side rose like waves of foaming green, one upon the other, as far as the eye could see. The light faded rapidly, and by the time he arrived at the camp he was finding his way by torchlight through the screeching darkness.

Next morning the fire in the docks was still burning. Twenty-five Japanese had been killed, two cargo ships damaged and the warehouse full of oil and gasoline destroyed. The fire had taken hold of latex and copra on the dockside and was raging out of control while shipping waited offshore.

There was no elation. Bill, James, Ibrahim and Lee Kuang Leong had all traveled steadily north up the Malayan peninsula for almost three months, planning and carrying out sabotage operations with increasing skill and success, moving on swiftly once each job was completed. Sometimes, when they were lucky enough to steal a boat, they could be dozens of miles away before any damage was done. The Japanese announced larger and larger bounties for the capture of white men, dead or alive, and the Malay police force was almost wholly under their control. The four men were forced to live in temporary camps in the jungle, and so had been weakened by illness and poor food; and in place of the schoolboy enthusiasm of their early days undercover they now shared a sense of living on borrowed time. Their success was their enemy; each strike against the Japanese put them in greater danger.

Cunningly, Bill had turned their fears into fuel for their endeavor. He had instituted a system of evaluating each operation and planning the next which kept the small group focused on their task and minimized the damage to their morale when things went wrong. The relentless pressure of activity left no fingerhold for terror in their minds.

Automatically, the four men began to consider their next target, the highway linking the East Coast with Kuala Lumpur and the west.

The road ran through a succession of mountain gorges where it appeared easy to lay explosives and cause a rockfall. Their stock of explosives, however, was so low that they first needed to find more. Their map showed an area close to Kuala Lumpur where there were two or three quarries, and on this unconfirmed promise they planned to steal dynamite.

"This job will be a real beaut." Bill traced the slender belt of the road across the map with the earpiece of his spectacles. "Everything the Japs have got is in the east and this is the only way across to the west of the peninsula. If that road is cut the Japs will have their hands tied, and all their troops will be held back there in the east or down here in Singapore. If only we could radio the Communists—between us we could give the Japs a hell of a beating before they got the road clear." They had heard that the Chinese Communists had also taken to the jungle and were gathering strength in several hidden camps in Perak. There were said to be several hundred of them, but with few arms and no radio contact with the outside world.

"If we could knock out the airfield at the same time, the Japs would be paralyzed.'' Ibrahim pointed to the only airstrip on the East Coast. ''If they wanted to send reinforcements they would have to come up from Shonan by train.''

''Shonan.'' James pronounced the new Japanese appellation with disdain. ''It won't be Shonan much longer; another six months and we'll be talking about Singapore again.''

There was an optimistic silence as Bill folded the map with care. Suddenly, without a word, James got to his feet and ran a few steps down the track leading out of the camp. His acute hearing had detected footsteps. He came back with a Malay girl about ten years old whom they recognized as the daughter of a village storekeeper who had been supplying them with food, an enchanting little sprite who normally laughed and teased her elders. Now, however, she was silent and lethargic.

''Where's your brother?'' Bill asked her. ''He was supposed to be here this morning—where is he?''

She looked blankly at them with her upturned brown eyes and said nothing. They offered her some food, but she made no move to take it.

''Well, she can't hang about here on her own.'' Bill unfolded his bony legs and stood up. ''One of you must take her back.''

''For Pete's sake, she's only ten. She's a child. What does it matter—she can take care of herself.'' James was eager to move on to the next objective.

''She's our responsibility, old man. Her parents wouldn't let her go anywhere unchaperoned. Maybe there's something wrong. And she could give us away to the Japs. Go on, James, get moving.''

''You don't go—better for me,'' suggested Ibrahim, taking the girl's arm. She gave a shriek and clung to James, shaking with the irrational fright of childhood. So James slowly walked her back to the outskirts of the village, and as they approached the site of the family's home he halted by a screen of shrubs.

Something was indeed wrong. The light wind that stirred the palm fronds above them carried the scent of smoke and scorching. The ground was black. The timber-built village store had been burned to the ground, and the neat stacks of dried fish, sacks of rice and tinned goods set out in front of it were reduced to smoking heaps. The fire had spread to the houses on either side, which were half destroyed; the village seemed deserted.

At the back of the gutted building James saw piles of sheeting on the ground. The air smelled of the charred goods and of something worse. James had never before smelled burnt human flesh but the obscene aroma, like roast meat but oddly sugary, was unmistakable.

He looked down at the child, who was clinging in panic to his leg, and spoke softly in Malay.

"What happened here, Sofiah? You must tell me."

Very slowly she mumbled the reply. First the Kempeitai, the Japanese secret police, who were already more feared than all the ghosts of the jungle together, had come and taken her father. Then the soldiers had come and killed everyone in the house—her mother, her grandmother, and her sister. They had found her brother hiding under the house, tied him to a tree and gathered all the neighbors to watch as they hacked him to death.

Then the Japanese took the cans of kerosene in the store, poured them over the building, and set fire to it.

"They did not find me because I was in my cousin's house," the girl finished, proud of the good luck that had saved her from the tragedy which was too big for her to understand. "The Japanese said it was because we helped the white men. They said the time of the white men was finished now and they would be killed like rats and so will anyone who helps them." James looked carefully at the quiet houses of the hamlet. Curtains of flowered cotton wavered in the breeze at the empty windows. A brown cow tethered under a group of palm trees raised its head and regarded them, flicking flies away with its tail. The stillness and silence of the scene were unnatural; he realized that at his approach the villagers had disappeared into their homes.

"Can you go to your cousin's house now, Sofiah?" She nodded, her lower lip wavering. "Go on then, and don't tell anyone I was here. You're a brave girl, I won't forget you."

She looked up at him with coy curiosity. "What will you do, *tuan*?"

"I don't know. Something. We will take revenge for the death of your family."

She released her hold on him and shook her head, then ran up the dirt road and vanished into the last dwelling.

As James turned to go, a stone fell beside him, then another hit him in the back. He heard angry adult voices raised indoors to stop the stone throwers. He walked steadily onward, suddenly feeling a stranger to himself inside his brown skin. His instincts told him that this was the end of their heroic career as saboteurs, but his conscious mind rejected the knowledge and searched desperately for absolution for the death of the storekeeper and his clan.

At the camp, Ibrahim brought the news that the Japanese had done more than massacre one family. They had executed the dockyard foreman and decimated the labor gangs for failing to inform on the saboteurs. They had launched a senseless attack on a settlement of Chinese smallholders, killing more than a hundred people; the innocent farmers were made to dig their own mass grave; then the entire community was lined up on the edge of the excavation and machine-gunned.

Bill at once ordered the camp to be struck and the traces of it hidden as much as possible.

"We must move out as fast as we can. The Japs will be looking for us with every man they can spare."

"Animals! They'll pay for this, we'll make them pay." James was almost shaking with rage as he began to dig the soft red earth. "When we do the KL road we'll take out half their bloody army."

"Have you gone raving mad?" the Australian's tone was malevolent. James looked at him with surprise, and saw fury in his friend's light-blue eyes.

"We are going to strike back, Bill. For Christ's sake, we can't let them get away with a bloody massacre."

"Why don't you think about it, mate? Or are you thinking with your dick now you've taken off your trousers?"

"What the hell do you mean?"

"God save us—you really don't know what I'm talking about, do you?" He paused as Ibrahim approached them.

"Shall we leave the stores, sir?" He pointed aloft, to the cache of supplies suspended one hundred feet above the forest floor.

"Get them down and break out all the quinine we've got, but leave the food," Bill ordered, and then resumed talking to James in a low fierce voice, not wanting the Malay to hear.

"Now listen, I'm speaking as your commanding officer. There can be no question of endangering the civilian population by any further activities—right? If we attack the KL road, the Japs will torch the town, it's as simple as that."

"Then what the hell are we doing here?"

"We're doing nothing more, *nothing*. The mere fact that we're at large in the country is a danger to the Malayan people. My orders are to escape, and make our way to Ceylon if we can."

"Run away—like all the rest? I won't do it. I won't betray this country." James was flinging spadefuls of earth aside in fury.

"For Christ's sake—if we stay now we might as well bayonet their children ourselves." Bill ran his hands through his hair with exasperation. "Why can't you see that? Which would you rather do—'betray' the people as you call it or fucking murder them?"

James remained silent, standing in the shallow excavation, his eyes cast down. Bill continued in an even lower voice.

"What's the matter with you, James? We're fucked, you can see that. We can't fight anymore. The party's over. Our orders are to quit."

"I know, but . . ." James did not dare continue. He sensed that the lives lost on their account did not weigh as heavily as they should have done with him, and that Bill was outraged by his lack of concern. ". . . it seems too damned cowardly," he finished.

"Ever heard that discretion was the better part of valor?" Bill stood up, relieved the discussion was over. "We'll live to fight another day, that's for sure."

Lee Kuang Leong, their radio operator, finished sweeping the fire's ashes into a banana leaf and tipped the debris into the hole dug by James.

"We take the wireless?" he asked Bill.

"We can't leave it. I grant you it'll slow us down."

"Can make in two parts, I think."

"Do it then—good idea."

In half an hour every trace of their habitation was gone and the ground covered in an innocent mantle of dead leaves and fallen branches. Bill fastened the leather money belt that contained their funds—several thousand dollars—around his waist, rolling his sarong over it to hide it.

"OK. Now my orders are to disband this unit in the event of reprisals against the civilian population. James and I will make our way to Port Swettenham and try to get off the peninsula and away to Ceylon. Any ideas, you two?"

"Better I go to Perak, join the Communist army." Lee spoke without hesitation. "Many camps in jungle. We can impede the Japanese by peaceful ways, just as we attack imperialists before invasion." He smiled, testing their tolerance. The Communists' commitment to controlling the country themselves was something he had frequently explained to the whites.

"Fair enough. Ibrahim?"

The Malay seemed undecided. "I go with him," he said at last. "If I go home, it will be bad for my family. Better to stay in the jungle."

"Right. We'll be traveling the same road for a few days. Best get started then."

James walked at the rear of the small column, feeling full of resentful anger.

As they marched westward, James and Bill barely spoke to each other. The Australian was racked with remorse that their adventure had brought tragedy to innocent people. He remembered their schoolboy excitement with a flood of shame which quenched his spirit and left him vulnerable to a formless despair.

Their physical condition, already debilitated, degenerated further with fearful speed. Within two weeks it was an effort to walk for more than an hour and the thorn scratches which crosshatched their arms and legs healed more and more slowly. Bill, with the weakest constitution, began to develop sores on his shins. They all grew thin and their bones seemed to stick through their skin. Lee Kuang Leong was the most distressed by this decline and began to avoid wounds from the savage jungle foliage with almost girlish hysteria.

The radio, useless since the batteries had died, slowed them down considerably, but Bill would not sanction its abandonment.

"The one thing we can do—the only function we've got left— is intelligence," he said. "As soon as we're among friends we must get the generator rigged somehow."

At first they avoided the villages, making temporary camps in the jungle at night, which only increased their misery. Day after day there was rain, which soaked their clothes, their equipment and every piece of fire material they found. Soon they were lightheaded with hunger and risked sending Ibrahim into a kampong to buy cooked rice. They stood at the roadside in the lashing rain and ate the food hastily from its wrapping of folded banana leaves, too famished to conceal themselves or seek shelter; they had scarcely swallowed more than a handful of grains when a jeep loaded with Malay police roared past, splattering them with mud. With crazy bravado born of physical weakness, James shouted curses after the vehicle.

"The villagers must have called them," Ibrahim said with disgust. "Next time we must choose a kampong with no telephone. They were driving too fast to get a close look at us, thank God."

They turned back into the jungle and traveled away from the danger as fast as they could until nightfall, when they halted, rigged a shelter from a waterproof groundsheet and spread another on the sodden earth below it. The rain was falling harder and faster; since their clothes and packs were already saturated the shelter was small comfort.

"Do you suppose we can eat the rest of the rice?" James asked Bill, looking hungrily at the squashed parcel of food he had taken from his pack.

"Survival training says never keep cooked food in this climate," the Australian replied, curling up his long legs as he sat down. His tone was uncertain.

Lee Kuang Leong screwed up his face and spat into the downpour. "The rice is only cooked a few hours—what harm can it do? I'm going to eat mine." With deft fingers he unfolded the creased leaf and began to gobble the food, and James and Ibrahim copied him at once. Bill paused, silently considering the bad feeling he would engender if he refused to eat and weighing it against the theoretical possibility that the stale food would give him a bellyache. Finally he, too, finished his rice.

In the dead of night they all vomited and lay groaning on the muddy ground while their guts writhed in rejection of the tainted rice. It had begun to ferment during the few hours they had carried it.

"God, it stinks." James inhaled the acrid half-digested mess amid the warm, humus smells of the jungle. "If the Japs had dogs they could sniff us ten miles away."

"At least it's stopped bloody raining," said Bill.

"That's right, old man, keep looking on the bright side." James pulled himself shakily upright on the stump of a fallen tree, then sat down hurriedly as his weak knees buckled.

"One more mistake like that and the Japs won't need to look for us anymore." Bill picked up his spectacles out of the mud, where they had fallen from his shirt pocket. Now he wore them only to look at the map and lived in terror that he would lose or break them.

The four men slumped shivering on the wet ground in the darkness and followed their own thoughts. Bill tried to plan the next day's march from what he remembered of the map, but every train of thought broke like a rotten thread and left his head full of meaningless information. James comforted himself with a reverie of his bed at Bourton, crisp and white with freshly laundered fine linen sheets and cozy from the warming pan. Lee thought of a feast he had enjoyed with his comrades when they heard the news of the Japanese invasion, of the sizzling morsels of pork and duck, the fragrant soups and the mounds of sweet, clean rice which his stomach had accepted with absolute contentment. Ibrahim dreamed of his home and the young wife he had married only a few months earlier, and the pleasure of sitting on the steps of his house in the cool of the evening with his father-in-law, discussing his new job in the district engineer's department while the women cooked the evening meal.

The strident calls of the night insects faded, and they heard nothing but the drips and trickles of water for a while, until the mournful gibbon whoops announced the dawn. Daylight brought new despair. Ibrahim was too weak to take more than a few steps, and James was hardly stronger. Bill ordered a morning's rest and sat apart from the others, desperately trying to order his thoughts. I'm getting too weak to think, he acknowledged to himself. But if I can't get us out of this, we'll just lie down and die right here.

Steam began to rise from the sticky ground and its thick mantle of vegetation as the heat of the day grew stronger. The Chinese, least affected by the rotten rice, paced slowly to and fro under the tree canopy, craning his neck with its prominent Adam's apple as he searched the foliage in vain for a bird, a squirrel, or even a frog—anything that could be killed for food.

Suddenly he halted in front of Bill. "What was the name of that village?" he asked. Bill shook his head to clear it and picked the damp map from his pack. Lee looked intently over his shoulder as he unfolded the tattered document and traced their pitiful progress. The Australian's stained brown finger and the Chinese's spatulate thumb traversed the plan slowly together; then Lee identified a name he evidently knew, and joyfully muttered a stream of curses in his own language.

"Maybe we will be OK," he announced with total certainty. "Here is a house I know." He pointed to a town a few miles farther down the road. "Very rich man, very good comrade. We can ask him help—I think at least he will give us food; maybe he can give us some place to sleep in the dry."

"It'll take you half a day to get there." Bill spoke with dawning hope. "If you leave now you'll make it by the evening."

"I can go?" The Chinese, bred to total obedience to authority, looked inquiringly at his commander. Bill nodded. "Get moving, Lee. I want you back here with all the dry food you can carry by this time tomorrow."

As Lee's squelching footsteps receded into the background noises of the jungle, James glanced weakly at the Australian, who stood gazing pointlessly in the direction of the Chinese's departure.

"He'll clear off," James predicted in a peevish voice. "You're nuts, Bill. We won't see hide or hair of him again."

Bill shrugged, the sharp edges of his shoulder blades clearly visible under his clammy green shirt. "So what? He was fit; if he saves himself, so much the better for him. No sense him sticking with us; you won't do the war effort any more good if an able man dies alongside you, eh?"

The three of them sat in silence, too feeble to argue. Ibrahim was feverish and rolled his head weakly from side to side, muttering to himself. James again conjured up the vibrant dream of his childhood home, and slipped away into the world of his imagination. Bill slept fretfully, fighting the desire to give in and resign himself of the hopelessness of their situation.

In the full heat of the next day they heard crashing footsteps approach; James, a little stronger, stood up and promptly sat down in surprise when he saw Lee tramping toward them, followed by three young Chinese, and with a gleaming native lunch pail in his hand.

"Ha-hah!" the Chinese shouted, his long, hollow-cheeked face radiant with a smile. "You think you not see Lee any more, heh? Happy to be wrong, sir? We will be all safe now, you see. Our friend makes you all welcome in his house."

The three-tiered lunch carrier was full of sticky cakes and dry biscuits, and there were bottles of warm fizzy lemonade to wash them down. Half carrying Ibrahim, they set off for the friendly house, a square mansion full of high-ceilinged rooms and heavy, dark furniture. Their host was a fat Chinese in a brown suit which creased around his spherical belly and strained at its shiny seams.

The man insisted that they sleep in his house, assured them that they would never be betrayed under his roof, and had his servants conduct them to two enormous box beds of carved black wood with embroidered curtains.

When they had washed, slept and regained their strength, he gave them a feast so rich and elaborate that they were stuffed after the first three courses and sat, fighting sleep and feeling uncomfortably bloated, while their host made long speeches reviling the Japanese and praising the valiant Communists and the coming revolution.

"And our allies," Lee Kuang Leong added, raising his bottle of beer to Bill and James, "who fight with us and share our struggle."

Later, when Ibrahim had fallen asleep and their host was swaying slowly and belching to himself, Lee leaned toward them again. "You are surprised I came back for you, heh? You know, we Communists will help you now, and you will help us, but when the Japanese are gone we will be enemies again. Our ambitions are not the same." He took a slow pull at the bottle. "But for this moment we want the same thing, to get the Japanese out."

The food and comfort revived their spirits, and with optimism came a sense of purpose. Their host had a great deal of information. The Japanese had interned thousands of aliens in prison camps all over the country, Indians as well as Europeans.

"I wonder if Gerald got away before the Japs took over Singapore." James stretched out a lazy hand for his half-finished bowl of soup.

"I can't see him going if he had the chance." Awkwardly, Bill picked up a few grains of rice with his chopsticks. "He'll be behind the wire, if he's still alive. What about undercover groups like us?" He turned inquiringly back to their host, who shook his head. Many Europeans who had been left behind the Japanese lines had given up and escaped by boat in the hope of reaching Ceylon, but a few remained. In the north, an Englishman was living with the Temiar aborigines: in the east three English soldiers were hiding in the house of a Malay Christian missionary; two English planters were living at the main Communist camp in Perak supervising weapon training.

"Are they attacking the Japanese?" Bill asked, mentally noting everything the fat man said. He kept a journal of their operations, but took care to record nothing in it that would be of use to the Japanese if he were captured.

"No, I think, no. We have no news. Only the bandits attack the Japanese."

"What bandits?" Eager for action once more, James and Bill gave him their concentrated attention.

"In the hills, at Pulai. Hakka bandits, sons of Kuan-Yin. Very bad men for women, gambling, everything like that, but they are still fighting."

The news reopened the discussion of their next course of action. Lee was intent on joining the main Communist camp, which was now called the 5th Division of the Malayan People's Liberation Army.

"How many are they?" Bill asked the fat man.

"One hundred, maybe two hundred. Not all in one place, but camps in the hills."

James saw that Bill was wavering.

"We're the only men trained and left behind with a working knowledge of native languages," he said slowly. "I'm the only Englishman I know of who can pass in the Asiatic population. Bill, we can't quit. It'd be madness. We're more good here than sweating over maps in Ceylon, eh?"

The Australian took off his spectacles and polished them on the tail of his fraying shirt. "You're right," he agreed at last. "If some of the other blokes can make out, so can we. Orders are clear that we should remain if there's work we can do in safety. Lee"—he turned to the sleepy Chinese—"we're with you." Lee nodded, his eyelids drooping, then he slumped gently sideways. "Now let's figure out a route."

PEARLS

The map, dimpled with the all-pervading damp, stained and falling apart along its creases, was once more spread before them. Bill took their protector's advice.

"Up the Ipoh road are many friends like me," he told them with plump self-satisfaction. "Best you take that road to here." His manicured finger, smooth and almost creaseless like a yellow sausage, stabbed down on to a faint red line on the map. "Then the river. Very easy."

And so it was; with their health restored, they marched easily along the road until they met a convoy of panic-stricken refugees and saw the distant smoke of a Japanese reprisal party which was massacring and burning its way southward down the highway.

They quit the road and tramped east, skirting the *padi* fields and the vast pools of slurry around the tin dredges. Much of this part of Perak was already an industrial wasteland, made gray and featureless by the concentration of open mine workings.

Bill then led them higher into the hills, choosing a route around the edges of rubber plantations where he could, because the going was easier although the risk of betrayal was greater. They saw the familiar sight of gangs of Tamil tappers about their work, oblivious of peace or war, uncaring whether the destination of the white juice yielded by the trees was Osaka or Detroit.

After one dreadful morning spent hacking their way through the dense jungle regrowth, when four hours of back-breaking labor gained them a mere twenty yards, they broke through to the dim, hot, calm of the virgin rain forest and made their way more easily.

In a few days they came to a river bordered by chrome-yellow sandspits, and they bathed in the crystal-clear water with relief. James washed the mud from his sarong and draped it over the great flanged roots of a tree to dry.

It was midday, and the forest was paralyzed by the heat. A profound stillness and silence, the calm of millions of years of undisturbed vegetable life, held them like an enchanter's spell.

"It's so still you think you can hear the trees growing." Bill sat on the bank, cleaning his glasses with the clear river water.

"You're whispering," James whispered back. They grinned at each other.

"You're a good mate, Jim."

"The best you'll get."

"Even if you ain't got a conscience."

"Can't all be perfect, can we?"

"It doesn't even worry you, does it?" Bill had been pondering his friend's peculiar moral deficiency ever since he had argued that they should continue sabotage work in spite of the Japanese reprisals.

"Never thought about it much, to tell you the truth." James was smiling up at the tree's gray trunk, and the small, almost colorless orchid blooming in a fissure of the bark.

"Would you really have carried on and blown the road?" The question was asked in the spirit of bland intellectual curiosity, but it made James uncomfortable.

"I thought that sabotage was what we were supposed to be doing," he grinned at his friend, uncertainty dulling his charm. "I thought it was the right thing to do."

The Australian put away his spectacles and regarded his comrade with genuine concern. James wasn't stupid, and he wasn't wicked. He was an honorable man, in many ways one of the best. But when he was enjoying something he was like a child, not wanting anything to spoil his pleasure, unable to tell right from wrong, utterly selfish. Being a soldier, especially in the role of a daring guerrilla fighter, powerfully titillated James's masculine vanity and blinded him to all other considerations. There was no point in arguing with him, Bill realized. He was enamored of a flawed ideal of manhood, a picture that was all show and violence, with no dimension of responsibility or care. For James, other people were mere objects to be disposed of according to his fancy.

"Well, maybe you'll get another chance with the commies." Bill lodged his spectacles safely in his shirt pocket once more and glanced downstream to where Lee was sitting in the shade rolling a cigarette.

"What do you reckon we'll find up at this camp?" James asked, grateful for the change of subject. He never understood Bill when he got into one of his sermonizing moods.

"I reckon we'll find a couple of dozen peasants who don't know their left foot from their right and a handful of political commissars filling them up with Marx."

"Can we trust them, Bill?"

"We have to trust them or we'll die. But as your commanding officer, my orders are to figure out a way to survive without them as fast as we can."

Another few hours' march led them to a track that had been freshly trodden, and a few hundred yards down it they were challenged by two young Chinese with guns, who brought them into the guerrilla camp at nightfall.

In a large bamboo house where twenty or so men and women were eating their evening meal, they were presented to the leader, Chang Heng, and his wife. He treated them like tiresome underlings barely deserving of his dismissal, and they were taken to another, smaller hut where they found two British men eating with a small group of Malays and one Indian.

"Well, this evens up the odds a bit—good to see you, I'm Robertson, this is Evans." The four men shook hands and Robertson introduced the rest of the party. "This, as you may gather, is the no-chopsticks mess. They've segregated us so our disgusting eating habits don't offend their revolutionary sensitivities. Tea?"

"Where are these running dogs now, without their money and the trappings of imperialist power? Here in the jungle, where all men are equal, see how pathetic the white men appear! Did they not scatter like fowl when the Japanese came? The time of the white men is over!" The speaker waved his fist, his whole arm trembling with tension, and the audience cheered. This was Chin Peng, a slender Chinese with a bad complexion and spectacles, the political commissar for Perak. James regarded him as the most dangerous of all the Communist leaders. He had a scholarly demeanor which automatically won him respect.

Only James understood the speech, and he translated it for the other Europeans, looking at them as he did so. After six months with the Communists they were a shabby spectacle. Bill was a walking skeleton, with a potbelly and a swelling below his prominent ribs—the enlarged spleen of a malaria sufferer. Evans was not with them in the bamboo meeting hut; he was dying rapidly of blackwater fever, the consequence of treating malaria with insufficient quinine. James and Robertson, both thin and half naked, were better off, although Robertson's legs were a mass of suppurating sores. James now wore the money belt, which hung loose around his wasted hips. He did not take it off even to sleep.

There was prolonged cheering at the end of Chin Peng's speech, followed by a commotion at the back of the hut. A white man wearing only brief khaki shorts, a gleaming jungle knife thrust through his black cummerbund, entered the hall, accompanied by six bare-chested Temiar braves. Chung Heng greeted him with respect.

"Noone!" Bill's lifeless eyes strained to see the newcomer. "My God, I hope he's brought us some drugs."

Noone was one of their few links with the outside world. He was a British anthropologist who had been living with the aborigines to study them; he was full of romantic admiration for their mystical, peace-loving ways, and at the onset of the war had opted to live among them, with a Temiar wife. The aborigines loved him as a brother, and in consequence he could move freely through the deep jungle, guided and fed and defended by them.

As soon as the meeting was over, the British gathered around Noone in the no-chopsticks mess. "I've got your quinine." He took a substantial package wrapped in banana leaves from one of his men and dumped it on the floor. "I've got tobacco, though it's only the native stuff. I've got disinfectant, and the boys shot you a bird or two."

They looked hungrily at the two glossy-feathered carcasses. The rations at the camp had dwindled to bad rice and tapioca chips with tiny amounts of sweet potato on special occasions. It sustained life, but afforded little enjoyment.

Jungle game, James said, was heard but not seen. He himself, the best hunter among them, had bagged nothing but a monkey in six months.

"Thanks, mate." Bill slapped Noone on the shoulder and shook hands with the Temiars to show his appreciation. "We've been eating snails for weeks, and there isn't a bamboo shoot round here for miles."

"There's no news on batteries for your wireless, though. Chapman sent you his newsletter." He gave Bill a sheet of schoolbook paper on which the officer in command of the men remaining in Malaya handwrote a jungle newspaper to keep the far-flung band informed. "The worst news isn't in there, though," He gave them cigarettes rolled the Temiar way, in pungent nipa leaves.

"What's that then?"

"Japs are using our men from Changi as slave labor up north. Word is they're dying like flies. I've seen them myself in cattle trucks heading over the Thai border—living skeletons already. A lot with dysentery, too. You three look fat in comparison."

They were so low in body and spirit that they barely reacted to the news. There was, after all, nothing they could do to help their comrades-in-arms.

Only two things were plentiful in the camp—time and talk. The Chinese were increasingly hostile to all the other races, and in the hours that remained after drilling the surly troops and scavenging for food, James, Bill and Ibrahim ran a desultory education scheme among themselves. James taught Cantonese,

Bill taught chess, and Ibrahim instructed them in the Koran—their only printed book.

Next morning the guerrillas put three Malays accused of spying on trial in the large hut. "You'd better be on parade for this," Bill told Noonen. "They stage these trials on the bread-and-circuses idea to give their people something to think about. We tried to boycott the last one on principle, but they attacked us for lack of solidarity. Pretty nasty, the whole affair."

The three accused, two old men and a girl, were charged before a tribunal of the guerrilla leaders and condemned by a succession of prosecutors. At least one of the men was well advanced in his second childhood; the girl was speechless with terror. "They're just peasants," James murmured.

Ibrahim nodded. "Nothing more than rattan cutters. Harmless."

The prosecutors worked themselves into a frenzy of anti-Malay rhetoric. A token defense was woodenly put forward by a young Chinese; then the tribunal made a show of consultation and delivered the verdict of guilty. The three Malays were taken out into the clearing, tied to trees, and bayoneted to death, amid much cheering.

"My job is to mold that rabble into a killing machine," Bill said with contempt. "They're so hostile they've even invented a 'Chinese' way of firing a goddam rifle. It's like a Mad Hatter's Tea Party—except I wouldn't fancy my chances very long after I left the table."

"We can't just sit here starving to death in the middle of a hundred crazy Communists. We've got to get out and do something." James felt as if frustration instead of hunger were eating his guts.

"For Christ's sake, man, what can we do? We've no equipment; hardly any arms, no wireless, not even enough to keep ourselves alive." Illness made Bill's normally reasonable tone sound weak and peevish.

"We've enough quinine now for months. Remember your orders, Bill? Find a way to survive without the Communists."

"So what? We *can't* survive without them. If they think we're betraying them they'll put us on trial like the other poor bastards. We're trapped. We'll just have to sit it out."

James flung his hair out of his eyes in an angry dismissal of this argument.

"What did you do in the war, Daddy? I *sat it out*, dear, in the jungle, and took lessons in Marxist dialectic. For God's sake, man, what's the matter with you?"

"Are you trying to call me yellow, mate?" Feeble rage

gleamed behind Bill's glasses. Ibrahim raised his half-moon eyebrows in amusement.

"Peace, my friends, let the birds do the squawking. What James is trying to tell you, in his heavy-handed European way, is that we have devised a strategy. Do you want to hear it?" Bill nodded grudgingly. "It is this. In my own state, Pahang, we have two very interesting things. One is the Japanese military HQ; two is a very loyal Malay population, and very few Chinese. We know the Sultan has helped Europeans escape to the jungle, and the police are reluctant to pursue the Japanese orders concerning security."

Ibrahim spoke with passion instead of with his normal Malay reserve. "Why do we not leave this place, where, as James says, we can do nothing and our lives may soon be in danger, and travel to Pahang? We should think about organizing a separate Malay resistance. Then we can perhaps recruit agents, start to gather information on the movement of troops and supplies, and pass it back to this camp, maybe to the British headquarters in India?"

Bill thoughtfully fingered his spectacles, which were now wired together where the tiny metal hinges had rusted through. "But we'll be informed on, for sure."

Ibrahim shrugged his bony shoulders; "The jungle will protect us. The jungle is neutral. I am sure the Japanese know the location of this camp, but they know also the difficulties of pursuing guerrillas through this kind of country."

"And just the three of us?"

James nodded. "We haven't talked to the others. Evans can't travel in his condition, and one of us must stay here in case they start sending men in from Ceylon. And I didn't think there was much point in talking to Lee." Their Chinese companion had become one of the most vociferous Communist officers.

They left the next day with Noone and his Temiars, arousing no immediate suspicion in the Chinese who did not believe the white men could live long in the forest. The aborigines guided them through the deep jungle, using their own tracks which were invisible to the untrained eye. In a week they reached the boundary of the state of Pahang.

"Arthur, my darling," wrote Jean Anderson, her pencil crawling slowly across the page of damp-roughened paper, "eighteen years ago today we were married. We never thought, we could never imagine, that we would spend this anniversary in such circumstances as this." She paused, exhausted by the effort, and looked around the room. The European women interned in Sumatra had been moved to an old prison house, a forbidding square building with heavy double doors and iron-barred cells like animal cages around a central courtyard. These enclosures, which were not locked, served as small dormitories and were furnished with bare platforms of bamboo on which the women slept.

The corner of this grim building that was occupied by Jean and Betty had been decorated with flowers by the other women for Jean's anniversary, and the vivid, succulent pinks of olean-ders and the purple-blue of the jungle convolvulus glowed in-congruously against the iron grille.

"Today, I think of you all the time . . ." she continued. It took all her strength to push the pencil across the page. Jean's wiry endurance had been sapped by more than a year of mal-nutrition and disease. Her legs, once skinny, were now bloated so that her ankles were almost obliterated. Her shoes had long ago disintegrated, and when she walked she wore rough wooden clogs, which were now arranged neatly, side by side, at the foot of her sleeping space.

". . . and I renew my vows to you, Arthur. When this night-mare is over we shall begin our married life anew in such a burst of happiness . . ." The pencil was now blunted and she paused again, looking for Betty. To sharpen the pencil, she needed to borrow a knife, and to borrow a knife she needed to walk to the kitchen, and to get up and walk she needed Betty's help.

There was a burst of giggling from across the dank courtyard. Four or five of the younger women, Betty among them, were amusing themselves by dressing a young Cockney girl as a bride, and now their creation was complete. The scrawny figure wore a veil of ragged mosquito net and carried an elaborate bouquet of wilting blooms and leathery leaves. Her dress was fashioned from an old sheet spotted with rust marks, and she skittishly pulled up the skirt to show a garter created from a perished rubber ring and a few shreds of gray lingerie lace.

"Pity about the bandages, Irene," Betty laughed, pointing to the ragged dressings covering the tropical ulcers on the girl's ankles. "Spoil the whole effect."

"Oh, I don't know—who'll be looking at my feet on my wed-ding day?"

"Betty," Jean called out apologetically, and the younger woman turned toward her.

"What is it?" she asked with a trace of irritation. Jean was struggling to get up, and clutching at the iron grille for support, but in her weakened condition she could not manage alone. Reluctantly, Betty left her entertainment and went to assist her friend.

"Can you help me to the kitchen, Betty? I need to get the pencil sharpened."

Betty hesitated. "Must you, Jean? It's pointless writing to Arthur; they'll never let us send the letters. You won't want to read them at the end of the war anyway."

The outlandish bride clattered across to them on her wooden clogs and picked up the two-inch length of pencil with which Jean had been writing. "I'll go for you," she offered cheerfully. "You sit down and take it easy, love. Save your strength."

Although the women were united in a close, almost cozy, alliance against adversity, and the more robust characters among them were at pains to outlaw pettiness and ill-feeling in the prison community, there was no doubt that every woman in the camp detested Betty. Her furtive, deceitful ways, her selfishness, and above all her conspicuous lack of care for the woman who had saved her life profoundly offended their charitable common morality.

Betty, completely obsessed with her own survival, barely noticed their hostility, and they never voiced it. It occasionally puzzled her that the other women did not extend their warm comradeship to her in the same terms as they did to Jean, but she put this down to the snobbery of the middle-class British women who formed the camp's unofficial leadership.

That evening, Jean fell asleep as if the effort of writing had exhausted her. In the middle of the night she began to mutter her husband's name and Betty, suddenly feeling helpless, went to the next-door cell to get help from Irene, the girl who had dressed up.

"Crikey!" she muttered, feeling Jean's forehead wet with sweat. "She's got a temperature all right. We'd better take her to the hospital straightaway. Hope it's not that swamp fever catching up with her."

They carried Jean's body, little more than skin and bone apart from the swollen legs, around to the hut that acted as a hospital and Betty, because she was no longer sleepy and had nothing else to do, sat and dabbed Jean's face with water for a few hours. The doctor's wife became more and more delirious and her temperature was soaring. Betty knew Jean was going to die. Many of the women with whom they had first been interned had contracted the same fever, and its progress was swift and inevitable. Another day, perhaps two, and Jean would be gone.

Betty slept a few hours before daybreak, then woke and queued for her morning cup of rice with a teaspoon of palm oil as a luxury. The Japanese officer in charge of the camp announced that there would be a distribution of mail that day, and most of the two hundred women in the prison eagerly gathered in a long line outside his office, talking excitedly as their captors slowly deciphered the addresses on the small bag of cards.

"Mrs. Rawlins?" Betty gave her name without much hope that there would be anything for her.

"Here." Into her hand was put a card addressed to Mrs. G. W. Rawlins (British Civilian Internee), Women's Camp, Palembang, Sumatra, c/o Japanese Red Cross, Tokyo, Japan. Up the side was stamped the number of the examiner who had verified that the message on it was no more than fifty words long and contained no mention of ill-treatment, food shortages or the progress of the war. Betty walked briskly back to her cell.

"Aren't you going to read it?" Next to Betty on the bare bamboo sleeping platform sat a curious Irene, who had no letter of her own. "Come on, Betty. You stood out there in the sun for an hour to sign for it, you must open it."

"I can't. I don't know the writing. It might say something awful."

The girl took the letter from Betty's hand. "Tell you what we'll do. I'll read it, and if I think you won't like it, I'll keep it for you."

Betty shook her head. An Englishwoman appeared at the doorway of the bamboo hut, her skeletal form silhouetted against the bright sunlight. "We need volunteers to bail out the latrines—either of you two?"

"I can't, the sores on my legs haven't healed," Betty said at once, drawing a contemptuous nod from the older woman. Betty never volunteered for anything unless there was a chance of extra food rations.

"I'll go." Irene scrambled off the platform and Betty was left alone in the dim heat of the hut. She turned the letter over, looking for a clue to its contents. Then she lay back and surrendered to the mental vacuum that was always waiting for her, narcotic, comforting nothingness.

"Sister Caterina—I didn't see you." The sweet-faced Dutch nun had entered the hut quietly. She was a respected leader among the camp women and had no doubt been sent to Betty by the others. Deftly she picked up the letter before Betty could reach it, and without a word opened it and read the card inside. Then she handed it to Betty with a smile.

"Not bad news, I think."

It was from an officer whose name Betty did not recognize, at Changi internment camp on Singapore Island, informing her that her husband had been alive two months earlier when he had left camp with a party of prisoners "sent north for an unknown purpose. We shall try to send news of your survival to him. I know he would wish to send you all his love," the message concluded.

"Happy now?" It was hard to tell. Betty's face was habitually vacant with very little expression. She had suffered, of course, a severe illness after childbirth; but by now they had all suffered as gravely, and many had died.

"Yes, I'm happy. Thank you, Sister. You're so kind." Betty folded the letter in two and tucked it into the old Bakelite soap dish that contained her remaining precious possessions, including the marcasite watch Gerald had given her on their engagement.

"The kitchen needs another person to pick rice, I think." The nun held out a hand to help her down from the sleeping platform.

"What day is it?" Betty asked her. "I can't keep track of time here."

"January twenty-fourth today."

"Good heavens, that's my birthday." I must tell them in the kitchen, she thought at once; perhaps they'll give me a treat.

"Well, now you can hope with God's help to spend your next birthday with your husband. How many years is it you have been married?"

"Let me count—it's 1943, and I was married in 1938—five years. My goodness."

"Congratulations, my dear, and bless you." To her embarrassment, the nun gave her a firm, clean kiss on each cheek. Even in the enforced intimacy of the internment camp Betty could not learn to like being touched.

"I wonder when that letter was written?" Betty reached out and opened the soap container to look. "Where's the date? February—oh." The nun looked over her shoulder.

"What's the matter?"

"It's more than a year old. That's no good. Gerald could still be dead and I not know." With anger, she threw the letter down and let the other woman put an arm around her shoulders.

"If God wills it he will be alive. Now come do some work and make yourself think of other things. Many women have no news at all, remember. At least, for you, there is still a chance.''

Later, as she sat outside the cooking hut with a wicker basket, picking out weevils, gravel and woodchippings from the prisoners' meager rice ration, Betty thought of the marcasite watch. If she sold it, she could buy eggs, or some sugar perhaps. If Gerald was dead, he couldn't mind, could he?

15

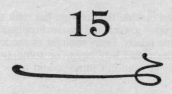

THERE WAS A NOISE IN THE DISTANCE, A LOW, TIRED ROAR THAT did not rise or fall but ground on remorselessly like a faraway ocean. It was the noise of London traffic.

Cathy opened her eyes and dissociated dots of light and color rushed painfully into her head. She shut her eyes again. She felt weightless, floating, heavy with nothingness.

At her side, something moved. A door opened and closed. The door was somewhere beyond her feet. Her throat was sore and there was a bad taste in her mouth. Her right arm felt awkward, as if it were being bent backward against the joint. Her foot hurt, her left foot. It was hot and tender, and the blankets were raised over it.

She opened her eyes again and willed the inrush of dots into a picture. A room, a window. She was lying flat and a tube was stuck into her right arm. The door opened and closed again, there was a rustle and a nurse was standing beside her.

"How do you feel?" She picked up the clipboard at the foot of the bed and made some notes on it.

"All right." Cathy tried to smile.

"Your sister's coming to see you. She'll be here soon, I expect."

The nurse's manner did not invite conversation. She left the room a few moments later, and Cathy tried to sit up. It was difficult. Obviously, she was very weak. There was a large, uncomfortable band of sticking plaster across her throat. Determined, Cathy pulled herself down the bed until she could reach the clipboard, and held it above her eyes to read it. It was Thursday. She had been admitted on Tuesday. Her temperature was normal, but it had been low when she was brought in.

She felt clearheaded but foolish. It was nice to feel so silly. Nothing was important. No one could hurt her. There was nothing to think about.

The door opened violently and Monty rushed to her.

"Darling, darling Cathy!" Monty's hair smelled smoky, reminding her of the world of pain outside the white walls. "It's all right, darling, I'm here. You're OK, you're going to be OK." Cathy tried to smile, but her mouth wouldn't obey. Although she felt inexpressibly happy to see her sister, her face was stretching into all sorts of grimaces. As Monty ripped a tissue from the box nearby and dabbed at her eyes, she realized that she was weeping. They hugged each other for a long time.

"Have they told you anything?" Monty asked her at last.

"What anything?"

"No, they haven't, have they, the shits. Your doctor's all right, but the nurses are absolute bitches. I don't think they approve of suicides, somehow."

The word "suicide" was puzzling. "Am I—did I . . . ?" her voice subsided in doubt.

"Don't you remember?"

Cathy tried to remember, and remembered that her husband had left her and wanted to divorce her. She began to cry again. She could remember nothing else. "Are there any pillows?" she asked. "I'd like to sit up."

Monty brought a pile of pillows from a chair and helped her sister upright, moving the cradle over her foot with care.

"Why have they put a tent over my foot? Is there anything to drink? My mouth tastes horrible."

Monty poured some water. "You've hurt your foot."

Slowly, Cathy began to remember. "But I took pills; I must have been unconscious. How could I have hurt my foot?" She smiled. It was ridiculous. She laughed. She couldn't stop laughing, it was so funny. Her face was wet; she was crying again.

Monty passed her some tissues. "I'll tell you everything later, when you're more together."

"Tell me now."

"No, Cathy, tomorrow."

"Don't be silly; you know me—I'll only worry about it."

"But you're out of your head."

"Considering the things I do when I'm in my right mind, that's probably as sane as I'll ever be."

Monty laughed, and Cathy laughed, and they hugged each other; then Cathy started crying again and Monty put the box of tissues by the hand that wasn't connected to a drip.

"OK—but it's heavy. You're in St. George's Hospital. You've been here two days. When we found you at home, you'd fallen off the bed. This"—she patted the sticking plaster across Cathy's throat—"is because they gave you a tracheotomy. You were in intensive care for a day."

"And that?" Cathy pointed at the hump over her foot.

"Does your foot hurt?"

"Throbs a bit, why?"

"You were lying so the blood supply in your leg was restricted, and no blood was getting through to your foot. They think part of your foot may be dead because it was deprived of oxygen for such a long time, and you might get gangrene."

"I thought that only happened in war films when they started amputating people's legs with blunt knives."

"Don't be silly." Monty squeezed her hand and tried to sound utterly reassuring. At one point the doctor had mentioned that amputating Cathy's leg was a possibility.

"Does anyone know I'm here?"

"I rang up Lord Shrewton. He was terrific. We agreed he'd tell Charlie, and now you've come around you can see him, if you want."

"And Jamie? Is Jamie all right?"

"He's fine."

"Mummy?"

"Yes, I told her. There's some bridge tournament on, so she said she'd only come up if you got worse. Didi went bananas but I told Caroline to tie her down." They laughed again.

Next day the crazy elation vanished and Cathy felt hopeless. The hospital psychiatrist came to see her, and a doctor.

"The shrink said I was a classic case," she told Monty. "His line was I was still grieving for Daddy. I told him he ought to try being married to someone like Charlie. I bet he wouldn't sit there looking so smug if his wife was screwing everything that moved."

"He's only worried that you'll try it again and get the hospital bad publicity. Did you tell him about the pills the doctor was giving you?"

Cathy shook her head. "They were only tranquilizers, nothing important." Her sister looked better, Monty thought. Her cheeks had a vague tinge of color and her eyes were no longer staring out of her head as if she'd seen a ghost.

"Any news on the foot—how does it feel?"

"Awful. It's agony and they won't give enough pain-killers because they say it's a good sign that it's hurting."

"Is it infected?"

Cathy nodded. "They gave me antibiotics too. If I could walk I'd probably rattle." They fell into a companionable silence. Cathy reached for the magazine that Monty had brought her and opened it without much interest.

"Did you really want to die?" Monty asked suddenly.

"Yes. It was all I could think about. I just knew it was what I had to do. I'd failed at everything so I had to die." Cathy spoke slowly, hardly able to remember how she had felt when she had planned her death with such meticulous care.

"Are you angry with me for stopping you from dying?"

Cathy considered the question. "No. I'm pleased to be alive now. I feel as if living means everything, when dying meant everything before. I feel awful about Jamie—how could I even think of leaving him?"

"You'd flipped, you didn't know what you were doing. You must have been junked up on tranquilizers for months."

"Do you know what I couldn't make the shrink understand, Monty? I wasn't *trying* anything, I *was* going to kill myself, and I failed and I feel bloody awful. I've failed at everything. I've lost my husband—I did everything I knew to keep him, and I lost." She sniveled and groped for the tissues.

"He doesn't know you, does he? He's used to seeing hysterical chicks who're trying the old emotional blackmail. He doesn't understand that you weren't just messing about." Cathy's tears began to burst uncontrollably from behind her closed eyelids. "You haven't failed," Monty consoled her. "You can't win anything if the deck's stacked against you."

"Other women do."

"Like who? Mummy? Didi? Mrs. Emanuel or the marchioness? What do you want to be like when you're fifty? Some harpy who fucks up Jamie's life because she hasn't got a life of her own?"

Cathy scraped tears from her eyes. "Jamie. Poor Jamie. Are you sure he's OK, Monty? Will you ask them to bring him to see me?"

With long hours in which to think, Cathy soon began to discover the significance of who visited her, and why. Monty came every day and treated the bleak little ward as if it were just another room in her own home, sitting gossiping and watching television. When she was there, Cathy forgot that she was injured.

Charlie sent her flowers, with a card promising a visit. His father, Lord Shrewton, visited quite regularly, despite the fact that he was obviously acutely uncomfortable in the presence of a woman who had been so appallingly wronged by his son. Cathy put him at his ease by encouraging him to talk business, and the reserved but sincere affection they held for each other deepened. The marchioness called once, briefly, twittering inanities.

Her most trying sympathizer was her grandmother, who wafted into the room in her new spring fur, a puff-sleeved honey mink, calling, "Where is the poor girl? My dear, how simply awful for you to be cooped up in this hideous room. You must make them move you at once. Those curtains! Too drab!"

She brought flowers, champagne, and a turquoise-silk negligee trimmed with fake *point de Venise* laçe. "Now, when Charlie comes you must be sure to look beautiful but fragile. Lie back on the pillows weakly and say almost nothing. Have you got some white makeup? I'll get some sent to you."

Cathy suddenly saw her grandmother as if she were a creature from another world, incapable of understanding how life on earth was lived. Here I am, she thought, lucky to be alive, lucky to have two legs and facing the possibility that I'll never be able to walk normally again, and Didi's only interested in teaching me to act like a courtesan so I can get Charlie back. If it wasn't for Charlie I wouldn't be in this mess.

Lady Davina at once sensed that her pupil's attention was wandering. "You've been very, very stupid," she hissed, her wrinkled, powder-caked face poking forward like a vulture's. "If you'd done as I told you, everything would have been absolutely fine. You've played right into that girl's hands and you'll have to work like a demon to get Charlie back in line now you've behaved like a silly little fool."

"I thought you said men liked women who acted like silly little fools?" Cathy saw that her sarcasm was completely lost on her grandmother, so she changed the subject. "Have you seen Jamie, Didi? I think the marchioness wants to keep him down at Coseley so he won't have to see me in the hospital."

The old woman glared at her through beads of blue mascara. "Have you gone completely mad? There's nothing more likely to put a man off than a sniveling brat about the place." Her bracelets clashed as she raised her arms in a gesture of despair. "I never could understand why you allowed Nanny to bring the little horror downstairs all the time and leave toys all over the house. Men can't stand children at any price."

Cathy sighed and leaned back on the pillows, letting her eyelids droop as if with exhaustion, exactly as her grandmother had counseled her to do with Charlie. "That's it! That's just how

you should look!'' the old woman exclaimed. ''Now remember
to look like that, say nothing, and make him feel guilty. He'll
soon come to heel.''

The next day the doctor decided to operate on Cathy's foot
and remove the dead tissue. Ten days later he operated again.
''You're going to be with us for some time yet,'' he told her
and she nodded, too woozy with drugs to take much interest.

Charlie at last came to see her with his usual bedraggled bunch
of flowers, bought as an afterthought from the stall in Belgrave
Square. ''I love you, Cathy, I'll always love you,'' he told her,
kissing her hands and fingering the wedding ring and the engagement ring as he did so. The rings were becoming loose
because she was losing weight.

''That's typical,'' Monty complained. ''You get skinny when
you're miserable and I just get fatter.''

''Well, you must be happy now, then.'' Cathy looked at her
sister with approval. Monty was decidedly slim. She was wearing a pair of topaz-velvet jeans and an antique cream-lace blouse
that veiled her breasts rather than merely covering them. Her
hair cascaded halfway down her back.

''Yeah.'' Monty suddenly realized that she was happy, but
could not find a reason and did not want to dwell on it in the
face of her sister's desolation. ''You'll be back on top of the
world once you get out of here.''

Was I ever happy? Cathy wondered when she was alone. She
remembered the frothy excitement of her honeymoon and wondered if a feeling based on so much self-delusion could rightly
be called happiness.

Charlie was soon appearing around the heavy hospital door
almost every day, and she was disturbed to realize that she felt
nothing at all for him; no love, no hate, not even contempt. She
felt a little sorry for him, because Lisa, the Texas nymphomaniac, was clearly keeping him on his toes.

''She's always giving parties and she expects me to be on time
and not get drunk,'' he complained. ''God, I miss you, darling.''

When she had been in the hospital a month, the plastic surgeon came to see her. He was suave and handsome, like a drawing from a woman's magazine romance, with humorous blue
eyes and very white teeth.

''What we're going to do,'' he explained, patting what was
left of her injured foot, ''is realign the bones and put a couple
of pins in to hold them straight. Then we'll take a skin graft,
and after that you should be able to start walking again.'' Cathy
sighed. She wanted very much to go home and hold Jamie in

her arms once more. She had begged to see him, but her father-in-law had gently but firmly declined to bring her son to the hospital.

Although the first operation was a success, the skin graft did not go so well.

"You've got unusually strong skin for a European. It's healing more as I would expect an Asian or African woman's skin to do," he told her. "Eventually I'm hopeful you'll get away with insignificant scars. But your general physical condition is so poor at the moment that you've no resistance to infection. We'll have to try again. I'm going to prescribe concentrated vitamins and some more iron for you."

Later that day the surgeon reappeared with a basket of strawberries. "First of the season," he announced, putting them on the table beside her bed. "No sense in missing all the good things in life while you're in here. Plenty of vitamin C. I've told Sister you're to eat the lot yourself."

"Do you give all your patients vitamins like this?" she asked him, enticed by the wonderful smell of the ripe fruit which spread toward her on the overheated hospital air.

"No—only the beautiful ones." He kissed her hand in a formal manner.

"You're a plastic surgeon—aren't they all beautiful by the time you've finished with them?"

"No. Not more than they were before I started anyway. Most women are beautiful; they just won't realize it." He sighed. He was a man who loved women and wished women loved themselves as much. "There's nothing I could do to make a woman beautiful if she doesn't see it herself. And there's nothing that could disfigure a woman who believed she was beautiful, whatever she looked like in the mirror. You're that sort. I don't treat many women like you."

Next day Monty came as usual, and remarked that Cathy looked better.

"I think I've got a crush on the plastic surgeon," Cathy confided, half serious.

"Steady on. Don't doctors get struck off the medical register and barred from practicing if they start carrying on with their patients? Can I have the last strawberry?" Monty peered into the almost-empty basket.

"He gave them to me last night. To be truthful, I think he's just trying to cheer me up."

Monty appraised her sister fondly, and noticed that the drawn look had gone from her face, and her hair, although it was limp and unstyled, had a hint of its former rich sheen. She was wearing the turquoise-silk negligee, but the color quarreled with the amber tints of her complexion.

"You look heaps better. What's happening? Are they letting you out?"

"No—I'm going to be in here for weeks and weeks." Cathy looked despondently at the rise in the blankets where the cradle still protected her foot. "I'm going to be crippled, Monty. I'm going to have to learn to walk all over again, and I'll never be able to run properly, or dance, or anything."

"Of course you will." Monty reached over and squeezed her sister's hand, noticing that the fingernails, which had been bitten to the quick during the anguished period before her suicide attempt, were a heroic millimeter in length. "You'll be able to do anything you want to do, just like you always could."

"There's one thing I'll never do again, and you're to have me committed to an asylum if I look as though I'm going to do it." Cathy held her sister's glance, and her eyes seemed deeper than ever with the shadow of pain behind them. "I'll never, ever fall in love again, not as long as I live."

Monty hesitated. Disclaiming love sounded like a heresy to her. She drew back. "Famous last words, I bet you," she said, with all the optimism she could command, which was not a great deal since Cathy never committed herself to anything without being prepared to follow it through to the end.

The next day, Charlie called to see Cathy with a bottle of champagne. He made her drink most of it, then said, "I've got a bit of business to sort out—just sign this, will you?" He put a pen in her hand and spread a sheet of paper on the table in front of her.

"What is it?"

"Nothing, just a trust document."

She started to read the paper.

"You don't have to read it, just sign it." She ignored him and read the legal paper to the end. It was a consent to a divorce from Charlie, giving him custody of Jamie. Cathy read it again to make sure, struggling to control her emotions. She wanted to kill him, claw out his eyes and trample on the corpse, but hatred, she swiftly realized, would not help her to defend herself.

"I suppose this is Lisa's idea?" she asked him cautiously, pressing the bell for the nurse in case he tried to hit her.

Charlie squirmed and tried to look appealing. "She wants to get married."

"More fool she. Why does she want my son as well?"

Charlie looked even more uncomfortable. "Well, you can't look after him in your condition, can you?"

The nurse came in and Cathy told him to leave. Then she telephoned Pasterns, her solicitors, and the battle commenced. First Charlie's lawyers sent a statement from him alleging that Cathy was mentally unstable and had ill-treated Jamie. Mr. Napier from Pasterns came to the hospital, looking most embarrassed.

"I didn't ill-treat Jamie," Cathy protested. "It was that awful senile old nanny the Coseleys insisted I should have."

"Can you prove this in any way? Anything written down, any doctor's letters or anything?"

"Well, our doctor will remember, I'm sure. And then there's the girl who came to look after him when Nanny Bunting was ill. And the psychiatrist here will tell you I'm not unstable."

They wrote to the Coseleys' doctor, who wrote back declining to give evidence. "It is my policy never to involve myself in the personal affairs of my patients," his letter said.

"Can't we subpoena him?" Monty demanded from her perch on the end of her sister's bed.

"This isn't Perry Mason, my dear. There's no such thing as a subpoena in English law. We might consider issuing a witness summons, but counsel will probably advise against it. Barristers are always very wary of a hostile witness. Can do more harm than good."

"How can he just refuse to give evidence, when they're trying to take my child away from me?" Cathy felt as if she were playing a game whose rules had not been explained to her.

"I think he's rather aware of which side his bread is buttered on," Mr. Napier said delicately. "He's the family's doctor, after all."

Cathy privately carried cynicism even further. Pasterns was sending her bills every two weeks, instead of following its usual sleepy accounting procedure; she rightly took this as a clear indication that they did not anticipate winning her case. She had a distinct impression that to fight the richest noble family in England was considered sheer folly by the superficially attentive but nonetheless venal professionals in her employ.

Her temporary nanny had already been approached by Charlie's solicitors, who sent her statement to Pasterns. It was very short, and simply said that her impression was that the Countess of Laxford took very little interest in her child.

"No one will believe that girl—she was having an affair with my husband. I found them making love on the stairs in the middle of the night," Cathy told her lawyer with confidence.

"Do you have any proof?"

"What proof could I possibly have? I saw them with my own

eyes and she ran off into the street half naked.'' Her lawyer was being very stupid, Cathy thought.

''My Lady, without proof there's nothing to stop your husband denying it, and then it's just your word against his.'' Mr. Napier, in his turn, felt his client was being uncharacteristically obtuse.

There was also a statement from Nanny Bunting, which stressed her credentials as a child-care expert of forty years' experience and described Cathy as ignorant, immature, a social butterfly and obessively jealous of her husband.

''The old . . .'' Cathy almost bit her tongue, trying to stop herself from swearing in front of the prim, overmature young man who was once more extracting a document from his bulging black case.

''And I'm afraid the trick cyclist isn't much help either.'' Mr. Napier handed her more papers with a warning tone in his voice. ''His opinion is that you're severely depressed, out of touch with reality and generally unable to cope.''

Angry enough to ignore the pain in her foot, Cathy pulled herself up in her bed and scanned the paper. She saw the words ''severe postnatal depression,'' ''unresolved grief reaction'' and ''probability of further attempts'' through a mist of rage.

''How dare he! He spent half an hour in here, and when I started telling him how Charlie had behaved he just cut me short and wouldn't listen. How dare he write that I'm unfit to care for my child?''

Mr. Napier avoided her angry gaze. ''We will, of course, get another opinion if you think . . .

''Yes! I certainly want another opinion and''—she forestalled his next point—''if you're concerned about the cost Mr. Napier, don't be. I can always sell my jewelry.''

Soon afterward the doctor said she could go home, and Cathy returned to an empty house. Charlie had come around to his former home while she was in the hospital; he had dismissed the servants and removed all his clothes and quite a lot of the furniture, including the contents of the nursery. At the sight of the empty room with its cheerful, toy-patterned wallpaper, Cathy broke down in angry tears.

''He's a drunken, promiscuous brute,'' she sobbed in Monty's arms. ''He's never taken a moment's interest in Jamie. If he'd killed his son he wouldn't have cared. He damn nearly did kill me. How can they think he's a better parent than I am?''

''Don't cry, darling Cathy,'' Monty soothed her. ''You'll only get lines around your eyes.''

''Lines around my eyes! Who'll notice them when there's *this* to look at?'' Cathy made a despairing gesture toward the ugly surgical boot that encased her injured foot. "And what's the point of looking beautiful if all it gets you is a man like Charlie? I wish I'd been born ugly, then he'd never have fancied me. Why aren't you saying 'I told you so'? You saw through him right from the start.''

Monty ignored her, and handed her the walking stick with which she could hobble unevenly along. The boot, heavy and unsightly as it was, at least made it possible to walk after a fashion. Within a few days, Cathy learned to balance well on her damaged foot. She had lost the tips of her first two toes, her muscles were weak from disuse and her foot ached after every effort.

Money was instantly a problem. She discovered that their bank had allowed Charlie to close their joint account, and requests for maintenance made through Pasterns were left unanswered for weeks. With icy composure Cathy took her jewelry to a well-stocked pawnshop in Victoria, and sold three large silver salvers she found in the pantry cupboard to a dealer in Chancery Lane. Two eighteenth-century French pastoral scenes, her wedding gift from Lady Davina, went to Sotheby's. She had enough to live on, to pay a daily cleaner to keep the echoing house decent, and to settle the bills from her lawyers.

There were more distasteful tasks ahead. Cathy swallowed her pride and her contempt and tracked down as many of her husband's lovers as she could—five in all, grubby artificial blondes living on the edges of Chelsea in curiously similar little apartments, with cuddly toys on their beds and the same odor, of long-term slovenly housekeeping optimistically smothered with expensive scent, lingering in their hallways.

Her first target was a bit-part actress, younger and more successful than April Hennessy, and much less infatuated with Charlie.

"You can count on me," she said at once, stubbing out a half-smoked cigarette. "I'll give evidence for you. I'll say whatever you want. I've always said I felt sorry for whoever was married to that flash bastard. He lost me the best part I ever had, you know—blacked my eye the day before shooting started. I'll never forgive him.''

"The case will probably get quite a bit of publicity," Cathy warned her.

"Right on!" The actress screwed her left eye into a theatrical wink which was emphasized by the rays of black eyeliner painted like eyelashes around the socket. "I hope you get a million, love, you deserve it."

The next day Cathy was amused to see in a gossip column a large picture of the woman in a plunge-necked gown, above the headline EARL'S SECRET LOVE.

With renewed confidence she visited the remaining four women, but they all instantly refused to make statements confirming their affairs with Charlie. At the last fetid little apartment, among the out-of-date copperplate invitations crowding the dusty mantelpiece, Cathy noticed a Coutts check for one thousand pounds, bearing Charlie's vestigial signature.

"I feel as if I'm trying to fight the Mafia," she told Monty in a weary tone. "It was the same with the couple who used to keep house for us—Charlie's just paid them all off. None of our friends will help, either. I thought they were my friends too, but they won't risk losing the Coseley money or the Coseley connections or the Coseley invitations just to help me get my son back."

"You miss him, don't you?"

"So much, Monty, so much. I hate being in that house. Every night I lie awake and think I can hear him upstairs in the nursery. Whenever the staircase creaks I think it's Jamie coming down to see me."

"Shall I come and stay with you for a while?" Cathy was thinner than ever now, Monty noticed.

"What about Simon?"

"He doesn't need me—you do."

By the time her divorce hearing was imminent Cathy could walk almost normally, and the surgical boot had been replaced by a pair of black patent shoes with grosgrain bows made for her with courteous care by her father's former bootmakers, Lobbs of St. James's. Her barrister, a jovial man with iron gray hair and a substantial belly that strained at the buttons of his striped waistcoat, eyed her with satisfaction.

"Very attractive, if I may say so. I like to see my clients looking their best. But if you take my advice you'll come to the court looking as plain as you can. Don't try to cover up your limp. Get rid of that Mona Lisa smile, too. Look as miserable as you can."

"Whatever for?" inquired Cathy, straightening the skirt of the demure navy-blue suit she had bought for the occasion. It had a small lace collar which, she thought, added the ideal touch of fragility and flattered the sallow tint of her neglected complexion.

"Setting aside the question of the custody of your son, any alimony you are awarded will be in a sum fixed by the judge according to his estimation of your prospects of remarriage. Look too pretty, or have a boyfriend waiting in the wings, and you'll get a mere pittance.''

Cathy nodded. "And what about my son—do you think we'll win?" Jamie was all she cared about. Talking about alimony was a waste of breath.

He answered too quickly to suggest confidence. "The courts always favor the mother in these affairs but . . . ah . . . I could wish we had more evidence in this case. Of course"—he looked at her with sudden concern—"you appreciate that this case isn't really about the boy at all, don't you?''

"Then what on earth is it about?"

"The money, My Lady. Your son inherits directly from the Coseley trust; he's a very rich young man, far richer than his father. Whoever gets him gets the loot.''

"But my husband is a wealthy man already, and Lisa's an heiress. . . .''

"Nothing rational about greed, in my experience. To him that hath shall more be given. The Good Book says it and it's the way of the world. One can never be too rich or too thin, eh?'' He stood up to show her out of his chambers, keeping to himself the opinion that his client was much too thin and had an air of angry, demented bewilderment which was not going to help him demonstrate her mental stability.

Cathy saw Charlie, with Lisa clinging to his arm and a team of lawyers leafing energetically through their documents, at the far end of the vaulted gothic corridor outside the court. His barrister was a clean-cut, expansive man whose air of authority immediately made Cathy's lawyers look tentative and shabby.

At the end of the first day of the hearing they were all despondent. The judge clearly accepted the picture Charlie's lawyers painted of Cathy as a neurotic, unstable woman. There was a purposeful scuffle in the press gallery, and next morning the headlines proclaimed CRUELTY TO EARL'S BABY and carried pictures of Charlie and Lisa looking loving and of Cathy with her bowed head and walking stick, looking like a witch.

The morning mail lay beside the newspaper, and Cathy looked at it without enthusiasm.

"All I ever get is wretched bills now." She finished her coffee and stood up.

"What's this?" Monty picked out from among the bills a thick gray envelope with a crackling lining of tissue paper.

"More bad news, I expect. Open it, if you like.''

Inside the envelope was one piece of paper, a page from *Texas Monthly* magazine, part of an article about European aristocracy visiting the state. There was a picture of Charlie playing polo, and beneath it the news that the Earl of Laxford was shortly to take up residence in Dallas with his American wife.

"Who sent it?" Cathy wondered, looking at the envelope. The postmark was smudged beyond interpretation.

"Who cares? It's amazing! That's just what we need—if we can prove they want to take Jamie out of the country, the whole situation changes. The judge will see what a shit Charlie really is. We can turn the tables on them!" Monty sprang to her feet and seized the large-brimmed hat of apricot felt which she wore to the court to hide her Jimi Hendrix explosion of hair and make her look sane, normal and trustworthy.

Although Cathy doubted that anything could prevail against the might of the Coseley clan, Monty was proved right. The actress testified for their side and was as good as her word, sturdily accusing Charlie of drinking, drugging and beating her up. When Charlie at last gave evidence and was forced to admit that he planned to live abroad, the judge adjourned the case to his chambers. Charlie began to bluster, as he always did when caught out in deception, and the judge's attitude toward Cathy became sympathetic.

In the small, oak-paneled room, the atmosphere grew tense as the lawyers worked out a compromise. Cathy listened intently and avoided Charlie's eyes. She was too afraid to hope, but inwardly she willed the judge to give Jamie back to her with every fiber of her being.

"I am inclined to think that the child will do best where he is, with his paternal grandparents." The judge at last looked up from his papers at Cathy, who at close quarters did not appear to him to have any potential for sadism or instability at all. She gasped with disappointment and he continued kindly, "But the court will be able to make another order in time, if you can demonstrate that your life is stable and that you are a fit person to care for your child."

He gave Cathy access to her son every weekend and for a fortnight in the school holidays, and made an order for twelve thousand pounds in lump-sum alimony which, Cathy saw from her barrister's face, was more than had been expected for her.

Charlie left the court hurriedly with Lisa on his arm.

"The pigs. Charlie never wanted Jamie, or the money, it's all that woman." Monty glared after the couple as they scurried into a taxi.

"That's about the size of it." Her lawyer took off his wig and smoothed his hair. "Men who argue about their children in court are usually arguing about money. No one has ever succeeded in putting a price on love."

"Charlie never cared about money." Cathy watched her ex-husband's taxi pull into the traffic in the Strand.

"I expect he cares enough about spending it and the new wife won't like that at all," the lawyer told her.

Her ex-father-in-law, Lord Shrewton, took her to lunch at his club the next week. Cathy had felt desolate and aimless for days and was grateful for his invitation.

"I want you to know that you'll always be welcome whenever you want to see little James," he said, his normal tone of dispassionate reason leaving no doubt that this was the complete truth. "And I'd also like to say that I don't much admire the way my son has acted over this."

"I think he had a certain amount of pressure on him." Cathy chose her words with care.

"That child-woman, yes. Very determined young lady. Of course, Charlie's been bullied by women all his life." From the marquess, this was an indiscretion. "Now, any idea what you're going to do?"

Cathy shook her head, aware that she felt comfortable in this male world of scuffed leather, polished wood and serious talk. The bleak days of anxiety were over, Jamie's future was settled and there was hope that she would one day be able to get him back. Cathy was also aware that by the time she had paid the final bill from Pasterns, her money would be barely enough to buy a small apartment. She would need to work, and she had never earned a penny in her life before, or seriously considered doing so.

"Why not come and work for me—for my company, rather? You can type a bit, can't you?" Her ex-father-in-law sounded sincere, almost eager to employ her.

"I've probably forgotten everything I learned in college," Cathy admitted.

"Soon pick it up. Nothing to it. You can start whenever you like—on Monday if it suits you?" He was trying to atone for Charlie's behavior. She agreed. No one else was likely to employ her.

Her divorce settlement was just enough to buy a cramped dark apartment in a huge building south of the Thames in Battersea. Prince of Wales Drive was crammed with every type of person who would have preferred to live across the water in Chelsea but could not afford it; there were many new divorcées like Cathy, fitting furniture meant for more grandiose homes into the narrow rooms, making their new lives with out-of-work actors, second-hand car salesmen and threadbare ex-service families as their neighbors.

PEARLS

At the end of Cathy's first week at work, Monty came around with a bottle of claret which she had selected for its pretty label, and they celebrated Cathy's independence.

Monty poured the wine into two of the enormous glasses that had been a wedding present from one of Charlie's hard-drinking friends.

"So what's it like?" she asked. Cathy's navy-blue suit looked businesslike and her shoulders, bony as they were, had lost the miserable droop that had crushed them in the past months.

"It's extremely boring," Cathy said, holding her glass to the light to appreciate the wine's color. "But I don't care, I won't be there long. I've made a decision, Monty. I'm going to make money, lots of it. I'm going to get Jamie back and I'm going to get so bloody rich I won't need a penny from the Coseley trust. It's what makes the world go around, money, and now I want my share."

"But how—what are you going to do?"

"Do? I shall do whatever I have to do." Cathy kicked off her shoes and put her feet up on the end of the oatmeal-tweed sofa that had been too small for Royal Avenue and was now too large for this poky apartment. She had no idea what she was going to do.

16

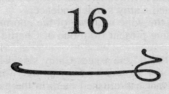

London in 1968 was the worst place in the world in which to fall out of love. The music from every boutique on the King's Road chanted "Love, love, love, love is all you need," at Monty as she made her way to Swallow's office.

Everyone thought that at last there was enough of everything; as much money, freedom, food, drugs, music and love as could possibly be necessary to live a perfect life. The remorseless spirit of the city was sweetened with a sense of abundance. If there was enough for everyone, the right thing to do was to give it away.

Kids boarded buses and handed out flowers to the startled, work-weary passengers, wishing them "love and peace." Swallow's clients seldom paid their bills. Girls with pre-Raphaelite hair set up free restaurants at every pop concert. People rolled joints and passed them out to the surrounding crowds to turn on strangers to the simple beauty of coexistence in a world of plenty.

Monty's existence was neither simple nor beautiful, because she could not, no matter now she tried, reawaken her love for Simon. She threw herself into supporting Cathy, finding a purpose for her own life in saving her sister's, but once Cathy was well again and working, Monty looked for something else to quiet her uneasy heart.

"Why aren't *you* playing with this group?" Rosanna Emanuel asked her over lunch one day. She saw Rosanna less and less frequently; their meetings were usually disrupted by her noisy year-old son, and they never seemed to have very much to say to each other.

Monty shrugged. "What could I do? I'm not really a musician."

"Yes, you are. You're incredibly talented, Monty, you know you are. My parents still talk about you. My mother keeps trying to make me take up singing again, and every time I refuse she says, 'Ah, if you had a voice like that Monty, your gift would call you to use it.' "

Monty shrugged and dug her fork into her *spaghetti vongole*, "I only write songs to amuse myself. I'd be embarrassed to show them to anybody." What she meant was that she loved her music with a passion that she did not want to share.

"There you are—that's your gift calling you."

"My voice is useless now, anyway. I smoke too much."

"Excuses, excuses." Rosanna decided to change the subject. She knew Monty well enough to appreciate that she would resist pressure with anger. "How's the group doing, anyway?"

"Not too bad. They play a couple of gigs a week, now, and Simon's getting bigger bookings. He's decided to book some studio time and cut a demo disc."

The studio had the latest four-track recording equipment, but the walls were cheaply soundproofed with egg boxes. Simon booked it for one night only—the nights were cheaper—and the first hour was wasted in an argument about what they were going to record. Simon wanted the A side to be "Don't Go Now," the best of their own songs. Rick complained that it was "doomy" and at last they compromised and decided on an old Chuck Berry number to back it.

At about 3:00 A.M., Monty was sitting beside the engineer watching in fascination as he flipped switches and pulled knobs on the mixing deck, when Simon came out of the studio to get her.

"We need a bit of piano," he told her, pulling her to her feet. "Come on, I'll show you what to play."

On the other side of the glass he sat her down at a scarred old upright piano and gave her a short phrase to play in the song's middle section.

They tried it a couple of times, then Rick suggested, "Do a bit more, Monty—play around with it a bit." She developed the phrase, and they nodded.

"Maybe a spot of echo . . ." The engineer reached forward for a knob at the far side of his desk.

"Hear it through the cans." Simon gave her his headphones and she heard her music played back.

"But it sounds awful," she protested, hating the bouncy, sentimental sound she had produced. The band shook their heads as one man.

"No, no, it's great," they reassured her, and Monty shrugged and smiled and played on to the end of the session, feeling embarrassed.

After that, they dragged her with them to every gig, sitting her down at a variety of beer-stained, cigarette-burned instruments where she tried her best to hide from the crowd out at the front of the stage. She did not like the packed, passive mass of people who stood waiting for the music to take them out of themselves, and began to take a perverse pleasure in playing with more and more aggression until she could see that she was getting through to them.

Rick insisted that she should sing too. "It looks pathetic having someone onstage who isn't singing with the others," he told her, refusing to argue. Monty sang, and loved it. The sound of her voice, rich, smoky and slightly ragged, complemented Rick's harsh tone to perfection.

"It's good having you with us, Monty," Rick said one night when they were momentarily on their own by the van. "It makes things kind of smoother with Simon, you know? It's easier to talk to him sometimes if you're around."

Before she could respond, Cy and Pete appeared, lugging one of the giant amps in its silver casing, and Rick ran over to help them; but Monty knew what he meant.

There was a permanent awkwardness between Simon and the others. Musically they were perfectly compatible, but socially Simon's wealth and upbringing created a gulf between them. Simon never walked into a bar expecting to be thrown out or saw a policeman and expected to be stopped and searched. Simon, like Monty, viewed the new era of love and peace with almost religious feeling as an opportunity to prove that human nature could change for the better.

The boys, particularly Rick and Cy, saw it simply as a golden opportunity to score—sex, drugs, or whatever was on offer from people too stupid to look after their own interests. One summer weekend they staged what they called a love-in at their house.

"It was great," Rick told them afterward. "We just went out on the street and stopped everyone we fancied and told them to come and join us. We had about twenty chicks in there at one point."

"Yeah, it was great." Cy nodded, his long hair swaying. "Every time some chick decided to split she'd start looking for her clothes. 'Course, we'd hidden them, hadn't we? Then she couldn't find them, then somebody'd grab hold of her, then that was it for another couple of hours."

Monty forced a smile. She and Simon still made love occasionally, but it was a hypocritical performance on her part. Within a year she had grown to detest everything about Simon, from the line of black hairs that grew down the nape of his neck to the way he always started his guitar solos the same way. She was profoundly shocked at the speed with which their love had degenerated to the kind of shell which she recognized as the embryo of her parents' icy sham of marriage. If love was the most important thing in the world, how could it just pop like a balloon, and vanish?

It was a punishing summer for all of them. Simon had twenty copies of their demo disc made, and sent them to every record company in London. There was no response whatsoever and so he patiently called every one of the executives to whom the disc had gone and swallowed dismissal, condescension and rejection with grim good humor as he tried and failed to make them come to hear the band. Monty spent more and more time with the others. The band was like a tribe now, always together, and it was somehow more tactful to go to Rick's filthy room than to invite the boys to Simon's luxurious apartment.

"I can't bear to listen to him," she told Rick. "He's so patient and so polite always, and they're such motherfuckers. . . ."

"Yeah. He's a trier, old Simon." Rick tipped sugar into his coffee and stirred it, looking at Monty at length while she, unaware of him, stared at the grimy, rain-streaked window.

The Juice played one or two gigs a week all through the winter, acquiring a group of supporters who crowded to the front of the stage to freak out in Simon's solos or roar at Rick as he baited them. Monty grew more confident on the stage as she realized people liked her; she even had a few fans who were specially her own, who sometimes left flowers on her piano or waited to talk to her at the end of the set.

Although the demo disc was a failure, The Juice's following grew and every call Simon made to book the band into a club was a little easier.

"We're getting through," Simon told them with reassurance.

"Yeah, but not fast enough. I don't wanna die before I cut

my first album,'' Cy snarled, spitting out of the van window for emphasis.

Toward the end of the following summer, word went around the pubs in London that there was to be a pop festival on the Isle of Wight, an idyllic fragment of farmland off the south coast of England, a white-cliffed holiday paradise. The summer had seen one or two small festivals already; a few thousand people had discovered the pleasure of sitting together peacefully under the stars to listen to music.

Simon abruptly canceled The Juice's bookings for the weekend and told them, ''We're going to the Isle of Wight for our holidays—we deserve it.''

From the outset the excursion was not the carefree picnic Simon intended it to be.

Cy grumbled ceaselessly in the van. ''Will somebody tell me why we're going to hear a lot of psychedelic garbage with this weekend hippie instead of staying in London to get smashed?'' he whined.

On the ferry to the island, he found a bottle of whiskey and drank most of it in forty minutes.

As they drove to the festival site he suddenly flung open the van door and started throwing out everything he could reach, shouting ''Free, free!'' to the amused villagers at the roadside.

The stage had been erected at the focal point of a natural amphitheater of green fields, behind which the sea gleamed in the sunlight like polished steel. The narrow lanes, their hedges gay with yellow toadflax and late foxgloves, were crowded with people who walked without haste to the concert ground to merge with the huge carpet of humanity.

Monty felt obscurely hopeful in the middle of the amiable crowd. Her blood tingled in her veins with a premonition of adventure, and as soon as she could, she escaped from the ominous atmosphere around Simon and spent a few hours with a group of French hippies, who had erected a Red Indian teepee at the edge of the site. They had expensive clothes and some powerful black hash. The children twined starry white camomile flowers in her hair and one of the women pulled off Monty's T-shirt with distaste and instead gave her an embroidered voile jacket which tied provocatively under her breasts.

''There you are,'' she heard Rick's voice in the crowd as the evening star was beginning to shine through the early shades of dusk. ''Where've you been? Simon's been going frantic.''

''It's so beautiful here—I couldn't stand the hassles anymore,'' she told him, feeling dreamy from the drugs. ''It's so heavy around Simon at the moment. It really brings me down. Where've you been?''

''Seeing the future.'' He jerked his thumb to the stage where a boy in a spangled caftan with a cloud of dark curls was singing something about children with stars in their hair. ''And I don't like it.''

They walked uphill in companionable silence, leaving the huge, peaceful crowd below them. At length they came to the cliff edge and sat down on the springy turf. The stage was a tiny illuminated picture in the distance, but the sound from the vast banks of speakers floated up to them clearly.

''Look—the chopper!'' Rick pointed to a helicopter which floated like a glowing spark over the sea. ''They said the Airplane would be flying in from a yacht—that must be them.'' They watched as the helicopter hovered at the rear of the stage, bringing in Jefferson Airplane, the headline band. It set down and became invisible as its lights were extinguished.

''That's what I want—I want to top the bill, make a million and fly in by helicopter, not be down here, groveling around in shit.'' Rick stubbed his cigarette out in a rabbit hole. ''You know that, don't you? I want it all. I'm hungry, Monty, we're all hungry. That's what all the trouble's about.''

''Simon's not hungry,'' she said, lying back and looking up at the indigo sky.

''Nah—he can't be, he's had it too soft all his life. It makes no odds to him whether he makes it this year, next year, sometime or never, but it does to us because making it's all there is for us, you know.'' He pulled his cigarettes from his shirt sleeve. He rolled his sleeves neatly above the elbow, like a soldier or a Boy Scout. He looked at her and tapped out two cigarettes from the crumpled packet.

''You're hungry too, aren't you? It don't make sense, but you are. Sometimes I think you're hungrier than all of us.''

He lit both cigarettes, threw the match away with too much energy and leaned over to put one cigarette between her lips. Then he tore it away again, threw both cigarettes aside and kissed her, almost biting her mouth with a desperate urgency that begged her not to reject him.

At once the rush of passion renewed within her, and she wound her arms around him.

Their eagerness made them clumsy as they struggled with their clothes and they were still half dressed as he thrust into her with cries that sounded half like triumph, half like a whimpering animal.

Afterward, when the sky was dark and the stars bright, she stroked his hair as he rested his head between her breasts.

"I wanted you for so long," he murmured. "You're a great chick. But I thought you were in love with Simon."

"I thought I was in love with Simon, too. I *was* in love with him once, but it just faded away." Was that really love? Monty wondered as she watched the moon struggle out from the clouds.

In the morning they slithered down the cliff to the beach and splashed naked in the waves. Then they left the island, hitch-hiked back to London and moved Monty's things into Rick's room. Monty left Simon a letter saying good-bye, and felt like a miserable coward.

Soon afterward Simon called a band meeting in the Wetherby Arms and announced that he was quitting and returning to his job in his father's firm. Monty came to the meeting, but she could not look at Simon, even when she wished him all the luck in the world.

Monty's life changed dramatically as soon as she moved into the decrepit gray house where Rick and Cy and Pete lived. The stucco was blistered and the windowsills rotted. Inside, Rick's room contained a bed, a table, and two chairs, one of which had no back. There was a gas fire which was connected to a meter, into which shilling coins had to be fed to heat the room.

When The Juice had a gig, they were paid twenty-five pounds. That worked out at five pounds each for Monty, Rick, Pete and Nasher, out of which Rick ran a kitty for gas for the van. It was not enough to live on, but both Rick and Cy insisted that they were musicians and needed no other job. Every Thursday they went up to the labor exchange to sign on for the dole. Monty was paid by Swallow on Friday, which was fortunate, because neither of the boys had any money left by then. After a month, she got a job in a small French restaurant near the office, waiting on tables for one pound an evening and tips. With this, the three of them had just enough money to get through the week, assuming that she stole some food in the restaurant.

One week when the restaurant was shut they went to the pub on Friday night and had three shillings and sixpence between them on Saturday morning, and no food.

"Party time," said Rick. They went back to the pub at lunch-time. "We're having a party at our place tonight—bring a bottle," he told everyone, not stopping at any table long enough to be obliged to buy a round of drinks.

Towards 11:00 P.M., people began to arrive, most of them

already drunk. They brought bottles of beer, wine and whiskey. Rick and Cy sat and strummed their guitars, and people drank. The people left, and in the morning Rick collected thirty-four empty bottles, which he took back to the shop on the corner. There was a deposit of tuppence on each bottle, and they then had more than a pound, enough to buy cornflakes, bread and jam.

This life delighted Monty. Being poor to her was like living in a free zone. There were no expectations, no constraints, no rules except survival. She wore the same pair of jeans every day for a year and got a bigger kick out of doing so than out of all the fabulous dresses Simon had bought her.

To her surprise, she also felt more loved by Rick than she ever had by Simon. He brought her tea in bed in the morning, and carried shopping for her, and washed up after she cooked meals on the rancid little stove on the landing, which the whole house shared. He was easy and relaxed around women, without the edginess inculcated for life by a single-sex boarding school.

"Go away," she said sleepily one morning as his hands slithered tenderly around her body. "I'm not fit to fuck this morning—my period's starting."

"That's nice, I must say. I wake up feeling all randy and you've got the painters in."

She giggled. "Have you got a pain?" he asked, closing his hand over her belly protectively.

"No. It's not that; it'll just be a bloody mess, that's all." He wriggled his erection hopefully against her.

"Tell you what—how about if I take the sheets to the Laundromat. Can't say fairer than that now, can I?"

"All right, it's a deal." Rich warm tingles were racing through her flesh. It was extremely messy and he took the sheets to the Laundromat just as he had promised, making tea for her first.

Rick could hardly believe he had been so lucky as to attract this beautiful, sexy, fantasy creature from another world—because the upper classes were a different world to him. Occasionally Monty would take him to a party given by one of her rich friends, and he would absorb, with resentful amazement, the truth about the life-style to which she was accustomed. As a point of pride he refused the champagne and was overly polite to everyone, at the same time swearing to himself that one day he too would have a big house in Chelsea, with servants and a sunken bath.

"You do love me, don't you?" he said to Monty one night,

as they walked home through Chelsea from another of these glittering interludes in their life of squalor.

"Of course I do." Monty slipped her hand down the back of his jeans.

"I never thought you would, you know. I thought you'd piss off after a weekend or two in that rathole."

"You don't think much of me, do you?"

"Yeah, I do, that's the trouble. You could have anyone. You could have one of them poncey stockbrokers with pots of money, and drive around in a Mercedes."

"You'll have a Mercedes, when we get our deal."

Rick kicked a tin can into the gutter. "*When* we get our deal. When pigs fly, you mean."

"We'll get it. The band's great now. Someone's bound to sign us."

"Well, I don't want a fuckin' Mercedes. I'll have a Roller. Got more class."

They walked on, following the meandering tail of the King's Road. A smell of frying fat from a fish and chip shop wafted toward them on the combination of brewery fumes, gasworks effluent and carbon monoxide that formed the atmosphere of Chelsea's outer limits.

"Got any money?"

Monty felt in her handbag, then in the pockets of her jean jacket. "Five, six, seven—seven and six. What for?"

"Get some chips, I'm starving."

"But, Rick, we've just been to a party with enough salmon and champagne to sink a battleship—didn't you eat anything?"

"No, I couldn't." She didn't ask him why, guessing at the peculiar inversion of pride that had made him refuse the food when he was hungry.

"Get me some—salt, no vinegar," she yelled after him as he crossed the road.

The Juice was a different band without Simon. Rick took control and they stopped playing the long, complex songs with enigmatic lyrics which Simon had preferred because they showed off his musicianship. Rick liked simple songs with a driving beat that would get the crowd on its feet. He could barely read music, let alone write it, and he relied heavily on Monty.

"Listen to this, love," he would say, playing a few chords on his guitar. "I had the next bit yesterday, but I can't remember it." And she would pick up the cheap acoustic guitar which he seldom used and take the fragment of melody and turn it into a song with all the pulsating, direct power that Rick knew he wanted but could not create by himself.

Words also came very easily to her. The poetry crammed into her head at school as a punishment had trained her mind superbly and, now that the ability was needed, the words tumbled out, thrusting and lunging at her listeners' emotions.

Rick was spellbound with admiration. "The things you know," he murmured, half mocking, when she suddenly decided to transpose a song into a different key so that it sounded completely different. She made him conscious that he was ill-equipped for his chosen world, capable of striking the pose of a musician but not of understanding his art.

Monty felt as if the working class was not so much another world as another planet. Rick, Cy and Pete had language and folklore and beliefs which were completely alien to her. They even looked different from the solid, well-nourished, upper-class boys she had known before. They were sparrow-boned and skinny. Pete had a slight spinal deformity. Cy's teeth leaned crazily like the tombstones in an old churchyard. All of them smoked heavily and coughed a great deal, especially in the winter.

They ate junk food, and drank only at the pub; buying alcohol to drink at home, she discovered, was tantamount to admitting to alcoholism.

While Rick kept his room as neat as a cabin on a ship, Cy's lair was stacked to the ceiling with debris and covered in a thick layer of dust. His bed was a mattress on the floor. His favorite occupation was smashing things, and he was never happier than when he found an abandoned car to wreck or a derelict house to attack as if he could tear it apart with his bare hands.

Next to destruction, Cy liked stealing. Every gig they played gave him the opportunity to steal something. Monty was embarrassed when he walked off with a piece of equipment belonging to another band.

At home, Cy plundered the gas meters with artistry, slowing down the clocks so that they would not register the gas consumed, and making it possible to run the fires all day in winter with a single shilling put through the slot again and again.

In supermarkets he stole food. He never paid his fare on the bus. He fiddled his dole money, and was outraged when the labor exchange official caught him and threatened to prosecute him.

"It's a fuckin rip-off," he yelled, kicking at a corrugated iron fence around a building site. "They got no right to say they'll get the law on me. I ain't done nothing."

"Yes, you have. You cashed your dole checks and claimed

you'd lost them, so they'd give you the money again," Monty pointed out. "That's fraud, you know it is."

"You can fuck off!" Cy shouted. "Nobody ever ripped you off, did they? What the fuck do you know about it?"

Monty walked on with Rick, leaving Cy pulling down the entire fence. "He's mad," she said in wonder. "Why's he so aggressive?"

"You don't understand." Rick pulled out his cigarettes and lit two of them, his hands cupped against the biting March wind. "All Cy knows is being ripped off, and being ripped off begins at home, like charity. If you've been ripped off all your life, well, that's all you know how to do, isn't it? So you just go out and do it back."

Monty took a cigarette from him and inhaled, thinking.

"People can know better. You can learn better. *You* don't rip everyone off all the time, and you and Cy grew up on the same street."

He looked at her, uncertain. "You don't know me, love." She did not react, so he continued, "Anyway, Cy's got nothing. He's got no way out. I'm his way out, because I can get onstage and act like a monkey and people will pay money to see me. That's the only way out for all of us."

They waited at the bus stop, cuddled together to keep warm in the raw cold.

Rick's ticket to fortune and fame was his ability to make himself into another person onstage, The Juice. Without his savage, raw-throated performance, The Juice was nothing but an average bunch of players. Rick was hardly a musician at all, a self-taught guitarist with a few laboriously acquired riffs which he played over and over again in different permutations. But the instant he ran onstage and pulled the microphone from its stand, he became a mad, mocking demon who dominated and excited the audience until they groveled at his feet, screaming for more.

One night after a gig they were packing up to leave when a man in a white suit, with a boyish face that looked prematurely aged and close-cropped blond hair, came over and spoke to Rick.

"I'd like to buy you a drink," he said.

"Thanks, mate." Rick finished coiling up his guitar lead and put it on top of an amplifier.

"Large Scotch for me." Cy sat down at a table at the edge of the half-empty room. Pete and Nasher, the drummer, followed him. Rick sat down last, pulling Monty beside him and putting his arm around her.

"I'm Dennis, Dennis Pointer." The blond man shook hands

with all of them and passed around his cigarettes. "Anyone aging you?"

"We split with our manager." It was almost true, since Simon had acted as their manager; Rick allowed the newcomer to light his cigarette.

"Got a deal yet?"

"Not exactly." Rick shook his head.

"I know you, don't I?" Nasher narrowed his eyes. "Didn't you have something to do with some horrible bunch of hippies."

"You mean Yellow Nebula—yeah, I managed them. Got them an outrageous deal with Virgin and they fucked off to the country to do all the acid they could carry and never came back." Dennis gave them a speculative look.

"We wouldn't do a thing like that to you." Rick grinned and blew smoke upward. "Pity. Jimmy Booker was a good singer."

"I'm still handling Jimmy. But I like you a lot—I've been following you around a few places."

"We'll think about it," Rick told him. The truth was they didn't need to think. They acted cool until the van was around the corner; then Rick and Monty shrieked with joy, Nasher beat a tattoo on the wheel arch and Cy put his feet on the dashboard and drummed his heels. They were singing their third chorus of "She'll Be Comin' Round the Mountain" when a police car howled up behind them and they were cautioned for reckless driving.

"Now I'll tell you how to get a deal," Dennis lectured them all a month later, in a café around the corner from the offices of Excellent Records. "Don't matter much what you sound like— that's for us to know and keep to ourselves, right? Your music won't cut any ice with that polecat you're going to see. What you gotta do is grab his imagination. You've got to let him know that you're the most filthy, steaming, obscene bunch of lads this side of Sodom and Gomorrah—got it?"

"Nah. What do you want us to do?" Cy screwed up his mouth in an obstinate line.

"Act natural," Dennis advised him.

The polecat's name was Les Lightfoot; his office was at the end of a long corridor lined with gold discs in gold frames. He had a Julius Caesar haircut and very clean jeans.

"Dennis has played me some of your stuff," Les began. "I like your sound. I think the kids'll go for it."

Cy gave him his most malevolent stare. "You want to watch your mouth, mate. I could go for you, 'nd all."

"Tell me about yourselves," Les invited them.

Cy got up and walked slowly around him, swiveling his high-backed leather chair. "I don't like you," he told him. "I'd consider killing you, if I thought you were alive."

The polecat swallowed, uncomfortably. This was not the way it was supposed to be. The artists were supposed to be respectful and polite, and wear their best gear. This gargoyle had moldy teeth and a four-inch rip in his jeans, through which the white flesh of his backside was clearly visible.

Pete also stood up and walked to the back of the office, up to a handsome potted palm. He pulled out an aerosol can and sprayed red paint on the fronds. It dripped onto the white shag-pile carpet.

"Look like blood, don't it?" he remarked.

Nasher appeared to be asleep. "Don't mind him," Rick advised the executive amiably. "He's a narcoleptic. Keeps dropping off. It's a form of epilepsy, apparently."

"I hope he doesn't do that onstage." Les Lightfoot loosened the knot in his satin tie.

"It's all right, we just keep on playing. Sometimes he has proper fits, of course. Then one of us has to jam one of his drum sticks between his teeth. Stops him biting his tongue."

Cy slowly unzipped his fly, and hauled out a semi-inflated pink balloon in the shape of a cock and balls. The balls were tinted an improbable purple. Cy picked a felt pen off the man's desk and began to paint hairs on the balls.

In desperation, the polecat turned to Monty and smiled.

"And what's your name, my dear?" he asked.

Monty had put on a collection of Victorian lace skirts and a camisole which, she knew, made her look gloriously hoydenish. She leaned forward, well aware that she was giving Les a clear view from her clavicle to her waist, down a tunnel of white lace frills.

"My name's Miranda," she said in her most languid, upper-class drawl. "But actually people usually call me Monty."

"Pleased to meet you," the man said foolishly.

Cy pulled out a switchblade knife and stabbed the inflatable penis with it.

Two weeks later Dennis brought them their contracts. Then they had money, but not time to spend it, because Les Lightfoot wanted their first album as soon as possible, and for three months Monty lived in a tunnel between the recording studio and their room. She bought herself a Moog synthesizer, but had no time to play with it. They were listening to the first number when Rick said, "I've been thinking—how about more girls' voices?

This sounds OK for the little clubs, but it isn't right for an album. It sounds thin.''

Their producer agreed. ''Monty's voice is terrific, but I think three girls would be better.''

Next day a black girl and a white girl joined them.

''I'm P.J., this is Maggie,'' the black girl said. She had enormous eyes and hair cropped flat against her skull. Maggie was squat and messy-looking, with clotted black mascara and a thick Scottish accent.

They were right, Monty thought, as she listened to the playback in the studio; three girls sounded better. It did not occur to her that her status in the group had been eroded, and her individual voice replaced by a mere sound.

Eight songs were recorded, one after the other. They represented the best of The Juice's repertoire, but the producer told them they needed at least three more to fill the album. Rick suggested another Chuck Berry standard, which was easily done, but then no one could agree on the final two songs. Les Lightfoot himself came down to the studio and listened to some of the material that the band had often performed, but he at once vetoed its inclusion on the record.

''Old-hat stuff,'' he announced. ''I'm sorry, boys, you'll have to come up with something new or the deal's off.''

The pressure acted like inspiration on Monty. The same night, as soon as she was alone with Rick, she burrowed into a box of papers and books she had brought from Simon's apartment and found the little notebook in which she used to write down the songs she composed for fun.

''Maybe we can use some of these.'' She seized the old acoustic guitar and began picking out a tune and humming the words.

Rick looked doubtful. ''I dunno—it's a pretty song, all right, but it's not our sort of a song, is it?''

Monty continued to play, developing the melody and changing the words until at last Rick came over and sat on the bed beside her, singing with her and making his own changes. Then they thought of a new idea, and Monty quickly put the outline of it down on paper.

Suddenly it was midday, and they stopped for an hour to go to the corner café for tea and bacon sandwiches. By the end of the day the first song was perfect, and Rick called the others to hear it.

Everyone was happy with the new song, and they worked on the second one in the studio, with everyone throwing in contributions.

The producer nodded with satisfaction. "This is the test," he said to Monty while the boys were running through the final version by themselves. "The band that gets to the top and stays there is the band that can get its own material together, and be good, and be consistent, and be professional. And there's not a lot of bands like that about."

By the time they had finished recording the album, all Monty and Rick wanted to do was sleep, but Dennis, their manager, had other plans.

"The real work's only starting," he told them. "You'll be doing interviews soon, and we gotta get some photographs done." Dennis's girlfriend was an assistant on a young-fashion magazine, and she took Monty on a very serious shopping expedition. They came back with antique lace knickerbockers, French blue jean jackets embroidered with colored glass beads and gloriously sexy high-heeled sandals of red and silver snakeskin. Merely wearing them made Monty feel excited and apprehensive. She hennaed her hair to a luscious mahogany and had it cut into layers of silky curls.

The interviews started and Rick came into his own. Shrewdly appreciating that his role on the world's stage was to outrage the spectators, he insulted reporters with complete abandon, turning up drunk, stoned, or very late—but never blowing out a press call completely. The Juice was offered one TV show in Newcastle, courtesy of Nasher's link with the area, and Rick and Cy wrecked the set. The *New Musical Express* called them the "The Terrible Twins of Rock," and Dennis squeezed Rick's shoulder with satisfaction.

"By George," he said. "I think he's got it."

"So now what?" Rick asked him, sitting on Dennis's desk. Dennis's office was one room with a telephone at the top of a listing staircase in Soho.

"Excellent ought to give you a tour." Dennis offered his cigarettes. "But they're waiting to see how much air play the album gets. Don't worry, I got a few tricks up my sleeve."

The tricks, they all knew, were two key disc jockeys who found Dennis a convenient supplier of cheap drugs and expensive women. *Freshly Squeezed*, The Juice's first album, entered the charts at number 63. The next week it rose to number 37, because Dennis hired a small army of kids from Swallow's agency to buy it at some of the stores whose sales figured in the charts. At 37, the album automatically went onto the play lists of all the radio stations, and Dennis's influence took it into the top 10.

Excellent Records hastily sent The Juice on a four-week tour of Britain on which they supported the label's biggest name, a psychedelic band called Crimson Lake. Halfway through the itinerary Dennis was called to London for a meeting with the record company, and returned smiling.

"After this, we're going to the States," he told them. "We've cracked it."

By the time they played their final three nights in London, Rick and Monty were lightheaded with exhaustion and Cy had done so much speed that nothing he said made any sense at all, even to Rick.

"I can't handle this," Rick said suddenly. They were sitting in their room at night. The house seemed cold and neglected, and after a month in hotel rooms the squalor was oppressive. "One minute I was hustling for a break, the next I'm being treated like I can walk on water. And I don't even know what day of the week it is. Thank God I've got you, love. You're the only thing that's keeping me sane."

The album's cover showed an oil-streaked man's hand with ragged fingernails squeezing a satin-covered woman's buttock. Its distinctive black-and-white design soon was repeated endlessly in the windows of music stores.

By the time the album was number 3 in the charts, Rick had given so many interviews nothing he said seemed real anymore.

"Every time they ask me where I come from, and I tell 'em Croydon, and Cy's mum and my mum worked in the same light-bulb factory, it's like you made it up for me to say, even though it's true," he told Dennis.

"There's some girl from *Rolling Stone* coming at half past two," the publicist replied, uncaring.

"But we're going to America today, aren't we?" Monty was starting to be wary of Rick after an interview, especially an interview with a girl.

He was always hyped up, arrogant and aggressive, as if his demonic stage personality had temporarily taken control.

"I've ordered a limo to take Rick to the airport and she'll ride out with him," the publicist countered. "Sign these, will you?"

Rick looked at the photographs with distaste. "Why don't you buy a rubber stamp?"

"You're out of date, mate. You sign the print and then we just duplicate the whole thing. Hurry up, the car's waiting."

In the limousine on the way to the airport, the girl from *Rolling Stone* pulled down all the blinds and took off all her clothes and set about giving Rick a blow job. He wasn't surprised. This sort of thing was happening all the time; the girls seemed to think it was expected and who was he to complain?

There were girls loitering in their hotels, girls hanging around the Excellent offices, girls finagling to get backstage at their gigs.

Within a matter of weeks it had become the ambition of every groupie who considered herself worthy of the name to lay Rick Brown of The Juice and Monty was astonished at their shameless ingenuity. One of them had even dressed herself up in an imitation of Monty's ruffles and denim and tricked a doorman into believing she was the real Monty and giving her a backstage pass.

In America, the girls who tried the interview scam claimed they worked for the BBC; they were much more persistent. Even the stupid ones, instead of hanging around the hotel lobby, gave head to the nearest bellhop, who would then let them into Rick's room. There they waited, until they got bored and tried Cy's room instead.

Rick slept with Monty, but few people outside the band realized this.

"Don't tell 'em you live together, for Chrissake," Les Lightfoot told him. "We're promoting you as the bad boys par excellence—none of that lovey-dovey crap, please keep the old lady out of sight."

Cy threw a television set off the twenty-second-floor balcony of the Hilton in Daytona Beach, Florida. In Memphis, he drove a hired Cadillac into the hotel swimming pool. Somewhere in Wisconsin a chambermaid claimed that he had raped her. The Juice was banned in Kansas.

Cy's room was always where the orgy was, and the mystique took root so fast they seldom needed to do anything more than open the door to a procession of bedraggled girls who wanted only to be able to say that they'd laid Rick Brown of The Juice. After them came the small-town jocks, the two-bit rock writers, the passersby and the hangers-on.

In Dallas, a pair of identical twins took over the scene and immediately sold their story to the *National Enquirer*. Cy read it with relish.

"Right dirty slags they were," he approved. "Fucked 'em both flat, and they couldn't get enough. Wanted me to do it all again with some spade chick. I told 'em it was all beyond me. I got 'em fuckin' each other's brains out with one of them dildo things. Incredible what some chicks'll do, innit?"

None of them wanted to lay Nasher, who passed blameless

evenings trying to phone his wife. Pete picked up a stunning blonde in Pasadena and dropped out of the action.

Monty did not realize that Rick was keeping Cy company with the endless flow of groupies until he leaned over the breakfast trolley in Los Angeles and sleepily scratched his brown curls. Two tiny gray insects, holding each other's grippers like square dancers, fell into his orange juice.

"Ugh." Monty fished them out with a teaspoon. Rick got up and washed the creatures down the lavatory, muttering something about the hotel being dirty. She did not find out what the insects were until she told P.J. about them.

"Crabs! Yeeuch! Men *are* so disgusting. Hope that's not all he's got—you'd better see a doctor."

The doctor, who was well known on the West Coast as a music business insider, gave Monty a blood test as well.

"You've got the clap," he told her as if he were telling her the time. "Better let me take a look at your boyfriend."

They went home full of penicillin, with orders not to drink alcohol. Cy had defiantly downed his first bottle of Scotch by the time they were flying over the North Pole.

On the way back to London they agreed that they could not face returning to their rotting house. Hotels were what they were newly accustomed to consider home.

"I reckon we should put up at the Savoy," Rick announced. "We can afford it, can't we, Dennis?"

"It's not my business how you spend your money. Sure, check into the Savoy and we'll start looking for proper homes next week." Dennis looked more wrinkled and colorless than ever. They were all tired and drawn after their weeks on tour, and Monty felt bloated from living on booze, coffee, drugs and hamburgers. She didn't like the fact that her breasts had enlarged, which Maggie confidently informed her was the inescapable result of singing every night.

In the peach-and-chrome Art Deco calm of the Savoy, Monty let Rick recover for a day and then went on the attack, determined to detach him from Cy and the groupie scene.

"Never, ever, again," she told him, her voice low and trembling with anger. "Never. No way. That tour was the most disgusting, humiliating experience of my life. How could you put me through all that, Rick? How could you come and get in my bed when you'd been down the corridor with Cy doing all those revolting things with those revolting groupies?"

He looked small, wretched and ashamed. "I'm sorry, love. I never realized you'd be hurt."

"Like hell. What was I supposed to do, join in?"

Rick squirmed unhappily. "You don't understand."

"I never do understand, do I? Whenever you and Cy want to wreck everything, somehow my understanding just isn't up to the occasion."

"Look—it's what rock 'n' roll is all about, being a big bad boy. Dope and sex groupies, and all that—we've got to have 'em for all the kids who'll never get the chance."

"Bullshit. You're having them because you want them. It hurts me, it's insulting, and I don't like it."

"Well, if you don't like it, you know what you can do about it, don't you?" Rick pulled the bathrobe around himself with a defensive gesture. "I ain't waited all my life to make it to have some jealous chick spoil it all. Go on, fuck off."

Monty shrugged and walked away. She felt very little, but she knew Rick would concede. She was the only stability he had. Without her to reassure him, support him, write his songs and lay down the ground rules of his life, he would simply fall apart in the crazy new world they had entered. She ought to feel sorry for him, but two months of continuous exhaustion had left her little capacity for feeling. She got dressed and went for a walk along the Thames Embankment.

When she got back, Rick was dressed, washed, shaved and contrite.

"I'm sorry, darling. I was a right pig." He put his arms around her. "I didn't realize how much you'd be hurt, honest, I didn't. Don't go, Monty. I need you, you know."

She saw tears glistening on his eyelashes. "We mustn't let this happen again," he said, holding her to him with all his strength. "We mustn't let all the crap come between us."

They kissed with real emotion for the first time since they signed their contracts, and made love like dying people, slow and naked.

They were into the second postcoital cigarette when Rick said, "Dennis phoned today."

"Mmn?"

"Just as well he did. I'd forgotten about the next album."

"What next album?"

"We signed a three-year deal for an album every six months."

Monty cleared the bliss out of her mind and thought about what he was saying. "That means we'll have to start recording in a month—shit!"

"Yeah. That's what I thought."

"We'd better write some songs."

Rick and Monty sat down, took up a guitar and tried to write new songs, but while Monty began to pick through the bits and pieces of melodies in the bottom of her mind and find words for the half-digested impressions of the last year, Rick kept getting up and walking around the room in agitation, making futile suggestions and getting angry with himself.

"My mind's a blank, I can't think of nothing," he admitted at last.

"I've got enough to work on here—why don't you take a break, go and find us somewhere to live?" Monty suggested.

Every two hours room service brought her black coffee, while Rick and Dennis drove around London looking at places. Dennis saw an apartment he liked on Knightsbridge and they tried to persuade Monty to come to see it.

"I can't, I've got to finish this song," she said. People had stopped staring at them in the Savoy Grill now, and the waiter brought her a broiled sole and a green salad every evening without being asked. She was trying to lose weight. The pictures from the American tour had not flattered any part of her body.

"Let's see." Rick took the note pad she used to write lyrics and looked at what she had written. It was a song about a man trying to call his wife, inspired by Nasher's hopeless battles with the transatlantic telephone cables.

"I can't sing this," he complained, "it's crap. All this I-miss-you stuff."

"No, it's good—you'll like it when you hear it," she promised him.

"No, I won't—why don't you come up with some good old rockers, eh?"

"You never like anything I do until it's on top of the Hot One Hundred." Monty meant the single from *Freshly Squeezed*, which was storming up the American charts.

"Oh, well, I suppose we can always shove in a few old Chuck Berry numbers to pad it out." Rick slashed his steak with disdain. He had ordered Chateaubriand, feeling that this grand name must mean an equally grand slab of meat. The neat little medallion sitting on a circle of soggy toast on his plate looked like some kind of trick played on a jumped-up nobody by a snobbish hotel.

Monty paid no attention to him. Her head was seething with ideas. She finished seven songs in a fortnight, and reworked three of the band's old numbers with some dutiful help from Rick. He had decided to buy a beautiful house in Chelsea very close to Cathy's old home, and was talking about getting a place in the country and keeping a few horses.

By the time The Juice went into the studios to record their

second album, Monty understood what Rosanna Emanuel's
mother had said about her talent being something from which
she could not escape. Music had claimed her as its willing
slave.

17

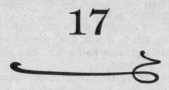

When Hussain Shahzdeh was nine years old, his father gave him a hammer and pulled up a brocade fauteil on which he could stand to reach the vast gilt-framed mirror over the marble fireplace of their apartment on the Avenue Foch.

"No Nazi will admire his face in my mirror," his father said. "Give it a good whack, my boy."

Father and son went from room to room, smashing the mirrors as they went. The floors, already dusty and bare of their carpets, were soon covered with silver fragments.

"Whatever are you doing with the boy—have you lost your mind?"

His mother fluttered in like an angry dove and swept him into her arms. He was tall for his age and sturdy. She was small and delicate, and Hussain felt himself to be almost as big as she was. Her black fox wrap was as richly glossy as her immaculately styled black hair. She moved in a cloud of Mitsouko fragrance.

"Now listen, my darling child, this is very serious." She held his hands in hers. "We are going on a long journey, and it will be very dangerous. You may be hungry and cold. There will be no more servants, no amusements, no luxury, at least for a while. You mustn't mind, my darling. I know you won't mind. You'll be a brave soldier, you always are." She kissed him and hugged him.

"Will there be school?" he asked, seeing some possibilities in the situation.

"No, no school for a while. That will be fun, won't it? We can play together all day." This sounded much better, not like any kind of deprivation at all.

They each had one suitcase and a gas mask.

"You can bring a toy, if you like; there's room for Tiger." Tiger, whiskerless and with half a tail, had slept with him all his life. He shook his head.

His father drove erratically, under a never-ending rain of exclamations and pleadings for care from his mother, down the long roads of the French countryside, through forests and cornfields; sometimes crowds of refugees clogged the highway, sometimes the road was all theirs.

As they traveled southward the wheat gave way to maize, and the elegant eighteenth-century chateaux of their friends turned into squat gray-stone castles with turrets and moats. Hussain was thrilled.

After four days they arrived at a romantic little fortress halfway up a Dordogne hillside which was wooded with sweet chestnut trees. Their host, a middle-aged nouveau riche, was flirting with Hussain's mother on the graveled terrace when a manservant appeared, empty-handed; he coughed for his master's attention, then said something to him in a low voice.

"They've crossed the Loire! Incredible! The filthy Boches have crossed the Loire. Dear God—what have we done that you should punish us this way?"

"We must be on our way immediately," his mother said, and within minutes they were back in the hot little Lagonda, waving good-bye to the regretful industrialist and his wife from inside a cloud of white dust.

By the time Marshal Pétain signed his shameful peace with Hitler they were aboard a sardine fishing boat on their way to Casablanca where, it was said, some units of the French army were organizing a counter-invasion.

His father at once reported to the office of the commandant of the regiment of the French army which he would have joined earlier had he not obtained an exemption from military service on the grounds of his mental health.

"My health is excellent—it is all a misunderstanding! I want to defend my country," he announced. He was put in jail while the commandant decided whether he should be prosecuted for desertion or for obtaining false papers.

Then Pétain ordered the army to disband, and after some show of reluctance, the HQ in Algiers enforced the order. His father was released, then rearrested and taken away in handcuffs.

At this time, Hussain acquired a healthy contempt for authority. He had also realized that he was not exactly French. One of the first actions of the collaborationist regime was to set up a committee to review all the naturalizations granted to foreigners in the previous twenty years, with the purpose of stripping "undesirables" of their French citizenship.

"Don't take any notice of that high-minded nonsense," his mother instructed him. "They don't give a damn about the citizenship. What Pétain wants is to strip the Rothschilds of their money to run his stinking little government."

In consequence, the French community in Casablanca divided into the pure French and the naturalized families. The latter, a group including Russians, Rumanians, Mexicans and a few Iranians like themselves, urgently discussed the best destination if they were made stateless—Switzerland? Portugal? America?

"Your father is a fool," one of his mother's friends told Hussain, straightening his collar with a gesture of pity. "He wants to run with the stag and hunt with the hounds at the same time. Of course both will pull him down."

"You are the man of the family now," another vivid Persian beauty explained. "It will be up to you to take care of your mother."

His father was transferred from prison to prison, and they trailed after him from one flea-bitten hotel to another, from Casablanca to Algiers, from Algiers to Marseilles, from Marseilles to Clermont-Ferrand.

His parents' naturalization was revoked, their property confiscated and their bank accounts closed. When the military authorities finally released his father from prison, Hussain was twelve years old, a fat boy who was silent and wary with adults and uninterested in children of his own age.

He accompanied his mother as she made friends in every new town. "Friends are the greatest asset you have in life," she said. "You can have everything you want if you have the right friends."

The adventure which his mother had promised him began, and they made their way to the Pyrenees, to a tiny village where the Resistance had guides who would take people across the mountains to Spain. Hitching rides in farm carts, meeting generosity in one village and treachery in the next, they at last reached Lisbon with nothing in the world but the clothes they had worn for a month and one diamond necklace, which was stitched into the waistband of Hussain's trousers.

"I shall go to London and fight with De Gaulle," his father announced as soon as his strength returned after the journey.

"You will not," his mother told his father in fury. "France

has taken everything we have; that lousy country isn't getting my husband as well. You will stay here. We shall go to America. The Americans don't grant citizenship one day and demand it back the next.''

With pitiful self-importance, his father took the diamond necklace and exchanged it for three tickets on a liner to America. Hussain looked forward to living in a country that was full of elegant women in satin dresses who sipped cocktails.

When they arrived at the dockside they discovered that the ship on which their passages were booked did not exist; the agency that had sold the tickets was nothing but a vacant room which, said the concierge, no one had ever rented.

Although she screamed and stormed at his father over little things, Hussain's mother did not fly into a rage over this catastrophe. Her liquid brown eyes were alive with thought. It was as if their total destitution was merely an amusing riddle with which she could occupy her mind.

They returned to their shabby hotel. His mother washed and pressed her clothes, pinned up her hair in elegant curls, brushed Hussain's jacket, made him polish his shoes and set out for the house of the wealthiest person of their acquaintance in Lisbon. She told him, ''Never give money to anyone who asks for it like a coward. They don't deserve it. People don't want to see ruin at their door—they want to see courage.''

With the dazzling dignity born of centuries of lineage from the noblest families in Persia, his mother explained to the marquesa that they had lost all their money and that she intended to make a living for her family by dressmaking. She mentioned, with a gay little smile, that she was well acquainted with the secrets of Patou, Lanvin and the other giants of haute couture. The marquesa smiled too.

''First I will need a sewing machine, of course, and I was wondering if perhaps there is such a thing in your household, an old machine for which your maid no longer has any use?''

They left with a sewing machine and a commission to copy two of the marquesa's favorite costumes in silk. There was a great deal of fine silk in Lisbon at the time; a whole ship's cargo of the glorious fabric had been off-loaded by a captain who preferred to get a bad price for it in Portugal than be sunk by a U-boat in the Bay of Biscay.

The city was full of such goods and while his mother sat day and night at her sewing machine, Hussain haunted the seamen's bars, finding out where he could procure worsted, linen or crisp cotton at rock-bottom prices.

The marquesa soon became one of the best-dressed women in

the city. Her friends sought out Hussain's mother in dozens. By the end of the war she was employing a young Portuguese girl to sew for her, and Hussain had learned all he would ever need to know about buying, selling, marketing and clinching a deal.

His father sat in a café all day with one glass of *fino* in front of him, speaking to no one. His weak mind was dawdling toward insanity. Before they left the city he took his son to a brothel and propelled him into a narrow room which contained a sofa covered in poor-quality pink satin. On it lolled a delicious little whore, hardly older than he was, who wriggled toward him and pounced on his penis as if she were opening a box of chocolates. After half an hour of hard work, Hussain's penis had not stirred and she withdrew, red in the face and bad-tempered.

Hussain returned to the salon and thanked his father with what he judged to be the appropriate mixture of filial gratitude and manly bonhomie. Privately he assumed that sex was just another of his father's foolish diversions.

The Paris to which they returned was a savage whirlpool of treachery and revenge, where the pickpockets and streetwalkers were being crowded out of the jails by hundreds of distinguished people accused of collaboration with the Nazis. Hundreds more were escaping to the country until the storm died down.

"Why are they doing that?" he asked his mother as they were pushed off the pavement by a crowd who had shaved the heads of two young girls and were spitting on them and tearing their clothes.

"They were whores for the Germans," she told him. "Crazy French. They are not denouncing the farmers who fed them or the shopkeepers who served them—oh no. You can't be a traitor if you sell cabbages. That's their idea of honesty."

"You will see," she told him later, "they will give the Rothschilds back everything, but when we ask for our property—well, you will see. There's no advantage to them in dealing fairly with us. French justice is only for the French."

It was exactly as she predicted. The Avenue Foch apartment belonged to a *haute bourgeoisie* family whose deeds were judged to be perfectly legal. Of the Shahzdeh bank accounts there was no trace. In due course a very small sum in compensation was granted to them.

"Give me the money!" his father demanded, swaying as he stood up. "I will make us rich again. I feel lucky, I shall go to the casino. . . ." His mother simply ignored her husband. Realism had become a conspiracy between her and her son.

In the angry city, there was no sugar, no coffee, no toilet paper, no soap, no petrol, no clothes.

"Naturally, they denounce everybody," his mother said. "What else is there to think about? Only hunger. If you can't have a full stomach you can always enjoy the execution of some petty official who used to eat too much."

Hussain ran into this maze of deceit like a hungry rat. His mother went from the house of one friend to another, drinking bitter coffee and gossiping. Hussain accompanied her and listened. This woman wanted tires for her automobile, that one needed a bigger apartment for her family, another had a daughter getting married and not so much as a meter of net for the wedding veil.

There was a bar in the Rue St.-Antoine where the racketeers gathered. They made a pet of Hussain, now a chubby adolescent with a fat backside and cheerful blackbird eyes. He had an air of trustworthiness which was partly due to his ignorance but increasingly due to the fact that he *was* trustworthy. What he promised, he delivered. If he could not deliver, he did not promise. There was no side to him, no pretension. Not for him the silk Italian ties and the alligator shoes, the pimplike accoutrements of his profession. He looked almost like a schoolboy, not quite deserving of his long trousers; thus even his sexual deficiency worked to his advantage.

Of course, there were bad types who thought they could put one over on the kid. Hussain sold a car for one of his mother's friends and was attacked in the labyrinthine passages of the St. Germain Metro by two men who stole the money. The same night the man who had bought the car was also attacked, and his face slashed from temple to chin with a straight razor. The scar needed thirty-two stitches, and ever afterward advertised the loyalty of Hussain's friends.

As well as blackmarket goods, Hussain dealt in influence. A *carte grise* for a stolen vehicle? "I've heard of a man who might be able to help—give me twenty-four hours." A good name for a cabaret dancer who performed for the Nazis? "Naturally, Mademoiselle did no such thing. People will say anything. I think I know someone who can help. . . ." Paris became a vast mosaic of needs and supplies, set in a symmetrical design by his avid memory.

His methods were so subtle he was nicknamed *Le p'tit gentilhomme*. To bribe a minor official, he would sit with him in a small bar in a part of town where the man was not known, and explain directly what he wanted. His watch would be on the table in front of him, as if he were timing the conversation. Hussain's watch was the only ostentatious thing about him; its heavy gold bracelet strap winked in the sunlight on a bright day.

PEARLS

A few minutes of polite conversation, some inquiries into the man's personal life and his own needs, then Hussain would pay and leave. His watch remained. If the man could not help, he would run after Hussain and return the watch. This happened only once.

Ceaseless activity made him thinner. By the time Hussain celebrated his twentieth birthday he still had a soft-bodied Middle Eastern fleshiness, with chubby cheeks and bright eyes, but he had acquired a certain elegance. He looked like what he was—a master fixer.

His father's last refuge from reality was religion and the old man passed his days in the coffee shop by the mosque behind the Jardin des Plantes, sitting at a hammered-brass table staring blankly ahead. At last he died, and Hussain bought an elegant apartment on the Quai d'Orsay.

"This is much too grand," his mother protested. "Whatever you are doing, it can't be honest. A boy of twenty shouldn't have such money. Hussain, promise me what you are doing, it isn't bad?"

"Of course not. All I do is bring together people who need things with the people who have them. There's nothing wrong, what could be wrong? I'm providing a service."

"I had no idea you had so much money." His mother looked in wonder around the empty room, savoring the luxury she had resigned herself to never enjoying again. The soft, blue light from the Seine streamed in at the long windows, highlighting the delicate plaster moldings around the ceiling.

Hussain now worked with his telephone; his deals were becoming bigger and bigger. In the French colony of Algeria, the communist FLN guerrillas had ambitions beyond bombing banks and assassinating individual administrators. They wanted war, and he spent much time eating couscous and drinking mint tea with men who were looking for guns. He derived the peculiar pleasure of revenge from supplying French army surplus arms to the Algerian revolutionaries, through Beirut.

His contacts—it was no longer possible to call all of them friends—were his lifeblood and he socialized relentlessly. In the evenings he would take his mother, always the picture of elegance in black crepe, to Procope, on the Left Bank, and watch her enjoy seeing Kirk Douglas or Vivien Leigh or Aly Khan. He would tell her she was still more beautiful than Bettina, Aly Khan's mannequin wife, which was almost true. Then, entertainment over, he would escort her home and begin his nightlong circuit of clubs and cabarets.

In the small hours of the morning, when the bakers' shops

were already perfuming the air with the aroma of the day's first croissants and baguettes, he would reach Le Bambou, a little dive with a fabulously perverse atmosphere which always inspired those of his contacts who nominated sex as the sweetener they preferred.

The entire room was paneled in bamboo, with bamboo stools at the bamboo bar and bamboo mugs for some of the special cocktails. It was a high room, and at one end of it there was a scaffolding of bamboo with cagelike alcoves for the girls. Each girl had a telephone in front of her on a bamboo table. A client could call up the hostess of his choice from the bar, and she would undulate down to dance with him. The lighting was a mixture of blue and ultraviolet, and some of the girls dressed so that their underwear would glow through their clothes in the ultraviolet beam.

Hussain sometimes bought cocaine or opium from Le Bambou's owner, Philippe Thoc, and often brought men there—the Germans and British in particular would sit with popping eyes, trying to decide which girl to call. The girls were mostly Asian or Eurasian, except for the two obligatory Swedish blondes.

One evening he entered Le Bambou and failed to get his usual delighted greeting from the manageress, Ayeshah. She was sitting at the bar with a face like thunder, a slender figure in a white ribbon-lace dress. The waiters, the barman and the hostesses were shooting nervous glances at her.

Hussain's experience was that other people's trouble was often his business, so he approached her.

"Why are men such idiots?" she demanded. Women often treated Hussain as if he were not really a man at all, sensing his complete lack of sexual interest.

"Which particular man is an idiot?" His eyes were frank and friendly.

"Philippe. Imbecile! You know there's a Chinese proverb— once a man has tasted the poppy he has no use for love? Well, I don't think Philippe has any use for anything. Love, money, his future, *our* future . . ." She glared around the room, her foot in its black-velvet shoe twitching with annoyance.

"He can't see what's in front of his nose," she went on. "I can't keep these girls long, now. Remember Pan-Pan?"

"The one with the long legs, who wore her hair in a chignon with a long fall?"

She nodded. Hussain always remembered women's looks in detail. "Well, she's going to strip at the Crazy Horse. And Helga, too, last month. I can't keep a blonde two weeks now. This city's too hot. It's jumping. And Philippe says we are quite happy how we are and why change it? Paris is the center of the world—Hollywood-sur-Seine! It's just a great big playground full of film stars and aristocrats, in their furs and their diamonds and their fancy cars. They have everything, they've done everything, they've been everywhere, they've met everyone and they're absolutely bored so they still chase every new thrill they see. How can anyone not want a piece of all that?'' She scowled. She was in a vile temper, but instead of diminishing her beauty, the malevolence added an unearthly aura of fascination to her features. Her French was heavily accented and inclined to break down completely under emotional stress.

Three men in expensively tailored gray suits with lapels an inch or so wider than elegance required came into the club and stood at the bar. Hussain raised one eyebrow in their direction. ''Know them?'' he asked her.

''Who are they?''

''The one in the middle is the deputy defense minister of Turkey. On his right is Martin, civil servant and developer of long-range arms strategy. The other one is with Dassault.'' She looked at him with an inquiring expression.

''They make the Mirage fighter, apart from anything else. I can guess what they're talking about.'' He gave the men a cheery salute, then turned back to Ayeshah. He had done business with all three men but appreciated that they might not wish to admit in public that they knew a small-time arms dealer.

Ayeshah left him and greeted the men, had the barman mix them complimentary cocktails, then vanished into the offices behind the bar. As she returned to the table, two tiny Thai girls dressed in fuchsia pink came out and negotiated the bamboo steps up to the cages with difficulty in their tight skirts.

''You like my Siamese twins?'' she was in a better temper now. ''They really are sisters, you know. Truthfully.''

''I believe you.''

The civil servant reached for the telephone and summoned the two girls to the bar. After some desultory dancing there was an intense conversation and all five left. Ayeshah's richly curved lips gave a small pout of satisfaction.

''I thought he'd go for them.''

''How do you know a thing like that?'' Hussain found sex fascinating because everything about it was outside his own experience.

''I don't know.'' She shrugged. ''I just know, that's all. I suppose you can read a man's sexuality in his face, if you know what you're looking for. But that's another thing—Philippe! I can't make him understand. There's no future in running a small-time operation like this.'' She waved her arm contemptuously around the smoky, noisy *boîte*. ''Sure, the club makes a profit, we make a living, but that's nothing compared to what I could do. A nightclub is like the center of a spider's web. People are attracted, then you catch and hold them, and after that . . . they are yours, you can take what you want from them.''

''What do you mean?'' He offered her a cigarette.

She shot him a shrewd glance from below her short, straight eyelashes. ''Listen. I did *that*''—she blew disparaging smoke toward the cages—''two years. I know a lot about men, things you wouldn't believe. And there's one thing *I* will never believe, that's what they will do for a piece of tail. A man will swim through a river of snot if he thinks there's a friendly pussy on the other side. And as for the bent ones . . .'' She shrugged, indicating that their idiocy was infinite. ''Completely crazy. It's the Achilles' heel—sex.'' The way she mispronounced ''Achilles'' was adorable, even while she was talking with savage cynicism. ''You know, you've seen it too. Even now, my Siamese twins could take photographs and that Turkish pervert would be in big trouble, and he'd pay big money to get out of it. That's better than two hundred francs a trick, wouldn't you say?''

Hussain nodded. ''Philippe doesn't agree?''

''Too much trouble, too big a risk . . . he's afraid. No, he's not afraid. He's just nothing.'' She folded her arms and sat back.

There had been many advantages for her in Phillipe's taste for opium; as their ambitions diverged, she had encouraged him to smoke as much as he liked to get him to the state of disinterest in which he would let her do what she wanted with the business. Now, however, his personality was beginning to disintegrate and he could no longer be controlled.

''What do you want to do, then—what are these plans for which Philippe has no enthusiasm?''

''Simple. We close this place, buy another, really chic. You see, we are getting some pretty flush clients. I've had Bardot in here with Vadim, Yves Montand . . . but they come here for fun, it's not their style, it's just a curiosity.''

''So, a smart club and . . .''

''The telephone is not a toy, you know. It's the future, I have seen that. Call girls. No more stupid little dolls who just want to shake their asses down at the Crazy Horse. Most of the business my girls do is with tourists, foreigners, out-of-town executives, parties . . . people who don't just want a fuck, they want a whole scene, a performance. They want to feel they've been where the action is, they want to feel they've been to *Paris*—

the Paris they all dream of, where *l'amour* is a great art, where women know more about love than anywhere else in the world.''

"So—you want simply to be the most famous madam in the world. Your ambitions aren't modest, are they?''

"Of course not; what would be the point of just a little ambition? No, you're wrong; I don't want to be a great madam. I want more than that.''

"What then?''

"What is there? As much as there is, that's as much as I want.'' Again, the look that stabbed his secret thoughts. She was like a panther, he decided. She could switch from kittenish play to the absolute concentration of a killer in the flicker of an eye.

"Does that frighten you?'' she asked him.

He considered. "No. I think you're right. A small ambition isn't worth having.''

"It frightens Philippe.'' Philippe had almost cowered when she tried to explain her plans to him. "He thinks I'm going to eat him up.''

"And are you?''

"How should I know? Yes, if it's necessary. He has no right to stand in my way.'' They fell silent and watched the dancers and drinkers, the buyers and sellers of flesh, as they circulated under the blue lights like languid fish in an aquarium.

"Shall I show you the place I have in mind?'' Ayeshah was a kitten now, soft and playful. She closed her hand over his wrist.

"Why not—is it far?''

She shook her head. "Just off the Champs—ten minutes if we go in your car.''

She took him to a four-story building with graceful wrought-iron balconies that was squeezed between taller buildings in a narrow street between the Champs-Elysées and the Rue St. Honoré.

"Wonderful location,'' he approved. "Your carriage trade will be gold-plated.''

"The Ritz is one minute away.'' She methodically sorted through a large bunch of keys until she found one that opened the door. The pearly dawn light of Paris flowed into a courtyard paved with ancient flagstones.

"I want to make a glass roof here.'' She waved both arms skyward, an ineffably beautiful gesture that emphasized the arrogant modeling of her breasts. "And this can be the dining room, like a conservatory. In the summer we can roll back the roof and eat under the stars. And then here inside, the bar, the dancing, perhaps a room for backgammon—like a library, with a good fire. You can have a lot of people here but, you see, it will still feel intimate, like a private house. I want it all very modern, with leather seating, but not cold, you understand? You can be chic and not intimidate people. No disgusting red plush.'' She gave a pout of disdain. ''And very nice flowers, looking as if the lady of the house has just done them with her own hands.''

He followed, spellbound, as she led him through the empty building, conjuring up visions which completely blotted out the tired cream paint and cheap partitioning.

''And upstairs—the girls?''

''Absolutely not. The girls somewhere else, maybe not too far. But no connection, no suspicion, ever. Who would come to my club if they thought the beautiful woman they were fortunate enough to meet there would be in the position to destroy their life the next morning?'' She raised one perfectly penciled black eyebrow as if inviting him to share a huge joke which only they could appreciate.

''Do you love Philippe?'' he asked her as he drove her back to Le Bambou in his discreet Peugeot convertible.

''No.''

''Did you ever love him?''

''No. I can't love any man.''

''Do you love anyone?''

''Yes.''

''Women?''

''I am not a lesbian, if that's what you mean. I don't think sex has anything to do with love; that's just stupid nonsense people make up because they feel dirty.''

''Why not answer my question—who do you love?''

She gave him a peculiar stare, for once uncertain how to respond. Then she said, ''I love children, because they are innocent.''

''Do you have any children?'' he asked suddenly, prompted by a premonition. He turned to look at her face as she replied, but a young man on a moped a few yards in front of the car suddenly swayed out into the roadway, and Hussain was forced to look back and steer to avoid him.

''I have had children,'' she answered quietly and with a finality which indicated that she did not want him to ask any more questions. ''And you? Whom do you love?''

''My mother. Don't all men love their mothers?'' They cruised over the Pont Neuf and Hussain halted at the crown of the bridge to admire the effect of the dawn on the white facade of the Sainte Chapelle.

"And who else?" she pressed him, as they drove on.

"No one. Passion is a distraction which I have been spared. I love to make deals, that's my great vice."

In a few minutes they reached the narrow street, whose crooked course had been unchanged since medieval times, where Le Bambou was situated.

"What would you say"—Hussain paused as he took the keys out of the ignition—"if I bought that lease for you? It would suit me to have the upper part of the building for my office."

"You mean, you want to back my club?"

"Yes."

"I need about half a million francs, I think."

"That's what I thought."

"OK." She spoke with care, mysteriously calm. "It's a deal." She put out her narrow, long-fingered hand and he shook it.

Scarcely a month later Hussain felt as if his destiny had been transferred from the care of one woman to another. His mother had a slight stroke, then a much more serious one, which left her partially paralyzed. In the hospital, X rays revealed a large tumor of the brain. She began rapidly to decline.

He hired three of the best nurses money could buy, and brought her infusions of verbena tea every two hours, really as an excuse to sit at the end of her bed and have her precious company for a little more time. Even at the door of death she was beautiful, her complexion as pale as a Christmas rose with violet shadows to highlight the proud swell of her cheekbones.

"Promise me something," she whispered to him one evening. "Promise me to live a good life, Hussain."

"Of course, mother, of course."

She shook her head, frustrated by her weakness. "I mean your business. You think I'm foolish, but bad money is the easiest money, I know that. Promise me you will never do anything which would have made me ashamed."

"I promise." He pressed her hand and kissed it, noticing tiny bruises where her frail capillaries had burst under the translucent skin.

"Another thing . . ."

"Anything—tell me."

"Your little Ayeshah—she must go to Givenchy. Tell her"— she paused for breath, her eyes sparkling with fun—"tell her it is my dying wish. Tell Hubert . . . no, I will tell him." She made him pass her the writing case and with a supreme effort to control her trembling hand she wrote to Hubert de Givenchy instructing him to give his personal attention to the new client she was recommending.

That night Hussain's mother died peacefully in her sleep. He cried like an infant for the first time in his life.

Barely a month later, early on a Tuesday evening when Ayeshah was still dressing upstairs and Le Bambou was almost empty, two uniformed gendarmes walked into the club and asked to see Philippe. He emerged smiling from his office at the rear of the premises, fearing nothing since he paid the police their graft like a prudent businessman. He was surprised when the gendarmes began to question him about his drug trafficking, since a substantial proportion of his wares was bought directly from the narcotics squad, a favor granted in return for the occasional betrayal of his customers.

When clattering boots resounded on the stairs from the back alley to the rear entrance of the club and police began swarming through every room, searching with unnecessarily destructive application, Philippe realized that he had become the prey of a predator bigger than himself. With a fatalism that was partly his nature and partly induced by opium, he shrugged his shoulders and allowed handcuffs to be locked around his wrists.

He was led away by the two officers; following them was a third who carried the sack of Moroccan *kif* from his desk. In the office, a police photographer's flashlight illuminated the desk top, the scales, the pharmacist's jar of white powder and the delicately folded paper packet of cocaine which Philippe had prepared for one of Hussain's acquaintances.

Ayeshah watched her lover's arrest with a curious expression of anticipation. Within an hour Hussain strolled through the door, punctual as ever for his appointment, and he saw at once from the suppressed excitement which was almost making her tremble that Ayeshah understood perfectly how he had accomplished the removal of his only possible rival.

He opened his mouth to speak and she instantly pressed two fingers to his lips to silence him.

"Let's talk about something interesting," she suggested lightly. "When will you take me to Givenchy?"

He escorted her to the salon the next day, where she was entertained by the great couturier himself and appointed the same fitter who had served Hussain's mother.

"Incredible!" the woman exclaimed, peering at the tape measure pinched between her bloodred fingernails. "Your measurements are *exactly* the same as the Princess's. Exactly!"

"Was she a princess? I did not know." Ayeshah was conscious that her slip was not of the best quality silk. It creased unattractively at the waist. There was still so much to learn.

PEARLS

"Why, yes, didn't you know? Very, very old Persian aristocracy, related to the Shah, the old Shah, that is. Shahzdeh isn't their real name. The Princess invented it because no one in Paris could pronounce their real name. So considerate. A true aristocrat."

"If your mother was a princess, you must be a prince?" she asked Hussain that afternoon.

"Yes, that's right. But believe me, if you are trying to find a home for three shiploads of contaminated tuna, it is no advantage to be a prince." He was exasperated. "Being a prince won't help me get these Nigerians to put their money into escrow. The Africans will buy anything, you know—they just have a little difficulty paying for it." She smiled. He was confiding in her more and more.

"But if you are backing a nightclub, being a prince would be a help, I think."

In a few weeks workmen were tearing down the flimsy partitions in Ayeshah's new premises and hacking holes in the brickwork to fit the glass roof.

Hussain went to see a doctor.

"As far as I am aware," he said, "I have never had any sexual feeling or completed the sexual act. Nevertheless, I would like to get married, and I would like to know if—if anything can be done."

The doctor sent him on a long pilgrimage to specialists, who did tests to investigate his hormones, his gland functions, his neurological fitness and his potential fertility.

Then the doctor faced him cheerfully across his desk.

"Physically you're in perfect health—well, almost perfect. Your testosterone level could be higher, but we can give you synthetic hormone treatment to counteract that. The major factor in your sexual deficiency is almost certainly psychological, and you would probably find that if you went into analysis for a few years, it would be possible to achieve some improvement."

"Could I have children?"

"You could have children now, if your future wife accepted artificial insemination. Your sperm count is quite normal."

That evening he called for Ayeshah with a corsage of white orchids and took her to dinner at Procope. Afterward they strolled in the moonlight by the side of the Seine, as lovers are supposed to do in Paris.

"What would you say . . ." Hussain began, halting opposite the curtains of an ancient creeper by the side of Notre Dame, "if I asked you to marry me?"

She took his hands but stepped away from him. Tonight the

white dress was of a rich brocaded satin, a Givenchy classic which swathed her body as if it were a Greek statue.

"I would make one condition only." This was the panther speaking; there was no flirtation in her manner.

"What would that be?"

"That you become a prince again."

"Is that all? What could be simpler? Then will you be my princess, Ayeshah?"

"One more thing—do you want children with me? Because I can't have them, I think. Anyway, I don't want them."

He shook his head, the moonlight glinting on the metal buttons of his double-breasted blue jacket. "I would not even want you to be my wife in the physical sense, unless you would like to be. The doctors say I can be treated, but I am reluctant to give up an advantage such as sexual disinterest. Unless it would make you happy, of course."

She smiled, childlike and happy. "I would not ask that. Let us have a marriage of ambitions."

"Ambitions and interests."

They shook hands once more on the deal, and he laughed.

"Of course, we will be the happiest couple in Paris."

"Why just Paris?"

"All right then, the happiest couple in Europe."

"Only Europe?"

"The world?"

She shook her head. "Primitive people are happy, you see. It never occurs to them to be unhappy. All they know is sick or well, old or young, enough to eat or not. We shall be the happiest *civilized* couple in the world."

They walked on, arm in arm, and Hussain realized that he had no idea where his bride came from. It was not important. She was a citizen of her place and time, just as he was. The rest was just excess baggage.

18

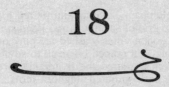

JAMES, BILL AND IBRAHIM FELT AS IF THEIR LUCK CHANGED AT the moment they crossed the state line into the smiling green territory of Pahang. After months of frustration, semistarvation and enduring the obstructive hostility of the Chinese Communists in Perak, they began to revive their hopes of hitting back at the Japanese.

A truck loaded with lumber met them at an appointed place on the road to Kuala Lumpur, and a young Malay flung open the unglazed door.

"Peace!" he greeted them joyfully. "What about a real cigarette? I know you want one—no Kensitas in the jungle, eh?" And James filled his lungs voluptuously with real Virginia tobacco.

The driver told them about the loyalty of the Pahang people. The Japanese had requisitioned a royal palace in the old state capital town of Pekan and made it their headquarters. Their cruelty and ruthlessness were an offense to God. The Sultan himself had issued a secret decree to his people to help the British.

"We are all of one blood," the driver shouted, hitting the steering wheel for emphasis.

"Drive us through Pekan," Ibrahim asked him. "I want to see my enemy." The red dirt road ran straight and unwavering, like the Roman roads on the Salisbury Plain which James's governesses had shown him. At an orderly angle of 90 degrees, it gave on to an equally straight metalled highway which, after an hour's driving, ran across a wide river and into the town of Pekan.

"It's like Cheltenham," James murmured to himself as they drove through the grid of spacious, tree-lined streets along which stood graceful wooden villas washed ice pink or lime yellow.

Bill said nothing, but craned his neck to admire the immense, ancient trees which bordered the riverbanks; from each fork or crack in the gray bark sprouted staghorn ferns. They passed the town mosque, a wooden building elaborately decorated with carvings and painted the cool, turquoise-green shade that is considered most pleasing to Allah. Pekan impressed him as a modest, gracious, peaceful settlement, and he recognized its character as being more purely Malay than the striving multiracial towns of George Town or KL. The place was full of the enduring spirit of the people—simple, industrious and harmonizing with both spiritual and earthly authority; it spoke directly to his heart and strengthened his resolve.

"Look there—Japanese HQ, formerly royal palace." The driver pointed to an imposing stone building in the heavy, neo-Victorian style of Anglo-Malay architecture. Its bulk dominated the tranquil elegance of the rest of the town. Around it a fine garden had evidently been razed to deny cover to any attacker. The red-and-white rising-sun flag flapped idly above the devastation, and a squad of soldiers, marching raggedly like marionettes, guarded the entrance.

Their rendezvous was at a coffee shop on the outskirts of the town, by a single-story suburban mosque whose minaret, crescent and star were silhouetted against the failing evening light. With Bill seated far back in the shadows, they talked with the stall owner, their driver, the man who owned the lumber company, a police inspector and a local lawyer. By the time the stall owner judged it prudent to put out the lamp, they had formulated their plan.

Bill left the next day with the driver and the lumber lorry, to hide out on a remote kampong at the apex of an inland lake three or four hours away. The Japanese had not even bothered to penetrate this poor rural area. He could operate a wireless without fear and train the volunteers the others recruited in safety.

James and Ibrahim rented a small kampong house from an elderly widow in a village an hour's drive away. It was the last of the houses which dotted a strip of fertile land between the river and the valley road. Their cover was driving trucks for the lumber company which dominated the area economically, an occupation which allowed them freely to ply the roads between

Pekan, the port, Kuala Lumpur and the distant jungle tracts where the trees were felled.

At once men began to seek them out. The first time a figure stepped out of the shadows of his balcony James hurled himself behind the single palm standing at the front of the house, expecting shots or an attack by jungle knife.

The stranger hesitated, cleared his throat and called out, "I am late, the road has been flooded."

James paused in bewilderment for a moment, then recognized their own password, suggested by Ibrahim. Tentatively he called back, "The road will be clear again by morning."

There was an awkward, distrustful pause before James boldly left the cover of the tree and walked forward. The youth waiting for him had been a student in peacetime and was now eager to fight the Japanese. James hid him in the house for two days, then drove him to Bill.

"Our first recruit," he announced in exultation, "first of many, you'll see."

They laundered their money a few hundred dollars at a time, exchanging the old bills issued under the British for the new ones printed by the Japanese. Bill sent a messenger to the house of the fat Chinese who had feasted and sheltered them on their journey to Perak. The house was a charred ruin and their former host and his family were dead; they had been betrayed to the Japanese very soon after the four men had left to find the Communists. By night, Bill's emissary dug into the earth below the ashes where he had been told to search, and retrieved the precious but cumbersome wireless which they had buried before leaving. A few weeks later James discovered a battery in a palm-leaf bag, stuffed under a tarpaulin on his truck by an anonymous well-wisher.

Bill assiduously practiced Morse code. They picked up weather forecasts from American warships and rejoiced. It was their first contact with the real war.

By Christmas, 1943, they had fifteen agents in training, and ten in the field. James appeared the picture of a cheery Malay truck driver, with a smooth skin the color of strong tea. He found he now needed to take only one Trisoralen tablet a day to maintain the color, if he kept in the sun. He drove his loads of timber the length and breadth of the state with messages and supplies concealed in hollowed-out billets of wood.

In the village, under Ibrahim's direction, he had been accepted along with all the other disruptive features of the occupation. Kampong Kechil was a village that hardly merited the name, a widely separated line of simple wooden houses, strung out along the valley road and distanced from each other by *padi* fields, open spaces or vegetable gardens. In consequence it lacked the intimate street life of villages where the houses were grouped closely around one or two wells.

James and Ibrahim spoke Malay all the time, even when alone. When Ibrahim talked to the villagers he derided James as a soft-living, Westernized "town boy," and made fun of his supposedly degenerate, irreligious ways.

"That way they won't care to get to know you," he laughed, "and if you forget your prayers no one will be surprised." He need not have worried. James's mutable nature adapted to the village ways with a naturalness which astonished his companion; the only aspect of his new life which he could not master was the mechanics of the truck.

"It's good of Allah to spare me from punctures," he remarked, looking perplexedly at the grimy engine. "I'd never manage to change a wheel."

"Allah in his mercy has given you me for a mechanic." Ibrahim delicately picked up a loose electrical lead which he reconnected to the starter motor. "Try if it will start now."

Their house was a simple building of old wood weathered to a reddish gray, with a tin roof. It was built in the traditional style on piles about two feet high, with some ornamental carving decorating the steps and the shuttered window openings. Bamboo guttering funneled rainwater into a large earthenware jar by the entrance.

A bridge, five planks wide, spanned the stream which flowed slowly between the house and the road. In the clear grassy space before the building, their landlady, Maimunah, sometimes sent her cow to graze. Her house was across the road, some twenty yards farther down, next to a long tin roof which sheltered the area where the villagers processed their latex. Every day Maimunah, a stately woman whose gray hair was bound up in a flower-printed, scarflike turban, set off for her small plantation of trees, and returned in the late morning with two full tins of latex bouncing on a bamboo pole over her shoulder.

She decanted the white sap into a rectangular trough and added formic acid to it, then sat in the shade for a quarter of an hour waiting for the mixture to harden. After that she tipped out the oblong of coagulated rubber onto a cloth and stamped on it to flatten it, before feeding it through an ancient iron mangle which still bore the gleaming brass plate naming its manufacturer in Sheffield.

The result of this procedure was a dirty yellowish-white blanket of latex which was draped over the fence to dry. Every week a Chinese dealer would visit the kampong with his truck, to buy what they produced.

Maimunah had one daughter living in the village with her husband; and their youngest child, a boy about four years old, sometimes helped her tread the latex, jumping on the stinking mat of resin with excitement. He was a mischievous child whose other delight was to sit in the cab of James's lorry pretending to drive it.

Frequently Maimunah's voice calling "Yusof! Yusof! Where are you? Stop teasing me! Come home now!" would float into the sleepy air, and perhaps later the old woman herself would saunter over the plank bridge to the house to ask James or Ibrahim if they had seen her grandson.

James was sitting on the steps one day when he saw the graceful form of a girl cross the bridge and approach him, hesitantly fumbling with her white scarf to veil her face. She was about fifteen years old.

Few of the village women bothered with the traditional Muslim ideals of modesty. The young, unmarried girls were the only ones who covered their heads, and in their shyness often made the business of hiding their faces from male eyes delightfully seductive.

"Peace," she greeted him hesitantly.

"Peace."

"I am looking for little Yusof—is he in your truck? I know he likes playing there." She darted a quick look at James from wide round eyes, then looked at the ground, embarrassed. As James walked to the truck, she followed him a respectful few paces behind. There was no sign of the child.

"I am sorry to disturb you." She turned to go.

"Wait—I'll see if he's hiding round the back." James jumped down from the cab and walked around to the tailgate. He heard a splutter under one of the canvas sheets on the platform; he flipped it back and Yusof leaped happily out and ran away down the road. The girl smiled, the whole of her pale, heart-shaped face relaxing with relief.

"Khatijah is my oldest granddaughter," Maimunah told him a few days later. "She has been living in Malacca where the people have poor manners, I think." James realized that she was apologizing for the girl's boldness. "Khatijah is a widow now," she added, as if in further mitigation. "The Japanese killed her husband before her own eyes because he was accused of helping the Communists. Less than a year, they had been married." She clucked her tongue as if reproving fate for its harshness. "But all young people must get used to hard times sooner or later."

In a few days, it became evident that Maimunah had more to be concerned about than her granddaughter's overfamiliar manner. The peace of the kampong was disrupted by a savage argument between Maimunah and her daughter, an overweight woman with a perpetually self-satisfied smile above her double chins. The slight figure of Khatijah soon afterward carried her small bag of belongings out of her mother's house and walked with some defiance down the road to Maimunah's home.

The two men watched with interest as the girl passed in front of their house. Ibrahim had been ordered by Bill to move south and set up a new center for the resistance; he finished crushing his clothes into a small brown fiber suitcase and knotted a loop of string around it tightly, shaking his head as he thought about Khatijah. "A young widow is as headstrong as a horse which has thrown its rider," he said, quoting a familiar proverb. "There'll be nothing but trouble on account of that girl, you see."

"She seemed quiet enough to me." James was taking Ibrahim's bicycle pump apart and preparing to hide inside it the precious sheet of paper on which their codes were written out.

"The women won't trust her; she won't be able to do anything right now her own mother's thrown her out."

James pulled the rusty spring out of the body of the pump. "What has she done?"

"It isn't a question of what she has done, my friend, but what she is. Women are the family's honor, after all. Her husband is dead, so she's come running back to her mother—that's natural. Where else could she go? But it's also natural that the village women will see her as a scarlet woman, all set to take away their own husbands now she has none of her own. She will bring shame on her family if they can't get her married again soon."

"Hardly her fault that her husband's dead, is it? She's so young." James realized that his British ideas of fairness would betray him if he questioned these customs publicly, but he felt sympathy for the persecuted girl and dislike for the villagers' narrow-minded callousness toward her. "What about her father? Shouldn't he take care of her until she's married again? That's what the Koran says, isn't it?"

"Ah—there you have it, my friend. Her father was a foreigner; he ran off and left her mother. Already a stain on the family's honor. And now her mother has a new husband and a new life and she doesn't want any living reminders of the mistakes of her wild youth around—understand?"

James nodded, folding up the code sheet and sliding it into the body of the bicycle pump. "Thank God we were not born

women, eh?'' Ibrahim laughed to hear him use this colloquial
platitude, giving James a playful punch in the ribs.

"You'll have no trouble without me around, I think.''

"Except with the damn truck.''

"I'll see if I can service it before I leave. My father would
weep if he saw me doing that, after paying so much for my
education.'' Ibrahim's father kept a garage on the other side of
the state, but had intended his son to become an engineer.

"You'll be building bridges again when the war's over,''
James told him.

After Ibrahim left, Maimunah became more friendly, taking a
maternal interest in her lonely tenant. Khatijah appeared often
to do James's washing for him or bring gifts of food. Sometimes
he ate with the two women. As Ibrahim had predicted, Khatijah
was shunned by the other villagers; when she was not helping
her grandmother she stayed indoors.

Bill designated their force the Liberation Army of Malaya.
They were almost a hundred strong, but still had no contact with
the British army commanders in Ceylon. Nevertheless, their optimism strengthened daily. When he was away from their headquarters at the head of the lake, James felt as if cast adrift. He
missed the excitement of making plans, the sense of purpose and
the companionship. Accustomed to having Bill make decisions
for him or to engage him in rigorous arguments over his actions,
he had a sense of his own incompetence when he operated independently.

Desire crept up on James so slowly he was taken by surprise.
It was eighteen months since he had had a woman, but poor
health and the sense of failure had lowered his libido. Now he
was fit again, and lived in a state of periodic elation as the
resistance operation gathered momentum. But there was, in truth,
very little action he could take, beyond traveling around to recruit men and keeping those already trained in contact with headquarters. Most of his time was unstructured. He was a man ready
for obsession.

He began to anticipate the sight of Khatijah's slender, tightly
wrapped shape sauntering along the roadside as he approached
the village. He saw her once at the riverbank, her wet sarong
clinging to her body and accentuating every curve as she poured
water over her bare shoulders, and afterward he looked for her
every time he passed the gap in the vegetation that gave him a
view of the river.

When James awoke sweating and aroused from a hectic dream
of lips and breasts and cascading black hair, he could no longer

deny his desire to himself. A few days later he made the seven-hour trip to Kuala Lumpur with a load of timber, and he went to Mary's, anxious to slake this inconvenient appetite before it led him into danger. But Mary's was crammed with Japanese officers, and he dared not enter. Instead he found a slatternly Chinese streetwalker, but as she squabbled over her price he was overcome with self-disgust and ran away.

He took terrible risks at the Kampong, talking openly to Khatijah as she worked and offering her rides down the road in his truck when she was loaded with latex. Then he took fright at his own rashness, and stayed away for days, prolonging a trip to Bill's headquarters.

"Marvelous news, Jim, bloody marvelous—Ceylon is sending men in at last." In the damp cool of the early morning, the tall Australian ducked out from under the low bamboo lintel of his hut. "They've dropped five blokes off the coast of Perak and they've met up with the Communists. It's happening, mate, it's happening at last." The Australian was also restored to fitness, his jungle pallor again roasted to Anglo-Saxon ruddiness.

"About bloody time." English came out of James's mouth awkwardly, and he had to struggle for the words. "Listen—do you need me in Kechil? Wouldn't I be more use over the other side, back in Perak, now?"

"I thought you loved the kampong life?"

"There's a problem."

"What kind of problem, for Christ's sake? Are they on to you?"

James shook his head. "There's a girl."

"So what. There's girls all over the place." Bill spoke with irritation.

"Bloody hell, man, you know what I mean. I'm fucking dreaming about her." He smiled involuntarily at his choice of words. Bill did not smile.

"I'm not going to blow this operation for the sake of your cock, mate. Use a bit of self-control, can't you?"

"It's not so easy, Bill." But he knew it was useless to go on. The Australian lived a life of cerebral pleasures that was virtually chaste. He had no understanding of the passion that was engulfing James's entire being.

"I've got to have a base near the Jap HQ, and you're the only man who can do it. You've said so yourself."

James drove angrily back to the kampong, thinking through the situation with as much calmness as he could. If he screwed the girl, the village would turn against him, especially if she got pregnant. He was not at all confident that the villagers believed his native disguise; he sensed that they had rapidly recognized him as British but chose not to acknowledge it openly, partly from loyalty to their cause and partly from natural reticence. He was at least certain that they suspected that he and Ibrahim were involved in anti-Japanese activities. If the village people became angry with him the whole operation would be in immediate danger of betrayal.

"I must move out," he said to himself in Malay as he slowed down along the rutted river road. "This can't be the only kampong where I can hide away. Tomorrow I'll go into Pekan and start asking around."

Even in the torrential rain he recognized the shape of the body walking along the roadside, holding a banana leaf over her head as an ineffectual umbrella. Even in the midst of planning his way out of danger, James stopped and leaned across to open the door of the truck. Khatijah climbed in with difficulty in her drenched clothes, smiling shy thanks.

I could do it now, James thought, and no one would know. You can't see twenty yards in this downpour. He felt breathless. Resolutely, he slammed the truck into gear and drove on as fast as he dared, nearly running down a group of water buffalo in his distraction. Neither of them spoke.

They reached the village and he stopped the truck on the area reinforced with stones where he usually parked it. I could do it here, he thought, seeing that the blinding rain still screened them.

Desire was like a hot pain squeezing his genitals. He drew the wide-eyed girl toward him and tugged at her sarong where it was folded above her breasts. He could feel her flesh warm and firm beneath the clammy fabric. The wetness of the cloth made it hard to unfold, and in that instant of difficulty James came to his senses. He threw himself out of the cab in panic and Khatijah scrambled out at her side and ran away in the sluicing rain.

Next morning he prepared to drive to Pekan as soon as he awoke, but Maimunah was watching for him and appeared at the foot of his steps. Her excuse for the visit was a dish of little cakes. Her greeting was friendly and her manner grave.

"The war has brought trouble into many people's lives," she began. "In times such as these, what can we do? Our destiny is changed by events just as the sands of the riverbed are shaped by deep waters."

James lit a cigarette to conceal his anxiety.

She rambled on through a tortuous series of observations about family life until James at last realized she had come to suggest that he marry Khatijah. The solution had not occurred to him before. It was simple, perfect. When she mentioned a sum suitable for bride wealth, he agreed to it at once.

The occupation was made the excuse for dispensing with most of the wedding formalities. Maimunah decorated her house with a few paper flowers; and as he sat beside Khatijah on the sacred carpet, his status of king-for-a-day perfunctorily indicated by a borrowed strip of gold-embroidered cloth and a hat similarly decorated, James realized that he was at least as satisfied with the marriage as most of Khatijah's relations were. Her mother beamed with pleasure, her stepfather, a massively fat and self-important man, grinned like a Buddha.

That night, James realized something else which had not crossed his mind before—Khatijah herself worshiped him, if only for restoring her status in the community. She clung to him with kittenish sensuality, giving him delicate caresses, then withdrawing, shocked by her own avidity. Naked, she was more beautiful than he had imagined in his most fervid dreams. Her breasts were high and round like pomegranates and her legs sinewy and slender.

He found he could not put her out of his mind by day, as he had been able to do with his Tamil woman. His flesh yearned for her unbearably every night he spent away from her, and at the kampong he idled away hours merely watching her prepare their food or cultivate her little plot of vegetables. He spent as much money as he dared buying her jewelry and clothes. When they had been married almost a year she told him she was pregnant, and he was childishly delighted.

He drove to the lakeside camp; there was a dazzling carpet of pink flowers on the pellucid water and Bill was alive with a new optimism.

"They've got through to Ceylon on the radio," he explained. "We're in business at last, Jim. Get me everything you can on troop movements, shipping, cargoes, communications, the lot. Spread the word. They're going to start to air-drop ammunition next week. Perak reckons they can raise a thousand men already."

He led James into his wood and bamboo hut and took away the back wall of woven palm leaves panel by panel; behind it was a secret room stacked with journals, papers, charts, the wireless and a map of Malaya showing the strength of the resistance. James looked at it, unmoved. Bill followed his thoughts at once.

"They'll come over to us in hundreds once the Japs are on the run in Burma," he said, rapidly assembling the false wall once more. "Shall we celebrate Christmas?"

"Is it Christmas now?"

"What's the matter, Jim? Can't you even count in English anymore?"

James grinned. Bill led him to the end of a listing jetty of planks where the fishermen tied up their small boats, and pulled up a string to which a bottle of champagne was attached.

"Best I could do to chill it." Bill slapped the label in appreciation and, loosened by its long soak in the water, it peeled away in his hand.

James had not touched alcohol for two years, and his tolerance had vanished. After two tiny glasses he was quite drunk.

"Congratulate me, old man," he invited Bill, "I'm going to be a father."

The blue eyes glared at him in cold perplexity.

"Perfect cover—what could be better?" James was grinning like an idiot.

"You'll be finished if it's born white."

"Won't be—just a lighter shade of brown, I should think. Mother's half-caste anyway.

The Australian shook his head. "For Christ's sake, man, there's a war on. You've got more important things to think about."

James's gaiety promptly deflated. "You're right. I'm sorry, Bill." He raised his glass. "Here's to victory."

By the time the child was due they had the news from Europe of Germany's surrender. In Burma, the Japanese were falling back. British aircraft could now reach Malaya and were dropping thousands of tons of arms and supplies, with more and more soldiers, to secret airstrips in Perak. Bill's concealed map showed that almost four thousand Malayan citizens could be called up and armed the instant a rebellion against the Japanese was ordered.

The signs that the Japanese were suffering on other fronts were everywhere. In the towns food was scarce, and Khatijah's little vegetable garden was feeding dozens of men in the field. Japanese requisition parties periodically raided the kampong, and the cattle, goats and chickens were sent to graze in jungle clearings far away from the road where there was less chance that they would be discovered.

On the docksides of the East and West Coast ports, the bales of latex piled up—no shipping could get through to take them away. The price Maimunah got for her latex dropped each week, and James advised her to stockpile the pressed sheets rather than sell them for next to nothing. He gave her money.

Supplies of gasoline dwindled, and James was forced to run his truck on a crude alcohol distilled from rubber, on which the gallant vehicle spluttered like a bronchitic pensioner.

The Japanese bounty for allied undercover agents was increased, but in the kampong James became aware of a subtle shift of loyalty toward him. The villagers' reserve warmed. His father-in-law, Osman, praised him openly before the other men and ventured a few words of English.

James's suspicion that the villagers had never been deceived by his false identity was confirmed when Maimunah presented him with his newborn daughter. The baby had large, round black eyes, and a faint down of black hair on her head. Her skin, James was relieved to notice, was a pleasant olive shade, and her tiny rosebud lips were cinnamon pink.

He knew that what he had to do was whisper the Moslem call to prayer in the newborn infant's ear, but as he prepared to do so, Osman took the quiet bundle and said the words for him. The baby snuffled, Osman gave a proprietorial smile and there was a murmur of surprise and approval in the small knot of people standing in the house to see the newborn.

"What will you do when the war ends?" Khatijah asked him a few weeks later, swinging the baby in a cradle made from a sarong suspended from the roof by two strings.

"I don't know," he said. With all his energy directed to the coming uprising, he had not thought beyond the struggle for liberation.

"Will there be fighting again?" she pressed him, curling her lips in the feline smile he could not resist.

"Yes, I think so. And we shall win, the Japanese will go."

"Will you leave?" She left the swinging cradle and nestled close to him.

"I may have to. I will have orders." Should he tell her just a little bit of the truth about himself? Would she be able to understand it? She was pitifully young and ignorant, only a peasant for all the intuitive cunning she used to give him pleasure.

"If you leave, will you take us? Say you will, please. I don't want to be left here without you. My stepfather resents me and my mother's always mean to me when he's around." She was warm and yielding in his arms and the faint vanilla smell of frangipani clung to her hair. No, he must not tell, he had said too much already.

"You mean you want to have an easy life in town and spend all day gossiping with other women instead of working, eh?" She lowered her eyes and pouted, and he leaned over and kissed the warm hollow of her neck, feeling the delicate pulse of the artery under his lips. "Don't worry," he murmured. "If I go back to the town, you will come with me—you are my wife." She giggled and teased him as he played with the braided-thread buttons of her tight blouse, caressing her breasts lovingly.

A few days later a distant, mechanical whine cut into the heavy silence of a cloudless noon, and James looked up to see three aircraft, like silver bullets, flying high overhead in the blue sky. Quickly the news came that the Americans were bombing Singapore, and Bill sent a message calling James to headquarters.

James told Khatijah that he might be away for some time, and set off for the lakeside in a state of high excitement, wondering what further news awaited him. As he jumped down from his cab in the clearing, he saw the Australian, with Ibrahim, three Chinese and two unfamiliar British men, sitting in the shade under the palm-thatched shelter beside the hut. Their poses were apathetic, and James at once sensed a peculiar atmosphere of shock.

Ibrahim looked up as he approached.

"It's all over," he said, his voice flat.

James looked from one face to another.

"What do you mean, it's all over? What's happened? Why all the gloom?"

"The Japanese have surrendered. The Americans dropped some big bombs on Hiroshima and Nagasaki. The war's finished."

James could think of nothing to say. He was shocked and disappointed; so were they all, bitterly downcast and feeling they had striven for nothing. But the enemy was vanquished, the war was over, and they knew they should be rejoicing.

"Just like that?" he asked at last.

They nodded. "They told us this morning."

"Have we got any orders?"

Bill unfolded his bony height and stood, aimlessly, his hands in his pockets. "Yes, we have orders. Special Operations Division is to join forces with American Strategic Services and the prisoner-of-war escape liaison to begin recovering our men in captivity. We are"—he picked the paper, on which the message had been taken down, out of his shirt pocket, unfolded his spectacles, and read—"to make no move at all until HQ are satisfied that the surrender is holding, but we should set about identifying POW camps in our area. We must under no circumstances approach a camp until we receive a signal."

"What about our men?"

"Stay in the jungle, do not engage the enemy, await orders to disband."

"What?"

Ibrahim nodded, his round, humorous face for once grim. "We've spent two years teaching them how to fight and now we've got to tell them the show's over before it started."

"Bad luck to sheath a knife before it has tasted blood." James quoted the Malay proverb with a weak smile, not expecting a response. The situation was beyond the power of charm to lighten.

"What's the truck running on? Jungle juice?" Bill straightened his shoulders and shook off his despondency, preparing to plan their next actions.

James nodded. "There's no gas for miles around Kechil."

"How much juice can you get hold of? I'll ask for supplies, but they'll be a while coming."

"As much as you want. Some guys from the kampong brew it up."

"Right. We'll get the map out and see if we can pinpoint locations for any camps we've heard about; then, since we've got transport, we might as well reconnoiter as much of the state as we can and find out exactly where they are."

They had a new map, printed in vivid green, blue and brown on a thick silk scarf. The two newly arrived Englishmen had brought it with them. During the Burmese campaign, the Special Operations Division had discovered that a map made of silk would not rot in the tropical climate, and could be concealed far more easily and put to many more uses than a conventional linen-backed paper chart.

In the next few days the skies filled with aircraft. Over Pekan leaflets were dropped announcing the Allied victory. The Japanese troops paraded in front of the palace under their commanding officers and surrendered without incident. In the country, the story was different, and there were many tales of Japanese attacks and Communist reprisals which Bill refused to commit to his journal.

They found three hundred Tamils in an internment camp in the south, hungry and diseased but not seriously debilitated. Another camp, inland, whose existence they had not suspected, contained over a thousand workers of mixed Asiatic races, mostly suffering from chronic malnutrition.

A detachment of Gurkha troops was sent to supplement their strength, followed by five Americans commanded by a major whose speech was brisk and clipped and who appeared about thirty-five years old. He had close-cropped, colorless hair and no sense of humor. James asked him his age, and discovered that he was twenty-four.

"You're younger than both of us," James told him.

"I guess if fighting your way across the Pacific an inch at a time doesn't make a man of you, nothing ever will," the major responded, blinking rapidly.

Now that they were working alongside seasoned troops, James and Bill had an uncomfortable sense of being amateurs. For three years they had lived in isolation, with no contact with the fighting which had, it seemed, engulfed the whole of the rest of the world. The task to which they had devoted themselves, of raising an underground army of resistance, suddenly seemed of marginal importance, almost as pointless as a game.

The war was over, and neither of them had fired a shot. They were not even versed in the requirements of army bureaucracy, and the mass of conventions, regulations and military practices which they had to assimilate dazed them in its complexity. Neither man shared his feelings with the other. Instead, they applied themselves to their new task with ferocious energy, trying to make up for wasted time. James eradicated from his mind every thought of Khatijah and his undercover life on the kampong.

The Americans in particular made them feel like boys. They were spare, scarred and brawny. They knew exactly where to stick a bayonet in a Japanese and twist it so that the man did not die at once. Through them, they learned of another camp, not twenty miles from Kuala Lumpur, where Europeans were held.

Bill ordered the wireless operator to send a signal requesting permission to enter the camp.

"What the hell are you doing that for?" the American major demanded.

"Orders—HQ has to send us a signal before we can go in."

"To hell with that. Men could be dying while you ask your CO's permission. Those guys in Changi looked like the living dead—we weren't a moment too soon. Get going."

With reluctance, Bill ordered James to take twenty men, find the camp and liberate it. The party set off in a Japanese truck whose markings had been obliterated with paint that was still wet.

They drove on dirt roads for half a day looking for the camp, finding it at last at the end of the afternoon, a stone's throw from the main Kuala Lumpur to Singapore railway line. James ordered his men to form a column and advanced on the raw concrete perimeter fence, the Gurkhas' footsteps resounding behind him with emphatic, parade-ground precision.

The gate opened at their approach, and the stocky Japanese commandant marched out, his sword already held before him. Drawn up behind him were sixteen soldiers. By his side was a skeletal Englishman, wearing only wire-rimmed spectacles and ragged shorts that had once been white.

"Captain Twyford, Royal Navy." They saluted.

"Captain Bourton. How many men are there here?"

"One hundred and eighty-two British, seventy-five other Europeans, two hundred and eleven Asiatics."

The sun was obliterated by low, dark clouds, which produced a lowering, premature twilight. It had already rained heavily that day, and a thick stratum of white steam was rising from the jungle-covered hillsides. James ordered the Japanese to be confined in one of the featureless, tin-roofed buildings, posted guards and set about assessing the camp's requirements.

"This was a transit camp," Twyford explained. "Men were billeted here on their way north to the labor camps, or on their way back. The only ones who stayed behind were so far gone the medics reckoned they wouldn't finish the journey. They didn't last long, most of them. After a while the Japs agreed to let us have a permanent medical team, which is how I ended up here. M.O., you see."

They found a room that contained unopened Red Cross mail dating back to 1942; beneath the higgledy-piggledy pile of cards was a cache of medical and food supplies, which James ordered to be distributed at once. He radioed Bill, giving him the numbers of internees and Japanese, and requesting more food and disinfectant. "And quicklime, if you can get it," he said. "They've been cremating the dead but it's rained so much there's no dry fuel. We've got half a dozen to bury; I've got the men digging graves, but there's only about four feet of earth before we reach bedrock."

Twyford brought him the list of internees who had passed through the camp, methodically divided into army and civilian, British, European and Asiatic, living and dead. In every division the list of the dead was four or five times longer than that of the living.

"We checked our list against the records in the main camps," he explained. "It was damn difficult to keep track. You'd see a group on the way north come through in eight trains, then a few months later they'd only need two trains to take what was left of them back. If a camp was hit by cholera, men would be dying so fast there'd be no one to record their names. Unless a man's mates survived to remember him, we'd lose all trace of him." He talked on, explaining the minutiae of the sad task with which he had filled his time for two years.

When Twyford had gone, James started to read through the

list, written in pencil in Twyford's meticulous, clerk's handwriting on several different qualities of paper.

"Rawlins, G. A. Capt.," he read at last. The record showed that Gerald had traveled north with his batallion in April 1943. The only other observation beside his name read: "Dec'd Burma railway? 1944." In his mind's eye James tried to imagine Gerald, emaciated, half naked, his honest eyes staring in his fleshless face like those of the other men in this isolated pocket of hell. His own robust limbs reproached him. He felt ashamed.

"Douglas Lovell, C. Major." That name was a recent entry. The old estate manager had traveled north with the last group of prisoners to be sent from Changi. James gathered up the papers and went to find Twyford in his makeshift dispensary, sorting through the newly opened Red Cross supplies of drugs with the help of two Indians.

"I know this man—I worked under him before the war. Is he still here? There's nothing written against his name."

"He'll be next door." Twyford handed one of his orderlies a large blue paper packet of lint dressings. "The last lot who came through were in terrible shape—all old and sick. They weren't fit to travel, but the Japs were getting desperate and sending out anyone who could hold a shovel. Here," he indicated to the Indians that they should continue the unpacking. "I'll show you."

They found the old man lying on the rusty remains of an iron bed without a mattress in the adjoining hospital building. The once vigorous, commanding figure was a shriveled carcass whose breath came slowly and noisily from its sunken mouth. Twyford left him; James, now accustomed to squat instead of sit, watched beside the dying man in silence.

"Can you do anything for him?" he asked one of the Indians who appeared with some of the new supplies and began dabbing red sulphonamide on another patient's ulcerated legs.

"There would be no point, sir. We were very surprised he did not die last night."

"What's he dying of?"

"Everything, sir. It's no good for a man of his age to do hard work and eat bad food. They had no drugs also. We needed this"—he gestured with the swab of antiseptic—"months ago but there was nothing. Nothing to buy even if we had money. He was a strong man, sir. Very strong heart. His men told us he had cholera and survived. This is a malarial seizure, Captain Twyford says."

"I knew him, before the war. I'd like to sit with him for a little while."

"Yes, sir."

James put his hand on the wrist, as thin as a bundle of sticks, and felt for a pulse. It was weak and halting. Tears pricked painfully at James's eyes and he let them fall.

Later it grew dark; the orderly brought in a hissing kerosene lamp and James watched the cloud of insects circulate around it, making faint sounds as they collided with the hot glass. In the deep stillness of night, he registered the moment at which the faint breath and the fluttering pulse stopped. James leaned over to listen for the heartbeat, retching with disgust at the smell of the body. The old man was dead.

James got up and left the building. He walked out of the camp gates, his mind numb. In the deepest night the jungle was nearly silent. All he could hear was a few churring insects and water dripping quietly from a million leaves, trickling in a thousand hidden channels.

Though that was all he ought to have heard, James's acute sense of hearing registered something else, he hardly knew what, something stealthy and metallic. Into his mind flashed the equation a more experienced man would have computed instantly—five hundred internees, hundreds more in transit, and they had found only a handful of Japanese.

James ran back to the gates, yelling to the guards to close them as the first shots rang out. The opening rounds settled quickly into a regular pattern of firing, and bullets ricocheted off the camp's blank concrete walls.

Part of his mind registered with relief that he could hear only rifle fire, no heavy guns or even a machine gun. In a blind haste, James tore into the hut where his men were billeted and roused them. The Gurkhas had slept in their clothes; and as they snatched up their weapons and darted into positions along the concrete perimeter fence, he blessed the fact that they were seasoned troops from the finest fighting force in the world.

"Lights!" he ordered. "Get the generator going!" Within a few moments there was a groan as the camp's primitive dynamo began to turn, and weak yellow illumination flooded the railway track. Half a dozen Japanese soldiers on the far side of the line hit the ground and crawled rapidly back into the cover of the vegetation beyond the embankment.

The Japanese outside the gates fired a ragged crackle of shots which died away as the defenders turned on the powerful searchlights mounted on the camp's two watchtowers. Without being ordered, the radio operator was calling their main base.

"They're sending up reinforcements, sir," he told James, who nodded, thinking with dismay of the hours it had taken him to find the camp in daylight, and wondering how long the relief force would take to trace them, traveling along the winding jungle tracks in the dark.

Twyford appeared at the door of his dispensary, a puzzled expression on his hollow-cheeked face.

James barked, "Get the arms store open and issue weapons to every man who's fit to fire a gun. Hurry, man!"

"What's happening?" The medical officer was plainly confused. "The Japanese can't attack us, they've surrendered."

"Go out there and tell 'em, why don't you?" In desperation, James was looking for a scapegoat for his own inexperience. He pushed Twyford's gaunt frame backward with an accusing finger. "You let us march into an ambush, you bloody fool," he snarled. "Why didn't you tell me the Japanese numbers? Didn't you realize what they were up to?"

"They all marched off yesterday." Twyford made a feeble gesture with his sticklike arms. "There were a couple of hundred of them. We thought they'd be going into KL to lay down their arms."

"Well, that was the last thing on their minds, by the sounds of it. What arms have they got?"

The exhausted man shook his head helplessly. "I don't know, rifles . . . small arms. We've seen nothing big. Maybe they've got some explosives."

"Let's hope you're right—if you are, we can hold them off for a few hours."

They could see nothing beyond the harsh glare of the camp lights, beyond which the jungle lay in darkness. There was no more shooting and the handful of soldiers waiting with weapons ready and fingers on their triggers shifted nervously in silence.

James decided to order the lights to be shut down, hoping to draw the enemy out into the open. Clouds covered the moon, and in the darkness he strained his ears to catch the smallest sound of men moving outside the camp's walls.

Suddenly there was screaming and some more gunfire from the Japanese. Immediately light flooded the area once more and James's men fired rapidly, killing two of the enemy who had been tempted out under the cover of the dark. One Japanese succeeded in hurling a grenade over the wall, but it fell in the center of the parade ground and exploded harmlessly.

Silence returned and they waited. James ordered the lights to be kept on, knowing the enemy would not fall for the same trick twice. There was a sudden crash of breaking wood, and an uproar of voices as the seventeen Japanese imprisoned in the camp broke out of the building where they were held and ran howling forward across the parade ground to attack the soldiers with their bare hands. The Gurkhas shot them down before James could even take aim with his pistol.

An hour later, the noise of a vehicle engine ripped apart the quiet and an armored car tore down the road, skidding and floundering on the irregular muddy surface, firing rapidly as it accelerated toward the gate. James's men opened fire. The vehicle began to weave crazily from side to side, bucking over the deep ruts until the driver lost control and it shot off the roadway and overturned. An instant later it exploded, and shreds of metal sliced the air.

"Suicide squad," James muttered to himself, blinking to keep his eyes straining past the glare of the burning car and into the dark jungle, searching for signs of another attack. He tried to put himself in the Japanese commander's position and guess what his enemy would do next, but his mind, crazed with dread and exhaustion, could produce no coherent idea.

The night wore on, the silence filled by the mechanical pounding of the generator. James barely moved. At length he heard the jungle insects begin their insistent chorus, and the first rounded notes of the gibbons calling in the forest canopy fell like bubbles of soft sound through the shrill cacophony. The black sky lightened to the east.

As dawn approached there were new sounds, a distant, muffled thud of gunfire which grew louder and closer, then ceased. A far-away roar of vehicles was followed by silence.

At last, James saw a truck like his own bumping slowly toward the camp on the rutted dirt road. There were others behind it, and as they advanced James saw that they were crammed with armed men.

"Thank God you got here in time," he said to the American major.

"We've been on the road all night. I knew you had trouble the minute you told us there were only a few Japs in this place. There must have been more. They had to be planning an ambush. We tried to raise you on the radio, but there was no answer, so we figured they'd attacked you already. You did well to hold them off, boy.

"Just as the sun came up we ran straight into them back on the road there. They weren't expecting anything to come down that track. A few of them tried to put up a fight but when they realized how many of us there were they just threw down their arms. It's all over."

James was suddenly aware of a pain like a bruise in his chest and of a dry taste in his mouth reminding him of the dentist. His tongue was sticky with blood.

"Is there a doctor who can take a look at you?" He heard the American ask, then sinewy arms caught him as he fell forward into blackness.

Although it always seemed to him afterward that the night had been a confusing, inconsequential sequence of events that made no sense at all, the citation for his decoration insisted that Captain James Bourton had courageously remained at his post and commanded his men with two broken ribs and a punctured lung. He had held off two hundred attacking Japanese, with a loss of only one of his own men.

Inwardly, James felt himself to be a sham. He recalled his emotions clearly and they did not correspond to his idea of heroic behavior. He had no recollection whatsoever of the shot that wounded him. But when Bill came to his hospital bedside in Singapore with news of the decoration, he did not voice his doubts, judging it better to be a phoney hero than an outright failure.

"We're going to London," Bill told him. The muddy ground on the other side of the hospital window was covered with row upon row of tents where sick and wounded men had been treated. The troops had left, and the rain-streaked canvas flapped heavily in the wind. "Then we'll be demobbed. Jesus, you look strange now you're a white man again."

James nodded and grinned as he rubbed his pale face from which all trace of the drug's brown tint had faded. In the hospital he had even lost his suntan. "It gives me a shock when I look in the mirror," he admitted. "What are you going to do when the army's finished with you, Bill?"

"What am *I* going to do? Come back, quick as I can. No offense, but I don't want to stay in good old England longer than I have to. Can't stand the climate. I'll see if I can get my old job in Perak again, or something else. There's bound to be a use for a guy with my background somewhere in this country. More important, what are you going to do?"

"Live off the family for a bit, I suppose." James, never in the habit of thinking very far ahead, had passed his weeks in the hospital in a pleasant mental limbo. "It'll be strange to come home after all these years."

The Australian eyed him with anger and resignation through his new, steel-framed spectacles. "What about the woman, Jim?"

"What woman?"

"The woman you married. You remember you married some woman in Kechil? You remember you've got a kid?"

"Of course I remember." James fidgeted, feeling uncomfortable under his friend's hard stare. The truth was that he had not thought of Khatijah or their child for weeks. "I'll send her some money, she'll have nothing to worry about. That sort of native girl can always get herself a new husband when it suits her."

"Suppose she's sitting there pining, waiting for you to come marching back down the road to take her away with you."

"Don't talk soft—more likely she's got a new boyfriend and they've already been down to the mosque to get her divorce fixed." James propped the telegram containing the news of his decoration against the empty waterglass on the table beside his bed and looked at it with satisfaction. "We never fooled those peasants for a minute, you know. They only helped us because they wanted to come out on the winning side and they knew they were on to a good thing. And they were right—the whole village would have starved if it hadn't been for our money. They knew we'd leave when the war ended."

A month later, his ribs still painful, James lowered himself into the narrow seat in the Dakota and winced. Once airborne, he saw the jungle-covered hills of Malaya slipping away below, the crown of each forest tree distinct even from the airplane's height. The sea sparkled in shades of turquoise; then the black expanse of Sumatra appeared and he sat back.

"Where are you going?" Beside him, a flight lieutenant held out a cigarette case.

"London—thanks. And you?"

"Colombo. Looking forward to going home?"

James nodded uncertainly. "Haven't really thought about it."

"Wish I was in your shoes." His companion put away his cigarettes and brought out a wallet. From it he took a photograph, neatly wrapped in cellophane, of a woman and a boy. "Haven't seen Junior here since I took that. He's in long trousers now, the wife says. You got family?"

"My father's very ill. I got a letter just a couple of days ago."

"Sorry to hear that. Any kids?"

"No—I'm not married." James spoke the truth, as he saw it. He did not regard a liaison with a woman of another race, contracted under a heathen religion, as having any legitimate status.

"Well, you'll be able to take your pick now, old boy." The other man gave the photograph a last look before replacing it in his worn black-leather wallet. James felt lonely. Ahead of him lay England, his family, his social position and the emotional desert laid waste by his mother. Behind him, although he had stifled the memory, he knew he was leaving a woman to whom he meant the whole world. And a child—nothing but an inanimate bundle, but a new life which he had created. Whenever he did think of them, he had an awesome sense that the child, the accidental product of his gratified carnal appetite, was the finest creation of his life.

19

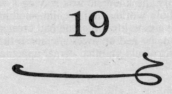

"I KNOW I SHOULD *NOT* BE SAYING THIS, MY LADY." IN THE nursery at Coseley, a spacious low-ceilinged room with a view out to the park, half obscured by the gray stone colonnade which decorated the upper story of the house, Nanny Barbara spoke to Cathy with embarrassment as she finished getting Jamie ready for his pony ride. "I do think it's a terrible shame you can't have Jamie with you. The poor mite just pines for you all the week. And your face is a sight to behold on a Friday when you go up to kiss him good night. I think that judge was very hard on the both of you."

Cathy sighed. "I know, Nanny. But at least Jamie's here and I can see him at weekends—his father might have wanted to take him off to New York now that he's married again."

"I suppose it's a mercy that he didn't, My Lady." She brushed the child's glossy dark hair, which was cut very short in an old-fashioned style, and carefully put on his hard black-velvet riding hat. "But Jamie cries as if his heart was breaking every week after you've gone."

"No, I don't, Mummy. I'm very brave, I never cry. Nanny's telling fibs." Jamie turned and hugged Cathy around the knees, his vivid blue eyes pleading for her to believe him. "Nanny, you're horrible. You promised you'd never tell."

Cathy picked up her son and hugged him. The truth was that she also wept at every parting, and then struggled through week after dreary week behind her typewriter at the Migatto Group offices, living for the moment when she would again be able to feel Jamie's small arms clutching her around the neck.

"I'm glad Nanny told me, darling. I miss you too, you know."

"Can I come and live with you soon, Mummy?"

"I hope so, darling. But you wouldn't be able to have your pony in London, would you?"

"Yes, I would."

"But where would you keep him?"

"I'd keep him . . ." The sooty smudges of his eyebrows rose as the little boy tried to think. "I know where—I'd keep him in my room with my toys. I'd get a special big box for him and he could have breakfast with me every morning." He chattered on eagerly as Cathy exchanged a sad smile with Nanny Barbara and led her son downstairs and off to the stables, where his black Shetland pony was irritably trying to chew its halter.

She lifted him onto the felt child's saddle, settled his legs in their diminutive jodphurs around the pony's barrel-shaped sides, shortened the stirrup leathers and led the pony and rider off for a lonely walk around the estate. The splendor of the house and grounds oppressed her and made her feel hopeless. How could she ever hope to give her son a good life when he was accustomed to so much luxury and all she could claim in the way of wealth was a puny salary and an apartment so small and grim that she felt as if she were living in a pair of upended coffins.

It was February and the grass had a grayish, exhausted look. A cutting wind swept across the Coseley estate from the chalk downs to the west. Cathy wondered if she would ever stop feeling guilty for the few moments of weakness that had made it possible for the divorce court to take her son away from her. She hated to feel guilty, not only because it was painful but because it was a waste of her emotional energy.

Encouraged by Lord Shrewton, she spent every weekend at Coseley with Jamie. The marchioness was charming to her now that she no longer had a place in Charlie's affections, and since Cathy had never discovered that the scheming woman had played a part in breaking up her marriage, she enjoyed a pleasant friendship with both the parents of her former husband. Charlie seemed to have no plans to return to England.

Monday morning was always the worst, because after the weekend at Coseley with Jamie the pain of parting was still fresh. Loving her son was the only happiness she had.

The hard facts were that Cathy's apartment consisted of only two rooms, and, as a secretary, Cathy hardly earned more than Nanny Barbara, given that the nanny's board and lodging were free.

"I've got to get them to promote me," she told Monty, as she finished basting the hem of a blue-and-white print dress she was making. She stabbed her needle into the fabric and snatched it out again so angrily that it made little clicking noises at every stitch. "It's maddening to work with all those men and know that they aren't any smarter than I am, and know that they're earning ten times what I make, even though Lord Shrewton's overpaying me for what I do."

"What have these guys got that you haven't?" Monty asked, handing her the scissors. Seeing her sister once more making her own dresses out of necessity, she felt awkward in her own lavish clothes. It was so easy to forget how other people lived now that Rick was a big star and they never seemed to go anywhere except by Rolls-Royce or private jet. She twitched the wide lapels of her kingfisher-blue St. Laurent satin blazer and wished she'd chosen something less ostentatious.

"The guys have got exams, degrees, old school ties . . . though now I think of it some of them haven't got any of those things. My boss is always saying that some of the traders are nothing but East End barrow boys." She finished stitching and moved to the ironing board to press the garment. "Clever old Monty—you're quite right. If they can do it, I can."

"But why the City, Cathy? Wouldn't it be easier doing something like private catering, cooking boardroom lunches and all that?"

"Oh, yes, it would be *easier*." Cathy's voice was harsh as she shook out the newly finished dress and held it up against her shoulders to show Monty how it looked. "It would be as easy as anything to make a living cooking, or sewing, or looking after children—but that's all I'd make, a living. This apartment block's full of gallant little divorcées like me, scraping together a few pounds every week out of cooking boardroom lunches and hoping they'll get married again pretty damn quick. Don't you understand, Monty? I need to make *money*, real money, big money, because that's what it will cost to make a home for Jamie. And the place to make real money is the City."

Cathy spoke with more confidence than she felt. The City, she knew well, was like a very large gentlemen's club which took pride in having no plans to admit women members. Thanks to her father, Cathy understood the unwritten rules very well, but changing them seemed an awesome task.

Everything about the building occupied by the Migatto Group impressed three cardinal qualities upon the visitor—prosperity, stability and masculinity.

The hallway through which Cathy walked four or more times

every day had massive porphyry columns, a marble floor checkered in black and gray and dark oak paneling with carved fruit embellishments by Grinling Gibbons.

The commissionaire sat before a large board telling visitors whether the directors and executives in the Migatto companies were in or not. The names had one of three prefixes—Lord, Sir or Mr.

Over the unused fireplace in the hallway hung a portrait of the founder, Samuel Migatto, in a beaver coat and a close-fitting black bonnet with flaps over his ears. He had a white beard, a shrewd eye and a hooked nose which the artist had highlighted.

The portrait dated from the late seventeenth century, when Samuel Migatto first appeared in the meticulous records of London trade. Below his portrait was a facsimile of the page of the *Cash and Commerce Journal* of the East India Company which registered his debut. Transaction number 309 at the end of *Januarie, Anno 1690,* showed that Samuel paid £7 for the privilege of importing 80 ounces of gold into London.

More portraits of men lined the gray stone staircase. The higher Cathy climbed, the shabbier the building became. Carved oak gave way to mahogany, which in turn was replaced by teak-veneer doors and polystyrene ceiling tiles at the top floor, where Cathy shared an office with one other secretary, Miss Finch. Miss Finch was a brisk little spinster with protruding teeth and white hair, who reminded Cathy of a West Highland terrier. She worked for a senior director on the second floor.

Cathy's boss, Mr. M. J. Gibson-Wright, had an office next to hers, indicating his lowly position in the pecking order.

"My dear, you have been sent to work for a dinosaur," he told her on her first day. "By rights I should have faded away three or four years ago, after the last takeover. I frequently leave my brains in my hip pocket, as you will discover. I'm still here because it will be cheaper to let me die than to sack me. Now where shall we go for lunch. Do you like fish?"

His hair was white at the temples and gray over the top, so he looked like a dapper seagull. Mr. Gibson-Wright had the perceptible flush of good living, and a combination of age, obesity and arthritis caused him to waddle as he walked. He looked at Cathy and saw a thin, intense girl with haunted eyes and a slight limp, who could, he thought, have been quite a beauty if she were not so steeped in unhappiness.

"I want you to call me G.W.—everybody else does." He smiled at her approvingly over the silver-plated condiment set. The restaurant was decorated in exactly the same ponderous style as the Migatto building, with a lot of dark wood and gilt-framed portraiture. "What would you say to the potted shrimps?"

"I'm afraid my typing's a little rusty," Cathy told him with anxiety. "But I've been practicing my shorthand and I'm sure I'll be able . . ."

He waved a glass of pale sherry at her to silence her.

"As far as I am concerned, my dear, your abilities are of no consequence. What I need is someone to buy my cigars, show me which bit of the paper to read, book my table for lunch and put me in my car at the end of the day—if not sooner. Apart from that your most important duty is to allow no one to disturb me when I am asleep. I take a little nap in the afternoons."

Cathy's face fell as she realized that there was no hope whatever that these trivial duties would lead her on to better things. Dutifully, she bought his cigars, made his bookings and marked his *Financial Times* every morning, highlighting the passages she thought he ought to read. G.W. took her to lunch several days a week, and told her indiscreet stories about the other men in the restaurant. There were no other women in the restaurants at all, except the waitresses.

Another burden from which Cathy could not escape was her grandmother, who relentlessly put her on the committees of her charity balls and pushed her into the arms of one prospective husband after another, while nagging her endlessly about her deteriorating appearance.

"You can't pine over Charlie for the rest of your life," advised Lady Davina, oblivious of the fact that Cathy never spoke of her former husband because the only thing she could think of to say about him was that he was a pitiful apology for a human being and, but for Jamie, she wished she had never set eyes on him. "It's the same for all of us, you know. Girls become women but every man remains a little boy. He was simply bound to lose interest in you once you were married. That's the trick of marriage, you see, dear. Maintaining the mystery. That way you keep the man interested in you. Next time, remember that."

"There isn't going to be a next time, Didi."

"Nonsense!" The old woman dismissed Cathy's opinion with a wave of her arm and a clash of her bracelets. "You say that now but you'll soon find life is quite impossible without a husband."

As much to deflect Lady Davina's interest as to please herself, Cathy began to date Rupert Lampeter, Charlie's one-time polo buddy and best man, who was the most personable of the small herd of her ex-husband's friends who gathered around her as soon as she was divorced, hoping to be infected with the glamor of the Coseley lineage.

Rupert entertained her. He was completely frivolous and largely uninterested in the boutique, the record company, the three restaurants and the property company in which his inheritance was rapidly trickling away. Tall, athletic, beautifully dressed, well-mannered, with wavy, pale blond hair and gray eyes, Rupert was also convinced that no scheming woman would ever entrap him into matrimony, which Cathy found reassuring. He flirted with her exuberantly and she felt herself bloom with his admiration.

Confidently, Rupert drove her home to Battersea one night, parked his neat little blue Mercedes under the leafy canopy of the plane trees, put his arm delicately around her shoulders and brushed her lips with his. Cathy instantly felt a wave of revulsion so violent that she thought she was going to be sick. Her body seemed to turn icy cold. A clammy film of sweat coated her skin; and her arms, which were tentatively returning Rupert's embrace, started to tremble.

"Steady," he murmured, sensing her strange reaction. "Poor little girl, you *are* in a state, aren't you? Better take it easy, eh?"

After two weeks, however, things were no better. Rupert was gentle, patient, humorous and desirable, but Cathy could feel nothing but acute physical distress in his arms. Sometimes it seemed as if every individual cell of her body was struggling to escape from the touch of a man.

"It's as if someone's playing some awful joke on me," she confided to Monty in despair. Rick and Monty had moved into a stucco-fronted house close to the Thames in Chelsea, and Cathy was helping her sister hang her cases full of multicolored clothes in the dressing room. "Rupert's perfect, everything I could want in a man; he's far, far kinder than Charlie." She handed Monty a chamois leather Minnehaha dress embroidered with beads. "I can't tell you how sweet and patient he's been. But as soon as he touches me, I freeze. It's horrible."

"Do you fancy him?" Monty demanded, stepping over five pairs of high-heeled boots which she had bought but never worn.

"Yes. I think I fancy him, anyway; he's good-looking and funny and I like his aftershave. What else is there?" Perhaps it was the bad light in the cramped room, but Cathy's speckled brown eyes seemed dull and unresponsive.

"Oh, not much—feeling your heart jump when you see him and your insides melt when you touch him and not being able to think about anything else for hours. . . . You can *think* you fancy someone, you know.''

Cathy's mobile upper lip twisted with contempt. "That's little girl hearts-and-flowers stuff. Do you feel that way about Rick?''

Monty paused with her arms full of her vivid chiffon stage dresses, trying to decide whether to hang them apart from her street clothes or not. The truth was that she cared for Rick, she felt fiercely protective of his vulnerability and insecurity, she liked making love with him, and sometimes it felt as if they fitted together like two halves of a single being, but she never felt on Rick's account any of the sensations she had described to Cathy.

"Yes, maybe you're right. Maybe it's only like that the first time and after that, everything else is just . . . toothpaste.'' Monty sighed, feeling much more than her twenty-two years. "Perhaps your body's being wiser than your mind,'' Monty suggested to her sister, finally closing the closet doors on her wardrobe. "Charlie must have really fucked up your head—perhaps you just aren't ready to love anyone else yet.''

"Do you think I've become frigid, Monty?'' Cathy could hardly say the word. Being frigid somehow meant being disqualified from being a woman.

"No, of course not,'' Monty reassured her sister at once with a warm hug. "You just need time to adjust, time to heal, that's all.''

Within herself, Cathy was not reassured. Now that she had experienced sexual repulsion, she noticed how many other areas of her life no longer gave her joy. She was uninterested in clothes, unable to taste food very well, unmoved by beauty in man, woman or art, easily bored and almost unable to laugh at things she knew she ought to have found funny. Every sensual faculty she possessed seemed to be frozen.

The man who finally rescued her from this bleak emotional prison was her boss. Although Cathy presumed that she had been assigned a valetudinarian has-been on account of her lack of secretarial skill, Lord Shrewton had deliberately sent her to Mr. Gibson-Wright's office in the hope that the old man's ingrained benevolence would find a way to revive her wounded spirit.

"You seem quite intelligent to me,'' Mr. Gibson-Wright told her one day, in tones of mild amazement. "Your father-in-law warned me you'd lost your marbles when young Charlie kicked over the traces. I thought any woman who took on young Coseley would need her head examined. Whatever did you do it for?''

"I was in love with him,'' she said.

"Next best thing to being out of your mind, I suppose."

She laughed, feeling the muscles in her cheeks, long accustomed to disuse, stretch around her smile.

"Don't laugh at my jokes, for heaven's sake. They'll all think you're the new popsy and I'll get no peace at home after that."

In her first three months at work Cathy typed just seven letters for G.W. Miss Finch suggested that she reorganize the filing room. Cathy suggested that she should instead relieve Miss Finch of the job of taking the minutes of the company's board meetings, but the older woman angrily refused. However, she then fell ill, and Cathy was asked to take over her work; and when Miss Finch returned she found that Cathy had laid a firm claim to her most important function, negotiating a small raise in salary in the process.

Every Thursday, a woman identical to Miss Finch came up from the Accounts Department with a tray full of brown paper envelopes and handed both of them a pay packet. Miss Finch snickered with disapproval at this point, making it clear she did not think Cathy deserved her pay.

"Wages!" G.W. trundled into the office as the accounts clerk was leaving. "Let's see what they're paying you for putting up with me—hmph! How long will it take you to get a new frock out of *that*, I wonder? Come into my office."

She followed him along the threadbare carpet.

"I wish they'd give you a decent office," she said, looking at the plain little room.

"Badge of rank, dear girl. They've demoted me, this is all I'm entitled to. When it's your turn, never be humble about the inessentials. Women always think status symbols are unimportant—they're not."

"What do you mean, when it's my turn?" Cathy sat on the ragged leather couch where G.W. took his afternoon nap.

G.W. plumped down in the room's only chair. "You've got twice the guts of most of the men in this building, and twice the brains. You may be hibernating now, young lady, but the day is at hand when you are going to want to use your abilities—and I'm going to show you how to start. Now give me your wages."

Cathy handed over the envelope and he tore it open with clumsy old fingers. "Thirty-four pounds, eh? And tenpence. There's the four pounds; that's your bus fares." He shoved the notes into her hand and picked up a telephone.

"We can't open an account for you at my broker's until you've got a bit more to play with, so I'll do your buying for you at first. Now what we want, if we're going to make money by

Tuesday, is something fairly lively. . . ." He glanced keenly down the list of share prices.

"But that's playing the stock market—I can't do that with my wages," Cathy protested.

"You don't *play* the stock market," he corrected her, mimicking her disapproving tone. "You *play* Monopoly, which is much more risky. You *invest* in the stock market. Now take this"—he put the tenpence coin in her hand—"and toss it. Heads we'll go for gold, tails for Fraser's Hill." The coin came down tails and G.W. telephoned his broker.

That weekend she impatiently scanned the share prices in the newspapers. Fraser's Hill, an Australian mining company, leaped up almost twenty pence in two days.

"You've made just over eleven pounds," G.W. told her on Tuesday morning. "So here's your wages back." More notes fluttered across his desk. "Now, shall we take your profit, hang on in there or what?"

Cathy considered. "If we'd put it in gold we'd have done better . . ." she ventured, picking at the hem of her navy-blue crepe dress; years with Charlie had made her wary of the consequences of questioning a man's judgment.

"Well done. Yes, we would. Want to switch?"

"Yes," she decided. "Fraser's Hill is really overpriced."

"Broker's commission will knock your profit down, of course. . . ."

G.W. made a tent with his fingertips and watched her indulgently.

"Shall we stay where we are, then?"

"It's your money, my dear."

"OK, let's stay." Cathy looked happier than she had at any time in the months since she had first entered the Migatto building. G.W. thought it odd that a young girl should bloom because she was making money and look wretched if she was wined, dined and paid compliments; but in the weeks that followed there was no denying the lightness of her step and the smile on her lips, the way the sheen on her hair returned and her complexion became ripe olive instead of a dull yellow. She grew bored with her demure print dresses and bought a bright-red wool frock. Little by little he introduced her to other markets—commodities, currencies and metals—and she almost always made a profit, except when she decided on a property company that immediately went bust.

"Could you have told me it was going to do that?" she asked G.W.

"Yes, my dear, I could. I got a whisper at the bar in the

Athenaeum last week. That'll be a problem for you, of course. It's not only who you know that's important in the City, it's what you know, who tells you, how close they are to the action and how up-to-date the information is. Never forget, money is only information in motion. I've made thousands over lunch when things were moving fast. *You*, my dear, can't stand at the bar at the Athenaeum,'' he said in tones of gentle regret. Then he looked at the gold watch that lived in his waistcoat pocket, its thick Georgian chain festooned across his stomach. ''Now, where shall we go for lunch?''

Miss Finch was in a permanent, hostile sulk.

''She thinks I'm gambling my money away,'' Cathy told G.W. as she helped him out of his car when they returned from lunch. ''She keeps saying 'A penny saved is a penny earned' and telling me about her pension.''

''Typical female attitude. Can't see beyond the end of the housekeeping money. Vision! Imagination! Courage! That's the stuff millionaires are made of!''

This seemed the perfect moment to show her hand. ''G.W., will you help me?'' He beamed at her with satisfaction.

''What with, my dear?''

''To leave you?''

''Ah, women—they always leave me in the end,'' he joked.

''I'm sick of being a secretary. I desperately need to make money, G.W., so I can apply for custody of my son. I need a real job, a career.''

His watery eyes looked startled. ''What—you mean, a career in the City?''

''Yes.'' Cathy smiled hopefully.

''Good heavens. Well, why not. A few women have done it. But why ask me? Why not ask Lord Shrewton?''

''Of course I could, and he'd probably find me something, but he'd be doing it out of kindness and feeling guilty and because it would be embarrassing for him to have to refuse me. And everyone would resent me, and I'd never get promoted on my own merit because they'd think I was just the boss's daughter-in-law.''

''I see you've given it some thought. Well now, let's see. You're quick-thinking, good with numbers, cool in a crisis— maybe they should try you down in Metals. These young metal traders make a pile if they're any good. But it's a gift, having the right temperament. You'll soon find out if you aren't any good. But if you want quick money, the Metal Exchange is the place.'' He appraised her thoughtfully, getting accustomed to the idea that she was serious. "I'll have a word with Henry Rose who runs the dealing room tomorrow."

They walked back to their office around the handsome sweep of Finsbury Circus, enjoying the summer sunshine. On the little white-painted bandstand in the gardens, a brass ensemble was playing a cheerful medley of tunes from *The Mikado*. For the first time in a very long while, Cathy felt happy.

As usual after lunch, G.W. was pleasantly drunk but not quite so far gone that he needed help up the stairs. He waved his cigar at the portrait of Samuel Migatto. "He never had a pension, did he? In his day, you could buy your gold and never know if you'd lose it to the Spanish Armada or the Barbary pirates the next week!" His free hand grabbed at the banister rail.

"Make no mistake, my girl. If it weren't for Jewish bankers, there'd be no English history to learn!" He paused for breath on the second-floor landing. "Bonnie Prince Charlie was seen off by a British army paid by a Migatto loan. Napoleon cost this country four hundred million pounds, most of it found right here in the City by Jews and Quakers!"

With a sigh of relief G.W. reached the top floor and headed for his office. Cathy opened the door and helped him take off his jacket. "Money's nothing to do with housekeeping and your pension. If you'd been taught history properly, dear girl, instead of by old tabbies like Miss Finch, you'd have realized that. Money's about power and freedom and the future." His eyelids closed blissfully and in a few seconds he was asleep. Cathy took off his shoes and tiptoed back to her office to while away the time until 4:30, when she would make G.W. his tea and call his chauffeur to take him home.

The next day she arrived at the Migatto building to find Miss Finch bustling in and out of G.W.'s office.

"It's all over," she announced. "He died at home last night. Merciful release. You're to help me clear the room and then you'll be working downstairs for young Mr. Migatto and Mr. Mainwaring."

Cathy collected her belongings from her desk, and packed the small collection of Mr. Gibson-Wright's personal things into a crate ready to be taken away by his family. She felt sad again, not only because she had lost the amiable, kind-hearted old man she had hoped would be her mentor, but because she knew that without him it would be that much more difficult to break out from behind her typewriter.

Mr. Migatto, a fifteenth-generation descendant of Samuel, was a Conservative member of parliament who very seldom appeared in the office. Mr. Mainwaring was bald and self-important. He patted her bottom on every possible occasion and Cathy started opening doors for herself whenever she could, to avoid giving him an excuse to get close enough to touch her.

Like G.W., Mr. Mainwaring did very little work. He also took her to lunch.

"My wife and I have led separate lives for some years," he announced on the first occasion.

"My position involves a considerable amount of entertaining," he said the second time. "Do you go out much in the evening?"

"Quite a lot." This was a lie, told to repel the man. Since Rupert had regretfully drifted away, Cathy seldom went out except to keep Monty company on evenings when Rick was raising hell with Cy.

"The gay divorcée, eh?" She moved her knee just in time to avoid his hand. Vengefully, Cathy ordered the most expensive dish on the menu. He took this as a sign of encouragement.

"I'll be off to Brussels on Thursday," he said, during their third lunch. "Might stay over the weekend. Nice trip—perhaps you'd care to come?"

"No, thank you," said Cathy.

"I suppose you think that because you were once married to Lord Shrewton's heir, you can behave how you please." He glared at her through his heavy spectacles.

"I don't see what my marriage has to do with it," she said. "Surely I can behave how I please whoever I am?"

"If I were you, I wouldn't rely too heavily on your connection with your former husband's family. In my experience such connections mean very little."

Cathy sipped her wine and tried to think of a way of making Mr. Mainwaring leave her alone without turning him into an implacable enemy. Already the men at the next table had stopped talking about the prospects for a Conservative victory in the imminent general election and were making small talk while they waited for the confrontation between her and her attacker.

"Tell me something"—she turned the wine bottle around and looked at the label—"why did you choose this? '62 was the worst year they had since the war. And St. Eustache is always on the thin side—that's why it's so cheap."

Mr. Mainwaring looked thunderous. "You'll find it doesn't pay to get clever with me, young lady. What are you, one of those women's libbers? Burned your bra, have you?"

There was a splutter of smothered laughter from the next table. "Take care, old boy, this animal bites!" advised a bibulous voice. Its owner was a tall, plump man with a young face belied

393

by his sober gray suit and shirt with wide blue stripes. From the many hours she had spent demurely taking minutes in Migatto's boardroom, Cathy recognized him as Henry Rose, a young junior director of the firm in the group that traded in metals and oil, and the man to whom G.W. had promised to speak about a job for her.

Giving Cathy an amiable wink, Rose whistled up a waiter and had the two tables amalgamated, putting an end for the rest of lunch to the persecution of Cathy. They split the bill four ways and Mr. Mainwaring slunk away to an appointment that Cathy knew was fictitious, leaving Henry to walk back with her through the narrow City streets.

"Good line, that, about St. Eustache. Must remember it. How do you come to know so much about wine?"

"My father taught me."

"Lucky girl. You must teach me; all I know is how to drink it. You used to work for old G.W. on the top floor, didn't you? Terrible shame—we shall all miss him."

It's now or never, Cathy told herself. "I'll miss him too. As a matter of fact, he promised me he was going to come and see you about me, but I don't suppose he had the chance before he died."

"Oh? Tell me more." The expression on his face was frank and friendly. Cathy noticed that he was happy to let her walk on the outside of the pavement, a technical discourtesy to a lady which none of the older men would have permitted themselves. Somehow it made her feel more comfortable. She felt that she was at last out of Lady Davina's sham world where men ruled and women manipulated.

Cathy took a deep breath. "I'd like to try my luck on the Metal Exchange," she told him as they approached Migatto's pompous pillared entrance.

He stopped and looked at her in silence for a few moments. "There's never been a woman on the Metal Exchange before," he said lightly, "but why not? It's a pretty tough place—do you think you're up to it?"

"Of course I do, or I wouldn't have asked you." Damn, Cathy thought, now I've blown it. Why couldn't I have been more tactful? But he did not seem offended.

"Tell me"—he looked her carefully up and down without a hint of lechery—"were you listening to my conversation in that restaurant while Mainwaring was making an ass of himself?"

Cathy nodded. "You were talking about the election and you said that if Harold Wilson wasn't thrown out, inflation would hit the sky and the country would be totally washed up."

He threw back his head and laughed, an uninhibited bellow of jocularity which echoed from the curved facade of Finsbury Circus. "You didn't miss much, did you?"

"I couldn't help . . ." began Cathy awkwardly as they entered the building and headed for the staircase.

"Don't apologize, that's just what I hoped. You've got the right ear, and the ability to concentrate on two things at once. At least two things at once. That's excellent. The ability to do that's the first thing you need to survive on the Metal Exchange. And you gotta be loud, sharp, quick and confident, good with figures. . . ." His voice had slight Cockney nuances; and from other details of his manner and clothing, which for English people amount to an encoded system of class recognition, Cathy placed him socially higher than what G.W. termed a barrow boy but definitely not from the upper classes, although his gold signet ring and solid-gold cuff links indicated his aspirations.

They paused on the first floor by the double doors to Migatto's dealing room. Inside she could hear the cacophony of fifty men shouting numbers into telephones.

"And you've got to be super-cool in that madhouse, and that's it, that's all you need." Henry Rose pushed the dealing-room door open a few inches to let her hear the frantic voices and clatter of activity. "You don't need breeding or education on the London Metal Exchange. Most of 'em burn out before they're thirty. But there's no rule says you have to wear trousers before you go on the floor. Anyone who can do that job can have it—but if you can't cut it, I'll fire you so fast you won't touch the sides on the way out. What d'you think? Still interested?"

Henry Rose was appealingly direct. Cathy liked his cynicism, his energy and the fact that he was looking her over quite differently from the way any man had appraised her before. She felt herself standing straighter as she talked to him, and sensed the door to her future opening wide.

"Well, you've got the primary requirements, including brass bloody nerve," he told her bluntly. "Mainwaring won't let you out of his sweaty hands so easily, and he outranks me, as it were, so you'll have to have a word with that ex-father-in-law of yours, get him to lean on the old creep from a great height."

He was correct. Mr. Mainwaring protested in the nastiest terms.

"You girls today, you'll chase anything in trousers. Certainly not. I won't allow it. A girl on the Metal Exchange—ridiculous. Oh, there are a few that've tried it—not a nice sort of girl at all. I know you're just dying to get down there with all those boys and have a good time, aren't you? It's out of the question, my dear. You'll thank me one day.''

So Cathy spoke to Lord Shrewton at Coseley that weekend.

"Young Rose has already had a word with me," he told her his pale eyes behind their spectacles glinting with approval. "One of his better ideas, if you ask me." This was his idea of a witticism. Lord Shrewton had many fine qualities, but his sense of humor was vestigial.

"Mr. Mainwaring says it's out of the question," Cathy told him.

"It's none of Mr. Mainwaring's business, is it?" Lord Shrewton stood with his back to the drawing-room fire, enjoying the heat. "If Rose has offered you a job, you can take it, can't you?"

The next week Henry Rose took her up to Whittington Avenue and into the Metal Exchange building, to the Visitors' Gallery. They looked down on a square, pillared room with a grimy skylight above a circle of worn red-leather benches which was pierced by four gangways.

"That's the Ring," he explained. "Thirty-six places, one for a dealer from each of the member firms. We trade the base metals—copper, tin, lead, zinc, silver, aluminum and nickel. Each metal is traded for five minutes at a time. You can tell which metal is being traded by the symbol on the board up there." He pointed to a display of signs above the calendar on the wall opposite them. "The midday session is just starting."

With a quiet bustle the room began to fill up with men—young men, mostly, wearing light-gray suits or dark-gray suits. Some had wide ties, some had narrow ties. Some had long hair, one or two were balding. Most of them had small notebooks, and all had an air of intense concentration.

Some of the men took seats around the Ring, the others manned the telephones against the walls, and a large proportion of them stood behind the seats. The lively buzz of conversation died away the instant the crescent-moon symbol on the signboard glowed with a red light.

There was intense activity at the telephones, and the men standing at the back of the chairs began gesturing like bookmakers in fast, idiosyncratic deaf-and-dumb language. The seated men leaned forward, calling out numbers in loud, urgent voices.

They spoke louder and faster until they were shouting, and the clerks behind them gesticulated as if they were going mad. Finally the dealers were yelling against each other at the tops of their voices. Then a bell rang, the red light died, the shouting stopped, and the men started making notes in their books.

PEARLS

"It's called dealing by open outcry," Henry told Cathy.

"I can see why. It sounds like a riot in a lunatic asylum. How on earth do they hear what they're saying to each other?"

"You just pick it up—you tune in to the guy you're interested in, tune out the others. This is a quiet day—it's usually twice as loud. There'll be a break now, and then they'll start the next metal—aluminum. They go right through twice, then there's a free-for-all when you trade the lot together. That's *really* noisy."

Cathy considered the possibility that she had made an error of judgment. She could already imagine her sweet, ladylike voice being drowned by the frenzied yelling of the other dealers.

"Of course, this is a tea party compared to what goes on in America," Henry Rose was saying. "In Chicago, where the traders stand jam-packed together in a small room, a man died of a heart attack in the middle of a session and nobody even noticed until they'd finished."

Cathy at once recognized his strategy. "Are you trying to scare me, Henry?" she asked with her sweetest smile.

"Of course I am," he announced, giving her a hearty slap on the shoulder which almost knocked her over. "If you can't take a little kidding from me, the guys down there will shred you. Seriously, you'll have plenty of time to get used to it. I'll start you on the telephone. Just listen to what the client wants and pass it on to the ticktack man—you *can* count your fingers, I presume?"

Despite the startled looks of the men in the Ring, Cathy's hesitancy left her as soon as she stood at the wall, surrounded by the peeling, ineffectual soundproofing of the Migatto booth with the telephone in her hand, waiting for the red light.

By her second day she was starting to enjoy the rhythm of the Ring and gaining confidence in her ability. Both her ears were sore from the telephone, and her shoes pinched unbearably by the afternoon, but as Henry had told her, there was little difficulty in the job as long as you could think quickly and clearly and not get flustered.

"It's a bit like skiing," she told Monty at the end of her first week. "You just have to let go and do it, and trust that you'll still be standing five minutes later."

"What are the blokes like with you?" Monty looked around Cathy's apartment. With the cool white furnishings, most of which Cathy had made herself, it had assumed a soothing elegance and a homeliness. Luxurious as it was, Monty and Rick's home still looked bare and untidy. The Juice were touring twice a year and spending six months in recording studios. There never seemed to be time for Monty to get anything done about the house.

"The guys are OK." Cathy considered. "We all go to the pub at the end of the day and I buy my round just like they do and it seems fine. They all look at me as if I were something from outer space, of course. I'm not the first woman to do the clerking jobs, but there's never been a woman trader before."

Monty's eyes widened. "Is that what you'll be?"

"Well—why not? Since I *can* do it, why shouldn't I?" Cathy was still uncomfortable with knowing how much of a thrill she got out of joining the stream of purposeful men who crowded the City's pavements, each one taking part in running the world. She tried to explain.

"Suppose I was the first woman trader? They'd remember me, I'd have really done something important. And I'm making money, Monty. Not a pile, not yet, but more, and I'll be coining it when I'm a trader. In three or four years, I'll be able to get Jamie back." Cathy, in her red wool dress, lay flat on the sofa; she had kicked off her handmade black patent shoes, something she only did when she was alone or with Monty because she was conscious of her sad, shortened toes.

"Then what?" Monty looked in the mirror, a Georgian relic of her sister's married days framed in slim gilt columns, and teased her hair absentmindedly with an Afro comb. She saw one square of pasteboard tucked into the frame. "The Belgravia Symphonia," she read. "Is this from Rosanna?" Rosanna Emanuel, who now had three children, was also a tireless promoter of her husband's career and organized the lavish functions that were connected with the work of his firm's charitable trust.

"Yes, she's always asking me to things, but I'm too tired to go, most of the time."

Monty sighed. "It's crazy, isn't it? On some days, I feel as if I've hardly touched the ground. We're still doing two albums a year and two tours a year, and it's killing me. Do you know, they nearly cut our electricity off last week, because I hadn't had time to open the bill and send it to Dennis to get it paid? We're supposed to be making millions, and yet we still can't pay our bills. I sometimes think it was easier when we were broke and Cy just fiddled the meters."

"What's happening to your money?"

"Dennis takes care of everything. If we need money, we just ask him."

"Who does your accounts?"

"Oh, some accountants." Monty noticed her sister's serene

expression curdling with exasperation. "Honestly, Cathy, don't worry. It's all being taken care of."

"I think you ought to check up and see some balance sheets. Do you know the Rolling Stones are leaving the country because there's *no way* they can pay their tax bill, even if they stay at the top the rest of their lives?"

"Well, when you're fed up with the Metal Exchange, you can go into business and manage money for superstars, starting with The Juice—OK?"

Cathy sat up and pushed a stray wisp of hair out of her face with impatience. "That's a great idea, Monty. That's just what I'll do. People like you and Rick will never get on with a straight City type who can't speak your language, and you're in real danger of getting ripped off because of it—not to mention the fact that you don't make the best use of your money. You need a financial consultant who'll take proper care of you."

Monty yawned, indifferent to her sister's criticism. Money did not interest her, and now that she had, she believed, more money than she could begin to count, even spending it seemed unexciting. "I think making money is the only thing that really turns you on," she told Cathy without malice.

Her sister smiled. "You could be right. Now I want you to do something for me. All the other women on the Metal Exchange didn't make it as traders because no one could hear them in all the shouting. Teach me how to develop my voice, Monty. There must be some exercises I can do."

Monty made her sister lie on the white wool rug on the floor. "Take a deep breath." Cathy gulped in as much air as she could.

"And let it out, and do it again, and feel yourself *here*." She put Cathy's hands over her ribs. "Feel your rib cage go in and out? That's what you don't want. You want to feel *this* go in and out." She prodded her sister's concave stomach.

Cathy breathed in and out again. "That's it," Monty approved. "Now practice that. You can't make a good sound if you don't breathe deeply. It calms you down too. Men breathe that way naturally. Women usually breathe from the upper chest."

"*Vive la différence.*"

"Louder—say it louder."

Six months later, Cathy moved up to doing the ticktack signs, which transmitted the message to buy or sell from the telephone to the clerk, who in turn shouted into the trader's ear from behind the red-leather bench. At day's end she had aching arms and an intoxicating sense that she was getting closer to the real action.

Her life, apart from Jamie, was lived between the Metal Exchange and the long, narrow Migatto dealing room, where two banks of positions faced each other in the center and Henry Rose's cheerful bellow occasionally sounded above the hubbub from his desk at the far end. High on the wall opposite him were four brass clocks, which recorded the time in London, New York, Tokyo and Penang. A Reuters printer chattered to itself in a corner, spewing reams of paper carrying the world's news and prices. The long windows were obscured by vertical strips of some white, synthetic material which allowed light in but obscured the view outside.

Sometimes Cathy felt as if the dealing room were a noisy, overcrowded, untidy spaceship thousands of miles away from the planet Earth. In her wounded emotional condition the all-consuming, high-pressure work was a relief.

Cathy was in the dealing room every morning at 7:00 A.M., for an hour of relative calm in which to catch up with the paperwork. Every transaction was recorded on a sheet of thin paper, color-coded according to the metal involved, from white for aluminum to yellow for zinc, and a heavy day's trading would generate a small mountain of multicolored sheets.

At around 8:00 A.M., the pre-market trading would begin and the fifty telephone switchboards became a mass of urgently winking lights. Shortly after eleven the traders and their clerks would hustle down the windswept pavements of London Wall and stream across Gracechurch Street and into Whittington Avenue in time to take their places for the morning market at 11:45.

Shortly after one o'clock, after the last session on silver and the announcement of the official metal prices for the day, Cathy would join the stream of men leaving the Ring and concluding "curb" deals as they emerged from the Metal Exchange building.

In thirsty streams they dispersed to the restaurants and drinking clubs in the adjoining streets of the City's Square Mile. Most of the Migatto people favored the Black Cat, a club that was almost an extension of the Metal Exchange. It was an establishment with no pretensions beyond cooling the throats of men who had been yelling themselves hoarse and meeting the idiosyncratic criteria for an establishment that could escape the tyranny of the British licensing laws.

The Black Cat was one of those rare enclaves where class did not count. Its wines were unremarkable, its food was hearty and its decor smoke-stained and dilapidated. Every new member went through a ritual in which the club committee cut off his tie and pinned it to the wall with a card on which he had to write a joke.

Here the golden-haired sons of the great banking dynasties rubbed shoulders with boys from East End dockers' families. Saville Row stood at the bar with Carnaby Street, and pure Cockney ordered at the same time as voices like cut glass.

"Once you've been in the markets it's hard to keep out," Henry told her, clutching a glass of claret in one hand and looking around the crowded basement room with satisfaction. "There's a cameraderie among the guys who do this job, which is like nothing else. It's a killer, the Metal Exchange, we all know that. It's something you can do when you're young and tough, something we'll all get out of in a few years—then everyone goes their separate ways."

Cathy enjoyed relaxing with the men for an hour or so after work, but was mystified by their liking for drinking contests and infantile mock fights. She felt accepted now, and was enjoying making friends, especially with Henry whose acute ambition she admired. It was, she discovered, pleasant to keep company with a man and feel no need to seduce him; and it was wonderful not to have to pretend you knew nothing about money or politics.

Lord Shrewton noted with approval that she thrived in this harsh but rewarding milieu, and for the first time in his life felt somewhat consoled for the disappointment of his son's inadequacy. At first tentatively, then with greater confidence as Cathy showed enthusiasm, he began to talk business with her on the weekends and show her, as he had once hoped to show Charlie, her way forward in the Group.

These developments flummoxed Lady Davina, who could conceive of no man who would invite a woman into his world and no woman who would welcome such an invitation. For Christmas, she gave Cathy a box of embroidered, lace-edged handkerchiefs and a blue Delft vase.

"If you're determined to stay at work, darling, you ought to have some little *feminine* touches about your office," she advised, trying to invoke Cathy's gratitude in place of the steely question in her granddaughter's chestnut eyes. "Why not have fresh flowers on your desk—the boys will soon get the idea and start bringing you little bouquets. And you can just drench a little hanky with scent and tuck it into your sleeve so the teeniest scrap of lace peeps out—never let them forget that you're a woman, darling. Or you could leave a handkerchief in your boss's office, just to make sure you're always on his mind—hey?"

"Lovely, Didi, super idea," Cathy said quickly, trying not to laugh as she imagined the vase being smashed in the first ten seconds of trading and the handkerchiefs engulfed in the jetsam of the dealing room. The old woman glowered, bitterly angry that her granddaughter had moved beyond her influence and jealous that the young woman had opportunities that had been denied to her.

"Your father would have died of shame if he could see you now," she said in a low, vicious voice. "You and your sister. You think you're very clever, don't you? I suppose it's the modern way but it's not what he would have wanted for his daughters, all this running around the world making fools of yourselves."

"Surely our father died of shame anyway?" Cathy returned calmly, suddenly hating the old woman and her insatiable need to make pawns of all her offspring. She wished Monty were there to side with her, but Monty had endless excuses about why she could never come to family gatherings at Bourton. She gave the vase to Jamie, who broke it at once, and the handkerchiefs to Nanny Barbara.

Henry moved Cathy up to the clerk's station behind the red-leather bench, and then, two years after she first set foot in the noisy room, Henry said, "Ready to go into the Ring, are you?"

"I thought you'd never ask me."

"There'll be quite a fracas, I should imagine. Press, and so forth." By now, she knew his mind in intimate detail. Henry Rose was an accomplished self-publicist who was blatantly encouraging the press to paint him as a bright, dynamic operator who was oriented fearlessly to the future and not afraid to make waves in a traditional City establishment. That very week he had achieved a few lines in the *Financial Times* by announcing formally that men would no longer be required to wear jackets in his dealing room, an innovation that had alarmed the older Migatto directors.

"You mean you've called up a few of your friends in Fleet Street?" she inquired.

"I might have."

"Maybe I should get my hair done?" For the past three years, Cathy had worn her hair in her favorite style, long but held back at the nape of her neck with a bow. She had ceased to be concerned with how it looked, and was mostly interested in keeping it out of the way. She decided, with a pang of guilt, to stay in London on Saturday and get her hair cut into a short, severe bob, which perversely made her look beautiful and almost girlish.

Cathy did Monty's deep-breathing exercises as she waited for her first session to begin. You can do this, she repeated over and over, it's easy. If those guys can do it, you can do it. She smoothed out the skirt of her clinging dress of claret-colored burgundy, which she had selected for its discreetly slit skirt, knowing that when she sat on the red-leather bench it would reveal a tantalizing glimpse of thigh.

She was trading tin. There was a hierarchy, even among the metals; the traders started with tin and moved up until they were seniors and could trade the most prestigious metal, copper.

Feeling calm, Cathy walked into the circle of red leather and sat down at seat number 27, Migatto's position. Thirty-three men also sat down. The red light glowed around the alchemist's symbol for tin, and one or two of the men spoke at once.

The nasal voice of Maurice, the clerk, sounded in Cathy's ear: "Thirty thousand at five."

Cathy drew a deep breath and opened her mouth to speak.

"Th . . . !" she got no further. Instantly there was a storm of cheering, shouting, stamping and catcalls. Men twirled football rattles, rang bells and blew whistles. Someone had a toy trumpet and somebody else was sounding calls on a beagling horn.

Cathy froze with shock. She felt paralyzed with embarrassment, and tried to remember, from way back, her first experience with mad prejudice, of people in the grip of uncontrolled reaction to somebody who was different. Straightening her shoulders, she looked around the Ring, and smiled. The noise died away to a few cheers, and then, as if nothing had happened, the men carried on trading.

Maurice was speaking again. "Buy three hundred thousand," he said.

It was a put-on, another test. *Nobody* could possibly be looking for such a colossal quantity of tin, or any other metal. They were trying to kid her. It was another of their infantile all-boys-together jokes. Cathy smiled and kept her mouth shut.

"Three hundred thousand," Maurice said, his voice rising with panic. Cathy did not respond. I'll show them they can't fool me, she thought with satisfaction.

"You s-s-s-stupid bitch—*three hundred thousand!*" Maurice, stammering in agitation, spoke loud enough for his voice to carry into the Ring. Several of the men looked at her with alarm and Cathy realized that she had made a mistake, this was not a joke, it was a serious order.

Two men offered fifty thousand at six.

"Five," she said, almost whispering with relief and dismay

that she had wasted precious seconds ignoring an order. I've got forty-two seconds to get the deal, she realized.

Just before the bell rang, she bought her last fifty thousand to make up the three hundred, at five. She felt ten pounds lighter and ten years older as she got up and walked out of the Ring. As she stood on the pavement outside finishing a couple of curb deals, she was blinded by a flash of light as a press photographer took her picture.

In the Black Cat, when the afternoon market had finished, Henry poured champagne over her head and the men slapped her on the back, shook her hand, kissed her. The club committee decided to make her a member.

"But I haven't got a tie for the wall," she protested.

"We'll find one for you."

"No—wait. Give me a card." She drew the outline of a tie in a dotted line on the card and wrote beside it, "You don't miss what you've never had." Then she signed underneath, "The Invisible Man." There was more cheering.

"Better drink some of that champagne," Henry suggested. "I don't want you catching cold in wet clothes. You'll lose your voice."

The next day, Cathy woke at 5:00 A.M. with a thundering hangover and an irritating idea that would not leave her mind.

In spite of knowing the other traders as friends—almost the only true friends she had now—she had been shocked by the noisy outcry with which they had welcomed her into the Ring. The catcalls, the hunting horns and the football rattles—it had seemed like innocent horseplay, but underneath she sensed real hostility to a stranger who had dared to penetrate the group. Suddenly Cathy remembered Rosanna Emanuel's first dinner at Benenden, when another girl had called out something about all Jews having horns. She remembered seeing her friend at first stunned, then defending herself with a submissive, placatory smile.

That incident had the same scent of mob prejudice, of people swayed by an emotion so violent they had broken their own rules of behavior in order to express it.

Cathy deprived Jamie of her company for another Saturday and went shopping. She bought herself a gray suit with a faint white stripe, a blue shirt and a bow tie. Thereafter her flowered dresses and colorful sweaters hung in the back of the wardrobe all week, as she tried to look as much as possible like the men with whom she worked. She traded her handbag for an Asprey briefcase and started drinking Scotch—with a lot of water.

"It worked for Rosanna, it'll work for me," she told herself. "I'll just blend in, until people forget I'm different."

Cathy had been trading for a year when she knew she had nothing more to prove to the men of the City of London. As she came up to the Visitors Gallery before the morning market, she heard her old boss, Mr. Mainwaring, showing some guests the Metal Exchange.

"Of course," he boasted, "Migatto have always been the most forward-looking of the Metal Exchange's members. Why, just recently we put the first woman trader in the Ring down there. Bright girl. Used to work for me, as a matter of fact."

Cathy smiled and wished him a pleasant good morning.

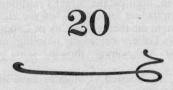

20

"CHRIST ALMIGHTY—LOOK AT THE STATE OF THAT!" A GIRL with no eyebrows, hair teased into vertical spikes and a black lightning flash painted down her face walked across King's Road in front of Rick's willow-green Rolls-Royce. She was wearing a torn black T-shirt, shiny black rubber tights that coated her legs like liquid, and a small padlock in her right earlobe.

"Get a move on, darlin'!" Rick shouted out of the car window. The girl paused in the center of the crossing and scraped her stilettoes as if she had trodden in some dog shit.

"Don't wind her up, Rick, or we'll never get there." They were already half an hour late for the awards ceremony and Monty knew that the strutting apparition in front of them was quite capable of spinning out the confrontation for another half hour. "Give her a grin and let's go," she urged Rick. "It's that girl from the punk shop—she'll piss about forever if she recognizes you."

She spoke too late. The girl had recognized the great Rick Brown of The Juice. He was old, rich and successful—everything that she despised.

For the punks Rick was a symbol of exploitation. He had made his millions from kids like them, peddling songs about their anger, their pain and their yearnings. But once the royalties started flowing, Rick and The Juice had sold out the great underclass of youth for whom they claimed to speak, and gone for all the trappings of privilege—the swanky cars, the country estates, the flashy women and the private jets. They had hired bodyguards and big dogs to keep away the kids who had put them at the top.

By 1976, the fat years were finished for Britain. Industries were collapsing like mushrooms rotting in autumn fields, leaving stinking pools of unemployment and deprivation. Kids finished school and signed on the dole, knowing the odds were that some of them would never be able to work in their lives. The future offered them nothing. They were angry.

The punk girl looked with loathing at the gleaming Rolls-Royce carrying people in evening clothes somewhere she could not follow. She raised a finger in the stick-it-up-yer-ass sign, and glowered, deliberately blocking the road.

Behind Rick's Rolls a tail of cars began to form along the winding length of King's Road. Just as their driver was opening his door to make the punk girl move, a pair of uniformed policemen strolled up and hustled her out of the road.

"Thanks, mate," Rick called to them.

The elder of the two constables reached into his tunic pocket for his notebook, walked up to the car and leaned down to talk to Rick.

"Any chance of an autograph, Rick? The old lady's a real fan of yours."

Rick wrote his name swiftly with the proffered pen and they drove on. From the pavement, the punk girl again gestured obscenely.

"Filthy scrubber. Who'd want to fuck anything like that?" Rick settled back in his seat and the car's tinted window rolled smoothly shut.

"She doesn't want to get fucked—that's the point. Why should a girl have to look attractive for men all the time?" The speaker was Cindy Moon, a columnist with *Hit Maker Magazine*, who was hosting the awards ceremony. Cindy was given to mouthing women's lib clichés but her own appearance belied her words. Her tinted blond curls were spun into a cloud of gold candyfloss around her shoulders, and her green chiffon dress, tightly cinched at the waist with a gold belt, revealed every feature of her anatomy. She looked like a Barbie doll with added nipples.

"Dunno why we're going to this party, anyway. We aren't nominated for anything, are we?" Rick ran his fingers through his floppy brown hair with a petulant gesture.

"Dennis says you've got to keep in the public eye," Monty reminded him.

"And they want you to present the award for best new vocalist," added Cindy, crossing her thin white legs.

"Oh, yeah. Who is it?"

"Bruce Springsteen."

"Fucking hell—not that one-hit wonder? Still, I suppose it could have been worse; they could've given it to some bunch of punks."

"They will, next year." Cindy had been one of the first of the rock establishment to take the new punk bands seriously. Rick gave her an angry look. "You can't fight it, Rick," she told him. "Things don't stand still anywhere, least of all in this business. Hits turn into has-beens quicker than beer turns to piss. The kids who're buying records now were spending their pocket money on penny sweets when you and The Juice had your first hits. They don't want the same old sounds."

Monty saw a fresh opportunity to talk Rick into taking the band in a new direction. In the beginning, when he had been insecure, he had always followed her advice. When the pressure had been on them to make two albums a year, he had relied on Monty's musical ability with a desperate gratitude. Then Dennis had got them a new and better deal with Excellent Records, and Rick's attitude had changed. He seemed to resent her talent, and avoided asking for her help.

Instead, he had fallen back into the safe, easy, rock 'n' roll style he had given the band at the beginning. Monty realized that he felt threatened when he had to rely on her, but she wanted to record her own songs, and she was bored with The Juice's output now, and so were the kids, who bought fewer of their records every year. Rick refused to change. Maybe, Monty thought, he'd listen to her if Cindy frightened him a little.

"Were we nominated for anything, Cindy?" she asked. "You were on the judging panel—what happened?"

Cindy's narrow, heavily glossed lips pouted as she thought. She knew at once why Monty was asking. Monty and Rick had had so many screaming rows in public that everyone in London knew what the tensions in their relationship were. "You want me to tell you the truth?"

"Of course, that's why I'm asking."

"I don't believe anyone ever mentioned The Juice. There are so many new bands now. . . ." Cindy fell into a studied silence of embarrassment and stared at her long red fingernails. Monty looked covertly at Rick. He was gazing out the car's dark window as if he were not listening.

The awards ceremony at the Savoy was an ordeal. Monty and Rick were not seated together; Dennis still insisted that their relationship should not be stressed in public. Instead, Rick and the rest of the band went around like a street gang of brawling

boys and Monty had to find her own level among the second
league of friends, engineers, roadies, gofers and publicists.

From her table at the back of the hall she watched Rick in his
old blue jean jacket standing with Cy, Pete and Nasher, reading
the nominations for Best New Vocalist. Cy had discovered heroin in the first month of The Juice's success. Now he looked a
little more gaunt every year, and one or two of his teeth had
dropped out. Pete was getting a distinct belly which bulged over
the top of his jeans. Nasher hardly seemed to change, except his
hair was thinning and he had taken to wearing a denim cap to
disguise his bald spot. The Juice looked middle-aged.

"Talk about the night of the living dead," sneered a boy sitting opposite her, as Rick mumbled an explanation about why
Bruce Springsteen was unable to accept his award in person. The
boy had a round bullet head covered with black hair which was
shaved to half an inch in length, and a small silver ring through
one of his nostrils.

"I thought Rick Brown *was* dead," his companion drawled,
peering at the stage through wraparound dark glasses an inch
wide.

"Be better for him if he was," the first speaker announced,
turning his back on the presentation ceremony. "Did you see
their last album didn't even make the top thirty? Aging savages,
that's what they are. Best argument for euthanasia I've seen for
years. Excellent will be dumping them at the end of their contract, that's for sure."

The man with dark glasses flicked them up and down like
Groucho Marx as he looked at Monty. "What's a place like this
doing in a girl like you? Don't I know you?"

Monty gave him a withering stare from below half-lowered
eyelids.

"Don't be stupid," the stubble headed boy told his friend.
"She's one of them. You sing with The Juice, don't you?"

"Yeah. I expect you saw me on TV when you were a baby."
Monty offered her cigarettes to show she wasn't offended by
what they had said about The Juice.

"That's your old man we're slagging off, innit?" the crop-
haired one challenged her.

"That's right."

"You don't seem too excited about him, neither."

Monty shrugged. "Nothing's exciting after seven years, is
it?"

"Dunno—I'll tell you when I'm old. Didn't someone tell me
you wrote some of their songs?"

"A lot of the early ones. I don't write the stuff they're doing now."

"Pity. They could do with some decent material, instead of doing all this plastic American crap. It's bad enough having people waste good money on Eagles albums without getting all that garbage from over there as well."

"Tell me about it. I think Rick wants to be the next Frank Sinatra or something."

He blew thick plumes of smoke from his wide nostrils and looked at her directly. "What about you, what do you want to do? Given up writing songs, or what?"

Monty shook her head, feeling her luxuriant dark curls, teased to a glistening mass with her Afro comb and tinted mahogany with henna, stir around her shoulders. Her black silk sweater embroidered with diamanté slipped off her shoulder and she pulled it back casually.

"I write stuff all the time," she told him.

"Good for you," he rejoined with a wink.

Onstage, Cindy Moon was breathlessly thanking everyone involved in the ceremony and saying good night to the TV audience. The floor manager waved his arms, everyone applauded and at last the TV lights dimmed.

Monty stood up to leave with the two young men, who were dressed entirely in black, with straps bound around their trouser legs.

"Tell you what," the short-haired one said to Monty as they left the overheated room, "when you get fed up with Frank Sinatra there, gimme a bell." He reached into the pocket of his studded leather jacket and gave her a card. "Sig Bear: Biffo Records" it said.

"I think you got great tits, 'n' all," he shouted to her outside the Savoy, as he walked away with his friend. Monty put the card in her silver snakeskin evening purse and forgot about it. She'd had the same conversation a dozen times in the past three years.

I wonder if Rick's having a scene with Cindy, she thought, watching him put his arm around the slender figure in green chiffon and face the TV camera with a smile for an interview. The idea of Rick with another woman—yet *another* woman— barely moved Monty now. In addition to the orgiastic style of The Juice's tours, Rick seemed to feel dutybound to jump every woman who came near him.

What worried Monty far more was the fact that, although she cared for Rick still, it was the vulnerable, hungry, insecure Rick she loved, not the arrogant monster he had chosen to become in public. Every now and then, when they were exhausted after one of their fights or wrecked at the end of a tour, they would find each other again, but then he would withdraw from her, turning into the taunting sadist he played onstage, and be lost to her. He did not want intimacy. It scared him.

Monty had learned a lot about men in the past seven years. She had begun with tit-for-tat affairs to kill the pain of Rick's unfaithfulness. Then she discovered that some men would come on to her to get at Rick; some—like Nasher—would make a pass out of sympathy for her; some—like Dennis—would attack out of pure greedy lust; and some—like Les Lightfoot, Excellent's A & R man, would try to lay her because they thought they deserved her as a perk of their jobs.

She had left Rick for three months and gone to Marrakesh with the effete lead singer of a glam-rock band, but he treated her like another accessory to his pose of ineffable style, and Rick, suddenly abject, had pleaded with her so passionately and abased himself so totally over the echoing Moroccan telephone line that she had felt cruel and gone back to him.

Monty watched as a couple of girls came up and asked Rick for his autograph. They tossed their blond hair and swung their hips as he talked to them, turned on just to be at the edge of a great star's sexual aura. If only they knew, Monty thought, what he's really like in bed. All the tenderness had gone; after seven years of nonstop promiscuity Rick fucked like a robot, giving no pleasure and probably getting none.

Next day there was a meeting with Dennis, their manager, who came to the graceful white-stucco house near the river in Chelsea where Rick and Monty lived when they were in London. Of all of them, he had aged most dramatically. His face was deeply lined and fleshless, like a monkey's, and his blond hair, now cut short, was almost white. With him came a fleshy young man in denims with long brown hair and an unshaven chin.

"This is Keith—he's going to direct our video," Dennis explained. "Excellent is gonna spend big money promoting the new album." He paused to take the gold toot-tube passed to him by Monty and snort a line of coke from the matching gold plate that was being passed around the table.

"D'you think Excellent is going to offer us another contract when this one ends?" Nasher was always the most practical member of The Juice.

"Could be. Could be they just want to get back what they lost on the last album."

"What do you mean, they lost?" Rick was roaming angrily around the room. "The album sold OK, didn't it?"

"It sold OK, Rick, but not great. And the tour was fucking expensive."

"Look, we don't wanna stay with Excellent, do we?" Rick leaned forward on the massive Odeon-style table of blond burr walnut and looked from one person to another. "They're old men, they're finished. We wanna move on, right?"

"I never wanted to sign a second deal with Excellent anyway." Cy gazed at the ceiling, his feet in their green boots propped against the mantelpiece. It was a beautiful white alabaster mantelpiece decorated with carved garlands, which Cy had already damaged with his habit of swinging up his legs and bringing his feet down against the soft stone with a careless crash. The eighteenth-century chandelier was also looking a little worse for wear. One afternoon Rick and Cy had passed the time shooting at the crystal drops with air pistols.

"If you want my opinion, Excellent is looking to save itself money by spending thirty thousand on a video and then making the tour much shorter—just a couple of big gigs here and in the States, no crazy sets or anything." Dennis closed one nostril and sniffed hard to encourage the last crystals of coke into his bloodstream. "We can make that work to our advantage. All we gotta do is something that'll cause a bit of a sensation. That shouldn't be too difficult, now should it?"

Keith, the plump young director, spoke for the first time, clearing his throat nervously. "I've had a few ideas and I thought maybe we could talk them through a bit and then I'll get a storyboard done and we can go into more detail."

"All right, Keith, tell us how you see us." There was a dangerous edge of sarcasm in Rick's voice.

"Well, it's a very alienated sort of feel, so I thought we'd maybe try a sort of urban landscape, lots of litter, brick walls, graffiti, trash in the gutters, weird kind of lighting. . . ."

The Juice, to a man, looked uninspired. Keith cleared his throat again.

"Or perhaps some bizarre sort of sci-fi scenario, with you all as extraterrestrials walking through the city, seeing it in all its freakiness. . . ."

"The earthlings won't understand," Nasher said, folding his arms.

There was an awkward pause. What none of them cared to admit was that they were scared of doing a video. Videos were very new; only a few of the biggest stars, like Bowie and the Stones had done one, and Bowie was a performing artist anyway, and Jagger still looked young.

Cy pulled his legs down the mantelpiece, scraping the fragile stone with his boots.

"How about a Roman orgy?" he suggested, running his pallid tongue over his sunken lips. "I could do with a few dancing girls and grapes and that."

"Ah—great—yes, a Roman orgy, mmmmmm. . . ." Keith fingered his stubble thoughtfully. Monty's heart sank.

They flew to Los Angeles to shoot the video, at the Bel-Air home of a TV talk-show host who was extremely proud of his classical-style pool. It was surrounded by white pillars, with a pediment at one end and a huge gold dolphin spouting water from its mouth at the other. The poolside area was covered in mosaics carefully copied from Pompeii, and a swing on gold ropes dangled over the semicircular flight of steps leading down into the water.

They started work at about 3:00 P.M. It had taken the rest of the day to dress the set as Keith wanted it, with garlands of roses wound around the swing, rose petals scattered ankle deep on the ground and gilt couches lined up by the poolside. He had the blue water tinted a glowing purple by the addition of some pink dye. There were ten dancers to shoot first, one with a python and one with a leopard on a gold chain. There was a cage full of doves. As twilight approached, flaming torches were fixed to the walls and there was a long pause for relighting.

Monty, Rick and the others sat watching with interest, occasionally dipping into the bowl of cocaine that Keith had thoughtfully ordered for them, along with four bottles of Jack Daniel's and some sandwiches.

"I hope nobody comes near me with that snake," Nasher shuddered. "I hate fuckin' snakes."

"Nobody's asked you to fuck it, Nasher," Rick told him. It was a feeble joke, indicating how nervous Rick was. He got up and walked away; Monty followed, and he put his arm around her without speaking. They walked along the gravel path at the side of the house. It was the mellow end of the day and the scent of the newmown lawn and blooming lavender mingled in the gentle air.

They paused at the crest of a slope of manicured turf which led away to a group of palms. The focus of the vista was a floodlit statue of Diana with a fawn and from the distance it was impossible to tell that it was made of fiberglass.

"What d'you reckon to all this?" Rick asked her suddenly.

"The video, you mean?"

"Yeah—are we right to do it, or what?"

"Rick—of course we're right to do it. It's the future. The

band's *got* to change, we can't go on doing the same old stuff the same old way forever. The kids who used to buy our records are grown-up now; there's a new audience coming along and they want something different.''

They sat down on the warm grass. Monty folded her arms around her knees like a little girl, watching her loose red-silk dress ripple as she moved. Her hair was a wild mass of dark tendrils into which the hairdresser had plaited some red-silk thread. Rick wrapped a curl around his finger, admiring its sheen.

''To tell the truth, I don't like what we're doing now,'' he admitted. ''We really need you, Monty. You've just got a way with music that I haven't. Oh, sure, I can leap around the stage and make a lot of noise and cause a lot of aggravation, but I can't hear a tune in my head and play it like you can. There were some fabulous songs on those first albums, eh?''

''Yes,'' she said simply, not daring to say more in case years of resentment sounded in her voice.

''When all this is over, how would you fancy doing your own album?'' he asked suddenly.

''Sending the old lady out to work?'' she teased him, delighted.

''Yeah, why not? You've got a better voice than I have, girl, and you know it. That's what I don't like, though. It's not how good you are, it's how big you're hyped. We'll just have to think of something to make 'em sit up and remember who's the boss, that's all.''

''It'll be OK, Rick. It's always OK.''

''I'm sick of it all, if you want the truth.'' He patted his pockets, looking for cigarettes. Monty had some in her purse, and gave them to him, but he continued, talking in a low, urgent voice. ''I'm sick of doing it all for them—making money for them, crashing the cars for them, fucking the chicks for them, being photographed for them, dressing up in fancy clothes for them, going round the clubs for them—I want to live my own life, not the life two hundred million people think I ought to live for their benefit.'' He shook a cigarette out of the pack, then offered her one, which she did not take. ''You're what I really care about, Monty, if you want the truth.'' He looked at her, his speckled gray eyes full of emotion. ''You do love me, girl?'' Discarding the unlit cigarette; he reached out for her hand and took hold of it.

''Oh, Rick, of course I love you. I'll always love you.''

''I haven't been very good to you, I know that.''

''You couldn't help it. It seems like we've both been out of control ever since the band made it. Suddenly it wasn't you and me anymore. It was the tours and the albums and the TV shows and the money and—oh, I don't know, everything.''

She thought of the endless days in anonymous rooms, of the nights in recording studios when she felt like just one more piece of technology in a high-powered machine for making money and pleasure—pleasure for other people, money they spent just to keep the horrors away long enough for the whole cycle to start all over again.

"What I want to know is—where was it? It, you know. The business, the real thing, the big O—whatever it is you're supposed to have made when you've made it.'' Rick stretched out his legs in their bleached jeans. "It's like it was always coming tomorrow and if we could just do another gig or another couple of songs, then they'd give it to us. Everything's hollow in the center, somehow.''

He looked at Monty; she was real all right, as real as life. Those huge black eyes, that velvet skin with its own rich musky scent that he loved. He remembered how the skin scent changed around her body, how rich and sweet it was down there between her legs, how delicate in the warm hollows of her neck. Rick knew every inch of her body, and wanted it now more than ever. It was the only prize he had won. He stretched out and held the warm heaviness of her breasts, savoring their texture, both soft and firm, the nipples hardening with desire under the fragile silk.

"Rick! Come on, we need you now. . . .'' the voice of the director's assistant broke into the private world of their intimacy.

"Can't it wait ten minutes?'' Rick yelled over Monty's head, his hands warm around her breasts.

There was silence. He leaned over to kiss her, but the mood was gone and the nerves had come back. They got up and returned to the set.

An hour later they were all dressed in shimmering tunics tied up with gold ribbons. Monty's was a soft turquoise, the other girls were in pink and white. Rick was in black with a gold key pattern around the hem. The hairdressers put plaits of gold braid around their heads and loaded Monty's wrists and ankles with wide brass bracelets. The makeup girl painted her eyes with sweeps of soft blue and gray, and dusted her golden shoulders with sparkling powder.

"Cocktail time,'' Keith announced, and his assistant appeared with a tray of champagne glasses filled with fizzing amber liquid. In the bottom of each glass a few crystals were dissolving.

"Heavens—real champagne cocktails,'' Monty muttered nervously. They gulped down the first one, took another, then a third.

A dry-ice machine spouted mist over the surface of the purple water. First Keith ordered shots of the band miming to the play-back of their new single, "Heart's Desire," which had a raunchy, almost disco beat. Three of the dancers crawled around their feet, lasciviously caressing the boys' legs, while two more dancers stood thigh high in the water and embraced.

Keith shot the boys lolling on the couches drinking whiskey and champagne, eating grapes (Cy insisted) and fondling the dancing girls.

"Now you girls." Keith pointed to Monty, P.J. and Maggie. "The swing." They lifted Monty onto the swing while the other two stood in the water pulling her to and fro. Keith ordered a hand-held camera to come in close on her face. It felt wonderful, swooping to and fro in the warm, steamy air, a little drunk, a little high and full of the sense of love and security she had from getting close to Rick.

"Fabulous, love, fabulous," Keith grunted. "Head back—further—further—don't worry, love, you're quite safe. Really let go and get into it." To and fro, back and forth she swung. The music pounded on, louder and louder. Rick and Keith talked intently.

"This is great—I want to do more of you looking really blissed-out and spacey," Keith told her, helping her off the swing. "Take this—it'll make your eyes wider." He gave her a white tablet from a tiny silver pillbox.

Suddenly one of the dancers in the water jumped out onto the poolside and ran toward the choreographer, complaining that the dye in the water was irritating her skin. Keith and the choreographer wrangled at length and the girls in the water were sent away to have cream smeared on their legs for protection. Monty began to feel hot and dreamy. She wanted to lie down somewhere.

At last they were ready to go again, and two of the girl dancers came forward, black girls with braided hair. Keith made Monty lie at the end of the water on her back. The music started again and the girls undulated their bodies over hers, shaking their shoulders frenetically until the gold ribbons holding their tunics unraveled and the light fabric fell away. Monty felt tingling excitement course through her and she writhed her body as Keith directed. A boy dancer held her feet to stop her from slipping toward the water; from the corners of her eyes she thought she could see Pete lying on a couch with a naked girl astride him.

It was misty and the light seemed to be growing dimmer. The trembling flames accentuated the dancers' movements. Monty felt her blood race in her limbs with the mixture of drugs and drink.

The music thundered on. A hand tore away the top half of her tunic and one of the girls bent over her, her red tongue flickering over her breasts. A shower of rose petals fell on them, caressing her skin, arousing her still further. The set was full of dancing bodies, mist, noise, flowers and flames.

Someone pulled her upright; two of the boys held her against their naked chests, tossing her from one to the other. Monty relaxed in their muscular arms—there was nothing else she could do. She realized, without concern, that she couldn't control her body. She felt like a swallow, swooping weightless through the air. Lips pressed her flesh, teeth nuzzled the softest parts of her body, teasing and toying and now and then threatening with a bite. Somewhere to her left she saw a white boy in a leopard skin kneel before a naked black boy and take his swelling erection in his mouth. They moved slowly together; everything was slow now, even the music.

She was carried, whirled around, thrown from one man to another. Her tunic unraveled and became nothing more than a drape of diaphanous silk which trailed between her thighs, around her waist, across one of her breasts. There was a girl eating fire, putting lighted brands in her mouth and closing her lips to extinguish them, then exhaling streams of flame.

Splashes. More people were in the water, dancing in the water, churning up the mist, sprinkling rainbow droplets through the air. Wet bodies were dancing together, moving together, hands cupping breasts, fingers sinking into buttocks. There were thighs on thighs, arms around arms.

Monty was lying on a couch on black-velvet cushions, raging desire in every atom of her body. Desire for what, for who? She couldn't remember. She wanted, wanted, wanted. She would die if she didn't get.

People were leaving the poolside and walking away. The light dimmed further, until the flickering flames from the torches were all that remained. The music died away, and she could hear the cicadas in the palm trees and the small liquid noises of the pool.

Rick was beside her, naked, with the gold fillet still holding back his hair. His arms reached under her and picked her up. He carried her to a pile of cushions in a warm, dim corner, laid her down and began to kiss her body.

"Beautiful, beautiful, so beautiful," he was murmuring as his hands pushed away the wisps of drapery. She reached toward him but he pushed her back, laughing. "We're on our own now, darling, and this is your treat. Don't do anything. Nothing. Lie back and enjoy yourself.''

She wanted him like a searing pain. Tremors, as light as moths' wings, ran over her skin as he touched her. She stroked his cheek as he sucked first one nipple, then the other, holding her breasts like precious fruit to his mouth.

"Please, Rick, now—now, darling Rick, *please*," she begged him, wriggling under his hard, narrow body. But he made her wait, still laughing, and finally sharp shudders of pleasure began before he had even entered her.

It was not enough. It was a stinging pleasure which lashed her senses like a whip, stirring them higher. He knelt between her legs and teased her with his mouth, his tongue stabbing, his lips stroking her taut wet flesh, lapping in the sweet moisture, avoiding, with cruel cunning, the one touch that would release her from the prison of passion. She writhed beneath him, abandoned, uncaring, wanting nothing but the vortex of hot darkness, and him within her as it whirled her away.

With demonic strength, his hands held her still, and then at last she felt him, hot and avid as she was, but moving into her flesh slowly, so slowly. She screamed as suddenly he withdrew and she clawed at his chest, and saw tracks of blood appear from her nails. Then he was on her, and in her, and they rolled over and over on the cushions, their faces wet with tears, but whose tears? They were on hard tiles, then grass, then half in the warm water. The darkness opened for her and she surrendered to it, wanting to melt or shatter or be destroyed utterly in a cataclysm of love.

"I love you, darling, I love you" were the last words she heard.

Rick disengaged; he stood up, holding out a hand for the towel Keith's assistant ran forward to give him. He wrapped it around his waist.

"I hope you got all that," he said to the director. "I don't think I could do it again."

"I got it, don't worry." Keith patted the camera casing. "Do that every night, do you?"

Rick grinned and gave him a kidding punch in the ribs. "Can't beat the old home cooking. Will she be all right?"

"Yeah, don't worry about it. They often zonk out on 'ludes. Take her home and put her to bed and she'll be fine in the morning. With any luck she won't remember anything."

"You *sure* she's all right?" Rick walked over to Monty's still body and felt her wrist. He hardly needed to. Her heartbeat was visible through her chest wall, like a flutter under the skin between her breasts where the distended artery was pumping.

"Quite sure, trust me. Don't worry about a thing. She won't remember what happened, most like. And by the time I've finished cutting it all together she won't even recognize herself."

"They're great, aren't they, them Quaaludes." Cy had been standing with the rest of the spectators behind the camera. "Got any spare?" Keith tipped the contents of his pillbox into his hand.

"Don't give 'em to anyone you don't like," he advised.

Rick looked at the young director curiously. "What's this to be, then—the first hard-core rock video?"

Keith shook his head. "Maybe I'll do you a special tape for private consumption only. But the one I do for Excellent will be OK, trust me. I'll cut around the naughty bits. But it'll be quite clear what's going on, all the same. The look on your old lady's face will be enough. Those eyes—incredible!"

When Monty regained consciousness the following afternoon she felt thirsty, she had a terrible headache, the skin of her legs and back had a rash in reaction to the dye in the pool water, and she remembered nothing of what had happened. Rick told her that the video was to be edited in New York, and that there would be no time for a private viewing of it by the band before it was rushed out to coincide with the release of "Heart's Desire." He was quiet, and very attentive to her, feeling guilty for what he had done.

Monty was taking a taxi home from her hairdresser in London one afternoon when a flickering screen in the window of a record store caught her attention. She made the driver stop, paid him and got out of the cab.

"That must be it, the 'Heart's Desire' promo," she thought, joining the small group of people watching the screen in the store window. She saw Rick's face below the gold headband, his jaw gaping with the mimed effort of singing. Then she saw one of the black girl dancers wriggling up his naked calf, then the snake, then herself singing with P.J. and Maggie. "Heavens, I look so fat," she wailed inwardly. The next shot was her own face, eyes languorously half closed.

She ran eagerly into the store and asked the man at the counter for a copy of the video.

"D'you want the regular version?" he asked her in a low voice.

"What regular version?"

"This one's a bit notorious. We've got the regular version you'll see on the TV, twenty-five quid; and just one or two copies of the special somebody put together from the outtakes. That's a bit pricey, of course.''

''What's in it?'' Suddenly it worried Monty that she had no memory at all of the shoot. She could usually remember something, no matter how smashed she got. Instinctively, she knew what the boy was going to say.

''Rick Brown getting it on with some chick. Hot stuff—there's life in the old dog yet. Take a look if you like—I think the lads are running it in the stock room. Can't get 'em out here serving customers, anyway.''

Monty opened the door he indicated at the back of the store, went down a short concrete corridor and peeked into a room at the end. One glance was enough. Three kids were sitting round the TV on crates, jacking off like monkeys. Monty had just time' to glimpse the screen before she withdrew, but the split-second view was enough for her to recognize her own body thrashing as Rick impaled her.

Numb and breathless with shock, she ran out of the store and blundered through the crowds of shoppers, looking for a pay phone. The first one she found had been vandalized. The second was out of order, and whined in her ear. The frustration made her angry, and the anger made her calm. From the third telephone she called Cathy's office.

''It's horrible, so horrible, Cathy—I can't tell you what they've done, the bastards. . . .'' Monty gulped, choked and started to cry.

Cathy's voice was firm and soothing. ''Where are you calling from? Tell me where you are and I'll be right over.''

Monty told her, then went to wait in a coffee shop. Twenty minutes later Cathy's steel-blue BMW swooped out of the traffic. The nearside wheels mounted the curb and it stopped with a jerk. Cathy's slim figure in a black-and-white tweed suit darted through the crowds and Monty flung herself into her sister's arms.

''The most awful thing, Cathy . . .''

Monty started shaking as she told Cathy about the video. As soon as she understood why her sister was so upset, Cathy said, ''OK. Now come and sit in the car and stop the cops covering it in tickets while I go and see how many copies of it I can find. It won't take long to check out Tottenham Court Road—will there be any more anywhere else, do you think?''

Monty shook her head and sniffed, still on the verge of tears. ''This is the place for hot tapes—let's hope they haven't sold too many of them.''

After she had settled her sister in the BMW's passenger seat,

Cathy calmly walked into one shop after another up the length of the road where London's principal hi-fi shops clustered. With her smart City suit and her commanding, upper-class voice she was an impressive figure, although the shop assistants were taken aback when she firmly asked outright for the bootleg version of the "Heart's Desire" video.

"What bootleg version? There ain't no bootleg version, and if there were I wouldn't sell it," blustered one greasy-haired, thickset man in shirt sleeves.

Cathy, cool and pleasant with the merest hint of a persuasive smile on her immaculate red lips, looked directly into his bloodshot eyes. "Either you sell them to me and make your profit now, or you keep them until tomorrow when we get our court injunction and get stuck with a load of hot tapes you'll never be able to sell at all. I know which I'd prefer."

Within half an hour she had bought every copy of the pornographic tape that she could find.

"Seventeen of them," she announced, dumping two bags full of tapes on the backseat. "And I got a copy of the official version too. Now let's get rid of them, shall we?" The powerful engine purred into life and the tires squealed as she pulled out into the traffic, heading north to Regent's Park. Cathy pulled up beside the canal close to the zoo, and the two sisters climbed out of the car with the bags which bulged awkwardly with the plastic cassette cases.

"I'll have to keep one," Monty said with resignation. "Rick won't be able to wriggle out of this if he has the evidence in front of his eyes." She took one tape out of her bag, then hurled the remainder over the wrought-iron railings into the water. Cathy threw her bag after it with both hands, and they watched the small pile of plastic evil vanish in the scummy green water.

"How could he do that to you? I could kill him, the filthy little creep." Cathy's voice was honed with anger and cut like a knife. "What's happened to him, Monty? He was always good to you, wasn't he? Or was he always a pile of shit, and now that he's rich and famous he can afford to act like a pile of shit?"

They walked back to the car and Monty paused, her hand on the door. "He's desperate, Cathy, that's all. Desperate, frightened and weak. He had to do something scandalous just to promote the band, get it back on top again. Of course he cares for me; he loves me in his way. But when he gets with the boys it's suddenly as if I don't exist. He just has to prove he's the boss. He'll do anything to stay in control."

"Pathetic." Cathy drove away fast. The trees were on the point of changing from the dry green of late summer to the gold of early autumn. The peaks of the huge aviary in the zoo towered above the foliage, and as they passed they saw a heron with a vast wingspan sail through the air inside the wire enclosure.

"It's a cage, in spite of everything, isn't it? It may be very big and very flashy, but it's still a cage." Monty looked tired and dejected.

"Time to break out, don't you think?" her sister suggested. "You're a big bird now."

"*What me, a swan?*" Monty squawked in imitation of the Ugly Duckling song, and gave a bitter little smile. "Yes, I know, I'm a swan and it's time I flew solo. Rick was going to do that, you know. He said he'd get me my own contract for my own album."

The car stopped at a red traffic light and Cathy turned to her sister and caressed her cheek. "Do you need Rick's permission or something?" she asked in a gentle voice.

When Monty got home, she ran the broadcast version of the video and noted with grim fury that although no sexual organs were visible and the action conformed to the laws on indecency, the TV viewers were to be treated to the sight of most of her naked body and—this was much the worst—her naked soul as well. She cringed with embarrassment at the sight of herself groveling for Rick.

He came in with Dennis just as the tape finished. Monty was afraid that the two men together would shout her down, but she didn't care. Misery had wrung out her mind, leaving it dry of judgment.

"You bastard—you filthy bastard!" she shouted, tearing down the staircase to attack him. "Is there anything you won't do—tell me? Why not just rip out my guts and eat them? That'll be a good stunt, eh? Coast-to-coast cannibalism, live by satellite?"

Rick looked at her, cold and domineering. "What in the world are you on about?"

"Don't act the innocent, Rick, not this time. I'm talking about the video."

She saw the flash of guilt in his eyes before he pulled back his shoulders and began to raise his voice. "So—there's a bit of skin in the video. So what?"

"So I don't exactly get off on the idea of a million little tykes all around the world wanking over the bit of skin in the video. It's my skin, Rick. And I don't care for the world to know how I look when I'm coming, or how you look when you're coming—although I don't suppose you care. And I don't want them to know that you and Keith got me out of it on some dope, and you went right ahead and got it on for the cameras while I was out of my head. *Now* do you know what I'm on about?''

"Oh, Jesus." To her surprise, Rick's aggressive tone disappeared and he suddenly looked very small and crushed. He came forward and put his arms around her.

"Look darlin', I won't blame you if you don't believe this, but I didn't know what I was doing either, truly I didn't. I was as out of it as you were. I don't remember anything, honest. All I can remember is sitting doing coke and booze all day, and''— he looked into her eyes, a twisted, painful stare—"and the way you looked," he finished. "That's all I remember."

Monty wanted to believe him, but she wanted to hurt him too. "Well, come upstairs and let me refresh your memory," she hissed. She grabbed his arm, pinching with spite, and pulled him up to the sitting room. Dennis padded after them, embarrassed and self-effacing in his sneakers. Fingers shaking with rage, she slammed the bootleg tape into the machine.

"What?" Rick sat down as if stunned, and Monty looked at him intently. Was he telling the truth? He watched in silence as their coupling filled the screen, cut to the music and lovingly interspersed with some extraordinary shots of a tumescent penis against the night panorama of Los Angeles.

"Scorpio rising," Dennis muttered.

"Get out of here," Rick ordered him in fury.

When the tape was finished Rick fumbled in the pocket of his jeans jacket for his cigarettes, lit two with automatic movements and passed one to her. She looked down at him without pity.

"Don't lie to me, Rick. You knew exactly what you were doing. Don't try to kid me."

"I swear to God I didn't know, Monty. For Chrissake, what do you think I'm made of?" He reached forward and ran the tape back to a close shot of her body with the flame light flickering over her golden skin. Shaded by the drifting cloud of her hair, her eyes were half closed and the lashes cast long shadows on her high, wide cheekbones. Her lips glistened and trembled; she was saying his name over and over again. Her arms were folded to cradle her breasts and the firm honey-smooth globes with their hard dark nipples gleamed in the hazy light.

"Take a look at yourself," he pleaded, his voice faltering. "What could I do? I couldn't help myself, I had to do it. You were begging me to fuck you and you're so fuckin' beautiful. . . ." He was hanging his head like a shamed child.

"But you didn't have to let them film you."

"Keith said he'd do a private tape, just for us. I never thought . . . some bastard must have pirated it. Oh God, darlin', I'm sorry.'' Suddenly he flung himself into her arms and she held him, feeling his irregular breathing as he haltingly begged her forgiveness.

"We've got to stop it," he said at last. "Where did you find this?"

"Tottenham Court Road—Cathy came and bought all she could find. A hundred quid each."

Rick called Dennis back into the room. "OK—what do we do now? How do we get these tapes off the streets?"

"Don't worry about it. I'll get some boys on to it right now and buy every one in the city, and we'll call the lawyers and do an injunction. Do you want to stop the regular video as well?"

Rick turned to Monty, implying that the decision was completely hers. She sighed, knowing that she was trapped. If she got the promotional video withdrawn, the record would lose TV exposure and they would have to write off a mint of money.

"No, it's too late now. At least nobody will know it's my bum." Monty herself had only recognized the buttock in question by her birthmark, and in the pile of unclothed bodies it had not seemed unduly prominent.

Dennis got on the telephone and gave orders, then left them to spend a sad evening together. The next day the newspapers were full of the story. They made the front pages of the two cheapest tabloids, and even *The Times* carried a report of the court application for an injunction.

That afternoon, the BBC banned the "Heart's Desire" video, announcing that it contravened normal standards of public decency and could not be shown without cuts. There were incessant telephone calls from newspapers, and Rick was invited to go on half a dozen mainstream talk shows as well as the rock shows for which The Juice was already booked. One show even wanted him to debate modern morality with a bishop.

Monty felt icy and detached. She wanted very much to be able to believe Rick, but it was impossible to ignore the chirruping confidence he now acquired as his old status of mouthpiece of the nation's youth was temporarily restored. Cathy condemned him outright.

"He used you," she said flatly. "You know he did, Monty, you must know. Why won't you accept it? It's not exactly a new situation, is it? He had a straight choice between protecting you and capitalizing on the fact you care for him, and when it came to the crunch you weren't as important as success."

Monty said nothing. She knew Cathy was right, but nonetheless yearned to believe that she was wrong. Cindy Moon offered her no comfort.

"It's typical of Rick—he didn't get to be one of the biggest rock stars in the world by taking care of everybody else, did he? He just saw his chance and took it. He's always had a genius for this kind of hype—the whole Juice mystique is built on that rape-and-pillage image."

Monty nodded, feeling miserable. "What I can't stand is everyone knowing." She shivered inside her thin white T-shirt. "Every time I meet anyone I'm wondering if they've seen me like that. I just want to hide under a stone until it's all forgotten. I'll die when I have to go out onstage."

Cindy looked at her with a speculative frown corrugating the arcs of pencil that signified her eyebrows. "Has Rick told you anything about the tour?"

"What's to tell—thirty-six gigs in forty-three days, starting next week. Then the States after that. If it's Tuesday it must be Oshkosh, Wisconsin." She shrugged.

"There's a rumor that Rick's changing the whole show."

"What do you mean?" Again, Monty half knew the answer.

"Just ask him," Cindy advised.

Monty asked him, and again Rick put his arms around her and started to talk in tones of desperate sincerity.

"We're dumping Excellent and we're dumping Dennis," he began. "It's all been coming for a long time, you know that, and this video business was just the end. He really fouled up. He's out. We're getting a new manager—and a new deal."

Monty pulled away from him and sat down on the edge of their king-size bed, a sleazy expanse of creased black satin.

"Thanks for asking me how I felt about it. I'm surprised you think the video business was such a wipeout—I thought it had come off rather well, myself."

"Oh, don't come the old acid drop, Monty." Petulantly, he turned away from her, pretending to look out of the window at the distant tourists flowing toward the punk quarter. In ten years the nerve center of Chelsea had shifted from the plush squares in the east to the tawdry new shops full of fetishistic leather in the west, only a few blocks from the run-down house where Rick and Monty had first lived.

"And what's all this about you changing the stage act?"

"What about it?"

"That's all I've heard."

"You've been on at me to change for years; I thought you'd be happy."

"Why not cut the crap and tell me what all this is about?"

"All right, I'll tell you." Mean and dangerous, he turned toward her, shoving his hair out of his eyes. "What it's about is—I'm not going down the tubes yet. None of us are. All those creeps like your *dear* friend Cindy, who've been trying so hard to bury The Juice, haven't reckoned with the fact that we aren't dead yet. I'm sick of being measured for my coffin.''

"Fair enough. What else?"

"Nothing else—except don't bother packing for the tour because you ain't coming. We're dumping all you girls. We're hard boys, always have been, and we're not having any more oohs and aahs and sha-la-las in the future. And I'm not having you on my back whining all the time for me to be good and act nice.''

Monty felt both angry and relieved. She had been dreading the tour, and despite the graceless way Rick had chosen to drop her she had a distinct, intoxicating sense of freedom.

"That's fine by me," she said, getting up and shaking out her hair as she thought through her next move. "I'll be much happier here in London working on my own songs than trailing around watching you on your Jack-the-lad trip every night."

"You'd better not be expecting me to have anything to do with them songs of yours either," he told her at once. "I'm not getting into anything you do, understand? What do you think you know about how the kids feel—born with a silver spoon in your mouth, talking in that cut-glass voice? It's all down to street credibility now. I can't afford to get involved with your music.''

"Anything else you'd like to say? Like 'So long, it's been good to know you' maybe?''

"Don't be daft, Monty. This has got nothing to do with us, it's business, music business, that's all. Don't take it so personal. I love you, girl, I'll always love you.'' He moved to take her in his arms again. "You've got the tape to prove it, eh?''

A fireball of rage exploded in Monty's mind. "What the fuck do *you* think you know about how the kids feel—you with your Roller and your big house in the country and your designer drugs and your gofers and your groupies and your hangers-on? Street credit? Don't make me laugh. You're not even a human being. You're just some robot that's built to sell records. You're a walking, talking ripoff machine, Rick—and you know it.''

He slapped her face, a quick, open-handed blow that barely hurt, a token of violence intended to remind her that he was the boss.

"You're getting hysterical," he announced. "Shut up if you can't talk sense."

Suddenly Monty felt very tired, too tired to hit him, too tired to reach for the Lalique vase on the night table and throw it at him—although the thought crossed her mind. Cathy was right, and Cindy was right. Rick cared for her, but he cared for himself so much more that his love was no longer worth having. And he was doomed, just like a vanishing species. He had lost touch with reality, even the reality of his own feelings, and he would not survive now that his environment was changing.

She pushed him away, went into the dressing room and found her new red acrylic-pile coat and a bag into which she pulled a haphazard selection of clothes.

"Oh, Monty, don't be stupid." His tone was wheedling as he followed her. "Come on, darlin'—now what are you doing."

"I'm leaving."

He pulled his hands out of his jeans pockets and took the bag out of her hand. "Don't be crazy. You're not going, you can't go. I need you. You're the only person I've ever loved, you know that."

"Heaven help the others then."

He tried to kiss her but she pushed him away, suddenly sickened by the smell of his breath. "I'll throw up if you touch me—I swear I will," she snarled. "You don't know what love means, Rick."

"That's not fair. That's a mean thing to say." He was playing the hurt little boy again, but this time Monty's heart did not warm to him.

Hearing at last that she was serious, he dropped his pose of humility and a venomous glare darkened his gray eyes.

"Suit yourself." His voice was cold. He dropped her bag at her feet and flung himself out of the room.

Without another word, Monty threw her notebooks, some tapes and a tape recorder into the bag and left, walking out into the exhausted warmth of a late September day. The early fallen leaves from the plane trees littered the ground. She hailed a taxi and drove to Cathy's immaculate white apartment in the Barbican.

Cathy opened a bottle of champagne and came to sit in the bathroom while her sister luxuriated in the warm tub scented with Floris lime.

"How do you feel?"

"Marvelous, Cathy. I feel as high as I did the day I ran out of the house when Mummy sold my piano, remember? I'm free again."

Cathy sipped the icy golden liquid thoughtfully. "What are you going to do now?"

"Call Cindy, because she'll tell the papers and then everyone will know I've split from Rick—otherwise, knowing him, he'll be on the phone to his bloody publicist telling the world that *he* dumped *me*. Then I'm going to buy some studio time and make a brilliant tape of some of my songs, and get myself a deal.''

''Can I help? What are you going to use for money?''

''Oh, I'll manage.'' Monty stretched luxuriously in the scented water, accidentally soaking some of her hair, which was twisted into an untidy knot on top of her head. ''And I might as well get my hair cut—one of those sexy *coup sauvage* jobs, don't you think?''

''I think you should go round to Dennis first thing tomorrow and get your money situation straight,'' Cathy told her firmly, retying the sash of her indigo silk robe.

''It is straight, darling. Our accountant took care of everything. My royalties always went straight into my bank account, my tax was deducted every year, it's all handled. Why should splitting with Rick make a difference?''

''You'd be surprised.'' Her sister stood up and reached for a thick white lavender-scented towel from the stack on the glass shelf, then wrapped it around Monty's dripping body as she splashed out of the bath. ''Whenever some man says he's taken care of everything, it usually means he's done bugger-all.''

As soon as the word was out that Monty and Rick had split, Cathy's telephones redoubled their insistent warbling as Monty's friends and acquaintances began to call—some to gossip, some to bitch, some to congratulate and some, the most gratifying of all, who wanted to work with her.

She recorded five new songs for her demo tape, plus one of The Juice's old hits to remind people of her credentials. Then, with a sense of devilment, she decided to add an old classic, ''Can't Get Used to Losing You,'' which she sang in a sarcastic whine and a maddening, incessant computer drum beat which sounded, the engineer said, like someone banging his head against a wall.

When the tape was finished, Monty took Cindy and went shopping in the new boutiques at the World's End, and bought a leather dress with a strapless top, which laced tightly down the back and was cut so low that it dipped almost to the crease of her buttocks.

''You look like a walking wet dream,'' Cindy told her, admiring the dress in the cracked mirror.

''Let's face it. I *am* a walking wet dream for half the kids in town," Monty replied. "Do you think I should cut my hair?"

"No—men like long hair."

Monty considered. It seemed a sound argument—the business of peddling your talent was largely the business of pleasing men. Cindy suggested she add a pair of red plastic stilettoes to the outfit, and some shiny black gloves that reached over her elbows.

"That ought to grab their imagination." Monty pouted with satisfaction and pulled down the top of the leather dress to exhibit a dangerous depth of bosom. I'd better buy an eyebrow pencil tomorrow, she thought. Nothing looks more sixties than the old arched eyebrows just a couple of hairs thick.

Sig Bear at Biffo Records never noticed her eyebrows when she arrived with the demo tape.

"Here she is, the body gorgeous!" he shouted, bursting out of his office into the dank corridor that was Biffo's reception area. His office had no furniture at all, only two telephones on the floor and a black 1950s statue of an Egyptian cat. I suppose, Monty thought, as she sat on the stained carpet, he's going to want to lay me on this at some point.

"Wash your mind out with soap and water," Sig suggested, ripping open a can of beer and offering it to her. He smiled like a frog, a wide, fat, self-satisfied grin.

"The bottom line," he told her, "is that I'd like to whack out a single from you straight away, then maybe another, then follow up with the album. So what I suggest is a two-year contract, with an option after that. We've got it drawn up somewhere—I'll get the girl to look for it."

"Did you know I'd be round, then?"

"No—but there's no harm in wishing, is there? That's the power of positive thinking. There's only one thing I don't like about you, to tell the truth."

"What's that?"

"The name. It's too real. We want a fantasy kind of a name."

To Monty's surprise, it was Christmas Eve before she got laid on the floor of Sig's office. Apart from the fact that they both skinned their knees on the harsh pile of the carpet, it was thoroughly satisfying. After a decade of sexual liberation, boys were a lot wiser about girls' intimate geography.

Afterward they sat on the floor sharing a beer, watching *The Wizard of Oz* on television. Judy Garland was putting on the ruby slippers. Suddenly Sig gulped down the mouthful of beer he had just swigged and gestured at the screen with the can.

"That's it," he announced.

"What's it?"

"Your name—Ruby Slippers."

"*Great!!* I love it!"

"Follow the yellow brick road," he gurgled, pushing up the leather skirt she had only just put on.

"Follow the yellow brick road. . . ." Luckily, he had not had time to put his trousers on at all.

"Follow, follow, follow, follow . . ." There was some snuffling, then silence, then a few grunts. The sightless ceramic eyes of the Egyptian cat looked disapproving. "Ah, Ruby," he breathed in Monty's ear. "I always wanted to fuck a chick called Ruby."

The rest of the winter was much less satisfactory. Because Cathy bullied her every day, Monty at last met Dennis to check out her financial position, and discovered that Rick had copyrighted all The Juice's songs in his name alone. She could claim no royalties, and since a new version of her old telephone song was climbing the Hot 100, and there were two disco versions of other songs doing well in Germany, this was a serious loss.

"You must sue him," Cathy told her. "Don't worry about whether you can afford to—you can't afford not to do it for your own self-respect. I'll handle the bills."

Monty hired a slick law firm with offices in Mayfair, but within a few months all her singing money from Biffo had been spent, and she was embarrassed at the amount Cathy was having to find to meet the lawyers' bills when it was plain that the case could drag on for years before coming to court. She also felt increasingly uncomfortable living in Cathy's apartment. She felt as if her big sister were taking over her life completely and so she moved into Cindy Moon's small apartment at the top of a big house in Notting Hill Gate. As Sig was quick to point out, this also gave her the advantage of an association with Cindy's neo-punk public profile.

Biffo released Ruby Slippers' first single, a fast, angry song called "Lies." Sig insisted that "Can't Get Used to Losing You" should be the B side, and Monty realized he was right when it tore up to Number 3 in the British charts. There was a lot of publicity and Monty gave endless interviews about her split with Rick and the video scandal.

She sat with Cindy watching herself on TV. The camera started at the red shoes and moved unsteadily up her body. The studio audience was trying to look animated.

"You've made it, kid. Congratulations." Cindy patted her ankle. "What's the matter, why aren't you jumping around being happy? You're a *star!*"

"I don't know." Monty saw herself on the TV, swinging her leather-swathed hips, her pouting lips jammy with gloss as she mimed to the sound of her own voice. "It doesn't feel like me, I guess. Not yet, anyway."

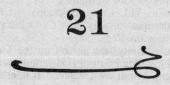

21

THE WINTER OF 1945 WAS ONE OF THE MOST BITTER BRITAIN
had ever endured. The cold was no worse than many other years;
the wind blew no more meanly through the streets of London
than it had before. What made the winter at the end of the war
so cruel was the climate of hopeless disappointment. There was
to be no reward for the years of suffering; instead there was to
be greater deprivation than ever—no food, no clothes, no fuel,
no homes, no work, no end to the brutalizing queuing for rations
and to making do. Victory had left Britain bankrupt, with nothing to take for comfort but illusions of glory.

The Bourton family's London home had been requisitioned by
the War Office, so James and Bill had no option but to take the
quarters to which they were ordered, in a shabby Pimlico terrace
where an assortment of officers from the less glamorous, more
unorthodox outfits in all three services were billeted. It was a
cold, dingy, sour-smelling building with dogeared exhortations
to economy stuck to every wall. Over the meager fire in the
lounge was a poem in pokerwork on a piece of packing case,
which was intended to prevent the occupants from using too
much coal. It read:

> *If it's warmth that you desire,*
> *Poke the wife and not the*
> *fire.*
> *And if you lead a single life,*

PEARLS

*Poke some other bugger's
wife.*

Since the trappings of grandeur were all that remained, their value was exaggerated. James, now Captain Lord James Bourton, D.S.O., quailed under the hearty praise for his supposed grit and courage, and tried to bury the memory of the chaotic fear-filled night in which he had been transformed from a failure to a hero.

By the time he stood with Bill Treadwell on a windy street corner by the side of Buckingham Palace, James was angry that so many people were so anxious to make him the embodiment of courage. He thought the heroes were the men who had died in Malaya, not the lucky ones like himself. The hideous memory of the charnel house by the railway track mocked him, but he could no more repudiate it than give back the medal he now held to his side in a cheap, black, mock-leather case. To do either would have been to declare himself a traitor.

"How's your father?" Bill asked as they walked cautiously toward the edge of the crowd. A pack of photographers was taking snapshots of the newly decorated men, who posed proudly in their uniforms with their medal cases open and their families around them. James paused and forced his own case into his coat pocket.

"He's slipping away. They thought he'd died last night, but he hung on. At least it means my mother couldn't come here with me—be grateful for small mercies."

Lady Davina had been the most vociferous barker of his valor. She proudly annexed to herself the admiration directed to her son, the triumphant warrior.

"What'll you do when he goes? Are you coming back to Malaya?" They turned into St. James's Park.

"Yes, I'd like to. My job's there, if I want it, though the company plans to run the estate with as few Europeans as they can. Still, that'll be more to my taste than lurking around at Bourton as the second son, and having to touch my brother for money. You're still set to go back?"

"For sure." The Australian stalked, heronlike, by the side of the concrete lake basin. The water in ornamental pools had been drained to prevent German bombers from taking bearings from such prominent landmarks. "Heaven knows what will happen, Jim. I went to a briefing at the Colonial Office yesterday and these Whitehall types haven't a clue. It's as plain as day to you and me that the Commies will just stay in the jungle and fight us instead of the Japs, but they can't see it. They think they can simply ask the Communists to surrender the guns they dropped, and that'll be that. My guess is there are thousands of arms hidden away in the jungle and the comrades are only waiting for the moment to use them."

He squinted up at the bleak sky. "My heart's in that country, somewhere, Jim. I feel I belong there. I certainly don't feel that England is home. Or Australia."

James did not feel that London was home either. He scarcely remembered anything about it, and the alien cityscape of bombed buildings and empty streets forcefully reminded him that his war had been a nursery game of make-believe in comparison with the ordeals of others.

At Bourton there were further reminders. The house had been requisitioned as a convalescent hospital; and although most of the wounded men had left already, there were enough wrecked bodies shuffling across the neglected lawns to taunt him with their misfortune.

The park was plowed with ambulance tire tracks, many of the great trees which had been the familiar friends of his boyhood had been felled, and the deer had gone.

The Duke of Witheram was dying by inches, his blood struggling through arteries silted with the fat of his own land. He had been barely conscious for several months, and three nurses attended him day and night.

James whiled away the gray days with shooting, but there was not much game since the gamekeepers had been called up to fight and every able man in the village had poached a bird when he could.

Shooting was James's cover for taking a walk and enjoying the domesticated contours of the English landscape, in which every tree that flourished did so with a landowner's approval and every field conformed to a farmer's imperative. Only among the immense beech trees of the West Wood did James feel the arcane force of free nature that animated the jungle. James had a sensitivity which would have equipped him to be an artist had he been born into a milieu that recognized art; he enjoyed the docile beauty of his ancestral land but felt confined by it. It was a claustrophobic world in which everything was limited, regulated and ordered, including himself.

At last the night nurse noticed that the old duke was no longer breathing and, at a decent hour in the early morning, tapped on Hugo's door to announce that his father was dead.

"I do not wish to be known as the Dowager," the widowed Davina told her family as they gathered for a subdued breakfast. "I shall revert to the title I had before my marriage—so much more attractive. I intend to put an announcement in *The Times* immediately.''

''Mother, I think you should wait a few days. We haven't announced Father's death yet, after all.'' Hugo's brown bullock's eyes quelled his mother with reproach.

''Of course, Hugo, you are the head of the family now. I shall do whatever you say,'' she conceded. ''Will you be talking to Pasterns about the will?''

''Naturally.''

The new duke did more than anyone expected him to do. In the greatest display of dynamism he was to muster in his lifetime, Hugo took the reins of the estate firmly from his mother's hands and applied himself to mastering the facts of the family's situation. Even his unimpressionable nature was moved by what he discovered.

''We're bust, as near as dammit,'' he confided to James in their father's study. ''Mother's run through a fortune without the slightest regard for the future, and there's no evidence that Father took much interest. He said as much to me himself—'There's enough to see me out; after that you can sink or swim on your own' was his line. There's been no maintenance, no investment, no planning of any kind.''

''What are you going to do?'' James was relieved that the inflexible law of primogeniture had absolved him of the responsibility for salvaging the family fortune.

''Sit down with some chap from Pasterns who's supposed to be an expert and see if we can cut our losses.''

A few weeks later the team of lawyers arrived, curious to poke around the estate, which most of them knew only through the bundles of documents that related to its disposition. Once they were present, Hugo announced a conference on the family's future.

''I want you to know, darling, that it's *all arranged*,'' Lady Davina whispered in James's ear as they made their way to the room set aside for the occasion.

''What's arranged?'' James pulled away his arm with irritation. He hated his mother's possessive caresses.

''Before your dear Papa went completely gaga, I had a word with him, and he agreed to something special for you,'' she told him, nodding with satisfaction at her own foresight. ''You'll see how clever I've been. You're a very lucky boy.''

When the will was read, there was an audible gasp from Hugo as the lawyer announced the codicil to which she referred. The duke had set up a trust for his younger son to provide a handsome endowment ''in the event that he should see fit to marry and sire issue.'' The bequest was in cash, and James knew enough to appreciate that it would be hard to find the money from the diminished estate.

Hugo passed the next two days with the lawyers. Lady Davina bustled about the north wing, harassing the hospital authorities to quit the main part of the house so she could repossess her kingdom and outlining to James their delectable future as she saw it. She replaced the Red Cross uniform she had affected during the war with a smart blue costume made up from black-market wool crepe, with stylish velvet revers.

''I thought you could have the London house, and I shall spend the winter there with you and the summer down here with Hugo. It'll be such fun, won't it, darling, when this dreary old rationing is over? You've missed some marvelous parties, of course, but there'll be so many more. London is simply crawling with pretty widows—you'll be able to take your pick.''

Hugo took visible pleasure in dashing her plans; discomfiting his mother's vain ambitions was now the only pleasurable aspect of his task.

''The best we can do is offer the house to the National Trust,'' he told them. ''They'll want an endowment with it, and to raise that I propose to sell the farms. The village will revert to the Rural District Council. The London house will have to go, though I'm advised to keep some stake up there so we may buy something smaller. All the property will have to be sold. Assuming that the Trust does buy the house, we will be allowed to remain in a part of it, and we can retain ownership of the home farm and some of the commercial holdings.''

''Hugo—this is outrageous! I will not allow it! This is my home. I can't possibly have charabancs and day trippers in my home.''

''Mother, you have no choice. I think you should know that the opinion of our advisers is that we would be in a considerably better position if you had not been determined to play the lady of the manor in quite such extravagant style.''

''You forget, Hugo darling, that if I had not refitted this dismal barn, it wouldn't be the showpiece it is today and you would have precious little chance of interesting the National Trust in it.''

Later she told James, ''See how lucky you are—you'll be living better than Hugo once you're married. Darling, do hurry up, I can't stand another minute in this place knowing I've got to lose it.''

Could she have been aware what the state of the family's affairs was? Of course she must have realized the truth better than anyone else had. James was haunted by the conviction that his mother had finagled his bequest only to assure her own future standard of living. He was terrified of the prospect of remaining forever in thrall to her insatiable ego, with a wife whom she would no doubt pick out for him and children who would be her cowed playthings just as he and Hugo had been. The image of a woman rocking a contented infant in a sarong cradle flashed into his mind, trailing with it the faint memory of spiritual peace.

What he craved was the sturdy sense of self-determination he had enjoyed in Malaya. What he feared was the humiliating role of his mother's pawn. James made up his mind. This bizarre legacy changed nothing. He would never claim it; instead, he would take the first passage he could get to Penang.

Within a month he was gone, and his last sight of England was a crowd of about five-hundred dockers at Southampton, fighting among themselves at the end of a demonstration against plans to close down half the dockyard and take away the jobs to which they had only just returned from the war.

James nearly cried with emotion as the train glided to a halt and the familiar red-dirt road through the jungle opened up before him. There was a small black car waiting at the leveled area beside the railway track, and beside it a figure he recognized with joy.

"Selambaram! I can't believe it—you're still here!"

"Where else, *tuan*?" The round eyes of his old conductor gleamed with happiness.

"My God, it's good to see you! How are things?"

"Pretty good, I think you will find. Bukit Helang was a lucky place because it was so difficult to reach that the Japanese mostly left us alone. You will see nothing much has changed, although with so few people to work we could keep only a small area of the estate properly cultivated."

James beamed with pleasure as they drove through the kampong. The dark hardwood houses with elaborately carved eaves seemed far more prosperous than the simpler houses of the Pahang village. Instead of the light green of the *padi* fields, the background was the rich emerald of the half-tamed vegetation—palms, glossy banana trees, durians and fruit bushes.

He noticed that the road was rutted; and as they approached the uphill sweep which led to the coolie lines and the estate buildings, there were more definite signs of neglect. The jungle grass had invaded the old rubber area, and the young plantings were completely overgrown. Half the coolie shacks were derelict and the handsome square pillars of the estate house were no longer as white as cricket flannels, but stained with the red dust. Many of the shutters at the windows were hanging loose and the signs of care upon which Douglas Lovell had insisted—the orchid pots, the well-swept steps, the furled bamboo blinds—had gone.

As the only conductor who had remained during the Japanese occupation, Selambaram had run the estate by giving priority to the clerkly observances of administration, which he understood, while holding blind faith that the forces of nature would cooperate. As a result, James found an immaculate record of chaos. Getting things to rights was to be a long, hard slog.

The rubber trees, which had not been tapped, had benefited from the rest and yielded generously. Labor began to return, old workers and new appearing daily as the word spread that the estate manager was hiring once more. James had the telephone lines and electricity cables restored.

For a while he would be the only European on the estate, and he elected to lodge in the estate house rather than go to the trouble of setting up his home in a bungalow. His former residence was now roofless, with creepers probing the wooden shingles of the walls. Gerald's bungalow was occupied by a new Malay assistant, and the nearby house used by Anderson, the doctor, was now Selambaram's home.

The greatest change was not in the overgrowth and decay which had seized the estate in three years, but the subtle shift in James's status—in the status of all white men—in the same period. The day the *tuans* fled and the years of rule by another Asian race had cracked belief in white superiority.

The colonial government was making grudging moves to Malaya's independence; and James found that, although his authority was accepted and he himself viewed with affection and respect, he was no longer looked upon as a permanent feature of the scene.

For the first time in his life he suffered loneliness. Not only was he isolated and exhausted at the end of each day by his work, but the growing uncertainty about the country's future distressed him. Needing always a mold in which to shape his responsive character, he found it difficult to be in such fluid circumstances.

His visitors were few. Dr. Anderson, who was now responsible for the health of the workers on nine adjoining estates, came once a month to hold a clinic. He was thinner, with sunburned skin wrinkled at his knees and elbows, and the horseshoe of hair around his bald crown was no longer brown but gray. James welcomed his company and kept the doctor's old Gilbert and Sullivan records and his wind-up gramophone in the sitting room to entertain him.

Occasionally a company inspector would appear to tell James he did not need another assistant. Bill Treadwell came when his new duties as adviser to a state ruler allowed.

"I'm not sure what I'm supposed to be advising him on exactly. Seems to be everything from diseases of oil palms to the likelihood of war with the Communists."

"How bad is it?" James asked him, narrowing his eyes in the brilliant sunlight as they drove up the road from the railway.

"As bad as it could be. Our old friend Chin Peng has been off to China to train with Mao Tse-tung and he's stirring his boys up like hornets. I never thought that all these months we wasted listening to him indoctrinate his men would be so useful. Once you've a few lessons on Lenin from Chin Peng it's quite clear what they're going to do. Attack the British. Start terrorizing the country the minute they're in a position of enough strength." He looked with approval around the estate.

"You did get off lightly, and no mistake. Business as usual already."

"The Malays have taken over the tennis court for badminton, but I've no one to play against anyway."

"Have you got any sandbags?" James looked at his friend with surprise. "I'm serious, Jim. You blokes on the isolated estates are going to be very easy targets. I'd think about digging in and defense, if I were you."

The Times arrived, as it had always done, three weeks late. It brought the news of the sale of Bourton House to the National Trust even before his brother's letter. The *Straits Times* also arrived every day, discussing in its awkward English the demands for the Malayanization of key industries, for national independence and for action against the Chinese bandits who were terrorizing rural areas.

Seeking action to cure his unease, James wrote to Pasterns asking for clarification of his father's will. Their reply did little more than restate the document's words. In the same post came a letter from the company announcing that the widow of Gerald Rawlins would be visiting the estate with Dr. Anderson in the near future.

At the quayside at George Town, Betty recalled her first sight of Penang. She felt a lifetime older than the girl who, nine years before, had stood beside an elderly missionary and scanned the multicolored crowd onshore for the half-forgotten face of her fiancé.

Now she was looking for another barely remembered face, the round, sun-reddened countenance of Dr. Anderson, which she at first overlooked in the throng because he was so changed by his years as a prisoner of war. He was no longer robust, but thin and stooping, although at the sight of him she felt a warm, enveloping rush of security. Changed as he was, his presence reassured her with an impression of continuity.

"Good trip?" he asked as his driver held open the door of his Rover.

"Not too bad. I'm not a very good sailor, I'm afraid. No sea legs at all."

"Good to be back to dry land again, eh?"

They continued in pleasant, trivial conversation until they reached the E & O Hotel, where they took tea on the terrace in the shade of a pink-and-white awning. They were both coming to terms with the horror of the past and the uncertainty of the future, and the only way to begin this work was with meaningless pleasantry.

Neither wanted to discuss what they would be obliged to discuss, sooner or later. In the women's internment camp in Sumatra, Betty had sat by Jean Anderson through long days in which she had talked distractedly for hours of her husband before she died of swamp fever; under a canvas canopy in the area called Cholera Hill in the labor camp on the Burma railway, the doctor had seen Gerald lose half his remaining body weight in a day and then die in violent convulsions as his emaciated body hurled out all its fluid in vomiting and diarrhea.

They ate together in the crowded dining room, while a Chinese string trio played Franz Lehár waltzes very slowly. Neither of them was hungry. Betty's pink-and-white bloom of freshness had subtly changed into an overall pallor with patches of high color on her cheeks. She wore a simple blue crepe dress. Her hair curled crisply, gilded with a strong new permanent wave, and her blue eyes were more misty than ever.

At last the doctor decided to breach the wall of silence. "Tell me about Jean," he asked simply.

"She was terribly, terribly brave," Betty began in a rush of embarrassment. "I'm sure she saved my life half a dozen times. I was dreadfully ill after I had the baby. It didn't live, you know. And she . . . ." She paused, groping in emptiness of her memory. Because Betty dealt with trauma by erasing it from her mind, she could recall very little of what had taken place in the women's camp, although it was only a short time ago. It was beyond her emotional strength to remember that she had sold Jean's wedding ring for three eggs and a pair of wooden pattens, and so the incident had been edited from her memory. "She was always so cheery," she finished vaguely. "She talked of you a lot . . ." It seemed unduly intimate to use his Christian name.

"Arthur," he supplied. "I thought of her too, of course." There was a heavy silence. "Gerald . . ." he began, but Betty interrupted at once.

"Don't tell me. I can't bear it, please. Don't tell me anything. I know that he's dead, that's all I need to know."

He nodded with understanding, touched by her frailty. "Have you any plans?"

"Not really. I must sort out our things, of course, that's why I'm here. But I've no home now, you see. Nothing to go back to in England. Our house was bombed, a direct hit." She looked wistfully away across the dance floor where two or three couples circulated below the languid ceiling fans.

He intended to pat her hand in sympathy, but found himself holding it, a small, soft thing that lay limply in his palm like a sick bird, with the wrist pulse fluttering like a heartbeat under the pale skin. Betty was comforted by his touch. It reminded her of the early days of her pregnancy, when the doctor alone had understood her fears.

"You're so good to me," she murmured. "I feel so lost without my husband. I just don't know what to do. Gerald was my whole life, you see."

After being sent back to England, she had returned to Malaya for one very simple reason. She not only felt lost without a man in her life, she also felt poor, and the prospect of returning to a life of genteel destitution on a small army pension dismayed her. It had seemed as if Britain were full of brassy, striding women who were thoroughly accustomed to competing for male attention. In the Crown Colony, Betty knew, women were more than ever in the minority and a husband should be easy to catch.

"It's been a rough time for us all," he consoled her, wanting very much to make sure that this dear, timid creature would never suffer again in her blameless life. She gave him a small, grateful smile, sensing that she had secured a suitor.

The next day they began the day's journey to Bukit Helang, and Arthur Anderson escorted her onto the ferry to Port Swettenham, the mainline train to Kuala Lumpur and the smaller train upcountry, from which they were driven to the estate in Gerald's old Model T Ford.

"Welcome, Betty, my dear, welcome. How very good to see you," James greeted them, noting the doctor's protective stance at once. "Isn't the old car magnificent? She started at the first turn of the ignition when we got her going again." He patted the vehicle's dusty black roof.

"What has happened to our bungalow?" she asked him, anxiety pinching two vertical lines between her eyebrows. "I must arrange for all Gerald's things to go back to George Town with me. If there is anything left, of course. There's been so much theft and vandalism, hasn't there, even on the estates the Japanese didn't bother with."

"We've got off lightly here. Selambaram says the Japs came, ordered him to continue production, then vanished. They shot a couple of men for show, that's all. We were very lucky."

"You're always lucky, aren't you, James?" It was a guileless observation. "You must have been born under a lucky star."

The three of them dined together, with a cluster of oleander blooms in a jam pot on the table and a new boy to bring out the soup, the curry and the ice cream.

"Your silver!" Betty exclaimed. "Dear Omar buried your silver. I can see him doing it in my mind's eye, I know exactly where it is. We'll go to find it tomorrow."

"It'll be gone by now, sure as eggs is eggs," Anderson observed, stretching his legs in the wicker lounger. "If you saw the hiding place, plenty of other people probably did too."

Betty and James fell easily into something like their old relationship, he courtly and charming, she happy in the security of his care. She mentally compared the doctor with the runaway aristocrat; Arthur would mean quietness and security, which she craved, but James, although the war had taken the edge of his fine, youthful confidence, could still dazzle her with his charm. He had about him the glow imparted by a wealthy background. Above all, perversely, she wanted James more because he seemed less interested in her.

Next morning Betty demanded a boy and set off in the direction of James's old home. A mere half hour later she burst in on him in the bare, stone-floored estate office.

"There!" she cried, dropping a tarpaulin bundle caked with moist red clay on his blotter. "Absolutely untouched. Please open it, James, I can't wait. It'll be like having all the lovely days of the past to look at."

Amused at her enthusiasm, he called for scissors and cut the half-rotted covering. Insects streamed away from their adopted home.

"Watch those red ants," he cautioned, pulling her back with his arm. "They bite like fury."

The sugar shaker, the salt, pepper and mustard pots, the coasters and the napkin rings and cutlery were all tarnished blue-black.

"I shall clean them myself!" she announced. "You've got some methylated spirit, haven't you? They'll be shining like new by suppertime."

And so they were, though it took her the whole afternoon to rub off the discoloration which clung stubbornly to the decoration and the engraved Witheram crests.

"It must be so nice to have a real family." Wistfully, she ran her rounded fingertips, gray with polish, over the heraldic device on a knife handle. "You know I have no one now, James? There's Gerald's family of course, but it isn't the same as your own blood kin, is it?"

"I suppose not." He felt tenderness as he leaned over her bent head, watching the humble, stained hands put the finishing touches on their work.

He was unaware that she had come to this house because of her shrewd female instinct for finding a provider, and had determined to ensure her future by fanning the ashes of their former closeness. James was also, for once, unaware of his own vulnerability. He never suspected that this little brown mouse of a woman had developed a capacity for selfish artifice quite comparable with that of his mother.

As the days of her visit passed, James lay awake at night, reasoning at random. If he stayed in Malaya, who better for a companion than Betty? If he returned to England, a wife would ensure his fortune, and Betty, dear little Betty, would never be the sort of managing minx he loathed. He would like to take care of Gerald's widow, as a kindness to his dead friend. He would like an outlet for his betraying sexuality, which had so often endangered his security in the past.

The only obstacle was Arthur Anderson, who had grown irritable with jealousy as soon as he sensed that he had lost his place in Betty's affections. However, the doctor had to continue his round of clinics elsewhere in the state, and within a few days he would be gone.

At the other end of the building, Betty also postponed sleep. Betty Bourton, she said to herself. Lady Betty Bourton—no, that would not do. Lady Bettina Bourton—much better. He will just have to call me Bettina, she resolved.

They were married three months later in the registry office at Kuala Lumpur with Anderson, who appeared to have accepted defeat gracefully, as a witness. James wrote at once to Pasterns advising them of the marriage and anticipating his legacy.

In due course the reply was delivered. "As you are no doubt

aware, the codicil relating to his bequest was drafted in your father's individual style rather than the legal form which is always preferable in such documents in the interests of precision. Taking into account that the will as a whole is drawn up in keeping with the trust documents existing in your family, it is our opinion that the true beneficiaries of this bequest are intended to be your offspring, rather than yourself. It also appears to us that your father intended this provision to apply only to your own natural children, since the wording precludes inheritance by any adopted heir.'' The writer then offered James congratulations on his marriage and assured him of the firm's best attentions.

They moved from the estate house into a large, newly built bungalow, with a room for a nursery and a woman servant, called an amah, to care for the child for which James now hoped.

Bettina, as it amused him to call her, bustled around arranging the furniture and drilling Ah Ching, the new boy, in the use of their latest luxury, an electric stove. She clung to James as she had clung to Gerald, wanting him back in the bungalow for every meal and interpreting every absence as a deliberate unkindness.

To James's dismay their sex life degenerated swiftly through a spiral of misunderstanding to the status of a disaster. Every element in his life combined to render him impotent. His work exhausted him. The clear fact that he needed to conceive a child to assure their future frightened him. Bettina's manipulative dependence angered him. Worst of all, the memory of sweet golden flesh, of kittenish sensuality and artless pleasing welled up in the darkness and he felt distaste for Bettina's passive white body and purse-lipped tolerance of his attempts on it.

He drank excessively, which made his flesh yet more wayward. He went to bed with dread in his bowels, frightened that he would not be able to achieve an erection, which was increasingly the case.

Worse was to come. If he overmastered his tiredness and distaste and achieved an ejaculation, a fierce pain flared up in his loins and persisted for some hours afterward.

On Anderson's next visit to Bukit Helang, James consulted the doctor about his sexual difficulties.

Anderson reacted with swift embarrassment. "Pain of that kind is very unusual in men," he said, as if he doubted James's word. "In women, it's quite common of course. Any trouble with your water, at all?"

"No."

"Ever had any—ah—venereal disease?"

"No."

"What about during the occupation, when you and Treadwell were living rough in the jungle—anything with the waterworks then?"

"Heavens, I couldn't begin to remember. We were going down with one illness after another in the beginning. We had no drugs, you see, and we had to eat whatever we could get. I'm a tough specimen and I got off lightly, but I was unconscious for three days once with one of the fevers that hit us."

"Mmn." The doctor examined him as if he could hardly bear to handle another man's body, putting on a thin rubber glove to feel the inside of his rectum with one finger. "Prostate seems a little enlarged"—he was plainly puzzled—"but it shouldn't be serious. There are no nodules, nothing. This may just be the result of an old urinary infection. Tell you what I'll do—we'll assume that this is another of these damn tropical bugs the boffins haven't caught up with yet and see how it likes some penicillin. Wonderful stuff, penicillin. Takes care of the clap too, you know." Anderson was not by nature a tactful man, but he would not have dreamed of telling James outright that he suspected that chronic untreated gonorrhea was the major cause of his problem.

Anderson came to dinner with them and stayed overnight, for which James was grateful since his presence diluted the tense atmosphere between himself and his wife. James's characteristic charm was waning; it was hard to radiate merriment with sexual failure, poverty and insecurity staring you in the face.

He saw no reason to confide his problems to Bettina. She was already whimpering "Don't you love me anymore?" and following him with reproachful eyes. They were squabbling with greater frequency. "You only married me for Gerald's sake," she would say, or "You married me because you felt sorry for me, didn't you?" She was terrified that he would divorce her; she felt as if the shame of that would kill her, that anything would be better than the misery of living as a stigmatized divorcée on a pittance—she was no longer entitled even to her widow's pension.

James at first argued, swearing, with the fluency of lifelong practice, that he loved her, but she began to be obsessed with her own inferiority and retreated beyond the reach of flattery.

"I'm no good," she told him. "I'm not your class, your family will laugh at me. They must be wondering what on earth possessed you to marry some common little woman with no money or family of her own."

The doctor returned in a week. "Thought it best to pop by,"

he told James, his bald head gleaming with a film of perspiration. "Penicillin doesn't agree with everyone. Besides, I'd like to see how it acts on your condition—very interesting, never come across anything like it before."

Anderson continued to make weekly trips to the estate for four or five months, eventually changing James's treatment to another drug, and always happy to stay the night. James was more glad of his company than anything else. Nothing seemed to affect his body one way or another. He never felt any sexual stirring toward his wife now, and she behaved to him with such coldness he seldom dared to make a move toward her.

One morning James left the bungalow in darkness as usual to take muster, then realized that he had forgotten to put on his wristwatch. Rather than risk turning the car on the pitch-dark narrow track, he left it and ran back through the silence that preceded the jungle dawn, when life seemed suspended, as if a thousand creatures were holding their breaths in anticipation.

James saw two figures in silhouette against the bamboo blinds and realized that his bedroom door was open and light from the kerosene lamp was streaming across the veranda outside. As he approached, he heard his wife's voice.

"I can't bear it when you're not here, Arthur. I feel so safe with you," she was saying. "I know I've made such a terrible mistake. You're the only person I can talk to. I just don't know what to do." The wicker lounger creaked as she sat down in a tense ball of distress.

"You mustn't blame yourself, Betty. He swept you off your feet, that's all. He's a good-looking chap, a real ladies' man. No girl could resist if he made up his mind to charm her."

"But he's so different now. He's . . ."

"He's seen me about it, you know."

"No, I didn't know." Her voice sank to an embarrassed whisper and James saw his wife bow her head.

"He and Gerald used to go down to that place called Mary's in KL before the war—did you know that?" The shadowy head was shaken and the face appeared in profile as Betty looked up. "I think he—ah—picked up something there that's the cause of some of this trouble. So you see, my dear, it's nothing to do with you."

"You mean, some disease?"

James smiled grimly to himself at her horrified tone.

The doctor put a reassuring hand on her shoulder. "No danger from it now, I'm certain. Cleared up long ago but there's probably some scarring. However, there's something else, my dear. I should have spotted it at once after all these years out East.

Occasionally a man gets accustomed to native women and can't
. . . well, if he takes up with a white woman afterward it's never
very successful. There's some fancy psychological explanation.
I've seen quite a few men like that in my time and I'm afraid I
think James is another one.''

"But he says he *must* have children, Arthur.''

"I'm afraid he has precious little hope of that at the moment.''

"I'm so glad you're here, Arthur. I couldn't go through all
this on my own.''

"Would you object if I suggested you should see a colleague
of mine in KL for some tests? There is just a possibility that
there's something that can be done, but we would need to know
that everything was all right with you too.''

"If I must,'' Bettina said slowly. "I suppose I owe it to him
to try everything.''

To James's surprise the doctor sat down beside Bettina, his
arm around her shoulders, and slowly kissed the top of her head.
Then Ah Ching appeared at the front of the bungalow and began
climbing the steps, and the two people drew apart.

James decided to send a boy to fetch his watch later and returned to his office, his mind in turmoil. Jealousy was the mild-
est of the emotions he felt. Uppermost was outrage—Anderson
had obviously deliberately prolonged his useless treatment in
order to have the excuse to be with Bettina, and had deceived
him about his sexual difficulties. Beyond his anger, however,
James saw that the situation could be turned to his advantage.
For the first time since the end of the war he allowed himself to
think of Khatijah and their child. He pulled out the letters from
the lawyers in London and read them again.

Bettina found that there were more and more occasions when
James could not be with her and suggested she should choose
Anderson's company instead. Swiftly her trust in the doctor grew
into a passionate affection, which he returned. She began to make
shopping trips to Kuala Lumpur, whose real purpose was to meet
Anderson in the tea room of Richard's department store.

She was an easy victim of romance. Impelled by the instinct
to find a protector and with any sensuality she might have
achieved blighted by the puritanical ignorance of her upbringing,
Bettina could adeptly arrange her emotions to suit her circumstances. Genuine passion was beyond her, but instead she felt
an equally powerful sensation, an artificial attachment created
from equal parts of expediency and fantasy.

James watched the couple carefully during the doctor's visits,
feeling contempt for their love affair, which seemed to him as
banal and sentimental as a cheap Hollywood romance. He took

a perverse satisfaction in their shared looks and the furtive, fingertip touches they exchanged behind his back.

He invited Anderson to spend the Christmas of 1946 at Bukit Helang. Bill Treadwell also joined them, and at once remarked upon James's grim, withdrawn mood.

"Not much goodwill to all men about you, Jim," he said with characteristic directness.

James rejected the invitation to confide his troubles. "Tell me about the prospects for peace on earth," he countered. "Have the Communists disbanded? I heard on Radio Malaya . . ."

The Australian made an expression of contempt. "Surely you're not still believing everything you hear on Radio Malaya?" They fell into a familiar discussion about the authorities' blindness to the communist threat and it was not until many hours later that Bill wondered why James was being so reticent about whatever was preying on his mind.

There were electric lights now to hang with the Chinese lanterns and Indian paper flowers on the young casuarina tree which was felled for the celebration, and a frozen turkey from the cold store in Kuala Lumpur replaced the suckling pig which had graced the board in Douglas Lovell's day.

Knowing that the lovers had formed the habit of meeting on the veranda in the morning after he had left for the muster ground, James set off in darkness as usual the day that work resumed on the estate, then turned back to spy on his wife.

Again he saw her with Anderson, two shadows on the blinds, who this time embraced and kissed awkwardly.

"I can't bear it, Arthur," Bettina spoke in a low, hopeless voice. "I've never known such happiness and I can't stand stealing it this way. I want to be with you for always."

"Leave him, darling, leave him, whyever won't you leave?"

Little as he cared for Bettina, now, James felt a stab of jealousy. The two figures sat down side by side and were evidently holding hands. James strained his ears to hear the rest of the conversation.

"I daren't run off, darling, I daren't," Bettina was saying. "Don't you see what he'd do? He'd finish you. I'm your patient too, don't forget, Arthur. If it was ever known that you had a love affair with a patient, and with the wife of one of your patients, there'd be a terrible scandal. The Medical Council would bar you from practicing ever again. You'd be struck off, and then what?"

"I could still practice out here—no one inquires too deeply into a fellow's credentials in the East."

"But we'd never be able to go *home*, Arthur." Bettina spoke with anguish. "I don't want us to be one of those awful, shady colonial couples. I want to be your wife, and to live with you in England, and have nothing to hide from anybody. I hate this beastly place, I've always hated it." They sighed and were silent and unhappy for a while.

James felt a surge of contempt. Like most aristocrats, he considered himself above snobbery, but the petit bourgeois tone of his wife's love affair disgusted him. Her craven preoccupation with professional status, respectability and what the neighbors would think, her automatic defense against a small-minded community which would spy from the camouflage of its lace curtains were anathema to his own values. Much as he despised the lovers' suburban dilemma, however, he appreciated its power to paralyze them.

"I've got to make him divorce me," his wife said at last. "Or catch him out with one of his native women. Then I'll be free. It won't be long now, I'm sure of it. If only he doesn't decide to go home with me. I couldn't bear to leave you."

"He won't go home until he's got his legacy, never fear. And he won't get that until he gets his child, which is impossible, so that's that. We're safe for a while."

Bettina gave a laugh, the cruel expression of a weak spirit's resentment which ignited hatred in James's heart.

"You're quite sure I can't get pregnant?" she asked the doctor. "Even if he could—do something?"

The man nodded. "I've seen the results of those tests you had in KL myself and it's exactly as I thought. When you were ill after your child was born, there was a lot of abdominal infection and of course in those circumstances with no treatment it probably continued unchecked a long time. There's no chance of the two of you ever having a child. So he'll never get his legacy, unless he settles for a native wife and a brood of half-castes—hardly the thing for the son of a duke, eh?"

"But don't you mind about me, Arthur? I wouldn't mind giving you children if you wanted them."

"I don't want them. I faced that a long time ago with Jean. All I want is you, my darling, and for us to be together always."

James drew back to avoid seeing their embrace. His head spun with the implications of what he had heard, and he walked back to his car in a trance.

When the morning's business was under way, he went into his office to consider a course of action. Then he called up Selambaram and announced that he would be going away for a few days, and after that telephoned an acquaintance in Kuala Lumpur to ask for a loan of his car.

* * *

He drove slowly down the straight, level road, red dust billowing from the tire tracks. It was like driving into a dream. The wooden houses slipped past, half hidden by thickets of bamboo. In the fields he could see people cutting rice—was she with them? He half expected Khatijah's graceful form to appear at the roadside and walk toward him, the steps confined to a seductive undulation by the tight dark-red sarong.

He was afraid of seeing her, afraid of her reaction when he proposed taking possession of their child. Better hope that she was harvesting rice with the others.

The cindery area of the roadside, where he had so often parked his truck, was waiting for the car. He walked to the house of his father-in-law, conscious of his stiff shorts and sturdy shoes.

They did not know him at once because of his pale skin and Western clothes, but he smiled and joked and reminded them of incidents during the war and at length they saw that he was the same person as the man who had married Khatijah and greeted him with a mixture of pride and wariness. Here, too, he realized, he had the name of a war hero.

"Your wife is well," Osman told him as they sat down on the wooden floor. Little Yusof fetched Maimunah, who arrived with a baby in her arms. Behind her trailed a watchful child with fine brown hair, dressed in a length of checked cotton which was tucked around her plump stomach. James noticed with relief that his daughter's skin tone was no more than olive, that her hair was not black but several shades of tobacco-brown, that her eyes were oval but not slanting.

"And you have another daughter." Maimunah was offering him the firmly swaddled bundle in her arms. With disbelief he took it, and looked down on the small face; a pair of dancing dark eyes scanned him with curiosity. The baby opened its tiny, toothless mouth and yawned. This child was also olive-skinned. He fancied that the eyes turned up at the corners, but could not be sure.

"Born six months ago," the grandmother told him. Mentally, he counted the months. Yes, it was possible. They must have conceived this child just before he left the village. "Very strong baby, laughing all the time." The tiny limbs struggled in their white wrapping and the baby gave a cooing gurgle.

He handed back the bundle and began negotiations, impatient with the delicate circumlocutions he knew he must phrase in order to persuade the grandparents. He wished to return to his own country with his children, and would make a gift of money to Khatijah and another to Osman. He proposed divorcing Khatijah under Muslim law. Their marriage in any case was not valid under the laws of Great Britain.

They had certainly expected something like this, and from the eagerness with which Osman began to discuss the terms of the deal James deduced that Khatijah had once more sunk to the status of an outcast in her family. "Of course," Osman observed pompously, "the Holy Koran decrees that children are the property of their father beyond the age of six. Of course, these circumstances are special, because their father wishes to travel so far away."

Maimunah, on the other hand, wrangled with unfeminine obduracy. "Khatijah's children are her only happiness, the only wealth she possesses. She will never give them up. She will fight like a tiger for her cubs." She glared around the dim, stuffy interior of the house. "Children as young as this need their mother. And besides, no honorable family would entertain such a suggestion."

Then there was a commotion among the crowd which had assembled outside, and Khatijah herself appeared, her red and brown skirts still wet from the *padi* fields. Obviously one of the children had run to tell her that her husband had reappeared at last and wanted the babies.

His heart turned over at the sight of her, vibrant with anguish, all modesty forgotten as her headcovering slipped off her braided black hair.

She flew at him, eyes as wild and staring as those of an angry cat.

"You shall never have them!" she screamed, clawing at his shirt. "I will die rather than give my babies to you! No other woman is going to raise my children. They belong to me. I love them. My children are all the world to me. If you take away my children I will die!"

Uncontrollable sobs tore at her lungs and she began to scream, cry after cry. She hurled herself at her stepfather, begging incoherently to keep the girls, and Maimunah spoke up again, arguing with Osman.

"It's not right to take such tiny children away from their mother. It's cruelty. How will the baby live happily without its mother? Khatijah should be able to raise her own children."

The women's opposition made up Osman's mind at once. He had no wish to cut the foolish figure of a family head whose womenfolk disregarded his authority.

"Be quiet, both of you. This man risked his life with the

Japanese for us. Are we now going to deny him what is right-fully his? I don't need two more mouths to feed, Khatijah—did you think of that?''

"No!" she screamed in fury, hammering her fists on the bare wooden floor. "No! No! I won't let you take my babies." She leaped up, snatched the swaddled baby from her grandmother's arms and ran to the steps, but at once two uncles restrained her and James flinched inwardly as he saw his child torn from its mother's arms.

The older girl, understanding what was to happen, began to scream and clutch Khatijah's skirts, but she, too, was pulled away.

"Take your granddaughter away," Osman told Maimunah. "This is best for everyone, and she will realize that when she has calmed herself." Khatijah's mother stepped forward, eager to remove the embarrassment of her disobedient girl from her husband's sight, but Khatijah halted at the head of the stairs and snarled at James.

"Never forget what you have done today—never! There is nowhere in the world you can take my children that I will not find them and come for them! And I will make you suffer for your cruelty."

After that, the affair was finished with the same furtive lack of ceremony that had characterized his wedding to Khatijah. Accompanied by Khatijah's mother and one of her uncles, James drove with the infants to Kuala Lumpur, where he sent the villagers back. Then he telephoned the estate and ordered his houseboy to bring the amah and meet him.

"What on earth is all this?" Bettina demanded as the amah carried the baby into the bungalow and James followed carrying the older child, who had at last screamed herself into an exhausted sleep.

"These are my children," he told her harshly.

She quickly crossed the room and inspected the baby, drawing back with her fingertips the cotton cloth in which it was wrapped. "What children? What are they? Native brats! I should have known! Not in there," she commanded the servant as she walked toward the room they had intended as a nursery. "They can live in the servants' quarters. I won't have you . . . I won't have them near me."

"Yes, you will, Bettina my dear." Wearily, James motioned her to sit down. She remained standing, arms folded, rigid with anger. "Yes, Ah Ching, that's the right room. The memsahib made a mistake." She opened her mouth to protest but he silenced her with a gesture. "Now tell me, Bettina—do you want your divorce?"

She stepped back as if he had hit her.

"What!"

"I'm too tired for any lies, Bettina. I've known what was going on between you and Anderson for a long time, so there's nothing you can deny. No need to panic." He smiled at her, summoning the remnants of his old charm to impose his will, and she approached as if drawn by a spell and sat down opposite him. "We can both have exactly what we want. I can have my inheritance if I have children—and I *have* children. You can have Anderson if I divorce you, and I will divorce you—all that's necessary is for you all to cooperate."

He got up and took a cheroot from the box on the black wooden sideboard, then lit it himself. Ah Ching and the amah were bustling to and fro with hot water and bed linen. He could hear the sleepy voice of the older child asking in Malay for her mother.

"Cooperate with what, James?" His wife was watching him with suspicion, torn between hope of a way out of the bleak emotional labyrinth in which she was trapped and fear of her husband.

"Making absolutely sure that there's no question about the legacy business, that's all. I can't take the chance that there'll be any question about the children's legitimacy."

"Have you taken leave of your senses?" she snapped, her voice almost cracking in fright. "They're your bastards, James, your *native* bastards. You can't make them any more than that. You don't seriously expect me to pass them off as my own children! You're mad! Two little niggers like that. It's absurd."

"That's where you are quite wrong. I've thought it out in great detail, Bettina, I'm not a fool. They're three-quarters white, and since my whole family is dark-haired I don't suppose they'll be in the least conspicuous. All I need are birth certificates, and all I need to get birth certificates are a couple of chits from the good doctor—do you see? No one will know any better by the time I get back to England—I'll wait a few years, of course."

"You've gone mad, James. You'll never pass them off as white children." He saw that her hands were shaking, and she clasped them together in the lap of her mauve print dress. She felt weak with tension.

"I don't see why not—they're no darker than I am. The older one's lighter, actually—you'll see tomorrow, she's got brown hair. Darker than you, lighter than me—what would be more likely?''

She looked at him in silence, hope and anxiety mingling in her misty blue eyes. "And you'll really let me go?"

"Yes."

"And you won't make any trouble for us?"

"Considering that you would be in a position to make trouble for me, I'd be foolish to even think of it. Of course, if Arthur didn't agree I would have to write to the Medical Council pointing out that he'd alienated my wife's affections, committed adultery with a patient, that sort of thing. You *are* my wife, Bettina. You haven't been a very good wife either, I should say."

A deep flush of shame darkened her pale face and her expression became anguished. "I didn't mean to, James, I swear it. I never intended to look at another man. I don't know what happened. The whole thing just grew and grew, day by day, until . . ."

"Until it was bigger than both of you?" He had intended to sneer, but checked himself. Like a horse, Bettina was uncontrollable when she was frightened. He would have to calm her to win her obedience.

"I think we both made a mistake." He put as much kindness in his voice as he could. "And we won't be the only ones. A lot of people were unsettled by the war. But there'll be no harm done if we keep our heads, I promise you." He took her hands and held them, looking into her eyes with the pleading expression which seldom failed to get him what he wanted. "Of course I was hurt, dreadfully hurt when I discovered . . ." She began to cry and he released one hand and gave her his handkerchief. "But when I thought about it, I realized that you're suited to Arthur, he's more your kind of chap than I am. Believe me, I don't want to stand in your way. But I must have my inheritance, don't you see? There's no future for any of us in this country. There'll be all-out war with the Communists soon, it's inevitable. And I'm damned if I'm going to go home to sponge off my brother for the rest of my life."

"We'd all go to jail if they found out," she protested, half convinced.

"Nonsense. They don't send people to jail for this sort of thing. And we'll never be found out, I promise you. The country's still in confusion, a few irregularities in paperwork aren't going to attract any attention. Why not talk to Arthur about it? Sleep on the idea, eh?" he suggested, patting her shoulder. "I'll take the guest room, shall I?"

The next morning, she agreed. By the end of the week Anderson had accepted the proposition with extremely bad grace, and filled in two dockets confirming the birth of girl babies to James and his wife. James chose the names Catherine and Miranda as a vain homage to Khatijah and Maimunah; he selected birth dates which cut the proper months off the children's real ages, in order that the births should not predate the wedding and that Pasterns should suspect nothing. For the same reason James also insisted that the divorce proceedings should wait the requisite time.

James decided to remain in Malaya for as long as he could, despite the news that some isolated rubber estates had been attacked by the Communists. They agreed that Bettina would leave as soon as Anderson found a temporary home for them. They planned to sail for Britain as soon as another doctor came out to replace him.

Bettina became sweet-tempered and friendly toward James. Once the log jam of their hostility had been breached, there was an atmosphere of good humor about the bungalow for the first time. James found it charming to return for his lunch and find the two infants sitting in the shade with their amah in their white romper suits and sunbonnets, and he acknowledged with pride that they were extraordinarily attractive children. The older girl was becoming sweetly attached to him and frequently toddled up to offer him a hibiscus flower, or a snail shell, or whatever treasure had most recently caught her fancy.

Bettina was surprised when he roused her one afternoon from her lie-down.

"Wake up, my dear, you must wake up. It's important."

Puzzled, she sat up and he passed her the silk wrapper she wore over her nightdress.

"Come into the other room." He did not want to tell her this in her bedroom.

"What is it—the Communists?"

"Yes, my dear, the Communists. There's been another attack, I'm afraid."

"Someone we know?"

"Up at Amblehurst." This was the English name of a rubber plantation almost as remote as theirs, farther to North Perak. "They killed the manager and his wife, and someone else who was with them." James paused, wretched in spite of his disdain for his wife's attachment, because he knew the news he had to give her would remove the only kind of happiness she had. "Be brave, my dear. It was Arthur. Arthur Anderson is dead."

She gave him a narrow, cringing look and said at once, "He

455

can't be. It wasn't his week to go to Amblehurst. It was someone else's.''

He mixed a strong gin *pahit* and put it in her hand.

"I'm sorry, Bettina. My poor Bettina. There isn't any mistake. He's gone."

Bettina did not cry. She was numbed with shock. "It isn't fair," she said, almost crossly. "I loved him. It isn't fair." As completely as if she had walked out of a door, she retreated into a distant, interior world and behaved like a sleepwalker for weeks. She never mentioned Arthur Anderson again, and never again exhibited any real cheerfulness or energy.

She stayed with James, because she had nowhere else to go. They rubbed along together amiably enough for a year or so, although she was unable to feel anything at all toward the two little girls. She drank a little more with each month that passed, and formed a bridge circle with three other planters' wives who relieved their fearful isolation with a day in Kuala Lumpur once a fortnight.

The Communist guerrillas, led by Chin Peng, picked off more and more of the Europeans who lived in isolation in the jungle, supervising the plunder of the country's resources. Five hundred Europeans died in the same year as Dr. Anderson. The Communists attacked in other ways as well; three hundred strikes hit the rubber estates and the tin mines. The British administration responded slowly, playing down the situation and gagging the press.

James found notices tacked to the trees on his plantation, proclaiming "Death to the Running Dogs." Their bungalow was fortified with sandbags, they were given a police guard and James toured the estate in an armored car with a shotgun at the ready.

In 1950, when the elder daughter was officially almost four years old, the British High Commissioner, Sir Henry Gurney, was assassinated beside his bullet-riddled Rolls-Royce en route to a hill station for the weekend. James decided it was time to take his wife and children home and claim his inheritance.

The war with the Communists in Malaya continued for twelve years, involving a hundred thousand British citizens. For the National Service conscripts in the fifties it was the posting they most feared because the fight was against two enemies, the Communists and the jungle; of these the jungle proved the more implacable enemy.

Malaya was granted independence in 1957; the war—which was always referred to as "the Emergency" by the British—

ended in 1960 with a victory parade in Kuala Lumpur, and the British military commander sat on the dignitaries' dais next to the American president of Pacific Tin. In London, James turned down invitations to the celebration cocktail parties and dinners. Malaya was a part of his life which he did not wish to emphasize.

In Penang, Bill Treadwell applied for citizenship in the new state of Malaya.

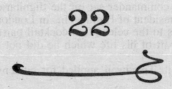

22

"GONNA SPEND MY WHOLE LIFE THROUGH . . ." MONTY
reached forward to the audience, stuck out one hip as far as the
tight leather dress would allow, and marked the beat. The stage
lights flashed. ". . . *lovin' you-u-u-u-u-u!*"

There was some desultory applause, and Monty and her band
made brief bows. A whine of feedback hurt their ears, as it had
done periodically right through the performance. The lights died.
Three or four beer cans sailed through the air and fell short of
the small stage.

"Thank you, Ruby Slippers. Thank you, everybody." The
DJ spun the new single by The Clash and the crowd pogo-ed
into life. Monty stumbled back to the cupboardlike dressing room
on shaking legs.

"Christ! That was awful." She slumped onto a hard chair and
looked at her face in the mirror. "And I look so vile. They hated
us, just hated us."

Her new band trailed after her—Winston, who'd done sessions
with The Juice when they'd wanted an extra drummer, Stas who
had been playing with another of Biffo Records' hopeful signings
when that band had split up, and Tony, who was really doing
her a favor, because he was one of the most sought-after session
guitarists in town. Monty admired Tony's effortless musicianship so fiercely that she felt overawed by his willingness to follow her into the succession of sleazy punk clubs which they had
played over the past few weeks.

They all looked defeated. One of the flying beer cans had caught Stas on the temple and he searched for a tissue to mop up the trickle of blood. There were no tissues. The dressing room at Dingwall's club was not equipped with such luxuries.

Sig shouldered through the door, full of energy. "Great, fuckin' great," he enthused, giving them all Cokes. "Isn't she lovely?" He squeezed Monty's ass and the leather dress squeaked under his sweaty hand.

"C'mon, Sig, it was a disaster. All these poxy clubs are disasters. We're not building a following doing this, we're just dying on our feet."

Sig picked Monty's coat off the hook on the wall, put his arm around her and led her out of the club into the damp night. Dingwall's was built on a cobbled courtyard by the side of a canal, and he supported her firmly as she stumbled over the uneven surface in her red stilettoes.

"Now get this straight, girl. You talk like a loser, you will *be* a loser. Nobody does great when they're starting out. You gotta give it time."

"There's a difference between doing great and having beer cans raining down from the ceiling, Sig."

"Ferchrissake, all these kids throw beer cans at all the bands they see. They also spit, yell and throw bricks if there are any bricks around. They want to be cool and be punks and stick safety pins through their noses, that's all. Don't mean nothin'. Not a thing. They liked you, you were good."

Monty squirmed inwardly; she was frightened of Sig. He was tough, physically strong and completely ruthless. He was also as stubborn as a pig and never conceded an inch when she argued with him. Instead, he would hit her if that was what would get her to do what he wanted, or bully her verbally, or, which was the most likely, simply argue her into a corner so that she obeyed him of her own free will but with fear seeping through her tissues as she did it.

The problem was that Monty was not only afraid of Sig. She was also afraid of every one of the boys in studded dog collars and girls with green hair who stood in a sullen mass on the other side of the microphone to hear her. Without The Juice to hide behind, without Rick to blame if they should fail, Monty was suffering a chronic case of stage fright.

"I can't stand it much longer," she told Cindy Moon when Sig allowed her to return home. It was high summer, and the faint pulse of reggae music from the West Indian club in the next street throbbed in the dusty air.

"He's a bastard." Cindy was sitting cross-legged in front of her typewriter. "Sig Bear has a heart of solid dirt. How can he push you so hard? If you crack up he'll never get his money out of you. Men are stupid." She uncoiled and put her arm around Monty. "You're good. You're a star. Keep hold of that and forget Sig."

"I'm not good though. I can write pretty songs, sure, and I can play well, but it takes more than that. I should never have let go in front of the band the way I did. I just don't know how to manage people. That was what Rick was so good at—OK, he was arrogant, but he knew how to put on a front for the rest of us, and how to talk people into things."

"He was just another dominating bastard." Cindy squeezed Monty's shoulders in a gesture of protection. "Men are all on total power trips. You don't have to grind other people to pieces in order to get on top of them."

Monty sat down on the black plastic-covered divan which was both their sofa and Cindy's bed. She felt as if she were being torn in two between Cindy and Sig, both of whom praised her talent but tried to push her into doing what they wanted.

At least Sig was easy to understand. He wanted her to finish the album and make him money. He did not pretend that he loved her—the word never crossed his thin red lips.

Cindy, on the other hand, smothered her with compliments and caresses, wrote her poetry and bought her presents. It was balm to her affection-starved soul. Monty had thought at first that Cindy was gay—there were plenty of rumors that she was.

She soon discovered that Cindy got her kicks going down to the reggae clubs and picking up black boys. Every month or so she would vanish for a few days of degradation with these contemptuous kids, who felt sexually exploited and abused her accordingly. Then Cindy would reappear in the apartment with a witchy, lopsided smile, show Monty her bruises and announce that white men didn't know the first thing about fucking. She had some surprising white boyfriends too—wealthy, straight business types, but Cindy seldom had a good word to say about any man, whatever his race or proclivity.

She would usually return with some cheap brown heroin powder as well, which she burned on a strip of silver foil to inhale the smoke. Smack was something else of which Monty was terrified, Cy had used it a lot, and it fitted with the nihilistic, destructive surrender to despair in his personality, which frightened her because she sensed the same chasm of nothingness in herself.

Cindy sometimes offered her some of the drug, but she always refused it.

"Tell you what," Cindy proposed suddenly, "come and see The Joe Jones Band with me tonight. That'll teach you everything you need to know about men on power trips."

"Aren't they big in Japan?" Monty inquired with a faint sneer. The British rock elite tended to look on bands that were big in Japan as soulless and commercial.

"Colossal. They're huge in the States, too. I liked a lot of their early stuff, it was sort of Dylan-ish, country rock. But now all they do is make a lot of noise and flash their equipment about."

Monty decided to go. She had nothing else to do except sit in the apartment in the heat fighting the fear in her heart.

Cindy took an hour and a half to get ready, at the end of which she looked stunning in another of her diaphanous chiffon dresses, this one striped electric blue and pink. She wore gilt stiletto-heeled sandals and a 1940s fox wrap with the animal's muzzle and paws worked into the design. Monty felt hopelessly dowdy in her leather dress, which was creasing and falling out of shape.

The Joe Jones Band took the stage between two mountains of speakers. With the first crashing chord they played, Monty felt as if she were lifted off her feet and dashed against the wall by a gigantic wave of sound. The volume made her bowels vibrate and her mind empty completely. It was impossible to do anything but give herself wholly to the ocean of noise and let it sweep her away.

They were lanky, long-haired American boys. Joe Jones was a mesmeric figure with raven-black hair which whipped about his naked torso. He wore nothing but a pair of skin-tight white-satin trousers which revealed every line of his magnificent thigh muscles, and a silver-buckled belt. He leaped around the stage, howling into the hand mike like a Red Indian warrior.

Cindy had backstage passes and insisted that they should be presented to the performers in their dressing room when the set was finished. She always took advantage of her position as a minor London celebrity to meet the top bands in town, but Monty hated the whole business of standing in a tiny concrete room wondering what to say next to people in whom she was not interested.

Raucous laughter greeted them from behind the dressing-room door. Joe Jones's legs seemed to fill half the room. He was sprawled in the only chair, a half-empty bottle of bourbon in his fist, his heaving chest mantled with sweat.

"Hi—I'm Cindy Moon from *Hit Maker*, and this is Ruby Slippers. How do you like London?" Cindy always introduced herself the same way.

The legs contracted, and Joe Jones shook Cindy's small hand, putting down the bottle in order to do so. At the intrusion of women the boys fell silent.

"I'd say 'sit down' but we're a little short of chairs. They showed me the review you gave our last album—you said some very nice things."

They continued to exchange pleasantries while Monty wished she were somewhere else. The problem was that there was nowhere Monty could look in the mirrored cell without her eyes being drawn to Joe's crotch. The white satin also outlined his cock, and he clearly found performing exciting. Even though the erection was subsiding slowly, the satin was so tight she could see the ridge of his penis.

As if he were aware of her attention, Joe Jones pulled a towel from around his neck and let it fall into his lap, modestly hiding everything. After another ten minutes of small talk Cindy said good-bye and left, with Monty trailing after her.

"See what I mean?" Cindy said as they hailed a cab. "They think they're so great, making all that noise, drinking all that whiskey, having all those chicks scream for them; they're just little boys, that's all. They were dying for us to come back to their hotel with them. Thank goodness we got out when we did."

"It might have been fun."

"You can't seriously *like* all that macho crap."

Monty said nothing; she was not quite sure how she felt. Of course she was repelled by all that aggressive sexuality. It was the same swaggering sham of maleness that she had hated so much in Rick.

"I've got a headache," she recognized at last.

"Poor, poor Monty. I'm so sorry."

At the apartment, Cindy insisted that she should not take an aspirin—"It makes your stomach bleed"—but instead put a dab of Tiger Balm on Monty's forehead. This did nothing. The pain spread down the left side of her face and settled in her teeth.

The next day was a Sunday and the pain in Monty's teeth became so bad that she felt as if she could hardly see.

"I know what would fix it," Cindy said with a curious reserve.

"What?"

"You won't take it."

"I'll take anything to stop this agony."

Cindy's lips twitched. "A whiff of smack would make the pain go away, I promise."

Monty shook her head. She went into her own room, and by the afternoon all she could do was lie down and moan.

"I can't bear seeing you like this," Cindy said, bringing her some camomile tea. "Just a tiny bit of smack and you'd be fine."

Monty pushed the mug away, nauseated by the idea of drinking anything.

"You're not thinking you'll get hooked on one hit, are you? It's not the same, inhaling. Look at me, I do it all the time and it's no big deal. You don't see me crawling round the room if I can't get any gear, do you? And believe me, Monty, the pain would go—it'd be there, but it'd be far away, where you could handle it."

Monty held out until the evening, then allowed Cindy to sprinkle some of the brown granules into a piece of foil and let her breathe in the smoke. It was a little sickly and acrid, but Monty was accustomed to bizarre chemicals.

"Now you'll know what it's all about," Cindy told her. "All the kids do smack now. It's nothing, just a good feeling."

Monty's stomach heaved and she dived for the bathroom to be sick. Then relief came, sweet and calming. As Cindy had predicted, the pain was still there, but it was not like pain, just a distant signal that she could ignore. The fear was far away too. Until the drug banished it, Monty had not realized how she had lived every day with terror disseminated throughout her being.

Three weeks later Ruby Slippers had another gig, and Monty asked Cindy for a hit to calm her the day before. It had worn off by the time she had to leave the apartment for the club, so Cindy gave her another one. She took the stage in complete confidence, performed well, kept a brave face in front of the band and let Sig say and do what he liked with no sensation of involvement at all.

They began recording the first Ruby Slippers album, and Monty found that she could get a faster hit by embedding a grain of smack into a cigarette. She still vomited every time; and since she was using the stuff more frequently, this was becoming a real inconvenience—and worse.

"I'm terrified Sig'll find out," she told Cindy. "He caught

me throwing up yesterday and I told him it was food poisoning, but he's too smart to believe that again. What'll I do? He'll kill me if he susses.''

''Use a needle,'' Cindy advised.

This did not seem nearly as alarming to Monty as it would have done three months earlier. True, she hated needles. But she hated the fear more. She allowed Cindy to inject her.

''You'd better lay off this Chinese stuff, though,'' her friend said as the lovely calm spread through her. ''It's not very pure. I'll see if I can find you some of the old white stuff. Pharmaceutical grade, that's what you need. Keep to your leg veins, if you can; then your arms will be clean.''

White heroin cost her about five times what the brown stuff did, but it was worth it. Monty had the money Cathy had loaned her for the lawyers' bills, and it slowly found its way into the pocket of the dealer whom Cindy met two or three times a week in a coffee shop near the *Hit Maker* office. Eventually, the money was gone.

''Can't you ask your sister for more?'' Cindy asked.

Monty shook her head. ''I can't lie to her. We're too close, we can practically read each other's thoughts.''

Cindy gave a pout of disapproval. ''I'm skint until the end of the month,'' she hinted.

''We'll just have to do without dope for a bit until I finish the album and Sig pays me some more of what's due from the single,'' Monty told her, offended that anyone should suggest that she deceive her sister.

The next night, when Monty returned late from the recording studio with Tony and Stas, intending to sit and talk for a while in the apartment, she found the door ajar.

''Cindy must have left it open,'' she said uncertainly. ''That's odd. She's always telling me to be careful to lock up.''

''Could be someone kicked it in.'' Tony showed her the lock, which seemed to have been loosened on its screws. ''Anything missing?''

At once Monty noticed that her tape recorder was gone, and almost all her expensive clothes. She opened the smart leather-covered case in which she kept her jewelry. It was empty. She felt behind the mirror where she kept a pair of flashy diamond-and-emerald earrings which Rick had given her, rolled up in a scrap of chamois leather. They too had gone.

''Oh, God, a break-in. That's all I need.'' She collapsed despondently on the black divan. ''Isn't it great the way life always hits you when you're down?'' The boys were sympathetic, and stayed with her until Cindy came home a few hours later. Cindy grew viciously angry when they told her that the apartment had been burgled, but Monty watched her with detachment. Cindy had suggested the hiding place behind the mirror for her precious earrings and Monty could not help reflecting that someone who had not known there was jewelry there would not have thought of looking for valuables in such an odd place.

Early the following morning, Cathy telephoned. "We've got to go down to Bourton at once—Didi's dying," she told her sister. "And I'm going to pick up Mummy first. Do you want to come with me?"

Monty had not seen her mother for years, and did not want to. Neither did she feel any compulsion to pay her last respects to her grandmother. "No—I don't want to come," she said. "It'll only bring me down."

There was a pause at the end of the telephone, and Monty suddenly felt guilty that she always dumped on Cathy the whole responsibility for their unlovable family. "Unless you'd like me to come, of course," she added.

"Please, Monty—I need you. It won't be a great day out, but I think it's something we should do together. Didi's part of our lives, after all."

Cathy's BMW hurtled like a silver bullet down to Brighton and drew quietly to the curb by the tall white house where their mother lived. Bettina seemed to have shrunk in stature, Monty thought. Her hair was inaccurately tinted honey-blond, with several inches of gray regrowth visible. The whites of her eyes were yellow, her skin was grayish and waxy, and the sisters noticed with horror that the backs of their mother's hands were spotted with small ulcers, the result of self-neglect and malnutrition aggravated by alcoholism.

Without the care of servants, Bettina's apartment was filthy. Piles of unwashed clothes and linen stank on the dusty floors and the kitchen was sticky with grease and crammed with putrid rubbish. Monty opened the bedroom door and recoiled at the stink. Their mother glared at them in mute defiance, challenging them to disapprove of the squalor.

At Bourton there was a peculiar air of furtive relief in the household. The servants were grave but lively. Hugo, their uncle, seemed to be taller; their cousins' children were quiet and cheerful; everyone in the house was trying to ignore the sense of relief that stole upon them as the tyrant lay dying.

"Darlings! So good of you to come to see an old woman," their grandmother called from the depths of her faded, chintz-curtained bed. "Forgive me, the doctor won't let me get up. But I've fixed him." She arranged her bedraggled pink-satin bed jacket trimmed with marabou. "I just happen to know the best man in London for my kind of cancer and he's coming down tomorrow to tell the old quack not to be so ridiculous. I'm remarkably fit for my age."

Dutifully they sat on the uncomfortable Louis XV gilt chairs and attempted to hold a conversation with the dying woman. Her hair was nothing but a few wisps of dull grayish brown tucked under a girlish velvet band. Her sagging eyelids were crusted with blue mascara and a coating of rouge clogged the fissures in her cheeks.

"I wondered, Catherine, when you are thinking of getting married again." She spoke with a conspiratorial gleam in her watery eyes, her hands with their joints knobbed by arthritis clutching at the satin quilt. "You must be quick, dear, before you lose your looks completely. Of course, you can't hope to compete with the young beauties of today, but you can always make a man fall in love with you if you know how it's done. This life you're leading can't possibly make you happy, and beauty just withers if you're unhappy, dear."

"Of course, Didi," murmured Cathy, stealing a glance in the shadowy ormolu-overhung looking glass to reassure herself that the creamy perfection of her complexion was still intact, that her hair still gleamed like burnished bronze, and that her black chalk-stripe suit did indeed enhance the delicacy of her build in the way she intended that it should.

"Don't say 'of course' to me like that!" The deformed hands clutched more convulsively as if to draw support from the exhausted glamour of the fabric. "You *must* take marriage seriously—that's been the trouble with you all along. Marriage is the only possible profession for a woman. The only point in this work nonsense is that you can meet the right kind of man. Otherwise you'll end up on the shelf like your sister."

Monty and Cathy exchanged glances of resignation, and Cathy steered the conversation back to Lady Davina's cleverness in seducing London's leading cancer specialist into attending her. This man appeared the next day, flustered and embarrassed, and spent an hour with the old woman after which he briskly took Hugo aside and advised him, "Nothing to be done, I doubt she'll last the night. She's having all sorts of delusions, don't take any notice of them."

It was difficult to ignore the demanding shrieks that soon sent the nurse scurrying downstairs to ask the family's advice.

"She wants to come down and make telephone calls," the alarmed woman explained. "She says she's got to telephone the

Prince of Wales and heaven knows who else. She says she can't stay in bed all day like a slut. She says she's organizing a ball and she simply must have royalty there.''

Hugo stumped upstairs and persuaded his mother to write letters instead of telephoning, and the old woman covered many pages of her rich blue writing paper with scrawled lines which tailed off midway down each page. Soon the bed was covered with half-written notes and she fell back into her pillows in a doze.

In the evening, Lady Davina awoke and said in apparently lucid tones, "I want to see my sons. My darling boys, I must see them."

Hugo left the dinner table and went up to his mother again.

"Where's James?" she demanded in anger, as if she suspected Hugo of hiding his brother.

"James isn't here, Mother," he sighed.

"Poor boy," she murmured. "He must miss all the fun we had at the embassy. He must be so desperately lonely out in the East. We must make him come home, darling, fix something up for him so he'll be able to stay, eh?" The cajoling inflections of the rasping old voice were almost obscene.

Later she demanded her jewel box; she spent the last of her strength raking through the jumbled trophies, occasionally holding up some glittering article to the spectral light of her chandelier, reflecting in silence on the hard-won attachment which it had symbolized.

At midnight the nurse gently removed a diamond bracelet from her patient's feeble grasp, rearranged the creased pillows and gave the semiconscious woman her medication. Lady Davina died quietly in her sleep a few hours later.

No one had thought to ask the Trust for permission to use the chapel for the funeral, so Lady Davina received her last respects in the village church before the burial. The sisters looked with interest around the little gray stone nave, wondering what the old woman's restless life of striving to have others do her bidding would bring her at the last. There were few guests: three elderly women who had outlived Didi, and one old man, one of those on whom she had never ceased to exercise her seductive skills, who left the graveyard with an unsteady step, deluded to the last that he had known a great lady.

As they walked back through the rain-sodden churchyard grass to their car, Monty asked: "Are you sorry she's gone, Cathy?"

They paused and watched the rest of their family as they dispersed. "No. She should have died at thirty, for her own sake."

Cathy spoke with surprising harshness. "I'm just sorry she made me waste so much time."

Caroline and Edward, with their stout spouses and beefy children in velvet-collared coats, moved slowly down the mossy path. They were sinking into the quagmire of small salaries and dying professions, led by the will-o'-the-wisp of landed-gentry life-style which would eventually lure them as if blindfolded into the anonymous middle classes. Caroline was married to an unprofitable farmer. Edward was the sales director of a small agricultural machinery firm. They were stolid, weatherbeaten and ignorant of any world that did not revolve around shooting seasons and bloodstock lineage.

Cathy suddenly gave an irritated sigh. "Wherever did we come from, Monty? We're not part of this tribe, are we? We want to change the world, not keep it as it is, pickled in vintage port and old school ties."

"Now you know how I've felt all my life," Monty walked briskly to the car and pulled open the door. There was never any need to lock a car in Bourton village. "We must have a rogue gene or something."

"Maybe Daddy was the same. It's hard to imagine what he would be like if he were still alive."

"I think he would have been a wonderful, wicked old man by now." Sadness settled on them, and they were silent as Cathy drove the short distance back to the big house. They both felt that Death had moved one generation closer to them. There was only Bettina ahead of them now, and they were both appalled at her rapid physical deterioration.

That evening Monty sank into black apathy, and Cathy looked at her with concern as she sat on the high brass fender by the drawing-room fire staring into the distance. She noticed that her sister had lost weight and was wearing a cheap army-surplus sweater over an old leather skirt.

"How's the court case going?" Cathy asked, hoping to draw Monty into a more cheerful mood.

"Great. We've got a fabulous barrister, a real shark. He looks as if he trains by biting the heads off live chickens before breakfast. I hope he's as good as the solicitor says he is—he's costing enough."

"What about the money?"

Monty gave a short, hard laugh. "That's going great, too. Don't worry about it, I'll cope."

"You're looking really slim." It was a sincere compliment and Monty nodded, smiling. "It must be the worry—look"— she pulled up her sweater and showed Cathy that she could put two hands between the waistband of her skirt and her body.

"Are you sure you're eating enough?"

"Cindy's always on a diet, so we don't eat much."

"What was the last thing you ate?"

"Cut it out, Cathy."

She watched in hurt surprise as Monty jumped off the fender and walked out of the room. When they got back to London, Cathy took Monty to lunch at a hearty, oak-paneled City carvery and gave her a check for five thousand pounds. Monty hugged her in guilty gratitude. She had not intended to ask Cathy for money, but now she and Cindy had debts and the gift would pay them off as well as buying them a substantial period of chemical peace of mind.

Monty became quite certain that Cindy herself had staged the burglary. She also realized that her roommate was making money on their deals, and that the heroin she bought was far from being pharmaceutical grade, but these things no longer seemed important.

Everything that had disturbed Monty now became gloriously unimportant. She was indifferent to the hostility of the band when she strolled into recording sessions an hour late or worse. Doing the publicity photographs was no cause for concern, although she used to feel absurd in the fetishistic outfits Sig ordered her to wear. Even though she had a crop of ugly pimples around her mouth, Monty faced the camera with no anxiety. She grew wonderfully thin.

Sig himself lost the power to scare her. She no longer launched herself into fucking with the desperate dread that if she did not please him she would be finished because he would dump her. She was just active enough to stop him from getting suspicious. But Monty's judgment was getting weak, and one night Sig suddenly rolled off her and sat up. He groped for his cigarettes and lit one with an angry gesture.

"What's the matter with you?" His voice was quiet but not friendly.

"Nothing. I just feel a bit weird tonight. I'll be OK in the morning."

"No, you won't. You'll be sniffing and strung out in the morning."

"No, I'll be fine."

"Sit up," he ordered. She did so. In the darkness she did not see him raise his arm and the blow was a shock. He knocked her off the bed. Her mouth filled with blood; she had bitten her tongue.

"Listen, you stupid bitch. I don't care if you fucking slit your wrists. You can jump off the Empire State Building for all you mean to me. But we've got a contract, you and I, I've paid you money, and I want my album, and it pisses me off that you ain't giving me an album because you're smacked out all the time."

"We've nearly finished the album."

"No you ain't. It's crap, what you've done. I heard the tapes yesterday. You'll have to start again."

She crawled to the far side of the room, swallowing the blood in her mouth.

"That's not true," she protested, wondering where her clothes were.

She heard him get up, walk over to the door and lock it. Then the lights snapped on and she blinked. He stabbed a blunt accusing finger at her as he got back into the bed.

"If I say it's true, it's true. Now come here. We've got unfinished business."

At first, she did not move, but she knew if she challenged him any further he would beat her up thoroughly. Hesitantly, she walked back to the bed and lay inert beside him. He killed his cigarette and pounced on her with furious violence, holding her to him like a doll. His penis was broad rather than long, and distended her delicate tissues painfully even when he was gentle. Sig was in no mood to be gentle now. Her weakness infuriated him because he knew it was her last hiding place. Instead of openly confronting him, she was seeming to comply with his will but contriving disobedience by making herself incapable of doing what he wanted. Overt defiance he could fight, passive resistance he could not; he rammed at her brutally as if his rage could spark the fight in her.

He paused and she felt a finger probing clumsily at her anus.

"No, please, Sig, that hurts," she whispered.

"It'll hurt a lot more if you don't get off the stuff," he answered. "Relax, stop fighting me. You'll get into it." He flipped her over as easily as if she were an insect, pulled apart her buttocks and crammed himself into her body. With his body weight pinning her down she was powerless and lay unresisting as the vicious strokes tore her flesh.

In the end she decided the quickest way to end the agony was to make him come, so she began to respond, faking all the passion she could. He was not fooled. She raked his flesh with her nails, gasped, purred in pretended ecstasy, her hips eagerly grinding, but she could almost feel his sarcastic smile.

After that calculated violation, heroin became as much a

way of taking revenge on Sig as anything else. The problem of the album took care of itself when Tony was offered two weeks with a big American producer in Los Angeles and found a loophole in his contract which meant that he could be released.

To Monty's surprise, Tony came to see her before he left, carrying a bunch of white chrysanthemums and a bottle of wine. He was a slim, quiet blond man with a self-effacing manner despite his honored status in the music business, and Monty was even more surprised when he told her: "Don't think we can't see what's happening with you and Sig, Monty. He's trying to make you over into some punk sex symbol, and that's just not your style. I've always liked your songs—they come right from the gut, they're honest, emotional. And you've got a fantastic gift for melody. Your music is grown-up music, not this gimmicky, get-rich-quick crap. Stas and Winston feel the same; we've all talked about it. You're dead right about doing the clubs—those kids aren't your audience at all."

Monty looked at him uncertainly, flattered but anxious. "I don't know. Sig's very smart about marketing, all of that. I just don't know anymore."

"Well, I know." Tony refilled their glasses. "I've had twelve years playing with the best, and I'd rather play with you smacked out than any other chick that's supposed to be together. Or most other blokes, come to think of it. In your place I'd run out on this album, and get another label to buy out your contract. Go for a producer who's into a really big, slick sound, that's what you need."

It was good advice, but Monty was unable to act on it. She felt powerless, a piece of flotsam carried along by a flood of events.

Her money ran out, and she made a deliberate attempt to play on Cathy's sympathy and get more, but Cathy looked shame-faced and shook her head. "It's a bad time, Monty. I've got a nasty few months ahead of me. You'll have to stall the bills for a bit—I wish I could help you but right now I'm in a jam myself."

Monty was so focused on her immediate problem of getting cash for drugs that she failed to notice an unaccustomed, haunted look in her sister's eyes, and the fact that she drank more Scotch than usual, throwing down the liquor with a desperation that was quite unlike her characteristic serenity.

The rent was due, and the telephone bill came in. "It's easy to get money if you know how," Cindy reassured her. "I'll ask some of my friends." She reached for the telephone and called someone named Roger who worked in a stockbroking firm. To Monty's amazement Cindy cajoled him into a dinner date, put on one of her alluring dresses and reappeared the next morning with a fistful of ten-pound notes.

"You can always get money from men like that," she told Monty. "Either they're bent or their wives are frigid little straights obsessed with the children. They're rich, and they're quite happy to pay for a bit of glamour and a few thrills."

Roger took Cindy to Frankfurt on a business trip the following week, and she returned with more money, but made it clear that she was not going to buy Monty's drugs with her earnings, or pay Monty's share of the rent and the bills which were mounting up.

"If I can do it, you can," she told Monty. "You're looking so beautiful, any man would get out his checkbook. All you have to do is a bit of the old voodoo—know what I mean?"

Monty knew exactly what she meant—the elaborate game of tease and make-believe that Lady Davina had taught Cathy, and which she herself had used on Sig in the days when she had kidded herself that she was using him, not the other way around.

Monty now had a permanent sense of degradation which she partly relished. There was a perverse kick to be had out of abasing herself. It was the only pleasure that remained to her. The drug was no longer enjoyable; it just kept her from feeling vile.

"They like double dates," Cindy told her. "It's less embarrassing for the blokes if they've got each other for company—means they don't have to make the effort to talk to the women. I'll see if Roger's got a friend."

Roger was short and thin, with sparse brown hair and very pale blue eyes. He wore the uniform Monty recognized from her voyages to the City with Cathy—a striped shirt, a diagonally striped tie and a dark-blue suit. The tie was tightly knotted. His friend was a little fatter, a little fairer in coloring and a little more nervous.

The four of them went to a very expensive restaurant in Mayfair. "Check it out," Cindy told her while Roger was in the lavatory. "Every woman in this place is on the game, except the owner."

Monty looked around the restaurant. It was full of sober-suited men, some of them famous politicians or film stars. The women were mostly past the first bloom of youth, dressed very discreetly in dull, good-taste silk pants suits, with a lot of gold jewelry. There was about them a telltale air of disinterest; it was the only difference Monty could detect between these women and any others.

"Roger's a real drag," Cindy confided. "He just wants everything he's ever read about in Harold Robbins. Let's blow their minds, shall we?"

Blowing the guys' minds meant going to a hotel around the corner and staging an elaborate pretense of lesbianism while the men sat awkwardly on the bed drinking vodka. Cindy kept the act going with a repertoire of outraged shrieks, protestations and compliments to Roger and his friend, which flattered them so lavishly that Monty nearly spoiled everything by laughing. Roger gave them one hundred and fifty pounds in clean ten-pound notes and seemed highly satisfied.

"You see?" Cindy laughed in their cab home. "They're perfectly happy, so where's the harm? They can tell all their mates about the two hot chicks who gave them a show last night, and feel like Genghis Khan—and we'll be OK for another three days."

Monty wondered uneasily about living beyond the three-day limit and was both relieved and dismayed when the telephone rang the next day and Cindy announced, "Roger wants to see you again—you're in business, kid."

"I don't want to go, Cindy. You go instead, if you like."

"Don't be stupid—where else are you going to get a hundred quid for practically nothing? And dinner."

"I feel I'm using them, Cindy, and I feel I'm being used, and I don't like it."

"But that's what it's all about, honey—trying to have sex without using somebody is like trying to eat without chewing."

"Come on, Cindy—suppose it's someone you love."

"Love? What's *that*?" She spoke as if she had seen a cockroach. "What's love about, except people getting their needs met? You are a hopeless old hippie, Monty."

"OK, so I'm a hippie. Right on, peace and love—bury me in my tie-dyed T-shirt. I still don't feel like fucking Roger or anyone else for money. The idea makes me want to throw up. Tell him I'm ill or something."

Privately, Monty decided it was time to pull herself out of this dangerous situation. She would cut down on smack, do it only on weekends, and find herself a job. Swallow Lamotte's company was still in business—maybe she could go back there. But cutting down made her feel ill—weak, tired, groggy and nauseated. Her gums ached and her eyes were sore.

She went to bed with a mug of sugary tea and tried to

watch television to take her mind away from the craving for a hit.

The doorbell rang and she did not answer it. Cindy was out, but she had her keys, Monty was sure of that. It might be someone coming to cut off the electricity.

When the bell went unanswered, someone began pounding the door.

"Monty! I know you're up there, I can hear the TV. Open up!" It was Sig, and he was angry. Fear grabbed Monty's guts. He can't get in, she told herself, he can't; the door is strong, he can't break it.

Sig yelled again from the street. "I'll get you, you slag. You owe me, don't forget. You owe me and I'll collect if it fucking kills you." He was throwing stones, but could not throw high enough to reach their windows. Instead, Monty heard a tinkle as a window in the floor below broke.

Eventually Sig went away. Monty was bathed in sweat, her heart leaping in her chest with terror. When Cindy came back she begged her for some gear, but Cindy would not agree to find some for her until Monty had herself telephoned Roger and made a date. After all, Monty told herself, it can't be worse than doing it with Sig.

This hope turned out to be true. Roger was easily satisfied with a straight fuck that barely made the two-minute mark. The hardest part was laughing at his jokes.

"Wowee!" rejoiced Cindy a few days later. "Roger wants to take you to Paris with him. You're a real hit!"

Not the sort of hit I ought to be, Monty mourned in silence.

Cindy loaned her a chiffon dress—Monty had become thin enough to wear her friend's clothes—and a suitably dull skirt and sweater. "You won't have any trouble with the customs if you look straight," she advised. "Just hang on Roger's arm and smile sweetly."

She took a pretty Art Deco compact for loose powder and washed it. Into the reservoir she tipped Monty's remaining packet of heroin, which was coarse enough to be held down by the small circle of stiff gauze which closed over it. She cut a circle of cellophane from a cigarette packet to fit inside the gauze. Then she dusted a green-ostrich-feather puff with face powder and put it on top.

"Blow away as much of the powder as you can," she told Monty. "It's so fine it'll fly away easily and you'll be left with the stuff underneath practically untouched." She snapped shut the blue enamel casing with a flourish. "Even if they do search you, which they won't, so much powder will come out of the compact when they open it they won't bother examining it any further. You can buy some disposable syringes in a *pharmacie*."

Monty waited at the airline check-in desk, hoping she would not meet anyone she knew and wondering if anyone would recognize her now, thickly made up in conventional tones, her hair tamed into balsam-conditioned curls, wearing a neat beige skirt and a simple angora sweater to match.

"Hello, Roger—my, you look great. I'm longing to see Paris. You are a darling to take me," she gushed, wishing she could spiel out this nonsense as easily as Cindy could. "I can't wait to get to the hotel," she breathed, pressing her thigh into his when they were seated.

"Why wait?" he asked. "Ever joined the mile-high club?" They fastened their seat belts.

"You wicked man," she giggled, trying to forget that she and Rick used to watch airline passengers from the sanctuary of the VIP lounge, trying to pick out from the shuffling herds at the boarding gates those who looked so incurably banal that they would find it exciting to screw in an aircraft toilet.

I mustn't think about all that, she told herself as she hurried up the aisle to the john. The days of private planes and being protected are finished forever. Rick really did love me, he just couldn't let himself show it, she thought, as Roger squeezed through the folding door, unzipping his fly and breathing hard.

Cindy had suggested that she should leave off her briefs, so there was nothing more to do than slide up the dismal skirt, find a way of propping one leg above the small washbasin, throw back her head and moan, "Baby, baby, my God, it's beautiful, Roger, darling Roger," until he had had enough.

Sex was becoming very uncomfortable. As Sig had predicted, she had developed permanent constipation. It felt as if someone had poured cement into her intestines and made her less inclined to eat than ever.

In Paris, she was careful not to utter one word of her excellent French, in case Roger should be intimidated by this superiority, although it was very hard not to intervene when he mispronounced the name of their hotel so disastrously that the taxi driver took them to the wrong side of the city.

Luckily Roger had business meetings all the next day, so Monty took a very thorough bath and strolled around aimlessly. She felt alienated to the point of mental paralysis. She could recognize that the city, leafless in the dead of winter, was beautiful, but the beauty could not touch her. It was just another irrelevance.

Monty had developed the drug user's sixth sense for recognizing other users. She shadowed two girls she saw meet by the St. Michel Metro and exchange a fold of paper for money. They separated and the one with the paper disappeared under the green-cross sign of a *pharmacie*. Monty waited for an hour, then went into the shop to get her syringes. She was ready for Roger by the time he returned, and listened with a decent show of attention while he explained what wankers his French clients were.

Although her mind was insulated by the smack, it exhausted her to be charming and acquiescent continuously, and she began to understand why call girls acquired their air of apathy. She recognized it again in one or two of the women in the restaurant to which they went for dinner. The aggressive stylishness of Frenchwomen was blunted in them; why bother to be chic for a trick?

"Your heart's not really in this, is it?" Roger sounded peevish. "Something on your mind? Worried about anything?" He thinks I'm angling for more money, she thought. Cindy had explained that the way to turn a date into a trick was to go moody, then tell him you were worried about a specific money problem like your telephone bill, then be deliciously grateful when he offered to take care of it.

"There's nothing on my mind, darling." She tried to smile and look seductive.

"Do you know who that is?" he asked her, indicating a spruce, dark man with heavy features sitting with an aristocratic-looking blonde in a peach-silk shirtwaist dress.

"Isn't he some sort of financier?"

"Some sort of financier? Isn't she cute? Darling, that's Umberto Ecole, he's in the middle of the biggest bribery scandal in Europe in the last ten years. If he goes back to Italy they'll clap him in jail the minute he gets off the plane."

"Heavens. Who's the girl?"

"Who knows—one of Madame Bernard's whores, I suppose."

A glow of animation entered Monty's lackluster eyes. "She really exists then, Madame Bernard? The most famous madam in the world?"

"Of course she does. Not my cup of tea, of course." One of Roger's most irritating foibles was pretending that he was a man who did not need to pay for sex but was merely generous to his women. "But I know a few chaps who've been to her little parties and they're apparently pretty memorable occasions."

Monty watched the couple under her eyelashes. They gossiped like an affectionate husband and wife. She looked at Roger, his chin greasy with butter from his asparagus, his eyes shining with the self-importance that she was there to enhance.

If I'm going to do this, she decided, I'll go the whole hog. If I'm going to be patronized, I'd rather it was by a bigger shit than Roger; and if I'm going to sell my body, I'd like it to be to the highest bidder, not for just enough to get me another couple of fifty-quid deals.

She shook off her depression and turned her attention to Roger, getting him bouncing with anticipation of the delights to come. Then, when the blonde with Umberto Ecole went to the ladies' room, she followed.

They were the only two women in there and there was no time to be diplomatic.

"Are you one of Madame Bernard's girls?" she asked quickly. The woman looked startled, then smiled.

"Do you want to go home and say you've met a real live call girl?" she asked with amusement.

"No," Monty declared with all the calmness she could command. "I want to *be* a real live call girl. I think"—she tossed her head with contempt toward the door, indicating her opinion of Roger—"that if something is worth doing, it's worth doing well."

"Are you staying in Paris?" the other woman asked, removing a smudge of lipstick from the corner of her mouth with a precise touch.

Monty gave her the name of the hotel, her own name and the name in which the room was booked. Then she steeled herself and returned to Roger.

She stayed in the room the next day and the call came at twelve. They met in Le Drugstore on the Champs Elysées; the blonde, Monty, and another, older blond woman who weighed, Monty judged, at least two hundred and fifty pounds. Her fat fingers were crowded with wide gold rings. Her name was Véronique.

They asked to see her passport, then chatted pleasantly about Monty's life, her family, her boyfriends and her interests. Monty effortlessly fabricated most of the information that she gave them.

"Let me see your hand," said fat Véronique, reaching for it with a motherly gesture. "Ah, yes, excellent, a very long life line—the other hand, if you please." In the pretense of reading her palms, Véronique pushed back Monty's sleeves and checked her arms for needle marks. Thanks to Cindy, there were none.

After an hour, Véronique gave her a level stare and said, "You realize much of this work is extremely tedious? You will be good if you look clean and arrive on time, first of all. In this business we don't like gypsies who are unreliable.''

Monty nodded and smiled, relieved. I've done it, she thought.

"We have to check you out, of course. How long will you be at this number?''

"We're supposed to be going home tomorrow.''

"So—ask him for your money and stay over a day or two.''

Véronique telephoned at noon again the next day and gave Monty an address in the exclusive Marais district.

"We have an apartment where you can stay until you are set up,'' she told her, "then this afternoon we will do some shopping.''

The apartment was in a tall, half-timbered building with a steeply pitched roof. Constructed in the seventeenth century, it now leaned back a few degrees from the quiet street. The ground floor was occupied by a discreetly tawdry *bijouterie* whose windows were half obscured with credit-card signs. The apartment was on the second and third floors, a slightly awkward assembly of spacious rooms decorated in white, glass and gilt—or perhaps it was gold plate, Monty speculated, as she put her unused syringes in the mirrored cabinet. She decided to celebrate her new success with a hit—just a small one to settle her nerves.

Véronique called half an hour later and took her to an Yves St. Laurent boutique, where she opened an account in Monty's name. Systematically she asked the manageress to bring out dresses, suits, two coats and innumerable accessories, working from memory of the current collection and disdaining to look through the racks.

Monty suggested a ravishing gypsy-style dress in purple lamé, with a laced bodice. Véronique shook her head. "Yves makes clothes for two types of woman, the good and the bad,'' she chuckled, "but you will find the bad women wear the quiet clothes and the good women dress like whores. I think he does it on purpose—it amuses him.''

"What's she like, Madame Bernard?'' Monty asked as their taxi waited in a queue of vehicles. The narrow street was lined with food shops, whose wares, in oval plywood baskets, were arranged in a fabulous display of color and texture along the crowded sidewalk.

"Nobody knows. No one. No one has ever met her.'' Véronique was gazing thoughtfully at heaps of oysters arranged on seaweed an arm's length from the car window.

"You must have met her,'' Monty insisted. The shop owner, seeing the fat woman's hungry glance and the beauty of her companion, called out to them and opened a pair of long, pale brown shells with his knife, passing them, one after the other, through the taxi window. *"Mes compliments, Mademoiselles,"* he called cheerfully as the taxi advanced a few meters.

"Never. Only one woman, in the beginning, spoke to her face to face. One day that woman disappeared, and now Madame Bernard speaks only on the telephone, with a disguised voice. Some electronic invention that makes her sound like Mickey Mouse." She threw back her head, displaying a plump, powdery pile of extra chins, and gulped down her oyster.

Monty, who hated oysters, offered Véronique hers as well, full of curiosity about her new employer. "You must be able to guess what she's like," she persisted. "You must have got some idea of her, if you've worked with her a long time."

"Certainly." Véronique slugged back the second oyster. "She has an extraordinary understanding of people, of personalities. She can always predict how someone will behave. But she is absolutely without pity. If you betray her, she will never forgive. Sometimes, if I have to give her bad news about somebody, I tremble, really tremble, because I know her reaction will be extreme and something terrible will happen." The older woman gave Monty a direct stare, making sure her point had been taken.

She's just trying to frighten me, Monty told herself. "Surely you have to be tough in this kind of business?"

"Naturally, but there is a difference between tough and cruel, *n'est-ce pas*? I think it's very strange, because a woman with so much understanding is usually tender. Madame Bernard is tough, yes; she's ruthless. At times the only thing one can say is that she is completely sadistic." The well-upholstered shoulders in their beige angora sweater shrugged and the long, twisted rope of pearls over Véronique's vast bosom rattled as she gave a sigh of incomprehension.

The next day Monty began to panic. The assurance of the whole operation intimidated her, and what had seemed like a fine adventure was looming as the final step toward self-destruction. What am I doing to myself? she wondered. I'm already doing smack, now I want to be a prostitute. It's time to get out before I'm in too deep.

She never doubted that Véronique would be sympathetic, and was shocked by the explosion that followed her confession that she had changed her mind.

"You don't play games with Madame Bernard, miss! All the trouble we've taken with you! Ungrateful piece of filth!"

"I'll give the clothes back, of course."

"Impossible! They will not accept them back! You must pay for them."

"But I don't want them. Of course they'll take them back; most of them are still in their bags, not even unpacked. I've returned clothes of St. Laurent dozens of times and they never make a fuss." Monty was angry now; she had been accustomed to treat the St. Laurent boutiques like chain stores during her days with Rick and they had always served her courteously no matter how many times she had changed her mind. "You're just trying to trick me, that's all."

Tingling with anger and a fearful foreboding that she was already in over her head, Monty folded the garments into their gleaming red and purple boxes and took them back to the boutique. The manageress was absolutely charming and regretted that it was a rule of the house that no clothes could be returned.

"You didn't have that rule when I shopped here before," Monty challenged her, praying that the woman might recognize her face.

"It is a rule for all Mademoiselle Véronique's friends," the girl replied with emphasis. From a drawer, she produced a bill for several thousand francs and trusted Monty would settle it soon. The friends of Mademoiselle Véronique always paid promptly, she said.

Monty considered simply leaving the clothes and taking a taxi to the airport. She opened her purse and checked that she had the air ticket Roger had bought for her in her wallet.

"That's stupid." The shop assistant put a confidential hand on her arm and spoke in a low voice. "They won't let you run away—you'll wind up floating down the Seine, just another 'suicide.' Paris is a serious place for a young woman, and these are serious people, do you understand? Thousands of girls come here every year and no one ever hears of them again." Monty then remembered that Véronique had not given her back her passport. Grimly she returned to the apartment.

"What do you think I'm doing, lying to you?" Véronique folded her bloated arms over her chest. "It's you who have lied to us, isn't it? You thought you would amuse yourself by playing at being wicked. You wanted to see if you were good-looking enough to be a top-class hooker, was that it? You thought we wouldn't see what you were the minute we laid eyes on you, eh? Don't you think I know what a junkie looks like? You stupid girls . . . you make me want to puke."

"I am not a junkie," Monty said with dignity. The late afternoon light was fading and she made a show of switching on the table lamps.

Moving with surprising speed for such a fat woman, Véronique snatched Monty's black-leather bag and tipped its contents out on the low glass table. Her pudgy hand pounced on the blue-enamel powder compact and opened it with care, evidently knowing what was inside. She picked up the powder puff between finger and thumb and discarded it, flipped up the gauze circle, snatched away the cellophane and waved the half-empty container of heroin under Monty's nose.

"What's this then? Sweet 'n Low? You haven't got much left, have you? What were you planning to do when you ran out?"

"It doesn't matter—I don't really need it. I just do a bit for fun now and then." How the hell did she know where to look? Monty wondered fearfully. She tried hard to think of a way to escape from the trap into which she had so stupidly walked, but her mind was blank.

An imperious ring sounded from the gilt-trimmed fake-antique telephone, and Monty jumped with alarm, wondering who could possibly know where she was. Véronique waddled across the room to answer and her whole body mass seemed to shrink as she listened. Monty's acute hearing detected a nasal twitter from the telephone line. That must be Madame Bernard, she told herself, folding her arms to stop herself from shivering.

Véronique replaced the telephone's earpiece and turned to Monty; her face had blanched under its thick beige makeup and her skin seemed almost green. She was obviously very frightened.

"Someone is coming to deal with you," she announced, gathering up her coat, gloves and bag with some agitation. "You are to wait here alone. Give me the apartment keys."

The fat woman unplugged the telephone and left the apartment, clutching it to her chest. Monty heard her turn the keys in the mortice locks at the top and bottom of the door. She at once ran from one window to another, hoping perhaps to find a way out, to a roof or a fire escape, but every window was sealed.

The window in the kitchen overlooked a lead-covered ledge about four feet wide, and although it was almost dark, she could see beyond it a typical Paris roofscape of parapets and flat-topped buildings over which it would be easy to climb. Monty resolved to smash the window and get away. She could go to the British Embassy; she would be safe there, and she could telephone Cathy to come and fetch her.

As she ran back into the kitchen with a gilt-legged velvet-covered stool from the bedroom, the lights in the apartment went out. She put down the stool and flipped the switches in desperation, but they were dead.

In the deep twilight, she saw the door of a tall kitchen cupboard open, and a small, black-clad woman in a dark mink jacket and a tailored suit, wearing a small round hat with a penny-spotted veil that masked her face, stepped through it.

With a movement as swift as a lizard's, the small woman closed the door behind her. Monty had just enough time to see the *escalier de service* beyond the thick wooden panels and sensed that there was at least one other person waiting out there.

"Who are you?" Monty demanded, frightened into truculence.

"Who I am is not important," the woman said. "What I want to talk about is who *you* are." She spoke in English, with a curious, clipped accent that gave her voice a metallic timber.

Slowly, the small dark woman advanced into the room. She was slim but her figure was rounded, and under the veil Monty could distinguish a heart-shaped, high-cheekboned face and a flat nose like a cat's. She could have been any age between twenty-five and fifty.

"You've no right to keep me here," Monty continued, retreating unconsciously as the woman advanced. "I want my passport back and I want to go home."

With another movement so quick it seemed like sleight of hand, the woman opened her black crocodile purse and gave Monty her passport with a black gloved hand.

"You can go when we've finished our little talk," she said, gesturing Monty into the drawing room. They sat on the white sofas and Monty felt the woman's eyes scanning her intently, probing every pore. Monty stared back, trying to see beyond the veil, feeling more and more intimidated.

"Who are you? Are you Madame Bernard?" Monty demanded.

"Madame Bernard does not exist."

"You would not be able to say that unless you knew who she was." A brief smile, like a gleam of winter sunshine, touched the perfectly painted cyclamen-pink lips.

"In your passport you call yourself a singer. Why do you want to be a whore?" The question was pitched in the kind of even, reasonable tone Monty had heard Cathy use when she was negotiating something difficult.

"I don't want to be a whore; I've changed my mind. Anyway, it didn't seem to be too different from what I was doing already."

To her surprise, the woman picked a malachite case from her purse and offered Monty a cigarette. There was a brief struggle over the stiff table lighter.

"Do you know what will happen to you if you live that way? Let me tell you." The cigarette was smoldering, unsmoked, between fingers tightly swathed in black suede. "You cannot sell love, and you cannot buy it either. It is not a commodity which can be traded. When you love you give *yourself*. If you try to trade yourself for money—or for security, or social position, whatever it may be—soon you can't love anymore."

Monty gave a short, hard, laugh. "Anything for a quiet life."

Suddenly the woman was very still, as immobile as a reptile on a rock. Monty sensed that she was very angry. "When you can't love, it's like death in life," she said slowly.

"A quick fuck's got nothing to do with love anyway," Monty argued, confused by the intense emotional atmosphere. The woman made no reply and the words echoed in the silence and mocked Monty with their truth.

"Why did you want money so much that you would do that to get it? You have talent, I think. You have a career, don't you?"

"No. Yes. The thing is . . . I just couldn't handle it. Everyone wanted me to do something I couldn't or be someone I wasn't and . . ." Monty suddenly found her tongue loosened and she talked, pouring out all the terror and pain and struggle of the last year. The woman sat as still as a statue, occasionally asking a short question in her strange cadenced voice.

"So, the drug made you forget how difficult your life was?" she said at last. Monty nodded. "What about the past—has life been that hard before?"

"A few times, not quite the same. Why are you asking?"

"Because I want to know. Continue, please, tell me what happened."

Now Monty was mesmerized by this steely personality and she talked on, about her songs, about Rick and The Juice, about Simon, about her father. When she began to relate the story of her abortion she felt tears beginning to run down her cheeks and wiped them away with her sleeve. Finally she faltered into silence, her heart stripped and raw, feeling drained and feeble. The apartment was completely dark.

"Why don't you stop taking this drug?" the woman asked in a neutral tone.

"I can stop easily," Monty said, believing this to be true with at least half her mind.

"Then why don't you? You're throwing your life away."

"No, I'm not."

"I think you are, my dear."

"You don't understand."

"I understand better than you. I hope you never need to understand the things which I have to know." The voice was suddenly as soft as silk. "Let me make you a proposition. I know a place in California where I can send you for treatment, and if you are prepared to accept their help, you will be able to stop."

Violently, Monty shook her head. "That's not necessary. That's ridiculous. Why would you do something like that—it will cost thousands?"

The voice changed, indicating a smile. "Let's just say I have made a lot of money and I can choose how I spend it."

"I'm not going to be your private charity." A tumult of old and new emotions was raging inside Monty. She felt exhausted, panic-stricken and ready to succumb to the sheer force of the woman's will.

The small, silhouetted figure stood up, walked to the apartment door and unlocked it. "You have no alternative," she announced, pulling the door open wide and admitting a dim light from the hallway. "Except to leave now, in which case you will not get as far as the end of the street. There are so many accidents just here."

The last shred of Monty's resistance parted. "But I don't understand," she protested in a weak voice. "Why would you want to do this? What am I to you?"

"One day, perhaps, you will discover."

As quickly as she had appeared, the woman left, and Monty heard her quick, light footfalls on the stairs. A few moments later the lights flickered into life, and she blinked in the brightness. She sat on the sofa in miserable apprehension until a heavy tread sounded outside and Véronique came through the door carrying a small Vuitton case.

"Come along," she said sternly, "get your things. We must not miss the flight."

This isn't happening to me, I don't believe this, Monty thought as she was steered out of the apartment, into a car, through the airport and into the first-class cabin of a Tri-Star. They were offered champagne, and she drank a lot of it and went to sleep.

The smoggy sprawl of Los Angeles seemed like a scene from a dream. Monty felt passive and controlled. Her deepest emotions were in turmoil after her conversation with the woman she was more and more convinced must have been Madame Bernard, and throughout the long, dull, uncomfortable flight the curious metallic voice asking the questions Monty had evaded for so long had echoed without ceasing in her head.

There was a limousine, chilly with air conditioning, at the airport, and after hours of driving they arrived at a substantial white-pillared mansion set in the center of a vivid green lawn.

Royal palms cast long shadows in the rich sunlight of the afternoon.

Véronique sat beside her like a watchful toad as she was interviewed by a young man with a dark, curling moustache.

"When did you last drink any alcohol?" he inquired.

"On the plane, champagne."

"Any idea how much? It's difficult, I know . . ."

"I suppose about a bottle." Her nose was running and she was starting to feel the lousiness of withdrawal.

"And your drug of choice is heroin, is that right?"

"Well, I use it sometimes." She did not like the routine way he used that expression, as if she were obviously just another junkie.

"When was the last time?"

"Heavens . . ." She tried to work out the time changes, and finally judged by how bad she was feeling.

"The day before yesterday. You want to know how much?" He nodded. "I'm not really sure," she lied. "I don't pay much attention."

She was to share a room with Véronique. They were directed to the laundry store to collect linen to make up the beds, after which Monty was allowed to telephone Cathy in London and tell her sister where she was. Monty looked at the other people in the center with curiosity; this is what addicts and alkies looked like. They seemed to be a mixed bunch, old and young, some obviously very wealthy. One of the women, tall with fair hair drawn severely back and a ravaged face, looked faintly familiar.

The next morning Monty attended her first therapy group. They had given her a shot to make the cramps stop, but she still felt shaky and sick as she looked around at the people taking their places in the circle of cheap plastic chairs.

"I'm John, and I'm an alcoholic," began a curly-haired young man.

"I'm Darren, and I'm an alcoholic and chemically dependent," followed a barrel-chested man in denims.

"I'm Mary-Louise and I'm chemically dependent," said the matron in a pants suit beside him.

"I'm Camilla, and I'm an alcoholic and chemically dependent," said the woman with the terrible face and fair hair. Monty stifled a gasp as she heard the assured English voice. It was Camilla Carstairs, the daughter of the judge, the lacrosse captain, the prettiest and most perfect of all the irreproachable girls in Benenden School. The last anyone had heard of her, she had been married to an ambassador. Monty suddenly lost the sense that this reality too was something from which she could escape.

Camilla looked at her with a weak but encouraging smile. The rest of the group had introduced themselves and now it was her turn.

"I'm . . ." she hesitated on her name, she seemed to have had so many names. "I'm Miranda, and I'm chemically dependent," she said at last.

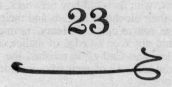

23

(faint mirrored text from previous page bleeding through)

"WE'RE PART OF A REVOLUTION, DO YOU REALIZE THAT?"
Henry Rose and Cathy were standing at the corner of St. Mary
Axe and Leadenhall Street at 7:00 P.M., waiting for a taxi to
take them to their dinner meeting at Trader Vic's.

"I never saw you as the Fidel Castro of Finsbury Circus,"
Cathy kidded him. They were both distinctly mellowed by early-
evening drinking. Henry had been been appointed to the board
of Migatto's banking division, and they had been celebrating
with the Black Cat's best champagne.

"You know what I mean," he said, sighting a black cab in
the distance. Across the road two elderly men, caricatures of the
City gentleman with furled umbrellas and pinstripe suits, had
also sighted the taxi. "We've got where we are on ability and
nothing else—we didn't go to Eton, we don't belong to the right
clubs, nobody pulled strings for us."

"Not for you, maybe, but I married the boss's son, don't
forget."

The taxi cruised past them and they hailed it, sprinting across
the street to get to the vehicle before the slow-moving, pinstriped
pair who glowered resentfully as they climbed into the vehicle.

"Shrewton hasn't given you any breaks you don't deserve,
you know that. If you couldn't hack it you'd be back in the
typing pool tomorrow." Henry settled into the corner of the cab,
waving cheerily at their disappointed rivals, one of whom made
a threatening gesture with his furled umbrella as they drove away.

"In ten years' time, they'll be laughing at the way those City types did business, with their old-boy networks, their deals done on a handshake, their alcoholic lunches and their chauffeurs taking them home at four o'clock." Henry, normally the soul of good humor, could not keep an edge of malice out of his voice. A few years older than Cathy, he relished the prospect of his own success at the expense of men who considered themselves his social superiors.

"If my father were still alive he'd never believe it. He spent his life telling me not to get ideas above my station. He was as fossilized as the nobs, in his way. Deep down he hated them, but it was all covered over with a veneer of respect." Henry's father had been a cutter in a Savile Row tailor's shop, a stooped, obsequious man who was ill-paid for his skill and who took refuge in a pedantic devotion to his craft. This allowed him to look down on the customers and disparage them for their inability to tell one weight of worsted cloth from another, however noble their lineage, weighty their influence or long their credit might be.

They sped past the new white Stock Exchange building, the symbol of the switched-on seventies, where women had been admitted to the floor a few weeks earlier. The optimistic sunshine of springtime glinted on the Gothic weathervanes and heraldic symbols which for centuries had shone above the Square Mile's gray temples of commerce. The medieval courts were lost in the evening shadows, and hundreds of feet above the time-scarred stonework of the ancient churches towered the new scaffolding around the City's first skyscraper, fifty-two stories of steel and glass which would house the headquarters of the National Westminster Bank.

Cathy rearranged the long rope of pearls which gleamed creamily in the folds of pink-striped silk between the lapels of her tailored gray jacket. She got a kick out of the oblique compliment Henry had paid her, but thought he was right for the wrong reasons.

"It's not because of us, is it, though? The real change is that the world's getting smaller, communications are getting better—the old boys can't adapt, that's all. You tell them we'll be trading in a twenty-four-hour market in ten years' time and it gives them a coronary just thinking about it."

He laughed, showing an expensive expanse of dentristry. "Go on, take some credit, Cathy. Modesty's out of fashion too, you know."

"I'm not being modest, I'm being accurate."

"You're being dumb. If someone gives you the chance to brag

a bit you should never turn it down. I didn't get where I am today by being accurate; I did it by making damn sure I grabbed all the glory that was going, whether I deserved it or not."

In the dealing room at Migatto Metals the revolution they were talking about was clearly in progress. It was scarcely a year since Cathy had first stepped into the Ring at the Metal Exchange, but already the Reuters teleprinter had disappeared from the dealing room and been replaced by a VDU on which the news was transmitted in luminous green. The sheaves of paper to which the traders had to refer grew smaller, as more and more information was electronically conveyed. People now sent telexes instead of written orders.

The pace of business was increasing too, and the more frantic it became the more Cathy loved it. The metals market was responding to the throes of the world's economy; when the dollar was devalued, when civil war broke out in Africa, or another major strike paralyzed Britain itself, prices soared or sank and a huge volume of metal changed hands. On those days the dealing room was a madhouse and the Ring complete pandemonium.

Cathy traded without a pause, wildly exhilarated by the pace, her mind a stream of figures, her ears burning from the telephone, her throat sore with incessant talking, barely pausing to eat or drink until the pressure shifted to New York at the end of the day. Then the priority was alcohol, a stiff drink—often several—before she went out to dinner, usually with clients, to massage contacts, sell Migatto's services and generally continue the social side of the business. Her mastery of her new profession delighted her, although it had startled some of Migatto's clients at first.

Only a few months ago earlier she had snapped "Migatto Metals" into a telephone during an averagely busy afternoon and heard a splutter at the other end of the line.

"May I speak with the trader, please?" She recognized the voice by its Swiss accent.

"This is the trader, Herr Feuer."

"No, I would like to speak with the trader, please."

"Herr Feuer, I *am* the trader. What can I do for you?"

The line went dead. Half a minute later she saw Henry leave his desk at the end of the room, throwing down his telephone with a gesture of anger. He bustled down the room to within earshot of her and yelled, "I'm putting Feuer back to you—he's having a fit because he's got to speak to a woman."

"I know," she shouted back, "he just hung up on me."

"Fucking Swiss. I told him to stuff it up his *lederhosen* and join the twentieth century." There was a surge of amusement from the men around her and the light on Cathy's switchboard winked inexorably once more.

"Yes, Herr Feuer. Certainly, Herr Feuer. No trouble at all. I'll be right back to you." She sold Herr Feuer's aluminum for him and thought no more about it.

That had been six months ago, and now Herr Feuer liked her to call him Heinz and had come around so much to the idea of doing business with a woman that he had invited Cathy to dinner. Since she was a minor celebrity, clients were often eager to meet her, but this time she had insisted that Henry come too because the flirtatious tone in the Swiss-accented voice was quite unmistakable.

Trader Vic's always made Cathy want to smile. For some reason the restaurant was the top favorite among the young City types and she had had to admit it was not at all an unpleasant place to be, and the food was delicious; but the mere idea was ridiculous—a phony Polynesian paradise with bamboo walls and a palm-thatched roof created in the basement of the Park Lane Hilton a few yards from the concrete, the tarmac and the carbon monoxide of central London.

Heinz Feuer was much younger than she had expected, a slim, tall man in his middle twenties; his butterscotch-colored hair flopped into his clear green eyes.

"You look much nicer than you sound on the telephone." The words were out of Cathy's mouth before she could stop them and once more she cursed herself for her unthinking rudeness.

"So do you," he returned with untroubled candor. "I thought you'd be an old witch of fifty who smoked cheroots."

"I thought *you'd* be at least sixty."

"A real gnome of Zurich, *ja*?"

He wore the kind of clothes that were almost a uniform among the young, rich Europeans who used the markets as just a more exciting way of gambling—brown Cerruti slacks and shirt, a plaid V-necked sweater in muted lovat green, Gucci loafers. Cathy was not at all surprised when he suggested that they accompany him to Crockford's to play roulette after dinner. She weighed the value of his business against the tedium of watching roulette and decided she should accept.

"Heinz isn't a bad sort," Henry said as they waited while he claimed his car from the Hilton's parking jockey. "Less of an android than the average Swiss, anyway." One of their large repertoire of private jokes involved a robot factory in Geneva where Swiss bankers, identically dull and prosaic, rolled off a production line.

Cathy yawned, then noticed that Feuer was waving to them from the depths of a white Lamborghini Espada. "Nice quiet taste in cars, too," she said with amiable sarcasm.

Since that night when her body had reacted violently against a man's touch, Cathy had gradually lost the sensation of icy physical detachment. She felt alive now, sensual and physical. She got a dizzying high from the thrill of the market, she felt melting tenderness toward her son, but what she had not yet felt was an attraction to a man.

The truth was that romance now had a very low priority in Cathy's life. She was making good money, and had thankfully sold her grim little apartment in Battersea and bought a much bigger and more luxurious home in the new Barbican development, a ten-minute walk from the Migatto office.

As soon as she moved in she realized that she had solved one problem and created another. She was working a fourteen-hour day, and although she now had the space and the means for Jamie to live with her, she would barely have seen him during the week. Passionately as she adored her son, she could see that it would be cruel to uproot him from the familiar comfort of his life at Coseley, where he attended the village school and ran riot all summer around the estate with a gang of local children, and expect him to flourish in the loneliness of a London apartment.

Lord Shrewton, thinner, grayer and wiser than ever, proposed a compromise as they drove down to Coseley together one Friday evening. "I expect you'd like to have young James to yourself a bit more now you're—ah—settled. Why don't we send him up to you sometimes for the weekend? No need to tamper with the custody arrangements and let Charlie know what's going on, just arrange things between ourselves, eh?"

"I think that would be ideal," she agreed at once. She had not seen her former husband since the miserable day at the divorce court when the judge had directed that Jamie should live with his grandparents. Charlie was working for an advertising agency which his new wife's father owned in Dallas, but every now and then she would hear, through Nanny Barbara or one of her old friends, that his affections were straying once more. It was not difficult to imagine that, when Charlie's current meal ticket threw him out, he would scuttle back to England and set about claiming Jamie and the money in trust for him. If she applied outright for custody of her son, she might even precipitate such an action. It seemed better to have Lord Shrewton firmly on her side than to have his loyalty once again split by a legal battle between herself and his son.

Lord Shrewton's solid, unostentatious Rover picked up speed

as the river of vehicles leaving the city flowed more freely once it passed the last junction on the Oxford road. The only sign that her former father-in-law was nearing his seventieth birthday was that he invariably fell asleep during the journey home, but Cathy decided to press her advantage while he was in the mood to talk family business.

"I'll be trading copper next week," she told him. The copper traders were considered the most senior.

"Excellent. I hope Rose gave you a decent raise before he moved on. Certainly deserve it."

"Thank you. Yes, he did."

"Nothing to beat the markets—great life if you don't weaken. You seem to thrive on all the ballyhoo. More than most, it strikes me. A lot of traders are in it just for the money, but you've got a taste for the job."

"I love it, but I don't want to do it forever."

"Got your eye on young Rose's desk, I suppose. Well, why not? Remind me when you've had enough of trading copper, eh? You'll have more time for the boy too, when you're a director. Good idea." She heard the gratification in his voice and realized he had already been planning to promote her.

In another year Cathy moved up to the position of junior director. She had gained the reputation of a baby tycoon in the making, but was amused to acknowledge that what her colleagues most resented about her was neither her ability nor her connections, but the mystery she preserved about her private life.

The fact that the beautiful Miss Bourton gracefully rejected all the approaches which were made to her, and yet seemed to have no man in her life, seemed to imply an insult to most of the male sex. This attitude was not very logical, but after a few years of watching the markets soar and plummet on waves of male emotion, she had realized that there was nothing very logical about the world of high finance.

Even her sister was mildly disbelieving. "Don't you get lonely?" Monty asked, sitting cross-legged on the oatmeal carpet in Cathy's Barbican apartment, playing dominoes with Jamie one rainy Sunday afternoon. Cathy was curled on the sofa in a red velour track suit, absorbed in reams of computer printout, analyzing the past quarter's business.

"No," she replied truthfully. "I'm totally blitzed with social life; I've got great mates I work with all day, I've hardly got time to see my old friends and I don't have a lot to say to them in any case. Jamie keeps me sane on the weekends, and I don't get enough time with him anyway. You're the only person I'd like to see whom I don't see enough.''

''But don't you yearn to be crushed in someone's manly arms?'' asked Monty in a vague tone, giving her sister a meaningful wink over the child's glossy dark head.

''No. I only yearn for the years and the energy I wasted thinking that being crushed in someone's manly arms was all there was to life. If you want the truth, Monty, I'm almost glad I walk with a limp because every step I take reminds me that I nearly lost everything I care about because I listened to Didi and believed all that junk.''

''I can crush you, Mummy,'' Jamie announced, rolling happily toward her across the floor. ''I'm stronger than King Kong and I can crush you to bits.''

''Why not crush your aunt instead?'' Cathy swiftly pulled the computer sheets away from his trampling feet as he climbed the sofa to embrace her. ''She's letting you win, I can see she is.''

''No she isn't, she's just stupid. Will you play with me now?''

''What is all that stuff anyway?'' Monty asked, indicating the printed columns of numbers.

''Sales figures, that sort of thing. Didn't you go to Japan with The Juice?''

''Uh-huh. Three nights at the Budokan.''

''What was it like?''

''Can't remember—booze, dope and jet lag. Story of my life. Why?''

''We're not doing enough business over there and I was thinking of setting up a trip,'' she answered, putting aside the printouts. ''Do we have to play dominoes, Jamie? Louis the Fourteenth was playing chess with grown-ups at your age.''

''Well, he was French,'' her son replied in a dismissive tone before somersaulting over the back of the sofa. ''And I bet they let him win, anyway.''

Later, when Jamie had gone to bed, Monty returned to the subject of her sister's lack of love life.

''There must be someone you fancy, surely? Just a little bit?''

''No. I walk into the City every day knowing that there are thousands of men all around me and I don't fancy any of them.'' Cathy wished Monty would stop nagging her. It was not quite true that she felt no attraction for any man. She was aware that now, when Heinz Feuer called, she felt a tiny but distinct thrill. But he was just a playboy, not the kind of man she wanted in her life at all.

On Monday Cathy approached the senior director for whom she worked, Nigel Fairwell. ''I think we ought to plan a trip to

Tokyo,'' she said. ''The Japanese traders don't make use of half what we can offer them, and since we need to establish ourselves in the options market before the competition gets really hot, someone ought to go over and sell them positively. I don't think options have been marketed as well as they could have been.''

''Fine,'' Nigel said without enthusiasm. ''Go ahead and set it up.'' He was a square-faced, blue-jowled man of about fifty, with broad shoulders and graying black hair.

''The Japanese will never accept you,'' Lord Shrewton told Cathy with amusement as she set off for her first trip to Tokyo. ''You'll have to sit back and let the men do the talking. Japanese won't do business with a woman.''

In Tokyo, she found that her chairman and former father-in-law had less faith in her than the men with whom she worked. The Migatto party comprised herself, Nigel and her former clerk, now her assistant, Maurice.

The day began with a breakfast meeting at 8:00 A.M. with the men smelling powerfully of aftershave and everybody damp-haired from their showers. They sat around the hotel table with Mr. Shimura, Mr. Matsuyama and Mr. Kodo, and Nigel, who had been to Tokyo before, introduced them all to each other. Everybody bowed.

''We're here to talk to you about options, a new product we've introduced at Migatto. This is Miss Bourton, who's our expert—she'll tell you all about them.''

While Nigel, in silence, attacked his eggs and bacon, Cathy went to work. ''Buying options allows you to limit your risk at times when the market is subject to short-term price fluctuations,'' she explained. ''The idea is that instead of buying a metal itself, you buy the right to buy it in the future—say in three months' time—but at the price it is quoted at today. Now obviously, if the price rises in the three months . . .''

Mr. Shimura, Mr. Matsuyama and Mr. Kodo listened intently.

Their next meeting was at 9:30 A.M., at a medium-sized brokerage house. Nigel again made the introductions. Everybody bowed. Their host led them to the boardroom, where twelve men sat around the table. At the head of the table stood a blackboard. Their host looked at Nigel with expectation.

''Miss Bourton is our expert—I'll hand you over to her,'' he said, taking a seat. Thank God I had a flip chart prepared, Cathy thought, and she picked up the chalk and wrote OPTIONS across the top of the board, then asked Maurice for a separate stand for the chart. She talked for half an hour, at the end of which the twelve Japanese executives bowed again.

Their next meeting was at eleven, followed by lunch. Cathy's voice was starting to sound rough, so she talked little while Nigel explained how to order a combination of raw fish that would be acceptable to a Western palate.

The first afternoon meeting was at the Hayasaka Corporation, which placed more business with Migatto than all the other Tokyo clients together. This time their host led them into a lecture hall where two hundred men were assembled. Everybody bowed.

"Off you go, Cathy," said Nigel, waving her toward the podium.

"Good afternoon," she began, noticing the interpreter in a glass booth at the back of the auditorium. Two hundred men reached for their headsets. "I'm Catherine Bourton from the Migatto Metals Company in London, and I'm here to talk to you about . . ." The interpreter was gesticulating. She tapped the head of the microphone in front of her; it made no sound. At once their host rushed on to the platform to apologize, and there was a five-minute break while a technician was found to restore the sound. Then she began again.

By seven o'clock, the three of them were in a whiskey bar with the last two clients of the day, men whom Nigel evidently knew well. A board of raw-fish snacks was in front of them, and a bottle of Japanese whiskey beside it. Cathy was the only woman in the bar apart from the waitresses, a situation to which she was completely accustomed in London, but here it was different, although she could not quite put her finger on the change.

She gave her spiel on options for the last time that day, answered the questions, then leaned back on the bar stool in relief as Nigel saw the clients to the door.

"Jolly well done," he said when he returned. "First class, Cathy."

"I thought they'd never go." She held out her glass and he poured the last round of whiskey. It tasted slightly tainted, but at least it was alcohol and put some kind of energy into her exhausted body. The mathematical facility in her mind, which never seemed to falter no matter how tired she was, calculated that she had now gone two full days and nights without sleep.

"They were a bit confused, I think. Normally the form is to drag us off to one of their godawful love hotels that they're so proud of. With you in charge they didn't quite know how to play it."

Cathy laughed. "Good heavens, I'm sorry if I've deprived you of a good time, Nigel. Don't mind me. I can always go back to the hotel and read a book."

"Please—you're our excuse! Those places are so tacky you've no idea—all fur-fabric love seats and heart-shaped Jacuzzis."

He ordered another bottle and the barman brought it with a bad grace, slamming it down on the bar in front of them.

"What's got into him?" Maurice, her assistant, a skinny, dark young man with greasy black hair, picked up the bottle to pour the next round. The barman bustled back and took the bottle from him, replacing it on the bar with a crash.

"Very bad!" he announced in barely comprehensible English. "Very bad! Woman make drink for man, no man make for woman."

"Oh—he's saying *you* ought to be serving us. Their women always pour the drinks. The geisha bit, you know," Nigel told her. He picked up the bottle himself. "Not to worry, old boy, we're English, don't you know—foreign devils, don't know the native customs."

The barman screeched with fury and seized the bottle before Nigel could pour it. He made a long speech in Japanese, then screwed the cap back on the bottle with an air of finality and pointed to the door. Nigel shrugged and led them out of the bar. They were all embarrassed by the incident.

"I'm awfully sorry," Cathy began, then stopped, wondering what she had to be sorry about.

"No, it's our fault, we should have slugged it out. We're paying, after all. The customer is always right." Maurice was looking intently at his feet as they threaded their way through the people on the crowded sidewalk.

"Let's find an honorable Nippon hamburger," Nigel suggested, leading them through the neon-harsh streets.

The following four days were exactly the same, except that they kept out of whiskey bars as much as they could. Nigel did nothing except make introductions, Cathy did all the talking and Maurice took care of the flip chart.

They flew back through Athens, where Cathy had learned to anticipate an air-traffic foulup on a scale that would make the Charge of the Light Brigade look like a sound decision. The plane was delayed four hours, and they wearily collected their briefcases and trailed into the transit lounge.

"Miz Caterina Button to information desk, pliz," The PA mumbled.

"That's you, Cathy," Nigel said, in a peevish tone which made it clear that he felt that if anyone from the Migatto party had been paged it should have been him. "Must be the office."

At the information desk they directed her to the VIP lounge where the receptionist called a steward who led her to a side room, a square concrete cell containing one table, four chairs and a telephone. She picked up the telephone and heard, through the whistling and hissing of a very bad line, the clipped tones of Lord Shrewton.

"I want you to break your journey and take a trip to one of the Aegean islands. There's a plane waiting for you, and I'll be joining you in three or four hours. I'm having a weekend meeting with Prince Hussain Shahzdeh at his wife's new place and she's apparently asked particularly for you to come along."

"Why me?" Cathy shouted into the receiver. She knew that the Prince dealt with Migatto's banking subsidiary occasionally, but was sure he had nothing to do with her side of the business.

"Your celebrity value, I expect," Lord Shrewton's dry laugh crackled in her ear. "The Princess collects interesting people, they're her stock-in-trade."

Cathy hesitated. She was exhausted, she wanted to write the report on the Tokyo trip for Nigel to sign as soon as possible, and she did not feel very much inclined to indulge the vulgar curiosity of a nightclub owner, albeit the most successful in the world.

"Can't you manage without me?" she asked.

"Absolutely not. This is an order. The place is being called L'Équipe Kalispera—you know her Paris club, L'Équipe? They're sending a courtesy plane; I expect the pilot will be paging you any moment. I'll see you later." There was a distant click and the line went dead.

An hour later, Cathy, who detested flying in small planes, bit her lips with alarm as the tiny Piper skimmed the ultramarine sea and swooped over the island, a kidney-shaped pile of brown-black rock, fringed with white foam. On the convex side the waves lapped at a sweeping silvery beach which, Cathy deduced at once, had been artificially created from imported sand. The plane hit the tiny runway at a sharp angle and slowed crazily to a halt. White-uniformed men ran forward to take her luggage and help her into a white mini-jeep.

L'Équipe Kalispera was an exquisite miniature paradise, rocky and bare with spectacular cliffs which plunged into the crystal sea. There was a white monastery building at the apex of the bare rocky hills and the meandering but newly surfaced perimeter road was dotted with the small shrines which the Greek islanders built to thank heaven for saintly protection from shipwreck.

She was driven to the village, a higgledy-piggledy pile of whitewashed buildings and stepped, cobbled alleys clustered around a circular harbor which contained two very large yachts and a flotilla of pleasure boats. Cathy had forgotten to reset her watch on the way back from Tokyo, but she judged the time to be around six o'clock in the evening.

The sky behind the rim of the rocky hills was tinged with lilac pink. She had the impression that the air was very clear and still; as the jeep drew up in front of a massive, studded door of dark wood, a single bell began to ring and the sound echoed back and forth across the harbor.

The village turned out to be a very carefully built fake, in fact a vast, rambling hotel which was furnished with massive pieces of dark antique furniture. Cathy was taken to a suite of white-walled rooms with low, beamed ceilings; the tall windows led out to a small balcony which overlooked the water.

She began to unwind, feeling the luxurious tranquillity smooth over her tiredness. The huge, dark wood armoire contained a wardrobe of blue-and-white silk resort clothes which, Cathy was surprised to see, bore the Valentino label. They were exactly the right size, even the delicately tailored bikini and the wide-brimmed hat of plaited natural straw. In the drawers beneath she found ivory crepe de chine underwear and some very plain gold Cartier jewelry.

On the floor of the closet was a pair of sling-back beach shoes of woven brown leather which caused her a pang of disappointment, because she still had to wear custommade footwear. She saw that they had been made by Lobb. Full of curiosity she slipped one on her maimed foot, and found that it was a perfect fit.

"They must have been made on my own last," she muttered aloud in astonishment.

A waiter appeared with a pitcher of a cold, frothy, pink beverage which she judged to be a cocktail of champagne and natural pomegranate juice. She sipped it from a chilled flute of paper-thin silver and felt deliciously refreshed. A maid arrived and drew her a bath which foamed with a milky essence and smelt very strongly of pure rose oil. She had just emerged from the fragrant water and put on a white robe of soft handwoven Greek cotton when the telephone buzzed and Lord Shrewton announced that he had arrived and would call to take her to dinner in an hour.

They dined on a sheltered terrace, enjoying the glimmering semicircle of lights reflected in the harbor water. There was a dish of golden Iranian caviar, some long-shelled razor clams steamed with herbs and *noisettes* of tender pink lamb.

"I'm so glad you ordered me on this trip," she told him. "I feel like a new woman."

"Thought you'd come around to the idea—first trip to Tokyo

is always a killer," he commented. The change of environment had not altered his bearing in the slightest. He had replaced his London uniform of a sober gray wool suit which always fitted rather badly with an identical lightweight ensemble and his stiffly braced shoulders and tight, tense jaw showed no sign of relaxation.

"Hasn't the Princess got another resort somewhere?" Cathy vaguely remembered reading in a magazine of the gala opening to a new chain of luxury hotels, but she had time to read magazines only at the hairdresser's and her sleek, simple bob required hardly half an hour to snip into shape every month.

"This is her second venture," Lord Shrewton explained. "The first was off the coast of Sardinia, L'Équipe Falcone. She's a clever woman. She picks the best architects and creates a first-class leisure complex in a completely natural environment. Then she makes sure she gets the best people to come to it—none of these—ah—what d'you call 'em, Marbella cowboys, Mayfair mercenaries, Palm Beach bums. Exiled royalty doesn't impress her either. The Princess invites only the *crème de la crème*."

"Such as ourselves."

"Such as ourselves. I wasn't surprised when she asked me to bring you. She likes beautiful women, but she likes them best if they're not making a career out of their looks."

The next day the Prince and Princess formally welcomed their guests at a reception on the yacht, which slowly backed out of the tiny harbor and cruised around the island, anchoring in a rocky bay below high, steep cliffs, a natural caldron where the waves churned white on the black rocks and the sea was so clear it was possible to see the sunlight playing on the pebbles of the seabed dozens of meters below the surface.

"She's like a mink," Cathy murmured as she watched the Princess's small white-clad figure moving among the throng of people. "She looks glossy and beautiful but sort of savage."

Shrewton nodded. "She can be a dangerous woman," he muttered from the side of his mouth. "The French papers call her The Queen of Darkness. Some of the things that have happened to people who've stood in her way cause a lot of unpleasant gossip. The old woman who owned this island, for instance. She didn't want to sell, and one day she just went for a walk in the hills and never came back. They never even found the body."

The Princess was moving toward them through the crowd, pausing to exchange a few words with each group of guests, her white silk dress rippling round her firm, slender body. Even in the deep shade of the yacht's canvas canopy the sun caught her diamond earrings and made them blaze. Her black hair was dressed in a simple chignon, revealing perfect bone structure and an unwrinkled, olive complexion.

In a short time she reached them and Cathy immediately complimented her on the island.

"This is the most exquisite place I've ever seen—and the clothes in my suite, and the *shoes*—they were such a wonderful surprise. . . ." She heard herself getting almost incoherent with enthusiasm.

The Princess's heart-shaped face was at once illuminated with satisfaction and Cathy was touched by the fact that this professional hostess, so full of hard, contrived graciousness, should have remained emotionally accessible.

"I was sure that you would have only business clothes with you, and would prefer to relax this weekend in something more appropriate." The full lips, painted fuchsia-pink, smiled widely but the Princess's black eyes were scanning Cathy's face intently. "You have done me a great honor by coming here. I wanted so much to meet you; I have heard a great deal about you. I know, of course, that you have to leave tomorrow, but would you care to come to have tea with me before you go? It would be nice to talk quietly alone together, don't you think?"

"Of course," Cathy agreed at once.

She spent most of the intervening period with the Prince and Lord Shrewton, listening and watching as they went through the pile of documentation prepared for a consortium which Migatto was forming with one of the Prince's companies. As her chairman had predicted, she found that she liked the Prince. He was direct, unpretentious and carried his wealth lightly, and while he systematically explored every area of potential weakness in the proposed deal, his patient courtesy never faltered.

Cathy sensed that the Prince liked her, too; he made sure she was able to follow the discussions by skillfully setting every decision in its context, and asked her opinion on several points with genuine interest. Cathy, who was accustomed to the way most Middle Eastern businessmen simply ignored any woman until she asserted herself, and then fell into confusion when they realized that they had to deal with her, decided that Prince Hussain was exceptionally astute.

The following afternoon a sparkling launch took her to meet the Princess aboard the yacht. Tea was served in a spacious salon furnished entirely in subtle off-white shades which somehow took the heat from the burning sun outside. Cathy and the Princess sat facing each other in a pair of deep-sided sofas, with the pale expanse of a silk Persian rug between them.

"Lord Shrewton tells me you're quite an ambitious woman,"

the Princess began, sipping her tea from a white bone-china cup that was almost translucent. "That's quite unusual for someone from your background, isn't it?"

"Yes, I suppose it is. But I don't think I had very many alternatives. I love my work and I need to be able to make a home for my son."

"But you come from a wealthy family, surely?"

"My people were wealthy once, but not anymore. When my father died there was nothing left but debts."

There was a pause and the Princess carefully put down her teacup, pursing her ripe lips in a momentary pout which made her look like a cat disdaining sour milk. "I heard something about your father, I think—some . . . was it . . ." She seemed unable to find the words, but Cathy had half a lifetime of experience in setting people at ease on the issue of her father, the Suicide Peer.

"There was a bit of a scandal at the time; perhaps you heard something about that. He committed suicide, you see. Then we found that he'd lost an awful lot of money, which was the reason. In the City in those days people set so much store on names and reputations—that sort of scandal would have been disastrous for him. Now, of course, people are much more accepting of that sort of thing. So many large companies in Britain are in trouble that an individual's problems aren't so important."

The Princess sat back, looking reassured. Cathy had expected that reaction, because she always tried to lighten the atmosphere when she was forced to talk about her father. She shivered slightly. The yacht's air conditioning was ferocious and she was wearing only a light blue-silk shift from the Valentino wardrobe.

"But it must have been a terrible tragedy in your life—you seem to have come to terms with it very well," the Princess prompted Cathy.

"There was nothing else to do but to come to terms with it. I loved my father very much but he was so full of vitality himself that he would never have wanted me to let the shadow of his death darken my life forever."

A soft-footed steward in a white uniform came to pour fresh tea. Reflectively, Cathy's gaze strayed across the glittering water to the hazy horizon beyond the harbor mouth. She was thinking of Daddy more and more, she admitted suddenly to herself. Maybe Monty was right, maybe she was lonely. What welled up in her mind increasingly was the echoing emptiness her father had left in her heart. The intense bond between them, that mixture of care and protectiveness, encouragement, spiritual closeness, the sense that the two of them were a thrilling conspiracy against the entire world—she would never find it again with any man.

It had been different from the warm attachment she shared with Monty; the magical element of sexual polarity had been there with her father. Their love had been the synthesis of two opposing life forces, strong, invincible; able, she had felt, to overcome anytning. It should have been strong enough to overcome death.

She shook her head quickly, dismissing the notion that Daddy would have lived if she had loved him more. With the unwavering clarity of vision that was pitiless even toward herself, Cathy recognized that her guilt stemmed from a different source. She had been a mere girl when her father had died. Now she was a woman, and she looked back on him with adult eyes, recognizing that if her father had still been living he would have been a man whom she held in slight regard, just as the rest of his business friends had done. She too would have considered him a foolish, charming man of little consequence.

"But you must think of your father sometimes?" the Princess insisted gently.

"Not very much. I don't have much time for reflection nowadays," Cathy returned at once, unwilling to open her heart to a stranger when, after so many years of pushing her emotions aside, she had barely discovered herself how she really felt.

The Princess asked her about Jamie, and Cathy talked about her son freely, with a sense of relief. Eventually she sensed that the Princess was uncomfortable, and remembered that her hostess was childless, and so she switched the conversation to the resort and the Princess's future business plans.

"And what about you? What do you see for yourself in the future?" the older woman asked, crossing her exquisitely modeled legs and rearranging the narrow pleats of her cream-silk skirt.

Cathy looked at her frankly and decided that there might be some percentage in flying a kite. "I'm not sure," she said. "I'm a junior director now and although Migatto has the reputation of being a dynamic outfit, it is rare for anyone to make it to senior director under the age of forty. I'm not sure I want to wait that long."

A sweetly humorous smile puckered the Princess's cheeks. "But Lord Shrewton thinks very highly of you; he's told me so. . . ."

"I've never known Lord Shrewton to act against his personal judgment, and he's got the rest of the group directors to consider. In any case, I think I'd prefer to be independent. In a few years I'd like to put my own team together and set up a financial consultancy." Cathy saw that the Princess was absorbing what she said with close attention and was encouraged to continue. "I plan to offer comprehensive advice across the whole financial spectrum. I want a base of business clients, but I'd like to specialize in high-profile private clients. My experience has been that the private client, because the volume of business is often small, is neglected by big institutions. I understood that very well when I thought about the tragedy of my father's death. He wasn't advised, he was exploited by people who were pretending to advise him, and it's a common experience among people with substantial personal wealth. No one's really geared to looking at finance in relation to individuals and their lives. Don't you agree, Princess?"

"Most certainly," the older woman said at once. "And when do you plan to make this move?"

"When I'm confident I've got the necessary expertise—three or four years, maybe."

"Well, I hope you will pay me the compliment of accepting me as your very first client? I am a wealthy woman in my own right, independently of the Prince, and I always feel as if I'm a nuisance to his people, someone they deal with as a favor to him, that's all. Promise me that you'll come to me when you are ready?"

"Of course—I should like that very much indeed." Cathy smiled with delight and congratulated herself on a successful sale. She, too, was interested in doing business with the Prince, but to deal with a man of such stupendous wealth would be out of the question for a young, unproven consultancy—unless, of course, there was a special reason why she should come to his attention.

A few moments later the steward announced that the launch was ready to take her back to the shore, and Cathy bade the Princess a warm farewell. She joined Lord Shrewton at the airstrip, and as their plane soared away into the rose-tinted dusk she felt a curious mixture of elation and sadness.

She had confided her ambition to only two people—to Monty, who had inspired her, and to Henry Rose, who she hoped would join her. In retrospect, she was surprised that she had opened up so readily to the Princess. She was rich, of course, but she was also more than a little sinister. It was not entirely the kind of involvement Cathy had wanted, even for the sake of a good platform from which to approach the Prince.

She was surprised also at the force of the feelings which had been unlocked in that casual conversation. Maybe she had been lulled by the Princess's thoughtful welcome, maybe softened by the wonderful completeness of L'Équipe Kalispera's conception. Her father would have loved the place, she thought. She would have loved to have been there with him. A light blanket of sorrow wrapped itself around her and, for the first time, Cathy confronted the enduring pain of her father's loss.

When she returned to London things began to happen which made Cathy wonder if it was not already time for her next move.

First of all, she sat down at a board meeting and listened in open-mouthed astonishment as Nigel Fairwell announced that the Japanese were now buying options as if they were going out of style, a phenomenon for which he smoothly took all the credit.

"Nigel—I did all the selling in Tokyo," she protested to him afterward.

All he said was, "Don't make a scene, Cathy. You did very well, but it was your first trip to Tokyo after all. Experience counts. You can't expect the Japs to take much notice of a woman."

"But they *did* take notice—if they're getting into options they must have. The only man we had any trouble with in the whole week was that barman."

Nigel put his heavy hand on her shoulder with a paternal gesture.

"I'm sorry if that's your reading of the situation, Cathy. It certainly wasn't mine, or Maurice's, I'm sure."

Maurice was shortly afterward made a director, of equal status to Cathy, and given most of her areas of responsibility. She was sent to Geneva for six months to work with the banking subsidiary there, then moved on to New York for another six months and given a position in the bank's research department, which was valuable experience for her but quite definitely a demotion.

The New York posting was doubly traumatic because that autumn Jamie, who was eight years old, was sent away to the boarding preparatory school which would precede his entry to Eton at the age of thirteen. The fact that she could not be with her son at this, his first important life passage, wrenched her emotions unbearably. She felt she had missed most of the golden years of his childhood, and that soon he would be on the threshold of maturity, ready to leave her just as she was ready to have him with her.

She flew back for several weekends to see Jamie, which her colleagues treated as further proof of her lack of commitment. Cathy did not care. Jamie needed her, and as she watched his carefree childishness develop in a matter of weeks into a serious, almost calculating, new wisdom, she did not regret for an instant investing in his security.

When she returned to London to live, Cathy was asked to work with the senior marketing director, taking special responsibility for public relations and administration. She was sent to a management course, a seminar on computer technology, and on another trip to Japan, this time to examine alternative corporate structures. These assignments were all tangential to the group's real business and Cathy realized at once that she was being moved sideways.

"Formally speaking, I'm supposed to be preparing a report on ways in which the group can be reorganized to meet the challenges of the future," she told Monty, sprawled on her old cream sofa at the end of another slow day. "But I know, and so does everybody else, that Migatto isn't the slightest bit interested in anything except plodding along in the same old way. So what the new job effectively means is that at the ripe old age of thirty I'm being put out to grass."

She presented this plan at another board meeting. "What I am proposing," she concluded, "is a system of network management in which all employees will be expected to participate in decision-making processes as equals. I want to institute a structure which will allow information to circulate from the front line in the dealing room back to the board as freely as possible. At present, half the human potential of this company is frustrated by a bureaucratic, hierarchical structure."

"But you're asking for a radical change, a long-term commitment to a new management style," Nigel Fairwell protested in tones of shocked disbelief.

"Of course I am," she said. "At present we're not growing fast enough and we're wasting our resources. I think that's a problem which needs a radical, long-term solution, don't you?"

There was an awkward pause and a lot of throat clearing.

"Should never have sent her to Japan," one of the men muttered under his breath.

"I thought they were all patting each other on the back for having the first woman on the board." Monty, Cathy thought, was looking thinner than she ever had in her life, but also rather gray and unhealthy.

"They just stuck me on the top of their crumbling outfit for decoration, like a cherry on a cake. I realize now that that's the only concession to change they're going to make. It'll be a job to make them accept that we've got to reequip the dealing room— five years ago it was the latest thing, but it's completely obsolete now. Lord Shrewton's the only one who can see beyond the end of tomorrow's lunchtime, but he's getting old, Monty, and he hasn't got the energy to take them on like he used to."

"Maybe that's why he likes having you around. Have you talked to him?"

"I'm sure that's why he likes having me around. Of course I've talked to him, but he's a chairman, Monty, not a dictator. He needs more than just me to drag that group into the twentieth century. The majority of the group directors aren't prepared to take me seriously at their level. And I'm not prepared to be shunted around the world, and separated from Jamie, because I'm slightly too famous to be fired without the group getting bad publicity out of it. It's time for me to move on, Monty."

Cathy spent the next six months discreetly sounding out three men who she knew thought the same way she did, having long discussions with Henry, and getting to know a useful number of financial journalists. She also rewrote most of Migatto's brochures and planned a new corporate structure which, she judged, would take care of most of the sources of inefficiency in the company and allow the employees to work together with better motivation and communication.

The meeting broke up with no commitment other than to read her proposal again. Four or five of the men, including Maurice, went through the dark oak door to the directors' washroom. They came out ten minutes later, laughing together.

When the minutes of the meeting were circulated, Cathy read with astonishment that the board had voted to reject her proposal.

"You were *there*," she said to Maurice. "They decided no such thing. They decided to keep it under consideration."

"Oh, maybe they decided to turn it down later," he said.

"But the meeting was over."

"I don't know—maybe they talked about it in the john. I don't remember. You didn't seriously expect them to go for it, did you?" She looked at him with dislike; Maurice was getting unbearably self-important. The mere idea of a sprat like him laughing and joining with the rest of the men in flushing six months of her work down the lavatory made her boil with rage.

"I'm never going to get any further at Migatto," She said to Monty that evening. "Sure, I can run off to Lord Shrewton and whine, but it won't crack the real problem. They treat me just like they used to treat our father, you know. Like someone of limited capabilities but a certain value, who has to be kidded that they're of some real consequence. They tolerate me, that's all."

She had a sad meeting with Lord Shrewton, which she deliberately chose to arrange in his office to indicate that, from now on, business would be business and family something different. She sat opposite him at the enormous Jacobean table he used instead of a desk and made her proposal.

"I'm very angry," she said with calculated weariness. "I should resign, I know, but there'll be a rumpus and the papers will want to know why."

"And you'll be severely tempted to tell them, I shouldn't wonder," he put in quickly, amusement glowing behind his spectacles. "That would never do, would it?"

"I see you're way ahead of me," she smiled.

"Damn shame. You're the best man among them if you want my opinion. I've been very pleased with our association. What shall we do, then? Let you go with a decent payoff? I suppose you've got another job lined up. Headhunter taken you up to a high place and showed you the world?"

"Not exactly—Henry and I want to set up on our own."

"Pinch all Migatto's business, I suppose. Serve us right." Her chairman looked thoroughly pleased with himself, as if her cleverness were entirely to his own credit. "What sort of severance figure did you have in mind?"

She told him, and he agreed to it after a token show of hesitation.

In addition to her handshake from Migatto, Cathy funded her company with a loan from Henry's bank and mortgages raised on her apartment and his house. They wanted offices that were equipped with the most modern technology they could buy, knowing that the faster they could get information, and the faster they reacted to it, the more effective they would be. They also needed a full complement of staff from the outset. Their clients would soon take their business elsewhere if there was any delay in processing instructions or drawing contracts.

Henry found the Pall Mall office, and redecorated it in a severe, modern style, which nevertheless shouted money at every visitor. The scheme was black and white, with classic Italian leather chairs, big black leather sofas, black marble tables and a vivid abstract painting, which Cathy privately disliked.

"I can see what you're thinking," he said as she helped him hang the vast canvas. "You're thinking we ought to have a nice set of sporting prints or maybe a few ancestral portraits. Shame on you. This company's a tough, fast-moving outfit geared for the twenty-first century, and I'm not having any gentlemanly British junk around the place."

Princess Ayeshah was true to her word and, within a week of Cathy's approach, switched a portfolio of several million francs to the company. She did not, however, achieve her ambition to be CBC's first private client. That privilege was claimed by Heinz Feuer, whose portfolio was even larger than the Princess's, though the Zurich bank that had invested it had done so much more cautiously than the Geneva firm the Princess had patronized. Feuer also sent Cathy a huge bouquet of lilies, highly scented trumpets with fantastically curled tips and crimson spots on their creamy petals blending to dark red throats.

"A man of taste after all," Henry approved as their new secretary put them on her desk under the abstract.

"I'm surprised he's got any money left, the way he throws it away at roulette." Cathy was aware that she sounded unnecessarily priggish.

"He doesn't bet more than he can afford, you know that."

"Hmn."

"And what does 'hmn' mean? I know what I think it means—it means you think Heinz is a little bit sweet on you and that's why he's given you the business, and that makes you feel all prickly and insulted because he ought to be dealing only from the purest commercial motives."

"Rubbish." Cathy folded her arms defensively and glared at Henry.

"Or it could mean that you're just a little bit sweet on Heinz. . . ."

"Absolute rubbish. He's a brat—immature, spoiled, too much money, too little sense. Yes, I think he's cute, of course I do. He's very amusing sometimes in a puppy-dog kind of way. . . ."

"He's good-looking, too."

"Yes, he is. So what?"

"Good family. Wall-to-wall *Almanach de Gotha* on both sides."

"Oh, really, I didn't know. Are you sure you're not sweet on him yourself, Henry? You seem to have taken a lot of interest. . . ."

At this point her business partner took a swipe at her with a rolled-up copy of the *Financial Times*. She dodged him and knocked the flower vase off the reception desk and the issue of Heinz Feuer was dropped while CBC's two senior directors discovered that their impeccably equipped office did not yet possess any cleaning cloths or a dustpan and brush.

In the next six months they discovered some more serious deficiencies. They were busy, and they should have been extremely successful. They did such an unexpectedly large volume of business that their computer system, which the salesman had assured them was more than adequate for their needs, could not cope with it. Three of their secretaries resigned in one week because they could not stand the pressure. Even their telephone installation proved inadequate. Soon the inevitable happened and one of their most important commercial clients, a small pension fund, regretfully announced that it planned to take its business elsewhere.

"We've got to get the office reequipped," Henry said with desperation as they sat alone together in the office on a stormy Friday evening. "The fact is we underestimated our success, and if we can't gear up almost immediately, we're going to lose a lot of business—and the best clients, too. They'll be the first to go."

"The computer salesman came today. We can install a new system over one weekend, but it won't be cheap."

"It won't be difficult to get a loan, Cathy, you know that— even though there's a credit squeeze right now there'd be plenty of people queuing up to back us. But they'd want a piece of the action—we'd lose our independence."

Cathy shook her head. "We'd be swallowed up in a year. I've thought it through already. My first reaction was to approach Migatto, because Lord Shrewton would swing a deal like this for me, I'm sure of it. But we'd become just another Migatto subsidiary, and in two years both you and I would be eased out of our own company—pfft! We'd be right back where we started."

"Yeah, that's how I read it too." Henry tipped back his black leather chair, put his hands behind his head and stared at the ceiling. He had lost weight in the hectic early days of the company, and was wearing loud yellow brocade braces to hold up the trousers of his navy-blue suit.

"We could try another way." Cathy pushed back her hair; it was overdue for a cut, but she had not had time for hairdressers lately. "Look for private finance."

"Mmn—that's the way my mind was working too."

"We'd have to be pretty stealthy about it—if word got out our clients would start leaving in droves."

"Any ideas?"

"D'you know a guy called Samir, Jason Samir?"

"You're not serious, Cathy. Samir Holdings? It's a house of cards; the whole group's based on overvalued property. Not exactly the model of a modern venture capitalist, is he? Now Slater Walker's crashed he'll be the next, if you ask me." Henry looked at Cathy's face and realized that she had already put her idea into practice. "Did he approach you?"

"Yes. Don't worry, I didn't tell him anything. I didn't tell him he was wasting his time, either. I was just neutral. I know you're right, Henry, but he's the best hope we've got. Let's think about it over the weekend—we'll have to make a move on Monday, one way or the other.''

She drove furiously across London to her apartment through lashing gusts of wind and rain, angry with herself for risking her success by making the classic mistake of undercapitalization. It's pride, she admitted to herself bitterly; I just wanted to do everything all by myself, do it my way, without any help. If I'd been smart enough to ask for help in the beginning I wouldn't be in this mess.

Monty came over; she looked strained and depressed, which intensified Cathy's gloom. She rambled on, talking about her problems with her new band, with her new manager and with Rick, and Cathy realized that her sister was hinting that she needed more money. Brusquely she refused, hating herself for doing it and for taking out her own bad temper on her sister.

"I'm sorry, Monty," she said, "it's a really bad time right now. I'm in a jam myself, and I've no one else to blame for it.''

"Forget it," Monty reassured her. "I shouldn't have asked, I didn't really want to. Don't worry about me, I'll handle it somehow.''

To Cathy's surprise, Lord Shrewton telephoned on Saturday. His normal telephone style was almost monosyllabic but now he made a distinct effort to be chatty.

"Just thought I'd give you a call to see how things were," he said, not able to sound in the least casual.

"Things are terrific," Cathy lied, at once alerted and wondering what lay behind his inquiry.

"That Samir fella's been putting it about he's going to move in and take you over." The dry old voice carried a trace of concern despite its owner's cool emotional temperature.

"Oh, is he?" Cathy felt angry and disappointed at the same time. Henry had been right about Samir; it had been a mistake ever to meet him.

"Heard you've parted company with that pension fund. . . .''

"They decided they needed a different kind of service. We weren't really geared for their needs. It was all quite amicable.''

"Bad news travels fast in the City, Cathy." She sensed that he was more than a little offended by her refusal to confide in him. "I hope that if you do have a problem of any kind you'll come to me first. I regard you as family, you know that.''

Even Jamie could not raise a smile from his mother over the rest of the weekend. She slept badly and on Monday she drove to the office early with a leaden heart and looked around the empty, luxurious suite of rooms without any sense of pride of ownership, only a grim appreciation of her own folly.

The telex was clattering, printing a message in its little room at the end of the corridor, and she went down to read it. To her surprise, she saw it was from Prince Hussain Shahzdeh, urgently requesting a meeting in Paris as soon as possible.

The tone of the message was emphatic and her mood lifted at once. With quick, deft fingers she acknowledged the communication, then tore off the printed slip of paper and considered her options. It was still two hours before Henry would be arriving, and if the Prince saw her that morning she could be back in the office in the afternoon.

Obeying a mad impulse to leave her problems behind her for half a day, she scrawled a note to Henry, grabbed her dark-blue wide-shouldered cashmere coat and ran out of the office and down to the street. She reclaimed her car from the startled attendant at the car park and drove to Heathrow airport. The early morning flights to Paris were always fully booked, she knew, but there were always cancellations too, and with luck she would be able to walk on a plane. Luck was with her this time, and from the departure lounge she asked her secretary to telephone the Prince and let him know she was on her way.

"This is magnificent; I never expected you to get here so quickly." The square, dark-suited figure of the Prince burst through the heavy oak doors of his office in a quiet street between the Opéra and the French stock exchange. He spoke in English and shook her hand in his fleshy, firm grip. A middle-aged, quietly elegant, ash-blond secretary brought them tea with a suppressed flutter of excitement.

"What can I do for you?" Cathy asked, hoping that she still projected the serene confidence which had always been one of her greatest assets. She smoothed the skirt of her navy-blue suit, feeling crumpled after the short flight.

"This is more a question of what I can do for *you*." His plump face with its thick black eyebrows bore a pleasant expression but he did not smile. Cathy was startled. This was not what she had been expecting.

"I've been paying close attention to the way you've been running my wife's money and I have to admit I'm most impressed," he continued. "You've had a very successful few months. It strikes me that just at the moment you could expand very fast if you had the necessary capitalization."

"There's no question about that," Cathy agreed. They had both seen through each other immediately. This conversation, Cathy understood with mingled relief and suspicion, was a formal minuet staged to save her face. He had heard of her trouble, in the same way that Lord Shrewton had—maybe even from Lord Shrewton himself—and was going to offer her the finance she needed. The only question that remained to be answered was—why?

"How would you respond if I offered you a loan which would allow you to expand your operation right now?"

"I would be curious to know why you would do such a thing."

"In my wife's interest—she feels she has an emotional investment in your success."

Cathy believed him. Apart from knowing the Prince to be a sincere man, she had sensed the peculiar quality of his relationship with the Princess. The woman fascinated him and had seemed to have the ability to dominate him when she needed to, tough and astute as he was. Cathy had also perceived that the Prince had a moral firmness which his wife did not; while she struck Cathy as the kind of woman who would give nothing without expecting a return of some kind, her husband would be unlikely to strike a deal with hidden strings attached to it.

"I'm flattered that the Princess should feel that way."

"We talked about you yesterday, and agreed that I should make an offer to you, since my business has rather more liquidity than hers at the moment."

As if he had all the time in the world, the Prince continued a leisurely conversation, in which the exact sum of the loan was never discussed—the implication being that no sum would be beyond his means. Cathy accepted an invitation to lunch with him and the Princess in their apartment. She returned to the office to collect the loan documents which had been drawn up in the interim, and the Prince's car took her to Charles de Gaulle airport.

Before the end of the day she was back in her office, her feet crossed jubilantly on the black marble top of her desk.

"We're saved," she told Henry, who stood in front of her looking anxious. "I found a fairy godmother. Or godfather. Both really—the Shahzdehs offered me a loan—look."

She passed him the loan agreement and he looked at it for a few seconds but could not concentrate on it.

"There's got to be a catch somewhere. There's nothing in it for them."

"They're charging a fair rate of interest."

"You could think of a hundred better uses for the money."

"Well, if there's a catch, Henry, I can't see it. It's a perfectly simple deal; it's watertight, unsinkable and copper-bottomed. Now, are you going to stand there like a dying duck in a thunderstorm all evening or are we going round to the Ritz for some champagne?''

They closed the office over a weekend for the new computer to be installed, and hired ten more staff to handle their business. Cathy sighed with relief as the first fortnight passed with only minor problems.

A slight figure marched into her office one blazing July morning as she was preparing to go out for lunch.

"Jamie! Of course—it's the school holidays already. But I thought you were going to Coseley first."

He was ten now, but in his gray school trousers and dark-green blazer he looked older. Jamie was not tall for his age; he was small and slender compared to his friends, but he had a self-possession which made him seem far more mature than they did.

"I got to Coseley and there was nobody there except Nanny Barbara," he told her. "There never is, and I'm tired of wandering around like a lost soul talking to the servants or mucking about with the village kids. And I don't want to take up hunting, shooting and fishing just to stop myself from dying of boredom. I've decided I want to come and live with you."

"Darling." Cathy walked round the black marble desk to sit beside him, using the wheedling tone all mothers adopt toward dangerous preteens. "You *can't* stay with me; there's nothing for you to do here either. It'll all be different when you go to Eton."

"I don't want to go to Eton." His vibrant blue eyes gazed calmly into hers.

"We'd better talk about this." She reached for the telephone console. "Can you call the Dorchester and tell them I've been delayed but I'm on my way? And hold all my calls, please. Now, Jamie, why don't you want to go to Eton?"

"Because all I'll learn is Latin and snobbery. . . . You can't deny that, Mummy, you've told me enough times yourself."

"But . . ." She was searching for arguments, and not finding any because she knew he was right, and that this was what she wanted, what she had longed for all these years. There was, in truth, no reason at all why he could not live with her full time now. Starting the business had simply wiped everything else from her mind.

"I want to come and live with you, Mum, and go to a regular school in London. I'll get my exams; I'm quite bright enough. Then I want to go to Oxford, then a business school in America, though I don't know about Harvard because they're *so* into management for short-term profits and in the situation in seven years' time I doubt that will be appropriate any longer, frankly.''

"You've got it all figured out, haven't you?"

"And I want to be a person like you, not like my father," he went on. "You've really made a mark, Mum. And you've done it all your way, not by marrying somebody or being somebody's daughter."

Cathy knew he was deliberately hitting the right buttons, and admired that too.

"Very well, you've convinced me. But I won't have much time for you—you'll have to take care of yourself."

"That's OK."

"You'd better speak to your grandfather," she suggested. "Just tell him exactly what you've told me, and I think he'll agree."

She was correct. Lord Shrewton, one of the few men she knew who always put common sense and his duty to his heritage before all other considerations, accepted Jamie's proposal with restrained but obvious pleasure. Charlie, who had been divorced by Lisa and was now living in Los Angeles with a new American wife, made no objection, and Cathy was at last granted legal custody of her son.

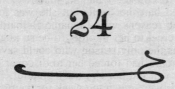

24

The California sunshine was as thick as syrup on the emerald velvet lawn. The driver put Véronique's Vuitton case and Monty's Turkish-carpet bag into the trunk of his car.

"We make just one promise to you here at the center. What you have to deal with now, Miranda, is living a normal life. We can only guarantee that if you don't go to your aftercare, you will go back to using drugs, or something else that alters your relationship to reality." The director with the curly moustache shook her hand. She and Véronique climbed into the car and drove away.

Véronique opened her purse and hunted in it.

"Here's your ticket." She handed the airline folder to Monty. "And what was left of your money when we were in Paris. I'll say good-bye to you at the airport."

Monty flipped open the air ticket and saw that it was for a one-way flight to London. "But you're sending me home—why?"

"Madame Bernard has no further wish to deal with you."

"But I owe her for the clothes. All those St. Laurent clothes you bought me—what about them?"

"They are of no consequence. Madame Bernard wishes you to return to your own life. She has instructed me to tell you never to attempt to contact her again."

Monty was stunned. The great shadow that had been hanging over her three months at the center was the knowledge that she

515

had to deal with her debt to the notorious Paris madam. She dreaded another encounter with the shadowy, ruthless woman who had stripped bare her soul, but she was grateful too and curious about the reasons why Madame Bernard had taken the trouble to be so cruel to her in order to be so kind. Monty knew now that she was the only person who could save her own life, but Madame Bernard had forced her to discover that.

"Perhaps you will tell her I'm truly grateful," she said, feeling that the words were much too weak for the profound emotion behind them. "I can't thank her enough. I feel I've been given the chance to start my life over again. Can't I even write to her?"

The fat blonde nodded. "You can give a letter to me. I'll see it reaches the woman you met—that's who you mean, isn't it?"

"Oh, stop pretending, Véronique. That was Madame Bernard, wasn't it?"

"Who knows? I have worked for her for twenty-five years and I've never met her. I never met the woman who talked to you either. I can tell you nothing. But I can tell you are absolutely unique in the history of this organization, miss. Anyone who tried what you did would have been taught a lesson she would never have forgotten. You're much luckier than you deserve to be."

Monty felt reborn after her weeks of therapy. For the first time in her life she had seen herself as she really was, faced herself honestly, reviewed her life and acknowledged that so far her only strategy for dealing with pain had been to blot it out with drugs or drink.

Cathy was waiting for her at Heathrow, looking deliciously severe in a black suit with white silk shirt and a bootlace tie.

"How did it go—are you OK?" she asked with concern as she hugged her sister.

"More OK than I've ever been in my life," Monty assured her. "But it's so good to see you—I've missed you so much."

"What kind of place was it—you just said it was something to do with drugs?" Cathy gave her sister a keen glance, aware that she had been deceived.

"It was a treatment center for addicts," Monty said bluntly.

"But you're not an addict—I mean, you've always taken things, I've known that, but . . ."

"Yes I am an addict, Cathy. Always have been and always will be. The only thing that's different is now I know how to live with it." Realizing that her sister would be anguished if she knew the whole truth of how she had been living for the past few months, Monty told her only the barest details.

516

As she anticipated, Cathy was full of remorseful sympathy. "How terrible. Oh, Monty, I'm so glad you're OK. If only I'd known what was going on. If only I hadn't been so obsessed with my business. Why on earth didn't you tell me you were in such trouble?" Inwardly she suddenly hated herself for her single-minded ambition. The signs had been there, Monty's pallor, her thinness, her behavior that seemed confident but had an undertone of lost hope—why hadn't she noticed, why had she failed the person she loved so much?

"I didn't want to tell you, Cathy. It was just something else I couldn't deal with. I was ashamed, I guess, I was sure you'd disapprove. I think I wanted to kill myself, too—you know when you wanted to kill yourself? You didn't tell me because you knew I'd have stopped you. I was determined to go over the edge."

Cathy held Monty to her, ignoring the crush of the crowded airport around them. "We must never, ever, do that to each other again. You're right, we're each other's lifelines. We keep each other afloat. If you ever let go of me again I'll know what's going on."

They walked to Cathy's car. "I was in a different world, too," Monty continued, not wanting to hurt her sister anymore. "I lied to everyone and most of all I lied to myself. I had no real idea how serious things were until I got to the center and had to do without the stuff. Then I realized I was totally dependent."

"I'll never forgive myself for deserting you."

"There's no way you could have known, Cathy. When it comes to people who're going down, it takes one to know one. That woman, Madame Bernard, knew where I was at because I suspect she's hit the bottom herself a few times. And I sensed it. If you'd tried to pack me off on a cure I'd have resisted like fury. Coming from her, though, I could accept it."

"It just doesn't make sense. Why would anyone do something like that for a total stranger?" Cathy shook her head, her thick brown hair swinging heavily as she did so. "Nothing is for nothing, Monty. That woman wants something from you and she'll call in the favor one day."

In London, Monty found that a lot had changed in twelve weeks. At the apartment she shared with Cindy, she found a note saying, "Dear Miss Bourton, please telephone this number when you return." It was signed with a man's name which she did not recognize. Monty steeled herself and called the number, and a man's voice answered. "I'm Cindy's brother," he explained.

"I didn't know she had a brother."

"She didn't talk about her family much, I gather." He sounded reserved, upper-class. Why was he using the past tense?

"Were you very close to my sister?" the man asked her. Monty thought about the question. It was quite obvious, now that she was free of a drug-induced disinterest, that Cindy had waited with the deadly patience of a predator to catch her at a weak moment and start her using heroin; then she had become her supplier and financed her own habit that way. How fond could one be of a friend who did something like that?

"I didn't really know her very well," Monty told him.

"I hope this won't distress you too much, then. My sister was found dead a couple of months ago. She had accidentally injected herself with too much of some drug—you knew she was an addict, I take it?"

Monty made all the appropriate noises of sympathy. It seemed Cindy's brother cared very little about her. Cruel and calculating as Cindy had been, Monty felt grief at the news of her death and at the back of her mind she was convinced that Cindy's death had been no accident. She had always had her habit so well under control; Cindy just wasn't the type to make a mistake about a dose, or get drunk and forget how much stuff she'd done.

She decided that she did not want to stay at the apartment. She could go to her sister's, but staying with Cathy would be fine for only a couple of days. Then the fact that Monty usually went to bed at 3:00 A.M. and Cathy usually got up at 5:00 A.M. would become more than even ties of blood could stand.

Instead, Monty called Swallow Lamotte, who at once suggested she stay with her and take up her old job. Since 1965 Swallow had rechristened the company three times, sold it twice and liquidated it once; its present title was Urban Survival Services. Everyone had white T-shirts with USS printed on them in red.

Swallow had also transformed herself, from a coltish good-time blonde to a dynamic woman with bright-red hennaed hair and the silhouette of an African fertility goddess. She still had fabulous legs and ripe, soft lips; obesity had not changed the way she dressed—she wore a purple boiler suit, a pink poncho and red cowboy boots.

"You're just in time," she announced to Monty. "We've got five people wanting punk waitresses for parties, and we've got to find a tank for a David Bowie concert in Battersea Park next week. And you're not staying with me, because we've got to look after the house Jack Nicholson's renting while he's away on location, so you're staying there. And next week the Joe Jones Band is flying in; the joint'll really be jumping then."

"I bet." Monty was depressed to find herself on the fringe of the music business, once more a kid outside the shop window of success looking wistfully at the good things she could not have.

"What's the Joe Jones Band here for—not another tour?"

"No, another album—they've decided to record at Paleward Priory. Now here's the card index. . . ." Swallow dumped a plastic box of file cards in front of Monty. "Find me six punks for Lady Swabo tonight, blondes if possible."

Within a year, the defiant punks had been swallowed up by the British propensity for absorbing dissidents into the social structure.

Tourists were starting to penetrate outer Chelsea, looking for the weird creatures with safety pins through their noses who obligingly dressed up on Saturday and left their homes in the suburbs for an outrageous *paseo* at the end of the King's Road.

Biffo Records had been taken over by a big American company and Sig Bear was being talked about as the first punk tycoon.

Swallow kept Monty so busy she had little time to think about anything but answering the telephones and getting out the mail. Once a week she went to a meeting in a room behind an Italian café, where for a couple of hours Monty again became Miranda who was chemically dependent, and she derived strength from knowing her own weakness. She needed strength to pick up the gift of her new life.

"Have a drink?" Swallow invited her, uncorking her daily bottle of Liebfraumilch.

"No, thank you. I don't drink alcohol anymore."

"Cigarette?" The pack passed under her nose twenty times a day, the smoke permeated the tiny red-and-white office next to the punk leatherwear boutique.

"I've stopped smoking."

"Fancy a line?" Swallow's friends were always borrowing her makeup mirror to chop up their cocaine.

"Girl, you come at just the right time, we just skin up right now," Winston greeted her with a joint the size of a half corona in his hand.

Monty decided to look up some old friends. "Let's meet for lunch," suggested Rosanna, and they went to San Lorenzo in Beauchamp Place, a choice Monty immediately regretted when she was greeted by half a dozen music-business types to whom she had to explain that, contrary to what Sig Bear had told them the week before, she had not just finished recording her album for Biffo in the South of France.

"You know the children and I are on our own now?" Rosanna mournfully tucked a shred of *radicchio* into her mouth and tore her eyes away from the sweet trolly. "Jonathan left us. I found out he'd been staying over with his secretary half the time when he was supposed to be abroad on business. Could anything so corny happen to me?"

"It seems to happen to all of us, sooner or later." Rosanna was distinctly plump, in a deliciously appetizing way. She wore a Karl Lagerfeld gray suit with a pink crepe de chine ruffled blouse.

"I've got the house, of course, and he's been very generous, but I'm not going to be another alimony drone, Monty. I've got an agent and he thinks he can get me some opera work."

"Terrific. You always had a better voice than I did."

"It's just a pity I didn't start using it when you did. I have to lie about my age, you know. My agent says none of the European opera houses will look at a singer under thirty. Do you think I look thirty, Monty? Tell me honestly."

"No, of course not," Monty lied. Rosanna sighed as she finished her salad.

"You're so lucky. You've got talent, Monty. I wish I had. And you'll have a proper career, while I'll just mess about amusing myself." The sweet trolly passed their table again. "How many calories do you think there are in a chocolate profiterole?"

"Millions. Let's have some." Monty waved to the waiter. She felt uncomfortable having Rosanna envy her when her career was becalmed and her talent seemed like a responsibility that was impossible to fulfill.

"What did they do with you at that center?" Swallow demanded when Monty came back from the office completely sober after lunch.

"We just sat around and talked. I've never felt so loved, Swallow. It was wonderful to be with people and show them who you really are and have them accept you."

"Well, at least your skin doesn't look like cold potatoes anymore. What about your clothes?"

Monty wore the USS T-shirt and jeans every day, with her old acrylic fur coat if it was cold.

"They're all at Cindy's, unless her brother's got rid of them. I don't want my old clothes anymore, Swallow. They weren't anything to do with me, only with the people I was posing as."

"That leather dress was fabulous."

"It made me feel like a whore."

"Fucking hell. I can't stand all this bloody purity. Why not join a convent?"

"Well, I felt ridiculous vamping around with my tits falling out everywhere."

"And what are you going to do—change your image?"

"I don't *know*, Swallow. I don't want to be Ruby Slippers anymore, that's for sure. That was just a bad dream."

"What are you going to tell Sig?"

"I don't know, I'll have to think about it."

"Well, you'd better hurry up, he's outside right now."

Monty gasped with fright, then made a determined effort to calm herself. She knew that she had been avoiding dealing with Sig, but Sig never avoided dealing with anything. His style was the preemptive strike. That was probably why he was a tycoon and she was a mess.

"Baby!" He stood in the doorway, fat and smiling, his black hair now cut with a Mohican scalp lock, wearing a very expensive-looking black-leather jacket. He held out his arms to her.

"Hello, Sig."

"Baby! Is that all—hello? No kiss for Siggy? Where've you been all this time? Not even a postcard! I missed you." He gave her a kiss on the cheek.

"I'll leave you two lovebirds together," Swallow told them, stomping out of the office. "I'll be in the pub."

This is a confrontation, Monty told herself. She tried to remember all the role plays she had done at the center, learning to be assertive in situations like this. First—check the body language. Why was she cowering behind her desk, allowing Sig to stand over her?

"What's this I hear—you're off the stuff?" Monty nodded. "Great, girl, just great. Now we'll really be back in business."

"Have a chair," she invited him, pulling out Swallow's seat for him and walking across the office to sit opposite. That was better. Now the eye contact. Monty wanted to look Sig in the eye as much as she wanted to kiss a cobra, but it had to be done, and she did it. His eyes were *rather* bloodshot, she noticed.

Now, say what you want in nice, cool language that isn't giving him a whole lot of emotive subtext.

"Sig, I don't want to be Ruby Slippers anymore. I felt that it wasn't working and I think I made a mistake about the direction I ought to go in. I know we have a contract, and I'm willing to fulfill it, but not like that." Now a touch of negative inquiry, just to top the whole thing off with a bit of style. "I expect that isn't what you wanted to hear?"

"You're dead right it isn't." He stood up and shoved his hands into his pockets with aggression. "I wanted to hear that you'd had the sense to sort yourself out, get off the stuff and

521

come back to reality, that you were gonna get down and finish my album.''

"I will finish your album, but not if it costs me my identity.''

"Your fucking identity! Don't give me that shit!''

Monty felt very much like throwing the card index at him, or lacerating him with sarcasm, or screaming. In an effort to stick to her game plan, she took a deep breath and told him.

"I feel frightened when you shout, Sig.''

"God, you're pathetic,'' he spat, walking around the office with stiff, angry strides. "All right then, have it your own way. I can't get blood out of a stone, I know that. You want to fuck up a brilliant career it's your business. You won't be so lucky again, you know.''

Monty said nothing; she felt better, not frightened anymore.

"You're definitely not coming back then?'' he asked her, leaning on his knuckles like a gorilla.

"I don't want to come back,'' she told him.

He flung round and grabbed the door handle. "I love you, girl,'' he said, "remember that.''

Then he was gone, and the door slammed behind him. A few minutes later Swallow reappeared.

"I saw him go—he didn't look too pleased,'' she announced.

"He said he loved me.'' Monty sounded doubtful.

"Obviously he loves you; it's written all over him. Why else would he come crawling round?''

Monty stood up and fluffed up her hair. "Well, if he loves me, he sure had a funny way of showing it. He did a fairly good job of wrecking me, after all. All he wanted was a custom-built artist to make him some money.''

"All men have a funny way of showing it,'' Swallow said, locking up the office and leading Monty off to the pub. "They don't want to make themselves vulnerable. They don't trust women. Sex is all down to power in the end, haven't you sussed that yet?''

It was a beautiful early evening in May, one of those evenings when London seems like a clean new city. Monty squared her shoulders as she crossed the road, feeling hopeful for no good reason other than that the air was fresh and she was free.

Next day, Swallow took a telephone call which made her give a low, dirty chuckle as she took notes.

"Here you are,'' she said to Monty, tearing a page off her notepad. "We want a boss vehicle for Joe Jones.''

The note said, "US car, big, customized???? Red pref.'' Monty picked up her handset and called London's custom-car king, who lived in a house behind the gasworks in Fulham.

"I might know where I can get my hands on just the thing," he told her. "Is the guy renting or buying?"

"Buying," called Swallow. "Up to fifteen thousand."

That afternoon the car arrived, a gleaming 1950s Chevrolet encrusted with chrome, with so many fins it looked like a pirated space shuttle. It was painted a glowing metallic variant of Chevrolet red, which would have been fine for a lipstick but was excessively vibrant for the ordinary London traffic jam. The price was £16,500.

Swallow and Monty had long ago perfected their car-buying act. Monty crawled inside, taking care not to scuff the white leather seats.

"The stereo doesn't work," she called out.

Swallow eyed the custom-car king bleakly. Monty opened one of the back doors.

"The other door doesn't open," she shouted.

"It's a beautiful job," the car king said, licking his lips. "Mechanically immaculate. Does 110 steady as a rock."

Monty tried the starter. The vehicle's response was sluggish.

"Reckon it could stand a new battery," she announced.

"Tell you what." Swallow said to the fidgeting customizer. "Get all that seen to, have it back here by this time tomorrow and let's say fifteen thousand." She turned away with finality. "Then you can drive it down to Paleward Priory," she told Monty.

The Priory was a massive gray-stone house which had been built in the fourteenth century, then added to over the generations until it was a comfortable L-shaped mass of masonry with Gothic windows and a fine view over a lush river valley. Behind the house was woodland, the tame, luxuriant forest of the Home Counties in which the trees looked as if they might be made of plastic.

The Priory had belonged to three major rock stars in the past decade, all of whom had embellished it according to their own taste. The first rock star had built the recording studio at the back of the house; the second had landscaped the garden to add a swimming pool, which was always too cold to use; the third had filled the park with fiberglass statues of African big game; Monty was startled to steer the red Chevy into the driveway and see a family of giraffe frozen under the chestnut trees.

The Joe Jones Band looked as boisterous and hairy as she remembered them. Even with his shirt on, Joe himself had a physical presence that made the air crackle. Contemptuous as she was of the big boys' delight in their new toy, Monty had to admit that the guy was *built*.

"How are you getting back to London?" he asked her. "Can I drive you to the station?" It would have been absurd to refuse, so Monty climbed in at the passenger door and Joe inched the oversprung, overcharged red monster out into the narrow country lane.

The car had a bench front seat, the kind that made you think about people petting at drive-in movies. How long before some dumb groupie gets another notch in her holster right here, Monty thought, stealing a sideways glance at Joe.

He took the car out to a major highway and bowled along in the fast lane, steering with two fingers. I suppose he thinks he's going to turn me on by scaring me to death, Monty told herself, shifting uncomfortably on the seat.

"I'm sorry—am I going too fast?" Joe swooped the car across to the slow lane and cut its speed to well below the limit. "I just wanted to see if it would go round the clock. I didn't intend to frighten you."

"What a patronizing *creep!*" she said to Swallow the next day. "Why are men so *infantile*? You should have seen them, crawling all over the stupid car, feeling mucho macho just because they had a hot rod in the driveway."

"How would you fancy keeping them in order for a few weeks?" Swallow had three telephone lines on hold and a handset in the hollow of each shoulder.

"Mussolini couldn't keep that lot in order, they're so into the old hot and nasty number."

Swallow snarled down one telephone, cut the other off and kept three lines flashing on hold.

"Well, they want a housekeeper and you're the best I've got."

Monty realized that she was being asked to spend the summer living at the Priory with five brawling studs.

"No, Swallow. Absolutely not."

"Absolutely yes. I can't trust this to anyone else. Jack Nicholson's raving about the way you watered his potted palms."

"I do not wish to spend the best summer of my life fending off passes from five oversexed morons who think they're God's gift to women."

"Oh, come on, Monty—you should be so lucky. What are you afraid of—getting raped?"

Swallow had shrewdly identified the source of Monty's uneasiness. She *did* feel sexually threatened by the aggressive masculinity of the Joe Jones setup.

"Is there really no one else you can send?" she asked Swallow with resignation.

Monty had been in Paleward Priory half a day when she realized that The Joe Jones Band was splitting up; the house was permeated with the atmosphere of recrimination. Joe and Al, the keyboards player, spent all day locked in the studio, while the other three members of the band floated around the house drinking and killing time with games of billiards.

She filled the icebox with the beer that made Milwaukee famous and went to the village stores to order steak, bacon and beans. Chili con carne, bacon sandwiches and barbecues usually took care of these he-man carnivores. The state of the house was not too bad, thanks to a cleaning woman who came in from the village daily.

There was a Blüthner grand piano in the music room, black and shiny, its surface like a mirror. Monty opened it and played a few chords, feeling that the keys were stiff. It had a glorious tone, particularly in the lower registers.

Monty ran through a half-remembered piece of Chopin, then tried "Are You Lonesome Tonight?" which was easier but sounded ludicrous on this well-bred instrument. Then she started picking out some of her own songs, listening to the way they sounded in the piano's rich, sweet texture. It was not quite in tune. The dissonance was almost an enhancement, rather like her sister's limp—the tiny flaw in a perfect beauty. A few phrases of melody floated into her mind and she sighed inwardly. Here it was again. No matter which road she chose, she ended up face to face with her own music at the end of it.

"I think the piano in the music room needs tuning," she told the boys at dinner. "Would it be OK if I called London for someone to come and fix it?"

Dinner was a most uncomfortable meal. Joe, Al, their engineer and Monty ate in the kitchen; the rest of the band took their food into another room.

"Sure, get the piano tuned," Joe agreed, reaching for the salad. She watched as he ignored her vat of chili and ate a heap of lettuce with most of the chopped egg and onion. There was an awkward silence.

"I guess I should tell you what's going on," he said at last, chewing rapidly. "This is the last album to which we're committed, and we were hoping to keep it together until it was finished but—ah—it isn't working out that way. We want to go different routes."

How arrogant of him to say "we" when he means himself, Monty observed in silence.

"So we've decided to give our record company a *fait accompli*. Al here is cutting a solo album, and I'm producing it for him."

Monty started clearing the plates and they got up to help her. "Won't they go bananas when they find out what you're doing?"

"Yeah. But I think they'll come around when they hear the tapes. I'll take a day out next week to meet some of the guys—they'll be in London then. I reckon we can square them."

She made coffee and the other two men drank theirs quickly and left the kitchen. Joe stayed; he put his feet on the table and picked his teeth, watching Monty as she finished stacking the dishwasher. She felt very uncomfortable under his gaze.

"You must have a very good ear to know that the piano is out of tune," he told her. She did not reply.

"I heard you playing this afternoon," he continued. "I'm sure I've heard you someplace before. Aren't you . . . didn't you have a record out sometime?"

"Yes, I did." She flicked the drying-up cloths as she folded them, wishing he would stop asking questions.

"Weren't you Rick Brown's old lady for a while?"

"Seven or eight years."

"Didn't we meet before, when we were playing in London?"

Monty wanted more and more to evade this interrogation. Why doesn't he just make a play for me and get on with it? she wondered. Joe's question lay in the air, a gauntlet she had to pick up.

"Yes. I was introduced to you with Cindy Moon."

His full, defined lips had the suggestion of a smile about them. He leaned forward, took his feet off the table and threw away the toothpick.

"Why didn't you say? I was sure I knew you."

"I was another person then. All that has nothing to do with who I am now." Why was she wasting her hard-learned honesty on this trash? Why didn't he shut up and get out of her kitchen? She felt she had to escape from the conversation, so she said, "If you've got everything you need, I'll go to bed."

"Sure." He stood up. "I'm sorry if I was keeping you up. That was a beautiful dinner you made."

"You didn't eat very much of it."

"I'm more or less vegetarian," he told her. "I guess I should have mentioned it."

She could not get to sleep. Her mind was full of disconnected thoughts that would not be calm, and her body felt uncomfortable. She stripped off the blankets and opened the windows, letting in the sweet air and the scent of the honeysuckle.

She sank into a restless unconsciousness, but woke again in

the dead of night, soaked in sweat, her skin burning. She had been dreaming about something, but could not remember what.

She turned over, and felt the old, familiar juiciness between her legs. So that was it. Monty ran her hands experimentally over her own body, feeling her breasts tingle and her skin come alive. It had been a long time since she had made love rather than submitting herself to sex.

The next day a familiar face appeared around the kitchen door. It was Tony, the guitarist who had played in her band when she was Ruby Slippers.

"Whatever are you doing here?" she asked, making him a cup of coffee.

"Joe called me, he wants me to do some sessions on this album." Tony hadn't changed. He was still neat, clean, albino-pale and matter-of-fact. Monty found that she was very happy to see him.

"Joe's off riding some horse," she said. "He's usually back by now, he won't be long."

"Do you like him?" Tony asked, direct as ever.

Monty gave a pout of indecision. "I can't figure him out," she told him. "I can't stand all that macho crap."

"Joe's nothing like that. He's been there and back. Fascinating bloke—I was sure you'd fall for him." Tony shook his head, implying that women's sexual preferences were chief among the great mysteries of the universe. "He was an orphan," Tony continued. "His mother abandoned him on an Indian reservation when he was a kid. He was an alcoholic when he was fourteen years old. Dried himself out and went into the Marines, got thrown out. Drifted off to New York, fell into a band, the rest is history."

"How old is he?" Monty asked, suddenly concerned that she might be older than he was.

"Thirty-ish."

"Has he ever been married?" OK, she admitted to herself, I care. I want to know.

"Yes, I think so. But, he's never really with anyone now. He knows too much about women, I reckon. It's amazing the way they come on to him."

There was a scrape of riding boots outside the door and Joe appeared, his jeans ripped at both knees. There were mud stains over half his T-shirt.

"This is what happens when your horse makes a unilateral decision to jump a fence," he explained. "I've busted my hand—is there anything to strap it up with?"

527

He took a shower and sat on the rim of the bathtub while Monty ran a taut bandage around his swelling hand.

She could no longer deny the message her body was giving her. She was aching with desire; just being close to that half-naked man, watching the water drip from his long wet hair down the muscular ridges of his abdomen, made her breathless.

She was captivated by the thought of his broad, bony hands, with long fingers and nails, holding her and caressing her and then having him dip into the hot center of her body, where her flesh was streaming wet with anticipation.

"What am I going to *do*?" she demanded of Swallow over the telephone. "My heart stops every time he comes into the room."

"Fuck him?" Swallow suggested in practical tones.

"What—and get hung up on another all-action superstud like Rick? Sign on for another term of abuse, like I did with Sig? Come on, Swallow—I need that like I need a hole in the head."

"So—don't get hung up on him. Fuck him and run," Swallow counseled.

"I can't."

"Why not? Everybody else does. With any luck he won't even notice."

"Thanks, Swallow, I really needed to hear that."

"Only trying to be helpful."

"For heaven's sake, this is *serious*."

Inactivity, the food of lust, fanned the flames. Monty found herself imagining what Joe was doing every idle minute of her day, tracking him through the mansion with sonar waves of erotic yearning. If he came near her she felt a visceral lurch which made her knees go weak and her mind a blank.

In a desperate attempt to stop him from permeating every cell in her body, she started spending afternoons at the piano, trying to write a song. It was miserably hard work, which dismayed her; was it possible that she might have lost her talent, the gift which she had always undervalued because it came so readily whenever she called it, which she had almost begun to hate because it demanded so much from her?

She wanted to write a song about the misery of living with a brutal, dominating man, and feeling the pain of subjugation to his selfish needs. She heard it in her head as something very down, bitter and Billie Holiday-like, but the beautiful piano simply could not produce the sound of suffering that she wanted.

Swallow's right, she decided at last. I've got to have Joe. Monty knew every trick of inviting a sexual approach and she began to use them unashamedly.

She stood too close to Joe, touched him and let her hand linger with unmistakable emphasis on his sinewy arm. She held contact with his deep black eyes longer than was proper, feeling thrilling palpitations as she dropped her gaze to his mouth and ran her eyes caressingly over his lips.

She flirted outrageously, until every conversation became a minefield of suggestive double-entendres. Joe was very polite, and she suspected with dismay that he tried to avoid being alone with her.

She took a walk in the rain, and came in breathless and be-draggled with her T-shirt clinging to her breasts and her erect nipples clearly revealed; in this irresistible condition she contrived to bump into Joe in a doorway, so she was held in his arms—or would have been, if Joe had not stepped back as if she were going to bite him, his hands held away from her.

It was tantalizing to be within the warm aura of the body she craved for a few seconds. Monty was considering more radical measures when Joe unexpectedly sought her out in the kitchen.

He avoided her eyes and said, "The goddam car's cracking up. Half the exhaust fell off this morning. Can you get it fixed for us?"

The custom-car king told Monty to take the Chevrolet to a garage in a narrow mews in north London where they specialized in American designs. The garage also specialized in reggae music, which pounded down the street from a colossal ghetto blaster.

Two mechanics in Rastafarian hats and blue overalls elevated the Chevy on a hydraulic platform and ripped out the old exhaust, moving in time to the beat. A third stood by and watched, a fat joint smoldering in his hand.

"Hey, man, don't stand around—get the torch over here," one of them called as they carried a new muffler out of the store and began to fit it, their spanners tinkling on the oil-stained concrete floor as they dropped them.

"Could you be, could you be, could you be loved?" sang Bob Marley and Monty lounged by the doorway, swinging her hips with the music.

The mechanic put out his joint and turned on the welding torch, laughing as he set an exuberant fall of sparks through the air. One of the other men made a joke and they all roared and fell about, the white flame wavering carelessly across the underside of the car. I hope they know where the gas tank is, Monty thought.

At the instant the premonition crossed her mind, there was a massive explosion. Jagged fragments of metal clattered on the ground all around her. The men screamed, their hair and clothes in flames, blood pouring from wounds cut by flying metal. All over the workshop floor, pools of oil were burning.

Monty whirled round, searching frantically for a fire extinguisher. It was too heavy for her, but a man ran out of the office to help her and they began putting out the fires. She ran to one mechanic who was yelling in agony, his back ablaze, and made him lie down to kill the flames.

When all the fires were out, Monty stood up and looked at the scene. The red Chevrolet was nothing but a mass of metal. Joe will be so angry, she thought in fear, putting her hands to her face.

Her face hurt. Her eyebrows rubbed off under her fingers, crisp crumbs of fried hair. Her hair smelled and was falling off in charred lumps. Her body hurt too. She was burned all over. As she looked at her hands, Monty saw they were as red as steaks.

Someone put a blanket around her. "Come on, girl, we're takin' you to the hospital," he said. Monty fell sideways, pain searing her body from the waist upward. "Joe's going to be so mad," she said.

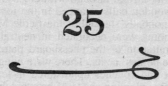

25

The name Princess Ayeshah chose for her nightclub was L'Équipe.

She selected it after weeks of turning names over and over in her mind, trying to decide on a single word which would have the right resonance. The name had to suggest exclusivity and elegance which were beyond the power of money to command. It had to have dignity, so that no taint of undue frivolity could attach to a head of state who included the club in his itinerary; at the same time the name of the club had to indicate that no woman to be found there would be less than memorably chic. Above all, the name had to embody the idea of an elite, an enclosed gathering of people with only one thing in common—their position in the highest international social echelon.

She found her inspiration in the game of polo, which had been a symbol of wealthy amusement familiar to her from childhood. Although she had crossed the world and attained a standing far higher than anything she could have dreamed of in the beginning, polo, she had remarked, always meant the same the world over—the most thrilling, beautiful and expensive pastime imaginable, in which horses so carefully bred and schooled that they were like living works of art were mastered by men with the riches, the leisure and the athletic skill to become superb horsemen.

The club's symbol was a polo pony, a tiny, prancing silhouette which was woven into the carpet, embossed on the menus, embroidered on the linen and engraved on the glasses. Beyond that, the motif was carried through with crossed mallets hung on the walls, and wooden balls arranged in the foyer in a pyramid, as were the cannonballs stacked at the École Militaire. The interconnecting rooms were decorated in neutral shades of wild silk woven in imitation of the chessboard patterns traditionally groomed into the ponies' coats. There were wing chairs of muted gray-gold velvet and couches upholstered in leather which was exactly the mature, glowing shade of brown achieved by a well-cared-for saddle.

Hussain, whose aesthetic sense had been honed for life during his childhood, added a collection of eighteenth-century French watercolors. The delicate, misty paintings, in their plain gold frames, assembled to please one individual eye, added to the impression that L'Équipe was nothing so vulgar as a nightclub, but a luxurious private home.

They compiled a guest list from a mixture of Hussain's mother's old friends, Ayeshah's most glamorous clients from Le Bambou and a selection made from Givenchy's address book. Ayeshah had plunged fearlessly into the new sphere of influence which a gilt chair at the Givenchy shows had opened up for her. The bitterness and frustrations of her years with Philippe lifted from her, and she once more became capable of warm but expedient charm. She exclaimed, she flattered, she alternated vibrant sympathy with effortless poise, she spent money lavishly and she made friends.

As she watched her secretary address the invitations to L'Équipe's opening by hand in her even, cultured script, with every title and decoration meticulously correct, Ayeshah was simultaneously thrilled and appalled by her own audacity. Her life seemed to have been a dizzying roller coaster of fortune which was now gathering speed for its final impact.

She had begun as a barefoot peasant girl dressed in a single strip of mud-spattered cloth, fit for nothing but the eternal chore of planting, harvesting and cooking rice; she had been betrayed, victimized and brutalized; she had endured a life of degradation that had been hell on earth; now she was a princess, dressed in couture clothes and planning confidently to impress the most elegant, the most snobbish and the most powerful people in the world. She, who was barely literate, was watching her secretary write invitations to members of half the royal houses of Europe.

She counted the years, and at once felt sad. Ten years had passed in her progress from nothing to everything, and it was too long. She had wasted time, and soon it would be too late for her to achieve her only remaining aim, the most important ambition of all. Ayeshah left the girl to finish the pile of thick cream cards and did what she always did whenever she felt the shadow of unhappiness; she went shopping. Hussain adored her spending money, and if a week went by in which no uniformed messenger boy delivered a stack of couturier's boxes to their apartment he would seriously suggest that she had been neglecting her health.

Rumors—skillfully created by Hussain who was adept at conjuring intriguing ideas in his listener's minds with barely spoken hints—filled the city before the new club opened, and in consequence not one member of that self-appointed governing body of style, *tout le Paris*, felt it advisable to refuse an invitation. Two leopards, restrained by jeweled black-leather collars and gold chains, patrolled outside at L'Équipe's opening, keeping order as well as any squad of security guards among the glittering crowd which clamored for entry.

From that spectacular beginning, there were never less than three photographers lurking with their Rolleiflexes under the spindly young plane trees outside the club, waiting patiently for famous faces. They never had to wait long. Sometimes the shy young Yves St. Laurent, Marc Bohan's assistant at Dior, would call in with a posy of models. Romy Schneider and Alain Delon, inseparable young lovers, came often. Princess Margaret, a tiny, erect young woman with eyes that flashed like fire opals, found she could sit down and play the piano for her friends in the backgammon room as easily as she could at Balmoral.

One evening the manager called Ayeshah at the apartment in a flurry of excitement. "Guess who we have a booking for tonight?"

"Margaret again?"

"No, better."

"Rainier and Grace?"

"Next week, maybe, the way we're going."

"Well *who*, for heaven's sake?"

"Edward Hardacre."

"Who the hell is Edward Hardacre?"

"Jackie Kennedy's detective, that's who."

"*Jackie's* coming to my nightclub?" She knew that the President and his young wife were paying their first official visit. For days the newspapers had talked of nothing else except Jackie's elegance, Jackie's pillbox hats and Jackie's political dilemma in patronizing the Paris fashion houses when she had worked so hard to demonstrate to the world that Washington also could lay a claim to elegance. The Kennedys seemed so much like demigods from a distant Olympus that Ayeshah had never dreamed that one of them would descend to the door of L'Équipe. She almost shrieked with delight at the news.

Hussain overheard her. As soon as she rang off, he made some telephone calls. In consequence, no paparazzi loitered outside L'Équipe that night, and the President's wife was very grateful for this thoughtfulness.

"This is nearly as good as being seventeen again," she said wistfully as she left.

The day after that, *France-Soir* had a large picture of Jackie at L'Équipe, taken from across the street with a telephoto lens, but by that time the victim was in Rome, innocently recommending the club to all her friends.

No one ever connected the exquisite Princess Ayeshah with Madame Bernard, whose name swiftly came to stand for the most beautiful women that money could buy. Those men who kept the REAumur telephone number in their address books under the letter B, most of whom had the discretion to choose not to write any name against that number, were never entirely sure that they were calling Madame Bernard, or that such a person really existed. Ayeshah herself never intended to be known by that name. It simply attached itself to the operation, a consensus nomination from her clientele.

The men who called Madame Bernard's number were answered by a woman's voice, which said "Locations Landon" on a pleasant, neutral note. The entire transaction was disguised as an inquiry about an apartment to rent. One room meant one girl, two rooms meant a pair, seven a small party; a north aspect meant a blonde, east a brunette, south a black woman. The price structure was encoded in the floor on which the fictitious apartment was to be located, with the first floor denoting the most expensive services. The clients' special requirements were ingeniously expressed in requests for particular features such as security locks, leather furniture or a view of a church. The code was passed on by word of mouth, along with the telephone number.

Agnes, the woman who answered the telephone, lived in a small room with a sloping ceiling on the top floor of an undistinguished apartment building. She had worked as a bookkeeper at Le Bambou, and Ayeshah valued her for her meticulous accounts and her complete avarice.

Agnes had worn the same gray-flannel skirt, winter and summer, for three years. Her long brown hair never felt the hand of a hairdresser; it was coiled around her head in braids, and once a month Agnes allowed herself the luxury of shampoo. Agnes rode to work on a moped and complained incessantly about its consumption of gasoline. She was ever alert to an opportunity to eat, drink or travel at someone else's expense. The only topic she discussed with any sign of pleasure was the bank account in which her savings accumulated. She regarded every extra half percent of interest as a personal victory over the Crédit Lyonnais.

Ayeshah explained to Agnes how she was to run the call-girl agency and then allowed the prim, sexless creature to name her salary, knowing that Agnes would not have the vision, let alone the courage, to ask for an unreasonable sum. She instructed her to keep two sets of books, one recording the fictitious business of Locations Landon, on which taxes were to be duly paid, and the other containing the true names of the clients and the women they hired, although the exact nature of the transactions was still to be disguised. The records, detailed as they were, would mean nothing to anyone except Agnes and Ayeshah.

The only remaining connection with her old life was Bastien the pimp, to whom Ayeshah directed that a generous monthly payment be made.

"That's not necessary," he protested when she outlined her plans to him, sitting at the scarred metal table in the depths of a street-corner *tabac* where he normally conducted his business during the daytime. Bastien had an expression of puzzled discomfort in his hard black eyes. "You don't want to forget your old friends, of course, but this is too much. I've no doubt we will be able to do business from time to time—naturally we will have interests in common—but we can always come to some arrangement. You know I've always been a reasonable man, Princess." He used her new title with ironic emphasis.

"I want to pay for more than your blessing and your support— I want silence, *absolute* silence," she told him. "There must never, ever be the smallest breath of suspicion about me, do you understand? I've made it look as if this agency is entirely Agnes's business, and I want you to make sure that is exactly what the girls take it to be. As far as the people who knew Ayeshah when she ran Le Bambou are concerned, she struck lucky with Hussain Shahzdeh, broke into the big time and now the arrogant bitch doesn't recognize her old associates on the street—do you understand?"

He gave her a nod and a smile which revealed his uneven yellow teeth, noticing that for this meeting she was wearing a cheap, blue suit and a wholly uncharacteristic blue-velveteen hat, an outfit so unstylish that she would scarcely be recognized by anyone who had encountered her at Givenchy. "And besides,'' she continued in an earnest tone, ''there is something else I will need you to arrange for me—but not yet.''

Before long, Agnes began to begrudge the hundreds of francs of excessive graft which she paid out each month. She was the kind of employee who was as mean with her employer's money as she was with her own, and the waste implied in every envelope stuffed with hundred franc bills which she handed to Bastien began to gnaw at her soul.

Only one girl connected with Le Bambou was accepted by Agnes—Pan-Pan, who had become a stripper at the Crazy Horse and who nightly wrapped her magnificent limbs in the rope meshes of a hammock for that establishment's most famous routine. Ayeshah decided to take a risk with Pan-Pan because she would undoubtedly attract other girls of the same caliber to the work. No one else who had known Ayeshah at Le Bambou was employed, but there was no lack of inquiries. When a woman's voice sounded on the telephone line, it might come from a haughty, high-class whore, a student who could not pay her book bill, a debutante looking for a thrill or a housewife who merely coveted a washing machine.

Within six months, Agnes complained that there was so much work she could not cope with it by herself any longer, and Ayeshah readily agreed to hire an assistant, choosing one of the poverty-stricken students, a round-eyed Canadian girl with a permanently startled expression. Shortly afterward, Agnes told Bastien, with inept insolence, that she intended to pay him less. Bastien informed Ayeshah, who made up the shortfall. Four weeks later, on her way home after making another payment to Bastien, Agnes was knocked off her moped on the Boulevard Sébastopol and killed outright by a lorry loaded with concrete slabs, whose steering was apparently defective.

The former student knew her employer only as a voice on the telephone, a woman's voice with a curious, unplaceable accent and a distinct, metallic quality. She was joined in the office by Véronique, a former house mannequin at Givenchy who had been dismissed because she could not control her weight. The timid young Canadian had hardly finished showing Véronique how the dual bookkeeping system worked when the voice on the telephone offered her several thousand francs plus her air ticket to go home. She agreed. Thereafter, none of Ayeshah's employees was ever to meet her. The little attic room was used only as an office. Money was paid into a bank account in the name of Locations Landon. Every week several ruled sheets of paper on which the agency's transactions were recorded with the clients' real names were posted to an address in the suburbs, from which they were posted again to addresses that were changed every few weeks. An elderly Iranian woman, who had once been a maid in Hussain's parents' household, was paid a small pension for the duty of collecting the large manila envelope each week and placing it personally in the princess's hands.

His wife's secret empire of vice troubled Hussain's conscience. He considered that the men whose names she recorded—many of them eminent, powerful and in positions of considerable public trust—were incomprehensibly foolish, but when he noticed the unnatural pleasure which Ayeshah took in her potential dominion over them he was disturbed.

"Don't you think this business could prove a danger to us, after all?" he suggested quietly one afternoon, as he watched her at the tiny Empire writing desk that had been his mother's, scanning the week's delivery of names.

"Of course not—whatever makes you say that?" She turned swiftly toward him, the color rushing into her heart-shaped face, her black eyes glittering with alarm. The triple necklace of graduated pearls around her throat rose and fell as she took a sharp breath. Hussain's cooperation was important and the idea that he might change his mind disturbed her.

"You're forced to deal with bad types like Bastien; you're making yourself vulnerable to scandal. . . ." he continued in tones of reasonable practicality.

"Nonsense. I know what I'm doing. No one will ever find out, I've made sure of that. And it's far better to have Bastien on our side than to try to cut him out—I've seen how those Marseillais operate, so have you. We've no choice but to involve him. Once you are operating outside the law the only people you can trust are those who have as much to lose as you do." Nervously she patted her hair, making sure that the pins which held her immaculate chignon were secure. "Besides, Hussain, think of the money—the girls make more than the club."

"But you don't need money. L'Équipe is an enormous success, you're planning to open another club in St. Tropez next year and that will be an enormous success too—speaking as your major backer, I'm delighted. Money isn't what you need now as much as prestige. If anyone ever connected you with Madame Bernard you would be ruined. You can achieve everything you want with clean hands, I'm sure of it. Why take such a risk?"

"But, Hussain, I thought you agreed!" She jumped up and crossed the room, moving sinuously in her clinging cream wool dress to where her husband stood leaning against the blue-white marble fireplace with one hand on the mantelpiece. She clung to his arm, pleading for understanding. "What about the things you want to do? Don't you see that the information we have will give you power? With what we know we will hold every institution in France in the palms of our hands. We could almost bring down the government if we wanted to. And not only France—we've had calls from all over Europe already. How can you tell me to back out when you will need the agency more than I do?''

He broke away from her with an irritated gesture, angry with himself as much as with her. He had never looked for the emotion which other people called love from Ayeshah. Hussain considered love to be nothing more than self-deception, a waste of energy, a weakness. She fascinated him in a way that was beyond sentiment, and she saw the world from the same perspective. Now, however, he was beginning to suspect that her life was directed to a point beyond their relationship. Could it be that she was attempting to use him in the way she had undoubtedly used Philippe?

"Don't try to make me responsible for what you're doing." He turned to face her, his face grave, the normal brightness of his glance extinguished. "I've told you my opinion; if you don't accept it there's nothing I can do about that. The fact remains I think you're being foolish, I think the agency is a weapon which can be used against you much too easily, and I think you should reconsider. That's all.''

"Very well. I think you are wrong and think time will prove me right." She followed him and caught hold of both his large, square hands in hers, the firm grip of her slim fingers almost pinching him. "Don't you realize that there are only two ways to do business, Hussain? Fine if you can keep everything straight and aboveboard, if you can trade on your spotless reputation and never touch one dirty centime—but if you start on the wrong side of the tracks, if you have to flirt with criminals and accommodate corruption, then you have to go on that way. I'm trapped, and so are you. The only thing to do is be the biggest gangsters of them all. That's the only freedom we have, don't you understand?''

He smoothed her hair affectionately, hoping she was wrong; his mother's injunction to live a good life never left him, although, like Ayeshah, Hussain's personal morality had been warped by the way in which he had been forced to survive. But Hussain was forced to admit that his own ambitions were maturing only slowly. He could always find a market for doubtful commodities, there were always desperate men who sought him out for his contacts in the arms trade, but the big business, the business which was legitimate, never came his way no matter what efforts he made to attract it.

The following year his persistent search for the deal that would open the door was at last successful. He was approached by the defense attaché of the embassy of the Central Sahara Republic, who wanted aircraft for Air-Sahara, the new national airline.

It was a natural development, the reward of years of discreet, successful trading. Sahara's defense minister had dealt with Hussain a few years earlier, when, as a guerrilla leader, he had bought guns and tanks for the revolution which finally ousted the French.

Hussain had talks with one French and one German aircraft manufacturer, and the French finally offered to pay him the larger fee for introducing the Sahara business. It took months of hard bargaining to get an agreement on a spare-parts contract, a period in which Hussain dropped eight kilos in weight and slept badly.

"Why not just take the Germans? They were prepared to play ball," Ayeshah asked him.

"There's more in it for us with the French, and I want to set a benchmark," he replied, "but if I can't get a good spare-parts agreement, I'll go back to the Germans, certainly. But if I sell Air-Sahara short now, the phone won't ring again on this kind of deal. The time to be truly greedy is when I can afford it."

The French at last agreed, the contracts were drawn, and then the storm broke. A disgruntled ex-Foreign Legion colonel on the aircraft firm's board denounced the deal as aid to the enemies of France and ruinous for the company itself. He also named Hussain, calling him a parasite. He accused Hussain of supplying the anti-French revolution with arms, and of a secret clause in the new deal to sell fighter planes to the new government, bombers which would be used against French interests in the rest of Africa.

"The filthy little liar!" Hussain raged, beside himself with both anger and fear that success would be snatched away from him at the last moment. "I wouldn't sell their lousy Rapier bomber even if I could—it's nothing but a jet-propelled coffin!"

The scandal exploded in August, the worst possible month, when there was no political news and all the politicians were at leisure to give the press sanctimonious statements. The story raged across the front pages of all the national newspapers and soon the most respected journal was calling for an official inquiry.

Ayeshah calmly took down the small oblong black box that housed the index cards on which the names of Madame Bernard's clients were noted. Her slender fingers, tipped with cyclamen-pink nails, flicked through the cards and she withdrew two of them and held them out to Hussain with an expression of inquiry. "Here is your enemy," she told him, showing him the name of the colonel, "and this man, I think, is on the board of the newspaper. Now it's your choice, Hussain—what's it to be? A good life and a failed one—or the success which you want, which you have worked for and which you deserve?"

He made a gesture of assent at once and with good grace. "You were right—I hoped not, but this proves it. How shall we handle it? Shall we start with the newspaperman—the old colonel is a complete fanatic and that type is always unpredictable."

"Leave it to me," Ayeshah said, giving her husband a smile which was intended to be reassuring, but which had precisely the opposite effect on him.

Within three days, the newspaper carried a lengthy statement of retraction from the colonel, which included a personal apology to Hussain. Beside it was a story from the paper's chief defense correspondent confirming that he had seen the Air-Sahara contract with his own eyes, that it was a superb confirmation of France's superiority in aviation and that it contained no clause in any way prejudicial to the national interest.

"Perfect," Hussain congratulated Ayeshah. "If I'd written it myself I couldn't have had a better vindication."

"It's only the truth, after all," she reminded him. "Do you understand what I mean now? In our situation we can't talk about right or wrong. There is no natural justice for us—we were wronged once, and we had to defend ourselves. Now it's impossible for either of us to leave our past behind—all we can do is go on in the same way, and fight fire with fire."

That week the manila envelope brought to Ayeshah by the aged domestic contained a spool of recording tape. Hussain awoke at 3:00 A.M. to hear a faint twitter of voices from the sitting room and reached for his black foulard robe. He and Ayeshah shared separate but adjoining bedrooms, and he went first into his wife's room, where he found that the bed, with its ivory-satin quilt and white-silk sheets, which were changed every day, bore no imprint of her body.

He walked quickly and silently down the corridor and listened for a few moments outside the double doors of the sitting room. He heard a woman's voice, harsh and threatening, and a man's voice, arrogant and aggressive at first, then cracking with emotion as it began to plead. The conversation at last concluded with mumbled words of agreement from the man. There was silence for an instant, then the chattering of reversed voices as the tape was rewound.

Hussain pushed open the door and saw his wife, a tiny, tense figure in her tightly sashed negligee of oyster satin, intently watching the tape recorder as the spools revolved. When the tape was completely rewound she touched the switch to play it again, sinking back in her chair to listen and reaching for a cigarette from the silver box on the table beside her. She caught sight of Hussain, gasped with shock, then jumped up to draw him into the room.

"Listen," she said, "it's priceless. Listen to this miserable little liar trying to deny everything. Then, when she starts giving him the dates and the times and the money, the girls' names, what they did—everything—he just goes to pieces. I swear he's almost crying—listen . . ."

"I don't want to hear it." Hussain gently made her sit down and turned off the tape, inwardly appalled at the enjoyment which had gleamed from her eyes as she described the colonel's collapse.

"Why not—don't you want at least to hear your enemy surrender?" She squared her shoulders defensively, sensing his disapproval. "Isn't this the moment you've been waiting for, Hussain?"

"Not I—you. You've been waiting for this, surely. This is the point to which your whole life has been leading you—all this time what you've wanted was to see someone destroyed. You were absolutely craving it."

"No—of course not, how could you suggest such a thing? It's natural to enjoy one's little victories, isn't it?" She smiled coquettishly and sat down, curling her legs under her, aware that she sounded evasive. His manner was not threatening, but Hussain was as cunning, as sensitive and as implacable as she was, and he was asking for an explanation. Ayeshah bit her lip and looked up at him, playing for time.

He looked down at her sadly, then slowly sat beside her and took her hands, making her turn to face him. "It isn't this man you really want to destroy, is it?" He gestured toward the tape recorder. "He was my enemy—but who is yours? Do you know what I think, Ayeshah? I have the sense that this whole operation is something you have created to attack one man, a man whose only vulnerable point is his sexuality, isn't that right?"

She swallowed, weighing the possible answers. She knew she could not lie to him, because he knew her too well to be deceived; to lie would be to undermine their relationship, perhaps beyond repair, and she needed him. If she told him the truth, perhaps he would help her. She decided to unfold for him the story which for so long she had hardly dared repeat to herself, fearing that the pain and bitterness which she had buried in her memory would once more engulf her.

When she had finished talking, Hussain continued to hold her hands in silence for a long while, understanding at last the weight of her hatred toward the man who had betrayed her. She did not cry. The pain was so keen, so strong, so close to the core of her spirit, that tears would not have eased it.

"You're still afraid of him, aren't you?" he said quietly, stroking her head over and over again.

It was true, although she had not recognized her fear before. She nodded. "He has everything, after all—wealth, position, power. He can't give me what I want without losing those things."

Hussain stood up and walked to and fro across the pool of light shed by the single lamp which illuminated the room. He ran his fingers through his short, curly black hair. "There's no point whatever in going to lawyers," he said at last. "My guess is that you could spend thousands and get nowhere. We'll ask him directly, and if he doesn't agree—yes, we'll destroy him. He'll be finished, I promise you."

On a fine spring morning, the spruce figure of an Englishman strode across the cobbles of the Place Vendôme, raising his hat to a pair of pretty shopgirls who pranced across his path clutching each other tightly for support as they walked awkwardly over the uneven stones in their high-heeled shoes.

Any Parisien could have identified his nationality at once; the immaculate camel-hair overcoat covered his shoulders like a second skin—only a Savile Row tailor could have molded cloth to flesh so exactly, without a wrinkle; his black-leather briefcase was ostentatiously scuffed, and the stitching was split at one corner—only an English gentleman would advertise his contempt for commerce so blatantly; there were the unmistakable, quasi-military features of his appearance, the severely cropped and parted black hair, the black shoes polished until they gleamed like mirrors; above all, there was the arrogant spring in his stride, the proprietorial width of his smile, the condescending courtesy of his gestures—in 1960, only an Englishman could have been so secure in the delusion that he was superior to the whole of the rest of the world.

Lord James Bourton left the Ritz behind him, crossed the Rue St.-Honoré and strolled through the Tuileries gardens, smiling benevolently at the children who scrambled onto the gaily painted merry-go-round under the watchful eyes of their nurses. The trees were mantled with the misty, pale green of their new foliage and beneath his feet the fine gravel was clotted with mud from the frequent squalls of the past few days. The rainy spell had passed, and the sky was the identical clear, carefree blue of a sky painted by Watteau.

He allowed himself a moment's unpatriotic reflection as he strolled across the Pont de la Concorde, acknowledging that the Seine embankment, with its heroic vistas of palaces and monuments, presented a far more inspiring landscape than the grimy borders of the Thames. But then, he reassured himself at once, the French excelled only at inessentials.

He mentally checked the address from the deep-blue pages of his pocket diary. The manservant who opened the door to him was absurdly well-dressed, and the Englishman smiled to himself at this typical sign of nouveau-riche ostentation. Still, he could find no fault with the waiting room into which he was shown. He had expected a vulgar riot of rococo, gilded, over-decorated and uncomfortable; instead, the furniture was mostly from the Directoire period, heavy and dark with severe, neo-classical lines. A Greek amphora, subtly illuminated in an alcove, emphasized the atmosphere of homage to antiquity. The heavy fringed curtains of pale-gray moiré enhanced the room's beautiful, watery radiance.

Curiosity had brought him to Paris this time. He was perfectly certain that his bank would not wish to be involved in any way with Prince Shahzdeh—or his wife. They were not the kind of people with whom a reputable City firm would wish to do business. The Prince was by all accounts an astute businessman, but his background was disreputable in the extreme. And the nightclub business, even at the exalted level of L'Équipe, was notoriously unstable and inseparable from the criminal element. However, when the Prince's letter had arrived at his office, describing a proposed resort development for which he was seeking finance and suggesting an exploratory meeting, James Bourton decided to agree simply because he wanted to take a look at the Shahzdeh couple.

There were so many rumors about them, about their origins, their wealth, their bizarre relationship. They were both presumed to be of Middle Eastern origin, and Hussain's title was often guessed by Europeans to be false. Many people who encountered the Prince and Princess sensed something unnatural about their liaison but could only express their suspicion in gossip and conjecture. James had heard that the Princess had been nothing but a cabaret dancer in Beirut when her husband had discovered her and fallen under the spell of her extraordinary beauty; he had been told that their bedroom was entirely paneled in mirrors, that the Princess hoarded clothes and owned three thousand pairs of shoes alone, that her exquisite face was entirely the creation of a famous Brazilian plastic surgeon. Naturally, no one would decline the opportunity to meet this legendary creature.

Time passed. A maid brought him the French interpretation of English tea, a watery, scented brew which was undrinkable. The room was very quiet, and James noticed that the continual roar of traffic was muffled by double windows. He looked at his watch and realized he had been waiting almost forty minutes. Still, discourtesy was to be expected from these marginal types. The wait only confirmed his opinion of them.

In her bedroom, Ayeshah wiped a smudge of lipstick from the corner of her mouth and redrew the line with a carmine pencil. With a tremendous effort of will she stilled the tremor of her hand, completed her makeup and rose to her feet, smoothing the tight skirt of her fawn and cream tweed suit and brushing imaginary grains of powder from the jabot of her white-silk blouse. The glistening dark sweep of her hair was furled immaculately into a pleat, revealing her small ears with their plain pearl studs. She twisted, checking in the mirror that the seams of her pale-beige stockings were straight.

Hussain kissed the top of her head. "He'll be at a disadvantage, because he is not on his own ground. Never fear, he can do nothing to hurt you. Don't forget that I will be directly outside the door—if you need me all you have to do is call. Are you sure that half an hour alone with him will be enough?"

"I don't know. It will be as much as I can stand, I'm sure." Her face was completely drained of color under its masklike maquillage. Together they walked down the long corridor. The manservant opened the double doors of the salon and closed them softly behind her. Hussain slowly lowered himself into an armchair beside the doorway.

James turned as he heard the doors open, and stood up as he saw the woman enter the room. She was as stunning as he had expected, a perfect beauty made awesome by her aura of power. The slender but rounded body, the exquisitely delicate legs, the full, sensual mouth and the flawless complexion would have made her irresistible, but her round black eyes with their heavy lids held a warning for anyone who dared to desire her. The Princess's beauty held the traces of corruption, like flaws in a jewel, which James recognized at once.

Ayeshah controlled herself with every ounce of strength she could summon. In the years since their parting she had trained

PEARLS

herself to imagine her one-time husband with a white skin, but
the shock of seeing him, standing here in her own home, a pale,
privileged Englishman, made her feel faint. She crossed the room
and sat down in the dark leather chair which Hussain usually
chose; its massive solidity reassured her.

She tried to speak, but for a few instants her mouth would not
open. Instead James spoke as he walked toward her.

"Have I the honor of addressing Princess Ayeshah herself?"
he inquired in French, expecting her to extend her hand. Realizing that he would touch her, she fixed him with a forbidding
stare.

"Do you recognize me?" she asked, feeling herself gain control of the situation.

"Why, of course; who could fail to recognize you, Princess?
You're famous. Even in England everyone has heard of L'É-
quipe and its beautiful owner." James was disconcerted, sensing
a peculiar electricity between the woman and himself.

"We met many years before L'Équipe ever existed. Look at
me carefully. You ought to remember."

"I'm sure I would never have forgotten such a charming personality. . . ."

"Think carefully," she warned, a cold, flat note in her voice.
He did as she asked with increasing unease. He certainly recognized the tone of her question; it was the kind of reproach
which a few women had made to him before, always as a prelude
to a clumsy attempt at blackmail.

What her question suggested was, of course, possible. In his
forty-four years James had experienced sexual encounters with
more women than he could possibly remember, most of them of
Asian or African origin. His youthful libido had survived the
brief trauma of his marriage and matured into a voracious sensual appetite which he had had the means and the leisure to
indulge as he pleased. Were it not for her imperious aura, the
Princess would have been precisely the exotic type he most enjoyed. But he had no recollection of her.

Besides, he reasoned swiftly, this woman was wealthy, successful and protected. She would have no need to resort to blackmail. Nevertheless, he followed the precepts of his class for
avoiding the possibility of embarrassment, and began courteously to negate her statements.

"Princess, I am quite certain you are mistaken," he told her,
returning to his seat. "I never forget a face, especially not a
beautiful face. Will your husband be joining us shortly? Or perhaps you would care to tell me a little about this development
that you are planning in London?"

545

"I'd prefer to wait for my husband, he will not be long." Fury began to roar through her mind like a fire. Now Ayeshah knew what his reaction would be; he would look down on her from the unassailable height of his race and standing, and dismiss her. She was sure that for the moment he genuinely did not remember her, and sure that when she forced him to recall everything he would flatly deny it. She racked her brains for a way in which to trap him.

"Tell me about your family, Lord Bourton." He was momentarily puzzled, then relieved that the conversation was taking a conventional tack.

"My family? Yes, well"—he coughed—"I'm a great family man of course. I've got two daughters, lovely girls, at school most of the time. . . ."

"May I ask what their names are?"

"The older one is Catherine, and the younger one was christened Miranda, although at home she's usually called by a sort of nickname." He smiled and there was an awkward silence.

Ayeshah walked to the writing desk and opened one of its small mahogany drawers. From the drawer she took a photograph, a curled monochrome print measuring two inches by two and a half. It was blurry, having been taken in sunlight too bright for the speed of the equipment, but it was possible to make out two infants in sunbonnets. One stood upright, the other, a mere baby, was held in the arms of a Chinese girl who wore a blouse and black trousers. They were posed in front of a single-story wooden building raised on piles.

"Then perhaps, if you do not remember me, you can at least tell me who these children are?"

He examined the indistinct photograph, screwing up his eyes. "Why, those are my girls, aren't they—with their amah? That looks very much like the house I used to have out in . . ." The word "Malaya" died on his lips as realization struck like lightning. He looked up at her with the fixed gaze of a doomed animal, terror curdling his blood.

She smiled, and he saw what he had not seen at first, the sweet, kittenish features of Khatijah, the wife he had married in the kampong in wartime. In mere appearance she had hardly changed at all, although her skin was pale, her clothes were European, and she wore makeup; but innocence had disappeared from her face and the yielding softness from her movements, effecting a chilling perversion of her allure. It was a spiritual change that had transformed her more completely than time or fashion could have done.

"No, I don't look quite the same, do I? Perhaps I shouldn't

blame you—I'm hardly a little native girl in a sarong any more, am I? And you don't look much like my handsome, brown-skinned husband either. But appearance isn't everything, is it?"

James had never considered the possibility that he would ever again see the woman who had borne his children. It had been unthinkable, and now that it had happened, and she was standing an arm's length away from him, he was paralyzed by fear. Some of his fear was rational—he was afraid for his rich comfortable life, for his impeccable reputation, for the love of his daughters, for his freedom, for his future. Deeper than these was an irrational fear, his old eternal fear of the female, personified in this angry woman who had the power to claim what he had selfishly stolen from her.

She saw his fear and it gave her courage. "Don't you want to know what I want? Don't you want to know why I've brought you here?"

He could not answer, so she continued. "You've taken so much from me, haven't you? My love, my happiness, my honor, my family, my home—everything that I had. When you took away my babies you took my whole life. This"—she indicated the room, and beyond it her existence in Paris—"this is nothing. It's just something that fills up the empty space, that's all."

She walked slowly around him as if looking for the place to deliver the coup de grâce. "I know everything about you, you know. I know much more about you now than when we were married—don't you think that's curious? Your Australian friend used to give me news of you. Until you left Malaya, of course. He didn't think you'd treated me very well, but I expect you knew that. And I've paid people to watch you, the last few years, Lord James Bourton. And the little Misses Bourton. They're lovely girls, you're right. And I'm their mother, and I want them back."

"Never." The double shock unlocked his tongue and James spoke almost before she had finished. "Never." The sound of his own voice emboldened him. "I love my daughters and I'll never let you have them. What kind of a life would you give them, anyway? If you dare . . ."

"Do you love them? Do you love them the way you loved me? Or do you just love the life they brought you? That's all you wanted them for, your inheritance, wasn't it? My God, you'd never even seen the little one before you snatched her away." She was still and tense, like a snake about to strike, hatred glittering in her black eyes. "I'd have done anything, you know. I'd have been my own children's amah for the sake of being with them."

He stood up, suddenly desperate to shatter the emotional web in which she was binding him. "I'm sure you would. You'd have done anything to get out of your little village, as I remember. You thought I was your ticket to a soft life and you still do. You don't love the girls, you don't know them, you've never known them—not the way I do, as people. They wouldn't even recognize you if they saw you. And if they knew what their mother was . . ."

She drew a sharp breath and he knew that he had found a weapon that was potent against her. He was sure, now, that her elegant facade overlay some evil of which, at the bottom of her heart, she was ashamed. The impression of vice he had read in her face was correct. It had been enough merely to allude to it.

The doors opened with a slight hesitation and a burly, olive-skinned man entered the room, taking command of the situation by his authoritative presence. He advanced toward James with a hand outstretched.

"Allow me to introduce myself—Hussain Shahzdeh." Dumbly James extended his own hand to meet the prince's fleshy grasp. Despite the gesture of friendly greeting, he had a momentary impression that the other man was going to hit him.

"Shall we sit down and discuss this situation like reasonable people?"

The three antagonists sat, the Prince and Princess side by side on a long gray sofa and James facing them, seated in the center of a black-leather couch. Ayeshah, desperately grateful that her husband had arrived to strengthen her attack just as she was faltering, slipped her arm through his.

"I'm sure you will agree that my wife's desire for her children is quite natural." James nodded. In the presence of another man his attitude was completely different, calculating and devoid of emotion.

"Your concern, naturally, is that you acquired your inheritance, in accordance with a codicil to your father's will, when you acquired your children. Of course, the children were legitimately conceived in wedlock and there is nothing at all to disqualify you from the bequest."

James nodded again, only partly reassured by the man's amiable tone. Hussain was a type he detested, a cheap market trader masquerading as a gentleman, a greasy Arab trying to ape European ways while at the same time eating away the fabric of the country which had given him shelter. James was not afraid of him, as he had been of Ayeshah. He had been lifted out of the quicksand of sexual guilt into which she had pushed him. Now that the whole affair was assuming the tenor of an irregular business deal, his concern was to find the most effective way to walk out.

"That's completely correct," he announced. "My concern is not financial, it is for the welfare of my daughters. If they were to learn, at this stage in their lives, that my wife, whom they have looked upon as their mother, was not in fact their mother at all, it would be a devastating blow. Absolutely devastating."

Equally, Hussain loathed James from the depths of his soul for being a threadbare, decadent aristocrat whose fine sentiments disguised utter emotional bankruptcy. He swallowed his dislike and continued, "Naturally. So how shall we resolve this situation?"

"There is nothing to resolve. I shall not permit any degree of interference in my children's lives, on any pretext whatever. That's all I have to say." He stood up, preparing to leave, and Hussain, ever conciliating, also rose, but made no move.

"As my wife mentioned, we have made some inquiries, Lord Bourton, and it seems to me that there might be certain advantages to you in coming to an agreement with us."

"What advantages?"

"You have a few small debts, I believe. Some of the arrangements which you have made with the trustees of your father's estate are perhaps what might be called . . ."

"Absolute nonsense." James was outraged that a man he considered to be little better than a racketeer was criticizing the probity of his own dealings. "I've never heard anything so absurd. You've no right to pry into my legal arrangements and when I find out who is responsible, whom you've been dealing with, there'll be hell to pay. Good God, do you think you can stand there and try to buy your way into my family?"

He advanced to the door as fast as he could without appearing to flee from the room. "As you yourself have pointed out, I've got nothing to fear, from you or from anyone. If you were ever foolish enough to try to embarrass me with this fantastic story you'd get nowhere, precisely nowhere. If you have any love at all for those children"—he looked directly at Ayeshah as he spoke and saw with satisfaction that her face was drawn with terrible distress—"you'll stay away from them, leave them as they are, for your own sake as well as theirs. They've been brought up as two nice, normal English girls; I'm sorry to speak bluntly, but a woman like you is everything they have been taught to despise. Good morning to you."

While his words still echoed in the room, James snatched his coat and hat from the hands of the startled servant and bolted through the door and out into the sweet fresh air and the safety of the street. His heart was hammering in his chest. At the street corner he hailed a taxi, suddenly feeling that he had no strength to walk any longer.

Anger and grief broke over Ayeshah like a wave. "I'll kill him," she screamed, "I'll kill him, kill him, kill him." Her face was skull-like and her eyes seemed to protrude with the force of the emotion which animated her. Protectively, her husband soothed her, setting aside his own violent feelings as he tried to calm her.

They had already discussed what they would do if James rejected their approach, but Hussain rehearsed the plan to her one last time. "Now I want you to think about one thing," he said, with the deepest gravity. "Which do you want—your children or to destroy their father? Because you must realize that if we succeed now—which we will—and if they ever discover what you have done—which they may—they will hate you."

"I'll make them love me," she answered.

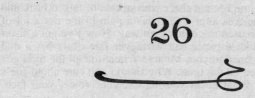

26

MONTY LOOKED AT HERSELF IN THE MIRROR; SHE WAS NOT AN alluring vision. Her hair was still long at the back, but scorched and frazzled, and it was mere stubble at the front. It also had a revolting singed smell. Her eyebrows were gone, and her eyelashes were less than a millimeter long.

Her face, neck, breasts and arms were all smeared with orange ointment. Her hands were bandaged. She had accepted four-hourly pain-killers to deal with the agony of her burns, which made her feel half stoned. This filled her with fretful anxiety that she was about to start using drugs again. There had been a substantial proportion of addicts at the center who had become dependent on substances prescribed by their doctors for the purest of motives.

"OK—that's enough bad news for one day," she said to Cathy, who helped her put her hospital gown on and get back into bed.

"When will they let you out?" her sister asked, plumping up the pillows.

"When I've got some skin on my tits, the doctor says. They think I may get away with no scars at all, as long as my hands don't get infected. They got the worst of it. I've got a few cuts from bits of metal, but I was lucky. You should have seen the car, Cathy—it was a total wreck. Joe must have gone bananas when he found out his darling Chevy was in bits all over Paddington."

Cathy shook her head, half exasperated and half sympathetic. "Once upon a time I had a sister who stood up, talked back and hit out when she was angry. She was a pain in the ass a lot of the time, but she used to get her own way. Now I've got a sister who crumples like a paper bag whenever fate deals her a dud card. What happened to you, Monty? Where did all the fight go? You're frightened all the time. Why should you care about Joe's darling Chevy? What about your hands, your voice, your face, your career?"

"It was the dope," Monty told her bleakly. "It was easier to find some drugs to make life bearable than to go out and fight for what I wanted. And it was easy for me to make a lot of noise when I was a kid and didn't have any real problems, but when the going got tough I got scared. Now I've got to start again from the beginning." Monty sighed and looked at her bandaged hands. "I'm just not as strong as you are, Cathy. And I can't work the same way. I need people, to be with me, to support me, to share my life, to love me. I can't thrive on fighting everyone the way you can."

Cathy tipped grapes into a bowl. "I'm sorry. I shouldn't bully you, darling. You're right, I know you are—we've got to do things our own different ways. Look"—she put a stack of paperbacks on the night table—"I brought you the complete works of Jilly Cooper—that should keep your spirits up. I'll come again tomorrow. Will you need a nurse or anything when they let you out?"

"I don't know—I might. My hands won't be any good for at least two weeks."

As Cathy left, Swallow arrived, and they squeezed past each other in the doorway, Swallow almost spherical in a purple jumpsuit and Cathy slender as ever in her new brown Armani.

"Christ, you look a mess." Swallow sat awkwardly on the end of the bed. "Joe Jones wants to come and pay his respects to the body—is that OK?"

"Oh, Lord. Is he very angry, Swallow?"

"He sounded absolutely choked when I told him."

Monty looked listlessly at the dingy ceiling. She was going to have to face Joe sometime and take whatever was coming; she didn't want anyone to see her the way she was, but maybe he wouldn't be too angry if he saw her looking pitiful. Monty smiled and winced with pain as her traumatized skin was stretched by the movement.

"Tell him he can come whenever he'd like," she said to Swallow. "Isn't life rich? To think I was going to make a pass at the guy and instead I go straight out and get his car blown up and end up looking like Mrs. Munster."

Joe came the next day, his face set. He brought a bunch of flowers and her tape player with some tapes.

"How bad is it?" he asked her, speaking low and fast as if he wanted to get the politeness over with as quickly as possible.

"Oh, not too bad," Monty lied. "I'll be fine as soon as my eyebrows grow back."

"You look like a Japanese mask," he told her. "Your eyes really turn up at the corners, don't they?"

OK, time to bite the bullet, Monty thought. "Joe, I'm so sorry about the car," she said, trembling inwardly. "I really didn't mean it to happen. It was an accident, there was nothing I could do about it. . . ."

He smiled, which he didn't do very often. "You hated that car, didn't you?"

"That doesn't matter—what matters is that it was yours, you liked it. I got it wrecked and I'm sorry."

"Why doesn't it matter—how *you* felt about it?"

"Well . . ." Monty was puzzled. This wasn't what was supposed to happen. He was supposed to call her an idiot, make some observation about the incompetence of women in general, then zap her with a mighty verbal punch designed to lay out her ego for the next six weeks. "Well, it wasn't my car, was it?" she offered uncertainly.

"It wasn't mine either. The boys wanted it, the record company paid for it, I only drove it. You're not lying here thinking about the goddam car, are you?" She felt stupid.

"There's nothing else I can do," she told him. "I can't read those books Cathy brought me because they make me laugh and it hurts to laugh. I can't even make phone calls because of my hands. Thanks for bringing the tapes, Joe; they'll be the main event of the day."

"As a matter of fact I wanted to ask you if you'd do something for me. I've brought a tape of some of the songs I've been doing with Al." He reached out to the table beside her bed and showed her an unmarked cassette. "Will you listen to it and tell me what you think of it? I'd particularly like to have your opinion of the third track. We've done it over and over again, and we can't seem to get it right. I know I've approached it wrong, but somehow, I just can't put my finger on it."

She was surprised. The amazing Joe Jones, big in Japan, colossal in the States, seldom out of the top thirty the world over, was asking her advice.

"Sure," she said, wary. Was this another rip-off in the making?

"Can I come to see you tomorrow?" he asked, taking his weight off the end of her bed. "Is there anything you need?"

"No, I'm fine," she told him.

"What's the food like in here?"

"Garbage. And I can't feed myself because of my hands, so I have to have some bloody nurse telling me to eat it all up."

"OK—why don't I invite you for dinner tomorrow?"

He arrived with more flowers, and some candles, and soon the room was transformed into a private world, flickering and fragrant. A waiter arrived from Mr. Chow bringing them a banquet packed into foil trays. Joe poured a tiny cup of transparent tea and held it to her lips.

"This is chrysanthemum," he told her. "I hope you like it—I thought it was right for you, more delicate than jasmine."

He picked up the chopsticks, broke the gold paper seal, and selected a morsel from one of the trays.

"This is melon stuffed with dreams." With the delicacy of a tiny bird feeding its chicks, he popped the food in her mouth.

When the meal was finished, she felt luxuriously drowsy. "Do you want to know what's wrong with your song?" she asked, looking up at his shadowed face as he rearranged her pillows.

"Not now," he said, pulling the sheet straight and tucking it under the hard hospital mattress. "Sing for your supper tomorrow."

Monty sighed as he blew out the candles and said good-bye. It seemed like the ultimate cruelty of fate to look like a nightmare and feel like hell and be cared for so tenderly by a man who could make her and several million other women melt with desire.

A powerful mood of what-the-hell settled on her the next day, inspired by the doctor who signed her discharge form and told her she could leave.

"The trouble with that song," she told him, recklessly tactless, "is that you've fucked it up; it's quarreling with itself. It's got a really strong melody but there's so much else going on you can't hear it. You don't need to dress up those harmonies with all that keyboard stuff you've put underneath—it'll speak for itself if you let it."

"Less is more, huh?"

"Right."

"Thanks, I'll do that." He was sitting on the end of her bed, his jeans stretched taut over the massive quadriceps muscles of his thighs. "Why don't you help me?"

Monty looked at him with suspicion. Was Joe just another man who wanted to make use of her talent?

"Will you credit me on the album and pay me a fee?"

"Of course. I'll get a contract drawn up for you at once if you agree."

He looked quite hurt that she should make such conditions, but Monty knew now that one of the tricks of a great exploiter is to create a world of upside-down values in which the victim is persuaded that whatever the predator wants is worthless. She had resolved in future to fix her price first.

"I'm not going to be much use around the house until my hands are healed." She held up her bandaged mitts to remind him.

"Don't worry about that, we'll take care of you. Now, what are you going to wear to come home? Your clothes must have been burned up."

"Of course, yes. I told the nurse to throw them away. I'll get Swallow to buy some for me later."

"Let me buy them—tell me what you want."

"Anything—jeans or something." There didn't seem much point in dreaming about lovely clothes when she hardly had any skin to wear underneath them.

"There are only two things a man can't do for a woman," Swallow predicted ominously when Monty telephoned her. "Have a baby and buy her jeans. Why doesn't he just bring up something from the Priory?"

"I think he wants to buy me a present and needs a good excuse," Monty told her. "Will you get someone to come and cut my hair? I'll scare the yokels to death looking like this."

The hairdresser cut her hair as short as a schoolboy's and showed her the effect in the mirror. Monty thought she looked younger and thinner. She had the impression of seeing her face properly for the first time, and she liked it. Joe brought the new jeans, which were two sizes too small.

"Do you really think my ass is that little?" she asked him, gesturing with her bandages.

"Isn't it?" he asked her with concern. "I reckoned it was about *this* size." He made a gesture in the air with his hands; it was unmistakably caressing and Monty began to smile but the pain stopped her.

"Damn you, Joe, will you stop making me laugh? Now get on the telephone and I'll talk to the shop."

All the shop had was a pair of black trousers that were severely tailored, with a jacket to match which Monty couldn't get on over her bandages. Joe helped her into the clothes and fastened the trousers for her.

"You're much more careful than the nurses," she told him. Monty was beginning to realize that she had been seriously wrong in assessing his character. He was the most gentle, thoughtful man she had ever met, nothing like the savage she had seen on stage. He could even change the dressings on her hands without hurting her, which was more than most of the nurses could.

At the Priory, she set to work at once in the studio, directing Joe and Al as they remixed the song on which he'd asked her help; then they went on to finish the remaining three tracks on the album. Her hands were still bandaged, but Joe was quick and subtle about doing what she told him. He was also full of cunning strategies to draw out her ideas and build her confidence.

"Love" was a word he used very cautiously, never entirely sure that he knew what it meant, but on careful consideration he thought he loved Monty. He was grateful that she was attracted to him, but most women responded the same way; he sensed that her heart had been broken so often it was mostly scar tissue; he knew with complete certainty that she would be able to love him only if she also found the strength to handle the rest of her life.

Joe was a good teacher, and to his delight Monty grabbed every opportunity he gave her. It was true that they complemented each other artistically. She was a much more sophisticated musician than Joe, but he had a raw power of expression which she did not.

"Aren't we a terrific team?" she asked as they listened to the last track when it finished. "Fred and Ginger, Tracy and Hepburn, you and me. We're magic."

He gave her a look that was startled but warm, and the little room seemed even smaller as their intimacy suddenly leaped into a new dimension. Monty felt light-headed and skittish. She trusted him now, and she trusted herself with him—after all, with half her skin still missing, what else could they do but talk? Al, the other musicians, and the engineer had already left—they were alone.

"Why do you always play so loud?" she demanded boldly, leaning back against the mixing deck.

He ran his hand through his silky black hair, thinking. "When I started out I used to feel this incredible *rage*, I wanted to kill everything and everyone. The place it came out was in my music. All I wanted to do was attack, destroy with noise, you know.''

"Don't you feel like that now?"

"No. That's really why the band is splitting up. I've become interested in music that's a whole lot more expressive. I've had it for communication on the Tarzan level. To tell the truth, I think the boys feel the same. But what we've gotten known for is that megaton fireball noise, and that's what our company wants us to go on doing. You can't blame them. They're in business to make money. People have got a lot of rage inside them and they're willing to pay to have it let out.''

"It was exciting, that killer sound.'' She wondered if he remembered just how excited he had been when they first met, and she hadn't been able to do anything but stare at his crotch. He dropped his eyes from her face at once, and she realized that he did remember, and he was embarrassed.

"What's excitement all about, though?'' He still couldn't look at her, she noticed. "Let me tell you something. I don't know if you'll understand but I'll try.'' He looked up, appealing to her. "I've had all the excitement I can stand, more than most people have in a lifetime. Thrillsville USA, that's my hometown. I've done dope, I've done booze, I've done jumping out of airplanes . . . and God knows what it is that I've got, but women have come on to me all my life. Once I was a big star and all, it was just ridiculous. It was like every chick in the world wanted my body. I know I laid four hundred and twenty-seven chicks in our first year, because we kept count, but after that I couldn't tell you. It got to be a game, seeing what I could get them to do.''

She nodded, remembering how Rick and Cy used to amuse themselves the same way.

"I was doing the same thing I was doing on stage—hitting back,'' he continued. "I realized I had to break the circle; OK, so women had used me, my mother had abandoned me, my wife had left me, so what? I couldn't stay on a revenge trip forever. I was the one who was suffering, I was the one who felt degraded. And I realized I was using fucking the same way I'd used alcohol, to cover up. It was something I could do to distract myself from everything I didn't like in my life. So I decided I'd let it go.''

"You mean you gave up fucking?'' Monty looked at him in amazement. A man who didn't fuck seemed an idea as bizarre as water that wasn't wet.

He nodded, searching her face to see if she understood. "It

wasn't at all difficult. I didn't give it up forever. I just wanted it to mean something. I felt it was time to take responsibility for my life. One day you have to admit that the buck stops with you."

Monty nodded. "I learned that at the center. I'm an addict, did you know that?" They talked on, trading secrets. She told him about her relationship with Rick, and with Sig Bear. "What I can't understand is that they both said they loved me, and they *did* love me, in their way—but all they did was take what they needed from me, and never think that they were destroying me."

He shook his head with emphasis. "They didn't love you, Monty. Nobody who loved you could ever use you."

She shrugged, wishing she could believe it was true.

After that they talked all the time, until it felt as if they knew each other like brother and sister. Somehow it became clear that they loved each other; they desired each other too—at least, Monty was almost sure Joe wanted her as much as she wanted him. He didn't flirt with her and he would not touch her, but their bodies were bonded mysteriously together.

Monty's new skin grew fast and flawlessly as she healed. Her face and body were fine—although rather pink—in a month. The bandages came off her hands and that skin too regenerated, at first as delicate as poppy petals, then thicker. By the beginning of August, only a slight puckering and discoloration on one hand remained to show that she'd been burned.

One by one the disaffected members of the band had left the Priory, and when the album was finished the technicians departed. Al was the last to go and Joe and Monty waved him good-bye from the driveway, like parents seeing off the youngest child to fly the nest. It was an uncertain summer evening, with towering columns of black cloud building up in the sky and the swallows flying very low above the lawn in front of the music-room windows.

They went into the empty house, made tea and took it into the sitting room. Joe sprawled on the chintz sofa that was so vast and shapeless it was like an ocean of printed roses. Monty walked to and fro in front of the narrow stone-framed windows, watching the unearthly dusk light in the valley.

Their silence was as heavy as the stormy air. The question "What now" hung between them like a sword. Monty could feel Joe's eyes following her as she paced the carpet.

"Can I play you something?" she asked him, desperate to cut the tension.

"Of course." He pulled in his legs and stood up, and she

led him into the music room, which was tall and narrow with French windows open to the garden and the valley below it. The eighteenth-century tapestry curtains stirred in a gust of warm wind.

"I haven't got any words for this yet"—she opened the piano and sat down—"but I think I've got the tune all figured out. Anyway . . ."

She raised her hands to the keys and began to play, finding the melody which had been lying at the back of her mind for a week. The notes seemed to arrange themselves by magic, until they were a tune that seemed a simple flowing line of sound with delicate harmonies reflected within it. She played it through three times, until she was sure that it was perfect.

"What do you think?" she asked him. Joe was sitting on a hard black-leather couch by the window.

"It's pretty," he nodded, approving.

"No, it isn't," she told him calmly, wondering why he was being so obtuse. "It's beautiful. It's the most beautiful thing I've ever written. If I never write anything better than that I'll die happy."

Of course. This was another of his games, a test to discover her true feelings, to see how sure of herself she was. He was sitting there, relaxed and expressionless, creating a climate of emotional neutrality in which she could express herself freely.

Monty walked across to Joe and stood looking down at his great sprawled body. His arms were spread out across the back of the couch, and she could see a sinew flickering in his left bicep.

"What I'd like to do is go into the studio tomorrow and record this. When my contract with Biffo ends, I want to start singing again, but this time the way I want, and I'd love it if you produced me, like you did Al."

She looked him squarely in the eyes. Inside her a chasm of fear opened. Suppose he said no? Suppose she had read him wrong? Suppose he made some slimy excuse and rejected her— now, when she had opened up to him and dared to say what she needed?

"OK," said Joe. "Let's do it." The flicker of nervous tension had moved to his lips. "Why start tomorrow?" he asked, knowing the answer. "Why not now?"

Outside big drops of rain were beginning to fall, leaving spots of moisture the size of pennies on the flagstones.

"We have something else to do now," she said, and stood astride him. Slowly, she sank down to sit across his lap. To her joy and relief, first one arm then the other left the back of the couch and he embraced her, his face pressed between her breasts. She felt the heat from his thighs strike up into her body, and hugged her knees around him.

Joe raised his face to hers and she took his lips, shutting her eyes to savor their harshness and the pleasure of the months of yearning coming to fruition at last. Lust as keen as anguish twisted inside her.

She plunged her hands into his thick black hair and strained him to her, feeling her blood catch fire. Their lips parted and their tongues met, flickering and darting around one another's mouths.

Monty felt fear again, knowing she was going to be vulnerable to this man as she had never been to any other, that he would possess her completely, but also make her the gift of himself. Soon there would be nowhere to hide, no escape from the demands of the life they would create together.

He sensed her fear and held her to him with as much strength as he thought she could bear.

"It's all right," he murmured, his lips brushing her ear. "We'll make it. We love each other. We'll always love each other."

She kissed his forehead, his eyelids, the sharp bridge of his nose, tasting the salt film of perspiration on his skin. Her lips explored the sinewy warmth of his neck, the firm swell of the shoulder muscles, the hollows behind the sharp collarbones, the tender membrane of his throat. With careful hands she pulled at the thin fabric of his T-shirt and pressed her mouth to the ridges of his chest.

"May I touch you?" he asked her in a soft voice. "Is your skin strong enough?"

"I think so." She pulled her own shirt over her head and threw aside the two garments together, offering him her breasts. This was the moment for which she had craved. His hands held her and his mouth closed over her flesh, trying the texture of the new skin with pressure as delicate as a falling leaf. His tongue, narrow and red, teased the swelling nipples and she heard a soft moan rise in her throat.

Outside the rain began to fall hard and fast, and the wind whipped wavelets in the sheets of water on the stones. A fierce gust blew back the glass doors and whipped the curtains. "Let's go upstairs," he whispered.

She shut the French windows, seeing the storm clouds circling above as if the sky were boiling. With their arms around each other's naked waists they walked slowly to the staircase and began to climb.

PEARLS

Joe was a full twelve inches taller than she and to walk this way was awkward. She slipped on the polished oak tread and he snatched her up protectively. The contact of their skin was electric; restraint abandoned them. Joe took off her jeans, then his own, and they stood clasped together below the stained-glass window at the half landing, glorying in their nakedness and wanting this first time to last forever.

It seemed to Monty that they stayed a lifetime on the staircase below the streaming window. Kneeling between his thighs she made love to him with her mouth, caressing the beautiful shaft of flesh that would soon be enveloped in the center of her. At last he asked her to stop, curled his long body between her legs and began to part the folds of her flesh with his fingers and tease with his tongue, coaxing the petals to swell and unfold and the sweet-smelling moisture to run. The small liquid noises echoed in the empty mansion.

Finally he drew her across him and their bodies locked slowly together. Monty curled her arms around his neck and let her pelvis rock gently. His hands on her hips slowed her almost to stillness and they rested together, listening to the rain and holding on to the moments of closeness as long as they could.

At last Joe said, "Darling, you're freezing—let's go to bed," and they separated and ran up to his room where they dived under the tangled quilt like romping children.

Their jeans lay discarded on the stairs, the sloughed-off skins of their old selves. In the warmth of the bed they set about the next phase of their union, acting like what they were, two sensual sophisticates showing off their skills.

At last they grew tired and fell asleep, while outside the storm continued in the darkness.

Monty woke some hours later, and lay still in Joe's arms listening to the thunder, which rolled like the balls in a giant's skittle-alley behind the distant Chiltern Hills. Lightning flickered at the far side of the valley, its blue radiance glowing briefly in their room.

She realized that Joe also was awake.

"I love you," she whispered, twisting toward him. "I feel like I've never loved anyone before."

"You never have loved anyone before," he told her, drawing her close. "And nobody has ever loved you."

The thunder sounded louder and closer. Monty counted the seconds between the noise and the light.

"Twelve," she said. "It's twelve miles away."

As if to mock her, a deafening clap sounded above the house, rattling the windows and shaking the floor below them. The lightning tore open the sky at the next instant, filling the room with white glare.

Obeying a primitive instinct to seek comfort, they searched for each other's lips and felt warm and moist and strong in their humanity as the tumult of angry elements continued outside.

She saw the whites of Joe's eyes gleam in the darkness and felt his hair fall around her face as he leaned over her, his breath coming faster than before. She sensed that now he was struggling to tame an impulse that was searing all his senses, and slid her hands under his, linking their fingers.

"Do it," she told him, "whatever it is, do it. I can take it."

He paused an instant, then fell upon her like a demon in the darkness, a mad spirit of the storm wanting to smash their bodies to atoms and let them recombine. With his strength unchecked, he held her, turned her, picked her up like a plaything, steadied her against his thrusts. At last he collapsed with an animal cry shuddering with the violence of release.

They slept again, and in the morning she took what she wanted from him, passing the dreamy dawn in a mist of ecstasy.

The sky was clear and the sunlight seemed as fresh-washed as the landscape. Chuckling rivers of rainwater ran down the pathways on the hillside and in the grove of chestnuts a wood pigeon called.

For the rest of the day, everything seemed like an intrusion between them. They did not want to get dressed, because it diminished their intimacy. When the telephone rang, they did not answer it. The mail lay untouched on the mat in the hallway. They walked through the rainwashed garden, picking currants from the bush trained against the wall and dipped their feet in the cold pool to wash off the mud. They made love when, where and how their bodies craved each other, prisoners of desire who did not want their freedom.

The next day, they were ready to admit the world into their universe. Joe made telephone calls, and at midday the engineer appeared, followed by Tony, her old guitarist. Winston arrived in the afternoon, by which time Monty had found words for her song. They began recording, and when it was finished the five of them listened to the playback in silence.

Winston laughed and slapped Monty's hand. "That is *the* most beautiful song I ever heard in my entire life, girl."

Joe rewound the tape and picked up a marker to label it. "What are we calling this?" he asked her.

" 'Broken Wings,' " she told him. "Now, shall I play you what I want to back it with?"

Eager to try her new plans out, Monty asked Sig Bear to release her from her Biffo contract.

"Not a chance," he told her. "Just because you've run off with some Hiawatha don't think you can come around here threatening to zap me with the old thunder-mittens and get everything you fancy. Any song you write now belongs to me, and don't you forget it."

So Joe took Monty to Arizona and they spent six months finding a site for their house and working with the architect to build it. His recording company offered her a new contract. The day her contract with Biffo expired, they went to Los Angeles to prepare her first album, and then make the video to promote it. It was a very simple film, with Monty in a black suit and white shirt, her hair cut short, and the band in their normal clothes, playing against a plain white background.

The company was nervous about "Broken Wings," saying it was too downbeat; instead they released "Man Beats Woman" as her first single. It climbed quickly to number three, and stayed in the top thirty for six weeks. In Britain, "Broken Wings," was a smash. Monty was called the new Joan Armatrading, the new Carly Simon, and the new Annie Lennox and a great new rock original. When the Grammy awards were announced, she won the category of the Best New Artist. The following year she won the Best Vocal Performance by a Female Artist; then it was Best Contemporary Female Solo Vocal Performance.

The next year, she was accused of dominating the award categories for female artists. Two years later she was asked to host the awards ceremony, but declined because she was expecting her baby. That year also she won her copyright action against Rick, The Juice and Excellent Music, and got her songs back at last.

Three months after Paloma was born, Monty telephoned her sister in New York.

"Hello," said Cathy's voice, "CBC Investment Corporation."

"What's the matter, Cathy—switchboard operator got the sack already?"

"Monty! What are you doing on the line?"

"Calling you, dummy, what do you think I'm doing?"

"Do you know what time it is?"

"Oh, no—have I fouled up again? I'm sorry, Cathy, I never can remember all the time changes." Cathy smiled to herself.

Monty could remember the most complex musical notations but the realities of time zones were beyond her.

"Good thing I was working late, huh? So how are you?"

"Terrific. Why aren't you coming over to see your niece?"

"I meant to, Monty, honestly I did. I'll be down on the weekend, OK? It's just been so hectic lately, the dollar's gone mad, and . . ."

Monty smiled to herself. Cathy always seemed to be busy. She had mailed Cathy articles from magazines about overcommitment and overwork being characteristic of the female tycoon, but it didn't do any good. Cathy only said they were characteristic of male tycoons as well. Monty had begun to suspect her sister must be happy working.

She arrived for the weekend as promised, and admired Paloma, who was three months old, feeling with a pang of regret all the long-forgotten emotions of early motherhood as she coaxed a wavering smile from the tiny red mouth and watched the big blue eyes focus slowly on her face.

What was the right thing to say about babies at this age—ah, yes, Cathy remembered.

"How is she at night?" she asked.

"Not too bad," Monty said with caution. "She sleeps about six hours, then wakes at five or six."

At 5:30 that morning Monty was sitting up in bed feeding Paloma, the pair of them pillowed comfortably against Joe's chest. She shifted uneasily. "Something's fallen into the bed, darling," she told Joe. "It feels like one of her toys or something. Can you get it? It's digging into me."

He slipped his hand over the surface of the sheet and pulled out the antique silver rattle attached to an ivory ring, which Cathy had brought as a gift for the baby. "Just a minute—there's something else." He felt under the pillow, and withdrew a small white leather jewel box, which he put on the shelf by the bedside.

When Paloma was asleep again, Monty noticed the box. "What's this?" she asked.

"Isn't it yours?"

"You know it isn't. I don't have any jewels except the ones you gave me." She looked at him with curiosity. He had already given her a huge heart-shaped diamond ring to mark Paloma's birth. "It's not from me," he said.

Monty opened the box. On a nest of black velvet sat an immense pink pearl.

At 6:00 A.M. on the same morning, Cathy stretched out like a starfish under the white comforter, and the fingertips of her right hand encountered a hard object under her pillow. It was a white-leather box, lined with black velvet, containing another very large pink pearl.

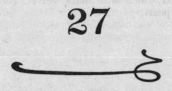

27

Cathy flew to Singapore at the beginning of September, for a conference called by the International Tin Federation. It was an exhausting three days of seminars in a featureless modern hotel, at which the four hundred delegates addressed the likelihood that the tin cartel would shortly collapse and the world price of the metal would fall drastically, a catastrophe for both its producers and the traders. The losses in London would be hundreds of millions of pounds.

The seminars had been tiring, and the knowledge that nothing could be done to avert the disaster gave her a sense of frustration. It should have been a relief to fly north to Penang to begin exploring her father's past, but Cathy could not shake her sense of foreboding as the small fifty-seater Fokker left the gleaming white skyscrapers of Singapore below and flew out of Changi airport. In less than an hour they would be in Kuala Lumpur.

Cathy was always intrigued that within so short a distance two cities could be so different: Singapore was a place with no memory, only a future. Among the mountain ranges of high-rise development the Raffles Hotel alone had retained an aura of the past. The fan-shaped traveler's palms and the pleasing white-pillared balconies were dwarfed by the sixty-story towers at either side. Now the Raffles too was unhurriedly preparing for the twenty-first century; and the shabby suites, which had reminded Cathy of the dank box rooms at Bourton, were being refurbished by David Hicks.

Forty minutes away from this anonymous international trade center, Kuala Lumpur had a sturdy sense of continuous time; respect for the past was part of the Malay national character. The city was dusty and chaotic, a sprawl of harsh modernity and Hollywood-Moorish monuments surrounded by endless green jungle.

Night fell quickly as she arrived, and there was nothing to do but check into the Hilton and plan the next day. She phoned her offices in New York and London, feeling restless and anxious.

She finally put through a call to Monty in Arizona, where it was early in the morning. "What's the matter?" her sister asked at once, sensing a note of agitation in her voice. "Are you all right, Cathy?"

"I'm OK," she said slowly, listening to her voice echo on the line. "I'm just not sure what I'm doing here. Do you think we're going about this the right way?"

"Who knows? We've got to do whatever we can. I wish I were with you, Cathy."

"Paloma needs you more than I do." She could hear the baby cooing in the background and guessed that Monty was holding her while she talked.

Cathy hung up and turned over in her mind the reasoning behind the trip, but felt the logic of it crumble. How could the pearls be connected with her father? She tried to talk herself into a more positive frame of mind. You're on your own, thousands of miles from home, dealing with the kind of problem you hate because it's formless and smells of irrationality—you're bound to feel anxious, she told herself.

Finding Treadwell had been simplicity itself. Her mother, as she expected, had been unable, or unwilling, to help. Bettina's physical and mental states were inexorably deteriorating and Cathy paid for a nurse to visit her every day, to keep her and her apartment tidy and clean, and to insist that her ulcers be dressed and the increasing number of tablets prescribed for her be taken. She still visited the bridge club two or three times a week, and apparently retained enough mental clarity to play the game and enough self-control not to appear drunk in front of her companions. The rest of the time, however, she lived in a state of complete alcoholic oblivion. Cathy occasionally tried to persuade her to move to a nursing home, but the old woman stubbornly refused.

When Cathy asked her about William Treadwell, all her mother said was "We knew nobody of that name in Malaya."

"But Daddy told me about him."

"You were a child, you must be mistaken," her mother replied, screwing up her colorless mouth in defiance. "No one of that name, I told you."

In her London office, Cathy's secretary acquired a set of Malaysian telephone directories with little trouble and found a William Treadwell listed in Penang with the title *Haji* added to his name, which Cathy knew indicated a Muslim who had made a pilgrimage to Mecca. Feeling that there could not be too many Muslims with Anglo-Saxon names on the island, Cathy dictated a letter which was answered at once, and then arranged a meeting for the day following the end of the Singapore conference.

After an overnight stay at Kuala Lumpur, she took another small plane to Penang, flying over the tops of the jungle trees and the glistening aquamarine sea of the Straits of Malacca until they touched down on Penang Island.

Treadwell met her at his office in George Town, an anonymous stone box in a stuffy Victorian building on King Street. The faint scent of cloves which emanated from his lightweight fawn suit hinted that he was now the proprietor of a small spice-trading business. The gold lettering on the door announced the Oriental Spice Company.

Thin, stooped and with spectacles, he looked more like a professor than a businessman. His hair was white, his face and neck red from the tropic sun. The hand which shook hers was bony, but its grip was strong.

"So it's not just your father that brings you out East?" he asked her.

"I had to come for a conference on the tin crisis in Singapore—it seemed a good opportunity."

"Mmm. That'll be a bad business for Malaysia. You're in that world, are you?"

"I'm in finance, yes. It's going to be a bad business for all of us by the looks of things, but the producers are the ones who'll suffer most, you're right. The world's very small; you can't really hide the way the North-South axis works, or pretend we aren't interdependent."

His faded blue eyes looked at her keenly. "Some things never change, do they? Here I am exporting spices just like the young men from the East India Company who came this way in the 1860s. In your father's day, of course, it was the price of rubber everyone got excited about down at the club. Now rubber's on the way out and they want everyone to produce palm oil, diversify the economy a bit."

There was a silence and Cathy knew she had to smooth the way for a conversation about her father.

"I expect you heard about my father's death," she began. "I

568

was seventeen when it happened. There was a terrible fuss, of course, because he'd left us so many debts. And we felt terrible, my sister and I, because when you're so young and money means nothing to you, you can't understand why a parent would commit suicide. It took us a long time to get over it. I can't believe it was more than twenty years ago."

An elderly Chinese secretary brought in a garish teaset on a tray and poured them two cups of strong Indian tea. Bill looked at the woman sitting across his scarred wooden desk and saw both strength and beauty. She had, he recognized, none of her father's weakness and all of her mother's beauty; he had not expected this. He had prepared himself for a typical upper-class Englishwoman in early middle age, perhaps with finer features than the norm, but with only the blundering force of the British temperament. Instead he found a clear-eyed intellectual toughness, which he sensed was like a core of steel in her character.

The Australian had anticipated this day for almost forty years, and had turned over and over in his mind the moral imperatives which should direct his conduct. He had at last resolved that he would assess the character of the woman who sought him out—if she ever did so—and then decide how to act. It would be wrong to ruin two good but limited lives, if that was what they proved to be, with truths which time had made irrelevant.

"I've always felt as if I hardly knew my father. Now I feel the time is right to get to know him, as much as I can."

"He was remarkable." Bill took her lead gratefully. "A remarkable man in every way. A cut above most of the fellas who came out East. Marvelous mind he had, when he chose to use it. Very amusing, a lot of charm, extraordinary gift for the Oriental languages. Never met anyone quite like him."

So far, just a standard eulogy. She couldn't expect more over a cup of tea from a perfect stranger.

"He said you taught him to play chess?"

"When we were guests of the Chinese Communists in the occupation. We used to play on a board scratched in the dirt, with the tops of beer bottles and little bits of bamboo for the pieces."

"Who won?"

"He did, when he put his mind to it."

"He taught me to play when I was a little girl. He could never concentrate though, so he always lost."

"That was about the size of it, yes. Always alert, you see, so he was easily distracted." Bill's hands, the fingers crooked with age, carefully removed his horn-rimmed spectacles, which he put down on the desktop in front of him.

"And is the rubber estate he worked on still producing? I'd love to see it."

He hesitated, looking at her with curiosity.

"We could drive out there tomorrow, if you like. I wouldn't mind seeing the place again myself. I'm told there's a road now; it'll be a day trip."

"Terrific."

She offered to drive and hired a car, then checked into the E & O Hotel, now much less than the finest hostelry in town, but, like the Raffles, full of evocative atmosphere. My father came here, she told herself, following the porter across the cool checkered marble floor. On the terrace where her father had inadvertently wooed foolish Lucy Kennedy, she looked out over the gray-blue waves and watched a fisherman in a narrow wooden skiff pull in his nets.

They drove aboard the slow iron ferry the next morning, and took a route south over a narrow but well-paved highway, through a landscape ravaged by tin mining, a succession of dreary gray workings interspersed with a harsh tangle of secondary jungle.

"This is Ipoh—they called it the town that tin built," Bill explained as they drove down the straight main street lined with shop-houses, slowly negotiating a throng of bicycles and trishaws. "Government housing." He waved his hand at an orderly estate of rectangular bungalows with zigzag ironwork balconies. "This was the first of their cheap housing schemes, designed to help people get off the land and into the industrial centers where there was work."

They sped on through village after village of ornate dark wood bungalows. Bill explained to her what the daily routine of the estate would have been, and how the planters' wives passed their days, and how hazardous life was during the Emergency. She realized that this gaunt old man was withholding the kind of information she wanted, and wondered why.

"When did you become a Muslim?" she asked him.

"When the country became independent. After that you couldn't hold a position of responsibility unless you were a Malayan citizen. I was working as a development officer in the state of Perak, helping to build the new country, give it a sound infrastructure. I loved the place, always have, and I decided to apply for citizenship so I could stay on. Quite a few Europeans did. I decided to take the religion too. I'm an all-or-nothing type, it appeals to me. There's nothing left to chance in Islam. And I thought it was not enough just to say you love a country. You have to commit yourself to it."

"How did my father react?"

"He thought I was mad, of course. Going native, he called it. The British thought that was the worst thing a man could do."

"I suppose if you believed all that God-is-an-Englishman stuff you wouldn't understand."

He watched her covertly as she reacted to his statement and was satisfied. "You don't buy that line, I take it?"

"That kind of thinking took the greatness out of Britain." Cathy swerved to avoid a truck full of oil-palm kernels which was driving down the center of the road. Treadwell gave a dry chuckle.

"Nothing in the Koran about the way a man's supposed to drive, of course."

After four hours the road began to climb through low, wooded hills. It followed a narrow railway line up a valley; then Treadwell directed her down a fork to the right. They drove through a village, slowing for a group of brown cows that were being driven down the road by a little girl in a cotton frock who idly tapped their rumps with a bamboo pole.

In time the walls of shimmering green jungle foliage gave way to orderly rows of gray-trunked rubber trees.

"This was just a beaten track in your father's day," he told her. "The rubber used to come down here on oxcarts to be loaded on to the train."

"Who owns the estate now?"

"Fella called Choy. Lives in Penang, great big house on Burmah road. The manager will be a Chinese, too, I expect."

They drove slowly past tin-roofed hardwood houses where the estate workers lived, pausing to let a man wheeling a bicycle loaded with cans of latex cross in front of them. The old estate house still dominated the landscape from the brow of the hill, although its stucco was peeling and the shutters, bare of paint, had lost some of their slats.

The estate manager was an Indian, a fleshy man of about thirty with heavy-framed spectacles, who told them to take their time and look around at their leisure. He had one of his assistants fetch a yellowed photograph album, and showed them pictures of the estate staff in the early days of the Emergency. Cathy had no trouble picking out her father by his beaming smile and perfect posture.

"I suppose that's my mother," she said, pointing to the figure in a cotton frock beside him, but standing apart.

"She's still alive, I take it?" Treadwell asked.

"She's very ill," Cathy told him, and although he expressed

regret she felt there was something in his manner which suggested he had not cared for her mother particularly.

The old bungalows had long since been razed, and a plantation of oil palms waved feathery fronds where Cathy and Monty had played as babies under their amah's watchful eye.

"Your father was a good manager, got on well with everybody." Bill stood awkwardly on the broken ground beside the track. "After the war, of course, he was a great hero to the Europeans out here. Not many of us stayed behind when the Japanese came and lived to tell the tale."

As they retraced their steps to the estate house, he told her about the days of the occupation, carefully testing her attitudes.

"I can't think of any other man who could have done what your father did. He passed himself off as a Malay, lived in a kampong, took some drug we'd been given to darken our skins. He blended in perfectly. In the turmoil of the occupation people got used to strangers, even in the villages. That was his nature, you see. Mercurial temperament, adapt to anything. The local people knew, I think, but by the time their suspicions had grown they were in danger themselves for harboring a European. We all had a price on our heads in those days."

Cathy turned the car and drove them back, feeling empty. She did not know what she had expected to find, but she was disappointed that she had felt no sense of recognition in this place at all, even though she had been born here. There was nothing more to see. It was as if her eyes had never before looked down this gentle slope of obedient vegetation. She had no recollection of the place at all.

"My father didn't talk about the past much." She let the car run smoothly over the bumpy track, then drove faster down the road to the railway. "He never even told us what he got his decoration for."

"I expect he was keen to get on with his life in England and put the war behind him. Our war didn't turn out as we planned, you see. When the Americans dropped the bomb it set everything we'd done here, recruiting and training men to overthrow the Japanese, at nothing. We risked our lives as well as any other man—more so, given the jungle. Quite a lot of fellas died of typhus or blackwater fever or some other tropical disease."

"Daddy was always very strong. He never seemed to get ill."

"He was a survivor. We both were. He was decorated for an incident after the war was officially over—only there were quite a few isolated Japanese units in the jungle who chose not to hear the news. He went to open up a prison camp down south somewhere, and they attacked in the night. Your father was quite badly wounded, but I don't believe he even knew it. Just fought them all off until we got there to relieve him. Oh, yes, he was a brave man—didn't know what fear was.''

On the long drive back he fell asleep, but woke as they approached the thronged streets of Butterworth, where they halted to wait for the ferry.

"It's curious,'' Cathy told him as they stood by the iron wall of the ferry looking out over the dark waves, "I feel as if I know my father less now, rather than more. None of this seems to be connected with him at all, and yet it must have been important to him.''

After years of practice in negotiation, she had a sixth sense for withheld information, and was sure that this man had chosen not to tell her something crucial about her father's past. Treadwell impressed her. He was thoughtful and intelligent, not at all the florid boon companion she had anticipated. But the man he had described to her was not her father. Cathy was too honest to have avoided the conclusion that her father had been a flawed man, and Treadwell had described a paragon. Perhaps if she appealed to him he would decide to be open with her.

"I always had the impression that you fell out with my father, or he fell out with you,'' she said with caution, wondering if he would choose to disinter a painful memory after so many years. They were walking back to the car.

"I think it's fair to say that I fell out with him,'' the old man said, picking his way on unsteady legs across the metal deck.

"What did you argue about?''

"If he never told you, then it isn't my place to fill you in.'' He opened the car door and sank wearily into the seat.

"You're a tough young lady, aren't you?'' he asked in a pleasant tone as the car bumped over the ferry gangway.

"Not so young anymore,'' she corrected him.

"Your sister, what's she like?''

"Absolutely different from me. She's more emotional than I am, more open to people. And she's always trying, testing, questioning—trying to find better ways to do things, better ways to live. More adventurous than I am, but more vulnerable too. She's a singer, you might have heard of her—Monty's her name.''

"Just Monty? I don't know much about singers, I'm afraid. What I mean is—is she tough?''

"She's strong. She'll never shut herself off from life, any part of life. She's got the kind of strength that comes from having lived, really lived. My kind of strength isn't the same.''

"Where is she?''

"America, She's just had her first child, a little girl."

"Would she come out here?"

Now Cathy knew that she had been right. There was more to tell, much more, and Treadwell had been sounding her out all day, seeing if it would be right to unlock the past.

"If it was important," she said.

"You'd better ask her, then."

Cathy delivered him to the door of his modern bungalow in a small village on the undeveloped side of Penang Island at 10:00 P.M. She drove back past the garish hotels along Batu Ferringhi beach, slowing down near the souvenir shops and restaurants which were decorated with strings of colored lights and thronged by wandering herds of tourists who strayed into the road. The highway twisted along the shoreline, overlooked by towers of condominiums, the milky sea lapping the large rocks below. Now, at last, she had a sense of accomplishing something.

Telephoning Monty was difficult. The line was persistently cut off and it was three hours before Cathy could get a connection. Her sister's voice was faint and almost inaudible.

"You've got to come out here right away," Cathy shouted. "I don't know what it is but he says it's important. I'm at the E & O Hotel in George Town. Cable me your flight time and I'll meet you."

"OK," she heard the indistinct voice say.

"She wants me to come," Monty told Joe, the telephone still in her hand. "I knew she would. I should have gone with her in the first place. Paloma will be fine with you."

"Are you sure you want to go alone?" He held her close, feeling protective but also disturbed. Although he tried hard, Joe felt jealous of Monty's bond with her sister. It was more than a mere emotion; it was an affinity of spirit that seemed as eternally strong as the force which held the earth in its orbit, and his own love could not compete with it.

"I feel I must," she said slowly. "It'll be awful without you, but whatever this is, it's something Cathy and I have to do together."

He nodded. They had not slept apart since the beginning of their relationship. "I'll miss you. We'll miss you. Don't worry about Paloma, she'll be OK."

When she arrived at the small, hot, crowded airport twenty hours later, Cathy was waiting, a still figure in a black silk dress; and as she kissed her sister, Monty suddenly felt as if they were children again, facing the world together.

The next day they drove to Treadwell's house, and sat side by side on the cushions of the sagging teak-framed sofa in his hot, dim sitting room, where the warm breeze from the sea a few hundred yards away barely stirred the curtains of blue and white flowered cotton. At home, Cathy noticed, Bill wore a *songkok*, the oval Malay fez, which contrasted with his craggy Anglo-Saxon features.

His Malay wife, a thin, yellow-skinned woman in a white blouse and blue skirt, brought them tea in thick white china cups, then withdrew to the rear of the building.

"What I'm going to tell you is going to shock you," he said, looking severe. "I've thought very carefully about whether I should do this, because it may not be for the best as far as your happiness is concerned. I'm not one of those who thinks we're put on earth to suffer, but I believe that there's more to life than happiness, and I suspect you may feel the same way."

He looked from one woman to the other, absorbing their faces. Now that he saw the younger one he was astonished that no one had ever questioned her origins before. The strong, curling black hair, the slightly flattened nose, the slanted eyes—the story was all there to be read.

"When we met the other day, I hadn't made up my mind what was the best course," he continued, talking to Cathy. "But I felt you'd come here with some kind of understanding already. My impression of you is that you're the man your father should have been. Maybe you've had a harder life than he did, in the beginning. Jim was my friend; I was attached to him as if he were my brother. But he'd been spoiled, somehow. Not indulged so much, but set on the wrong path, as it were. It was as if he saw the world the other way up. You're right, we fell out in the end. You've got all of his charm and none of his weakness. He would have been a terrible ladies' man, if he had been inclined that way."

"And he wasn't?" Cathy heard her voice sound uncertain. She had never considered the question of her father's sexuality.

"Not in the modern way, no. Quite a few of the old colonial types preferred native women—I think your father was one of them." He looked at them carefully to see if they were shocked, but met the steady gaze of two brown and two black eyes.

"Are you telling us that he had a mistress?" Cathy prompted gently.

"Several, I shouldn't be surprised. He also had a wife. During the war, when we lived undercover, he married a Malay girl. He was completely crazy about her. I didn't understand it. She was a beautiful girl, but I thought he was mad, told him so. Of course it helped his cover, no doubt about that. It was a lot harder for the people he hid with to turn in one of their own."

"What happened to her?" Monty felt hot, despite her loose red-silk dress; she tried to imagine her father making love, but no image would come to her mind. It was as if they were talking about another person.

"He left her flat at the end of the war—never gave her a second thought. I went to see her a few times, gave her some money." He paused, wondering if he had chosen the best way to unfold the story. Now that the two women were sitting in his house he could hardly believe it was true himself.

"There were children," he said at last, looking from one to another with fierce intensity.

"You mean we've got brothers and sisters somewhere?" Cathy felt her pleated white skirt sticking to the backs of her thighs in the heat, and shifted uncomfortably on the low sofa.

"No." His pale tongue moistened his lips and she saw his Adam's apple bob as he swallowed. "He had two girl children with this Malay woman. When he came back after the war he married—that woman in the photograph." Plainly, he could hardly speak Bettina's name. "Do you know very much about your family's financial arrangements?"

"We know that the money he lost was really ours, intended to be in trust for us," Cathy told him.

"That was all the money your father had. He needed to marry and start a family before it would be released. When it was clear that our old life here was finished, your father was desperate. And he found he couldn't have children with that woman—so he went looking for his Malay wife."

Monty's dark, velvet eyes widened in surprise. *"You mean Cathy and I . . ."*

"He brought you back to the estate and passed you off as the children of his new marriage. False birth certificates, the lot. I never thought he'd get away with it. Obviously, he did."

"So we aren't—we aren't Bettina's children, his wife's children, at all?" They looked at each other at the same instant and drew together, then they looked back to him, questioning with their eyes.

"British law didn't recognize his first marriage. There'll be a record at the mosque, perhaps. Did you ever . . . did anyone ever tell you anything about all that?"

They shook their heads. "I don't believe the rest of the family knew. My grandmother was a very difficult woman, but my father was her favorite and she could never keep any kind of secret. If she knew anything she'd have let it out one day."

"Your mother—Betty, the woman you thought was your mother . . ."

"She never told us anything. She never even told us where babies come from, let alone anything about ourselves." Monty had never stopped hating Bettina, and now she felt an enormous sense of release, knowing that she was justified. "I didn't get on with her, you see. I used to dream of something like this."

Cathy nodded agreement. "All we ever had was this feeling that we didn't belong, that we were different somehow."

"Well." He gave a gentle smile, looking from one face to another, seeing that they had not yet fully absorbed the impact of what he had told them. "Now you know that you really are different."

"So what was she like, our real mother?" asked Monty.

"Sweet little thing. Worshiped the ground below his feet. Enchanting. Like a kitten." Treadwell's red-rimmed eyes were glistening. "She used to break my heart, asking me when he was going to come back. And she loved you so—of course, all the Malays love children, but she adored you, just adored you." He looked away through the window at the sparkling sea and the misty horizon.

"I hit him when I found out what he'd done. I'll never forget coming up to the bungalow and there you both were, in all the little white togs they used to do their babies up in in those days. And you"—again he spoke to Cathy—"you were the image of him at that age. Went straight in and floored him, knocked the corner off one of his teeth. I couldn't have anything to do with him after that. I went straight down to see your real mother and she was in a terrible state. The whole family was arguing about whether to get the doctor for her—not a real doctor, the medicine man they call in to deal with evil spirits. She was just lying there, eyes open, not seeing anything, as if she were in a trance. She was ill, nothing more than skin and bones; she had a fever of some sort, but they weren't interested in that, they were afraid some ghost had taken possession of her. Only the grandmother was prepared to accept she was sick."

He sighed and took a mouthful of his tea, which was almost cold. The sisters sat in silence as he continued, "It wasn't the best situation for her. Her mother was a selfish woman, she'd been left by the girl's father—incidentally, they said he was a white man, English-speaking but not from England—and frankly she just wanted to get rid of her however she could. I took the girl to a hospital I knew, and the grandmother with her. And I made sure to get the money, or what was left of it, because your father paid them off. It took about three months before she was better, and then she decided to go and seek her fortune in Singapore. She had some idea of being an amah in an English family and then getting him to take her on in his household so that she could be with you that way.''

Cathy sat in silence, vaguely aware of the waves splashing on the distant purple rocks. She remembered the anguish she had felt at being parted from Jamie when he was a baby, and tears of sympathy for the mother she had never known pricked her eyelids.

''Don't blame him,'' Treadwell said suddenly. ''I blamed him, but really he couldn't help himself. In some things your father just couldn't tell right from wrong. I don't think he ever realized what a terrible thing he'd done. He was like a coolie, you know. You couldn't ever get through to the coolies not to lie, or steal or cheat on their quotas or do their work right. That kind of morality was a luxury to them, a luxury they couldn't afford. No sense in being a fine individual if someone else owns you, is there? Your father was just the same about women. I'd argue with him, but he couldn't see what I was going on about.''

He blew his nose into a large white handkerchief, then reached for a worn document case on the checkered cloth that covered the table, and handed it to them. Cathy took the heavy leather folder from him. ''That's my journal, that I kept during the occupation. You might be interested to read it.''

''What happened to our mother when she went to Singapore—where is she now?'' Monty pressed him. He looked away, unwilling to continue and afraid of their reaction.

''We should know,'' Cathy urged him in even tones. ''Even if you think we might not thank you for telling us.''

''Well, you may not thank me, but there it is. You're right, you must know. She was tricked, trapped by a few Chinese who ran a cheap dance hall, and she became what they called a taxidancer. Little better than a prostitute really. A lot of the girls who were abandoned by Europeans drifted to the towns and ended up that way—the Malays are very strait-laced and their families wouldn't take them back. Then she began to change, she got hard, eaten up with hatred, obsessed with getting money from the British soldiers—there were thousands of them in Singapore then.''

''You kept in touch?'' Cathy inquired.

''For as long as I could. She used to ask me for news of you, any little detail I could tell her she'd lap up. I brought her photographs. He never knew, or he'd have tried to stop me. Then she took up with a Eurasian boyfriend, regular lounge lizard, and started running with the fast set in Singapore. Your father left when the Emergency started, took you back to England, and shortly afterward she persuaded this man to take her to France. They planned to open a nightclub in Paris.''

There was a worn manila folder on the table, and he opened it, sorting through the few scraps of paper it contained. He slowly selected a narrow blue card and passed it to Cathy. It bore the name ''Le Bambou'' in white, pseudo-Chinese lettering. She turned it over and saw some smudged, barely legible writing. ''We are a great suces. Soon I can get my children. My thank to you for everything,'' it read, above an elaborately scrawled signature.

''She could barely write,'' he said. ''That was the last I heard of her.''

''How terrible.'' Cathy turned the card over again, then passed it to Monty. ''She must have suffered so much. How could our father have done such a thing?''

''He didn't really believe she was an ordinary human being, with genuine human feelings—finer feelings than his own, as it turned out. The British Empire was built on the assumption that the natives weren't quite full members of the human race, don't forget.''

He could see that the older one was taking it harder than her sister. Looking dazed, she was gazing around the room as if seeing it for the first time.

''The village is still there of course; I'll take you to it if you like. But the family left. The grandmother died, the mother and her husband moved out to Malacca where his people were, then they moved again and I lost track of them. This was, oh, twenty years ago.''

''I'd like to see the village,'' Cathy said, feeling suddenly as if her voice were sounding far away.

''Tomorrow, if you like. Best plan would be to fly over to Kuantan, on the far side of the peninsula, the East Coast. From there it's a couple of hours drive.''

As they drove back to George Town Monty felt as if she had been released from a prison that had confined her all her life.

''Of course, of course.'' She shook her head as she drove, ''Didn't you always feel it? Of course Bettina couldn't care for us—my God, I feel almost sorry for her. Keeping a secret like that all those years, no wonder she hit the bottle. She never loved us, why should she? And do you think Daddy died because the secret was going to come out?''

''Please, Monty, please—don't let's think about it too much, not yet.'' Cathy slid wearily from the car outside the hotel and they walked into the empty hallway which mysteriously held the scent of old wood and polish characteristic of an English country house.

"Don't you want to telephone Joe?" she asked Monty, suddenly wanting to be alone with the turmoil of her emotions. Her sister spent an hour reassuring herself that Paloma had accepted her absence with insulting lack of distress, then appeared in Cathy's room.

"You're really turned over, aren't you?" Monty said, noticing that Cathy was still sitting in the same dejected pose by her window.

"I don't know how I feel, to be honest, Monty. I'm just confused. Will you sleep in here tonight? I don't want to be alone."

They woke early and drank some coffee, which had the unpleasant, chicory aftertaste of the drink everywhere it was served in Malaysia. Treadwell arrived as soon as they had finished, in his own battered Morris, and drove them to the airport. The small plane rose swiftly above the mantle of cloud which blotted out the endless treetops below, and was buffeted by turbulence above the mountainous spine of the peninsula.

As it made its descent, Monty peered through the window and saw that the country was an endless expanse of vivid green with a handful of buildings and a few roads, like gleaming threads, winding through it. There were none of the deep gray wounds in the jungle which the tin workings had made in the West, and no large, sprawling towns.

At the airport they rented a Datsun, and Treadwell directed Monty, who was at the wheel, along a wide trunk road which was crowded with trucks and cars. At the outskirts of Kuantan itself, they turned along the arterial road to Kuala Lumpur, then branched off after an hour.

The road they followed was absolutely straight and barely wide enough for one vehicle. It ran across low hills, between plantations of young rubber and oil palms, and they encountered only one car coming in the opposite direction in forty minutes of fast driving.

"Here—turn right," Treadwell directed as they crossed a wide iron bridge over a muddy brown river. Monty obediently swung the wheel, and drove slowly along a wide, rutted track fringed with gleaming foliage which rose to a height of eight or nine feet. There were deep ditches on either side of the road, full of rushes whose leaves reflected the bright sunlight like sword blades.

They stopped for a group of half a dozen water buffalo ungraciously loitering across the road, their gray muzzles lifted and horns swept back as they gazed curiously at the car. One truck, weighed down with massive tree trunks, rolled slowly past them, leaving a choking cloud of red dust behind.

The natural hedge of vegetation gave way to *padi* fields, small enclosures of bright green young rice, with a few bungalows grouped at the far side.

"This is the beginning of the village," he told them. "Your house is a little farther along."

Two or three chickens strayed into the road, and again Monty stopped, to let them run to safety. They passed the rubber-processing plant, where three old cast-iron mangles stood under a rusting tin roof and dirty blankets of latex hung drying on the fence.

"Has it changed?" Monty asked their guide.

He shook his head. "Hardly at all. People have left, houses have fallen down, the village is smaller than it was—but this kind of life never changes. It's gone on the same way for hundreds of years. The rubber came, about the turn of the century, that was a change, I suppose. But a village is a village the world over. Pull in here." He indicated a gravel bay at the roadside.

There was a broad stream beside the road, and some houses, with fifty yards or so between them, which were reached by bridges made of wooden planks. Treadwell approached a woman in a tight-fitting yellow blouse and a turquoise and gold sarong, who was draping some freshly washed shirts on a low wire line. After a short conversation he returned to them.

"The house is empty, has been for a few years. Come on, I'll show it to you."

The houses on this side of the peninsula were simpler than those in the West, Cathy noticed. They were square bungalows of weathered wood, mostly undecorated, built on piles, with unglazed windows and roofs of corrugated iron streaked with rust. There was a straggling, half-dead pomegranate bush in front of the house to which Bill led them, which was almost hidden by shimmering palms.

The interior was bare and empty. Monty, oblivious of the dust which might stain her white cotton dress, sat in the doorway and looked down the short flight of steps and away to the plank bridge, sensing the tranquil spirit of the place. Simple people living simple lives had, she thought, created an air of peace there. She tried to imagine herself like the woman Bill had spoken to, hanging out the clothes she had washed in the river.

Cathy's uneven footsteps on the board floor echoed in the deep silence of the clearing around the house. To her this village represented the beginning of the long chain of trade, industry and finance. She herself was placed at the far end of the chain, the rich end, the end that controlled the whole length below it. Here in the village most of the people were trapped in subsistence agriculture, their whole lives given over to mere survival. They had nothing to bargain with in their dealings with the rest of the world. They were powerless and expendable.

"The house where we were born," she said to Monty, feeling unable to relate anything she saw to herself, or to the memory of her father.

"Did she ever have any other children?" Monty asked Treadwell suddenly.

"No, not as far as I know. I don't think she wanted any, she was so absorbed with you, with the loss of you, her memories of you, her dreams about you. And most of the taxi-dance girls got infections of one sort or another."

They decided to stay in the area for a few days, and drove back to Kuantan. Treadwell returned to Penang, leaving them with the folder containing a few hazy snapshots of themselves as infants, some old addresses and one or two scrawled notes from their mother. They checked into the Hyatt and spent most of the evening sitting side by side on the long silver beach, watching the waves of the South China Sea, strong and eerily phosphorescent, rolling in and crashing against the steep bank of sand.

"I was happy the way I was," Cathy said, her chin resting on her knees like a little girl. "And now I feel that I'm becoming someone else. It's as if someone were digging up my foundations; I feel as if I'm going to crumble."

"You'll be all right, Cathy, I'm with you, I'm always with you. You aren't going to crumble; you're going to be stronger when you've taken this in, and happier, too."

Monty took the number of a detective agency in Singapore, which Cathy had obtained, and a Chinese woman with a reassuringly unemotional manner flew up to meet them. Monty gave her the manila folder and she agreed to start work tracing their mother's family.

After a week, visiting the village every day seemed futile. They decided they had absorbed as much as they could of the atmosphere of their birthplace, and together they traveled to London.

"So—the return of the prodigal boss. What's the news on the pearls?" Henry greeted Cathy with a hug and a kiss on both cheeks as she walked into her office. He was surprised to see that she did not look in the least refreshed by her break but seemed instead to be tense and distracted.

"The pearls?" She had almost forgotten about them. "Oh, the pearls. Nothing, Henry, unless information's come in while I was away. We discovered something much more serious, but I can't tell you anything about it yet. I've got to see Jamie first. I must drive to Oxford this afternoon."

Her son, as she expected, was boyishly excited by the idea that his mother had acquired a secret identity. She did not tell him what had become of his newly discovered grandmother and played down the vileness of James's actions, in the process reassuring herself. That's what I can't accept, she mused as she drove back to London. I can't believe my father did those terrible things. I know he was the sort of man who could be foolish and who lacked judgment, but I can't believe he would be so callous as to rob a mother of her children.

When she told Henry he gave her a penetrating, startled look and at once said, "Take another week off, Cathy. This is too big for you to handle while you're working. Leave everything to me; I'll cancel my meetings and cover yours."

She shook her head emphatically. "No, I'd rather work; it's a relief to have something else to think about. Do you know what the hardest part is? Feeling I don't know my father, that I never knew him, that he conned me into loving him. I was young when he died, and it's maddening to think he was gone before I had a chance to understand him."

The next day Henry gave her a dusty brown envelope about nine inches square, stuffed with yellowed scraps of newspaper. Stamped across it was the order "Do not remove from library."

"That's your father's file from *The Daily Telegraph*," he told her. "I asked a friend to get hold of it for me. Maybe that'll be some use—there are a lot of stories about him."

The file made sad reading. Cathy stayed late in the office smoothing out the crumpled scraps of paper and following reports of her father's failed business ventures and visits to race meetings.

One of the characteristics of *The Daily Telegraph*, besides its staid conservatism, is that from its unassailable moral height it looks down on the scandals of the day and records them in far greater detail than *The Times*, or any other quality newspaper. When she began to read the newspaper reports of her father's death and the inquest that followed, Cathy at last found something to add to her new understanding of her father.

All the newspaper reports mentioned his debts. *The Telegraph*, in addition, carried a paragraph which read: *Speculation in the Continental Press has continued for some months about Lord James Bourton's connection with the Paris call girl known as Nadine, who is believed to have been murdered at the beginning of October last year.*

Cathy had moved to a penthouse apartment in the Barbican, where Monty was waiting for her. They had agreed that for the moment, they would tell Treadwell's story only to Joe, Jamie and Henry.

"There's more to this, I'm sure of it now," Cathy said, showing Monty the press cuttings. "I still don't think Treadwell told us everything. He was afraid to. Maybe it's something he only suspects."

"Daddy went to Paris regularly," Monty said, puzzled by the passion in her sister's manner. "The European scandal sheets print stories about me all the time, too. There's never anything in them. They said I was dying of leukemia last year."

"Well, I'm going to fly over and get someone to go through the newspaper archives anyway. Something may come up, who knows. I can't stand not knowing about Daddy, Monty. It's suddenly as if we've got no parents—we can't remember our real mother at all, and our father was a totally different person from the man we thought we knew."

Monty murmured sympathetic agreement, but realized that she saw the situation from a different perspective than her sister did. I'm not disturbed by the past because I live in the present, she thought. I rejected my family—or what I thought was my family—at the outset, but Cathy's still connected to it all. Now she's got to work through everything I did in all those years, the pain and struggle of knowing who you are, in a few weeks.

"We're supposed to be going to the Shahzdehs' new resort in two days," she reminded her sister gently. "Had you forgotten?"

"Damn. Yes, I had forgotten." Cathy was suddenly irritated because, lovely as she anticipated that the new L'Équipe Créole would be, the last thing she wanted to do right now was to fret away a long weekend on business entertaining. She sighed. She would have to go. Both the Prince and the Princess were important clients, and the Princess had particularly asked Cathy to introduce her sister.

The resort was an island in the Caribbean near Martinique, and Joe and Paloma flew out to join them there, which lightened the atmosphere. A gulf was opening between Cathy and Monty, and they both sensed it and were the more distressed because the discovery of the circumstances of their birth seemed to be separating them, when it should have united them. Cathy's attitude was opposed to Monty's in every respect. She could not stop thinking about her father, while Monty was impatient for news of her mother. Before leaving London she hired a second detective to search for the woman in Paris, and at the same time to pursue the rumors which had surrounded their father before his death. Joe made things easier. He took the weight of Monty's impetuous curiosity, and soothed Cathy's distress.

L'Équipe Créole was the sixth of Princess Ayeshah's resorts and one of the most beautiful. It was a large coral island fringed with natural beaches of pink and white sand which ran gently into clear water thronged with electric-bright colored fish. The central buildings, of local gray-brown honeycomb stone, were at the crest of the island's central hill, and the Princess's guests were accommodated in bungalows in the traditional Caribbean style, with soaring steep-pitched roofs of pale pickled pine, under which pockets of cool air were created.

A thicket of frangipani had been planted downwind of the central hall, and as the guests assembled for the welcoming reception, its sweet vanillalike fragrance was carried to them on the warm breeze. Despite the beauty and luxury around them, Cathy was unable to relax, and felt her exhausted emotions assaulted by the hedonistic atmosphere.

Princess Ayeshah was not accompanied by her husband, who had been detained in Paris on business. She wore a high-necked, long-sleeved gown of ruched white crepe de chine, and her hair, as always, was styled in a French pleat, which had grown fuller and more shapely in response to changing fashion. When she saw Cathy she gave her a warm welcome.

"May I introduce my sister?" Cathy stepped back to present Monty, who shook the Princess's hand and began to praise the beauty of the island just as Cathy had done when she had first met the woman in Greece.

"I'm delighted you could come, I have wanted to meet you for so long," the older woman rejoined, giving Monty a formal embrace of welcome. "I was hoping we would have time for a private talk before you leave?"

"Yes, of course," Monty said, and they agreed to meet the next morning. Monty then attached herself to the Princess and followed her as she made her way graciously around the room. Cathy felt tired, unnaturally so, and she soon left the party and went back to her bungalow. There she lay on the bed but could not sleep, tossing and turning unhappily for a couple of hours until Monty appeared.

"Oh, Cathy, I'm sorry—I was enjoying myself, I didn't think that you might not be up to it."

"I can't stop thinking." Cathy sat up against the cool white linen pillows. "I keep thinking about Mummy and Daddy, the

585

people we called Mummy and Daddy, anyway. Who knows what they really are to us?''

"Cheer up, Cathy, please. Aren't you just a little bit glad that you aren't Bettina's daughter? She wasn't the best of mothers, was she, such a selfish, cruel woman.''

"You don't understand!'' Cathy, who seldom raised her voice, almost shouted at her sister. "We can't say that, we've no right to make that kind of judgment, we don't know anything about her. But Bettina isn't important to me, it's Daddy I care about—I can't accept that he lied to us all those years. How could he look at me every day of his life and *know* and never tell us?''

She fretted sleeplessly all night. At last she slept, but badly; she dreamed vividly but could remember nothing, and woke as the birds were calling at the beginning of the sudden Caribbean dawn.

She called for coffee, and was surprised when the telephone rang again almost as soon as she put it down.

"We have a telex for you, Miss Bourton; it came in overnight. Would you like us to send it round with the coffee?''

"Yes, please.''

The telex was from Mr. Phillips at Garrard's. BINGO, it read. PEARLS ANSWERING DESCRIPTION OF YOURS FISHED JANUARY SMALL INDONESIA COMPANY. SAWA TRADING FLORES SUNDA. LAST SEEN IN POSSESSION OF COMPANY OWNER. PURSUING FURTHER INQUIRIES. PHILLIPS.

Cathy had again almost forgotten about the pearls, but now her interest revived. She and Monty had tried to unravel a trivial mystery and discovered something far more serious, perhaps fatal to her own inner serenity. The question of the pearls was something which might drive away the brooding clouds in her mind, for a while at least.

Her new toy, her portable telex, invited her to action. She sent a message to Henry in London asking for everything he could find out about the Sawa Trading Company, then paced her terrace with impatience, planning to wait until Paloma was awake and she could decently invade the intimacy of her sister's family.

To calm her nerves, she put on her new white bikini and the white crushed-silk robe which matched it, checking the effect approvingly in the mirror before setting out to stroll to the pool for a swim. A hummingbird, like a flying emerald, was breakfasting among the yellow alamanda flowers.

The island's pièce de résistance was the swimming pool, a gleaming blue-green lake landscaped to resemble a jungle rock basin, with a high waterfall at one end and ferns gushing from hollows in the gray-black rocks. Someone else was already in the water and, vast as the inviting expanse of aquamarine was, Cathy had wanted it all to herself. She paused, irritated. A woman, also in a white bikini, was swimming lazily where the water was deepest.

Cathy recognized the Princess, and was at once intrigued. The Princess was so elusive, so protective of her own privacy, that the opportunity to watch her like this was like the chance of watching a cheetah at a watering hole.

How extraordinary her body was, Cathy noticed. The princess's age was another of the great mysteries about her. From what one knew of her, she must be around fifty at least, yet she was as firm-fleshed and graceful as a polo pony. Cathy watched in admiration as the high-breasted figure pulled itself out of the water and walked, with an indefinably seductive waver, to the springboard at Cathy's side of the pool.

The Princess made a showy swallow dive, then swam around to the poolside and began to walk toward the board a second time. Cathy had the overpowering impression of watching herself, just as she had in the dream she remembered from the time she stayed with Monty in Arizona. All that seemed very long ago now.

This time the Princess stood poised at the end of the board, an erect figure full of energy like an Art Deco statuette. Cathy noticed that there was a dark shadow just above the back of the right knee, and her hand unconsciously strayed to her own birthmark. I must remember to point out to Monty that the Princess has a mark like that, she told herself. Maybe then she'll stop worrying about Paloma.

At length she grew tired of spying on her hostess, and took a buggy down to a cove where the sea swimming was not impeded by the inconvenience of coral close to the surface. She swam for almost an hour, enjoying the physical and mental relaxation, then showered, changed and went to find her sister.

The atmosphere in Monty's bungalow was electric. From the way that Joe looked sharply up as she entered, Cathy knew that they had been talking about her, and at once felt resentment.

Monty was ravishing this morning, vibrant and completely alive, but she was anxious as well and kissed Cathy with more than usual warmth. She wore a loose white dress with white leggings, and was cradling Paloma against one hip.

"You needn't worry about Paloma's birthmark, because Princess Ayeshah has one just like it," Cathy told her in a cheerful tone.

The words were like bullets. As soon as she had said them Cathy realized the implication. Both Joe and Monty looked at her intently, then Monty, without speaking, put Paloma down on the floor and passed two slips of perforated paper to her sister, a pair of telexes—the one from Garrard's and the one she had not seen, from Henry in London.

"Apologies for invading the privacy of your mail—I came to find you this morning and met the boy delivering that." Monty indicated the new message. "And then I read the other one."

The telex was from Henry. NO PROBLEM RE SAWA TRADING PART OF SHAHZDEH GROUP SUBSIDIARY OF QUADRANT HOLDINGS. SMALL IMPORT EXPORT OUTFIT ACTIVITIES INCLUDE FISHING PEARLS, TORTOISESHELL, ETC REGISTERED UK 1980. A list of directors followed, and the message ended WHAT GIVES HENRY.

Cathy raised her eyes to her sister's, all at once feeling cold and weak. "She couldn't possibly be. Impossible. *Impossible*. No, Monty, I won't believe it. Anyway, she's Iranian."

"The Prince is Iranian," Joe pointed out. "She could be anything. Does she ever talk about Iran?"

"We've got to see her, ask her—at least, there isn't much doubt that we have her to thank for the pearls," Monty said, "But there's something else, Cathy."

"What?" She saw the somber look in her sister's eyes and felt afraid.

"I talked to the Princess a long time last night. The minute she spoke to me I knew there was something I recognized about her. I thought it was just the sort of recognition you get from seeing a face in the papers. But it wasn't. It was her voice. I know it, I'd know it anywhere, I'll never forget it. That woman may have given us the pearls, and that woman may be our mother, but she's also Madame Bernard—or whoever that woman was who so generously decided to save a perfect stranger's life when she met me in Paris."

Cathy leaned back against the wooden rail of the balcony, the brilliant sea glittering behind her, and rubbed her eyes. Rapidly her quick, analytical mind assembled the new information beside what she already knew, and she began to see the shape of the truth which was yet to be discovered.

"We must be sure," she said.

"I *am* sure, Cathy. I could never forget that voice. It sounds like metal."

"No, no, we need proof, absolute proof."

"I think you're right," Joe said. "You've uncovered so much already, but you need to be certain before you do anything."

"I want to see her, I want to go to her now—think of all the time we've already wasted. . . ." Monty said.

"Yes—think of it," snapped Cathy suddenly, "and ask yourself why? She's known me for years and never said anything. She knew you, too, and never said anything. Oh, maybe she hinted, but she didn't come out with it. There must be a reason for that, and it can't be a pleasant one.''

''But look what she did for us—my life, your business—she saved them both. Doesn't that prove that she loved us all along.''

Cathy shook her head violently, her wet hair swinging against her cheeks. ''No—all it proves to me is that she wanted us to love her.''

''You're frightened of her,'' Monty accused.

''No, I'm not—I'm only frightened for us.'' Cathy walked into the cool of the room, away from the harsh morning sunlight. ''I want to leave here now, go back to London, and find out everything else, until I'm satisfied that the whole thing is out in the open.''

Monty followed her sister, feeling bewildered and angry. ''But why don't we simply meet her and ask her?''

''For the same reason that she never met us, and told us— twenty years ago, when our father died.''

''I think you need to know more, Monty.'' Joe swept Paloma into his arms as she marched unsteadily toward the balcony. ''The way this woman has acted to you is ambivalent, like she wants one thing but her nerve fails her when she goes for it.''

Reluctantly, Monty agreed to return to London. They prepared to leave immediately, and Monty sat down to write the Princess a note to explain why she could not keep her appointment.

''What shall I say?'' she asked Cathy, her mind blank.

''Urgent family business,'' Cathy suggested, her face hard.

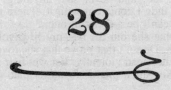

SUNDAY, THE SIXTH OF OCTOBER, 1963, WAS A DULL, OVERCAST and humid day. At Longchamp racecourse, the glittering crowd assembled for the Prix de l'Arc de Triomphe sweated slightly in their formal dress. The dazzling gaiety which normally pervaded the world's most brilliant race meeting seemed to be subdued by the sulky climate. The towering figure of President de Gaulle was, unusually, absent from the scene, as was his dapper foreign minister who was in Washington enduring a distinctly cool reception by President Kennedy.

There was no British horse in the race, which was also unusual, and in consequence very few British accents were to be heard among the crowd's excited clamor. The British were staying away for a reason in addition to their lack of national interest in the race. An immense scandal, involving prostitutes, politicians, aristocrats and a Russian spy, had toppled the Conservative government. A display of hedonistic behavior a few months after the Profumo affair was considered by most of Longchamp's British devotees to be in bad taste.

One Englishman remained oblivious to the sensitive moral climate in his country.

"Time to take a look at the runners, don't you think?" Lord James Bourton put down his champagne and reached for his field glasses, indicating to the twelve men who had accepted his invitation to share his bank's box at Longchamp that he intended to move down to the paddock and watch the horses parade before the race.

"Good idea," assented a clipped voice, and the narrow frame of Eddie Shrewton appeared between the glass doors which separated the box's seats from the hospitality area behind.

"Right—anyone else?" James beamed his jagged smile, disguising his resentment at having to waste his talents as a host on a man so difficult to amuse. Shrewton had come to Paris with three other directors from the old-established Migatto group, whom James knew well. He was more than ten years older than James and was being spoken of as the group's next chairman.

James already knew him, of course, in the distant manner in which every British aristocrat knew the others, as a name, a title, a face and a set of connections. After twenty-four hours of close personal acquaintanceship, however, James disliked the man; not seriously, because James did nothing seriously, but distinctly. Eddie Shrewton was joyless, earnest and reserved. He seemed older than he was, not only because his hair was prematurely gray but also because his tall, thin body was ungainly. In addition, his morning suit looked shabby and hung badly from his stiff shoulders, and he rarely smiled.

He had not placed a bet on the race, barely entered into the lengthy discussions about the riders' abilities, the horses' forms, the going on the course and the hopes of the owners, and was only now showing enthusiasm for the stroll to the paddock because, James plainly recognized, he was bored by the entire proceedings. The man had no gift for frivolity; furthermore—and this was the nub of James's distaste—he had an air of substance and consequence which James knew he himself would never be able to acquire. Most of the time, James was able to distract himself from the knowledge that he was a failure, but it was a difficult trick to pull off with a man like Eddie Shrewton nearby.

As they joined the crowd which streamed through the starkly graceful interior of the new grandstand James did his best to make conversation.

"Nasty business with Relko after the Derby," he said.

"Was there? I didn't know."

"Devil of a fuss about it—dope test was positive. Jockey Club inquiry only finished last week."

"Oh, really." James gave up. The man knew nothing of the sport of kings, and showed no inclination to learn. The only course left was elementary instruction.

"There he is now," he said, indicating Relko on the far side of the white-railed enclosure. The horse was dancing nervously sideways as if on tiptoe, his gleaming brown sides already darkened with sweat. "Brilliant horse in his day, made a very good showing at the Prix Royal Oak here a few weeks ago. Crowd cheered him all the way to the unsaddling enclosure—not surprising he's the favorite today."

James watched with interest as the horses were led into the ring one by one. His passion for the turf had amused him now for seven years or so, but his interest was waning now that two of his London bookmakers would no longer allow him credit.

However, he found the Arc, as the British called France's most important international race, impossible to miss. The whole of Paris seemed to stream into the Bois de Boulogne and gather in the hope, often rewarded, of celebrating the supremacy of French bloodstock. The women were so impeccably elegant; the course in its light woodland setting made such a charming picture; the *turfistes* were so passionately partisan as they told each other that Relko was the finest horse ever ridden; even the jockeys' silks seemed to have a clarity of color which was missing at the English meetings. Longchamp was more than ever the scene of beauty, breeding and high emotion which Raoul Dufy had delighted to paint.

Since that unpleasant day three years ago when he had been tricked into a meeting with the Princess Ayeshah, James had avoided Paris, but the lure of the Arc finally proved irresistible. Nevertheless, he looked around with unease, fearing the sight of his enemy among the ferociously chic women who preened like fabulous birds of paradise beside their dark-garbed escorts. The custom at Longchamp was that while the horses paraded inside the paddock, a parallel display of impeccably groomed, highly bred and savagely competitive animals took place outside the rails.

Lord James Bourton was so unassailably secure in his sense of social and racial superiority to the woman who had borne his children that he had dealt with her threat by ignoring it. The notion that a peasant woman, an ignorant, primitive, heathen creature, no matter how well-dressed she might appear, could possibly cause him damage, seemed quite impossible. He could not believe it; he could barely acknowledge the facts of their distant association. His confidence was a quicksand which swallowed up the truth and left no trace of it to disturb his mental equilibrium.

Only a deeply buried core of guilt remained to undermine his pleasure, and it produced merely a momentary tremor of discomfort which passed as soon as James noticed that the horse on which he had placed a substantial sum, Le Mesnil, was being led into the paddock. He had had a tip that the three-year-old had recovered his form after losing badly at Chantilly in the spring, and had put three bets of a thousand pounds on him to win with separate bookmakers. With odds of 13 to 1, Le Mesnil could make him a useful sum.

In the sixteen years since he had claimed his inheritance, James had sunk rapidly into debt. His spending on pleasure and debauchery had been high and his business judgment poor. After Ayeshah and Hussain had indicated that they knew of his precarious financial position he had been sufficiently frightened to take the final step of mortgaging his home and consolidating his debts with a single loan company. Money had no real significance for James, and he would apply his mind to his finances only when forced.

Recently he had found a more attractive way to redeem his position and that had added to his desire to visit Paris again this year. Through his racing friends he had met a young Frenchman whose family was trapped in Algeria by the new government's vicious restrictions on foreign exchange. A French national who wished to leave the new-hatched state could take only the equivalent of thirty U.S. dollars with him. All the French bank accounts in Algeria had been frozen.

After a very successful day at the Cheltenham Gold Cup the previous year, James had spent a long night drinking with the anguished young man, consoling him for the fact that his family, after seventy years of planting olive groves and growing oranges in the colony they had loved, was now to be trapped in poverty in a hostile new country.

At last the Frenchman had asked for his help, and James had agreed to import a succession of Berber carpets, which would make their way to Casablanca from the family's most southerly estate in Algeria. Stitched into the center of each tightly rolled bundle was a long paper-wrapped cylinder, a cache of gold napoleons.

James opened an account in a false name at a small private bank in London, and stored the gold in the vault, ready for the *pieds-noirs* whenever they chose to quit Algeria, and far from the scrutiny of the French or Algerian authorities. In the meantime, he took a handsome rake-off from each consignment. The transaction allowed him to service his debts and enjoy his normal lavish life-style without extending his attenuated credit any further.

Le Mesnil sauntered gracefully around the paddock, swishing his tail and mouthing his bit, showing the confident, settled air of a winner in every step. His groom had sensibly separated him from his bay stablemate Sanctus, who was playing up nervously as usual. Behind Sanctus walked Baron Guy de Rothschild's Exbury, a small, light-framed chestnut with three white socks, who calmly ignored the restless prancing ahead of him. James smiled to himself, reminded of his daughters by the contrasting demeanor of the two colts; Sanctus, full of ability which his jockey could barely control, was like Monty, while Exbury, a pretty animal, ostentatiously cool, with a steady, level gaze, had exactly Cathy's temperament.

"They'll be off down the course soon—last chance to put some money on," James prompted his prim companion. Eddie Shrewton was gazing at the horses with little interest. "See anything you fancy, Eddie?"

"Little chestnut looks useful," he answered, indicating Exbury, who was standing quietly while his jockey mounted.

"Rothschild hasn't had a winner since 1934, but Exbury's beaten last year's champion so I'd say he's a likely contender," James advised. "He ran very well in the Coronation Cup, too. Whether he's got the quality to pass Relko's another matter—but you could back worse, I'd say."

They returned to the box and Shrewton telephoned a modest bet on Exbury.

Sanctus had to be led down to the start, and Relko tore past him in a lather of sweat. Exbury, James noticed with irritation, strode out well as he passed the *moulin*. He considered a last-minute bet on the Rothschild chestnut, but his dislike of Eddie Shrewton held him back.

"They'll be starting them in stalls next year," he informed his party as the race began. "The French will try anything new."

"Makes sense to improve the course as much as possible. Why not if they've got the money to invest in the sport? The stand is superb—makes Longchamp a lot more pleasant than Ascot," Shrewton observed as the runners, led by Relko, approached the gentle hill near the beginning of the course.

James did not answer him and followed the horses intently with his binoculars. Relko dropped back and another horse, a pacemaker rather than a serious contender, took the lead as they crested the hill. Sanctus faltered on the downhill run, and as they approached the straight, Le Mesnil took the lead and the crowd gave a roar.

"He's well on his way home now," shouted James in delight as Le Mesnil drew away from the tightly grouped horses behind him.

Two furlongs from the finish Relko's jockey asked his mount for a final effort, but the favorite had spent his force too early in the race and had nothing left to give. Le Mesnil led by a clear distance of eight lengths. With an unfaltering, strong stride, his head up, his nostrils flared and his jockey barely needing to encourage him with an occasional sight of the whip, he bore down on the finish.

Exbury's jockey at last gave his horse a light, backhanded touch which set the little chestnut alight. The horse running alongside him also surged ahead, but Exbury, as if moving into an extra gear, pulled away from the rest, showing an astonishing surge of acceleration. He reached the darker horse a hundred meters from the line, amid hysterical cheering from the crowd. James sat down in silence as Exbury streaked past the winning post, a clear two lengths ahead of his horse, Le Mesnil.

"Good show," he said to Shrewton, shaking his hand and disguising his own keen disappointment with the ease of a lifetime's training. "Damn good show. Genuine champion, magnificent race. I'll take your lead in the future, Eddie."

A pink flush of embarrassed pleasure colored Eddie Shrewton's monochrome complexion as he accepted the rest of the party's congratulations. Relko, the favorite, who had lost his backers millions of francs, galloped home to jeers and catcalls from the crowd.

"Bloody Frogs—no sense of sportsmanship," said James. "Come on, let's go and see Guy in his moment of glory."

That evening James led his party to a hostelry close to the Bois which was celebrated for its discretion rather than its cuisine. It was an ugly Belle Epoque mansion with a large but ill-kept garden. Kitchen aromas percolated into the high-ceilinged dining room, which echoed with the clatter of plates and cutlery, while upstairs the bedrooms were furnished with massive four-poster beds whose once-opulent hangings never lost their odor of damp, moth and stale cigar smoke. James's custom was to finish the Longchamp weekend with a dinner in the private salon, a room with French doors to the garden and a high, vaulted ceiling supported by exposed beams, which had a vaguely ecclesiastical ambiance.

His guests would be joined around the oval table by a dozen of Madame Bernard's girls; after supper the waiters would withdraw and leave them completely alone; there would be more drinking, teasing, shrieks of laughter, perhaps a little performance if one of the girls had a specialty, and then the party would disperse according to their individual tastes. The only rule James imposed was that no one should lapse so far from decency as to try to take one of the hookers back to the Ritz; James liked to be known at the Ritz, and did not care to risk his standing by inviting a scandal.

The girls arrived in four low-riding black Citroëns. They had been taking Benzedrine and were raucously gay, swooping on the men with cries of delight, winding their slender arms around their necks and demanding their names while they nibbled earlobes and loosened ties. Madame Bernard's people knew James's tastes and the last out of the cars was a tall, lissom girl in a gold-lamé sheath dress, carrying a white-leather bandbox. She had a matt-brown skin and aquiline features which proclaimed her North African origin as clearly as the harsh intonations of her accent. She had evidently been told to pay him particular attention, and took no interest in the other men.

"Nadine is superb at the *danse du ventre*," the brunette hanging on Shrewton's arm whispered to James through scarlet lips. "It's something you should not miss. I'm sure she has brought her costume."

"No doubt she has." James smiled into Nadine's sloe eyes and gave her slim waist a squeeze, but he felt boredom steal upon him like the autumn mist that was rising from the cold dew-pearled lawn that encircled the building. The evening would be entirely predictable and he found that he had little appetite for any feature of it.

The truth was that James had aged since his encounter with the Princess; it was as if a decade or more had caught up with him all at once. The change was barely visible in his springy black hair or his dark eyes which sparkled in their network of deepening wrinkles. The force of his charm was undimmed.

Inside, however, his spirit was faltering. The sustained mental effort of canceling the aggressively renewed memory of Khatijah was draining him. His infectious enthusiasm had waned; sexual gratification seemed barely worth the effort and he could be turned off by the merest unpleasant detail of an encounter—cheap scent, the impression that he was being watched or a woman's offhand manner.

For the past eighteen months James had been keeping a West Indian prostitute in Bayswater, for comfort as much as for sex. She was a cheerful woman who amused him with her down-to-earth manner and was so plump she made him think of a dark-brown Michelin man. His mistrust of women was increasing with age; more and more he preferred the familiar, if coarse, pleasure of the whore he knew to the more refined delights which might be promised by a stranger.

He had drunk champagne all day and had a strong thirst. Instead of wine he drank brandy and soda with the meal, finally emptying the siphon. He handed the empty container in its wire-mesh covering to a waiter and demanded another, but it was slow to arrive and he continued to drink the cognac neat, telling himself it was fine vintage spirit and not as injurious to his constitution as cheap brandy would have been. Before long he had an ugly headache.

He noticed Eddie Shrewton at the far end of the expanse of white damask that was now stained with claret and littered with cigar ash. He was as withdrawn and disinterested as ever and would no doubt shortly slip away back to the hotel. James pursed his lips with contempt for the thin-blooded creature whose favor he was required to court.

Nadine emerged through the service door, and was greeted with whoops of delight from the diners. She had exchanged her gold sheath for her dance costume, a lurid wrapping of chiffon veils over a green sequined girdle, and her wrists and ankles clashed with heavy brass bracelets. Two waiters swiftly removed the tablecloth, and she climbed onto the scarred oak surface beneath and began to undulate slowly from one man to another, twisting her wrists and twitching her pelvis rhythmically. Whining Arab music sounded from the walnut Gramophone cabinet.

James leaned back in his chair, an uncomfortable carved Gothic affair upholstered in red plush, and gazed vacantly toward the gyrating body through the dense pall of blue smoke that hung above the table. He realized that he was very drunk. He closed his eyes for a moment and had the sensation that the room was swinging to and fro.

Two or three of the men were on their feet, tucking hundred-franc notes beneath the slight overhang of taut brown flesh at the rim of the sequined girdle. Not to be outdone, James flourished a thousand francs and advanced upon her. He crushed the money against her shimmering belly and the girl sank to her knees on the table in front of him, her supple brown body shuddering lasciviously as she began to lean backward. Her small, high breasts shivered in the confines of their sequined harness.

The tempo of the music increased and another whisper of transparent fabric dropped from the girl's coral-tipped fingers. Now there were only three left, two tied in loose knots over her hipbones to accentuate their movement, and one draped between them.

The dance was probably as old as lust itself, and James had seen it too many times to be moved, even by this accomplished and nubile artist. He closed his eyes once more and let boredom and brandy submerge his consciousness.

He came around to feel the cool, damp nighttime air in his

face and his feet dragging awkwardly across the gravel of the driveway. Concerned not to scratch his black patent shoes he coordinated his legs sufficiently to stumble between the two people who, with his arms around their shoulders, were half carrying him.

A car door was opened and he fell into the rear seat of the vehicle. His legs were inert again, but someone lifted them inside the car and shut the door. There were voices, then other men got into the front of the car. He heard the staccato voice of Eddie Shrewton telling the driver to take them to the Ritz, then lost consciousness once more.

The noise of the traffic in Paris is distinctive. While in most cities the individual notes of the vehicles on the streets blend into one chord, in Paris every engine has its individual voice; like the cacophony of jungle insects, the engines shrill and grate in defense of their territory. Against the background hum of distant cars it is possible to pick out the prosperous sound of a Peugeot, like the belching of a well-fed lion, or the unmistakable sewing-machine clatter of a *Deux-chevaux*, accompanied often by a screech of brakes, a squeal of tires and the clapping of the side vents as another little Citroën bucks awkwardly away from a near-collision.

The traffic sound can be heard even in the hushed depths of the Ritz, and James knew where he was before he opened his eyes. He could tell, by the rosy glow of blood through his closed lids, that it was daytime. He felt as if his skull were being crushed in a red-hot vise. That was the brandy. He had been a fool to drink so much of it. He was getting too old to drink as he used to.

He became aware of two other sources of discomfort; his mouth was hideously dry and his dessicated lips were sticking to his teeth, and his bladder was full. James lay still as long as he could, trying to summon some saliva to moisten his lips. At last he decided he must move, and rolled off the bed onto his hands and knees on the thick carpet. He gained his feet shakily and walked to the bathroom.

When he had urinated and drunk some water, he decided to clean his teeth. That done he felt better and walked back to the bedroom, where the girl on the bed beside him lay spread-eagled on her stomach in a pose of abandoned relaxation, her arms flung out above her head. Her naked body was completely uncovered and with automatic thoughtfulness, he tucked the gold satin quilt around her; the girl was quite chilled. She must have kicked the cover off hours ago.

PEARLS

He sat for a long time on the chaise longue at the foot of the bed, sipping water and collecting his devastated wits. Finally he checked his watch. It was 1:15 in the afternoon. There was no particular need to hurry, but he had chartered a private plane for his party, and they would need to be on their way by 3:30.

There was a knock at the door, an imperious double rap which commanded James to rise to his feet and cross the small, oval sitting room of his suite to answer it.

"Ah—you're up and about at last." Eddie Shrewton, in a dark blue suit which fitted no better than his morning dress, swayed awkwardly from one foot to another outside the door. "How are you feeling?"

"Bloody awful," James smiled broadly. "I think I have a pneumatic drill in my head. Come in, come in. I was just going to order some coffee."

"I'll do it." The older man called room service with an air of authority, then turned to the pitiful creature beside him.

Lord Shrewton had no more admiration for James than James had for him, but expended less energy on such emotional considerations. Bourton was an amusing fellow, he could see that, but he made an ass of himself so often over women, drink or money that Shrewton's sense of humor was unequal to the task of appreciating him. Worse, there was something unsound about him. The older man's instinct was that James was not to be trusted but, since he had no facts to support the hunch, he kept it strictly to himself.

"If you tell me what the orders of the day are I'll start getting things moving," Shrewton said, seeing that James was unshaven and still in his evening clothes. "The other fellas are downstairs having a spot of lunch."

"Not to worry, old man. We've got all the time in the world." Now that his senses were returning to normal, James felt nauseated. He was aware that his hands were shaking.

Eddie Shrewton was irritated. Bourton was certainly in no state to cope with the travel arrangements and although he clearly had no work of any consequence to be doing in London, that was not the case with most of his guests.

James felt that he was being discourteous and collected what strength remained. "I'll get the cars laid on for two hours' time." He stood up and looked distractedly around the room for his itinerary. "Damn. I know I put it down somewhere."

Briskly, Shrewton began to lift cushions and open drawers. They moved into the bedroom, and James again saw the sleeping girl. Bewilderment halted him in his search for the travel documents—he had no recollection of taking the girl back to the hotel—indeed he could remember very little about the previous night—but one of the iron rules of his life was that he never took girls back to the Ritz.

He did not care to court Eddie Shrewton's disapproval by asking him if the girl had ridden back with him in the car. However she had got there, getting her out of the hotel unseen was an important priority. She had slept enough.

James sat heavily on the bed and shook the girl's shoulder. "Nadine. Nadine, my dear. Wake up, Nadine. Time to go home now."

She did not stir.

"Nadine. Come along, dear. Wake up, now. Nadine."

Eddie Shrewton overcame his distaste and embarrassment and crossed the room to stand over James and the woman.

"Didn't you give us some sermon about not taking girls back to the hotel?" he asked, trying not to phrase the question as an accusation.

"Damn right. It's just not done, in my book."

The older man's pale hand reached out and pulled the tangle of hair off the girl's face. He touched her cheek with his fingertips, then her neck.

"You fool, Bourton. You bloody fool. She's dead—can't you see?"

James jumped off the bed and stared in horror at the body. "But I didn't . . . But I was . . . Oh God, I never . . . I couldn't . . . Eddie, I hope you don't think . . ."

"No. I don't. You were blind drunk. You couldn't lift a finger. You couldn't have screwed a rat in that condition, much less done this."

With a gesture that was so careful it was almost tender, he swept the girl's waterfall of dark hair to one side and tried to turn her over, but her left arm, which was hanging over the edge of the bed, would not move. When he investigated, Shrewton found that it was fixed to the iron frame of the bed by a pair of steel handcuffs. Around her neck, tightly embedded in the horribly contused flesh, was James's black-satin tie, which he removed and put in his pocket.

There was a discreet tap at the door of the suite and Shrewton sprinted to it immediately, closing the bedroom door deftly as he went. He took the tray with coffee from the waiter, glanced at the bill, then said in English, raising his voice to impress his meaning upon the foreigner, "This is charged to the wrong room. I asked you to charge it to my room—change the number on the bill, will you? Here." He gave the number, and watched while the man altered the figure on the top right-hand corner of the slip of paper, gave him a tip of exactly 15 percent and shut the door without undue haste.

"Where did those girls come from? D'you call someone, know someone?"

James was standing against the wall by the bedroom door, as if trying to get as far away as possible from the dead girl. "What?"

"Don't you see what this is?" James looked at him with a dull expression, and Shrewton realized that between his hang-over and the shock he was completely stupefied. With firm gentleness, he led the younger man out of the bedroom, shut the door, and made him sit on the gray sofa in the little salon.

"You didn't touch that woman, but we'll have a devil of a job proving it. This is a setup. Someone wants to blackmail you, or maybe me, or maybe all of us. They killed the girl and put her in bed with you. Now—where did she come from?"

"That's it—Madame Bernard." James's slumped body straightened. "I'll call her number—they'll know what to do; they must have got out of this kind of jam before, or worse, I shouldn't wonder."

He tried to stand up and reached toward the telephone on a side table, but Shrewton pushed him firmly back into the depths of the sofa. "Don't be a complete ass, Bourton. That madam, whoever she is, must be involved in this, don't you see? She or someone she's working with. Have you—ah—have you had dealings with her in the past?"

James nodded.

"Any trouble? A grudge, a vendetta, some kind of deal that didn't work out . . . ?" His voice tailed off. Eddie Shrewton could not imagine what kind of transaction with a call-girl agency could have gone so sour that the guilty party would be framed for murder. He could, however, imagine that there was no degree of stupidity of which James would be incapable.

James shook his head. "Nothing. Always a very amicable association. Absolutely confidential, never a whisper. Not cheap of course . . ."

The other man made a gesture of impatience. Shrewton knew there was only one thing he could do, and it must be done quickly before the hotel staff became aware of the situation. He left James with instructions not to open the door to anyone except him, ran down the corridor to his own suite and made one telephone call, to the ambassador's private line at the British Embassy.

The ambassador, his contemporary at Eton, understood instantly the implications of the call. "I'd better get round there now," he said, as calmly as if agreeing to an impromptu game of tennis.

"Is there an embassy physician—trustworthy sort?"

"Certainly. I'll hunt him out and be over within the hour."

The two men were announced forty minutes later, and Shrewton took them to James's suite. The ambassador was small, plump and neatly made; his waist was so much wider than the lower part of his body, and his feet so small, that he had the appearance of a toy clown. The doctor, who was French, was older than Shrewton had expected, white-haired, slow-moving and hesitant.

With difficulty because the corpse was stiffening, they turned the girl onto her back and the four men instantly averted their eyes as her torn, bloody stomach was revealed. The smooth-skinned belly that had rippled sensuously twelve hours earlier was a mass of thin, precise cuts.

"Ritual murder," the doctor explained as he carefully patted the shredded flesh with febrile fingers. "Very common among the Algerians, Tunisians, a lot of the Africans. But it wasn't done here, there isn't enough blood. There's an artery nicked. She'd have poured blood when it was done. But you can see the sheets." He spread the crumpled linen flat, showing them the extent of the bloodstains. "They'd have been soaked if that had been done here."

"She died from being strangled?" inquired Shrewton, his voice hushed by the horror of the sight.

"Hard to say definitely without a postmortem, but I should imagine so. And she was moved quickly—I can tell that because the body fat changes after a certain time and retains the traces of pressure from the way the body was lying at the time of death. She was killed somewhere else, then brought here. A very clever job, but it won't stand up in court."

"Whose name is the suite booked in?" The ambassador stood up and walked to the windows to draw the curtain, then dropped his short arms to his sides, realizing that there was no point.

"Bourton here. He was with me all night."

"In your suite?"

"Eventually. We were out drinking until late. He keeled over in the corridor and I put him to bed on the couch in my room."

James, still stunned by the shock, stared dumbly at his feet to cover his amazement. He had expected Eddie Shrewton to be earnestly, pedantically, faithfully and maliciously truthful about the entire affair.

"So he was with you the whole time?"

"Until we came here this morning and found her."

"All night?"

"I couldn't sleep so I was pretty much awake all the time. I give you my word as a gentleman, he was under my eyes the entire period."

The ambassador nodded, apparently satisfied. "I'll call the Minister, see what we can do. Don't touch anything and stay where I can get you on the telephone at once."

Shrewton led James back to his own suite and began patiently to phone London, calling his own office, his home and James's office with news of their delayed return. Cars were organized and the rest of the party was sent home knowing nothing of what had taken place. By the end of the afternoon half a dozen men in white overalls arrived with a stretcher, an ambulance and a hacksaw, and removed the body of the girl under the doctor's direction.

The two men spent a somber evening together. James, still numb with shock, was moved to a room connected to his companion's suite and fell into a deep sleep just after nine o'clock. In the morning the ambassador's car called for them, and they had a meeting at the embassy with an unsmiling civil servant, who regretted, at length but without much sincerity, that such a crime could have been committed on French soil.

By the following afternoon they were on their way to the airport.

"Eddie—you saved me. You don't know what kind of mess . . ."

"I can guess. I don't want you to tell me. And don't thank me. I was in as much trouble as you were and anything I did was for myself as much as you. From what I hear, you haven't got much more to lose in life, but I'm not quite in the same position." The man was so lacking in humor that when he did make an attempt at levity it passed almost unnoticed.

James fell silent in the corner of the car and forced himself to look at the gray streets. Whenever he shut his eyes the ghastly sight of the girl's lacerated flesh projected itself into his mind. He could not banish the image.

The doctor had been wrong. The tracery of cuts was not an indication of an Arab ritual murder. The sliced skin had fallen into a pattern which James recognized instantly, a pattern which he had seen every day of his life; the Bourton coat of arms had been carved into the woman's body.

For three months James was overpowered by the certainty that a vengeful destiny was pursuing him. The girl he had thoughtlessly abandoned seventeen years ago had transformed herself into a pitiless Nemesis. The deepest terror of his subconscious, the female destroyer seeking to consume him, had become flesh. His years of carefree, forgetful pleasure were at an end and the final reckoning was inescapable.

James had no doubt at all that Ayeshah had arranged the girl's murder, that she had tried to frame him and would then perhaps have offered to procure his liberty in exchange for her children. He had escaped her only by the good fortune of Eddie Shrewton's concern, but he was still in danger.

Two days after his return to England the French papers reported that the mutilated body of a prostitute had been found on waste ground on the outskirts of Paris. This was such a common occurrence that it merited only a few lines in *Le Monde*.

The rumors began immediately and they were accurate, specific and aimed at James. An English *milord* had been involved in the prostitute's murder; she had been killed at a debauched private party attended by a dozen prominent Englishmen at the end of the Longchamp weekend, and he had carved his armorial bearings on her body. Coming so soon after the Profumo scandal, the stories confirmed the long-established European conception of a degenerate British aristocracy and the Continental newspapers took them up with enthusiasm.

Then a photograph appeared, a blurred but recognizable shot of a disheveled James brandishing a thousand-franc note under the dancing girl's bare stomach.

Clippings from the scandal sheets began to arrive in the mail at James's office, and he ordered his secretary not to open his letters. He tried to telephone Eddie Shrewton, but could not get through; the secretary was embarrassed, but had clearly been told to block James's calls.

James lived every day on the edge of panic. His heart beat irregularly, shuddering in painful palpitations which left him breathless. He felt constantly cold and tired, sweaty flushes would strike him without warning. He lost weight and his complexion grew waxy and bloated. He tried to drink to blot out his anxiety, but his tolerance for alcohol vanished and he began to black out whenever he drank to excess.

In November, two officers of the City Police Fraud Squad asked him for a meeting. Their manner was diffident and professionally neutral. They were pursuing investigations at the request of Interpol into an alleged violation of the Algerian exchange-control regulations. James felt crushed by the heavy yoke of destiny.

Only his daughters had the ability to mitigate his distress and when he collected them from school at the end of the winter term it was with a wave of relief. The mere sight of them running eagerly toward him, their young eyes undimmed by sadness, their faces full of pure emotion, their limbs full of innocent grace, warmed his heart. He hugged them, wrapped in their heavy winter clothes, and felt restored.

He soon noticed how in a few weeks they had both moved so much closer to womanhood. Monty already had a bosom of mature proportions, and Cathy's demure beauty had lost its girlishness. James told himself that even in loving his daughters he had lived in a fool's paradise; before long other men would take possession of them, leaving him bereft.

For Christmas he bought them each a string of pearls, perfect, creamy jewels as flawless as their clear young complexions. He wanted to give his girls jewelry to be sure of being the first man to pay that tribute to their burgeoning femininity.

A resigned, defeated peace replaced his earlier distress and he found emotional sanctuary in the family festival at Bourton, tainted as it was by his mother's dominating presence and the waspish coldness of his wife. Guilt, like a vampire, had sucked him dry of every emotion except the love of his girls.

In May the Fraud Squad visited him again, accompanied by a French detective. They had traced the bank account he had opened in a false name, and although James wearily denied any knowledge of it, or of the gold allegedly smuggled out of Algeria in the carpets he had imported, all four men knew that the case was proved and that a prosecution would follow in a few weeks.

He brought the girls to London at half-term, and heaped them with presents on the pretext that they needed summer clothes.

"Your father must love you very much," the saleswoman at Fortnum and Mason remarked as she folded two neat, slim evening purses of black patent leather in sheets of crackling tissue. "There aren't many men who would take such an interest in what their daughters wear."

"I suppose he does," Cathy replied, wondering if she dared ask for some new shoes. She was used to people remarking on the rapport between her father and her, but never understood why. Her father's love was like the air she breathed, invisible all around her. She would not appreciate how vital it was until she had to live without it.

He took them back to school, kissed them and said good-bye, resolving that it would be for the last time. His own life was ruined, but he could still save theirs from his own selfish stupidity and from Ayeshah's mad desire to possess them.

He flew to Paris and met the Princess once more at her apartment. This time there was no delay before the double doors opened and she appeared. A cold, echoing calm, like the icy silence of the high Alps, had settled on James and he felt nothing as she approached him. He was at an emotional altitude above fear.

She wore a white Chanel suit trimmed with gold braid which, for the first time that James could recall, gave a slight impression of vulgarity to her appearance. Her eyes glittered with pleasure under their heavy lids.

"You have delayed much too long," she said to him at once. "You should have come to me last year, then I could have done something. Now things have gone too far."

"Yes, they have. You've finished me, you can congratulate yourself."

The secrets which they shared were so grave that the atmosphere between them became intimate. Ayeshah was disconcerted; she had not expected this feeling of a bond with the man she hated.

"Last time I was here you invited me on a false pretext." He had difficulty focusing his eyes on her. "Now I must apologize, because I am here under false pretenses. I've got nothing to discuss with you. I'm not asking you for anything. I have come only to tell you that you will never get the children. Never."

"Are you going to keep me away from them when you are in jail?" Complacently, she crossed her legs and reached for the silver cigarette box on a side table.

"If you had any notion of love, you would have gone to them long ago. But I don't think you do." He screwed up his eyes as if looking at a bright light, the deep wrinkles spreading across his face. " 'Queen of Darkness' is the right name for you. You don't understand love. And you can take your children, and you can stand before them as their mother, but they'll never love you. I've made sure of that." With deliberate absence of chivalry, he allowed her to light her own cigarette.

"You're so confident, *Lord* James Bourton. You think you can make the world and everything in it be exactly the way you want it to be, as if you were God. You think that if you can't see me, I don't exist, and that if you can't understand me, I must be evil. And you think you can create your children exactly as you want them to be, as if they have no will, no characters of their own." She stood up and walked to the mantelpiece, blowing cigarette smoke sharply upward. "In a sense you are right, of course. Whatever I am, that's what you made me, but it's not I who have destroyed you. You've destroyed yourself."

"You're still a peasant, aren't you? Nothing's your responsibility, nothing's your fault, you're just the innocent victim of it all.'' Anger was slowly penetrating James' anesthetized senses and he felt light-headed with the force of the emotion. "I didn't make you what you are. That was your choice. But I've made damn sure my daughters won't follow you. They'll be fine young women soon, and when they find out that you're their mother— if they find out—they'll have more contempt for you than I do.''

"I don't think so.'' Ayeshah was suddenly anxious. This was not how she had envisaged the final encounter with the man who had stolen her children from her. She had wanted to see his ineffable pride devastated, to watch him wallow in humiliation, to hear him beg her to save him from ruin; this half-insane state of defiance was something she had not imagined, and his words hurt her. "Anyway, how will you know? When I am together with my children you will be in prison.''

"That's another thing you're wrong about,'' he told her in a quiet voice. "I'll be somewhere where you can't reach me, when you meet—if you're ever misguided enough to make yourself known to them. In a way I wish I could be there. You will lose them twice. I did you wrong in the beginning, I admit that. But you've betrayed yourself just as much as I betrayed you. That's what they won't accept.'' She stared at him angrily, unable to find the words to reply. James stood up, paused for an instant because he felt dizzy, then walked to the door. "I've said everything I have to say to you.'' Authority was at last returning to his voice. "You've made too many mistakes. It's too late to win your daughters' love. It was all for nothing, Princess. You'll realize that soon.''

He strolled back to the Ritz feeling physically weak but mentally euphoric. The account was square. There would be a scandal, of course, but not a big one—his brother and Eddie Shrewton between them would see to that. And then his fight with Ayeshah would be taken up by Cathy and Monty, his beloved daughters, in whom he had perfect confidence.

29

Monty tried not to sulk, but she felt as if Cathy had dragged her down from a sublime emotional peak, and she responded with violent resentment. Full of passionate impatience for the solution to the mystery of her life, she could not bear to be forced to wait. The idea of her real mother, a new and important force in her life, filled her with deep joy and she was afraid that the delay, and the information which they were seeking, would somehow mar the perfect pleasure which lay ahead of her. When they returned to London she was rough with Paloma, and withdrew from Joe, who immediately flared into such uncharacteristic anger that she was startled.

"I'm sorry," she said, "it's Cathy, she's the one who's upset me, not you. Let's do something, get out of here—I can't stand being in her apartment when I feel like this."

They took Paloma to the zoo, but it was windswept and bleak; the sight of the confined animals depressed them both and Paloma screamed with terror when one of the goats in the children's enclosure tried to nibble her sleeve. They left and walked down to the rose garden in Regent's Park, where the last of the season's blooms, blemished by the weather, hung limply from their stems.

"Why are you angry?" he asked her quietly, drawing her to a wooden bench where they sat down.

"I don't know. I feel that something's been snatched away from me, something important. I think Cathy's being selfish. I hate her when she acts like the almighty older sister who's always right about everything. I suppose it's the world she works in, but she's so dominating sometimes, her way has to be the only way. . . ." Monty was aware that she sounded weak. "Oh, I don't know. What's the matter with me, Joe? I did very well without the mother I thought I had for so long—why am I so attracted to this woman I hardly know?"

"What is it that draws you to her?" Joe asked, putting his great protective arm around her and ruffling the pile of her spotted fur coat.

"I didn't like her when I met her as Madame Bernard," Monty told him. "I was grateful, of course, terribly grateful, but she made my blood freeze, she was so sinister. I didn't want to meet her when I knew her as Princess Ayeshah—Cathy had to persuade me. You know I hate those glittery, nighttime people."

He nodded, the gusting autumn wind blowing a strand of his long black hair across his face. "I remember, you said you'd meet her for Cathy's sake but you wouldn't have crossed the street for her if anyone else had asked you."

Monty laughed. "Oh dear, did I really? But you're right— what's the difference now I know that she's my mother? Maybe I'm being romantic, idealizing her in my mind already."

"What do you think?"

She knew he had once again talked her into seeing herself clearly, but just for once she wanted him to order her around.

"You're a man, you're supposed to tell me what I think," she kidded him. "Anyway, stop hiding behind being a guru as usual. What do *you* think?"

"I think you're a wicked, immoral woman." His full lips curled in a smile and he ruffled her fur collar.

"Why?"

"What are you doing wearing a coat like this—don't you know that the acrylic is a protected species?"

"Why, that's sentimental garbage, Mr. Jones. The acrylic is a nasty, ratlike little animal, no better than vermin, and anyway, this one's ranched."

They laughed into the wind together and felt reunited.

"You know what?" Monty continued as they walked back through the light scattering of yellow early-autumn leaves on the pathway. "She isn't real to me, even though I know her. I can't really imagine my real mother, or her being my real mother. It's just too big for me to get my head around. But all the time, when I was a kid, I had this feeling that there was something missing in my life, like a lost piece of the puzzle. When I fell in love for the first time I felt complete somehow, like I'd found the missing piece. Then when the love died there was that great hole there again."

"I know. I used to feel that way too." Joe paused to fasten the studs on Paloma's pink quilted baby suit. "I never knew my mother, couldn't remember anything about her, and I used to think if only I could find her I'd be OK, like the other kids. Then one day I just decided that was dumb, I didn't want to be like the other kids. . . ."

". . . . and they weren't the way you thought they were anyway," Monty finished, as they walked on. "I realized that when Cathy's marriage broke up and she wasn't my perfect sister anymore, but just as weak as I was in her way. But now I've got that stupid feeling again, that maybe this time there *is* a missing piece after all and I've finally found it. I think my real mother is going to make everything I don't like about myself OK—but when I think about who she really is and what she really is . . . Oh, Joe—why is life so damn difficult?"

Cathy ordered the man who was investigating the European press coverage of her father's death to send whatever he had discovered to London immediately, and as an afterthought asked if he could get a copy of the marriage certificate of Prince Hussain Shahzdeh.

The next day a courier delivered a bulky packet to her apartment, and she and Monty sat down at the round Georgian table, made from a single piece of yew wood, which was used for work more than entertaining, and began to spread out the copies of long-forgotten newspaper articles. There had been no time to translate them, and as neither of them spoke German, Dutch or more than a few words of Italian, they concentrated on the French stories.

Cathy's face was set as she read over and over again the accusation that her father had been found in bed with a dead call girl beside him.

"I don't believe it," she said at once. "It's a lie. Someone tried to frame him."

"There's dozens of articles, this must have gone on for months," Monty said in a small voice, stunned by the lurid implications of the rumors.

"Now you see why I wanted to wait." Cathy pulled a large sheet of paper toward her. It was folded in half. As she opened it she saw the smudged but unmistakable picture of her father waving money against a woman's half-naked body. She gasped, and Monty snatched the page from her and spread it out.

"Jesus." She gulped with the shock of the image, violently repelled by it. Nevertheless, Monty forced herself to absorb every detail of her father's face. He looked drunk and disheveled, and there was something so redolent of habitual corruption in the gesture of the arm that was outstretched with the note in it that the picture branded Monty's mind. She suddenly connected her father to the men she had courted when she too had tried to sell herself, and realized that he must have been nothing more than another of those contemptible lechers whom she had despised so much.

Cathy's mind relentlessly imposed a pattern on the confusion of vile information in front of her. Somehow it all seemed so much more horrifying in French. The passionate, precise language, well-adapted for sexual innuendo, conjured up visions of debauchery far worse than the evidence of the poorly focused photograph.

She began to stack the reports in date order. "You're right, there are too many of them," she said to Monty. "Look, here are two from the same rag, saying almost the same thing, within two weeks of each other. And here, the same thing again . . . and look, his name is the only one mentioned but there are half a dozen other men in this picture. This isn't genuine reporting, this is an orchestrated campaign." She sat back from the table and made a tent out of her fingers while she thought, a pompous gesture which she usually tried to avoid. "If you're right and she is also this Madame Bernard . . ."

"And I am right, Cathy."

"I think you are. It makes sense, though it's horrible to think about. Then she must be mixed up in this somehow. I cannot, I just cannot, believe our father would kill someone like that."

Monty was studying the photograph, trying to make out the other men's faces. "Does he look familiar to you?" She pointed to the most distant figure. All that could be made out was that the man was wearing spectacles.

"No. It could be anyone. Let's look through the other stories, see if there are any names."

At last Monty found a whole page from a German magazine which contained, next to a story that the Queen was divorcing Prince Philip, a small update on the scandal with three names in addition to their father's. Two of them Cathy recognized, but knew that the men were dead. The third was "Shroeton."

"Shrewton?" Monty inquired. "*E* and *W* are next to each other on the typewriter—easy mistake to make."

"If it *is* him . . ." Cathy began, and then checked herself. "Why am I pretending—it's him. As a matter of fact I'm glad. It looks as if Lord Shrewton's almost the only man in my life who hasn't lied to me for years. Whatever the bottom line is, he'll give it to me, and he'll make it quick and clean.''

Cathy telephoned her former father-in-law and calmly pressed him into seeing them that afternoon in his office. He worked in the Migatto building only two days a week now, and was preparing to retire the following year.

"You remember my sister?" Monty, sleek in a wide-shouldered black jacket and tapered trousers, shook the old man's soft hand, and they sat on the hard Jacobean chairs beside his table.

"This must be very important," he said, offering them drinks which his secretary poured.

When she had left the room, Cathy came directly to the point. "This isn't going to be easy for you, but you've always paid me the compliment of being direct with me, and I hope you'll be able to do that now. Monty and I decided to investigate the circumstances surrounding our father's death. We became aware that because we were so young at the time we hadn't been told the whole truth."

Lord Shrewton drew a breath of anticipation, and Cathy continued. "We've discovered that there was a scandal involving him with the killing of a prostitute in Paris a few months before he died. I wondered if you knew anything about it?"

"You've a good idea that I do know something or you wouldn't be here." He sipped pale malt whiskey neat from a crystal tumbler. "You've a right to the truth, now you've read all the lies. I was with your father right through the night that it happened. He was unconscious. He'd been drinking. We found the girl in his room the next morning; she'd been horribly cut up and strangled."

He paused, giving the two women time to take in what he was saying. Now completely white-haired, Lord Shrewton seemed as pale as death itself, but he was as incorruptible as a diamond and Cathy felt relief that she was at last getting a full account of her father's affairs.

"It was a setup," he announced, his voice crackling with outrage still, more than twenty years after the event. "Someone wanted to blackmail him, and I stopped them. I got our ambassador in and had the whole affair hushed up. For my own good as much as his, I have to admit."

"I don't suppose you got on with him very well," Cathy prompted.

"You have to get on with all sorts of people in business, but yes, you're right, your father wasn't my type. Not that I didn't have sympathy for him. Second son—that's a hard row to hoe. He'd done better than many of 'em."

"If you hushed it up, where did these rumors come from?"

"From her, from the woman who was after him. The woman he used to find all these party girls for his private celebrations. At least, I presumed it was she and he thought it likely. Lord knows what he'd done to deserve it, but hell certainly had no fury like her."

"So you were never really sure who was behind it?" Monty asked, feeling disappointed that there was still so much uncertainty.

"Not at the time, but later I found out because she contacted me. The only time I ever spoke to her was on the telephone, never met her." Behind his spectacles, which were dusty and needed polishing, the astute old eyes flickered from one face to another. "I don't suppose you think too much of your father now, eh? Natural, of course. It's not a pretty story, even though he was absolutely innocent."

"But apart from the fact that it was the woman who sent him the girls, you never knew who she was?"

"Never gave a name, of course not. The only thing I remember that was distinctive was the funny nasal voice she had."

"What did she want from him—did you ever discover?" Cathy was fitting together the final pieces of the jigsaw.

"No, I never even inquired. Nothing to do with me, the less I knew the better. But he had other troubles as well, I think it was the combination that brought him down. Debts, as you know, and he was mixed up in an exchange-control fraud of some kind. He was desperate, you see."

"And what did she want from you?" Monty demanded, and Cathy turned toward her sister as she spoke, astonished that she had not thought to ask the question herself.

"Curious. Extraordinarily curious, considering the way things turned out. She said she didn't want two innocent girls to suffer for their father's wickedness, and wanted me to promise that I'd take care of you two if anything happened to him."

"*What?*" the two women spoke in unison, amazement on their faces.

"Yes. Cathy, my dear, I hope you know me well enough to trust me in this. Of course, when my son brought you to our house barely a year later I was suspicious, highly suspicious, but I saw at once that you were as innocent as a newborn lamb and that Charlie was mad about you—and no one could order my son's affections, whatever was at stake. I don't have to tell you, you know it well enough, I daresay." He slowly rose to his feet and walked around the table to take a chair close to her. "I expect you'll go away now and feel that everything I've done for you I did because someone was twisting my arm, and it's very important that you shouldn't think that. After that first attempt, this woman never got in touch with me again. I was, as you know, disgusted with the way my son treated you, and after the divorce I felt sorry for you and I felt it would be right to offer you a chance to rebuild the life he had destroyed. But after that, my dear, you were on your own. I gave you nothing but what you thoroughly deserved, you must believe me when I tell you that.''

Cathy nodded, feeling the prickling rush of tears again. She reached out and squeezed the pale hands which were spotted with brown age marks.

"And you are absolutely certain you don't know who this woman was, apart from having something to do with the girls? Did he ever give you a name?''

"The girls came through that organization called Madame Bernard. He talked about her as if she were one woman, but she might have been a whole business. Everyone knew about her in those days.''

"And did you ever think all of this might possibly have had any connection with the Princess Ayeshah?''

He gave her a quick, hard look of inquiry, then shook his head. "The Princess? No. Never occurred to me. She knows all sorts, the Princess, no doubt some of them not very savory people, but I never had any reason to believe she was mixed up in this sort of thing. Her husband started doing business with me two or three years later, and . . .'' He paused, searching for words.

"And what?'' Cathy urged, tingling with anticipation. Now she could see everything clearly, and her way ahead was open.

"It always puzzled me, our association. He'd have been far better off with some of the other merchant banks. We weren't really in his line. I was surprised when he approached us. But it was a happy business relationship, as long as it lasted.''

"One last question.'' Cathy remembered that she too had two fingers of whiskey waiting to be drunk, and drained half of it in one gulp, thankful for the fiery spirit's warmth in her throat, which was dry and tight with tension. "You hushed up this affair at the time. . . .''

"I was about to become chairman here, last thing I needed . . .''

"Of course. But now—if I tried to revive the investigation, how would you feel?''

"Are you thinking of doing that?''

"We haven't discussed it together.'' Cathy looked at Monty,

who stared back at her with unmistakable anger in her black eyes.

"You'd be taking a perfectly right and proper course if you did," he rapped with something like his old severity. "I can't say I'd welcome it, raking over old coals, but I'd support you, give whatever evidence was necessary. Ambassador's dead now, so are most of the other fellas. To some extent I suppose it's been on my conscience."

They thanked him and left, walking back to the Barbican in a stunned silence. The apartment was quiet and empty, because Joe had taken Paloma out.

They sat at opposite ends of the square black-leather sofa.

"I can see why you like him—he's a fine man," Monty said at last, running her hands through her short hair.

"There aren't enough like him," Cathy replied, easing her shoulders out of the jacket of her dark-red suit. It was tightly fitted in the new season's style, with a long narrow skirt that flared below her knees. She kicked off her plain black-leather pumps and smoothed her stockings, black with a scattering of tiny dots, over her tired feet. "Do you realize what it all means, Monty?"

"She must have been trying to get us back somehow." Monty propped her head in her hand and looked at her sister. Cathy was very white, but her characteristic serenity had returned and, with her perpetually smiling mouth, she looked almost contented.

"Was she? Or was she simply trying to contact him for her own reasons?"

Monty shook her head emphatically. "What reasons? Hussain must have been loaded, even in those days. She can't have needed money."

"I'd guess Hussain's business was still semi-covert in those days; maybe she was trying to get Daddy's support for one of his deals. . . ." While she was speaking, thinking aloud, Cathy regretfully admitted that her father's support in business would scarcely have been worth such an effort. "No, you're right. But if she had wanted us, wanted to see us or meet us, she could have done that at any time. She could have just driven to the ferry and been on our doorstep in a few hours, if that was all she wanted."

"Maybe she was afraid. She was nothing when he left her, don't forget. OK, she'd come a long way from that village, but she must have felt intimidated by the power and the money all around him." Monty gave a short, bitter laugh. "She wasn't to know our father was broke."

''Wasn't she? My guess is she had a damn good idea. She was trying to finish him. She wanted to kill him, she just didn't have the nerve to do it herself. Do you know why I think he killed himself?''

''Poor Daddy—he must have been so miserable. He knew he was going to hit the bottom. He had to lose us or lose everything else. No one can make a choice like that.''

''Uh-uh.'' Cathy shook her head with maddening certainty. ''That wasn't it. He'd have found something to enjoy in being poor, you know. His friends would have rallied round and paid his debts, people always do in that situation. A scandal wouldn't have killed him, he'd have almost enjoyed it for the grief it would have caused Didi and our . . . and Bettina. No, he didn't just give up hope, despair and die. You remember Treadwell called him a survivor—he should have known if anyone did. I think Treadwell did know.''

''Know what?'' Irritably, Monty crossed her legs, pinching the creases in her trousers to have an excuse not to look at Cathy. She was beginning to feel very angry with her sister.

''He killed himself for our sake,'' Cathy reached across and took Monty's hand, which held hers with distinct reserve. ''He wanted to make absolutely sure that that woman would never have any claim to us. He wanted to make sure that we'd hate her, that even if she tried to deceive us we'd be able to find out, put two and two together, and realize what she was. She's pure evil, Monty.''

''You can't say that, she's our mother. Look what he did to her, look what they all did to her—what chance did she have? Wouldn't you have hated any man who did that to you?''

''Would you make those excuses for yourself? Between us we had the same breaks as she did, don't forget. They took Jamie away from me; you were nearly put on the game yourself. And if Madame Bernard let you go, how many other girls do you think she trapped that way, sending them down to St. Laurent to run up a bill they couldn't pay? And you didn't have to pull your life around; she only gave you the opportunity, it was your strength, your motivation. We've both suffered what she suffered, but we made different choices. She could have done the same.''

''But she did save me, Cathy, and you too, when you'd just started and you needed money. She was there when we needed her, she was trying to be a mother to us.''

Cathy released Monty's hand. She felt absolutely calm, as if she were high above the world looking down on the meaningless affairs of people below her. "No, she wasn't. She was trying to buy us, trying to buy our love."

"You're very hard," Monty told her. "She was a pathetic little girl from a peasant village, virtually illiterate, not smart, not even street-smart. You know what happens to girls like that. They're natural victims. Big cities eat them up. But she survived; she did better than survive, she won out, she's on top of the heap. Don't you admire that? Can't you at least find some sympathy for her?"

Cathy shook her head. "I'm being hard, yes, but not cruel, Monty. Yes, she started with nothing and her achievement is fantastic. And I suspect that in the beginning at least, it was the thought of us which sustained her. But look at what she's done. She's killed people; she killed that girl, she had her cut up, sliced like salami and put in bed next to our father. She's probably killed dozens of other people. She's a criminal, a psychopath. She's played with us for years, deceived us, lied to us, spied on us, manipulated us, tried to draw us into her web, make us grateful, force our love—can't you see that? Sympathy? No, I haven't any sympathy. She's a monster, and that's what she's made herself."

Monty gave her sister a stony look. "You just don't like to admit that you might owe her a few things—like the great success that you're so proud of. Suddenly there's a possibility that you had a little help with your life and you can't take it." Swept by a wave of anger, Monty jumped up and stood over her sister. "Why don't you examine your own motives before you start judging other people? You're still in love with Daddy, you won't blame him for anything. Instead you're trying to blame her."

"Why are you always so stupid and emotional? It's all there, Monty, as plain as the nose on your face. You're the one who can't face the truth, not me!"

Like a brush fire after a drought, fury set their exhausted emotions blazing. Suddenly they were arguing, shouting at each other as they had never done in their lives before, saying things that they knew were untrue only in order to wound.

"You're just a frigid, dominating bitch, Cathy! All you care about is money and power, so you can't understand anyone who doesn't think the same way. You're wrong, you're wrong—why can't you accept it?"

"Don't scream at me as if I was one of your bloody entourage. You're on a total ego trip, you've been on it for years, you want everyone to obey you instantly, believe whatever you believe, do whatever you say. Well, I'm your sister, I'm the one you can't fool—don't forget that! You'll never be a big star to me, just a sniveling brat who's always in trouble.''

The terrible tension of the past few weeks was breaking at last and rage swept through them, destroying everything in its path. Like children they were terrified by the power of their own anger, but unable to stop.

"You can't handle this because it's about fucking—and that's something you don't like because in that area you're a total *failure*.'' Monty snarled. "But fucking was all there was between our mother and father; and she made her fortune from it and he died because of it. What's the matter, Cathy—can't you face the facts of life?''

Cathy jumped up, shoving her sister furiously away from her. "What facts can't I handle? I'm pretty damn clear on the fact that that woman killed our father.''

"Yes, but she's our mother too, don't forget, our own flesh and blood. Whatever she is, she's part of us, flesh of our flesh. Now I think about it you look quite like her. . . .''

There was a sharp crack as Cathy hit Monty full in the face, then hit her again, grabbing her by the lapel of her jacket to stop her from moving away. Monty seized Cathy's wrists and wrenched them furiously. "You don't want to know—you can't take it, can you? You want to be little Miss Perfect, all your life as tidy as your school cupboard, no dirt in any of the corners. We came from dirt, we were born in it, our whole lives are down to nothing but the worst things two people could ever do to each other. . . .''

Viciously Monty pulled Cathy's hair and Cathy struck out again. The two of them were standing face to face, flushed scarlet with anger and trembling with the force of the emotion, when there was a rattle of keys and the noise of the front door opening at the lower level of the duplex, announcing Joe's return.

Suddenly Cathy's face crumpled in tears and she collapsed in a miserable heap on the floor. Monty, at once full of horror at her sister's pain, flew downstairs to ask Joe to leave them alone for a while, and ran back to Cathy, quivering with remorse.

"I'm sorry, I'm sorry, darling Cathy,'' she murmured, her arms around the heaving shoulders, feeling their warmth through the thin gray-satin blouse. "I didn't mean it, any of it, I didn't mean to be so cruel.''

"No, no, Monty—you're right really. So am I. Neither of us can bear it, now we know the truth.'' A sob tore her throat, and Cathy cried until her face ached, but still more tears came and she could not stop them. She cried for the tragedy of both their parents' lives, for the pain of her father's loss which she suppressed every day, and most of all for the fear of losing Monty, who held her until at last the storm of weeping was ended.

They were silent for a long while, then at last Monty said, "I didn't mean it. I can't handle this either. It's too much."

"We can do anything if we do it together." Cathy wiped her wet cheeks with her sleeves, oblivious of the marks on the silk.

"Did you mean that about reopening the inquest?" Monty helped her to get up.

"I don't know, I can't decide. Yes, she ought to be charged with murder, for killing that girl if not for killing our father. But that's not why I want to call in the police—I want revenge for what she did to Daddy, just like she wanted revenge for what he did to her. And I don't want revenge for Daddy's sake, either, I can't pretend that. I want it for me, because I can't believe in him anymore as my wonderful adorable father. I'm no better than she is, am I? And I'm frightened, I just want to stop her, Monty. I am so scared that she'll destroy our lives like she did his—she's so full of hate."

"What do we do—call Scotland Yard?"

"I couldn't do it, Monty—could you?"

"No. I couldn't turn her in; she is our mother, whatever else she might be. And we can't be absolutely certain, either. We're guessing, that's all. We need to be sure."

"Lord Shrewton's the only one who's acted decently. I'd like to have his advice," Cathy decided at last.

As she had anticipated, her former father-in-law declined to make any decisions for them, but calmly suggested that they first assemble all the evidence against the Princess and seek the advice of lawyers before proceeding any further.

At Pasterns Mr. Napier, now a portly, balding man with a red face and pinstripe trousers, tried to talk them out of taking any official action. "It'll be a beastly affair, a stain on your own children's lives. . . ."

"No, it won't," Monty told him with irritation. "Our children's lives are their own to create as they choose. They'll be responsible for what they are, just as we are."

"What about the stains on our lives, Mr. Napier?" Cathy asked in her most reasonable voice. "It wasn't very pleasant, coming out as the daughter of the Suicide Peer, hearing everybody whispering every time I came into a room. I loved my father, Mr. Napier, and this woman took him away from me just when I needed him most. I can't put that right, I can't turn the clock back and have my life over again." Until she spoke those painful words, Cathy had never admitted, even to herself, how painful it had been to face publicly the scandal of her father's death. She had been brave, and thought only of making good his loss by marrying gloriously. At last she could acknowledge the pain she had felt.

"You certainly have an immense volume of evidence here, but the final connection between the murder, this Madame person—if she exists—and the Princess is not, in my opinion, proved at all. You are correct in suggesting that the first move would have to be to apply for a new inquest on the prostitute's death, in the hope that the court would recommend that this woman be prosecuted. But without some kind of admission from her you would really have no case," he announced with finality, dismissing the stack of gray document boxes which contained sworn statements by Bill Treadwell in Penang, Lord Shrewton, and the sisters themselves, as well as reports from the two investigators they had briefed. Feeling almost superstitiously afraid, Cathy had copied the entire file and lodged a duplicate volume in a bank vault.

"He's being cautious, that's a lawyer's job," Lord Shrewton observed. "And he's right—you'll need concrete evidence if you're hoping to reopen the case and then proceed to a prosecution. And I'm not sure what you would achieve, even then."

Cathy shook her head. "Neither am I."

"I made a few inquiries for you through an old friend in the City police," he continued, leaning back awkwardly in his immense dark oak chair. "Your mother, assuming she is your mother, is quite a formidable woman. I doubt it would be easy to bring a successful prosecution against her for anything. She's not unknown to the police—as the Madame figure, that side of her operations at least. They've investigated two or three other cases like that of your father—similar in that there was an intention to blackmail. They didn't get very far. I've little doubt that she has very highly placed contacts with the French authorities. My chap suggested that you might persuade her to come to London, perhaps play on her feelings to get a confession out of her, and then let the police hold her on a passport offense while . . ." He stopped talking, aware that he was not being heard with much sympathy.

Cathy and Monty looked at each other in silence for an instant, and then Monty straightened her shoulders. "We couldn't do anything like that. Cathy—don't you think we're just avoiding the issue? What we must do is see her, talk to her face to face, meet her as our mother and hear her side of the story at least.''

''I don't understand why she hasn't confronted us already,'' Cathy agreed. ''She must have known we were discovering who she was when we left L'Équipe Créole so quickly.''

''Don't you think she's scared?'' Monty asked quietly. ''That's why she sent us the pearls—she wants us to come to her. She's scared we'll reject her if she makes the first move.''

They arranged the meeting exactly as Cathy always fixed meetings with her most important clients. Her secretary telephoned the Princess's secretary and asked for the earliest possible date on which the Princess could come to London on an urgent matter. The reply came within half an hour, and the Princess arranged to arrive two days later and asked for a car to meet her private plane at Lydd Airport and bring her to London.

''Don't go,'' Hussain advised Ayeshah at once. ''Ask them to come here. They must be planning some kind of trap if they want you to come to London. Ayeshah, think, I beg you. We know they know almost everything now. You've had them followed out to Penang, you know they've seen Treadwell; they found the scent of the Nadine affair, followed that up. The older one at least is a very intelligent woman, and she has a high moral character, I think. They know who you are, what you are, to them as well as what you are in yourself. This meeting can't bring you any good.''

''The younger one is different—warmer, more emotional. She may have persuaded her sister, who knows? She can't wish me any harm. Don't forget I know a few things about her.'' Ayeshah was perfectly composed, although her elation was so strong that he saw her hands were trembling. Nothing, he realized, would now stop her pursuing this final meeting with her daughters.

Hussain shook his graying head with exasperation. A hundred times in the past two decades he had seen his wife's steely determination waver when confronted by the reality of her daughters. From the day when they heard the news of James Bourton's suicide Ayeshah had begun to talk about the girls in a dreamy, sentimental way which was quite unlike her. She had taken no action. Every few years or so she would plan a grand visit to London to make herself known to her daughters, but the scheme would linger, be postponed from month to month, and finally she would discover a reason to change her mind. This neurotic indecision disturbed Hussain deeply.

The pearls had presented the Princess with a perfect solution. The discovery of the two matching jewels had itself seemed like the hand of destiny pushing her toward the climax of her life.

"For the last time, I implore you, Ayeshah—don't go. It's a trap."

She laughed, a bitter joyless sound which grated on his open heart. "They couldn't trap me, Hussain. How, what could they do? Nothing without blackening their own names, and that of their father, and giving their own children a scandal to live down the rest of their lives."

"Maybe they are brave enough to do that."

"Brave! Don't talk like a child. Stupid is what it would be and you say yourself they're not stupid. You will see that I'm right. I've waited so long, Hussain, and now I shall have my girls at last. They are my children, they love me."

A few days later the golden Rolls-Royce which met the Princess left the tiny airfield and began its journey to London across the flat gray expanse of Romney Marsh. As the road meandered northward Ayeshah struggled with an uncontrollable apprehension which made her feel almost nauseated. The unfamiliarity of the wintry countryside increased her anxiety. Because there was no L'Équipe club in London, she seldom visited England. As the car approached the grimy wasteland of the city's southeastern fringes, Ayeshah remembered the many conversations at which she had rejected the idea of a London club, using all manner of rational excuses to disguise the fact that she had been afraid even to be in the same town as her two lost children. The car's progress was halting, from one queue of traffic to the next, until it crossed the Thames at Westminster and quit the main flow of automobiles to speed along Horseguards Parade.

It was a keen, cold morning a few days before Christmas and London was packed with shoppers. The streets were jammed with slow-moving traffic, and in Regent Street and Oxford Street the illuminated decorations were reflected in the plate-glass windows of the busy stores. In St. James's Park the trees raised leafless branches to the gunmetal sky, and office workers walked hurriedly to their lunchtime destinations, their arms folded over their coats for warmth.

Cathy stood by the window in her office, looking down at the traffic-clogged street below. She too felt fearful, a sensation to which she was not accustomed. Apprehension was like a pain under her ribs, burning intensely and spreading out through her limbs. The more she tried to suppress her fear, the stronger it grew. In the adjoining office Joe, Henry and Lord Shrewton waited, but Cathy found she could draw no comfort from their presence, although she was grateful for it.

"Are you scared?" Monty asked, from her perch on the edge of Cathy's marble-topped table. She was dressed unusually smartly, with a crisp white piqué shirt under her black suit and a small diamond brooch at the collar.

"Yes. I'm terrified of her, isn't it strange? I know that I've got the right to do this, that this is the right thing to do, but I can't get rid of the feeling that something terrible is going to happen. Isn't it ridiculous?"

"I'm scared too, scared that when I see her I won't be able to handle it. I'm all churned up, I can't think properly. Suppose we've got it wrong and she isn't our mother at all?"

"I can't stop thinking about what she did to our father, and to heaven knows how many other people. How can she be my— our—mother? And yet she is, she must be." Resolutely, Cathy turned away from the window, the skirt of her dark-gray suit swinging with each decisive step. "I've seen the car at the end of the street—she'll be here in a minute." The golden Rolls-Royce at last crawled to the curb outside the building's entrance below, and the doorman went to open the door.

Rapidly, Cathy crossed the room and pressed one of the buttons on the console of a black telephone on a low table in the conversation area.

"She's on her way up now," she told the men in the next room.

From the instrument's small speaker, she heard Lord Shrewton's voice, unemotional as ever. "Good luck."

"Have you seen her yet?" asked Joe's rich American voice.

"Uh-uh. She's just getting out of the car," Monty told him, calling across the room from the window. In the street below the small figure of the Princess, moving with its characteristic reptilian quickness and half buried in a close-fitting blond-mink coat, stepped out of the car. Rain, so light it was almost mist, fell through the cold air.

Ten minutes later the Princess Ayeshah was standing in front of them, the force of her personality filling the room. She was plainly in the grip of high emotion which was held in check by her uncertainty. She did not know what to expect, and was unable to take control of the situation. Cathy at once seized the initiative; cool out, she told herself, make it normal, get the situation mastered before it explodes in our faces.

"Good morning, Princess, I hope you had a pleasant journey?" Cathy herself took the blond-mink coat, damp from the rain, and handed it to her secretary. In a severe white gabardine dress which tapered from wide shoulders to a narrow skirt, the Princess relaxed a little, and greeted Cathy with dry kisses on both cheeks and exclaimed at the pleasure of meeting Monty again.

They sat at one end of Cathy's office, around a low black-lacquer table on which the telephone stood innocently behind a small sweet-scented gardenia bush, a wide black ashtray and copies of the *Financial Times* and *The Wall Street Journal*. The Princess at once lit a cigarette which Cathy took as an encouraging sign of her nervousness.

"I must apologize," she said pleasantly. "I've nothing to discuss with you in the way of business. This is a personal affair, that's why we're both here. I'm sure you can guess what it's about."

The Princess's tense mask of a face at once blossomed into a smile and she put down the cigarette. "You know who I am." She looked at the two sisters and tried, as she had tried many times before when one or other of them was with her, not knowing of their relationship, to feel love. Nothing happened. She felt nothing at all. It will come later, she promised herself.

"We think that you are our mother, our real mother," Monty took up the conversation, ignoring the Princess's stare and the peculiar, flat quality of her eyes. They should have been alive with animation, that was what the rest of her tense, mobile body suggested, but they seemed to be opaque, with no light in them. "We know that we are the children of a woman my father married in Malaya during the war, whose name was Khatijah binti Ahmad, and we think that you are the same person." Monty, too, searched her heart for emotion but found none.

"Yes, I am Khatijah. I am your mother. You have found me at last." The words sounded very large now that they had finally been spoken. Monty was suddenly frightened that the older woman was going to embrace her, and she pulled back. The three women looked at each other as if surprised by their own frankness.

"You found us a long time ago, didn't you? Why didn't you ever tell us you were our mother?" Cathy tried to keep the telltale note of concern from her voice. She was touched by the sight of the Princess in a way which she had not anticipated.

"I was afraid you would laugh at me, or turn away from me— you were already quite old by the time I came to Europe, you realize. Tell me honestly, if a strange half-Oriental woman had come to you when you were twelve years old and said she was your mother, what do you think you would have done?''

As her mother talked, she analyzed her features, trying to find herself in the heart-shaped, olive-skinned face and the perfectly painted bow of the mouth. She looked across to Monty, and saw more likeness there, in the straight, broad, catlike nose and the sensual modeling of the face. But, Cathy realized as she crossed her knees under the pleated gray skirt, she had her mother's legs.

"I don't suppose we would have believed you," smiled Monty.

"Even up to now I was never certain that you would want me. That's why I sent you the pearls. I know how clever you are"—she smiled at Cathy—"and I knew you would soon find me, and put the whole story together. Then it was up to you, what you wanted to do. But your father would have done everything he could to prevent our reunion," she continued, blowing cigarette smoke fiercely from her pursed lips.

"Did he ever try?" asked Cathy, trying to disguise her wish to condemn this woman for her father's death. More than anything, she wanted to be satisfied that she was hearing the truth, but she knew that she would have to hunt for it with a certain amount of cunning. People lied when they were frightened, and Cathy saw that the older woman was afraid.

"He told me you would never accept me, that you were proper little English ladies and that I was everything you had been taught to despise." The bitter emotion behind her words was unmistakable, but Cathy, with a poignant vision of her father in her mind, was not moved. She led her mother onward, probing deeper and deeper into her heart.

By instinct, Monty moved the conversation to the subject of Bettina and confided her own feelings of alienation from the woman she had believed was her mother.

"How I hated that woman," Ayeshah almost spat. "I used to dream of her hands touching you, holding you, picking you up . . . can you imagine how I wanted to touch you both, all those years?''

"She didn't like us at all, she almost never touched us," Monty remembered sadly. As she said the words, her childhood feelings no longer seemed important. "I don't think our father even noticed us very much until we were old enough to answer him back.''

"Such a waste, such a waste of love." Ayeshah looked down, wanting to weep, but finding that she had no tears. Instead, she had a sense of inner emptiness which was welling up like cold liquid and drowning her emotions.

Cathy forced herself to pursue the facts of her father's death. "When did you contact him after you had made your way to Europe?"

"In 1959. I remember it as if it were yesterday. His face—you could not imagine the expression. He thought he had left me in the mud of the *padi* field, that he was completely safe, that a little peasant woman could never, ever, follow him across the world to take her revenge."

"I can imagine he would have been surprised. But what did you ask him for?"

"Why, for you, of course. I wanted you with me, I wanted us to be together, I wanted at least for you to know me as your mother."

Monty felt as if she were taking part in a dream. With her real mother actually in front of her, the fear that some overpowering natural emotion would overwhelm her seemed ridiculous. Instead, she found she felt pity for the small, fiercely elegant woman before her. With the insight acquired in exploring her own weaknesses, Monty recognized the sly justifications, the maze of self-deceptions, the elaborate tapestry of lies which the Princess had woven in order to rationalize her own impulse toward evil. She saw her mother as nothing but a weak, bitter woman whose triumphant success had been acquired at the expense of her own character. Rage had driven her, but it had also eaten her up. Now the Princess was balanced at a tragic fulcrum, about to fall into a spiritual void.

"Tell me," the Princess continued, "didn't you always know in some part of you that you were different?"

"Oh, yes," Monty agreed, hoping to kindle more positive feelings in her mother. "I used to think I was a changeling, you know, a fairy child who'd been exchanged in the cradle."

"What did our father say when you asked for us?" Cathy also sensed that the Princess was searching desperately for feelings to match her long-held illusion of love. Cathy found that she pitied her mother, and it was an uncomfortable emotion. Part of her suddenly wanted this traumatic meeting over with as soon as possible.

"He laughed. He threatened me, and then he began to pretend I did not exist. He always did that. When we were married he would start to think about his war, the fighting he imagined would come. He would not even know I was with him. He did the same thing later. He thought about you, about his life, his business, his money, his social position—pfft! I disappeared, he made me vanish, just like smoke." She ground out her cigarette with unmistakable anger, leaving the butt, stained with cyclamen-pink lipstick, crushed almost flat in the ashtray.

"You must have been very angry?" Monty prompted.

"I have never been so angry in my life, never. Not even in the beginning—you"—she pointed at Monty with a stabbing gesture—"you were a tiny baby, just a few months old, and you were taken right out of my arms, but even then I was not as angry as I was when I saw he was denying I even existed."

"So what did you do?"

She paused before replying, scared that they would condemn her but wanting to confess. And she was still angry. The anger, she realized, was a ghost she could never exorcise. "I did what I had to do. It was so easy. Men are so weak, aren't they? They can never resist . . ." She looked from one face to another. Cathy heard this contemptuous opinion expressed of her father without her usual protective feeling for his memory.

"So that story about the call girl who was found dead in bed . . ."

"He walked right into the whole thing. He had those tastes, you know, your father. He always liked those exotic girls. He might just as well have hanged himself with his own hands. And then of course the shame of it was more than he could bear. That was something he could not deny, he could not hide from."

"You mean our father really killed that woman?"

The Princess hesitated, suddenly aware of the snare which James had laid for her. She heard his voice, harsh and accusing, echoing in her head, telling her that she was everything her daughters despised, that they would never accept her. Now that they were beside her, she saw that it was not true. Her daughters were wise, strong, adult women. They were listening to her without judgment. It was she who could not accept them. Try as she would, she felt nothing for them.

Ayeshah was stricken with panic, like a cornered animal. The trap was so intricate, so precise, so carefully framed, so inescapable that she could admire its workmanship even as she twisted within it. She had walked into it because it was constructed of love and loyalty, feelings which she no longer had and could no longer recognize. The camouflage had deceived her perfectly.

Cathy and Monty saw the Princess falter and willed themselves to stay calm and not alarm her on the brink of confession.

"Did he really kill her?" Monty asked the question again, as softly as she could.

Ayeshah realized with terrifying clarity that the whole of her life was at the point of implosion. Within a few seconds everything would fall in on itself in a useless ugly mass, like an overripe fruit which has been eaten from within by insects. She felt powerless to stop the inevitable collapse. But she decided to tell them the truth, all of it. That at least she could give them.

"No. No, he didn't kill her; she was dead when she was put there. They told me he was so drunk he would not have awakened if the Ritz had burned down around him." She looked up, making a final appeal. "But you realize that I did it for you? Everything I've done, I did for you. I wanted you so much. . . ."

The Princess's voice died away and she regarded the two women blankly, acknowledging at last that she had wanted revenge on their father more than their love.

"You saved me from destroying myself and I'll always owe you for that," Monty said suddenly, looking down sadly at the small white figure.

Ayeshah nodded, and remembered lecturing Monty about love. It was the nearest she had ever come to admitting that she herself could not love anyone anymore. Now she could not escape that knowledge any longer.

Ayeshah stood up, a pitifully tiny figure in the room of large, solid furniture. She had a sense of being unreal and stumbled against the edge of the table. Cathy saw that her mother was disoriented and gently took her arm.

"Why don't you stay in London for a while?" she suggested to her mother. "I had a hotel reservation made for you. We all need time to take everything in."

"No, I think I had better go now." The Princess was struggling to regain her composure, and Cathy at once reached for the telephone and called her secretary, asking for the Princess's coat. They walked with her to the glass outer door of the office.

Tentatively, the Princess lifted her face to be kissed and they both coldly pressed their lips to her smooth cheeks. Monty saw she had left a smudge of her rose-pink lipstick behind, and wiped it off with her fingertips, a gesture that might have been thought of as tender.

After she had gone, the two women stood silently together for a few moments, sharing an atmosphere of anticlimax. Then Monty asked, "Did we do the right thing, Cathy? She looked so miserable."

"I don't know. What else could we have done? Maybe it's too late for her to be happy. You were right, Monty, she never had a chance."

They went back to the office and looked out of the window again at the street below. The gold Rolls-Royce was moving slowly along the curb; Princess Ayeshah was walking slowly beside it in the rain.

a few moments, sharing the uncertainty of each other. Then Moody asked, "Did you do the right thing, Carla?" She looked so miserable.

"I don't know. What else could we have done, Major?" too late for her to be honest." Major' he now had a chance—

They went back to the office and logged out of the shadow again at one small laptop. The soft Rolls Royce her moved slowly along the curbs between Avenbury, was waiting slowly, leaving it in the rain.

About the Author

CELIA BRAYFIELD contributes to a wide variety of British publications and is now TV critic on the newly launched *London Daily News*. In America she is best known for her collaborations on Shirley Conran's books, LACE and LACE II. She lives in a Victorian cottage with her seven-year-old daughter, Chloe, and three very old cats.